PUBLICATIONS OF THE NEW CHAUCER SOCIETY

THE NEW CHAUCER SOCIETY

Studies in the Age of Chaucer, the yearbook of The New Chaucer Society, is published annually. Each issue contains substantial articles on all aspects of Chaucer and his age, book reviews, and an annotated Chaucer bibliography. Manuscripts should follow the *Chicago Manual of Style*, 16th edition. Unsolicited reviews are not accepted. All correspondence regarding manuscript submissions should be directed to the Editors, Michelle Karnes and Misty Schieberle, studiesintheageofchaucer@gmail.com. Subscriptions to The New Chaucer Society and information about the Society's activities should be directed to Sif Ríkharðsdóttir, chaucer@newchaucersociety.org. Back issues of the journal may be ordered from University of Notre Dame Press, c/o Longleaf Services, Inc., 116 S. Boundary St., Chapel Hill, N.C. 27514-3808; email: orders@longleafservices.org; phone: 800-848-6224; fax: 800-272-6817; from outside the United States, phone: 919-966-7449; fax: 919-962-2704.

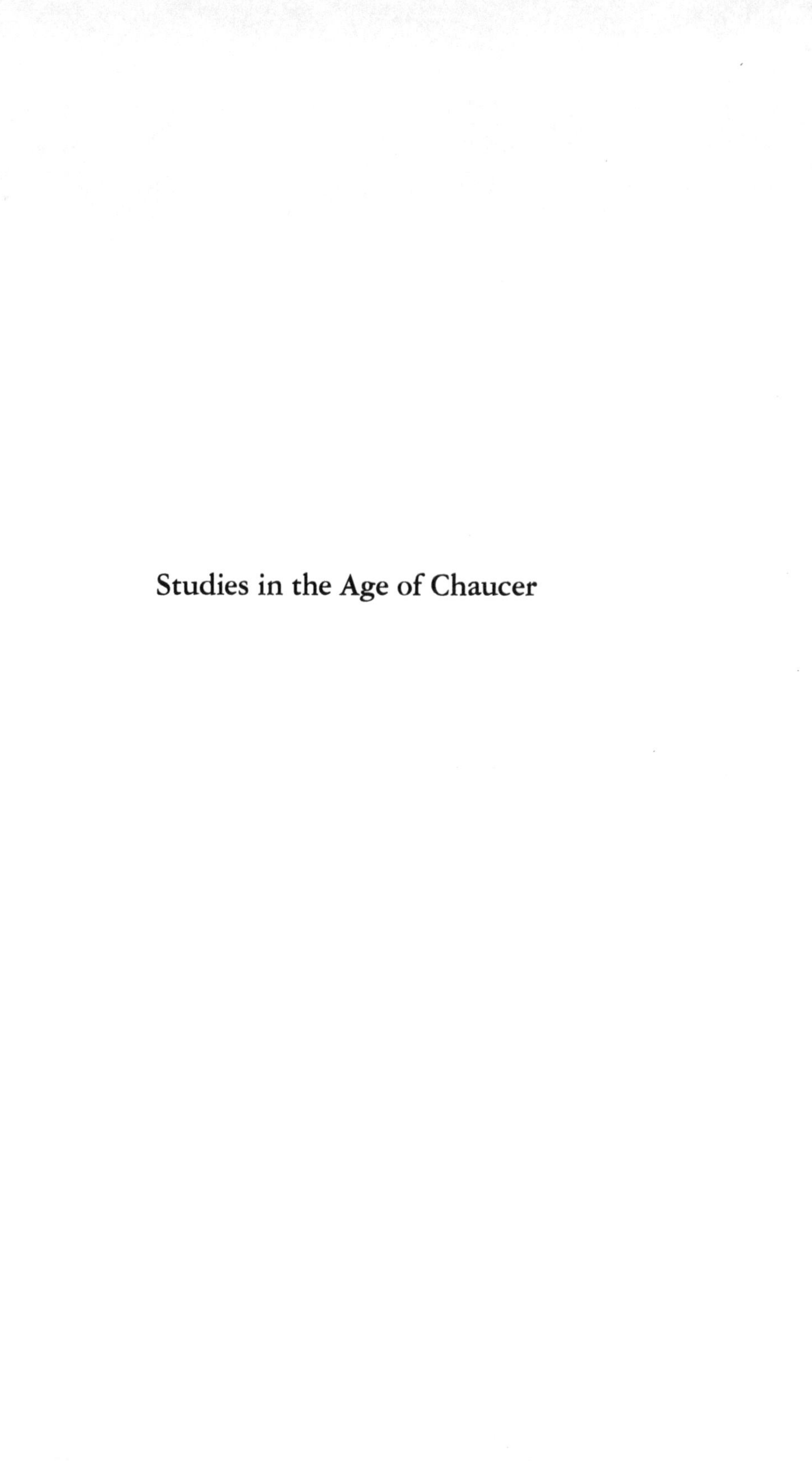

Studies in the Age of Chaucer

Studies in the Age of Chaucer

Volume 46
2024

EDITORS

MICHELLE KARNES AND MISTY SCHIEBERLE

PUBLISHED ANNUALLY BY THE NEW CHAUCER SOCIETY
UNIVERSITY OF ICELAND IN REYKJAVIK, ICELAND

The frontispiece design, showing the Pilgrims at the Tabard Inn, is adapted from the woodcut in Caxton's second edition of the *Canterbury Tales*.

First edition. Published by University of Notre Dame Press for The New Chaucer Society.

ISBN-10 0-933784-48-1
ISBN-13 978-0-933784-48-2
ISSN 0190-2407

GPSR Compliance Inquiries:
Lightning Source France,
1 Av. Johannes Gutenberg,
78310 Maurepas, France
compliance@lightningsource.fr
Phone: +33 1 30 49 23 42

CONTENTS

ARTICLES

COLLOQUIUM. Reconsidering the Subject

REVIEWS

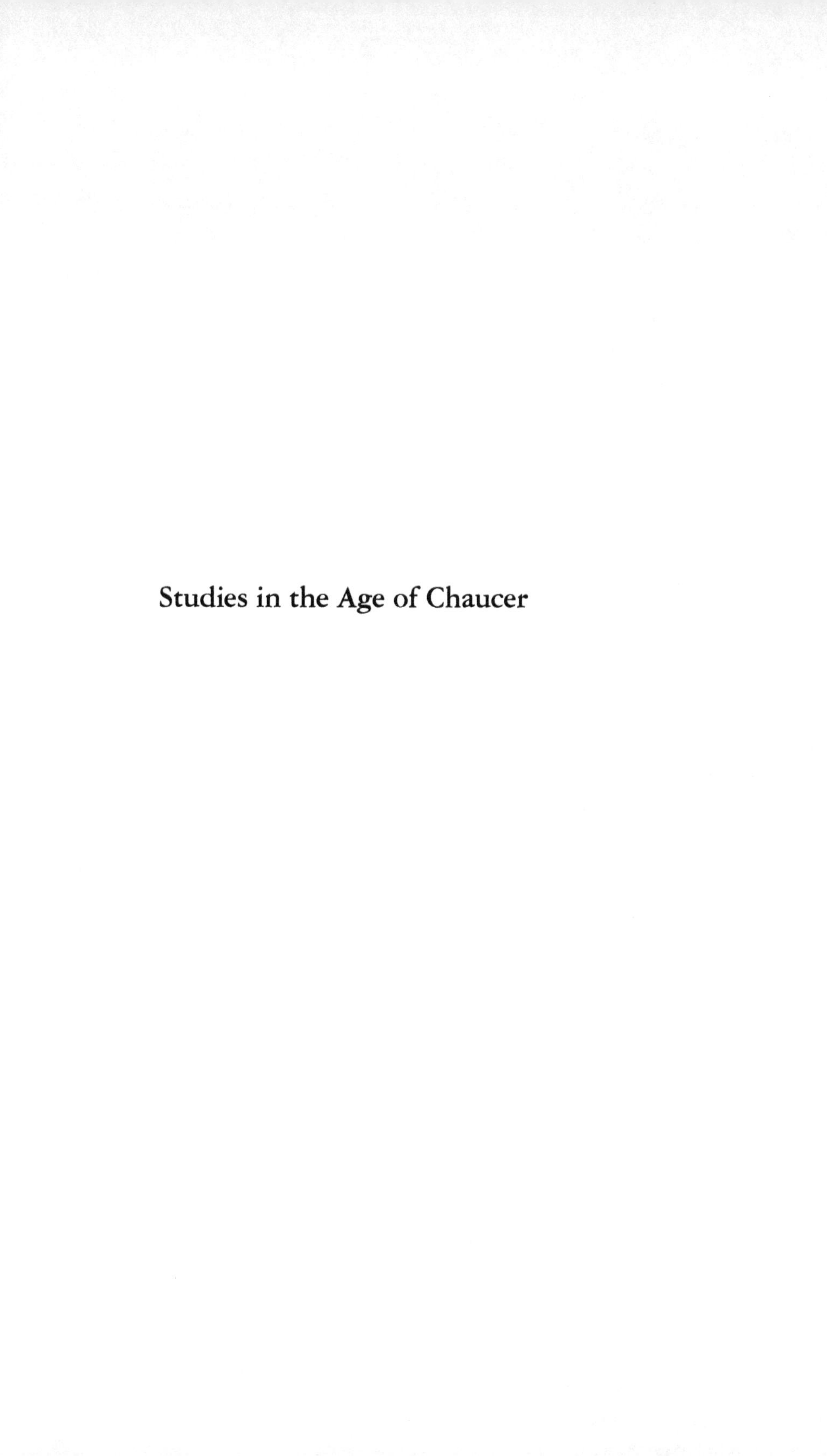

Studies in the Age of Chaucer

Marriage Counseling: *The Merchant's Tale*, the Book of Esther, and Medieval Medical Advice

Noa Nikolsky
University of Miami

Abstract

This article argues that Chaucer's *Merchant's Tale* draws heavily on the biblical Book of Esther in its portrayal of May and Januarie's marriage. The tale's interest in medical healing and counsel is indebted to late medieval readings of the Esther story in both Christian and Jewish traditions. By the time Chaucer was writing, Queen Esther was seen as a wife who could skillfully manipulate her husband by using medical knowledge and presenting herself as a wise counselor. Januarie and May's final confrontation in the tale is presented as a parody of Esther's intervention with Ahasuerus, and the tale's use of the Esther motif thus points to unease surrounding the story of the wily and manipulative Jewish wife.

Keywords

Chaucer; *Canterbury Tales*; *The Merchant's Tale*; Chaucer's sources; Book of Esther; medieval medicine; counsel; biblical criticism; antisemitism

CHAUCER'S *MERCHANT'S TALE* invites its readers to think about medicine. Its plot unfolds within its protagonists' corporeal boundaries—dependent upon their carnal desires, bodily changes, and physical shortcomings. The tale is interested in the failings and ailments of its characters'

This article has greatly benefited from the advice and support of Rita Copeland and Emily Steiner, who read and commented on several early drafts. I also wish to thank Jonathan Stavsky, for his help with tracing biblical reception in late medieval Europe, and David Wallace, for his insights into *The Merchant's Tale*. Thanks to the two anonymous reviewers for their comments and suggestions. Thanks also to Muriel Bernardi, Emma Dyson, Aylin Malcolm, and Lefteris Paparounas for reading drafts of this article. Finally, I wish to thank Michelle Karnes for her constant support in elevating the article to its current state and for her invaluable feedback throughout the process.

Studies in the Age of Chaucer 46 (2024): 1–35

bodies as well as in their potential to be healed, and the language used to talk about the bodies of Januarie, May, and Damyan is that of the medieval science of medicine. From the reference to Constantinus Africanus's medical treatise *De coitu*, to May's claim of experiencing pregnancy cravings (a symptom known in medieval medical literature as *pica*), Damyan's lovesickness, Januarie's blindness, and May's impromptu lecture on ophthalmology, *The Merchant's Tale* playfully engages a number of medical and scientific concepts. The mutual exchange between medical and literary writing is not a new topic in critical scholarship, and medievalists have long been interested in the links between the poetic and the medical.[1] This article likewise takes this relationship as its subject, but it argues for the relevance of a new source in thinking about the medical material in *The Merchant's Tale*: the biblical Book of Esther. Although the tale contains both explicit and implicit references to the Book of Esther, the relationship between the two works has largely gone unnoticed. I argue that the Book of Esther should be considered part of the medical discourse that permeates *The Merchant's Tale*. The interweaving of the story from the Hebrew Bible throughout the tale serves to connect its interest in both medical healing and the gendered politics of counsel, as well as to foreshadow its conclusion in which these two themes coalesce. By modeling Januarie and May's marriage after the story in the Book of Esther, the tale teaches its audience to read the final interaction between May and Januarie as a type of medical encounter in which a wife heals her husband through her extensive scientific knowledge and excellent medical advice. It is the same kind of medical encounter that the later Middle Ages imagined took place between Queen Esther and King Ahasuerus, and Chaucer draws on these postbiblical readings in order to underscore the scene's ironic subversion of the biblical story.

My argument here unfolds in four parts: first, I show that Chaucer draws inspiration from the Book of Esther for *The Merchant's Tale* and models May and Januarie's marriage on the marriage of Queen Esther and King Ahasuerus. To my knowledge, the relationship between the two texts has been hitherto unexplored in scholarship, with the notable

[1]See, for only a few examples concerning England, Caroline Batten, *Health and the Body in Early Medieval England* (Cambridge: Cambridge University Press, 2024); Hannah Bower, *Middle English Medical Recipes and Literary Play, 1375–1500* (Oxford: Oxford University Press, 2022); and Julie Orlemanski, *Symptomatic Subjects: Bodies, Medicine, and Causation in the Literature of Late Medieval England* (Philadelphia: University of Pennsylvania Press, 2019).

exception of Kevin J. Harty, who mentions *The Merchant's Tale*'s explicit references to the Book.[2] Second, I examine the ways in which the tale uses medicine and counsel to thematize its view of marriage as the site of medical encounters between husband and wife. Third, I show that the Book of Esther was likewise read as a story about both medicine and counsel within the context of marriage in the later Middle Ages: Esther was seen as a wife who could manipulate her husband using both her rhetorical powers and her scientific and medical knowledge. Finally, I restate the similarities between *The Merchant's Tale* and the biblical book in order to reexamine the way in which the Esther motif changes our understanding of the tale.

The Book of Esther

The Book of Esther was probably written around the fourth century BCE. In the Hebrew Bible it is considered one of the five *megillot*, or scrolls, which are read liturgically at Jewish festivals, a practice that continues to this day as the Book is read during the festival of Purim. In the Septuagint, the Book of Esther is grouped with the historical books, and the Christian Middle Ages received it as canonical. The Book tells the story of Judeans living in fifth-century BCE Persia, under King Ahasuerus (sometimes identified as Xerxes I, who reigned from 486 BCE to 465 BCE). The story begins with the deposition of Ahasuerus's first queen, Vashti, because of her disobedience to the king, and the king's search for her replacement. Ahasuerus chooses Esther, a young Jewish girl who initially hides her heritage from everyone in the palace. Esther's uncle and guardian, Mordecai, becomes involved in a power struggle with the king's chief counselor, Haman, who, as an act of revenge, convinces King Ahasuerus to approve an edict calling for the killing of all the Jews of the kingdom. Esther eventually convinces the king to reverse this edict, Haman is executed, and the Jews' enemies are killed instead.

For Jewish communities in medieval Europe, the Book of Esther provided many points of interest and inspiration: the story about diasporic Jews saved from annihilation could offer comfort to communities that were themselves often persecuted and expelled from their homes. Medieval Jews translated the Book of Esther into a variety of vernaculars, and these

[2]Kevin J. Harty, "The Reputation of Queen Esther in the Middle Ages: *The Merchant's Tale*, IV [E]. 1742–45," *Ball State University Forum* 19 (1978): 65–68.

translations were read during the festival of Purim alongside the Hebrew original. The story also served as rich source material for adaptation and parody, and many texts engaging with the Book of Esther in this way survive from the later Middle Ages, especially in Provence.[3] The Book of Esther is known for not mentioning God's name once, and the festival of Purim is colored by bawdiness, drunkenness, and an emphasis on role reversal. The story of Esther and Ahasuerus thus also carries with it an interest in the illicit and the carnivalesque.[4]

Christian audiences would have likewise encountered the Book of Esther in a variety of adaptations and media: it was a popular story for inclusion in sermons, literature, and art. The Book does not receive extensive theological commentary in the writings of the early Church fathers, but later theologians devote more attention to the story of the Persian king and queen.[5] The first full Christian commentary on the book is by Rhabanus Maurus (ninth century), and later medieval commentators included Hugh of St. Victor (twelfth century) and Nicholas of Lyra (late thirteenth and early fourteenth century).[6] Queen Esther is also frequently portrayed in the visual arts: her story is depicted in sculpture at Chartres Cathedral, and in stained glass at Sainte-Chapelle in Paris (both mid-thirteenth century). In the fifteenth century, Esther can be found painted on marriage chests common in Florentine art from the workshops of masters such as Sandro Botticelli and Filippino Lippi, emphasizing her role as a bride and wife. Ahasuerus's banquet, too, was often depicted in the visual arts,

[3]For more see Susan L. Einbinder, "A Proper Diet: Medicine and History in Crescas Caslari's 'Esther,'" *Speculum* 80 (2005): 437–63; Jaclyn Tzvia Piudik, "Hybridity in the Fourteenth-Century Esther Poems of Israel Caslari," Ph.D. diss. (University of Toronto, 2014); Erica Baricci, *The Ma'aśe-Ester: A Judeo-Provençal Poem about Queen Esther. A Critical Edition with Commentary* (Leiden: Brill, 2022); and Susan Milner Silberstein, "The Provençal Esther Poem Written in Hebrew Characters c. 1327 by Crescas de Caylar: Critical Edition," Ph.D. diss. (University of Pennsylvania, 1973).

[4]For more on Jewish exegesis and political and theological concerns see Barry Walfish, *Esther in Medieval Garb: Jewish Interpretation of the Book of Esther in the Middle Ages* (Albany: State University of New York Press, 1993).

[5]For an overview of references to Esther in patristic writers see Agnethe Siquans, "Esther in der Interpretation der Kirchenväter: Königin, Vorbild der Tapferkeit oder Typus der Kirche?," *Zeitschrift für Antikes Christentum* 12 (2008): 414–32.

[6]For more information on the theological reception of the Book of Esther by medieval Christians see Mark E. Biddle, "Christian Interpretation of Esther before the Reformation," *Review & Expositor* 118 (2021): 149–60; Jo Carruthers, *Esther through the Centuries* (Oxford: Blackwell, 2008); and Kimberly Vrudny, "Medieval Fascination with the Queen: Queen Esther as the Queen of Heaven and Host of the Messianic Banquet," *ARTS* 11 (1999): 36–43.

and its luxuries and splendor inspired many literary and artistic representations.[7]

Christian readings have traditionally treated the Book of Esther as historically true, and Esther's intervention to save the Jewish people as part of Christian salvation history, since her actions would eventually lead to the birth of Christ. The story was also read typologically, and Queen Esther was interpreted as a type of church—saving the people of God from death and servitude—or as a prototype for the Virgin Mary, another Jewish woman who was chosen for a position of great importance. Iconographic depictions often contrasted Esther and Mary, although other characters from the Book were not ascribed such consistent antitypes from the New Testament. The Book of Esther was to become the subject of popular theatrical adaptations in the sixteenth and seventeenth centuries, but no such treatments of the full story survive from the Middle Ages.[8] Authors in late medieval Europe did, however, frequently engage with the Esther story in popular literature, poetry, and sermons.[9] The Book's thematization of gender roles and marital relations was picked up by Christian authors, who were interested in Esther as both a female Jewish heroine and an obedient and devoted wife. She is often invoked in the same breath as other female protagonists from the Hebrew Bible, such as Judith or Susannah, but her role as a good wife to King Ahasuerus is also frequently emphasized. She is sometimes contrasted with her predecessor—Queen

[7] Aloysius Bernardus Josef Maria Goosen, "Ester," in Van Abraham Tot Zacharia, *Thema's uit het Oude Testament in religie, beeldende kunst, literatuur, muziek en theater* (Nijmegen: SUN, 1990), 82–87; Carruthers, *Esther through the Centuries*; and Nirit Ben-Aryeh Debby, "Bride, Court Lady, Oriental Princess, Virgin Mary, Jewess: The Many Faces of Queen Esther in Early Modern Florence," *I Tatti Studies in the Italian Renaissance* 24 (2021): 345–76.

[8] Early modern theatrical adaptations of the Book of Esther include the anonymous Florentine *Della regina Ester* (dated to 1490–95), Hans Sachs's *Die gantze hystori der Hester* (1536), Valten Voith's *Esther* (1537), the anonymous English *Interlude of the Virtuous and Godly Queen Hester* (1561), the Yiddish *Ein Schön Purim Shpil* (1697), and Jean Racine's *Esther* (1689). See also Chanita Goodblatt, "To Play the Fool: The Book of Esther in Early Modern Biblical Drama," in *Enacting the Bible in Medieval and Early Modern Drama*, ed. Eva von Contzen and Goodblatt (Manchester: Manchester University Press, 2020), 232–52; and Michele Osherow, "Crafting Queens: Early Modern Readings of Esther," in *Queens and Power in Medieval and Early Modern England*, ed. Carole Levin and R. O. Bucholz (Lincoln: University of Nebraska Press, 2009), 141–57. For the ways in which Esther figures in medieval and early modern French literature and culture see Nicole Hochner, "Imagining Esther in Early Modern France," *The Sixteenth Century Journal* 41 (2010): 757–87.

[9] Nirit Ben-Aryeh Debby explores in a recent article the rise in interest in Queen Esther in fifteenth-century Florence. See Ben-Aryeh Debby, "Bride, Court Lady, Oriental Princess, Virgin Mary, Jewess."

Vashti—in stories that feature examples of good and bad wifely behavior.[10]

This is also the way in which Esther is first introduced within *The Merchant's Tale*. Chaucer emphasizes Esther's role as a wife when he references the biblical story at the beginning of the tale. She is mentioned in the so-called "marriage encomium," in which the narrator sarcastically exults the virtues of wives and women. The narrator of the encomium pleads with husbands to listen to their wives' advice and to follow their counsel:

> He may nat be deceyved, as I gesse,
> So that he werke after his wyves reed.
> Thanne may he boldely beren up his heed,
> They been so trewe and therwithal so wyse;
> For which, if thou wolt werken as the wyse,
> Do alwey so as wommen wol thee rede.
> (*MerT*, 1356–61)[11]

The narrator then follows up with examples of the "wyse" men who, he claims, have benefited from their wives' counsel. The examples are all taken from the Hebrew Bible:

> Lo, how that Jacob, as thise clerkes rede,
> By good conseil of his mooder Rebekke,
> Boond the kydes skyn aboute his nekke,
> For which his fadres benyson he wan.
> Lo Judith, as the storie eek telle kan,
> By wys conseil she Goddes peple kepte,
> And slow hym Olofernus, whil he slepte.
> Lo Abigayl, by good conseil how she
> Saved hir housbonde Nabal whan that he
> Sholde han be slayn; and looke, Ester also
> By good conseil delyvered out of wo
> The peple of God, and made hym Mardochee
> Of Assuere enhaunced for to be.
> (1362–74)

[10]See for example the reference to both women in Eustache Deschamps, *Le miroir de mariage*, lines 9124–52, in Monique Dufournaud-Engel, "'Le miroir de mariage' d'Eustache Deschamps: Edition critique accompagnée d'une étude littéraire et linguistique," Ph.D. diss. (McGill University, 1975).

[11]All Chaucer quotations are from *The Riverside Chaucer*, gen. ed. Larry D. Benson, 3rd ed. (Boston, Mass.: Houghton Mifflin, 1987).

Chaucerian scholarship has long struggled with the question of how to interpret this list of biblical heroines: Christian theology upheld Rebecca, Judith, Abigail, and Esther as examples of virtuous women, who aided in the unfolding of Christian history and God's plan for humanity's salvation. At the same time, as Chaucerian critics have pointed out, all four women mentioned in the passage tricked and deceived their male partners in order to bring about this salvation.[12] As examples of the felicity of female counsel, then, these biblical stories appear to be a contentious choice. Despite the biblical heroines' mostly clean theological reputation, most scholars agree that the placement of the passage within the ironic encomium serves to underscore May's deception of Januarie, rather than offer a flattering comparison between the tale's couple and biblical antecedents.

Another enigmatic feature of the passage—which has, to my knowledge, not yet been addressed in criticism—is the speaker's claim that the biblical stories are examples of good *wifely* advice. In fact, only three of these biblical women are wives, and not one of them can be said straightforwardly to provide her husband with advice. Judith, of course, is a widow; Rebecca is indeed married, but is here mentioned as helping not her husband, Isaac, but her son, Jacob; and although Abigail is praised by David for her wise counsel in the Bible (1 Samuel 25:33), she is here linked explicitly to her first husband, Nabal, whom she does not provide with counsel and whose orders she disobeys. The only wife who could arguably be said to provide her husband with counsel is Esther, although the narrator only praises her actions insofar as they benefit the Jewish people and her uncle, Mordecai, not her husband, King Ahasuerus.[13] The reference to the Esther story thus also foreshadows the way in which May's actions will ultimately benefit her own interests, rather than her husband's.[14]

[12]For some of the scholarship on the tension between the condemnatory and laudatory reading of this passage see Emerson Brown, "Biblical Women in the Merchant's Tale: Feminism, Antifeminism, and Beyond," *Viator* 5 (1974): 387–412; Charlotte F. Otten, "Proserpine: Liberatrix Suae Gentis," *ChauR* 5 (1971): 277–87; W. Arthur Turner, "Biblical Women in 'The Merchant's Tale' and 'The Tale of Melibee,'" *ELN* 3 (1965): 92–95; and Amanda Walling, "Placebo Effects: Flattery and Antifeminism in Chaucer's *Merchant's Tale* and the *Tale of Melibee*," *SP* 115 (2018): 1–24.

[13]*The Merchant's Tale* shares its interest in the topos of female counselors with the *Melibee*. Both tales adapt the same biblical heroines passage from Albertanus of Brescia's *Liber de consolationis et consilii*, and its French translation by Renaud de Louens. In the *Melibee*, Prudence introduces the examples in order to illustrate the merits of women's counsel rather than wives' counsel, and in this she is more in line with Albertanus's original version. *The Merchant's Tale*'s insistence on wives' counsel thus seems like a deliberate choice.

[14]For the Jewish tradition that saw Mordecai as Esther's husband see Barry Walfish, "Kosher Adultery? The Mordecai–Esther–Ahasuerus Triangle in Midrash and Exegesis,"

Moreover, Chaucer singles out the story of Esther and Ahasuerus and further cements the comparison between the couples later on in the tale. During May and Januarie's wedding feast, the newlyweds are again compared to their biblical counterparts:

> Mayus, that sit with so benyngne a chiere,
> Hire to biholde it semed fayerye.
> Queene Ester looked nevere with swich an ye
> On Assuer, so meke a look hath she.
> (1742–45)

The Merchant's Tale goes to great lengths to make the comparisons between May and Januarie and Queen Esther and King Ahasuerus explicit, but its medieval readers would have likewise picked up on the implicit similarities between the two stories: both tell of a sovereign who decides to choose a bride, and both chosen wives will come to unsettle the household into which they are incorporated. King Ahasuerus and the knight Januarie both choose a wife whose origins are unknown to them. Queen Esther hides her Jewish ethnicity from everyone in Ahasuerus's palace, and only reveals her identity at the end of the book in order to save the Jewish people. Like Esther, May is chosen among many other candidates because of her beauty and attractiveness, and little is known about her family history despite Justinus's warnings that one must inquire after a wife's background before marrying.

Both stories likewise begin with a contemplation on the relationship between husbands and wives: when his first wife disobeys him, King Ahasuerus seeks advice from his counselors, who are worried that her behavior will set a bad precedent for wives throughout the kingdom. One advisor suggests the king send out an edict decreeing that wives must always submit to their husbands (Esther 1:16-20). *The Merchant's Tale* also opens with a reflection on the role of wives within a marriage: the narrator of the satiric encomium praises wives' obedience and submission to their husbands: "Al that hire housbonde lust, hire liketh weel; / She seit nat ones 'nay,' whan he seith 'ye.'" (1344–45).

Prooftexts 22 (2002): 305–33. Although there does not seem to be any evidence to suggest that this is what Chaucer had in mind, the tradition could have permeated into popular understanding. It is also possible that Christian readers would have independently understood the relationship between Mordecai and Esther as more than familial.

Finally, both stories are interested in illicit sexuality. Both set their narrative climax in gardens—a setting that invites carnality and transgression: when confronted with Haman's treachery, King Ahasuerus escapes into his royal gardens to deliberate on what to do with his evil counselor. Upon reentering the palace, however, he finds Haman lying at Esther's bed and assumes the counselor is intent on assaulting the queen. The enraged king then orders Haman to be hanged. The garden in *The Merchant's Tale*, which Januarie had built so that "[h]is housynge, his array, as honestly / To his degree was maked as a kynges" (2026–27), is the place where May and Damyan finally consummate their love. The parallel with the Garden of Eden is prominent, but Januarie's wish that his garden be "as a kynges" marks the setting as more royal than heavenly.

Explicit and implicit parallels to the Book of Esther are thus woven into *The Merchant's Tale*, from the encomium in its beginning, to the garden scene at its end. What was it about the story of Esther and Ahasuerus that enticed Chaucer to include it in his own tale about a mismatched married couple? To understand the use of the Book of Esther I propose two ways in which the biblical book was read in the later Middle Ages: as a story about a wife counseling her husband, and as a story about medical knowledge and healing. Advice and medicine are tightly interwoven concepts in both medieval readings of the Book of Esther and *The Merchant's Tale*, and marriage is the arena in which the power dynamics inherent to both healing and counsel are played out. Medieval readers of the Book were drawn to the scene in which Esther changes Ahasuerus's mind and convinces him to reverse his edict, and Esther was seen as a wise and shrewd wife, who uses her powers as a counselor as well as her knowledge of medicine to convince her husband to do the right thing. At the same time, readers understood Esther's intervention as performative and manipulative: her counsel was provided not for the benefit of her husband and his kingdom, but in order to save herself and her people. Her knowledge of medicine was used to manipulate her husband and change his mood. Chaucer is playing with this understanding of the Book when he models May and Januarie after the Persian king and queen. In what follows, I first examine the ways in which medicine and counsel are integral to both *The Merchant's Tale* and the Book of Esther, before showing how Chaucer uses the Esther motif to examine the gendered power dynamics inherent to both medicine and counsel in the tale.

Medicine and Counsel in *The Merchant's Tale*

Chaucerian critics agree about the importance of both counsel and medicine for *The Merchant's Tale*. They cite the debate between Justinus and Placebo as an example of the former, and Januarie's use of aphrodisiacs or Damyan's lovesickness as examples of the latter. While counsel and medicine both have distinct learned traditions, it is not uncommon for them to emerge as twinned discourses in late medieval culture and literature. The association is seen, for example, in the expectation that medieval physicians offer their patients not just medicaments but medical advice, too, and in the proliferation of medical advice literature in the later Middle Ages. Genres of political advice literature, such as those derived from the *Secretum secretorum*, in turn, often incorporate sections on health and medicine.

Moreover, both counsel and medicine emerge as particularly gendered discourses in the medieval imagination. Female healers in the romance tradition are often tasked with curing and taking care of male protagonists.[15] Female and feminized counselors also frequently feature in political writing and advice literature.[16] These women's gender is often presented as directly linked to their ability to perform both roles: either because of their devotion to their male partners and the gendered expectations of caretaking, or because their gender allows them to critique a male figure from a socially inferior position. Literary examples of wise women in the Boethian tradition, who both impart counsel and heal their male interlocutors, either literally or figuratively, are also common in European literature and in Chaucer's own oeuvre.[17] In *The Merchant's Tale*, Januarie likewise expects his wife to care for him and his body, and to advise him as a counselor, while May happily pretends to fulfill both roles. But the young May is not a courtly healer or a political strategist; she is a trickster who plays on these gendered expectations in order to facilitate her adulterous desires.

[15]For example, Nicolette from the late twelfth-/early thirteenth-century *Aucassin et Nicolette* fixes Aucassin's dislocated shoulder. Chrétien de Troyes's late twelfth-century *Erec et Enide* features a scene in which Enide nurses her husband back to health.

[16]For a thorough discussion of the gender dynamics of counsel and female-coded counselors see Misty Schieberle, *Feminized Counsel and the Literature of Advice in England, 1380–1500* (Turnhout: Brepols, 2014).

[17]Alain de Lille's Natura and John Gower's Venus are two famous examples. Chaucer's Prudence is likewise a wife who counsels her husband and, in the process, competes with the surgeons and physicians who were brought in to advise Melibee.

The way in which the two thematic interests intersect and play out between May and Januarie was noticed by one of Chaucer's earliest readers: the author of the "Prohemy of a Mariage betwixt an Olde Man and a Yonge Wife, and the Counsail."[18] This poem, found in London, British Library, MS Harley 372 and sometimes attributed to John Lydgate, is worth dwelling on here because it is a good example of the way in which *The Merchant's Tale* was read by late medieval audiences. The poem is framed as a written response to a letter from a friend, who has asked the narrator for advice about whether he should marry a young wife. It is a homage to *The Merchant's Tale*, and repeats parts of the story with similar protagonists and a similar narrative frame. The poem presents marriage as a continuous process of attempt and failure to heal one's spouse, and therefore as a series of medical encounters between husband and wife, a theme that it also picks up from *The Merchant's Tale*, as will become evident.

The narrator of most of the "Prohemy" addresses a "frend that sumwhat was aged" (2), and cautions him against marrying at his advanced age. The narrator warns the friend to "[r]emembre wele on olde January, / Which mayster Chauuceres ful seriously descryveth, / And on fressh May, and how Justyne did vary / Fro Placebo, but yet the olde man wyveth" (29–32). The reasons for such warnings are made more explicit than in *The Merchant's Tale*, as the narrator explains that his friend may not be able to satisfy a young wife's sexual desires. The language is steeped in the vocabulary of disease and medicine:

> War the siknesse that called is the pank,
> A terme of court for the tide bitte no man,
> A maladie called "male de flank,"
> A bocche that nedeth a good cirurgian;
> And but he be, she wol have men that can,
> That hath the crafte and the kunnyng pure,
> To make a parfytt and a redy cure.
>
> (113–19)

[18] All references to this poem are to John Lydgate(?), "Prohemy of a Mariage betwixt an Olde Man and a Yonge Wife, and the Counsail," in *The Trials and Joys of Marriage*, ed. Mary Elizabeth Ellzey, Douglass Moffatt, and Eve Salisbury (Kalamazoo: published for TEAMS in association with the University of Rochester by Medieval Institute Publications, Western Michigan University, 2002), https://d.lib.rochester.edu/teams/text/salisbury-trials-and-joys-prohemy-of-a-mariage-betwixt-an-olde-man-and-a-yonge-wife-and-the-counsail (accessed July 28, 2024).

The young wife's desire for sex, characterized as a "siknesse," "maladie," and "bocche" (a type of swelling or boil), requires a "good cirurgian," which the old husband is clearly not. She will therefore inevitably turn elsewhere for her cure. Marriage is here presented as a medical relationship, in which the husband must take on the role of healer. If the wife's "siknesse" is not cured, the marriage will fail through adultery.

The narrator of the "Prohemy" proceeds to tell of a rich man called Decembre, who, in his old age, weds the young but poor July. As he is courting her, Decembre confesses that he suffers from three ailments for which there is no cure: first, he is quick to anger. Second, he is often angry without a cause. Before he can finish his list, however, the young July interrupts to assuage him:

> Quod she, "Good lorde, can ye no remedye
> For these two poyntes, that bene easy and smale?
> In good feith, sire, I cane ful sone aspye
> Salve for such sores; she is a feble female,
> That lakketh such read; good lorde, telle on your tale
> Of your thrid poynt, myn herte mery to make,
> And up my soule I shal al undirtake."
>
> (330–36)

Once again, their marriage is presented as a medical encounter, this time with the roles of patient and healer reversed. Now it is the husband who assumes the role of the patient, and the wife who sees it as her responsibility to find a "remedye." The patient/healer dichotomy is clearly gendered: July's assertion that it is only a "feble female, / That lakketh such read" maps the giving and receiving of medical counsel onto the gendered expectations of the marriage: it is a female virtue to find remedy for a husband's malady, and the failure to do so means a failure to live up to gendered expectations. This encounter is also one in which medical advice is exchanged: the "salve" July offers is likened to advice or "read." Women's healing, then, is not only judged by their ability to cure their husbands' bodies, but also by their ability successfully to transmit medical knowledge to their husbands and to convince them of the effectiveness of the treatment.

Decembre now proceeds to disclose his final "poynt": he is impotent and will therefore have to remain chaste—a great departure from Januarie's assessments of his own sexual capabilities. July offers to cure all three of his flaws, as she reassures him once again that it is a wifely duty to provide good medical counsel in such matters: "I make warant, for ful onwise is she / That cannot counsel in such juparté" (354–55). Of course, as in *The Merchant's Tale*, her "remedy" turns out to be merely a clever rhetorical trick: once the marriage is legalized, July "cures" Decembre's first "poynt" by promising that she will always be more wrathful than he is; the second by saying that she will give him cause for all his anger,; and finally, in addressing his impotence, she makes the legal argument that Decembre must hire someone who can pay the marital debt in his place.

The "Prohemy" presents Decembre and July's marital negotiations not only as a legal dialogue, but as a medical one as well. Marriage becomes a relationship in which medical care and advice can and should be exchanged, and in which husband and wife are responsible for each other's health.[19] The roles of physician and patient and those of counselor and counselee map precisely onto the gender dichotomy presented in the poem. Yet while either spouse can assume the role of a patient, the role of the dispenser of medical advice is marked as exclusively feminine: while the narrator warns his friend that a husband should be able to act as a "good cirurgian" in order to cure his wife's swelling (with a nod to the intrusive and penetrative aspects of surgery), the healing skills ascribed to a wife center mainly on providing her husband with good "read" and "counsel" in order to effect his remedy. Of course, this skill proves rather dangerous when a wife's rhetorical expertise is used to advance her own pleasure rather than curing her husband's ailments, and her ability to counsel devolves into mere sophistry. This is precisely why, the narrator argues, it is important to choose a good wife. While there is no more hope for Decembre, the prospective husband to whom the "Prohemy" is addressed

[19]Much excellent scholarship has been devoted to the study of medieval female medical practitioners. See, for a foundational example, Monica H. Green, "Documenting Medieval Women's Medical Practice," in *Practical Medicine from Salerno to the Black Death*, ed. Luis García Ballester (Cambridge: Cambridge University Press, 1994), 322–52. The idea that a woman had caring responsibilities toward her male partner is also present in much medieval literature, especially romance and conduct manuals for women. For example, *Le ménagier de Paris*, an anonymous French conduct manual written in the fourteenth century, instructs a future wife on how to manage her husband's household, sleep, and toilette in order to make him healthy and comfortable. It also includes recipes for common medical afflictions. See Gina L. Greco and Christine M. Rose, eds., *The Good Wife's Guide: Le Ménagier de Paris. A Medieval Household Book* (Ithaca: Cornell University Press, 2009). For an overview of female healers in literature see April Harper, "The Image of the Female Healer in Western Vernacular Literature of the Middle Ages," *Social History of Medicine* 24 (2011): 108–24.

can still preempt such a scenario: he can choose to privilege the male narrator's "counsail" over the temptations of marriage and give up the endeavor altogether.

Reading *The Merchant's Tale* "back" through the lens of the "Prohemy"'s homage sheds some further light on the tale's concern with healing and medicine. Januarie and May's marriage, too, is rife with medical encounters in which husband and wife act as healer and patient, employ medical language, and dispense medical advice. Justinus's claim that "[a] wyf axeth ful many an observaunce" (1564) contains social as well as medical connotations: an "observaunce" refers to the practice of observing laws, rituals, or ceremonies, but it can also mean an attendance to or care and treatment of the body.[20] Januarie proves unable to provide May with appropriate "observaunce," since, despite his laborious amorous efforts, she famously does not think "his pleyyng worth a bene" (1854). Damyan, on the other hand, the younger man who is brought in to perform this "observaunce" just as July had suggested in the "Prohemy," is a very skilled healer. As pointed out by Emerson Brown, Damyan's link to medical practice is established nominally, through his connection to St. Damian, patron saint of physicians. Brown additionally notes Chaucer's subtle punning on the word "lechour" (meaning both a lecherous person and a healer) when Pluto points out Damyan's hiding place by exclaiming: "Lo, where he sit, the lechour, in the tree!" (2257).[21] Damyan thus performs the healing role that Januarie is unable to fulfill within his marriage: he takes care of May's "*male de flank*."[22]

Januarie may not be the skilled surgeon that May desires, but May, on her end, is an expert at convincing Januarie that she has healed him. Her role in "curing" Januarie is anticipated by the narrator of the encomium, whose ironic praise of marriage commends wives on their ability to act as caregivers for their husbands when they are sick:

[20] *MED*, s.v. *observaunce*, def. 1(a, g).

[21] Emerson Brown, "The 'Merchant's Tale': Why Is May Called Mayus?," *ChauR* 2 (1968): 273–77.

[22] Although Chaucer does not mention May's sexual insatiability in such direct terms as the author of the "Prohemy," this type of wifely insatiability is precisely what Justinus warns Januarie against when he advises him not to marry a young wife. Samantha Katz Seal has moreover shown that May's sexual desires are very much embedded in the plot of *The Merchant's Tale* through the narrative focus on sight and imagination. See Samantha Katz Seal, "Pregnant Desire: Eyes and Appetites in the *Merchant's Tale*," *ChauR* 48 (2014): 284–306.

For who kan be so buxom as a wyf?
Who is so trewe, and eek so ententyf
To kepe hym, syk and hool, as is his make?
For wele or wo she wole hym nat forsake;
She nys nat wery hym to love and serve,
Though that he lye bedrede til he sterve.
(1287–92)

The idea of a wife caring for her bedridden husband must have appealed to Januarie, whose insistence on marrying a woman much younger than himself would ensure that his wife is able to support him in old age.[23] May capitalizes on this expectation when she convinces her husband that she is the one responsible for the sudden return of his eyesight. The reader knows, of course, that Januarie's miraculous recovery is the work of the god Pluto, but May insists that it was her and Damyan's encounter that brought on this cure:

And she answerde, "Sire, what eyleth yow?
Have pacience and resoun in youre mynde.
I have yow holpe on bothe youre eyen blynde.
Up peril of my soule, I shal nat lyen,
As me was taught, to heele with youre eyen,
Was no thyng bet, to make yow to see,
Than strugle with a man upon a tree."
(2368–74)

May's answer makes sense only if the couple does indeed conceive of their marriage as a site where medical healing can occur, and it is only persuasive if Januarie agrees that his health can in some way be May's responsibility—in other words, if he accepts the idea of marriage as a site fit for medical encounters. May certainly plays into the role of the wifely healer in the tale's final scene. To Januarie's protest that he had caught her and Damyan having sex in the tree she responds: "[t]hanne is . . . my medicyne

[23] *Kepen* here reads ambiguously to me. The verb can mean "to protect" or "to preserve," in which case the phrase means that no one is better at caring for a husband than his spouse. However, *kepen* can also imply that a wife keeps or remains by her husband's side in sickness and health. Finally, the verb can also mean "to desire" or "to wish," an ironic eventuality in which a wife wishes her husband sick or healthy, and the sentence is resultative. See *MED*, s.v. *kēpen* (v.), defs. 11(a), 6, 2.

fals; / For certeinly, if that ye myghte se, / Ye wolde nat seyn thise wordes unto me" (2380–82).

May implies that she cured Januarie's blindness through her "strugle" with Damyan, but her words are offered to him in the form of advice as she tells him to "[h]ave pacience and resoun in youre mynde." Like in the "Prohemy," the young wife is tasked with providing her husband with advice or counsel. This expectation is also set up in the beginning of the tale: as noted above, the narrator of the encomium draws on stories from the Hebrew Bible to implore husbands to listen to their wives' advice. The encomium's ironic tone, of course, foreshadows the way in which Januarie—like Decembre and the biblical husbands—will be tricked by his wife's counsel, but the tale does take care to present May as an effective counselor.

Like in the "Prohemy," the act of counsel in *The Merchant's Tale* is gendered, and male counsel is contrasted with female, wifely advice.[24] The male homosocial society, which Januarie calls together in the first part of the tale, is unable to influence the stubborn knight. While the flatterer Placebo gives up any pretense of counsel and tells Januarie that "youre owene conseil is the beste" (1490), even the righteous Justinus is unable to sway Januarie from his decision to marry the mysterious May. The young wife, on the other hand, will succeed where her male counterparts have failed. She is the only character who will be able to convince her husband of anything. May not only convinces Januarie that she was the one to heal his eyesight, she also manages to rationalize away his seeing of her and Damyan in the tree: she explains—in very scientific terms—that a long period of blindness could lead to an incorrect interpretation of one's visual perceptions, and that Januarie has experienced an optical illusion. May then concludes with one final piece of advice: "He that mysconceyveth, he mysdemeth" (2410). Her "healing" is thus reliant on a scientific and material interpretation of events, and on persuading her husband of this scientific reality.[25] The reader is aware of the supernatural

[24]Amanda Walling argues that the two realms of advice-giving in *The Merchant's Tale* are linked, since Placebo manages to flatter Januarie in a way reminiscent of the encomium's faux-praise of obedient wives; see Walling, "Placebo Effects," 13–15. I am convinced by Walling's assertion, but my argument here is interested in the differences between the two. Since May will turn out to be the only counselor capable of changing Januarie's mind, I maintain that the tale sets her up as a more successful foil to the two male counselors.

[25]For an account of the ways in which Chaucer weaves the scientific language of optics into his version of the story of a deceived husband see Peter Brown, "An Optical Theme in *The Merchant's Tale*," *SAC* 1 (1984): 231–43.

cause behind the cure of Januarie's eyesight: the intervention of Pluto and Prosperpina, of which both Januarie and May remain ignorant. The scientific explanation that May offers, although in line with contemporary medical thinking, is therefore misleading, and her cure and counsel prove to be the same kind of "medicyne" that July offers Decembre: nothing but a rhetorical trick that assures her husband he has been healed yet makes him look foolish in the process.

Like her intervention as a healer, May's powers of persuasion are presented as a strikingly gendered feature: we know her rhetorical prowess has been divinely granted by Proserpina only a few lines earlier:

> . . . I shall yeven hire suffisant answere,
> And alle wommen after, for hir sake,
> That, though they be in any gilt ytake,
> With face boold they shulle hemself excuse,
> And bere hem doun that wolden hem accuse.
> For lak of answere noon of hem shal dyen.
> Al hadde man seyn a thyng with bothe his yen,
> Yit shul we wommen visage it hardily
> And wepe, and swere, and chyde subtilly
> So that ye men shul been as lewed as gees.
> (2266–75)

The reluctant queen of the underworld grants not only May but "alle wommen" the rhetorical skills necessary to defend themselves against their husbands' accusations, even if this is done through deception, and even if their arguments are contradicted by visual evidence.[26] The final scene of the tale is thus presented not only as a medical encounter, but as a hermeneutic act of counsel-giving, in which both rhetorical skill and the ability to be persuaded are markers of gender. In granting May her powers, Proserpina in fact creates the very figure of the manipulative female counselor conceived by the tale's antifeminist discourse.

The world of *The Merchant's Tale* imagines a wife who is tasked with healing her husband, but whose medical healing is related to her dispensing of counsel and to her powers of persuasion. Choosing the wrong kind

[26]Proserpina makes sure to emphasize that such skills could be employed in self-defense. The reality she proposes, one in which a woman could die for "lak of answere," is very different from the one Pluto sees, in which wives are the main perpetrators of violence or "vileynye" (*MerT*, 2261).

of wife thus becomes a dangerous prospect for a potential husband, not just because a trickster wife can make him look foolish, but also because a wife is ideally positioned to manipulate his body and his health. Justinus, who embodies much of the male anxiety surrounding women and wives in the tale, warns Januarie about the stakes of a bad marriage: "And syn I oghte avyse me right wel / To whom I yeve my good awey fro me, / Wel muchel moore I oghte avysed be / To whom I yeve my body for alwey" (1526–29). A wife's influence over her husband's body is what underlies the anxiety surrounding female healers and counselors in the tale: husband and wife are corporeally linked through the sacrament of marriage, and a wife's counsel can thus have serious consequences for a husband's body. A wifely counselor, *The Merchant's Tale* suggests, is uniquely suited to manipulate her husband's body and to cause it a great deal of good or ill.

The Merchant's Tale is not the only place where such dangerous wives are found. *The Nun's Priest's Tale*'s Pertelote, for example, dispenses unlicensed medical advice littered with scientific language, which similarly endangers her husband's life because of her incorrect interpretation of his dream. Both tales include a wife whose medical and materialist explanation of events, and her ability to convince her husband to take her advice and ignore his own intuition makes her husband into the butt of the tale's joke. But while Pertelote is acting sincerely in her limited capacity as a non-Latinate and female amateur physician, May uses her scientific lecture to deceive and trick her husband: she capitalizes on the image of the wifely counselor and the wifely healer, and Januarie, who believes that wives are effective caregivers, and that their advice is beneficial for their husbands, is duped. In manipulating her husband in this way, the young May is not only subverting the expectations set up by the tale, but also mirroring the behavior of her biblical double, Queen Esther.

Esther as Medical Counselor

In her manipulation of her husband, both in leading him into the garden to play and in convincing him that she has cured his vision with her "strugle," May takes a page out of the playbook of her queenly predecessor. The fourteenth-century Esther had amassed a reputation as a clever wife, who was able to bend her husband to her will through her medical knowledge and her wifely counsel. Unlike the sincere female counselors from the Boethian tradition, or the trustworthy female healers of romance, Esther had a reputation as a particularly manipulative and dishonest wife, and her powers lay in her talent for tricking her husband and influencing his body and mood. Esther's ability to persuade King Ahasuerus to countermand his edict for killing the Jews of the kingdom captured the medieval Christian imagination. In various biblical adaptations Esther is depicted as a mediatrix, interceding before the king on behalf of her people, and she is therefore often compared to the Virgin Mary, that paradigm of female intercession on behalf of Christians. Some versions of the *Speculum humanae salvationis*, for example, showcase these iconographic similarities: Queen Esther is depicted on her knees, pleading with her husband to spare the Jews. She is juxtaposed with Mary, who, on the opposite page, is baring her breast before Christ in a similar pose.[27]

Esther was also held up as an example for medieval queens in political writing, in order to illustrate ways by which a queen could petition her husband on behalf of her people. Paul Strohm and Lois L. Huneycutt have shown how both Matilda of Scotland, queen to Henry I in the twelfth century, and Anne of Bohemia, queen to Richard II in the fourteenth, were compared to Esther in contemporary writing because of their intercessions with their respective husbands on behalf of their subjects.[28] Strohm identifies two tropes associated with female intercessors in political and historical writing: the abject intercessor, a humble self-abasing woman who pleads for her lord to show pity and mercy for his subjects, and the shrewd female counselor, whose relationship to male authority is more critical and who imparts good arguments and sharp analysis in her persuasive speeches. Strohm argues that in the later Middle Ages the figure of Esther could embody both of these topoi: she was seen both as a sage counselor and as an abject intercessor. Depictions of Esther, and subsequently depictions of queenship and queenly authority that made use of the Esther trope, existed in a system where power hierarchies could be destabilized and reversed, and in which authority, humility, shrewd persuasion, and compassion could all be ascribed to the same queenly signifier. Queen Esther could be both shrewd and obsequious, stubborn and

[27]See, for example, the woodcuts in Avril Henry, ed., *"The Mirour of Mans Saluacioune": A Middle English Translation of "Speculum humanae salvationis." A Critical Edition of the Fifteenth-Century Manuscript Illustrated from "Der Spiegel der Menschen Behaltnis, Speyer, Drach," c. 1475* (Philadelphia: University of Pennsylvania Press, 1987), 196.

[28]See Paul Strohm, *Hochon's Arrow: The Social Imagination of Fourteenth-Century Texts* (Princeton, N.J.: Princeton University Press, 1992), esp. Chap. 5; and Lois L. Huneycutt, "Intercession and the High-Medieval Queen: The Esther Topos," in *Power of the Weak: Studies on Medieval Women*, ed. Jennifer Carpenter and Sally-Beth MacLean (Urbana: University of Illinois Press, 1995), 126–46.

submissive. As an intercessor, she could be at once accepting and suspicious of male spousal authority. She could be argument-driven and also invoke mercy.[29]

Accounts that imagine several possible, interchangeable Esthers are reminiscent of Jewish exegetical traditions that highlight Esther's two-faced nature. The *Midrash Esther Rabbah*, a rabbinic exegetical work probably combined in the twelfth or thirteenth century (with several parts written much earlier), explains Esther's second name, Hadassah (the Hebrew name for myrtle), thus: "just as the myrtle's scent is sweet, but its taste is bitter, so was Esther sweet to Mordecai and bitter to Haman."[30] The tradition of Esther's two-facedness—albeit in the name of the Jewish cause—dates back at least to the Talmud, which emphasizes the secrecy surrounding her Jewish origins,[31] and was likely part of the Christian reception of Esther's story, both in theological and in popular writing. Esther, then, was often regarded as somewhat inscrutable: she could be sweet to some, but bitter to others. Her meekness could be a front for wiliness and cleverness. As we will soon see, she was also a skilled performer and could use her twinned identities in order to manipulate her husband into taking her advice.

Such an unstable signifier, especially in the form of a Jewish queen, was likely to engender at least some unease. The anxiety about a potential disruption to male authority in Esther's story and its afterlives is perhaps the reason that some medieval authors choose to be explicit about what kind of Esther they depict. Some authors strongly emphasize the Persian queen's obedience and submissiveness to her husband's authority. Middle English poets, for example, often refer to Esther as meek, humble, or mild. The Middle English translation of Roger d'Argenteuil's *Bible en François* explains that it was "by the mekenes of the good quene Hester that was of the lyne of Iuwes, whom weddid a Sarazine prince" that the Jews were

[29] While both the abject intercessor and the sage counselor could work to establish the existing political authority of the lord or to depict female power over the lord, they are not often used interchangeably. Strohm notes that the only other examples of these tropes used together occur in depictions of the Virgin Mary.

[30] *Esther Rabbah* 6:5: "מה הדסה ריחה מתוק וטעמה מר, כך היתה אסתר מתוקה למרדכי ומרה להמן." In Joseph Tabory and Arnon Atzmon, eds., *Midrash Ester Rabah* (Jerusalem: Schechter Institute of Jewish Studies, 2014), 115. The same idea is found in *Midrash Tehillim* and *Midrash Abba Gorion*, both likely written before 1050 CE.

[31] Babylonian Talmud, Megillah, 13a:11.

saved.[32] French poets show the same tendency: Mauchaut's *Le Remede de Fortune*, for example, praises Esther's "umilité."[33]

At other times, however, Esther's ability to embody both meekness and shrewdness, humility and cunning, is embraced in all its complexity. Christine de Pizan recounts Esther's story in her *Book of the City of Ladies* in the context of a section that should by now sound familiar: Christine's dialogue with Rectitude on the merits of female counselors. In Christine's rephrasing of the story, Haman is a "deceitful flatterer" who turns the king against the Jews.[34] Esther's mediation on behalf of the Jews looks at first like the meek self-abasing plea for mercy that Strohm discusses, but Christine makes sure to emphasize that this display is strictly performative:

The queen was so upset by this that she dressed and adorned herself as nobly as she could and went into the garden, accompanied by her ladies as though seeking diversion, at a time when she knew the king would be at his window; and as she was returning, she passed the king's chamber, giving the appearance that this was totally unstudied on her part, and upon seeing the king at the window, she immediately fell to her knees and, completely prostrate on her face, she greeted him. The king, greatly pleased with her humility and viewing with enormous pleasure the magnificent beauty which she radiated, called to her and said that should she ask for anything, she would have it.[35]

[32] Roger and Phyllis Moe, *The ME Prose Translation of Roger d'Argenteuil's Bible en François, ed. from Cleveland Public Library, MS W q 091.92–C 468* (Heidelberg: UWH, 1977), 50.

[33] "Et s'eüsse autretant d'onnour / Comme ot Godefroy de Buillon . . . Et avec ce l'umilité / Qu'Ester ot, et la loiauté / D'Abraham, a verité dire, / Ne peüsse je pas souffire / Pour dame amer de tel affaire" (lines 114–27). See Guillaume de Machaut, "Le Remede de Fortune," in *Guillaume de Machaut: The Complete Poetry and Music*, ed. Uri Smilansky and Domenic Leo, trans. R. Barton Palmer (Kalamazoo: published for TEAMS in association with the University of Rochester by Medieval Institute Publications, Western Michigan University, 2019), 2, https://d.lib.rochester.edu/teams/publication/guillaume-de-machaut-complete-poetry-and-music-volume2 (accessed July 28, 2024).

[34] A "faulx flatteur" in Maureen Cheney Curnow, "The *Livre la Cité des Dames* of Christine de Pisan: A Critical Edition," Ph.D. diss. (Vanderbilt University, 1975), 861.

[35] Translation by Earl Jeffrey Richards. See Christine de Pizan, *The Book of the City of Ladies*, trans. Earl Jeffrey Richards (New York: Persea Books, 1982), 146. The French reads: "De ceste chose fu moult dollente la royne. Si se vesti et para le plus noblement que elle pot et ala, ses femmes avecques elles comme pour soy esbatre, en un jardin ou elle savoit que le roy estoit aux fenestres; et quant vint au retour vers la chambre du roy comme se elle n'y penssast point et elle veist le roy aux fenestres, tantost celle se laissa cheoir a genoulz et, toute estanue sur sa face, le salua. Et le roy, a qui moult plus son humilité et qui a grant plausance regarda la grant biauté dont elle resplandissoit, l'appella et luy dist qu'elle demandast quelconques chose qu'elle vouldroitet elle l'aroit." Cheney Curnow, "The *Livre de la Cité des Dames*," 861–62.

In Christine's account, Esther deliberately performs meekness: she waits for the right time to approach the king and acts out a carefully studied routine as though it was spontaneous. Her double reputation allows her to play both parts at once: she appears to the king as meek, but is shown to the reader as shrewd and tactical.

The same interest in Esther's double act is found in conduct literature, where she is sometimes used as a model for the exemplary behavior of wives. Esther appears twice in the *Book of the Knight of the Tower*, where the author praises her wifely discretion. In Chapter 17 of the *Book*, which is titled "How a good woman ought not to stryue with her husbond," the narrator invokes Esther as he explains the correct way to go about marital strife. Caxton's Middle English translation of the text reads:

> For right so shold a wyse woman do/ by thensample of the wyse quene hester/ wyf of the kyng Assuere/ whiche was moche melancolyque and hasty/ But the good lady answerd not to his yre/ But after when she sawe hym well attempryd/ place/ and tyme/ thenne dyde she what she wold/ And it was grete wysedom of a woman.[36]

The Esther depicted in the *Book of the Knight of the Tower* also wears multiple hats: she is able to perform the role of the meek wife in front of her husband, but the narrator praises her wisdom and cleverness. Wives are encouraged to follow Esther's example and maintain performative behavior that keeps the public-facing hierarchies of the married couple intact, but which does not preclude them from chastising their husbands in the way Justinus dreads. Esther thus becomes a figure who can be cast in a double

[36]Geoffroy de la Tour Landry and William Caxton, *The Book of the Knight of the Tower*, ed. M. Y. Offord, EETS s.s. 2 (London: Oxford University Press, 1971), 35. The French reads: "Cy parle de la bourgoise que se fist ferir par son oultraige: Car tout ainsy le doit faire preude femme à l'exemple de la sage dame la royne Hester, femme du roy Surie, qui moult estoit colorique et hatif; mais sa bonne dame ne lui respondoit riens en son yre; maiz après, quant elle véoit son lieu, elle faisoit tout ce qu'elle vouloit, et c'estoit grant senz de dames." Geoffroy de La Tour Landry, *Le Livre Du Chevalier de La Tour Landry, Pour l'enseignement de Ses Filles. Pub. d'aprés Les Manuscrits de Paris et de Londres*, ed. Anatole de Montaiglon (Paris: P. Jannet, 1854), 41. It is hard to pinpoint exactly which, if any, of the episodes in the Book of Esther these descriptions refer to. The biblical account features Ahasuerus becoming angry with his first wife, Vashti, and perhaps Esther's correct manipulation of her husband's anger was interpreted as a prescriptive account of correct wifely behavior, as opposed to Vashti's. In the biblical story, Esther is prompted several times by Ahasuerus to ask him for anything, and, abiding by storytelling rules, she does not mention the king's order for killing the Jews until the third time she is asked. By then the king is mollified enough to grant Esther whatever she wants.

role, and who can capitalize on her double reputation in order to achieve "what she wold." Despite her manipulative streak, Esther is not blamed by any of these authors. Instead, she is praised as an effective counselor because her goals are noble and aligned with Christian morality: by interceding on behalf of the Jewish people, she will eventually contribute to Christian salvation, even though the way through which she achieves her goals undermined male royal authority, and would be seen as suspect if emulated by any medieval European wife.

The medieval Esther also had a specific skillset that she used for this intercession: she was especially talented at manipulating her husband's body and his mood, and she did this by using basic medical techniques to manipulate his balance of primary qualities. Medieval medical theory, broadly speaking, maintained that a body's balance of primary qualities (i.e., heat, coldness, wetness, and dryness) determined its state of health. Such a balance was unique to every body and was called *complexio*, and since the boundaries between the physiological, the psychological, and the emotional were often seen as porous, one's balance of primary qualities could also determine one's temperament or disposition. A *complexio* could be balanced, or dominated by one of the four humors (choleric, melancholic, sanguine, or phlegmatic). The best way to manipulate one's *complexio* was through the use of the *res non naturales*, or the non-natural things. These are usually six in number and include, in their most ubiquitous form: air, food and drink, sleep and wakefulness, exercise and rest, evacuation and repletion, and the passions of the soul.[37]

The accounts of the Esther story above present Esther's intervention as driven by her accurate reading of her husband's body, and the language used is overtly physical and medical. Christine's Esther knows how to present her beauty and humility before the king in order to bring her husband the kind of "enormous pleasure" that will make him amenable

[37]These six things are "non-natural" because they are extrinsic to the body, while the *res naturales* are intrinsic (these include, for example, humors, spirits, or body parts). For a summary of the non-naturals see Luis García-Ballester, "On the Origin of the 'Six Non-Natural Things' in Galen," in *Galen and Galenism: Theory and Medical Practice from Antiquity to the European Renaissance* (Aldershot: Ashgate, 2002), 105–15; and for a history of the term *complexio* see Danielle Jacquart, "De crasis à complexio: Note sur le vocabulaire du tempérament en latin médiéval," in *Mémoires V: Textes médicaux latins antiques*, ed. Guy Sabbah (Saint-Etienne: Université de Saint-Etienne, 1984), 71–76. For a comprehensive account of the medical and theological writings on the relationship between body and soul, and the question of whether the body can influence the soul, see Naama Cohen-Hanegbi, *Caring for the Living Soul: Emotions, Medicine and Penance in the Late Medieval Mediterranean* (Leiden: Brill, 2017), esp. Chap. 5.

to her request. In the *Book of the Knight of the Tower*, Esther observes Ahasuerus's unbalanced *complexio*, and waits until he is "well attempryd" in order to approach him. The king's anger has roots in humoral imbalance: Caxton's description of Ahasuerus as "moche melancolyque and hasty" [38] (rendered in the original as "colorique et hatif") locates the king's ire in physical imbalance and humoral excess.[39] Esther correctly diagnoses her husband's pathological physical state, and therefore waits to speak to him until he is "well attempryd," meaning both emotionally restrained and humorally balanced. Her knowledge of medicine and her ability to diagnose Ahasuerus's body correctly mean that Esther's counsel can be delivered in an effective and convincing manner, at a time when Ahasuerus is emotionally susceptible to such an intervention.

The biblical account of Esther's intervention emphasizes the careful way in which the queen entices her husband before asking for mercy for her people. She appears in front of him in regalia, and invites him to two consecutive banquets before putting forth her request. When he has been sufficiently wined-and-dined, Esther implores her husband to save her people and to punish Haman (Esther 5–7). The medieval retellings of the story retain the emphasis on the physical manipulation Esther manages to exert over her husband, but they often add details from contemporary medical thought: authors emphasize the physiological effects of Esther's beauty, which she takes care to flaunt before the king; her diagnosis of Ahasuerus's *complexio*; and, as discussed below, the food and drink that alter the king's temperament. Esther's success as a counselor and her knowledge of medicine are thus intertwined within medieval retellings of

[38] "Melancholy" is a term so broadly used that citing one medical definition in an attempt to define it often proves counterproductive. Medieval medical texts used it to indicate different things: it could refer to one's complexional balance or one's complexional predisposition, but also to an illness of the soul or an illness originating in the brain. Within the Greek humoral system, melancholy was, among other usages, used to refer to black bile: a cold and dry substance. For the purposes of this article, I take mention of melancholy in literary works to refer to a medicalized way of describing Ahasuerus's body and disposition.

[39] Melancholy and choler are normally used to refer to different humors. Caxton may have been thinking about "black choler," another name for black bile, when he translated the text. See, for example, Henry Daniel's *Liber uricrisiarum*, where Daniel states that "blak colre & melancolie ar al one." Henry Daniel, *Liber uricrisiarum: A Reading Edition*, ed. E. Ruth Harvey, M. Teresa Tavormina, Sarah Star, Jessica Henderson, and C. E. M. Henderson (Toronto: University of Toronto Press, 2020), 47. The text of the *Book of the Knight of the Tower* in London, British Library, MS Harley 1764, which is dated to the middle of the fifteenth century, has "hote and hasti," which sounds more like yellow bile to me.

the story. Moreover, the medieval Ahasuerus proved to be the perfect foil for such a manipulative queen, and medieval retellings present him as a perfectly amenable patient to Esther's medical interventions.

Hasty King Ahasuerus

The reason Esther manages to counsel her husband effectively is that the king allows himself to be swayed by her rhetorical and medical knowledge. King Ahasuerus is often depicted in medieval retellings as an unstable and fickle ruler, who is easily influenced by food, drink, women, and flatterers. The biblical account depicts King Ahasuerus as quick to anger, especially as he is dining at some of the lavish banquets in the story, and the image of the drunken, feasting, and angry king was happily adopted by medieval readers of the Book, who were interested in the king's pathological *complexio.* While some theological traditions glorified the king's banquet in Esther 1, interpreting the passage as referring to spiritual rather than material wealth and excess, other readers, both Christian and Jewish, were more interested in the physiological effects of the food and drink described in the book. Israel ben Joseph Caslari, a fourteenth-century Jewish physician from Avignon, wrote two adaptations of the Esther story.[40] His poems depict King Ahasuerus as an angry and melancholic ruler, whose excessive consumption of wine renders him emotionally and humorally unstable. In one account the king's banquet is described at length, and the foods served are said to have, alongside their status as delicacies, an explicitly medicinal purpose:

> They served stews
> which came in filled cauldrons;
> beef and mutton came with pepper-sauce,
> With arugula and mustard
> [. . .]
> They ate tarts for their health

[40]Caslari was versed in both medicine and Jewish learning. He is known to historians of medicine as the translator of Arnau de Villanova's *Regimen sanitatis ad inclitum regem Aragonum* into Hebrew (most likely from a Catalan version). His translation of Arnau's *Regimen* was completed in 1327. The Judéo-Provençal poem is likewise dated to 1327, and the Hebrew poem is extant in two early manuscripts: one from Provence dated 1402, and one from Italy dated 1447–55, as well as a few later copies. For more on Caslari and the two Esther poems see Einbinder, "A Proper Diet"; Piudik, "Hybridity"; and Silberstein, "The Provençal Esther Poem"

Just as medicine prescribes.
Finally, he gave them rice with sumac
To calm their stomachs,
[. . .]
besides that he served new wine.
Galen said: "I will have to
get used to water rather than wine."[41]

The entire passage describing the food served at the banquet spans about thirty lines and ends with the medicalized descriptions of the wines served. As the feast comes to an end after seven days, Ahasuerus is found completely unable to control his consumption: "The King was so unable to strive / that he not get himself drunk, / by the end of the week / he was light-headed from the wine; / from it he was truly demented, / he was so completely inebriated."[42]

The king's drunkenness then sets off his immodest request for Queen Vashti to appear in front of him, and when she refuses, his anger is once again described in humoral terms:

The King was filled with melancholy.
He said: "What shall we do with this devil?"
And in his great wrath
He said to all his barons,
"Know ye, barons, by my crown
That I have never met anyone
Who made me so angry."[43]

[41]Originally in Judéo-Provençal, translation from Einbinder, "A Proper Diet," 453–54, which is adapted from Silberstein, "The Provençal Esther Poem," 194–95. Silberstein's critical edition (transcribed into the Roman alphabet) reads: "Ministreren morteirols / Aquels vengron plens pairols / Bueu e mouton venc am prebrada / Amb eruga e am mostarda . . . Mangeron tartas per fizica / Aisi con medicina poblica. / En reedier det ris am sumac / Per confortar lor estomac . . . Mais aiso mes vin novel / Galenus o dis: 'De l'aiga mes / Dal vin escaira que ieu m'ais.'" The Galen quotation is corrupt and thus not fully transcribed. It has not been traced by any of the scholars who have written on the poem.

[42]Translation from Silberstein, "The Provençal Esther Poem," 195. Silberstein's transcription reads: "Tat non se saup estudiar / Que non s'anes enubriar / Lo rei, al cap de la semana / El ac dal vin la testa vana; / En fon erai enrabiat, / Tant fort se fon enibriat."

[43]Translation from Einbinder, "A Proper Diet," 446, with reference to Silberstein, "The Provençal Esther Poem," 197. Silberstein's edition reads: "Lo rei fon plen de malenconi. / Dis: 'Que farem d'aquest demoni?' / E am sa gran felonia / Dis a tota sa baronia: / 'Sapias, barons, per ma corona, / Que ieu non atrobiei mais persona / Que tant me fezes airat.'"

Ahasuerus's "malenconi" is directly linked to his immoderate consumption of food and wine, and Caslari presents him as a medically unstable subject.[44]

Caslari was not the only author who read Ahasuerus's banquet as a medicalized event. The theological commentator Nicholas of Lyra, in his *Postilla super totam bibliam*, explains why Vashti threw a separate banquet for women in Esther 1:

> First, because women are weaker in *complexio* than men, they therefore also have less food and drink. And that is why they used to eat in a more regulated fashion than men. Secondly, because there was a habit among the Persians that the wives of the most noble men did not subject themselves to the looks of other men.[45]

Nicholas of Lyra explains that the banquets in Esther 1 are medically tailored to their participants and connects the discussion to contemporary medical theory, which stated that women's *complexio* was different than men's.[46] In another passage Nicholas discusses the beauty regimen to which the candidates for the position of future queen were subjected, and he is similarly concerned with the king's medical state and its relationship to women's bodies. He explains why the virgins were anointed with oil for six months and perfume for another six:

> These make a woman's flesh attractive by suppressing the bad smells that are in women. All these things were done according to the counsel of the king's

---

Caslari's Hebrew poem is less medical in its description: "חמת המלך בערה בקרבו \ ותפעם רוחו ויתעצב אל לבו" (The king's anger grew in his insides / and his spirit throbbed and his heart grew sad {my translation}).

[44]Einbinder suggests that the king's melancholic complexion may be the result of some of the foods served at the feast (for example beef, venison, and geese), since they were thought not to be suitable for someone who inclines toward a melancholy constitution or complexion but rather to be for a "mean" (i.e., balanced) complexion. Einbinder suggests that Caslari may have been interested in the question of the personalization of regimens of health, an interest that likely emerged from his translation of Arnau de Villanova's *Regimen sanitatis*; Einbinder, "A Proper Diet."

[45]The Latin reads: "Primo quod mulieres sunt debiliores {*or* debilioris} complexionis quam viri, sunt etiam minoris potus et cibi. Et ideo ordinatior comedebant per se quaecum viris. Secundo, quod consuetudo erat apud persas quod coniuges maxime nobilium non dabant se aspectibus aliorum virorum." Nicholas of Lyra, *Postilla super totam bibliam* (Venice: Bonetus Locatellus, 1488), fol. 314r.

[46]Women were thought to have a balance that tended toward the wet and cold, while men tended toward the hot and dry. According to some medical theorists they would therefore require different diets, although very few medical regimens did in fact account for gender differences in a systematic way.

physicians, so that he might find greater pleasure in the women, or at least in some of them, and in this way the ensuing greater pleasure would cast aside the sorrow that has gone before.[47]

The description of the virgins' beauty regimen, which has embarrassed commentators for a few centuries because of its explicit sensual nature, is here attributed to the effect of women's bodies and their smells on Ahasuerus. The king's sorrow is once again medicalized and becomes the subject of medical intervention, while the pleasure Ahasuerus receives from women's bodies is presented as a medical remedy, prescribed by the court physicians. Whatever benefit Ahasuerus gains from meeting Esther, then, is medical as well as sensual.

But as noted above, Esther was not only understood as presenting a passive cure for the king's melancholy, she was an active participant in the manipulation of his physiology and mood. Medieval reimaginings of Esther 7, in which Esther throws an elaborate banquet for the king and his counselor, capitalized on Ahasuerus's reputation to explain how he was able to be manipulated by his wife. The *Middle English Metrical Paraphrase of the Old Testament* describes Esther's banquet in vivid detail:

Þe qweyne was fayn þem forto fyll
with alkyn bestes and fowls fyne,
with spycery to spare or spyll;
And when þe king was glade with wyne,
þe king sayd þen þe qweyn vntyll,
"wyf, aske of me oght þat is myne;
ffor half my kingdom yf þou wyll,
aske yt and yt sal be þine."[48]

The anonymous author describes the minutiae and materiality of the banquet in ways we have seen before, but the effect that the food and wine

[47] "[F]aciunt carnem mulieris suavem et redolentem ad reprimendum fetores qui in mulieribus solent esse. Omnia ista fiebant de consilio medicorum regis ut sic maiorem delectationem inveniret in eis, vel saltem in aliqua earum et sic maior delectatio superveniens dolorem abijceret precedentem." Nicholas of Lyra, *Postilla super totam bibliam*, fol. 314v.

[48] Michael Livingston, ed., *The Middle English Metrical Paraphrase of the Old Testament* (Kalamazoo: published for TEAMS in association with the University of Rochester by Medieval Institute Publications, Western Michigan University, 2011), https://d.lib.rochester.edu/teams/publication/livingston-middle-english-metrical-paraphrase-of-the-old-testament (accessed July 28, 2024), lines 16873–80.

have on the king's disposition now serves an additional purpose: it makes the king amenable to Esther's requests. The relationship between the Persian king and queen has now come full circle: Queen Esther's medical knowledge and her ability to read her husband's humoral state mean she can effectively manipulate him into taking her counsel and advice, while King Ahasuerus's propensity for emotional and material excess makes him vulnerable to such manipulations.

With so much medical language attached to the Book of Esther in the late medieval tradition, it is perhaps not surprising that the Book itself became a source for medical knowledge and understanding. We see an example of this in the work of the thirteenth-century scholastic encyclopedist Bartholomaeus Anglicus, who was clearly interested in the medical properties of Ahasuerus's banquet. He makes several references to the Persian king's feasts in his *De proprietatibus rerum* in order to describe the rules of a good meal. The passage is embedded in Book VI of the encyclopedia, within a section on the preservation of health. Bartholomaeus gives a list of the *res non naturales*, a common feature of medical texts on prevention, and quotes a variety of medical authorities on the matter: Hippocrates, Galen, Avicenna, and Constantine the African all make an appearance, but in Chapter 23, "De cena" ("On the Meal"), Bartholomeus turns to the Book of Esther, rather than to medical writers, in order to talk about what makes a good meal:[49]

> The þridde [thing that enhances the meal] is þe herte and glad chere of hym þat make þe feste; þe sopere is noȝt worthe ȝif þe lord of þe hous is heuycherid, *Hester 1*: *Whanne he wexith hoot, et cetera*. Þe ferþe is many diuers messes, so þat who þat wole not [of] on, taste of anothir, *Hester 1*: [In oþir and oþir. Þe fifþe is diuers wynes and drinkes, *Hester primo*]: *Wyn was ibrouȝt, et cetera.*[50]

[49]The quotations below are taken from John Trevisa's Middle English translation: John Trevisa, *On the Properties of Things: John Trevisa's Translation of Bartholomaeus Anglicus De Proprietatibus Rerum. A Critical Text*, ed. M. C. Seymour (Oxford: Clarendon Press, 1975). Bartholomaeus also quotes the Book of Esther when describing the properties of a good lord in the same book, Chapter 18.

[50]Ibid., 330. The Latin reads: "Tertium est invitantis liberalitas, quo ad vultus hylaritatem, nihil enim valet cena ubi facies hospitis cernitur turbulenta. Hester 1: 'cum incaluisset, etc.' Quartum est ferculorum multiplicitas, ut qui non vult de uno, gustat saltem de alio. Hester 1: 'in alijs et alijs.' Quintum est vinorum et poculorum diversitas, unde in Hester 1 dicitur: 'vinum etiam inferabatur,' etc." The Latin is taken from Bartholomaeus Anglicus, *De proprietatibus rerum* (Lyons: Petrus Ungarus, 1482), n.p., and checked against Bartholomaeus Anglicus, *Liber de proprietatibus rerum* (Strassburg: G. Husner, 1505).

Bartholomaeus connects the food and drink served to the king's emotional disposition and emphasizes the wine's effect on his body. The reference here is to Esther 1:10, which only makes a short mention of the king's disposition. The verse reads: "Now on the seventh day, when the king was merry, and after very much drinking was well warmed with wine . . . ."[51] Amid Bartholomaeus's section on the *res non naturales*, however, it is food and wine's psychosomatic quality that is emphasized. King Ahasuerus is again presented as a medical subject, who is especially susceptible to the effects of wines and medicines. This use of the Book of Esther alongside medical authorities suggests that the Book was mined for its medical knowledge and interpretation of physical reality, as well as theological and topological interest.

The Merchant's Esther

It should come as no surprise that *The Merchant's Tale*, which is so preoccupied with medical language and medical healing, makes use of the Esther motif in order to explore its protagonists' marital dynamics. As I have shown, the Book of Esther was often used by physicians, commentators, and learned authors to learn and think about medicine and medical ideas. *The Merchant's Tale*'s interest in medical encounters and the way in which medical knowledge can be used and abused within the context of marriage thus finds a perfect parallel in the Esther story, which likewise highlights the power dynamics inherent in the gendered medical encounter. The Esther story should therefore be viewed as part of the medical discourse that Chaucer incorporates into his tale. The incorporation of the Esther motif likewise sheds more light on the tale's own staging of the medical encounter between the knight and his young wife.

When May and Januarie are first compared to Esther and Ahasuerus, they are situated within a long tradition of marital dynamics embodied by their biblical predecessors. Like Ahasuerus, the "hastif" Januarie is quick-tempered and excessive in his consumption, and is very susceptible to food, drink, and sexual pleasures. Januarie is clear about his intention

[51]References are to the Douay-Rheims Bible, *The Holy Bible: Douay-Rheims Version, Challoner Revision, the Old and New Testaments* (Cleveland: Duke Classics, 2012). The Vulgate reads: "Itaque die septimo, cum rex esset hilarior, et post nimiam potationem incaluisset mero." A similar phrase occurs in the Latin translation of Esther 7:2 (although not in the Hebrew), where the Vulgate reads: "Dixitque ei rex etiam secunda die, *postquam vino incaluerat*: Quae est petitio tua, Esther, ut detur tibi? et quid vis fieri? etiam si dimidiam partem regni mei petieris, impetrabis" (emphasis mine).

to indulge in pleasure and resist any kind of moderation when he explains why he does not want to marry a wife appropriate for him in age:

> ". . . She shal nat passe twenty yeer, certayn;
> Oold fissh and yong flessh wolde I have fayn.
> Bet is," quod he, "a pyk than a pykerel,
> And bet than old boef is the tendre veel.
> I wol no womman thritty yeer of age;
> It is but bene-straw and greet forage."
> (*MerT*, 1417–22)

The conflation of sexual and culinary pleasures underscores both Januarie's taste for bodily delicacies and his physical susceptibility to women's influence. The comparison of women who are more appropriate for him in age to "bene-straw and greet forage" presents him as unable to follow a physically moderate and healthy regimen. As he attempts to "heat up" his complexional balance with wine and spices, Januarie likewise betrays himself to be vulnerable to physical manipulation. The aged knight is also quick to anger: he dismisses Justinus's concerns about his marital intentions with another food-based comparison: "Straw for thy Senek, and for thy proverbes! / I counte nat a panyer ful of herbes / Of scole-termes" (1567–68).

Similarly, May resembles the medieval Queen Esther in a number of ways. She will turn out to be clever and manipulative, but her husband will be unable to see this side of her and will maintain his belief in her obedience and submissiveness. The narrator carefully crafts this development from the beginning of the tale. May's first attribute, when she is finally introduced, is her inscrutability. The reader is not granted access to May's desires or thoughts. While the narrator is very explicit in his description of Januarie's interiority, May is chiefly described in terms of her appearance. As Januarie is preparing for his wedding night, the narrator takes pains to explain his internal turmoil: "But in his herte he gan hire to manace / That he that nyght in armes wolde hire streyne / Harder than evere Parys dide Eleyne. / But nathelees yet hadde he greet pitee / That thilke nyght offended hire moste he" (1752–55). May, by contrast, is brought to her wedding bed "as stille as stoon" (1818). And although Januarie's advances on the wedding night are described in greatly unfavorable terms, the narrator famously refuses to grant the reader a look inside May's mind at the time: "But lest that precious folk be with me wrooth, / How that he wroghte, I dar nat to yow tell, / Or wheither hire thoughte it paradys or helle" (1962–64).

May's inscrutability endows her with the same type of narrative power we have seen attributed to Esther: because it is difficult to know what she is thinking, she is able to make a distinction between how she appears to the intratextual audience and how she will appear to the reader, and she is able to draw on different topoi of female behavior. When Chaucer compares her to the biblical queen during the wedding, he makes sure to emphasize her external appearance and her "meke look" as he explains that "hire to biholde it semed fayerye." The emphasis is again on what can be observed from the outside. Just like Esther, then, May has a surface and an interior, a sweetness and a potential for bitterness. Like Esther, she is able to juggle both in order to advance her own desires.

May's ability to present as both passive and assertive has been noted by critics before. Holly Crocker, for example, reads May's lack of reaction to her husband's amorous advances as a type of agented and performative passivity, meant to undermine the male fantasy of a hierarchy of masculinities based on men's ability to control women. Crocker argues that May's passivity makes a mockery of the gender fantasies entertained by the male characters in the tale, including the narrator. She points especially to the final interaction between May and Januarie, in which May convinces her husband that her agency in healing his sight is, in fact, another expression of a socially sanctioned feminine passivity.[52] This "double act" also has, as I suggested above, a prominent precedent in the figure of Queen Esther.

Like the biblical queen, May is skilled at both reading and manipulating her husband's *complexio*. She learns how to provoke in her husband the kind of pleasure that will make him amenable to her request. Chaucer makes clear that it is May who generates Januarie's desire to play in the garden:

> . . . er that days eighte
> Were passed [of] the month of [Juyn], bifil
> That Januarie hath caught so greet a wil
> Thrugh egging of his wyf, hym for to pleye
> In his gardyn, and no wight but they tweye.
> (2132–36)

[52] Holly A. Crocker, "Performative Passivity and Fantasies of Masculinity in the Merchant's Tale," *ChauR* 38 (2003): 178–98.

The "wil" that Januarie catches is incited by May, who, like Esther, arranges to meet her husband in his enclosed garden. The young wife, who has hitherto been seen to observe her husband's behavior closely and keenly, is able to use Januarie's propensity for excess and his inability to control himself for her own devices. She does the same thing when she convinces him to let her climb upon the pear tree as she claims to experience pregnancy cravings, and the way in which Januarie's body bends itself to May's will is emphasized in his response: "'Certes,' quod he, 'theron shal be no lak / Might I yow helpen with myn herte blood'" (2346–47). May knows how to manipulate her husband's mood and *complexio*, and by doing this she is able to orchestrate the perfect circumstances for her and Damyan to consummate their love.

When Januarie's eyes are opened and he catches the young lovers in the act, May does not hesitate to use her knowledge of medicine and science and her ability to manipulate her husband in order to talk herself out of the bind. In doing so she embarks on a burlesque reenactment of Esther's intercession before Ahasuerus: the accused wife, with the help of Proserpina, draws upon her biblical predecessor's reputation as a wifely healer and counselor and convinces Januarie that her actions were performed purely for the benefit of his health: "As me was taught, to heele with youre eyen / Was no thing bet, to make yow to see / Than strugle with a man upon a tree. God woot, I dide it in ful good entente" (2372–75). Januarie, who cannot understand the narrator's sarcasm, truly believes that his wife's medical care and her counsel will serve his best interests. He also cannot see past May's "meke look." The old knight, who aspires to be like a king, can easily mistake himself for Ahasuerus and his wife for Esther. But he has failed to see that the biblical queen's meekness is merely performative, and that the ultimate beneficiaries in the biblical story are not the Persian king and his kingdom, but the Jewish queen and the Jewish people. If Januarie believes his wife to be as meek as Esther, he has clearly not understood the full extent of the biblical story.

While Esther's intentions may align with Christian morality in medieval readings of the Book, May's desires are a product of the fabliau universe that she inhabits. In other words, she does not imitate the Persian queen in virtue or motive. Nevertheless, she is able to mimic Esther and convince her husband to trust her as he would trust the biblical heroine. The irony of the final scene comes from the subversion of the lofty biblical story, in which a wife saves her people by pleading with her husband, and its portrayal as the bawdy tale of a cuckolded husband and an adulteress wife.

The way in which Chaucer weaves the Esther story into the Merchant's grumpy tale sheds more light on how the biblical story was read by its medieval readers. Although Esther had a good reputation in Christian readings of the Book, Chaucer's subversion of the story suggests that she nevertheless provoked some anxiety in the medieval imagination. Her ability to counsel her husband effectively and the medical knowledge that allowed her to manipulate his body may have served the greater Christian good, but the same qualities within a young, lusty wife could undermine the patriarchal household and serve more sinful ends. Similarly, although Ahasuerus could be read as a useful idiot for the cause of salvation in the biblical story, in Januarie's "paradys terrestre," the foolish husband who allows himself to be swayed by food, wine, and women only makes himself vulnerable to his wife's adulterous desires.

Conclusions

I have argued that *The Merchant's Tale*'s ironic treatment of the Esther story can be read as indicative of a discomfort with the kinds of power wives can wield over their husbands, and the ways in which both medical knowledge and effective counsel could, in the wrong hands, be misused by trickster wives. To this unease about powerful and deceptive women we can perhaps add another layer: the anxiety about non-Christian social actors and the ways in which they can trick or manipulate Christians. Although the Book of Esther was comfortably integrated into the Christian biblical canon of the fourteenth century, its status as a good Christian story would come to be unsettled and its popularity among Christian readers would soon come to dwindle. Martin Luther's complaint that the Book was "too Jewish" in its nature and too beloved by Jews would be echoed by Protestant readers of the Book into the nineteenth and twentieth centuries, and the story of Esther, Mordecai, and Ahasuerus would come to be associated with early modern Christian notions of Jews and Jewishness.[53] The violent ending of the Book, especially, would give rise to antisemitic rhetoric that would last until the present day. Although the

[53]See Martin Luther, *D. Martin Luthers Werke: Kritische Gesammtausgabe*, Vol. 1, *Tischreden aus der ersten Hälfte der dreiziger Jahre* (Weimar: Hermann Böhlaus, 1912), 208, https://archive.org/details/werketischreden10201luthuoft/page/208/mode/2up (accessed July 28, 2024).

Book is still canonical in both Catholic and Protestant Bibles, its popularity among Christian readers and commentators did not last.[54]

Chaucer's playful use of the Book of Esther, though written at a time in which the Book was still popular among Christian readers, nevertheless seems to reflect some similar interests in the Jewish characteristics of the biblical story. Edward Wheatley, in his analysis of *The Merchant's Tale*, points out that Januarie embodies several antisemitic stereotypes including both his physical and metaphorical blindness, his love of material goods, and his sexual transgressions.[55] May's ability successfully to parody Queen Esther's behavior without the context of correct Christian morality, as well as the presence of the pagan gods at the moment of deception, could likewise be seen as reflecting fears about non-Christian actors and their influence on Christian society. I do not mean to suggest here that any one character in *The Merchant's Tale* should be interpreted as Jewish, but rather that the tale invokes a number of tropes and stereotypes that medieval Christian society would have associated with Jews. In Chaucer's use of the Book of Esther, we can therefore see a soft precursor to the way in which Reformation writers such as Luther would come to read the Book.

Queen Esther was not often used to exemplify antisemitic or antifeminist discourses in the fourteenth century, but in her integration into *The Merchant's Tale* we see that her story was not devoid of conflict, either. The male voices of the tale showcase two different ways of reading the Book of Esther: Januarie knows it as a story about a meek and wise wife who counsels her husband, while the ironic narrator of the encomium implies that it is a story about a trickster, who manipulates her husband through her knowledge of medicine. As we have seen above, the difference lies in how the reader understands Esther's intention: Does she act within the context of Christian morality, which will eventually lead to salvation, or does she act purely out of self-interest, to promote her family and her people? In Chaucer's world, Esther may have acted within the correct moral framework, but May certainly does not.

[54]On Esther's fall from grace in Luther's eyes see Isaac Kalimi, "Martin Luther, the Jews, and Esther: Biblical Interpretation in the Shadow of Judeophobia," *The Journal of Religion* 100 (2020): 42–74. On Luther's legacy see Elliott S. Horowitz, *Reckless Rites: Purim and the Legacy of Jewish Violence* (Princeton, N.J.: Princeton University Press, 2008) esp. introduction and Chapter 1.

[55]See Edward Wheatley, *Stumbling Blocks before the Blind: Medieval Constructions of a Disability* (Ann Arbor: University of Michigan Press, 2010), esp. chaps. 5 and 6. Wheatley also points out that the setting of the tale in Lombardy likewise alludes to the Italians who, in the fourteenth century, had replaced Jews as the main moneylenders in northern Europe.

Corruption, Consumption, and Chaucer's Reenchantment of Craft in *The Canon's Yeoman's Tale*

Adin E. Lears
Virginia Commonwealth University

Abstract

With its emphasis on alchemy's deadening effects on the alchemist's body, *The Canon's Yeoman's Tale* expresses a preoccupation with "the world grown old": the corrupting change of postlapsarian life. Through this topos, the tale raises questions about human labor and about the consumption of materials and bodies as resources. In doing so, it reveals a little-acknowledged ecological perspective in the poem that augments the emphasis on waste emerging in medieval ecocriticism. Scholarship on the tale has persistently emphasized a suspicious or melancholic perspective on the Yeoman's devitalized or wasted body, interpreting it as a warning against the alchemists' misplaced faith or misplaced work. Yet the tale's ecological imaginary also lies in its critique of a form of scientific materialism, dramatized in the Canon's dismissal of his apprentice's "amase[ment]," which cultivates the supremacy of the knower over the known world. More pointedly, its ecocritical perspective is evident in its gesture toward an alternative to such materialism: a form of craft knowledge evident in the Yeoman's lists, redundancies, and asides, through which the artisan could come to an understanding of natural philosophy through a materially poetic engagement with the world. With this gesture, Chaucer's Yeoman offers a reenchantment of craft that endows the Yeoman with a form of subjectivity open to wonder at the mutability and flux of earthly life.

Keywords

craft; vitality; medicine; labor; wonder; alchemy; science; natural philosophy; authorship; ecocriticism

I would like to thank the Cornell Society for the Humanities and the VCU Humanities Research Center for supporting this work at crucial stages of its development. I am grateful to all the colleagues and friends, including Michelle Karnes and the anonymous readers for *SAC*, who offered guidance and encouragement. I also want to acknowledge the creatures around me as I wrote, especially Violet, whose wordless presence sustained me invaluably, and without whom this work would not be. This essay is for her.

Studies in the Age of Chaucer 46 (2024): 37–65

"WHY ARTOW SO DISCOLOURED of thy face?," the Host of the Canterbury pilgrims asks the Yeoman, when he and the Canon have caught up to the travelers near the close of the *Canterbury Tales*.[1] In response, the Yeoman describes his frenzied years of alchemical laboring, "blond[ering] and pour[ing] in the fir" (670) in pursuit of the Philosophers' Stone, all of which has sapped his strength and tarnished his complexion to "a wan and . . . leden hewe" (728). The Yeoman's turn to describe the processes and materials of alchemy and their effects on his body and interior life introduces and ultimately forms the basis of the entire *prima pars* of his tale, a confession of craft secrets. His confession leads directly into the *secunda pars*, a moralized fable of a canon crookedly selling the "secrets" of alchemy to a priest. In the unfolding of *The Yeoman's Prologue* and *Tale* there is a curious conjunction between the Yeoman's vital fluctuations and his self-fabrication through poetry, as if his words in confession and storytelling address the deficiencies of his body and soul.

Such attention to vital fluctuation demonstrates a Chaucerian preoccupation with what James Dean has called "the world grown old": the notion that the Fall of Adam and Eve initiated a conflict between body and soul that sapped the vital forces of the body, making it vulnerable to decay and death.[2] In this context, which accentuated a distinction between pre- and postlapsarian life, the decreasing vitality of the body also bespoke a concern with the problem of an emergent present—one in which the human body, as well as the natural world writ large, existed in a state of ever-progressing corruption and decay. This idea is perhaps most forcefully expressed in Chaucer's short poem *The Former Age*, which exhibits what Andrew Galloway has called "the habits of a fallen mind," lamenting a devolution from an Edenic social and environmental unity into one fractured by greed and "doublenesse" (*Form Age*, 62) with its own irony and

[1]*CYP*, 664, in *The Riverside Chaucer*, gen. ed. Larry D. Benson, 3rd ed. (Oxford: Oxford University Press, 2008). All subsequent references to Chaucer's works will be cited parenthetically in-text from this edition by line number.

[2]James Dean, *The World Grown Old in Later Medieval Literature* (Cambridge, Mass.: Medieval Academy of America, 1997), 1 and throughout. See also Adin E. Lears and Tekla Bude, "Matter and Meaning: Early English New Materialisms," *Exemplaria* 35 (2023): 91–108 (95–99); and Gillian Adler and Paul Strohm, *Alle Thyng Hath Tyme: Time and Medieval Life* (London: Reaktion Books, 2023), 182–88.

linguistic multivalence.[3] Traces of the habits of thought that define the world-grown-old topos appear throughout the *Canterbury Tales* in various guises, as Chaucer's pilgrims express both anxiety and grudging acceptance of the human susceptibility to physical degeneration and death. In *The Knight's Tale*, for example, a vividly extended passage on the physiology of Arcite's wounded body (*KnT*, 2743–56) ultimately prompts Theseus, duke of Athens, to deliver a consolation speech that situates the vulnerability of human bodies within a divine order originating with a "Firste Moevere" (2987) who allots a specific lifespan to all creatures. While the First Mover is "stable . . . and eterne" (3004), all natural things, according to Theseus, exist in a state of "descendynge so til it be corrumpable" (3010). The corruptibility of the human body is more comically presented in gendered terms in the Prologue to *The Monk's Tale*, in which the Host compares the Monk to a "tredefowel" (*MkP*, 1945), or breeding rooster, and laments the loss of the Monk's virility to the chastity required by religious orders. Because the most potent men—"the corn / of tredyng" (1954–55)—are committing themselves to religious orders, the Host suggests, laymen are becoming progressively punier "shrympes" (1955), just as "feeble" trees produce "wretched" offshoots (1956). Though these and other examples differ in purpose and tone, they all bespeak a worldview that defines the human body in terms of its susceptibility to corrupting change and considers Chaucer's medieval present as a precarious world of diminished vitality.

The Canon's Yeoman's Tale both extends these Chaucerian preoccupations and attempts to negotiate them. By illuminating the physically devitalizing effects of alchemy, *The Canon's Yeoman's Tale* raises questions about the consumption of materials and bodies as resources, revealing a little-acknowledged ecological perspective in the poem that augments the emphasis on waste emerging in medieval ecocriticism.[4] Eleanor Johnson argues that *The Canon's Yeoman's Tale* foregrounds a mode of "ecosystemic thought" by accentuating the wasting of the Yeoman's body.[5] Yet the tale's ecocritical perspective also lies in its critique of a form of scientific materialism

[3]Andrew Galloway, "Chaucer's 'Former Age' and the Fourteenth-Century Anthropology of Craft: The Social Logic of a Premodernist Lyric," *ELH* 63 (1996): 535–53 (538).

[4]See, for example, Eleanor Johnson, "The Poetics of Waste: Medieval English Ecocriticism," *PMLA* 127 (2012): 460–76; and more recently Johnson's book-length study *Waste and the Wasters: Poetry and Medieval Ecosystemic Thought in Medieval England* (Chicago: University of Chicago Press, 2023). See also Susan Signe Morrison, *The Literature of Waste: Medieval Ecopoetics and Ethical Matter* (New York: Palgrave, 2015).

[5]Johnson, *Waste and the Wasters*, 102–25.

that cultivates the supremacy of the knower over the known world, and in its gesture toward an alternative: a form of craft practice through which the artisan came to an understanding of natural philosophy through a materially poetic engagement with the world.[6]

Though *The Canon's Yeoman's Tale* was long interpreted as a warning against the corrupting effects of alchemy, more recently scholars have argued for a more positive, or at least ambivalent, valence in the Yeoman's treatment of alchemy, particularly as the social, physical, and linguistic devolution brought about by craft knowledge and practice offered Chaucer a means to articulate new forms of authorial subjectivity.[7] These accounts frame the idea of the author in terms of what Lee Patterson calls "the ideology of individualism—the enabling fiction of modern culture."[8] Here I trace an alternative vision of authorship and subjectivity grounded in physical receptivity and imaginative openness to the wonders and possibilities of the material world.[9] For the Yeoman, the Canon's emphasis on

[6]Pamela Smith locates such artisanship-as-natural philosophy in the naturalism of sixteenth- and seventeenth-century northern European painters, alchemists, and other craftspeople. Ultimately, she identifies such embodied epistemologies as crucial to the development of the Scientific Revolution. See Pamela Smith, *The Body of the Artisan: Art and Experience in the Scientific Revolution* (Chicago: University of Chicago Press, 2004), esp. 17–20. Lisa H. Cooper has detailed how Chaucer probed the overlaps and divergences between material and poetic making; see Lisa H. Cooper, *Artisans and Narrative Craft in Late Medieval England* (Cambridge: Cambridge University Press, 2011), 11–14 and throughout.

[7]Patricia Ingham, for example, argues that the Yeoman's use of alchemical jargon accentuates an overlap between alchemical and poetic invention in ways that anticipate modern conceptions of the author as a subject defined by intellectual ownership of ideas or techniques. Similarly, Nicola Masciandaro locates Fragment VIII within the shifting labor landscape of post-plague England, where medieval thinkers debated the perils and pleasures of "subjective" work: its capacity to shape the worker's sense of individual subjectivity. See Patricia Ingham, *The Medieval New: Ambivalence in an Age of Innovation* (Philadelphia: University of Pennsylvania Press, 2015), 143–66 (163–64). See also Nicola Masciandaro, *The Voice of the Hammer: The Meaning of Work in Middle English Literature* (Notre Dame: University of Notre Dame Press, 2007), 125–44.

[8]Ingham and Masciandaro's readings resonate with Patterson's influential interpretation of the tale, which viewed alchemy as the site of a "modernizing impulse" different from mere scientific materialism in late medieval culture: an urge toward human creation and improvement coupled with a fear of what would be lost with such progress. For Patterson, alchemy offered a means of constructing an identity as a philosopher and intellectual, and provided Chaucer ways to articulate an "awareness of *himself* as a modern poet oriented toward a dynamic future." Lee Patterson, "Perpetual Motion: Alchemy and the Technology of the Self," *SAC* 15 (1993): 25–57 (31 [emphasis original], 56). For another interpretation of *The Canon's Yeoman's Tale* in terms of Chaucer's self-fashioning as an author see Samantha Katz Seal, *Father Chaucer: Generating Authority in the Canterbury Tales* (Oxford: Oxford University Press, 2019), 110–20.

[9]Chaucerians such as Holly Crocker have highlighted Chaucer's preoccupation with other forms of subjectivity that understand the human in terms beyond the individual

"siker[ness]" and intellectual mastery raises questions about the sustainability of alchemical labor, for both the laborer and his materials. Yet while scholars such as Johnson read the tale to be a commentary on wasteful effects of wrongheaded labor, my reading asks if and how the poem offers a means for the Yeoman's healing, illuminating how the Yeoman's poetic creation revivifies his wasting body in a way that amplifies his material enmeshment with the nonhuman world.[10] Thus, the Yeoman finds a way out of the deadening effects of alchemical labor through his own process of creation, which relies on what Mary Carruthers has called the "craft of thought."[11] For the Yeoman, such thoughtcraft is a form of invention through a state of mental suspension—amazement and imaginative forgetfulness—that the contemporary political theorist and critic Jane Bennett might call enchantment.[12] With such enchanted invention the

and self-governing. Though Crocker's account does not explicitly engage with the world-grown-old topos, it emphasizes "vulnerability" and "endurance" as key aspects of the "material virtue" through which late medieval and early modern women exercised ethical action. In doing so, Crocker invites us to ask how medieval thinkers understood the ways that the "fallen" condition—the human body's openness and susceptibility to other matter, for example—might offer a form of strength, even force. *The Canon's Yeoman's Tale*, I argue, is persistently preoccupied with such "fallen" states of being and imagines what might happen if they formed the basis of poetic making. Holly Crocker, *The Matter of Virtue: Women's Ethical Action from Chaucer to Shakespeare* (Philadelphia: University of Pennsylvania Press, 2019), 2–6.

[10]Johnson, *Waste and the Wasters*, 103–6.

[11]Mary Carruthers, *The Craft of Thought: Meditation, Rhetoric, and the Making of Images 400–1200* (Cambridge: Cambridge University Press, 2000).

[12]Jane Bennett, *The Enchantment of Modern Life: Attachments, Crossings, and Ethics* (Princeton: Princeton University Press, 2001), 5–6 and throughout. Since Max Weber's vocation lectures, the idea of modernity has been entangled with notions of disenchantment: "modern" life allows for wonder no longer; such a feeling belongs instead to a superstitious and religious past. Yet Bennett has amplified the forms of enchantment that pervade modern and contemporary life—in human encounters with nature and also, unexpectedly, with technological and bureaucratic processes—and has further shown how to cultivate through such enchantment an ethics of generosity and forms of subjectivity open to matter outside the self. H. Marshall Leicester influentially adapted a Weberian notion of disenchantment as "discursive consciousness" to argue that Chaucer's *Canterbury Tales*, and fourteenth-century western European thought more broadly, evince an awareness of the social construction of ecclesiastic and secular authority, hierarchical social organization, and other matters previously attributed to divine agency and order. Max Weber, *Charisma and Disenchantment: The Vocation Lectures*, ed. Paul Reitter and Chad Wellmon, trans. Damien Searls (New York: NYRB Classics, 2020); H. Marshall Leicester, *The Disenchanted Self: Representing the Subject in the Canterbury Tales* (Berkeley: University of California Press, 1990). In addition to Bennett's, other critiques of Weberian disenchantment and accounts of the survival of enchantment in modern life include Michael Saler, "Modernity and Enchantment: A Historiographic Review," *The American Historical Review* (June 2006); and Joshua T. Landy and Michael Saler, eds., *The Re-Enchantment of the World: Secular Magic in a Rational Age* (Stanford: Stanford University Press, 2009).

Yeoman shifts away from the dogmatic authority that has defined his worldview as an apprentice alchemist toward a poetic and experiential relationship to his materials. This shift in perspective endows him with a form of subjectivity that is open to wonder at the mutability and flux of earthly life.[13]

"Be ye no thing amased": Wonder and Philosophy in the Alchemical Workshop

At the core of Chaucer's ecological imagination in *The Canon's Yeoman's Tale* is the cognitive and physiological experience of wonder, a vexed affective category in medieval natural philosophy. Historians have emphasized how medieval natural philosophers understood wonder as a state that could incite and ultimately be quenched by philosophical inquiry. As Caroline Walker Bynum aptly puts it, the scholastics held that "If philosophers are diligent enough, wonders will cease."[14] This inclination lent itself to a perspective that stressed knowledge of the natural world as a form of command over it. Influenced by an Aristotelian emphasis on cause, the scholastics stressed the dominion of natural order, holding that God created the physical world and the causal principles that moved it, all of which could be learned and known by the natural philosopher.[15]

Yet natural philosophy was not only or exclusively about satisfying wonder with knowledge. Michelle Karnes has detailed how both Arabic and western traditions of natural philosophy emphasized the "ontological uncertainty"of marvels—the objects and processes that produced wonder—understanding them to incite creativity in a hypothetical, speculative mode. Because marvels transgressed conceptual boundaries, resisting easy classification, many natural philosophers acknowledged how they pricked

[13]The closest parallel to the vision of authorial subjectivity in *The Canon's Yeoman's Tale* comes in *The House of Fame*, a poem that at its core seeks to dismantle the voices of literate authorities into a maelstrom of rumor and, with it, sonic and sensory experience. This melee is the basis of what Rebecca Davis has called Chaucer's "fugitive poetics" in *The House of Fame*. For Davis, *The House of Fame* acknowledges poetry's material agency and seeks to accommodate its volatility in stable yet dynamic poetic forms. Rebecca Davis, "Fugitive Poetics in Chaucer's *House of Fame*," *SAC* 37 (2015): 101–32.

[14]Caroline Walker Bynum, *Metamorphosis and Identity* (New York: Zone Books, 2001), 49.

[15]Lorraine Daston and Katharine Park, *Wonders and the Order of Nature 1150–1750* (New York: Zone Books, 1998), 109–33.

the imagination, inciting fuller and deeper investigation.[16] Nature produced wonders—indeed, it *was* a wonder—and for many medieval thinkers, the study of natural wonders through the analytical techniques of philosophy was less concerned with ascertaining truth than with generating imaginative possibilities about the world of nature and humankind alike.[17] Far from accentuating humankind's dominion over the inert matter of the natural world, this perspective on wonder amplified the prodigious force of nature upon human life.[18]

In sum, natural philosophy was ambivalent about wonder. On the one hand, it could incite imaginative speculation on God's creation, provoking an intellectual creativity and abundance predicated on cognitive uncertainty. On the other hand, and particularly in the context of university education, such uncertainty needed to be pinned down. Chaucer draws on both of these perspectives on wonder in *The Canon's Yeoman's Tale*, critiquing a dogmatic insistence on cause and accentuating how imaginative and amazed engagement with nature might be a revivifying force on a devitalized mind.

Chaucer's critique is apparent in the Canon's response to his apprentices' experimentation. At a culminating moment in his confessional account of the alchemical workshop, the Yeoman recalls a failed experiment in which a pot used to heat metals over a fire breaks suddenly and violently. "[G]reet strif" (*CYT*, 931) breaks out in the workroom as the alchemists speculate on the cause of the failed experiment: the straw was not mixed as it should be; the fire was made of undesirable beech wood. Responding to this commotion, the Canon silences their speculation, telling them:

> I am right siker that the pot was crased.
> Be as be may, be ye no thing amased;
> As usage is, lat swepe the floor as swithe,
> Plukke up youre hertes and beeth glad and blithe.
>
> (934–37)

Here, the Canon's dismissal of amazement begins to suggest an attitude toward wonder that viewed it as a preliminary affect in need of resolution through philosophical certainty. This suggestion is not transparent or

[16] Michelle Karnes, *Medieval Marvels and Fictions in the Latin West and Islamic World* (Chicago: University of Chicago Press, 2022), esp. 16.
[17] Ibid., 83–111.
[18] See also Lears and Bude, "Matter and Meaning," 91–95.

straightforward, however. Though wonder and amazement are significantly imbricated in modern English, their overlap was not as well established in Middle English. The *Riverside* glosses this instance of "amased" as "dismayed," following the *Middle English Dictionary*, which offers "stunned," "dazed," "bewildered," or "alarmed/frightened" as definitions.[19] The first attested usage of "amazed" in its modern sense—"filled with wonder, astonishment or great surprise; astounded"—comes in the sixteenth-century historian Edward Hall's royal chronicle of the Lancaster and York families, in which Hall describes a crowd who "wer not a little amased, & marueled muche."[20] Hall's pairing of "amazed" with the verb "marvel" suggests that the word's connotations had begun to shift to accommodate wonder as well as stupefaction and alarm.

The voice of Chaucer's Canon, I suggest, offers an earlier example of this gradual shift in meaning, beginning to move the idea of amazement toward the semantic field of wonder. Crucial to this interpretation is the cardiac physiology invoked in the Canon's command that his apprentices "[p]lukke up {their} hertes," an injunction that chimes with medieval natural philosophy on the *physiology* of wonder, i.e., what happens to the organs and viscera of the body during the experience. The thirteenth-century scholastic Albertus Magnus was the first to articulate wonder as a physiological condition, framing it as an innervated state of effeminate and animalistic precarity. In his commentary on Aristotle's *Metaphysics*, Albert followed Aristotle in defining the drive to understand as a distinctly human attribute, for "all men by nature desire to know."[21] He extended this Aristotelian definition by describing the physiology of wonder, declaring "Now wonder we call an *agonia* and *suspensio* of the heart in insensibility at a great portent apparent to sense, thus so because the heart undergoes a systole."[22]

The twinned terms Albert used to characterize the state of wonder—*agonia* ("suffering") and *suspensio* ("suspension," "hanging")—suggest a condition of physical and cognitive precarity: an experience of vulnerability in which the desire for knowledge was suspended, depriving the wonderer

[19] *MED*, s.v. *amased* (ppl.).

[20] *OED*, s.v. *amazed* (adj.), https://doi.org/10.1093/OED/8054448512 (accessed March 23, 2024).

[21] Albertus Magnus, *Metaphysica*, 1.1.4, ed. Bernard Geyer, in Albertus Magnus, *Opera omnia*, ed. Cologne Institute of Albert the Great (Cologne: Monasterium Westfalorum, 1951–); translation by Marjorie O'Rourke Boyle, "The Wonder of the Heart: Albert the Great on the Origin of Philosophy," *Viator* 2 (2014): 149–72 (149).

[22] Albertus Magnus, *Metaphysica* 1.2.6, trans. Boyle, "The Wonder of the Heart," 150.

of a drive that marked his humanity. This state came to be subtly gendered in Albert's elaboration on wonder's physiological nature as a "systole of the heart." Albert's physiology of wonder was grounded in what Marjorie O'Rourke Boyle calls a "caloric principle of animation" drawn from Aristotle.[23] Aristotelian theories of vitalism located vital spirit in the heart, which heated up the blood and pushed it out to the rest of the body in a cardiac expansion called a *diastole*. As it cooled, the blood was contracted back into the heart in a *systole*. Because medieval medicine generally held that cardiac heat generated a humoral state associated with masculine intelligence, to experience a state of systole-in-wonder was to exist in a state of diminished masculinity.[24] Philosophy offered an antidote to this condition. As Boyle writes, "To philosophize was to attain figuratively the male constitution that for Aristotle was hot, ablaze with the vital spirit . . . to move physically beyond cardiac *systole*, contraction, to cardiac *diastole*, expansion."[25]

Chaucer's Canon echoes this treatment of the physiology of wonder. The Canon's command to "be [not] amased" is, in part, a command to reinvigorate their mental energy, "plukk[ing] up [their] hertes" (937) from the state of cardiac *suspensio* that characterizes wonder. As Boyle shows, throughout his corpus Albert associates *agonia* not only with "suffering" but also with an ignorance of cause that amounted to fear.[26] In Middle English, "to pluck up the heart" was an idiom for summoning courage, suggesting that the Canon's command that the apprentices "[p]lukke up" their hearts is also a command to eliminate fear.[27] The Canon's response to his apprentices' speculation, in other words, may read as an attempt to comfort them in their uncertainty (i.e., "don't be dismayed; the pot was cracked, that's all"). Or, it may be read more grimly as a command to "man up" and replace their wonder with the security of epistemological certainty. Whether we interpret the tone of the Canon's response as kindness or beration, its effect is the same: it shuts down the apprentice's imaginative speculation and asserts the Canon's own authority, secure in his knowledge of cause.

[23]Boyle, "The Wonder of the Heart," 157–62 (157).

[24]Joan Cadden, *The Meanings of Sex Difference in the Middle Ages: Medicine, Science, and Culture* (Cambridge: Cambridge University Press, 1995), 171–73.

[25]Boyle, "The Wonder of the Heart," 171.

[26]Ibid., 152–53.

[27]*MED*, s.v. *plukken* (v.), def. 3.

This self-authorization suggests that the Canon's knowledge of alchemy has come, at least in part, through university education. Through the thirteenth century, as universities and schools were established and the curriculum developed and standardized, medieval scholars increasingly privileged intellectual certainty as a defining feature of the academic discipline of philosophy, relegating the passion of wonder to the role of the student rather than the philosopher.[28] The impulse to reduce wonder within medieval scholasticism had two important effects, which ultimately undergirded a deep epistemological divide between "authority" and "experience." First, the reduction of wonder concentrated authority within a small group of university-educated thinkers. Second, it declared the supremacy of a certain kind of knowledge, as well as a particular doctrinal method for acquiring that knowledge through the institutional authority of established texts and thinkers, namely *doctores* and masters.[29] This wonder-theory established the philosopher as an authority, both among humans and within the natural world, positing that most events inciting wonder had natural explanations that might be deciphered by those with knowledge of the order of the world. This perspective assured the supremacy of the knower over the known world, reinforcing hard distinctions between the subjective knower and the object of knowledge. Such a view of authority was established on the dismissal of other ways of knowing—knowledge from experience, for example—by associating them with marginal figures such as women and children. As Lorraine Daston and Katharine Park remark, "In the medieval scholastic analysis, wonder became a taboo passion: the mark of the ignorant, the non-philosopher, the old woman, the empiric, all of whom were only one step up . . . from animals and children."[30]

Indeed, throughout Chaucer's corpus, it is often women and laypeople who experience wonder and amazement. The Middle English word "amased" and related terms appear rarely in the *Canterbury Tales*, and persistently in the context of feminine suffering. In *The Man of Law's Tale*, Custance tells her Northumbrian rescuer that she was "so mazed in the see," drifting alone in a rudderless boat, "That she forgat hir mynde" (*MLT*, 526–27). In response to the "mervaille" of a divine voice

[28]Daston and Park, *Wonders and the Order of Nature*, 110–20; see also Bynum, *Metamorphosis and Identity*, 48–51.

[29]Daston and Park, *Wonders and the Order of Nature*, 118; see also William Eamon, *Science and the Secrets of Nature: Books of Secrets in Medieval and Early Modern Culture* (Princeton: Princeton University Press, 1994), 53–58.

[30]Daston and Park, *Wonders and the Order of Nature*, 118.

reprimanding the steward's false testimony condemning Custance, the court stands "As mazed folk" (678). And in *The Clerk's Tale*, when Walter reveals his marriage tests, his suffering wife Griselda

> for wonder took of it no keep;
> She herde nat what thyng he to hire seyde;
> She ferde as she had stert out of a sleep,
> Til she out of hire mazednesse abreyde.
> (*ClT*, 1058–61)

These examples emphasize the physio-cognitive experience of amazement, linking it to states of deep embodiment: to forgetting, to unknowing, and to sleep. It is significant that one of the definitions of the verb *masen* includes "stunned, faint, senseless, weak, exhausted," citing the melancholic, insomniac, and arguably emasculated narrator of Chaucer's *Book of the Duchess*, who calls himself a "mased thyng."[31] Chaucer's invocations of amazed wonder, then, hew toward mental suspension without resolution through philosophy.

Up to this point, I have accentuated the Canon's skeptical treatment of the ignorance associated with wonder.[32] Karnes, however, has argued that for Chaucer, medieval wonder was not without the influence of the mind, showing how imagination is a crucial aspect of wonder in *The Squire's Tale*. For Karnes, Chaucer acknowledges a form of mental engagement particular to wonder, thus granting a certain agency to the laypeople who wonder at the mechanical *mirabilia* of the court.[33] *The Canon's Yeoman's Tale*, I argue, is similarly sensitive to forms of bodily and experiential knowledge, critically scrutinizing the academic philosopher's emphasis on rational epistemological security. Instead, the tale amplifies matter as a foundation for poetry, and so proposes an experiential agency for the poet or wordsmith who is open to the material world. Such force emerges from the receptivity of the body, a dynamic that, as Holly Crocker has shown, Chaucer associated with women's experience. Feminine agency and subjectivity emerge in unexpected ways for Chaucer. When Custance and Griselda

[31]*BD*, 12. *MED*, s.v. *masen*, def. 2(c).

[32]See, for example, Scott Lightsey, "Chaucer's Secular Marvels and the Medieval Economy of Wonder," *SAC* 23 (2001): 311–12. For a similar perspective see John Fyler, "Domesticating the Exotic in the *Squire's Tale*," *ELH* 55 (1988): 1–26 (6).

[33]Michelle Karnes, "Wonder, Marvels, and Metaphor in the *Squire's Tale*," *ELH* 82 (2015): 461–90, esp. 469–74.

relinquish themselves to the shifting currents of fate, for example, they both seem to enact a commitment to an idealized form of feminine virtue based in a passivity bereft of interior life. Yet Crocker shows how Chaucer's perspective on feminine virtue was far more complex than this, accentuating how the suffering endurance of Chaucer's Custance and Griselda puts pressure on the idea that virtue is always accomplished by an individual subject. Such endurance, she argues, effectively illuminates how ethical agency does not just come from within but also emerges from *reactions* to external forces stemming from God and humankind alike. For Crocker, Chaucer's accounts of virtuous women have social effects, offering implicit critiques of patriarchal family structures and Christianity's drive toward universal dominion, for example, and presenting alternative visions of feminist ethics in which the suffering protagonists must enter into networks of cooperation and care with entities both human and nonhuman.[34] The Canon's philosophical impulse to establish secure epistemological authority is foundational to Chaucer's critique of alchemy's desperate and fruitless labor.

"Slidynge science": Consumptive Work and the Problem of Alchemical Jargon

In *The Canon's Yeoman's Tale*, the alchemists' pursuit of the Philosophers' Stone is not a process of vitalization through the elimination of wonder and the attainment of philosophical understanding, but the opposite: a gradual and dangerous depletion of the alchemists' vivifying qualities. For Chaucer, the alchemists' endless pursuit of the Philosophers' Stone traps them in a cycle of fruitless scientific inquiry through which a fixation on a specific end only leads back to a preoccupation with cause, in a futile cycle that extends into their opaque language. Patterson has shown how medieval alchemical texts disclose an awareness of the murkiness of their own jargon as each clarifying gloss must in turn be glossed, concealing even as it attempts to reveal. As such, alchemy and its jargon revealed their own failures and so "unwittingly encourag[ed] a certain disenchantment" and became a space of "modern" self-awareness and values, enabling Chaucer to articulate his own subjectivity as a poet.[35] Rather than celebrating Chaucer's modernizing impulse toward individual subjectivity, here I

[34]Crocker, *The Matter of Virtue*, 111–53, 197–250.
[35]Patterson, "Perpetual Motion," 48.

linger on the ways that the Yeoman's devitalization calls attention to the alchemists' enmeshment with matter outside themselves. In expressing this, the Yeoman critiques a model of labor that is unsustainable for both artisans and their materials, and indicts a corresponding language that creates and reinforces the supremacy of the knowing philosopher over all others.

This critique reveals itself in the complex experience of time articulated in the Yeoman's account of alchemical practice. He amplifies the yeoman-alchemists' laborious orientation toward the future as they pursue the production of wealth, declaring:

> He [the Philosophers' Stone] hath ymaad us spenden muchel good,
> For sorwe of which almoost we wexen wood,
> But that good hope crepeth in oure herte,
> Supposynge evere though we sore smerte,
> To be releeved by hym afterward.
> Swich supposing and hope is sharp and hard;
> I warne yow wel, it is to seken evere.
> That future temps hath maad men to dissevere,
> In trust therof, from al that evere they hadde.
>
> (*CYT*, 868–76)

As the Yeoman lays bare the keen cost of hope in the successful creation of the Philosophers' Stone, he emphasizes its material toll in the alchemist's present. Such desperate labor wears down the body so that it "sore smerte" and "dissevere[s]" the alchemical laborer from "al that evere [he] hadde." There is a sensitive slippage between economic and emotional value in this passage. In the Yeoman's assertion that pursuit of the Philosophers' Stone causes the alchemist to "spenden muchel good" he implies that the expense of goods and possessions is a wasted investment in the service of funding an alchemical payout that never yields a return. This formulation also implies an expenditure of the broader interior condition of what is "good" in the alchemist: his spiritual "value" or "virtue."[36] With a similarly multivalent invocation of economic and physical loss, the Yeoman's complaint that the alchemists' orientation toward a future product "dissevere[s]" him from "al that evere [he] hadde" implies the loss of material possessions and accumulated economic wealth in funding the pursuit of the Philosophers'

[36] *MED*, s.v. *god* (n.[2]), def. 1.

Stone. In tandem with this economic loss is a loss of life force evident in the changes that have taken place in the Yeoman's complexion, which, he tells us, has gone from "fressh and reed" to "wan and of a leden hewe" (727–28). The alchemists' pursuit of a complete product has had a corrosive and debilitating effect on their bodies.

Indeed, the Yeoman's descriptions of the alchemical workshop begin to suggest not a positive generativity but an endless cycle of depletion and loss. The alchemists' orientation toward production turns alchemical generation into a repeating process of use and consumption. As we have seen, when the pot breaks, the Canon chalks the entire experiment up to a loss:

> "What," quod my lord, "ther is namoore to done;
> Of thise perils I wol be war eftsoone.
> I am right siker that the pot was crased.
> Be as be may, be ye no thing amased;
> As usage is, lat swepe the floor as swithe,
> Plukke up youre hertes and beeth glad and blithe."
> (932–37)

The Canon's perspective, which seeks to reassert mastery by eliminating amazement, in turn suggests a careless attitude toward the materials of his craft. He commands the apprentices to sweep the floor "as usage is," a term that evokes habit, the repeated performance of an action for the purpose of acquiring skill, even a habit that had the force of law.[37] In response to this command the apprentices turn to cleaning up:

> The mullok on an heep ysweped was,
> And on the floor ycast a canevas,
> And al this mullok in a syve ythrowe,
> And sifted and ypiked many a throwe.
> (938–41)

These lines describe the standard activity of an alchemical workshop: the apprentices sweep up the bits of broken pot, remnants of a failed alchemical experiment, and press them through a sieve, sifting and sorting, as they have on many occasions. Yet the passive grammar of the sentence along with the violent connotations of the verbs places the experimental

[37] *MED*, s.v. *usage*.

materials at the center of attention and accentuates the human force visited upon them. The Middle English *throuen*, for example, was used in martial contexts referring to thrusting a weapon or hurling a missile.[38] Similarly, *piken* often referred to agricultural and infrastructural work, in which earth was dug and broken up for the purpose of planting or building.[39] It could also refer to "seiz[ing]" or "plunder[ing]" in the context of war.[40] These connotations of human force combine with the term "mullok" (938, 940), a rare term that is thought to stem from *molle*, denoting dust, waste, or ash: in other words, the refuse of materials that have been used up. Together, such language calls attention to the ways that rigid obedience to the laws of craft might go hand in hand with an instrumentalist disregard for nature, one that views the material world solely in terms of its capacity as matter for the alchemist's use.

The root of such instrumentalization is a forceful orientation toward the future and an assertion of the Canon's own will over the process of experimentation. His unwavering vision of the experiment's end thwarts its outcome, rendering experimentation into a cyclical process without dynamism or change. Silencing the apprentice alchemists, the Canon declares:

> "Pees! . . . the nexte tyme I wil fonde
> To bryngen oure craft al in another plite,
> And but I do, sires, lat me han the wite.
> Ther was defaute in somewhat, wel I woot."
> (951–54)

As the Canon seeks to bring about a different outcome, his focus is on "the next time" they undertake the experiment. With the assertion that he "*wil* fonde" or "strive," his future tense points to his own will or desire, suggesting a perspective whereby the Canon can bring about an outcome by the sheer force of his own intention. With this persistent orientation to the future, which renders alchemical experimentation into a linear trajectory pointing to a final end, the Canon's emphasis is on shaping the experiment to his own will, not adapting to chance or circumstances.

This ruthless pursuit of the future is, moreover, a specifically masculine endeavor. Samantha Seal demonstrates the impulse toward queer generation at the core of this scene: in the private space of the alchemists' workshop,

[38] *MED*, s.v. *throuen* (v.[1]), defs. 1(b) and (c).
[39] *MED*, s.v. *piken* (v.[1]), def. 1.
[40] *MED*, s.v. *piken* (v.[1]), def. 8.

the men come together in order to bring about an alchemical process that fails, ultimately showing Chaucer's suspicion of such "unnatural" processes of creation.[41] I suggest that we read the Yeoman's descriptions of the masculine space of the workshop not simply as Chaucer's critique of "improper" generation between men but also as an interrogation of a masculine philosophical model of creation more broadly: one that excludes the experiential knowledge that philosophers associated with women and the laity. The homosociality in this scene serves to underscore the ways that the philosopher's approach to creation is dominated by a small group of men. While Chaucer's satirical take on their fruitless labor is suggestive of a suspicion toward erotic generation between men, as I will show in a later section, it ultimately offers a glimpse of an alternative model of creation grounded in a craft knowledge that accentuates the imaginative possibilities embedded in an embodied experience of craft.

Yet at this moment in the text, the Canon's myopic and self-serving will to influence the future leads him counterintuitively back to analyzing the "defaute," or mistake, in the experiment. As the desperate press of "futur temps" (875) makes itself felt in the alchemists' bodies, they are continually returned to an orientation toward cause. As a result, they live simultaneously in the past and the future, seeking to ascertain how to redo the alchemical experiment with the desired result: the creation of the Philosophers' Stone. In this way, the Yeoman dramatizes his characterization of alchemy as a "slidynge science" (732): a self-perpetuating, though static, mechanism of labor whose toll is a loss of physical and spiritual vitality.

Understanding the Canon's "slidynge science" in these terms illuminates the specialized language of the alchemist's craft as a senseless mode of communication that reinforces the knowledge of a select few. The alchemist's circular return to cause from an orientation toward product only produces the ranting of lunacy or, as the Yeoman puts it, "We faille of that which that we wolden have, / And in oure madnesse everemoore we rave" (958–59). *The Canon's Yeoman's Tale* has long been acknowledged as a critique of technical language, largely because of its uses and commentary on alchemical jargon.[42] The Yeoman rails at the speech of philosopher-alchemists, complaining about its "clergial and queynte" (752) terminology and likening it to the "chiter[ing]" of jays (1397). Their speech, like their

[41]Seal, *Father Chaucer*, 110–20.

[42]John Fyler, *Language and the Declining World in Chaucer, Dante, and Jean de Meun* (Cambridge: Cambridge University Press, 2007), 155–79.

alchemical generation, is thwarted, its limited intelligibility serving to concentrate and reinforce the power of a small group of knowers.

With this emphasis on the unintelligibility of the alchemists, the Yeoman comments on the issue of craft secrecy, a practice that was intimately related to authority and ultimately to authorship, among both natural philosophers and craftspeople throughout the Middle Ages. In order to guard the professional secrets of their craft, many artisans developed a specialized vocabulary in order to facilitate the transmission and circulation of craft knowledge among insiders. Karma Lochrie traces this kind of "covert operation" as an example of "men's ways of knowing" in the later Middle Ages, highlighting its presence both in the literature of secrets that formed the basis of natural philosophy and in the discourse of technical secrecy governing craft guilds.[43] While the increasing emphasis on secrecy within guilds may have been partially motivated by economic pressures, it also had the same effect as in the natural philosophical discourse of secrets: as Lochrie writes, "the air of secrecy surrounding craft technologies also increase[d] the value of the material that [was] placed under its veil."[44]

Such secrecy around specialized knowledge produced a range of social, legal, and ultimately literary effects. Describing the rhetorical operations of the *Secret of Secrets* and related texts on natural philosophy attributed to Aristotle, Lochrie sums up how secrecy works "to assert the power of the master's knowledge, exclude the reader, and, at the same time, always defer the text's meaning."[45] The Yeoman criticizes this aspect of alchemy, attributing such inaccessible language to philosophers, whose "termes" are so "myst[y]" that "men kan nat come therby" (1398, 1394–950). To use such jargon establishes a tyrannical power imbalance between the philosopher and everyone else; in John Fyler's view, the philosophers of the Yeoman's account are modeled in part on medieval figurations of the biblical tyrant Nimrod, originator of the Tower of Babel.[46] The Yeoman's contempt for the confounding obscurity of alchemical jargon is consistent with the tale's critique of the masculine philosophical impulse to know cause in order to produce a desired product. For the Yeoman, these impulses exist

[43]Karma Lochrie, *Covert Operations: The Medieval Uses of Secrecy* (Philadelphia: University of Pennsylvania Press, 1999), 98–118. For a book-length study of medieval and early modern craft knowledge as an antecedent to notions of authorship see Pamela Long, *Openness, Secrecy, Authorship: Technical Arts and the Culture of Knowledge from Antiquity to the Renaissance* (Baltimore: Johns Hopkins University Press, 2001).

[44]Lochrie, *Covert Operations*, 107.

[45]Ibid., 106.

[46]Fyler, *Language and the Declining World*, 174–76.

to construct and maintain a form of masculine authority that has a ruinous effect on the objects and people around it, asserting a vital spirit only to expend it in ways that sap the liveliness of the individual and social whole.

But this model is challenged when one of the apprentices addresses the Canon directly, speaking up for a mode of experimentation grounded in chance and transformation. This lone voice of dissent within the workshop draws attention to the present—to the metal that "yet is ther heere." He gestures not to the "nexte tyme," a specific point in the future, but more generally to "another tyme" when the metal they have might transform from "mysshap[en]" to "well" (942–50). The dissenting apprentice's call to put faith in "aventure" (946)—in the forces of fate or chance occurrence—contrasts with the Canon's preoccupation with "sikerness."

With this emphasis on chance, the apprentice effectively acknowledges what Jane Bennett calls the "vibrancy" of the material world: its agency and force on human bodies, minds, and experiences. Drawing from the work of Michel Serres, Bennett describes a way of being based in collaboration between material bodies. She articulates a vibrant ontology that "conforms to [a] strange logic of vortices, spirals, and eddies"; this is a dance between human and environment that reveals "the strange structuralism of vital materiality, a structuralism that includes the aleatory."[47] Chaucer's dissenting apprentice shifts the tale's account of creation away from a linear trajectory of cause and effect toward one grounded in the "spirals" and "eddies" of *aventure*. By seeking to accommodate the contingencies of the material world, the dissenting apprentice invites the other alchemists to focus on the process and experience of making, with all its transformations and flux, rather than on the end product.

For Bennett, the idea of vibrant matter follows from the notion of enchantment. Both emphasize affect: the force of nonhuman matter on the human. But whereas enchantment places focus on the human experiencing the feeling, vibrant matter centers the nonhuman that affects human experience. Chaucer's dissenting Yeoman gestures to the ways Chaucer recognizes the vibrancy of objects and things—an acknowledgment that is also evident in the Yeoman's description of the alchemical burlesque of the workshop: the alchemists struggle to contain the volatile metals that "pierce," "sink," and "leap" about their environment so that the walls of the pot cannot "make hem resistence" against their force

[47] Jane Bennett, *Vibrant Matter: A Political Ecology of Things* (Durham, N.C.: Duke University Press, 2010), 118–19.

(908–17).[48] Yet if the Yeoman's account accentuates how his alchemical education has reinforced an antagonism between human minds and metallic matter, he is also preoccupied with the ways they can work in tandem: with the subtle shifts in embodiment, cognition, and subjectivity brought about through experience in the workshop, and with the ways that such fluctuations could produce modes of enchantment, even within a mind disenchanted by the corruptions of time.

Out of "Kynde": Reenchantment and the Yeoman's Craft of Thought

The dissenting apprentice's model of making-by-*aventure* chimes with the Yeoman's own approach to listing the alchemical materials of the workshop, not in order of "kynde" but, instead, "as they come to mynde" (788–89). For many scholars, the Yeoman's speech, including his lists, underscores the problems of alchemy and of postlapsarian life in general.[49] At best, they convey the extent to which he has become habituated to the obscure technical jargon of his trade.[50] At worst, they suggest a mind disordered by toil and desperation.[51] Yet other scholars have found in the Yeoman's lists a liveliness and skill that belie his devitalization and grim conclusions about the problems of alchemy. For Patricia Ingham, the Yeoman's use of alchemical jargon accentuates an overlap between alchemical and poetic invention in ways that gesture toward a Chaucerian conception of authorship—one that developed in tandem with the first stirrings of the notion of proprietary knowledge in medieval craft guilds.[52] With her emphasis on invention, Ingham privileges the final end of making. Here I draw attention instead to Chaucer's focus on transformation—on flux or flow—rather than invention, accentuating the tale's attention to the process of creation rather than its end result. Ultimately the tale acknowledges transformation as a process of creation as much as corruption.[53] If the

[48]Ingham, *The Medieval New*, 160.

[49]Fyler, *Language and the Declining World*, 155–88.

[50]Stephen A. Barney, "Chaucer's Lists," in *The Wisdom of Poetry: Essays in Early English Literature in Honor of Morton W. Bloomfield*, ed. Larry D. Benson and Siegfried Wenzel (Kalamazoo: Medieval Institute Publications, 1982), 214–16.

[51]Eleanor Johnson, "Chaucer and the Consolation of Prosimetrum" *ChauR* 43 (2009): 455–72 (465). See also Johnson, *Waste and the Wasters*, 113–22.

[52]Ingham, *The Medieval New*, 163–64.

[53]For interpretations emphasizing transformation as corruption see Seal, *Father Chaucer*, 114–15; and Richard Firth Green, "Changing Chaucer," *SAC* 25 (2003): 27–52.

Yeoman highlights the murky obscurity of alchemical jargon as an extension of the alchemists' all-consuming cycle between product and cause, his poetics offer a way out, if only momentarily.

The Yeoman's recalibration of creation emerges explicitly against the authority of the Canon as the Yeoman turns to an extended description of the materials and processes of the alchemical workshop. Here, the Yeoman apologizes for his "lewed" inability to recall the materials of his alchemical recipes in the proper taxonomical order of "kynde." Some have taken the Yeoman's profession of ignorance at face value.[54] In my view, though, the Yeoman's declaration that he will recite out of order signals that he is moving away from a dogmatic relationship to the materials and practices of his craft, which center on secure knowledge and mastery. Instead, he is beginning to embrace a poetic relationship to them, a perspective on making that hews toward imagination and a suspension in present sense experience. By embracing a poetic relationship to his materials, the Yeoman adopts a form of what Pamela Smith calls "vernacular science," that is, craft knowledge as an embodied form of natural philosophy, which she finds among alchemists of sixteenth- and seventeenth-century south Germany.[55] Significantly, however, Chaucer's "vernacular science" is articulated, in part, through a bodily relationship to the *language* of matter as much as to matter's physical manipulation.

Key to this interpretation is the Yeoman's assertion that he cannot "reherce" the words of the Canon exactly. A. J. Minnis accentuates how this term undergirds a Chaucerian theory of authorship grounded in a principle of compilation—in *recitatio* rather than *assertio.* Rather than fashioning himself as an efficient cause of his own writing, as other medieval authors were inclined to do, Chaucer repeatedly reminds readers that he is simply rehearsing or reiterating the material of others. In this way, his theory of authorship is backward-facing, grounded in authority that has already been established. By declaring that he cannot draw from the established authority of the Canon, the Yeoman turns away from the forms of authorship grounded in compilation that Minnis finds throughout Chaucer's body of work.[56]

With its connotations of repetition and recollection, the word *rehersen* is also reminiscent of Mary Carruthers's mnemonic theory of *inventio.*

[54]Fyler, *Language and the Declining World*, 172.

[55]Smith, *The Body of the Artisan*, 26, 129–51.

[56]A. J. Minnis, *Medieval Theory of Authorship*, 2nd ed. (Philadelphia: University of Pennsylvania Press, 1988), 190–210.

Carruthers distinguishes between rote memorization and what she calls the medieval "craft of thought." She draws attention to the ways that memory and forgetting were used creatively in early and high medieval rhetorical traditions, so that poetic invention from the storehouse of memory was paradoxically *enabled* by forgetting. First, a student learned the rules and traditional interpretations and commentary, then the student forgot them in order to enable creative mental play.[57] Carruthers addresses how these ancient rhetorical techniques made their way into monasticism, showing how meditation, informed by rhetoric, became a creative pursuit. Yet, as she notes, such mnemonic techniques were not limited to monasticism but constituted a broader mode of craft knowledge, fundamental to other creative processes and experiences.[58]

In *The Canon's Yeoman's Tale*, the Yeoman's craft knowledge of alchemy—his experience or skill in the processes of the discipline—informs a perspective on poetic creation. The Yeoman employs his craft knowledge in a model of creative forgetting that is emphatically sensual, embodied, and accommodating to the material world. For Carruthers, one mode of creative "forgetting" is that which occurs when "the semantic link between words and images was *suspended*, wholly or in part . . . enabl[ing] someone to hear a word solely as sounds, see an image solely as shapes, or isolate a phrase or image from a conventional context, and thus free herself to make her own intended associations with them."[59]

By slowing the narrative progression of the tale and lingering on a sensuous relationship to his materials through language, the Yeoman's lists of alchemical materials and techniques envelop him in an unfolding present: a way of experiencing time outside the pursuit of product and cause. David Raybin has argued that the *prima pars* of *The Canon's Yeoman's Tale* articulates a "humane artistry" through which Chaucer explores how to create beauty even within the limitations of mortal life. For Raybin, the Yeoman's account betrays a "fascination" with alchemical processes, an "intellectual excitement" that refuses to occupy a space of dispassionate objectivity.[60] Such fascinated excitement is a space of enchantment. Bennett characterizes

[57]Carruthers, *The Craft of Thought*, 29–31.

[58]Ibid., 1–3.

[59]Ibid., 30 (emphasis added).

[60]David Raybin, "'And Pave It Al of Silver and Gold': The Humane Artistry of the *Canon's Yeoman's Tale*," in *Rebels and Rivals: The Congestive Spirit in "The Canterbury Tales,"* ed. Susannah Freer Fein, David Raybin, and Peter C. Braeger (Kalamazoo: Medieval Institute Publications, 1991), 189–212 (197).

enchantment as "a state of wonder" defined in part by "the temporary suspension of chronological time and bodily movement." Building from the aesthetic theory of Philip Fisher, she notes the somatic effects of wonder and enchantment: "Thoughts . . . [and] limbs are brought to rest even as the senses continue to operate, indeed, in high gear."[61] It is worth noting that this contemporary perception of wonder partially diverges from some medieval wonder theory, which often emphasized the stupor or insensibility of wonder.[62] Yet, as Karnes reminds us, the ambiguous cognitive state produced by marvels—they might possibly be true, or they might not—was a "state of suspension" which invited a creative leap.[63] Here, in his treatment of the Yeoman's poetic lists, Chaucer aligns such cognitive quiescence not with insensibility but with physical sensitivity and imaginative attunement. This enchanted and vibrant state of making is grounded in the spark of imagination that emerges from material embodiment and sense experience, resulting in a poetic suspension of narrative progress that amplifies the force matter visits upon the human mind. Here, Chaucer's forgetful Yeoman is, perhaps, a bit like his "mazed" Custance, who "forgat hir mynde" (*MLT*, 526–27), drifting alone at sea. For the Yeoman, such a physio-cognitive state produces a tremendous outpouring of imaginative work.

After apologizing that he cannot recite the ingredients of alchemy in proper taxonomic order, according to the Canon, the Yeoman goes on to recite them anyway "as they come to mynde" (*CYT*, 788):

> As boole armonyak, verdegrees, boras,
> And sondry vessels made of erthe and glas
> Oure urynales and oure descensories,
> Violes, crosletz, and sublymatories,
> Curcurbites and alambikes eek,
> And othere swiche, deere ynough a leek—
> Nat nedeth it for to reherce hem alle—
> Watres rubifying, and boles galle,
> Arsenyk, sal armonyak, and brymstoon;
> And herbes koude I telle eek many oon,
> As egremoyne, valerian, and lunarie,
> And othere swiche, if that me liste tarie;

[61]Bennett, *The Enchantment*, 5.
[62]Boyle, "The Wonder of the Heart," 160.
[63]Karnes, *Medieval Marvels and Fictions*, 25, 112–41.

Oure lampes brennyng bothe nyght and day,
To brynge aboute oure purpos, if we may;
Oure fourneys eek of calcinacioun,
And of waters albificacioun;
Unslekked lym, chalk, and gleyre of an ey,
Poudres diverse, asshes, donge, pisse, and cley,
Cered pokkets, sal peter, vitriole,
And diverse fires maad of wode and cole;
Sal tartre, alkaly, and sal preparat,
And combust materes and coagulat;
Cley maad with hors or mannes heer, and oille
Of tartre, alum glas, berme, wort, and argoille,
Resalgar, and oure materes enbibyng,
And eek of oure materes encorporyng,
And of oure silver citrinacioun,
Oure cementyng and fermentacioun,
Oure yngottes, testes, and many mo.
(790–818)

At this moment, the Yeoman's lists offer a formal means of accommodating the vibrancy of his materials.[64] Here matter moves. Over the course of his recitation, the Yeoman shifts from one category of matter to another: minerals such as "gum ammoniac" and "verdigris"; then vessels such as "violes" and "crosletz," or crucibles; then back again to minerals, to herbs "valerian" and "lunarie; to other organic matter: "asshes, donge, pisse, and cley." By naming materials such as bones, dung, "mannes heer" and piss, the Yeoman includes, in Raybin's words, "not simply the dregs, but . . . also the substance of the human body." Doing so diminishes the distance between the knower and the known world and calls attention to the matter of the human and its entanglement with the physical cosmos.[65]

Indeed, the material body undergirds the very structure of the Yeoman's vibrant catalogue, which is held together not by correct taxonomical organization, but by the sounds of the poetic line, the lilt—alternately fluid and jarring—of stressed and unstressed syllables. Bennett describes the sonorous aspects of enchantment, a term linked to the French verb *chanter*, or "sing," accentuating how the repetition of word sounds has the capacity to turn a meaningful phrase into nonsense and also incite new ideas, points

[64]Davis, "Fugitive Poetics," 103–5.
[65]Raybin, "And Pave It Al of Silver and Gold," 199.

of view, and self-conceptions.[66] Bennett's focus is on the refrain, but her point about the uses of sonic repetition might apply to metrical poetry more broadly. In recounting the materials and techniques of alchemy, the Yeoman not only creates poetry, but also begins to find a new form of labor—one that departs from the deadening pursuit of product and cause that has defined his work for the Canon.

The Yeoman's emphasis on the experience of poetic making offers a new way of conceiving of his subjectivity as well. In its sense of unstoppable momentum, the Yeoman's list offers a form of material abundance, even excess. Johnson calls it "wasting verse," arguing that it is a way Chaucer makes his critique of waste *felt* by readers.[67] Yet in the context of a poem so sensitive to the deadening effects of the pursuit of a creative product, another reading emerges: an emphasis on process and flux. Through his poetic lists, the Yeoman offers an alternative way of being in the world, different from mercantile accumulation. Crucially, the Yeoman's poetic flow is interrupted, revealing its own imperfection, and so grounding the Yeoman within a dynamic process of his own. By integrating hyper-accented lines such as "Arsenyk, sal armonyak, and brymstoon," the Yeoman's lists toggle back and forth between a fluid expression that accentuates the sensuous and material nature of his authorship, and moments of halting or jerky texture. Even when the Yeoman does shift briefly, claiming to recite other alchemical components in accordance with the order he was taught, his poetry remains imperfect. Coupled with his fraught relation to authority, such inconsistencies of meter signal that the Yeoman is in the *process* of making: his poetry is not a polished product, but an ever-emerging form.

"Bigynnen for to glowe": Subjective Transformation and the Yeoman's Lapsarian Poetics

By giving voice to this emerging form, the Yeoman charts a revitalized sense of self grounded in imaginative play as much as work. In Fyler's view, Chaucer's turn to playfulness and pleasure in language is a concession to the cosmic tragedy of the declining world and its dissemination of meaning.[68] But, in my reading, Chaucer's focus on play is far more important

[66]Bennett, *The Enchantment*, 6, 159–74.

[67]Johnson, *Waste and the Wasters*, 118.

[68]R. W. Hanning, "'And countrefete the speche of every man / He koude, whan he sholde telle a tale': Towards a Lapsarian Poetics for *The Canterbury Tales*," *SAC* 21 (1999): 29–58; Fyler, *Language and the Declining World*, 177.

than this formulation implies. For Chaucer, play with language is integral to making a sense of self and world. In sum, the Yeoman offers what R. W. Hanning has called a "lapsarian poetic," glossed by Fyler as "the poetic delight, even revelling, in the centrifugal forces of multiplicity, and the difficulty of reining that multiplicity in, of reducing it to a single, unifying message—in effect of condensing the profusion of words to a single Word."[69] As this description suggests, this material orientation to language embraces its slippery, somatic properties and the insights and pleasure such engagement produces. It also resists a dogmatic insistence on linguistic certainty or the possession of knowledge that follows from such certainty.

In his discussion of Chaucer's "lapsarian poetic" Hanning underscores how much of the socially minded complaint literature and social satire of Chaucer's day had its roots in penitential literature.[70] The doctrine of penance was founded on the idea that individuals reexperience the Fall daily through sin. Confession became a tool for restoring a manner of prelapsarian perfection to humankind. Its efficacy hinged on a perfect alignment among thought, word, and deed: to receive absolution, one must demonstrate truly, through the external signs of words and actions, a full interior feeling of contrition. With its confessional structure and its sense of pressing effort and urgency—nearing the end of the day, the Canon and the Yeoman catch up with the rest of the pilgrims, but barely and with great effort—*The Canon's Yeoman's Tale* is also undergirded by the medieval literature of penance. Yet the Yeoman's confession incorporates personal experience with an exuberant flair for language and story. In other words, his confession moves away from perfect alignment of thought, word, and deed, and toward poetic fabrication.

In his simultaneous impulses toward self-revelation and self-creation, the Yeoman, in his tale, walks a fine line between confession and gossip.[71] Michel Foucault alludes to the unstoppable, self-mining creativity in the act of confession in "the infinite task of extracting from the depths of oneself . . . a truth which the very form of gossip holds out like a shimmering mirage."[72] In Lochrie's terms, confession is "the secret that is dedicated to

[69]Fyler, *Language and the Declining World*, 52.

[70]Hanning, "And countrefete the speche of every man," 40–47.

[71]Susan E. Phillips, "Gossip and (Un)official Writing," in *Middle English: Oxford Twenty-First Century Approaches to Literature*, ed. Paul Strohm (Oxford: Oxford University Press, 2007), 476–90.

[72]Michel Foucault, *History of Sexuality*, Vol. 1, trans. Robert Hurley (New York: Vintage Books, 1990), 59.

speaking its name *ad infinitum*."[73] In the manner of a penitent *and* a gossip, the Yeoman's confession of craft secrets is irrepressible. Yet such an uncontainable flux of language is quite different from the endless multiplication of terms the Yeoman criticizes in the jargon of philosophers. Rather than asserting a secure possession of knowledge, it proceeds with a kind of joy in the sounds and textures of his trade in a way that proposes a mode of being-in-transformation. Rather than focusing attention on the past by examining first cause or fixating on the eventual creation of a future product, the Yeoman occupies an ever unfolding present.

The ontological space opened in the course of the Yeoman's fabulation has both a physically and ethically transformative effect on the Yeoman himself. We have seen how the Yeoman has admitted to the corrupting influence of his labor in the alchemical workshop, in the change in his complexion. As scholars have long acknowledged, the metamorphosis of the Yeoman's complexion from red to lead is the opposite of the desired effects of alchemy, in which a white elixir was transformed into the red elixir, which would purify base metals such as lead into precious metals such as silver or gold.[74] Yet in the midst of his story of a wily canon gulling a naïve priest, the Yeoman inserts a telling aside:

> Evere whan that I speke of his [the Priest's] falshede
> For shame of hym my chekes wexen rede.
> Algates they bigynnen for to glowe,
> For reednesse have I noon, right wel I knowe,
> In my visage[.]
>
> (1094–98)

Speaking of another canon's falsehood again transforms the Yeoman's complexion, this time inflaming his cheeks with the heat of shame. The Yeoman claims that his cheeks "wexen rede," then adjusts his terminology to say they "bigynnen for to glowe," acknowledging that, as he knows well and has already mentioned, "reednesse have I noon." Fyler has read this passage as a joke that reveals a melancholic sense of loss and existence in a fallen world.[75] Yet there is an undeniable sense of linguistic excess in this brief passage—one that, like the Yeoman's lists, calls attention to the physical enmeshment of the human alchemist with his nonhuman

[73]Lochrie, *Covert Operations*, 43.

[74]John Reidy, "Explanatory Notes to *The Canon's Yeoman's Prologue and Tale*," in Benson, *The Riverside Chaucer*, 947.

[75]Fyler, *Language and the Declining World*, 171–72.

materials. The Yeoman replaces his initial descriptor for the external sign of his shame—*reed*—with another—*glowe*—that means virtually the same thing. The Middle English verb *glouen* referred to bright coloration and was specifically used to describe a person inflamed with emotion. It also specifically applied to the transformation occurring in heated metal, so the Yeoman's suggestion that his cheeks "glowe" renders the effects of his tale-telling—his own form of falsehood—like those desired effects of alchemy: his poetic fictions have begun a process of purifying transformation.[76] What seems like a disambiguation that accentuates what the Yeoman has lost—his cheeks glow, they are not red—appears instead to be simply a reiteration of the same physical and emotional reaction in different terms, a poetic pile-on that takes pleasure in the expansion of thought and exploration of affinity between human and nonhuman matter.

At this moment, the Yeoman acknowledges that he himself is in the process of transformation. Something has been lost—his goods and his good, perhaps—through the product-oriented alchemical work he has desperately undertaken. But in language, through the exuberant material slipperiness of words and poetic fictions, it has begun to shift back again. Here, as with his halting meter and imperfect poetic production, the Yeoman's emphasis is on the beginning of a change rather than the end: his cheeks "wexen" red and "bigynnen" to glow. This emphasis on beginnings accentuates the process of transformation, not its end result, a product that can be owned and sold. This is not a superficial change, but instead a transformation that spans the Yeoman's exterior physiology and interior conscience. The Yeoman evokes the religious domain of confession, which measured the efficacy of penitents' confession in their experience of shame, made visible through signs such as a blush. Yet significantly, this change in the Yeoman takes place not in the confessional *prima pars* of his tale, but in the story itself. Thus, though this detail was surely informed by the theological dogma of confession, it cannot be narrowly reduced to its influence.

At the close of his tale, the Yeoman moves away from fabulation and ends on a conservative note, an apparent return to the "sentence" of his own doctrinal teaching. Condemning the mystifying jargon of the philosopher and the fruitless "multiplicacioun" of alchemical labor, he calls for an end to the alchemist's pursuit of the Philosophers' Stone:

[76] *MED*, s.v. *glouen* (v.).

> Thanne conclude I thus, sith that God of hevene
> Ne wil nat that the philosophres nevene
> How that a man shal come unto this stoon,
> I rede, as for the beste, lete it goon.
> For whoso maketh God his adversarie,
> As for to werken any thing in contrarie
> Of his wil, certes, never shal he thryve,
> Thogh that he multiplie terme of his lyve.
> And there a poynte, for ended is my tale.
> God sende every trewe man boot of his bale!
> (1472–81)

The Yeoman's final word is that alchemy is against the will of God and will only lead the alchemist to "multiplie" his pursuit. Yet throughout this passage, the Yeoman strains to rein in his own multiplication of language, stating that he has concluded multiple times in the course of nine lines. Patterson calls the final section of the tale a "closure [that] fails by excess": the Yeoman's inability to conclude reveals a "negative knowledge" by which every attempt to express the truths of nature presents the need for further explanation.[77] For Patterson, such verbal multiplication, punctuated with the Yeoman's declaration that he has found a "poynte," is a testament to his desire to escape his "vibrantly oral performance" through the fixity of script.[78] I have suggested that we need not read failure or a desire to escape in the Yeoman's verbal multiplications, whether they emerge as lists or redundant asides or conclusions. The overall sense of these last lines is conservative: don't bother going against God's will by seeking to know the Philosophers' Stone. Yet the Yeoman's performance as a whole registers a persistent zigzag between this secure dogma and self-fabrication that belies the apparent conclusiveness of his account and suggests a form of subjectivity that continues to shimmer in a state of flux and change. Thus, despite its apparent conservatism, *The Canon's Yeoman's Tale* actually ends with a rejection of "sikerness" and an embrace—however tentative—of the precarity that approximates amazement.

In an influential essay, "The Trouble with Wilderness," which anticipates Bennett's treatment of enchantment in many ways, the environmental historian William Cronon identified the sublime, a category dependent on

[77] Patterson, "Perpetual Motion," 34–35.
[78] Ibid., 35.

wonder, as an aesthetic and cultural construct that has helped to define our understanding of the idea of wilderness. For Cronon, the Romantic sublime imbued nature with an element of the supernatural that inspired awe, making the aesthetic sensations of the sublime into a kind of numinous experience of divine spirit, an attitude ultimately contributing to the "quasi-religious values of modern environmentalism" that seeks to protect the purity of nature in its most pristine forms. Such a fetishistic approach to nature, which places value only in those spaces perceived to be untouched by human artifice, points to a desire to "fl[ee] from history," a habit of thought at the core of Cronon's "trouble" with the idea of wilderness. As Cronon explains, the desire to exist outside history "represents the false hope of an escape from responsibility" and "the fantasy of people who have never themselves had to work the land for a living."[79] It is a paradox that is impossible to realize in actuality, for if the value of nature depends on its distance from human influence, "the only way to save nature is to kill ourselves."[80] The better solution, for Cronon, is to nourish wilderness as a state of mind: to encourage in *cultivated* environments and landscapes the same senses of awe, wonder, and humility that emerge from abandoning rational subjectivity to an experience of sublimity.

I have argued that, in its critique of epistemological security and its embrace of the precarious suspension of amazement and the unruly unfolding of the present, *The Canon's Yeoman's Tale* grounds itself in historical change and dramatizes the pursuit of just such a wilderness of the mind. Though it is emphatically situated in the present, the Yeoman's wilderness of the mind does not seek to exist outside history. Its suspension is slowness, not stasis: an experience of time focused on dynamic change. For the Yeoman, such change is most keenly felt in and through language—in the embodied joys of poetic expression and in the subtle shifts of conscience enacted in such expression, which make possible new ways of being and knowing in relation to other matter.

[79]William Cronon, "The Trouble with Wilderness; or, Getting Back to the Wrong Nature," *Environmental History* 1 (January 1996): 7–28 (16).

[80]Ibid., 19.

Property and Pessimism: The Problem of Land in *The Tale of Gamelyn*

Alexis Kellner Becker
Ithaca College

Abstract

This article argues that the fourteenth-century Middle English outlaw narrative *The Tale of Gamelyn* is a romance against the future. *The Tale of Gamelyn* insists upon both the impossibility of futures and the dangers of future-oriented societies, especially when these futures depend upon landed property. *Gamelyn* begins with a controversy over traditions of primogeniture and partible inheritance, both of which, the poem goes on to show, contravene their intended purpose of ensuring the continued investment of familial social and economic power in land, leading instead to various forms of waste. When the outlawed youngest son Gamelyn flees to the forest and becomes the king of the outlaws, the poem presents a functional, harmonious society, without familial relationships, or property, but this society is predicated on its own ephemerality. Unlike the protagonists of other comparable Middle English romances, Gamelyn does not reproduce. I consider this anti-futurity in conversation with Lee Edelman's conceptualization of "reproductive futurism" in *No Future* (2004). Edelman, however, does not consider the reproduction of property relations. *The Tale of Gamelyn* is a critique of reproductive futurity that focuses on the futility of land as a locus for social reproduction; it surveys a set of possibilities but reveals them all to be hopeless.

Keywords

The Tale of Gamelyn; inheritance; land; Middle English romance; anti-futurity; waste; outlawry; forests

An early version of this essay was presented at the Medieval Insular Romance Conference in Cardiff in 2018, in a session on "Family Geographies" that I organized with Michelle de Groot and Stella Wang. I am grateful to Megan Leitch and Victoria Flood for their patient early feedback, as well as to Masha Raskolnikov, my Ithaca writing group, and the anonymous reviewers and editorial team at *SAC*.

Studies in the Age of Chaucer 46 (2024): 67–96

THE *TALE OF GAMELYN* (c. 1350) makes its way to present-day readers as a codical hitchhiker.[1] It is is available for us to read because of its "fortuitous survival"[2] in twenty-five manuscripts of the *cd* version of the *Canterbury Tales*.[3] *Gamelyn* was reproduced almost despite itself, staking accidental claim to Chaucerian territory in which it did not properly belong. This is fitting because *Gamelyn* is a romance against reproduction; it vitiates the project of long-term survival, especially the long-term survival of property. Within the comedic paradigm of the Middle English romance, *Gamelyn* unties the relationship between land and reproductive futurity.[4]

In its 898 lines, the poem follows youngest son Gamelyn through his disinheritance by his malicious eldest brother, his time as deputy king and then king of the outlaws in the forest, and his violent comeuppance against his brother and the corrupt local representatives of the law. *The Tale of Gamelyn* begins with a knight, Sir John of Boundys, leaving his property to all three of his sons—with particular concern for his youngest, Gamelyn. After Sir John dies, the eldest brother, also named John, tricks Gamelyn out of his lands and takes guardianship of Gamelyn himself; he wastes and mismanages Gamelyn's lands and clothes and feeds him poorly. Once Gamelyn hits puberty, he becomes upset by the state of his lands and confronts John. After winning a wrestling contest, Gamelyn returns home to find that John has locked him out; in response, Gamelyn throws the porter in a well, makes his way in, and holds a week-long feast while John

[1]Stephen Knight and Thomas H. Ohlgren, "The Tale of Gamelyn: Introduction," in *Robin Hood and Other Outlaw Tales*, TEAMS Middle English Texts (1997), https://d.lib.rochester.edu/teams/text/tale-of-gamelyn-introduction (accessed May 8, 2024). Quotations in the text are from this edition, with line numbers provided in parentheses. See also Franklin R. Rogers, "The *Tale of Gamelyn* and the Editing of the *Canterbury Tales*," *JEGP* 58 (January 1959): 49–59.

[2]Nancy Mason Bradbury, "Gamelyn," in *The Encyclopedia of Medieval Literature in Britain*, ed. Siân Echard and Robert Rouse (Hoboken, N.J.: John Wiley and Sons, 2017), 1.

[3]See also Jacob Thaisen, "Gamelyn's Place among the Early Exemplars for Chaucer's *Canterbury Tales*," *Neophilologus* 97 (2013): 395–415; and A. S. G. Edwards, "The *Canterbury Tales* and *Gamelyn*," in *Medieval Latin and Middle English Literature: Essays in Honor of Jill Mann*, ed. Christopher Cannon and Maura Nolan (Woodbridge: Boydell and Brewer, 2011), 76–90.

[4]On romance as comic see James Simpson, *Reform and Cultural Revolution* (Oxford: Oxford University Press, 2002), 257–309.

hides. When the guests finally depart, John tricks Gamelyn into being fettered to a post in the middle of the hall. After two days and two nights, Gamelyn convinces the household spencer, Adam, to free him in exchange for a promise of land. Gamelyn pretends still to be bound as John hosts a feast for a group of "men of holy church." Gamelyn and Adam fetter John and flee to the forest where they encounter and join a group of outlaws whose king Gamelyn eventually becomes. Some of Gamelyn's loyal tenants come to the forest to tell him that John has become the sheriff and declared Gamelyn an outlaw. Gamelyn returns to the court, where his middle brother, Sir Ote, agrees to stand in surety for him. While Gamelyn goes back to the forest, Sheriff John bribes the judge and jury to hang Gamelyn. Gamelyn returns, takes the judge's place, and installs his outlaws as the jury. They sentence the corrupt judge, jurors, and Sheriff John to be hanged. After this, the king pardons the outlaws, makes Ote Justice, and makes Gamelyn Chief Justice of the King's Free Forest. Gamelyn's lands are restored to him, and Ote makes him his heir.

The romance's restoration of order at the end, its corrupt legal officials dead, its outlaws pardoned, and Gamelyn transformed from outlaw king to arbiter of forest law itself, appears initially to be in keeping with the tendency of Middle English romance to usher all disruptive or chaotic forces back within its ambit.[5] Yet the poem's "restoration" of an order that may never have existed, alongside its nearly constant pessimism about the possibility of any kind of lasting order, suggests an orientation toward the future that differs both from most of its peers in Middle English romance and from the Robin Hood oeuvre of outlaw literature.[6] It does not operate along the reformist, "cybernetic" logics that animate many other Middle

[5]See ibid.; James Simpson, "Derek Brewer's Romance," in *Traditions and Innovations in the Study of Medieval English Literature: The Influence of Derek Brewer*, ed. Charlotte Brewer and Barry Windeatt (Cambridge: D. S. Brewer, 2013), 154–72; and Alexis Kellner Becker, "Sustainability Romance: *Havelok the Dane*'s Political Ecology," *NML* 16 (2016): 83–108.

[6]In the 1950s, a debate over the class interests of medieval outlaw literature, in particular that of Robin Hood, took place in the pages of the journal *Past & Present*. *The Tale of Gamelyn* is mentioned as another example of outlaw literature, despite its divergent form. Most readers of *Gamelyn* now seem to agree with J. C. Holt and T. H. Aston that it is a romance of the lesser gentry, but very likely with a mixed audience. This debate is reproduced in R. H. Hilton, ed., *Peasants, Knights and Heretics: Studies in Medieval English Social History* (Cambridge: Cambridge University Press, 1976), 221–72. See also Phillipp R. Schofield's discussion of the exchange in *Peasants and Historians: Debating the Medieval English Peasantry* (Manchester: Manchester University Press, 2016), 225–26. For the relationship between the diffusion of Middle English romance and the *Gest of Robin Hood* see P. R. Coss, "Aspects of Cultural Diffusion in Medieval England: The Early Romances, Local Society and Robin Hood," *Past & Present* 108 (1985): 35–79.

English romances.[7] The order restored at the end of the romance is highly provisional. Gamelyn's reappropriation of unjust systems is futureless. *The Tale of Gamelyn* insists upon both the impossibility of futures and the dangers of future-oriented societies. It does so by critiquing inheritance traditions; offering conflicting ideas of waste and wastefulness; presenting a functional alternative society that is predicated on its own ephemerality; and, finally, having its hero not reproduce. Although Gamelyn and his brother Sir Ote triumph over usurpation and mismanagement, neither, as far as we are aware, has children; land justice and good management stop with them. Inheritance, as Tom Johnson has pointed out, is "deathly" or spectral; property was "understood to pass from one generation to the next in a continuous motion," a motion that depended on both the desires of the dead and the claims of the unborn.[8] *Gamelyn* posits an immense problem with the transfer of generational landed wealth, and then solves it, with a high body count, for exactly one generation.

The best-known academic theorization of anti-futurity is Lee Edelman's *No Future: Queer Theory and the Death Drive* (2004), in which he argues that the political and narrative fixation on reproductive futurity cathects on the figure of "the Child" and makes a case for refusing this orientation toward the future.[9] Edelman's conceptualization of "reproductive futurism," however, does not consider the reproduction of property relations. Among medieval and, indeed, much later elites, inheritance, which entailed anxieties about land, children, power, and mortality, was a locus of textual and legal attention. Eve Salisbury discusses the fourteenth-century relevance of Edelman's "reproductive futurity" in *Chaucer and the Child*.[10] "Considering the allegations leveled against Richard II, the ubiquitous presence of the plague, and a social environment rife with discontent and despair, Edelman's insights, however removed from the fourteenth century by time, provide a means by which we might understand attitudes that tie a pervasive fear of procreative failure to the political *zeitgeist* in England."[11] Salisbury is writing about Chaucer's own attitudes toward the figure of the child and toward reproductive futurity in his writing here.

[7]See Simpson, "Derek Brewer's Romance."

[8]Tom Johnson, "Byland Revisited; or, Spectres of Inheritance," *Journal of Medieval History* 48 (2022): 439–56 (455).

[9]Lee Edelman, *No Future: Queer Theory and the Death Drive* (Durham, N.H.: Duke University Press, 2004).

[10]Eve Salisbury, *Chaucer and the Child* (New York: Palgrave Macmillan, 2017), 14–16.

[11]Ibid., 15.

Gamelyn was likely written well before Richard II's reign, but Salisbury's other observations about the attitudinal tenor of the fourteenth century hold. *The Tale of Gamelyn*, however, is not a narrative that is afraid of procreative failure; rather, it simply posits its possibility and, perhaps, its inevitability.

For a minor gentry landholder like Sir John, children are meant to ensure the continuation of the investments—emotional, laborious, or financial—that he has made in land. Although we are informed of Gamelyn's helplessness during his wardship, by the time we first properly meet him he is stroking his beard. There are no children in the outlaw forest. There are no children in the courtroom. There are no children in Gamelyn's future, and there is no propertied future in Gamelyn's land. *The Tale of Gamelyn* uses its plot of inheritance controversy, usurpation, and outlawry to reveal a deep skepticism about law, family, and social forms.

Gamelyn is often thought of as a genre-mate with *Havelok the Dane*, an earlier Middle English usurpation romance, written in Lincolnshire (*Gamelyn*'s possible place of origin). After Havelok and his wife, Goldeboru, have won back and reunited their usurped kingdoms of Denmark and England (and killed their usurpers), we are told that they had fifteen children, all of whom became kings or queens.[12] Gamelyn, on the other hand, marries near the end of the poem and dies a few lines later. The poem's failure to provide a future is not just initial (the problems of Sir John's property and its inheritance) but total (both Gamelyn and Ote's failure to reproduce).[13] After the violence and labor that go into reappropriating Gamelyn's lands from John, both Gamelyn and Ote's lack of heirs is conspicuous. John is also childless, a fact made explicit when he tricks Gamelyn into believing that he will make Gamelyn his heir. Because he apparently never married, John's execution at the end of the poem leaves no one bereft. In the words of Felicity Riddy, many of the Middle English romances' "plots are derived from the crises and hiatuses of the nuclear family and the lineage."[14] Susan Crane includes *Gamelyn*

[12]For similarities between *Gamelyn* and *Havelok* see Kenneth Eckert, "'He Clothed Him and Fedde Him Evell': Narrative and Thematic 'Vulnerability' in *Gamelyn*," *Medieval and Early Modern English Studies* 23 (2015): 131–46.

[13]In a recent article, Angela Florschuetz shows how the Middle English romance *William of Palerne* is haunted by the fragility of having "one true heir." "Bad Blood: Patrilineal Inheritance and the Body of the Heir in *William of Palerne*," *SAC* 42 (2020), 147–82.

[14]Felicity Riddy, "Middle English Romance: Family, Marriage, Intimacy," in *The Cambridge Companion to Medieval Romance*, ed. Roberta L. Krueger (Cambridge: Cambridge University Press, 2000), 235–52 (235).

among the insular romances that "share the narrative pattern of departure and return, which usually takes the specific form of dispossession and reinstatement."[15] Yet *Gamelyn*, in which the "confidence in the law" expressed in earlier romances "breaks down,"[16] troubles romance's conservatism, in which "landed stability can be threatened but will endure."[17] In the romances, Crane argues, "the idea that children double their parents' lives, by stressing continuity rather than disjunction between generations, validates the principle of land inheritance. Thus the stability won by the hero through his appeals to justice will outlive the hero himself."[18] In many ways, *Gamelyn* does the exact opposite of this. Neither the titular character nor either of his siblings produce heirs; Gamelyn's disruption of the corrupt legal system, rather than winning stability, underscores the fundamental, and continuing, instability of a system perpetually vulnerable to corruption. Not only is the system vulnerable to corruption, the poem shows, but its premises are contradictory, perhaps even incoherent. Yet the poem does not propose an alternative; it is pessimistic rather than radical or even reformist in its outlook.

In *Gamelyn*, family, land, and power are irrevocably at odds; the only harmonious landscape is the forest polity of the outlaws, which, by definition, cannot last. In Marion Turner's discussion of coats of arms as spatial distillations of a family's genealogical history, she claims that "space and time were . . . family matters at their essence."[19] But in *Gamelyn*, neither space nor time can, ultimately, be supported by or remain in the family. The space *outside the law* is presented as an alternative to the problems posed by the elder Sir John's partible threat to the Norman inheritance of primogeniture, the optimal inheritance tradition for consolidation of power. The greenwood is not a societal model with a sustainable future; it is without reproductive capacity (or heritable land), and it requires the continued expulsion of individuals from the law for its continuation. *Gamelyn* only valorizes transient social formations. Laws or processes oriented toward longevity are doomed.

It is tempting, and perhaps correct, to associate *Gamelyn*'s anti-futurity with a thirteenth- and fourteenth-century societal structure in which local

[15]Susan Crane, *Insular Romance: Politics, Faith, and Culture in Anglo-Norman and Middle English Literature* (Berkeley: University of California Press, 1986), 86–87.

[16]Ibid., 54.

[17]Ibid., 88.

[18]Ibid., 89.

[19]Marion Turner, *Chaucer: A European Life* (Princeton: Princeton University Press, 2019), 233.

governance was increasingly prone to corruption.[20] *Gamelyn*'s legal "realism," and its author's apparent legal knowledge, have often been commented upon.[21] This legal specificity contrasts with the poem's temporal and spatial placelessness.[22] The poet is careful not to name the king who appears at the end, the town where Gamelyn's family lives, or the forest to which he flees. This has the effect of placing the poem inside the law (at least, when Gamelyn is inside the law) and outside time. It translates extralocal concerns (the sweep and longevity of power, what land can mean) into a local context, without ever geographically locating that context. John Scattergood calls *Gamelyn* "provincial" in its concerns; it is, indeed, concerned with minor landed gentry and local administration.[23] But unlike, say, the firmly geographically situated *Gest of Robyn Hood*, *Gamelyn* refuses to reveal its province. The temporal and spatial placelessness is striking in light of the poem's resistance to continuity and its pessimism about land's ability to retain its meaning or value. No land in the poem can carry even the amount of meaning that comes with a name. If, in Turner's words, "space and time" are "family matters," *Gamelyn*'s unspecified setting points toward its pessimism about the relationship between family and space.

Inheritance and Its Discontents

By beginning the narrative with a controversial bequest, the *Gamelyn* poet establishes the inherent difficulties of land's futurity. On his deathbed, Sir John of Boundys announces that he would like to divide his land equally among his three sons, with particular instruction not to forget his youngest son, Gamelyn (lines 35–40). We cannot know what the predominant

[20]See particularly T. A. Shippey, "The Tale of Gamelyn: Class Warfare and the Embarrassments of Genre," in *The Spirit of Medieval Popular Romance*, ed. Ad Putter and Jane Gilbert (Abingdon: Routledge, 2000), 78–96.

[21]See especially Richard W. Kaueper, "An Historian's Reading of *The Tale of Gamelyn*," *MÆ* 52 (1983): 51–62; and Edward F. Shannon, "Mediaeval Law in *The Tale of Gamelyn*," *Speculum* 28 (1951): 458–64.

[22]John C. Ford has argued that it takes place earlier than its fourteenth-century composition, possibly the thirteenth century; Dominique Battles, on the other hand, reads the poem as taking place around the time of its composition. John C. Ford, "Land Tenure in *The Tale of Gamelyn*," *MÆ* 89 (2020): 23–49; Dominique Battles, *Cultural Difference and Material Culture in Middle English Romance: Normans and Saxons* (New York: Routledge, 2013).

[23]John Scattergood, "*The Tale of Gamelyn:* Noble Robber as Provincial Hero," in *Readings in Medieval English Romance*, ed. Carol M. Meale (Cambridge: Brewer, 1994), 159–94 (184).

customs of inheritance were—or what the *Gamelyn* author imagined them to be—in the poem's nonspecific setting. Although primogeniture was the predominant inheritance tradition in post-Conquest England—and the inheritance tradition followed, for the most part, by the Crown—inheritance customs in England were relatively diverse. Indeed, the poem's placelessness leaves its reader without a sense of which inheritance model is normative and which outlandish. The poem's dialect is north Midlands, likely the northeast Midlands; Nottinghamshire, Lincolnshire, and Leicestershire have all been suggested as possible homes of its author.[24] Although Kent, with its well-known partible inheritance tradition of *gavelkind*, was too far south,[25] partible inheritance was also common in East Anglia, particularly in Norwich.[26] Sir John's desires might have come off as anachronistically early medieval, as partible inheritance was dominant in pre-Conquest England; alternatively, they might have seemed geopolitically distant, resonant (for instance) of the Welsh custom of *cyfran*. Dominique Battles sees the poem's conflict between coparcenary and primogeniture as a conflict between native, pre-Conquest custom and knowledge and Norman custom and knowledge. Alex Davis locates the primary conflict in the poem as one between the will of a testator and the dominant custom of primogeniture.[27] On the other hand, as Edgar Shannon, among others, has pointed out, Sir John's desire for a partible estate may not have been quite as radical as it appears to readers unfamiliar with the regional variation in medieval English inheritance traditions.[28] However unusual or usual it was, coparcenary offers a relationship to land and power that differs from the Crown's, as it confuses and diffuses how landed power is centralized.

In counsel, Sir John's executors, his knights, land upon a compromise between Sir John's wish for three-way partition and their own investment in primogeniture: the land will be split between the two elder brothers, "and for Gamelyn was yongest he shulde have nought" (44). Sir John demurs and composes an oral will that splits the land among the three sons, dividing these inheritances not by amount but by method of

[24]Knight and Ohlgren, "Introduction."

[25]Interestingly, Franklin R. Rogers has argued persuasively that some of the dialect forms in *Gamelyn* reflect a Kentish copyist. Rogers, "The *Tale of Gamelyn* and the Editing of the *Canterbury Tales*."

[26]Barbara Dodwell, "Holdings and Inheritance in Medieval East Anglia." *The Economic History Review* 20 (1967): 53–66.

[27]See Battles, *Cultural Difference*; and Alex Davis, *Imagining Inheritance from Chaucer to Shakespeare* (Oxford: Oxford University Press, 2020).

[28]Shannon, "Mediaeval Law in *The Tale of Gamelyn*."

acquisition. He leaves his eldest son, John, "plowes five / That was my faders heritage whan he was alyve" (57–58). To his "myddelest sone" he leaves "fyve plowes of londe, / That I halpe forto gete with my right honde" (59–60). And, finally,

> . . . al myn other purchace of londes and ledes
> That I biquethe Gamelyne and alle my good stedes.
> And I biseche you, good men that lawe conne of londe,
> For Gamelynes love that my quest stonde.
>
> (61–64)

This system may well have made more sense to a fourteenth-century minor baron than Sir John's initial plan to divide the lands equally.[29] We do not know whether Sir John was, himself, the eldest of his family; we do know he inherited five plowlands from his father and that these plowlands were his father's own inheritance. He leaves these to his eldest son, making sure that his inheritance from his own father subscribes to the tradition of primogeniture in its bequest, and that John Jr.'s inheritance is unsullied by purchase or work. John C. Ford has recently shown how this inheritance would have been held in fee tail.[30] Thus, Sir John's five acres could not have gone to any but the eldest male heir, and they would have been indivisible.

The middle son, later identified as Sir Ote, gets five plowlands that Sir John "halpe forto gete" with his "right honde." Ote's inheritance is the same amount as his elder brother's, but Sir John acquired it through work rather than the accident of birth. Ford suggests that these plowlands were "earned as a fief by Sir John for military service," either to the king or to a lord.[31] In either case, these lands would have been accompanied by an honor of knighthood, which would have been conferred along with these specific lands. These, too, would have been indivisible. When the knights attempt to override Sir John's original nuncupative will, their program would give the younger John both his father's ancestral inheritance and his military fief/knighthood; Ote would inherit the rest, leaving young Gamelyn landless.

[29]Splitting the lands equally would also have required that his twenty-five plowlands be divided into fractions.

[30]Ford, "Land Tenure," 29.

[31]Ford also suggests the possibility of subinfeudation, if the poem takes place before 1290; ibid.

Regional inheritance customs may illuminate why Sir John's choices were controversial for his executors. Barbara Dodwell has found that, in Norfolk, Suffolk, and parts of Cambridgeshire, where partible inheritance was common, "the custom [of partible inheritance] applied to land held by socage, that is, by a money-rent, but did not apply to military tenures."[32] If *Gamelyn* takes place in one of these East Anglian regions, customs of primogeniture would apply to exactly the portion of land, a military tenure, that Sir John leaves to his middle son. If that is so, this configuration uncustomarily (perhaps illegally) supplants the eldest heir with the middle son. Sir John's method is a reversal of the existing custom that was recorded for the forested manor of Brigstock in Northamptonshire: "the deceased's properties were divided between the elder son, who received all the lands the father had purchased in his life, and the younger son, who claimed the lands that his father had inherited."[33] His elder son, John, receives the lands Sir John inherited; his middle son receives his military fief (and the honor of knighthood); and his youngest son, Gamelyn, is meant to receive all the other lands and tenants he has purchased, as well as all of his good steeds.

Gamelyn's inheritance is larger than either of his brothers'. Ultimogeniture was a rare but existing custom in which the younger son inherited over the elders; it was an infrequent borough or manorial custom (often referred to as "borough English") and was especially unusual among the wealthy or heavily landed. The knights' reaction may have been due their desire to keep wealth undivided, but they may have also worried about Sir John not appropriately performing aristocratic behavior.[34] One of the conventional models for the form of partible transmission that Sir John of Boundys initially desired was inheritance by daughters in the absence of sons. Even where primogeniture was the norm, it did not apply to female heirs; where there were multiple daughters, they inherited equal portions of the property.[35] This might be one element of the knights' horror at Sir

[32]Dodwell, "Holdings and Inheritance," 59.

[33]Judith Bennett, *Women in the English Countryside: Gender and Household in Brigstock before the Plague* (Oxford: Oxford University Press, 1987), 14.

[34]See Richard Britnell, "Social Bonds and Economic Change," in *The Short Oxford History of the British Isles: The Twelftth and Thirteenth Centuries, 1066–c. 1280*, ed. Barbara Harvey (Oxford: Oxford University Press, 2001), 101–13 (124).

[35]For inheritance by daughters see, for example, J. H. Baker, *An Introduction to English Legal History* (Oxford: Oxford University Press, 2007), 267; and Bennett, *Women in the English Countryside*.

John's testamentary decree; it could, in their community, be an upending of gender norms.

While the impossibility of knowing precisely when *The Tale of Gamelyn*'s events are meant to be set—or if they are even meant to be set precisely somewhere—makes it difficult to understand the relationship between Sir John's dying wishes and existing norms, we do know that by the thirteenth century primogeniture was the most common inheritance custom in England.[36] The knights, for whom it seems to be the default inheritance tradition, are concerned with maintaining consolidation of landed power for the eldest son. The possibility of continued and endless subdivision of land reduces, with each generation, the amount of profit any individual can gain from his land. In the view of the knights, it seems, Sir John's commitment to coparcenary is a kind of class traitorism. Sir John's will commits his three sons to being less wealthy than their father was, unless they, like their father, acquire land throughout their lifetimes. The very beginning of *Gamelyn* proposes a chivalric context (a tale "of a doughty knight" [2]) but moves us out of that context: our hero is not a knight, and neither is our villain. The only named knights are the dying (then dead) father whose nuncupative will sets the plot in action, and his middle son, Sir Ote. Both John C. Ford and Geert van Iersel interpret the knights' concerns with John's inheritance as concerns about his knighthood.[37] Van Iersel sees the knights' proposal as a compromise that "historically would have put the two brothers within comfortable reach of the income range associated with knighthood."[38] Thus, there is incentive for John's later appropriation of Gamelyn's land: "without additional land, John cannot retain a position in society which is comparable with that of his father."[39]

[36]Baker, *An Introduction*, 268: "By [Ranulf de] Glanvill's time (c. 1190) knights' fees had ceased to be partible and all went to the firstborn, but land held in socage was still partible if it had been so of old . . . During the next century, primogeniture spread to most free tenures, and enabled great landowners to keep their estates intact, whatever the form of tenure. It nevertheless remained far from universal at the manorial level until 1925." See also Sam Worby, *Law and Kinship in Thirteenth-Century England* (Woodbridge: Boydell and Brewer, 2010).

[37]Ford, "Land Tenure." Sir John's executors are, apparently, a group of local knights, his peers.

[38]Geert van Iersel, "The Twenty-Five Acres of Sir John: *The Tale of Gamelyn* and the Implications of Acreage," in *People and Texts: Relationships in Medieval Literature*, ed. Thea Summerfield and Ken Busby (Amsterdam: Rodopi, 2007), 111–22 (120).

[39]Ibid., 119. See also Alexis Kellner Becker, "Subsistence (Land and Food) in the *Squire's Tale*," in *The Open Access Companion to the "Canterbury Tales,"* ed. Candace Barrington, Brantley L. Bryant, Richard H. Godden, Daniel T. Kline, and Myra Seaman

Ford's argument is similar, although it hinges on land tenure rather than knights' fees. John Jr.'s bad behavior, on which much of the plot of *Gamelyn* hinges, may be motivated by his father's choice to distribute, rather than reproduce, his wealth and social status.

Primogeniture is the method of inheritance that reflects post-Conquest regnal succession. Although the real fourteenth-century context of the poem saw holdings divided in multiple ways, the fantasy of primogeniture promised land that maintained its power over time, centralized in the proprietary rights of the eldest son. It was, then, a fantasy of the nation. Coparcenary, on the other hand, with its constant threat of further morcellation, was not only a tradition more common in Ireland, Wales, and parts of northern and western Scotland than in England—it also resembled the way in which, in those places, power was distributed into what R. R. Davies has called "little worlds."[40] Sir John of Boundys's name—John of the Boundaries or Borders—could suggest that, regardless of its location of composition, the poem might be meant to take place at some kind of borderland. Although the *Gamelyn* author was likely writing in the east Midlands, relatively distant from, say, the Welsh or Scottish border, the poem is carefully nonspecific about its locale, and aside from the ambiguous "Boundys" there are no place names.

"Boundys" could refer to the boundaries of a property—what differentiates, or should differentiate, Gamelyn's share, for example, from John's. And *boundys* are also limits—perhaps the temporal limit that the text ultimately claims for Gamelyn's family's control over any land at all. Nancy Mason Bradbury sees "Boundys" as referring to Sir John's status as a member of the minor gentry: "its apparent denotation, 'of the boundaries' or 'of the borders,' suits Sir John's position at the very margins of medieval elite society."[41] Another possibility for the *boundys* is that they refer to the boundary between forest and arable or pastureland in forested parts of England. This boundary or border, often less than stable in practice, constituted a zone in which those crossing the border experienced a reconfiguration, a translation, of their relationship to the law. The forest reconfigured legal subjects. Assart, forest land that has been converted

(2017), and its bibliography, at https://opencanterburytales.dsl.lsu.edu/sqt1/ (accessed May 8, 2024).

[40]R. R. Davies, *The First English Empire: Power and Identities in the British Isles 1093–1343* (Oxford: Oxford University Press, 2000), 95.

[41]Nancy Mason Bradbury, "Gamelyn," in *Heroes and Anti-Heroes in Medieval Romance*, ed. Neil Cartlidge (Woodbridge: Boydell and Brewer, 2012), 129–44 (131).

into arable, is a translation from one eco-legal mode of being into another; in the late eleventh through the thirteenth century, wastes were afforested, in another act of eco-legal translation. As I will discuss, when Gamelyn eventually enters the outlaw forest, even without the knowledge that he is an outlaw himself, he is immediately incorporated into the outlaws' extra-legal mini-polity.

At the same time, the poem frequently exploits the pun on *bound*: Gamelyn is "bounde" or put "in bonde" by his brother (lines 348, 372, 378, 383, 391, 393, 397, 405, 774); he pretends to be bound after Adam the spencer frees him (433, 435); after their attack on the monks, Gamelyn and Adam are accused of having "boundon and wounded men, ayeinst the kingges pees" (544); when Adam suggests to Gamelyn that they take to the forest he says it will be better to be "there louse than in the toune bounde" (602); and when Sir Ote stands in surety for Gamelyn, he is "in thi stede ibounde" (758, 814).[42] By associating borders or boundaries with restraint or imprisonment, *Gamelyn* points toward the critique of property that will echo in the poem's ultimate pessimism about its future. The poem's only included place name, *Boundys*, possibly refers to a limitation or a *limen*.

Sir John's partible will gives rise to violence, division between family members, and wild misappropriations of power. At the same time, given that the eldest son will be the most proximal cause of these outcomes, as well as, it turns out, a poor manager of land, the poem also asserts a fundamental problem with primogeniture as an inheritance norm. James Simpson has written that "in a society that practices primogeniture, younger brothers will always be an energetic and potentially disruptive social force."[43] Primogeniture has its disruption baked into it, but so, in *Gamelyn*, does coparcenary. Inheritance, we see, is an impossible problem, a "deep strangeness."[44] Sir John of Boundys has managed his estates well, but, even with the legal power of his will, he cannot ensure anything about them for the future.

[42]Knight and Ohlgren point out that the family name appears to be spelled *Bonndes* in the manuscript, "but in line 348 *ybounde* is written in just the same way." *The Tale of Gamelyn*, ed. Stephen Knight and Thomas H. Ohlgren, in *Robin Hood and Other Outlaw Tales*, https://d.lib.rochester.edu/teams/text/tale-of-gamelyn (accessed May 8, 2024), note to line 3. Marybeth Ruether-Wu discusses the multivalent "bounds" at length in her doctoral dissertation "Revel, Reiving, and Outlawry: Regulating the Body Politic in Late Medieval Popular Literature," Ph.D. diss. (Cornell University, 2017), 88–91, in which she associates them with broken bodily boundaries.

[43]Simpson, *Reform and Cultural Revolution*, 276–67.

[44]Johnson, "Byland Revisited," 440.

Mismanagement

Inheritance, which has already been established as a problem, immediately fails to establish the kind of lineal continuity it aims for. As soon as Sir John is in the ground, his eldest son, John, takes over young Gamelyn's inheritance.

Sone the elder brother   giled the yonge knave;
He toke into his honde   his londe and his lede,
And Gamelyne him selven   to clothe and to fede.
He clothed him and fedde him   evell and eke wroth,
And lete his londes forfare   and his houses bothe,
His parkes and his wodes   and did no thing welle;
And sithen he it abought   on his owne felle.
(70–76)

John takes care of Gamelyn inadequately; he clothes and feeds him poorly. Furthermore, and perhaps more importantly, he lets his lands, houses, parks, and woods *forfare*: go to ruin or be *wasted*. It is this waste that makes John's behavior usurpation rather than wardship.[45] Gamelyn's first action, upon coming of age, is to recoil at his brother's mismanagement of Gamelyn's inheritance—not only did he waste, he failed to exploit:

Gamelyne stood on a day   in his brotheres yerde,
And byganne with his hond   to handel his berde;
He thought on his landes   that lay unsowe,
And his fare okes   that doune were ydrawe;
His parkes were broken   and his deer reved;
Of alle his good stedes   noon was hym byleved;
His hous were unhilled   and ful evell dight;
Tho thought Gamelyne   it went not aright.
(181–88)

[45]See Noel James Menuge, *Medieval English Wardship in Romance and Law* (Woodbridge: D. S. Brewer, 2001). At the same time, John is an unusual choice of guardian; in gentry families, wardship of an heir under twenty-one, and their land, would revert to the superior lord; among freeholders, the guardian would be a member of the family, but "not a potential inheritor, likely to harm the child or its interests." See also Nicholas Orme, *Medieval Children* (New Haven: Yale University Press, 2001), 326–28.

His lands are "unsowe," while his oaks have been felled; his parks are unsecured and his deer stolen. And his steeds, which his father had left particularly to him, are gone. His house has been unroofed, and only cursorily repaired, if repaired at all. Gamelyn's response to this waste and disrepair is to think "it went not aright." The usurpation itself is not exactly what is vexing Gamelyn—the poor stewardship is.[46]

The poet clarifies that Gamelyn is in "his brotheres yerde," not on his own usurped property. A *yerde* is a landscaped or managed area: the grounds of an estate, like our contemporary yard, a parcel of a field, or a plot set aside for cultivation or recreation. It consistently refers to a piece of land that has been maintained. From his brother's well-managed yerde he thinks about his own "landes," which "lay unsowe"; as well as his trees, which were cut down; his unsecured parks and his stolen deer; his steeds; his roof. Not only are his lands not being preserved for him; they are going to ruin, leached of their economic and social value from a combination of hostile neglect, overuse, and underuse. And these wasted lands are within close sight of John's own rightfully inherited, well-preserved land.

In a way, Gamelyn's response to the mismanagement of his lands echoes the neighboring knights' response to Sir John's wish for a partible will: both want to see land held, controlled, and treated in a way that generates profit over time. While partibility disrupts the centralization of power in land over time, neglect empties land of its power immediately. Sir John and the younger John's goals seem to be at cross-purposes; the father wants to distribute his lands fairly to the younger generation, while the son is primarily interested in exercising power within his lifetime. But the outcomes are similar: land's future is curtailed.

When Gamelyn expresses his anger at the state of his holdings to his brother, he emphasizes his parks, his deer, his arms, and his steeds:

> By feithe, seide Gamelyne   now me thenketh nede;
> Of al the harmes that I have   I toke never yit hede.
> My parkes bene broken   and my dere reved,

[46]John has behaved like Waster in the fourteenth-century allegorical poem *Winner and Waster*, whose "londes liggen alle ley, his lomes aren solde, / Downn bene his dowfehowses, drye bene his poles; / The devyll wounder one the wele he weldys at home, / Bot hugere and heghe howses and howndes full kene" (lines 234–37). *Wynnere and Wastere and The Parliament of the Thre Ages*, ed. Warren Ginsberg, TEAMS Middle English Texts (1992), https://d.lib.rochester.edu/teams/text/ginsberg-wynnere-and-wastoure-and-the-parlement-of-the-thre-ages-introduction (accessed May 8, 2024). See Scattergood, "*The Tale of Gamelyn*," 188.

Of myn armes ne my stedes   nought is byleved;
Alle that my fader me byquathe   al goth to shame,
And therfor have thou Goddes curs   brother be thi name!
(95–100)

He leaves out specific mention of the unplowed fields, the drawn-down oaks, and his unroofed house, and he focuses on the more knightly, less managerial parts of his holdings: parks rather than fields; and deer, arms, and steeds, associated with leisure or military service, not productivity. He newly adds the detail about his arms. Although his initial despair was largely about land drained of resources, here he reorganizes it into a complaint about social status. In other words, he is emphasizing one form of *norture* over another.

At the beginning of the poem we are told that their father, Sir John, knew "of norture and muchel of game" (4).[47] The word *norture*, much like present-day English "nurture," was used in three distinct senses in the fourteenth century: nourishment or food; the upbringing of a child; and breeding, manners, courtesy, or gentility.[48] When Gamelyn is John's ward, John denies him *norture* (first definition) while publicly questioning his *norture* (third definition).

Despite the care Gamelyn takes to perform noble priorities in his complaint, John replies:

Stond stille, gadlynge   and holde thi pees;
Thou shalt be fayn to have   thi mete and thi wede;
What spekest thow, gadelinge   of londe or of lede?
(101–3)

We can see why, when speaking to John, Gamelyn did not prioritize food or shelter. We see John's defense: why worry about food and shelter? John

[47]For a reading of the "game" in *Gamelyn* see Alex Davis, "'Game' in *The Tale of Gamelyn*," *MÆ* 85 (2016): 97–117.

[48]See *MED*, s.v. *norture* (n.), defs 1, 2(a), 3(a). London, British Library, MS Harley 7334 uniquely provides the word "ynough" after "norture." In that version of the poem, the word "ynough" introduces an ambiguity: it might simply mean the same thing as *muchel*, putting "norture" and "game," both being sites of Sir John's great knowledge, in apposition. On the other hand, it also had the same meaning as present-day English "enough": adequate, sufficient. Here, then, "norture" and "game" could be in contrast: Sir John knew *enough* about nurture to get by raising three sons, while he knew a great deal about *game*. Gamelyn has been poorly fed, even as he is put to work providing nourishment for John's household. When he complains to John, he emphasizes "game" over "norture."

provides him with those (although not, as the poem makes clear, very well). As a "gadlyng," a person of low or perhaps illegitimate birth, Gamelyn, John claims, has no standing to speak "of londe or of lede," of landed and tenanted property.[49] John makes the issue one of class or of *norture* in its third definition, even though Gamelyn had already tried to circumvent this with his performed knowledge of aristocratic priorities.

Gamelyn responds that he is "no wors gadeling ne no worse wight, / But born of a lady and gete of a knyght": *I am no worse a gadlyng, no worse a guy, than you are.* Gamelyn is explicitly defending his social status: his parents, like John's, were a lady and a knight (although, as he does not specify *which* lady and *which* knight, he has not necessarily asserted his legitimacy). A "bastard" cannot inherit,[50] so John attempts to reframe Gamelyn as a presumptuous upstart rather than his ward, since "Magna Carta forbade guardians to commit waste in their wards' lands."[51] In John C. Ford's reading of the central conflict of the poem, what Sir John's executor-knights wanted was for both John's plot and Ote's (knighthood-conferring) plot to be left to John, leaving the plot that went to Gamelyn (which John has now usurped) to Ote, and leaving Gamelyn with nothing.[52] Their father's prioritization of Gamelyn, then, is the reason for John's lack of knightly status; if Gamelyn had no inheritance, the younger John would also be Sir John by merit of his inheritance. But taking Gamelyn's lands, treating Gamelyn poorly, or even attempting to demote Gamelyn socially cannot solve this problem for John. Gamelyn's land cannot confer knighthood, since it was purchased rather than granted; only Sir Ote's can (and does, for Ote). Gamelyn's land produces meaning and power incorrectly. As Ote seems to be an adult by the time his father dies, his land would be significantly more difficult to usurp; there would be no guise of wardship under which to do so. Instead, John's usurpation is wasteful and impotent.

The prohibitions of land waste initiated in the thirteenth century, beginning with Magna Carta, expressly forbade what John has done here.[53]

[49]"Lede" comes from the old English *leode*, people or citizens, so the implication of the idiomatic "londe and lede" is tenanted land. Someone with "londe and lede" is a manorial lord. See *MED*, s.v. *lede* (n.[2]).

[50]Frederick Pollock and Frederic William Maitland, *The History of English Law before the Time of Edward I* (Cambridge: Cambridge University Press, 1968), 2:397–98.

[51]Baker, *An Introduction*, 240.

[52]Ford, "Land Tenure."

[53]Eleanor Johnson, "The Poetics of Waste: Medieval English Ecocriticism," *PMLA* 127 (2012): 460–76 (462).

The 1278 Statute of Gloucester clarified that overuse of land by any temporary holder was waste. Waste law, in Eleanor Johnson's words, is "designed to keep arable land viable and available for future generations at a broad scale."[54] Land inheritance customs are designed to do this at a smaller, local, familial scale, but these two legal traditions butt up against one another in surprising ways in *Gamelyn*.

In response to John's mistreatment of his lands, Gamelyn exacts a revenge that stages a debate between the two of them about waste. After he returns from winning a wrestling competition to find himself locked out (and after killing the porter and throwing him in a well), Gamelyn's eventual revenge is to perform a caricature of gentility by inviting absolutely everyone to a week-long feast at his brother's house:

> He lete inne alle that gone wolde or ride,
> And seide, "Ye be welcome without eny greve,
> For we wil be maisters here and axe no man leve.
> Yusterday I lefte," seide yonge Gamelyne,
> "In my brothers seler fyve tonne of wyne;
> I wil not this company partyn atwynne,
> And ye wil done after me while sope is therinne."
> (310–16)

"We wil spende largely," he says, "that he hath spared yore" (322).[55] If John's neglect permanently ruined Gamelyn's fields, John owes him monetary recompense. Young Gamelyn knows the law here, as he will know the processes of juridical law later in the poem. In keeping with Gamelyn's penchant for extra-legal violence, anyone who complains will join the porter in the well. John lies hidden in a turret during this, "and see him waast his good, and dorst no worde speke" (328). This moment sets up a contrast between John and Gamelyn's ideas about what it means to waste. For John, food fed to the public is wasted. For Gamelyn, food never grown is.

John asks "who made the so bold for to stroien the stoor of myn household?" (352–53). Gamelyn explains that the feast was paid for by the land John usurped (353–60). At this point, he does mention the fifteen plowlands and the beasts bred from those Sir John bequeathed to him, which

[54]Ibid.

[55]For more on feasts in *Gamelyn* see Renée Ward, "The Social Contracts of 'Mete and Drink' in *The Tale of Gamelyn*," in *Food and Feast in Premodern Outlaw Tales*, ed. Melissa Ridley Elmes and Kristen Boivard-Abbo (Abingdon: Routledge, 2021), 30–54.

he omitted from his initial outburst at John; they either have generated profit or ought to have generated profit that Gamelyn has now spent on the feast. If John had been cultivating his land and breeding his animals appropriately, the substance of the feast would not have been a loss to him; if it is a loss to him, as it clearly is, then he is guilty of waste.

These conflicting notions of "waste" are especially striking in light of the brothers' earlier argument about status. If Gamelyn's claim to the land were illegitimate, as John tries to claim, John would not be legally guilty of land waste. As if to prove his legitimate status and his right to his own resources, Gamelyn responds with an over-the-top performance of conviviality and hospitality that matches his absent deer, steeds, and arms, but which John interprets as waste. From John's perspective, Gamelyn's feast is both waste and theft; from Gamelyn's perspective, it generated food, sociality, and meaning. Both of these contradictory meanings of waste leave nothing for the future.

Greenwood

After a spree of anti-ecclesiastical violence during another feast, Gamelyn and his new ally Adam the Spencer run away to the forest. In this space outside of the law, Gamelyn and Adam join the outlaw community, where conflicts over property do not exist because landed property does not exist. Eventually, upon the current outlaw king's return to the inside of the law, Gamelyn becomes the king of the outlaws.

After the poem's focus on property, its ownership, its treatment, and its productivity, the change of location is striking. The medieval forest, as Jacques Le Goff and Corinne Saunders have argued, was ambiguous, requiring "multiple perspectives," and marginal.[56] The forest of *Gamelyn* is a conceptual and geophysical periphery; the real English forest was also a territory of particular centralized legal focus. In both outlaw literature and real life, the forest was often conceptualized as a space outside the law where the king, according to Richard fitz Nigel, leaves behind "the

[56]See Jacques Le Goff, *The Medieval Imagination*, trans. Arthur Goldhammer (Chicago: University of Chicago Press, 1988), 52–56; and Corinne Saunders, "Margins," in *A Handbook of Middle English Studies*, ed. Marion Turner (Chichester: Wiley-Blackwell, 2013), 332–33. See also Lesley Coote, "Journeys to the Edge: Self-Identity, Salvation, and Outlaw(ed) Space," in *Robin Hood in Greenwood Stood: Alterity and Context in the English Outlaw Tradition*, ed. Stephen Knight (Turnhout: Brepols, 2011), 47–66, for a reading of the greenwood as "margin" in the sense of medieval manuscript margin.

jurisdiction of other courts of the realm,"[57] even as, in Barbara Hanawalt's words, "royal foresters were England's first contact with a policing force that had a regular beat and made regular rounds."[58] The forest is a liminal space, outside the bounds of normal property law but also hyper-legislated. In the quest narratives of Arthurian romance, the forest is marginal to quotidian political life; it is the landscape of chivalric adventure. In romance, "the forest comes to function not just as a negative setting or darkly resonant symbol, but in a far more complex manner, as the focus of narrative resolution, and hence as a landscape which may be essential to the progression and construction of the narrative."[59] The forest of *Gamelyn* is, rather than "the focus of narrative resolution," an alternative model of society that rejects narrative's forward projection into the future. Among the outlaws in the forest, Gamelyn and Adam find a harmonious society, without property, heirs, or families. The forest is the only location in *Gamelyn* where no violence occurs. The outlaw society is also predicated on its own lack of a future: despite the social harmony and apparent abundance of the forest, the outlaws wish to be pardoned and to return to society, to return to the inside of the law.

Gamelyn and Adam enter the forest with the generic expectations of romance. Adam is apprehensive, even though it was his idea to flee to the forest in the first place. He fears, it seems, that they have entered the forest of romance, "a place of mystery, fear, or danger," or "destiny, wonder and *aventure*."[60]

> Gamelyn into the wode stalked stille,
> And Adam Spensere liked right ille;
> Adam swore to Gamelyn, "By Seint Richere,
> Now I see it is mery to be a spencere,
> Yit lever me were kayes to bere
> Than walken in this wilde wode my clothes to tere."
> (612–17)

[57]Karl Steel, "Biopolitics in the Forest," in *The Politics of Ecology: Land, Life, and Law in Medieval Britain*, ed. Randy P. Schiff and Joseph Taylor (Columbus: The Ohio State University Press, 2016): 33–55 (33); and Barbara A. Hanawalt, "Men's Games, King's Deer: Poaching in Medieval England," *Journal of Medieval and Renaissance Studies* 18 (1988): 175–93 (176).

[58]Steel, "Biopolitics," 48.

[59]Corinne Saunders, *The Forest of Medieval Romance: Avernus, Broceliande, Arden* (Woodbridge: D. S. Brewer, 1993), x.

[60]Ibid., 3, 57.

Adam is, perhaps, expecting a supernatural, wild, or violent encounter; he longs for his former life of safe domestic labor.[61] He may be expecting a "romance forest"—and, because he is not a romance protagonist, this expectation makes him feel misplaced. The pair do, after Gamelyn fails to comfort Adam, encounter a sort of wonder:

> As thei stode talkinge   bothen in fere,
> Adam herd talking of men   and right nyghe hem thei were.
> Tho Gamelyn under wode   loked aright,
> Sevene score of yonge men   he seye wel ydight;
> Alle satte at the mete   compas aboute.
>
> (620–24)

The wonder they encounter is a tableau of social harmony: 140 young men, sharing food. A feast of large scale, like the week-long one Gamelyn organized after his wrestling match (and at which he begged his guests to stay after they had eaten and drunk their fill), is a daily occurrence in the outlaw kingdom. Although the outlaws are not explicitly described as poachers—unlike in many of the later Robin Hood texts, which thematize poaching as a central activity of outlaw forest life—it is hard to imagine where else they could have acquired their food.[62] The elision of where and how the outlaws acquired their food draws attention to the suspended state of resources and social life in the forest: land is there, but not in the same way that it is inside of the law; food is just there. All of the problems attendant to inheritance and estate management are resolved in the greenwood. Outlaw society makes a virtue of futurelessness; with no land to entail or power structures to organize into the future, the outlaws find uncorrupted and seemingly incorruptible order. *Gamelyn* presents the inside of the law as a space that is corruptible in ways that the space outside of the law is not.

Gamelyn's time in the forest provides a snapshot of things actually working, an alternative way of governing and being. Here, he is not only outside of unjust judgments of corrupt legal authorities; he is outside of inheritance law. Because membership in this social universe is based on

[61] It is of note here that John's household employees were hardly safe or secure; Gamelyn kills the porter just for doing his job as instructed (lines 285–304).

[62] See Stephen Knight, "Robin Hood and the Forest Laws," *The Bulletin of the International Society for Robin Hood Studies* 1 (2017): 1–14. If the outlaws' forest is the royal forest, even foraging would have been a legally dodgy activity.

outlawry—and contingent on continued expulsion from the outlaw's other community—the family is not a structuring unit of society, and succession is non-hereditary. The greenwood's land is unmanaged but habitable and plentiful. But this alternative society, of which Gamelyn becomes king, is interrupted by Gamelyn's loyal tenants, who have come to tell him that his brother has become sheriff and Gamelyn has been declared "wolfesheed" (705–6). An outlaw was called the wolf's head because he "had no more rights than a hunted beast"; he could be hunted with impunity.[63] Legally, only the king (or those to whom he had given explicit permission) was allowed to hunt game in the king's forest; thus, hunting in the king's forest was a kind of performative gentility that, itself, was a form of criminality. This real forest situation sees itself reflected in the gentility of *Gamelyn*'s forest-dwelling outlaws. In the limited monarchy of the outlaws, we see the "appropriation of the state's language, symbols, and processes by outlaws."[64] This performative gentility includes both the outlaws' pronounced hospitality and their sociopolitical structure. When Gamelyn first meets the band of outlaws, he asks "What man is your maister, that ye with be?" The outlaws respond "Oure maister is crowned of outlawe king." Having learned that the outlaws are governed by a *king*, Gamelyn knows he and Adam will be fed hospitably and treated well "if that he be hende and come of royal blood" (653–59). On the other hand, from Gamelyn's tenants' place within the law, things are *not* working; John, having newly become sheriff, is a bad landlord in every sense of the word.

Outlaw society does not revolve around or even include property. Outlaws cannot reproduce outlaw subjects themselves; their population is reproduced through the corruption inside the law. Outlaw society requires the law for the generation of its subjects; in order to generate the particularly noble denizens of the outlaw kingdom in the forest, it is implied, the law must be corrupt. There are no women (or children) in *Gamelyn*'s forest. The greenwood's existence as a social society is always contingent on its denizens' eviction from the norms and power structures that manage and organize land and its meanings; legal violence predicates its order.

The implicit goal of outlaw life seems to be to make it back inside of the law. Despite the ways in which life in the greenwood is demonstrably

[63]Saunders, *The Forest of Medieval Romance*, 3.

[64]W. M. Ormrod, "Law in the Landscape: Criminality, Outlawry and Regional Identity in Late Medieval England," in *Boundaries of the Law: Geography, Gender and Jurisdiction in Medieval and Early Modern Europe*, ed. Anthony Musson (London: Routledge, 2005), 7–20.

better than life inside of the law, no one questions the King of the Outlaws when he is pardoned and returns inside the law, leaving his throne to Gamelyn. Outlaw society's ideal form is its own obsolescence: not the eradication of the law (they are monarchists, not anarchists), but the resolution of the law's problems and corruptions and their reincorporation into its fold. The best society we see in *The Tale of Gamelyn* is predicated on the dream of its own dissolution. Because the outlaw kingdom's perfect order depends on its collective dream of its own obsolescence, of its members' hoped-for reincorporation into the law, the social order and harmony found there are provisional and transient, contingent on the society's formal hierarchy in the absence of property, family, and investment in a future.

The outlaw court is more orderly and less corrupt than the legal spaces its members want to return to; the romance's three feasts are exemplary of this. Gamelyn's week-long feast is so extreme as to be a parody of hospitality; John's feast results in Gamelyn's and Adam's gruesome attack on his ecclesiastical guests. But when, at the outlaw feast, Gamelyn and Adam are brought to the "mayster outlawe" and tell their story,

> He bad hem sitte doun   for to take rest;
> And bad hem ete and drink   and that of the best.
> As they eten and drunken   wel and fine,
> Than seie on to another,   "This is Gamelyne."
> (675–78)

Outlaw hospitality is sincere and without affectation. The inherent nobility in Gamelyn—and in the outlaws in general—is recognized in the absence of possessions. The outlaws have a social hierarchy; it is undisputed. As Jamie Taylor has pointed out, "outlaw justice both resists and reflects orthodox forms of legal community."[65] Social power here is not accompanied or informed by land. The death of an outlaw's outlaw self—their reincorporation into the law (and, usually, back into the possession of land)—leaves no outlaw inheritance and no outlaw heirs. Where heirs to the English crown acquire both power and land, successors to the outlaw crown (such as Gamelyn) acquire only a kind of power and status.[66]

[65]Jamie K. Taylor, *Fictions of Evidence: Witnessing, Literature, and Community in the Late Middle Ages* (Columbus: The Ohio State University Press, 2013), 110.

[66]The king, of course, had technical ownership of all of the land, and practical ownership of the royal demesne, which included, for example, the royal forests.

When Gamelyn and his outlaw colleagues are finally exonerated at the end of the romance, Gamelyn's position of greenwood authority is translated from King of the Outlaws to Chief Justice of the King's Free Forest. In the poem, the forest is at odds with the landed gentry because it houses the outlaws that threaten its (corrupt) order. In reality, the king's forest officials and the landed nobility clashed over land usage and imposition of different forms of law.[67] In 1175, Henry II "made a controversial decision to subject even earls, barons, and clergy to the forest law."[68] Many communities in royal forests were part of ancient demesne, which meant that their lands had once been the direct property of the king and that they had special legal rights of access to the king.[69] In its relationship to customary law and to the king's law, the forest is simultaneously center and periphery. For the corrupt clergy and legal officials of *Gamelyn*'s countryside, the forest is a periphery, an afterthought; its land means nothing because it cannot be acquired unless, through assarting (the process of turning forest into arable land), it becomes a different kind of land.

The Tale of Gamelyn's image of the greenwood as a space outside the law suspends the existence of the forest law, of the forest as a space that was just as juridical as the village, and where, just as in the village and the manor, local officials were delegated power from the Crown. At the end of the romance, the outlaws take over the law; almost immediately, they are pardoned and reincorporated into it. And when, at the end of the poem, Gamelyn is named Chief Justice of the King's Free Forest, the fantasy of the forest as an extrajuridical space evaporates. With Gamelyn's legitimated position, the fictional outlaw-greenwood slides into being the real medieval king's forest. Gamelyn will continue to walk his circuit "under the wode shawes," but now he will be responsible for interpreting the forest on behalf of the English king.

Gamelyn's response to being formally excised from the law when he is declared wolf's head is to physically reenter it, promising his tenants that he will go to the next shire court. Gamelyn goes to the court briefly, before returning to the forest while Ote stands in surety for him. One day, he stands looking out over "the wodes and the shawes and the wilde feelde" (784), thinking about his eldest brother who has bribed the inquest to rule to hang Ote. Early in the poem, he looked from his brother's managed

[67]See Simon Schama, *Landscape and Memory* (New York: Vintage, 1996), 147.
[68]Steel, "Biopolitics," 33.
[69]Bennett, *Women in the English Countryside*, 15.

"yerd" out over his own ill-managed lands. Here, in his final moment as King of the Outlaws, he looks out over his "own" unmanaged lands. When, upon his welcome by the king back into the law, he becomes the Chief Justice of the King's Free Forest, he will be responsible for managing the forest into the law, doing work such as preventing poaching and assessing the profitability of forest resources.

The Chief Justice of the Forest was, beginning in the early thirteenth century, the top administrator of a large and complex system of forest administration.[70] In the fourteenth century, these roles went from terms served to lifetime offices that were generally regarded as "property" and which "often, in practice, became hereditary."[71] *Gamelyn* was being written at a time when the office of the chief forester, the Justice of the King's Forest, the very office which Gamelyn would hold, was transitioning from being considered a set of *duties* to being considered property, subject to property disputes.[72] The poem has already shown a deep skepticism about the futures and possibilities of property. Early in the poem, we see John waste Gamelyn's holding. Here, near the end, amidst the "resolution" of Gamelyn's and the outlaws' and the forest's reincorporation into the law, we see all of the possibilities of the outlaw forest, including its alternative relationship to the land and to governance, wasted *into* the legal regime.

No Future

When Gamelyn and his fellow outlaws get to the court, they fetter John, the justice, and the twelve jurors. Then Gamelyn ordains his own inquest; the twelve corrupt jurors have been replaced by twelve jurors from the outlaw community. The justice, the sheriff, and the twelve original jurors are all hanged. The processes of law are corrected by being turned inside out; those living outside of the law are now not only inside the law, but authoritatively so. Justice having been restored (by the full-scale eradication of the practitioners of corruption), Gamelyn and Ote make peace with the king. The king pardons all of the outlaws. Ote is made justice; Gamelyn is made Chief Justice of the King's Free Forest. Ultimately, in the words of Maurice Keen, this "solution is not a new dispensation, but

[70]Charles R. Young, *The Royal Forest of Medieval England* (Philadelphia: University of Pennsylvania Press, 1979).

[71]Ibid., 159.

[72]Ibid., 160.

a change of personnel."[73] By the end of the poem, the organization of Sir John's lands is just as the knights at the beginning wanted it to be: split between two brothers. The elder brother, Ote, has both the ancestral and military fees; Gamelyn is heir to these and holds his own "land and his lede" (891). The text does not linger on his lands' waste earlier in the poem. The poem, with its bad eldest brother, takes up a critique of primogeniture only to settle back into a revised version of it. Upon Ote's death, should Gamelyn survive him, Sir John's entire estate would be reunified. "Gamelyn can thus anticipate succeeding to all his father's wealth and status, something neither of his older siblings could ever normally have hoped to do."[74] But this possibility of future reunification is delicate: should Ote have a son, for example, the five plowlands that were originally Ote's elder brother's must, by necessity, be left to his son. In fact, any production of heirs on the part of either Ote or Gamelyn threatens to repeat the mess *The Tale of Gamelyn* relates; on the other hand, a failure to reproduce halts the reproduction of their already limited familial power.

As the poem ends, Gamelyn has no heir, and the poem does not suggest one:

> And Sire Ote his brother made him his heire,
> And sithen wedded Gamelyn a wif good and faire;
> They lyved togidere the while that Crist wolde,
> And sithen was Gamelyn graven under molde.
> (893–96)

The Boundys lands will fall out of that immediate family upon Gamelyn's inevitable death. The search for a proper heir might be difficult and even more divisive than Sir John's will; the land might revert to the superior lord, whoever that might be. The text's conflict between partibility and primogeniture is the vehicle for its pessimism about the very project of heir-inheritance, of land's continuity. *Gamelyn* does not present an alternative model for the disastrous social forms it lays bare. For a moment the greenwood outlaw society appears to be this model, but that society is not only futureless but defined by its futurelessness. When the outlaws

[73] Maurice Keen, *The Outlaws of Medieval Legend* (Berkeley: University of California Press, 1961), 93.

[74] Ford, "Land Tenure," 39.

are reincorporated en masse back into the law, their peaceful court is disbanded.

Gamelyn begins with the messiness and controversy over Sir John's nuncupative will, and it goes on to reveal the problems inherent in every possible method of retaining power and value in land over time and for following generations. E. P. Thompson has pointed out that, historically, "intentions in inheritance systems, as in other matters, often eventuate in conclusions very different from those intended."[75] Well aware of this fact, the *Gamelyn*-poet undermines attachments to symbols of futurity such as land and the child, showing one of the primary goals of the medieval nobility and landed gentry—the continued investment of wealth and power in land—to be for nought.[76]

Beowulf, in an English text from several centuries prior to *Gamelyn*, also, famously, does not produce an heir. By the end of the poem, Beowulf's non-reproductiveness, his failure (and apparent lack of effort) to produce an heir, is regarded with grief, presaging the eradication of the Geat people. Beowulf's refusal of futurity—a model of governance that is temporally delimited to his reign as king—is something that the poem refuses to blame him for, even as it forms itself into an elegy for this loss.[77] Unlike Beowulf, Gamelyn does marry, although he does not appear to reproduce, and neither *Gamelyn* nor any of its characters mourns his nonexistent heir. This contrasts with *Gamelyn*'s clear and evident mourning of his wasted land, discussed earlier. The melancholy of, for example, *Beowulf* is that a single person cannot promise or create a future. The optimism of *Havelok the Dane*, with its joint Danish-English kingdom and its fecund protagonists, is that a single person—or, at least, a pair of disinherited orphans—can. *The Tale of Gamelyn*'s in-the-law gentry or elite or ecclesiastical

[75] E. P. Thompson, "The Grid of Inheritance: A Comment," in *Family and Inheritance: Rural Society in Western Europe, 1200–1800*, ed. Jack Goody, Joan Thirsk, and E. P. Thompson (Cambridge: Cambridge University Press, 1976), 328–60 (328).

[76] Language that gestured toward a distant or infinite future was common in legal decisions about land rights in the thirteenth and fourteenth centuries, but the impetus behind this language was complex and often contradictory. See Paul Brand, "*In perpetuum*: The Rhetoric and Reality of Attempts to Control the Future in English Medieval Common Law," in *Medieval Futures: Attitudes toward the Future in the Middle Ages*, ed. J. A. Burrow and Ian P. Wei (Woodbridge: Boydell, 2000), 101–14.

[77] *Beowulf* also begins with a narrative of successful inheritance, as opposed to the heirless death of Beowulf at the end. In contrast, *Gamelyn* begins with a narrative of problematic inheritance. For inheritances in *Beowulf*, see Michael D. C. Drout, "Blood and Deeds: The Inheritance Systems in *Beowulf*," *SP* 104 (2007), 199–226. Also worth noting is the distinct presence of mothers—including a particularly monstrous one—in *Beowulf*.

characters are invested in power's inherence in land over time (in the form of inheritance, disinheritance, usurpation, being paid off or enriched by landowners); its outlaws desire, eventually, to return to the legal space where these things matter. But the poem steadfastly refuses to offer any models that work, stick, or are worth fighting for.

For a text so concerned with family and the household, the total absence of women (until three lines from the end of the poem) is striking. The outlaw community in the greenwood is a homosocial, masculine environment, as are the chivalric and juridical communities at the beginning and end of the poem respectively. The only hint of a mother, or more than one mother, is when John suggests that Gamelyn may be illegitimate. Similarly, Sir John's desired partible inheritance might evoke, briefly, a feminized relationship to land. But there are no women in any of the spaces *Gamelyn* occupies. While we are told that Gamelyn marries, directly before the poem ends, we never occupy the same space as this nameless wife. Women occupy a spectral role in *Gamelyn*, resonant in their absence. In Gillian Adler's discussion of Chaucer's *Wife of Bath's Prologue*, she writes "while male and female lives operate according to the same trajectory, the emphasis on bloodline enables masculine linearism to locate triumph in futurity."[78] In *Gamelyn,* there is no triumph in futurity; the absence of women emphasizes this lack.

Homosocial environments can be sinister and corrupt, like John's courtroom; they can also be fair and harmonious, like the outlaw kingdom. Both versions are non-reproductive. The end of the poem undoes both of these homosocial spaces through the execution of John and the corrupt judge and jury, and the king's pardoning of the outlaws. The outlaws, now no longer outlaws, disperse throughout the inside of the law. Andrew James Johnston has argued that another homosocial scene in *Gamelyn*, that of the wrestling competition, operates as a failed utopian space.[79] According to Johnston, "the homosocial and even homoerotic aspects of a seminude wrestling match are employed to engender a utopian space of a supposedly classless masculinity seeking to erase the narrative's intense

[78]Gillian Adler, *Chaucer and the Ethics of Time* (Cardiff: University of Wales Press, 2022), 156.

[79]Andrew James Johnston, "Wrestling in the Moonlight: The Politics of Masculinity in the Middle English Popular Romance *Gamelyn*," in *Constructions of Masculinity from the Middle Ages through the Present*, ed. Stefan Horlacher (New York: Palgrave Macmillan, 2011), 51–67.

ideological contradictions."[80] Where I read the outlaw forest as the poem's space of idealized sociality, Johnston also sees the wrestling, because of, rather than in spite of, its inherent violence, as a temporary glimpse of a kind of classless utopia focused on men's bodies. The outlaw society's harmony is predicated on its own future obsolescence; likewise, the wrestling's harmony depends both on its play-acting violence and on its status as an event, with a clear end and a clear winner. Gamelyn's defeat of the champion avenges the harm done to the two sons of the franklin Gamelyn meets on the way to the wrestling.[81] A franklin is defined by his status in relationship to land; he is a non-noble landowner, a person with property but no aristocratic status. If his heirs predecease him, as may be the case here, the transmission of his property is paused or confused.

Lee Edelman, in his conceptualization of reproductive futurism, is not interested in property relations or their reproduction. For the *Gamelyn* poet, reproduction of members of its gentry class is part and parcel of the reproduction of their landed interests. At the same time, the poem's structures of family, inheritance, and landed wealth have their own failure embedded within them. The outlaw forest, which is by definition non-reproductive, is the poem's only example of civic harmony.

Fantasies of the future, Edelman claims, circulate around the figure of the Child and the social and symbolic mandate of reproductive futurity. Fantasies of the no-future, in *Gamelyn*, circulate around the haunted and fractured conjunction between people and their land. In other words, rather than seeing the *child* as the structuring component of future-oriented narrative, *Gamelyn* takes land as the structuring component of its futureless narrative. But, as Noel James Menuge reminds us, in the medieval wardship romance, land and child are continuous categories. The vulnerability of land—its susceptibility to waste—is illuminated by Gamelyn's despair over John's mismanagement of Gamelyn's portion. At first glance, it is striking that a narrative so deeply pessimistic about property's future should be so invested in its management. At the same time, the form of the wardship romance, which includes *Gamelyn* as well

[80]Ibid., 51.

[81]The text is ambiguous—or inconsistent—about whether the champion has slain, or has simply threatened to slay, the franklin's sons. The Middle English word *scleyn* can mean to "slay"—but also to "beat" or "cause damage to"; *MED*, s.v. *slēn* (v.). Knight and Ohlgren argue that the franklin's sons are with him after Gamelyn defeats the champion (*The Tale of Gamelyn*, note to line 197): "Than seide the frankeleyn that had the sones ther" (line 251). It is possible, however, that "ther" is modifying the franklin himself, not his sons.

as earlier Middle English romances such as *King Horn* and *Havelok the Dane*, as Menuge has argued, revolves around the wasteful misappropriation of an underage heir's land by a legally appointed or self-appointed guardian.[82] Wardship, and the abuse of wardship, necessitate a child whose relationship to the land that should be his is vulnerable to waste, as in *Gamelyn*. Menuge sees Gamelyn's wasted land and his subsequent outlaw exile as coextensive with his legal childhood. "As the action of waste is the external correlative of the legal vulnerability of the ward, so too is the wilderness period within each of these romances a signifier of legal infancy."[83] When the adult Gamelyn violently returns to the inside of the law, the reformed world is one without wards, guardians, or child heirs.

The refusal of land's future is the refusal of land's ultimate incorporation into narrative. As the narrative of *Gamelyn* demonstrates, the project of inheritance, in which the dead fill land with ongoing social power and meaning, is too contradictory to survive indefinitely. In his argument for the radical potential of romance—calling it the "genre of contradiction par excellence"—Andrew Cole claims that romance "helps you think outside yourself while its contradictions keep you from escapism."[84] I have argued that *Gamelyn*'s pessimism is not exactly radical; the poem restores what looks like order and makes sure that there are no viable alternatives. *Gamelyn*, with its excavation of the long-term failure of both norms and alternatives, is, as José Esteban Muñoz has characterized the "anti-social thesis in queer studies," exemplified by Edelman's *No Future*, a "romance of negativity."[85]

The end of the poem discards its corrupt enemies and incorporates Gamelyn and the outlaws back into the law—this time the royal law—and back into royal land like the forest, but it leaves no excess for the future. We do not even know if Adam the Spencer, who, before his defection from John's household, was the steward responsible for provisioning it, receives the land Gamelyn promised him; even his future is foreclosed.

[82] Menuge, *Medieval English Wardship.*

[83] Ibid., 65.

[84] Andrew Cole, "Romance and Commitment," *PMLA* 137 (May 2022): 510–26 (515).

[85] José Esteban Muñoz, "Thinking beyond Antirelationality and Antiutopianism in Queer Critique," *PMLA* 121 (May 2006), 825–26. See also José Esteban Muñoz, *Cruising Utopia: The Then and There of Queer Futurity* (New York: NYU Press, 2009).

Five Strokes of the Axe: Patronage and the *Gawain*-Poet

Helen Cooper
Magdalene College, University of Cambridge

Abstract

There have been numerous attempts to identify the poet of the four poems in British Library, MS Cotton Nero A.x, or, failing an identification for the author, a patron or household from the right dialect area, or with the right dialect affiliations, who might have commissioned or at least taken an interest in the poems. Working from the widely favoured hypothesis that one man wrote all four poems, but with a concentration on *Sir Gawain and the Green Knight*, this paper considers the combined evidence for the cultural backgrounds of the possible poet and patron. In place of earlier suggestions, which have ranged from the royal court to the gentry, it explores the possibility of episcopal patronage. A plausible contender for such a role would be Richard Scrope, bishop of Coventry and Lichfield, the diocese that included the dialect area of the poet. Lichfield was a major centre for the copying of devotional texts; the Scropes had emerged from the gentry class not long before, and Richard was closely associated with the king, who stayed on occasion in the bishop's palace at Lichfield. Other details, including his devotion to the Five Wounds of Christ and the family coat of arms, suggest a more specific link. Scrope's involvement with the royal council might also provide a missing London link with *Saint Erkenwald*. After his elevation to the archbishopric of York, he was involved in the Northumberland rebellion against Henry IV, and is reported as having requested execution with five blows of the axe. An English carol on what was perceived as his martyrdom resonates imaginatively with the romance, and perhaps contains faint echoes of it recast for a religious text.

Keywords

Gawain-poet; MS Cotton Nero A.x, romance authorship; episcopal patronage; Richard Scrope; Five Wounds; *Saint Erkenwald*; Lichfield; quadrivium

My thanks to King's College London, who invited me to give the Gollancz Lecture on which this paper is based. More personal thanks go to Mary Carruthers, Richard Firth Green, and William A. Quinn for sharing their unpublished work with me; to Michael J. Bennett, for discussion of the Scropes; to Christopher Page, for information about music; and not least to Ad Putter, for being on the other end of email on many occasions.

Having kept both his protagonist and his readers in the dark as to just what is going on in *Sir Gawain and the Green Knight*, a few lines before the end the poet seems to solve the mystery by revealing the identity of the mysterious Green Knight. The figure who has up to this point seemed to be the villain of the story, or at the very least the antagonist of both Gawain and the Arthurian court, names himself as Bertilak de Hautdesert, and declares that he is the same person as the previously unnamed host of the castle where Gawain has been staying. That is not quite the end of the poem, however, and not quite the end of the Green Knight either; for just as we think we know who he is, our last sight of him is not as Sir Bertilak, nor as the host returning home. Instead, he rides off "whiderwarde-so-euer he wolde," and still green (2478–79).[1] On his previous disappearance from the action, at the end of the opening court scene and some time after Gawain had given him his own name and asked for his, he had declared himself to be known as "þe kny3t of þe grene chapel" (454); and we have no way of knowing which is correct, or if both are right—one's name, after all, is not necessarily the same as what one is called.[2] His declaration that Morgan le Fay gave him his present appearance is equally unhelpful. If it was designed to scare Guinevere to death, as he states, it was singularly unsuccessful, and he never suggests that Morgan had anything to do with the tempting of Gawain, which he claims for himself (2358–63). Readers, and no doubt the original audience of the poem, tend to construct a single coherent plot from all this, increasingly now to make Morgan the central figure; but that is as much a fiction as the poem itself. The way it is written seems designed to prevent any such

[1]Editions consulted for this paper are *The Works of the Gawain Poet*, ed. Ad Putter and Myra Stokes (London: Penguin, 2014); *The Poems of the Pearl Manuscript*, ed. Malcolm Andrew and Ronald Waldron, 5th ed. (Exeter: Exeter University Press, 2007); and *Sir Gawain and the Green Knight*, ed. J. R. R. Tolkien and E. V. Gordon, rev. Norman Davis, 2nd ed. (1968; Oxford: Oxford University Press, 2012). Also consulted is the digitized copy of the manuscript on the British Library website, https://www.bl.uk/manuscripts/FullDisplay.aspx?ref=Cotton_MS_Nero_A_X/2 (accessed January 31, 2023), and the introduction given there. The digitized version is also available on the University of Calgary website, digitalcollections.ucalgary.ca/Browse/Collections/Gawain-Manuscript/ (accessed July 26, 2024).

[2]On different ways of naming and their usages see Jane Bliss, *Naming and Namelessness in Medieval Romance* (Cambridge: D. S. Brewer, 2008).

fiction cohering into reliable fact; and since the work is equally fictional, there is no underlying fact to appeal to. It is as if the Green Knight's main function is to remain mysterious.

Poems, however, even anonymous ones, do not write themselves, and there have been plenty of attempts to identify the poet; but attempts to do so can begin to seem like the continuing quest to find the "real" author of Shakespeare's plays: Christopher Marlowe? Francis Bacon? the earl of Oxford? Elizabeth I?—and plenty of others. The question of who wrote them has inevitably been taken as an invitation to speculation, though without the evidence offered by the testimony of Shakespeare's contemporaries and the title pages of his works. Neither the *Gawain*-poet nor the scribe put his name on the manuscript, nor do we have any records that would enable us to give the author a reliable name or a life; we do not even know if a single author wrote all four of the poems in the manuscript, British Library, MS Cotton Nero A.x, or if *Saint Erkenwald*, which survives only in a late fifteenth-century manuscript, should be ascribed to the same person. That shares composition in alliterative meter and some phrasing with the Cotton poems, appears to be closely contemporary with them, and is written in a similar dialect; but its action and its interests are firmly located in London. The probable deduction as to where the *Gawain*-poet lived has likewise been based on the dialect of the manuscript, which is generally agreed to be that of the northwest Midlands, most likely Cheshire or the adjoining Staffordshire border; but some of its features may belong to the copyist rather than the poet. The presence of the Cotton poems in a single manuscript indicates some sort of association between them, but many medieval poems appear in multi-author miscellanies that likewise combine religious and secular texts. Their date of composition can be estimated only approximately. The date of their language would be affected by unrecorded oral usages of particular words, by the age of the poet or poets when he or they were writing, and by the impression of modernity or archaism they wanted to convey. The favoured age for the script is the later fourteenth century, though that would not give a firm date for the poems' composition; and the illustrations of dress, armour, and architecture were added after the copying. Almost any date from the mid-fourteenth to the early fifteenth century has been canvassed and can claim supporting evidence,[3] though the

[3]Examples of the ranges of date proposed include, at the early end, Francis Ingledew, *"Sir Gawain and the Green Knight" and the Order of the Garter* (Notre Dame: Notre Dame University Press, 2006), and a meticulously argued chapter on language in a forthcoming book on the *Gawain*-poet by Richard Firth Green. Joel Fredell cautiously favours a late

use in *Cleanness* of Mandeville's *Travels*, written in 1356 or 1367, would militate against the earliest suggested dates.[4] The uncertainties of all such evidence have in turn encouraged many scholars to date the poems to match their own theories as to the particular context or occasion for which the poems (in particular *Gawain* or *Pearl*) might have been written.[5]

What follows here is a comparable set of related speculations, starting from a series of working assumptions in line with the majority of editorial scholarship on the four poems contained in the Cotton manuscript, here reinforced by a further theory as to their possible patronage and context—a patronage that could bring *Saint Erkenwald* into the same line of sight. The most widely shared assumption of the last few decades is that a single author wrote the four Cotton poems: they share the same dialect, a comparable grasp of the possibilities of alliterative poetics, and a common alertness to the humanity of his characters. The next assumption, widely agreed despite dissenting voices, is that he was working in the late fourteenth century, a proposition for which this paper will offer further support. That he was male is indicated by the evidence for his education in Latin. The closest guess as to what he was, as distinct from who he was, has been that he was a clerically trained man working in an aristocratic or substantial gentry household.[6] That brings us no nearer to his identity, however, and the northwest Midlands is a large enough haystack to make finding a needle very difficult.

Identifying a patron, however, or a household that could provide a likely or plausible context for the composition and reception of such poems, cuts down the number of options substantially, and a number of possible candidates from the later fourteenth century have been canvassed, from the

---

date to bring them closer to his fifteenth-century dating of the manuscript ("The *Pearl*-Poet Manuscript in York," *SAC* 36 [2014]: 1–39).

[4]See Putter and Stokes's introduction to *Cleanness* in *The Works of the Gawain Poet*, ix. The earliest surviving Mandeville manuscript dates from 1371.

[5]Recent suggestions for topical reference include Sarah McNamer in a paper to the New Chaucer Society conference in 2022 (with a follow-up book planned), "Did the *Pearl* Poet Write at the Court of Edward III?," in which she proposed that the poem was written for Edward's son Lionel and his wife for their Christmas in Dublin in 1362, in connection with the death of their infant daughter; and Andrew Breeze, who claims to have found "proof" of a connection to Richard II's favourite Robert de Vere, earl of Oxford, on the basis of the appearance of the word "ver" (spring) in the poem (866). Extrapolating from that, he claims a date for the poem of 1386–87 (*The Historical Arthur and the "Gawain" Poet* [Lanham, MD: Lexington Books, 2023]).

[6]See for instance Ad Putter, *An Introduction to the Gawain-Poet* (London: Routledge, 2014), 14–23.

royal court to local gentry.[7] The apparent disparity of dialect between the poems and the court can be elided by the presence there of Richard II's entourage of Cheshire archers, and therefore the possibility that even the king might have been sufficiently acquainted with the poems' dialect to have understood them without undue difficulty; the Cheshire bodyguard was formed only in 1397, however, which gives little time for the poems to have been written before the king's deposition.[8] A number of English monarchs, including Richard, are known to have possessed French romances, but no royal owners of English ones are recorded until the fifteenth century.[9] *Sir Gawain* itself has many of the qualities of courtly romance of a kind unusual in Middle English: the critical habit of describing the metrical romances as popular may be misleading (the gentry, merchants, and citizens who seem to have been their major patrons would not be pleased to be classed with the peasantry, and that many of the texts have sources in French romance likewise suggests higher social origins for them), but *Gawain* nonetheless seems to be an altogether more sophisticated production. Unlike many of the English romances, it does not have a single French source, but its exploitation of motifs drawn from French suggests both an author and an audience who could appreciate them. That might suggest an aristocratic patron, but there is negligible evidence for such patronage of Middle English romance. The main exception (though the date, the language, the locality, and the degree of originality do not exactly match up with the Cotton Nero poems) would be the commissioning in the 1350s of a translation of *William of Palerne* by Humphrey de Bohun, sixth earl of Hereford and a grandson of Edward I, for the anglophone members of his household: an alliterative work that generally keeps

[7]The royal court was proposed by Gervase Matthew, *The Court of Richard II* (London: John Murray, 1968), 166, and has been much canvassed since, not least by John M. Bowers: see in particular his *An Introduction to the "Gawain" Poet* (Gainesville: University of Florida Press, 2012), which includes a consideration of *Saint Erkenwald*. Discussions of patronage include Michael J. Bennett's "The Historical Background," in *A Companion to the Gawain-Poet*, ed. Derek Brewer and Jonathan Gibson (Cambridge: D. S. Brewer, 1997), 71–90.

[8]Christopher Given-Wilson, *The Royal Household and the King's Affinity: Service, Politics, and Finance in England, 1360–1413* (New Haven, CT: Yale University Press, 1986), 217–26 and Appendix V, 282–90.

[9]For a conspectus of royal and aristocratic book ownership at this period see V. J. Scattergood, "Literary Culture at the Court of Richard II," in *English Court Culture in the Later Middle Ages*, ed. Scattergood and J. W. Sherborne (London: Duckworth, 1983), 29–43. The books recorded are largely devotional, many in Latin; the remainder are in French, either informational or romances. The *Roman de la Rose* appears frequently; the majority of the romances are Arthurian.

close to its impeccably aristocratic French source, composed for Countess Yolande of Hainault in the thirteenth century.[10] High aristocrats were, however, thin on the ground in the Cheshire area, not least because as a palatinate county it came under the direct control of the king. At the early end of the possible date range for *Gawain* was Henry of Grosmont, duke of Lancaster and earl of Derby, the author of the pious Anglo-French *Livre des saints medicines*, who had interests in the northwest Midlands and who would offer a fit with the three devotional poems; but he spent much of his career fighting in France, and died in 1361.[11]

The best attested interest in Middle English romance was focused on the gentry, who supply some of the handful of known names of both owners and copyists, many from the north or north Midlands, not so far from the Cotton Nero area: families such as the network around the Finderns of Derbyshire, or individuals such as the Yorkshireman Robert Thornton.[12] The name most often proposed for association with *Sir Gawain* belongs to this group, though his career soon raised him to its higher levels: Sir John Stanley. The younger son of a Cheshire family, he has been proposed both as patron and as author of the work. He entered the records after he murdered a cousin, and retained something of a reputation as a bruiser. He prospered in royal service under Richard II in connection with the Cheshire archers, and more under Henry IV and Henry V, becoming lieutenant of Ireland in 1399 and lord of the Isle of Man in 1405; that same year he was made a Knight of the Garter, so providing a possible link with the Garter motto, "Hony soyt qui mal pence," added to the end of the poem. He was a man who attracted legends to himself. Various family traditions had his wife's father rescued from an eagle's nest as a baby (turned into the family badge, it is the origin of the many Eagle and Child pubs, the name predating the later association with Jove and Ganymede), then having a liaison with the daughter of the Grand Turk and leaving

[10] *William of Palerne: An Alliterative Romance*, ed. G. H. V. Bunt (Groningen: Bouma's Boekhuis, 1985).

[11] See W. G. Cooke and D'A. J. D. Boulton, "*Sir Gawain and the Green Knight*: A Poem for Henry of Grosmont?," *MÆ* 68 (1999): 42–54.

[12] On the circulation of vernacular romance in this area in the later Middle Ages see Michael Johnston, *Romance and the Gentry in Late Medieval England* (Oxford: Oxford University Press, 2014). On Thornton, see Michael Johnston and Susanna Fein, eds, *Robert Thornton and His Books* (Cambridge: D. S. Brewer, 2014); and on the Findern Manuscript, *The Findern Manuscript (Cambridge University Library MS CUL Ff.1.6)*, facsimile, ed. Richard Beadle and A. E. B. Owen (London: Scolar Press, 1977).

her pregnant, and finally dying in 1414 as the result of an Irish lampoon.[13] The Stanleys acquired literary associations in the fifteenth century, but there is no record of any such connections as early as 1400; nor, if one man wrote all the Cotton Nero poems, does he seem a good fit as patron (and even less as author) of the religious ones, however romantically attractive a link with *Sir Gawain* may be.

There is, however, one further group beside the royal court or the gentry that has rarely been considered for patronage, but which can provide equally good circumstantial evidence for such a role: the episcopacy. Bishops figure on occasion in romances—Bishop Turpin of the Charlemagne romances is a notable example—and the *Gawain*-poet makes a point of seating a bishop alongside the king at the opening feast (112). In England, bishops were typically of gentry origin, so brought up in the class associated with anglophone romance; they were largely appointed for their administrative abilities, not least in connection with royal business, so had a generous interest in the secular world. This commonly meant a focus on Westminster, and several owned property in or near London.[14] On occasion leading aristocrats sent their heirs to be educated in episcopal households as an alternative to education by the king or other nobles, presumably with an equivalent expectation of social, martial, and some intellectual training.[15] The class range of the episcopacy is most fully indicated by William of Wykeham, bishop of Winchester, who was the son of a well-to-do villager yet rose to be briefly appointed as chancellor of the realm under both Edward III and Richard II; highly experienced in both management and finance, he made up for his few academic credentials with a keen interest in education, founding both Winchester College and New College, Oxford.[16] The lives of some bishops themselves included military activities, most notably in the case of Henry le Despenser, bishop of Norwich, leader

[13]An account of the facts of his life is given by Michael J. Bennett, "Stanley, Sir John (c. 1350–1414)," in the *Oxford Dictionary of National Biography* (*ODNB*). For the legends see "The Stanley Poem" of c. 1562, in *The Palatine Anthology*, ed. James Orchard Halliwell (1850; repr., London: Bibliolife, 2009), 208–71.

[14]Caroline M. Barron, "Centres of Conspicuous Consumption: The Aristocratic Town House in London 1200–1500," *London Journal* 20 (1995): 1–16.

[15]For examples (mostly from the fifteenth century) see Nicholas Orme, "The Education of the Courtier," in Scattergood and Sherborne, *English Court Culture*, 63–85 (75–76), where he notes that there was "much in common between the establishment of a prelate and that of a lay magnate."

[16]See Peter Partner, "Wykeham, William (c. 1324–1404)," in *ODNB*.

of the Despenser Crusade of 1383. They typically had the Latin and French education that would have equipped them to appreciate the range of reference and sources shown in the Cotton Nero poems, as did many of the clerks in their households such as might have composed them. The most striking example of their literary patronage in this period comes slightly late for the *Gawain*-poet, when Robert Hallum, together with the other leading English delegate at the Council of Constance in 1415, commissioned a Latin translation of Dante's *Divine Comedy* to make it available to non-Italian speakers.[17] Born in Cheshire and elevated to the diocese of Salisbury in 1406, Hallum brought a number of Cheshiremen with him to staff his bishopric. There is no specific evidence for his interest in English-language romance, apart from what might be suggested by his origins, but to judge from the contents of late medieval miscellanies, the same people had comparable interests in both secular and religious literature. There are a good number of records of monasteries owning French romances, and although some of these texts bordered on the pious (the Grail romances, for instance, or *Gui de Warewic*), by no means all of them could claim any devotional elements.[18] Evidence for episcopal interest in English poetry is strongest for lyrics, such as those of Bishop Ledrede of Kilkenny's collection of Latin versions of existing English songs, with their original tunes noted; and diocesan influence behind the anthology of British Library, MS Harley 2253, is now being suggested.[19] Evidence for

[17]Hallum is discussed as offering a hypothetical illustrative alternative biography for the unknown poet in my introduction to Keith Harrison's translation of *Sir Gawain and the Green Knight*, Oxford World's Classics (Oxford: Oxford University Press, 1998), xiii–xiv (the series format requires a biography of the author). He is also mentioned by Cecilia A. Hatt, *God and the Gawain Poet* (Cambridge: Cambridge University Press, 2015), 228–31, though she concludes that "it is tempting but probably unwise to speculate" that he was the poet's actual patron.

[18]For details, see C. Barranu, "Multilingualism and Knowledge Exchange in English Manuscripts, c. 1215–c. 1415," Ph.D. diss. (University of Cambridge, 2022), 116–21. The best-known example is that of Bordesley Abbey, which was given an assortment of French saints' lives and romances, including a *Lancelot*, by the earl of Warwick early in the fourteenth century: see Madeleine Blaess, "L'Abbaye de Bordesley et les livres de Guy de Beauchamp," *Romania* 78 (1957): 511–18. Derek Pearsall also discusses the possibility of ecclesiastical patronage in "The Origins of the Alliterative Revival," in *The Alliterative Tradition in the Fourteenth Century*, ed. B. S. Levy and P. E. Szarmach (Kent, Ohio: Kent State University Press, 1981) 1–24; and "The Alliterative Revival: Origins and Social Backgrounds," in *Middle English Alliterative Poetry and Its Literary Background: Seven Essays*, ed. David Lawton (Cambridge: D. S. Brewer, 1982), 34–53.

[19]Discussed by Kathryn Kerby-Fulton, *The Clerical Proletariat and the Resurgence of Medieval English Poetry* (Philadelphia: University of Pennsylvania Press, 2021), 184–87, 192–93; and see the digitized Red Book of Ossory, https://issuu.com/churchofireland/docs/redbookossory (accessed May 1, 2023).

romance from the later fourteenth century is harder to locate, but there are a handful of records that could suggest links. One instance is the author of *Sir Ferumbras*, who may well have had a connection to the household of John Grandison, bishop of Exeter (died 1369). The *Ferumbras* text survives in both draft and finished form on the cover of two papal documents relating to the diocese between 1357 and 1377, with the handwriting of the second document apparently matching that of the romance.[20] Grandison himself collected a large library and had a particular interest in Cornish saints' lives, though those would most likely have been in Latin. Kathryn Kerby-Fulton has recently argued strongly for the importance of the "clerical proletariat"—unbeneficed clerks working with the administration of dioceses or similarly large-scale institutions, or as chapel clerks or vicars choral—as key people in the composition of Middle English poetry. *Saint Erkenwald* itself, a poem specifically linked to St. Paul's, could well be an example.[21] It is by no means too far a stretch to consider the episcopacy as a source of patronage for the Cotton Nero poems.

The possibility of such patronage would fit with the inferences it is possible to make about the poems' author, and by extension his patron, from internal evidence. The poet was presumably writing for an audience who would understand his dialect, or at least be familiar with northern speech. He knew French, his work showing traces of familiarity in *Cleanness* with Mandeville's *Travels* and the *Roman de la Rose*, and in *Gawain* with French Arthurian romances, including the prose ones.[22] He not only knew

[20]See the description of the manuscript (Oxford, Bodleian Library, MS Ashmole 33) in *Sir Ferumbras*, ed. Sidney J. Herrtage, EETS e.s. 34 (London: Trübner, 1879), pp. xv–xvi, and the digitized reproduction on the Bodleian website (https://medieval.bodleian.ox.ac.uk/catalog/manuscript_319 [accessed July 26, 2024]). An association of the Harley Lyrics with the diocese of Hereford has been proposed by Daniel Birkholz, *Harley Manuscript Geographies: Literary History and the Medieval Miscellany* (Manchester: Manchester University Press, 2020), 66–70, but it probably remained at the level of an overlap of networks between the diocesan household and the patrons or scribes of Harley 2253 (see Ralph Hanna, "Poetic Sites," in *The Oxford History of Poetry in English*, Vol. 2, *1100–1400*, ed. Helen Cooper and Robert R. Edwards [Oxford: Oxford University Press, 2023], 28–53).

[21]Kerby-Fulton, *The Clerical Proletariat*, 262–97.

[22]Analogues to the beheading game are found in French romances including the Caradoc section of the *Perceval* continuations and *La mule sans frain*; it may ultimately be Celtic in origin. See Elisabeth Brewer, "Sources I: The Sources of *Sir Gawain and the Green Knight*," in Brewer and Gibson, *A Companion*, 240–56, and her *Sir Gawain and the Green Knight: Sources and Analogues* (Cambridge: Boydell and Brewer, 1973). There is no comprehensive study of the prose romances in relation to *Gawain*, though the nearest analogue to the name Bertilak and the epithet "Goddes" for Morgan (2452) are both found in the Vulgate cycle (see Carolyne Larrington, *King Arthur's Enchantresses: Morgan and Her Sisters*

Latin but had a good familiarity with the Vulgate, as is evident in the biblical grounding of the three religious poems. That he had an education that went beyond the basics of clerical training is further indicated by the sophistication of his interest in numbers, based on the recurrent twelves of the Apocalypse in *Pearl* and of fives in *Gawain*—a topic that has fascinated critics, and on which more below. Although his clerical education is evident, however, there are also indications that he was not fully ordained, though such inferences are less certain. What Middle English poets say about themselves, when it is possible to check, is generally based on fact: their very first audiences, after all, would usually have been personally acquainted with them. So in *Patience*, he listens to sermons rather than giving them (9–10); and if the infant in *Pearl* was indeed his daughter, as is implied but without unequivocal commitment, he was not under a vow of celibacy. The same point is apparently confirmed by his insistence in *Cleanness* that God created sexual activity for pleasure (700–708), a rare sentiment to find in medieval religious writings. He seems to know enough about sea travel, in the generous detail of ships' tackle in both *Cleanness* and *Patience*, to indicate that he had some experience of it. This experience might be connected with his complaint about having to travel to Rome at his lord's orders (*Patience*, 51–56), though that is phrased in general rather than solely personal terms.[23] He might well have had generous cosmopolitan experience: men from Cheshire, both secular and ecclesiastical, had abundant links with administration in the court, the country, and English-occupied Gascony. Alliterative verse may have been geographically associated with the west and the north, but the cultural reach on display in the poems is far more than provincial in scope.

The cultural hinterland of both *Pearl* and *Gawain* is also inherent in their numerology, as part not of their local but of their Latin intellectual context. Numerology, as distinct from counting, or indeed anything domestic or pragmatic, was an academic matter, and so also suggestive for possible episcopal, or at least clerical, patronage; and that raises questions as to who would have appreciated it. Numerology was important in

in Arthurian Tradition [London: I.B. Tauris, 2006], 12–14). Ad Putter's *"Sir Gawain and the Green Knight" and French Arthurian Romance* (Oxford: Clarendon Press, 1995) concentrates on the verse romances of Chrétien de Troyes.

[23]Green notes in his forthcoming book that the phrase the poet uses for this, "liege lord," appears in the *Middle English Dictionary* as referring only to the king; but that would still hold good here if the speaker's more immediate lord was himself traveling on the king's business, as discussed further below.

biblical exegesis whenever actual numbers are mentioned, as with the fives and twelves of *Gawain* and *Pearl*, but more complex forms of number symbolism worked somewhat differently. There was no standardized numbering of biblical verses until the sixteenth century, and the number of the constituent parts of a poem was rarely significant in any text that expected a count beyond three (for the Trinity) or five (for the joys or sorrows of the Virgin). The hymn to the Virgin in Chaucer's *Prioress's Prologue* has five stanzas, but its source in Dante's St. Bernard (*Paradiso*, XXXIII.1–21) has no such connection, and even with a poet as sophisticated as Chaucer it is hard to rule out coincidence.[24] There is no evidence for anyone counting lines, nor does any vernacular manuscript note them or suggest that they are of significance in composition. There are a couple of instances in fifteenth-century German texts where the scribes noted the line totals of what they were copying, but that was because they were working on a piecework basis, paid by the line.[25] Larger units, such as the passūs of *Piers Plowman*, might be numbered, but there is no indication there that the count matters symbolically, and the numbering changes with the various versions of the text. The *Divine Comedy* is clearly very different, its meanings being symbolically conveyed in part by the explicit numbering of its cantos and *cantiche*, but even there the line count has no apparent significance.[26] There are a few earlier Latin texts in which the poet or patron notes the line count, but none of the medieval *artes poeticae* mentions numbers as a principle of composition.[27] Number became important, not in the preliminary trivium with its concentration on grammar, rhetoric, and logical argument, but in the more advanced quadrivium, which included geometry (number in space) and music (number in

[24]There seems to be no preference for five stanzas among Middle English lyrics to the Virgin except where the five joys are the subject, and in the case of *The Prioress's Prologue*; otherwise the number is random.

[25]The same has also been suggested for British Library, MS Harley 862, a manuscript of the poems of Charles d'Orléans, though the efforts at counting are both perfunctory and incomplete. My thanks to Ad Putter for the German references.

[26]An acquaintance with Dante has on occasion been proposed for *Pearl*, though the common elements do not go beyond what is found elsewhere in religious literature. A closer analogue in subject would be Boccaccio's Latin eclogue *Olympia*, on his dead daughter, but that is even less likely to have been known in England at this date: see further David Carlson, "The *Pearl*-Poet's *Olympia*," *Manuscripta* 31 (1987): 181–89.

[27]See E. R. Curtius, *European Literature and the Latin Middle Ages*, trans. Willard R. Trask (1953; Princeton University Press, 2013), 506–9. Vernacular evidence is much harder to come by. Proportion, rather than counting, was central to Boethius's treatise on arithmetic, widely disseminated as a textbook: see Michael Masi, *Boethian Number Theory* (Amsterdam: Rodopi, 1983).

time).[28] The study of number was the study of proportion and numerical relations, and it was here that its symbolic qualities could emerge.

It would be possible for readers, or indeed listeners, to notice the twelve-line stanza form of *Pearl*, and its congruence with the twelves of the Apocalypse that are emphasized later. Harder to spot would be its total of 1,212 lines across 101 stanzas, where roman numerals (MCCXII), almost universally used for written numerals, offer a less instantly recognizable payoff. They might also notice, independently of the totals, that the section with the extra stanza, six instead of five, is the one that has the refrain line "more and never the less" in a direct reference to increase (Section XV in numbered modern editions). Whether they would have thought to do the count is another question, which becomes more acute in *Gawain*. The stanzas there have irregular numbers of lines, totalling 2,530, or 2,525 (MMDXXV) if the final bob and wheel are omitted; but even on the page they are very hard to count, as the bob is always written to the right of the rest of the verse, and often opposite a random line late in the stanza.[29] There were ingenious ways of counting on one's fingers and knuckles, but the sheer interest of the stories would be a serious distraction from counting. The relation of the cited numbers to the proportions of the text would have appealed most directly to someone of more advanced education than most of the gentry or aristocracy could have provided.

The numerology of *Pearl* and *Gawain* is not just a matter of counting lines. Quite apart from the lack of evidence for such a practice, there were differences between cardinal numbers, what they could be chosen to symbolize (five for either the Virgin or the Five Wounds, for instance), and the way their relations showed up the proportions and harmonies underlying God's workings. Even in *Pearl*, most readers or listeners were unlikely ever to have counted the lines or thought the number might be of interest, and the more significant meanings emerge only as a step beyond the line count alone. The twelves of *Pearl* are explicitly drawn from Revelation, so the numerical basis of the poem can participate in that apocalyptic significance: the bare number can acquire a spiritual dimension. The reason for

[28]On the numerological connections between them see Mary Carruthers, "Of Notes and Unfolding Sounds: Perspectives from Grammar and Geometry," *European Drama and Performance Studies* 19 (2022): 59–63.

[29]See the digital facsimiles of the manuscript cited in my first note. One distinctive feature for the line count at the end of the poem is that whereas the bob, "Ywisse" (2526), is elsewhere attached syntactically to the preceding stanza, here it links the stanza with the wheel, so that it can be counted in either direction.

the fives of *Gawain* is far from being so explicit. They are obviously connected to the pentangle; but why the pentangle? It was much less usual in medieval culture than the six-pointed star, the two superimposed triangles rather than the single continuous line of the pentangle. Rarely used in heraldry, its most common function seems to have been as an apotropaic magic talisman, hence its occasional appearance in graffiti.[30] Gawain could do with some apotropaic magic, but that is not what gets commentary in the poem. One possible answer would be that in its quadrivial interpretation, geometric rather than linear, it offers five as a number in space, as something more extensive and more complete than a number alone, a form at the root of cosmic harmonies.[31] The first thing we are told about the pentangle is that it is a unit, and its unbroken line brings together the five fives enumerated in his arming into a single representation of *trawþe* (626). In medieval number theory, cardinal numbers did not so much form a sequence as they were expressed outwards from the monad, from one, just as here the single unbroken line produces the geometric series of fives. It was a basic principle of the first of the arts of the quadrivium, arithmetic, and is accordingly given first place in Alan of Lille's outline of the subject in his *Anticlaudianus*:

> Principium numeri fons mater origo
> est monas, et numeri de se parit unica turbam.

> The monad is the beginning of number, its fount, mother, origin,
> and of itself alone
> gives birth to the host of numbers.[32]

In Mary Carruthers's words, "the idea of the Monad generates all the creating cosmic harmonies and ratios . . . the point isn't just that the boundary line of the pentagon is unbroken, it's that what's inside is a single harmonious unit. That idea is as much social and ethical as it is

[30] The pentangle is discussed in Putter and Stokes's note to lines 619–65; its use as a talisman and for graffiti, apparently with apotropaic meanings, is discussed extensively in Chapter 4 of Green's forthcoming work.

[31] For the mathematical complexities of the pentangle, including its relation to the golden ratio (though the term came into use only later), see N. M. Davis, "Gawain's Rationalist Pentangle," *Arthurian Literature* 12 (1993): 37–62.

[32] Alan of Lille, *Anticlaudianus*, III.311–12, in *Works: Alan of Lille*, ed. and trans. Winthrop Wetherbee (Cambridge, Mass.: Harvard University Press, 2013).

mathematical."[33] In the scene of his second arming as he sets out for the Green Chapel, the girdle that Gawain ties over the badge on his surcoat replaces the unity of the pentangle with the linear belt with its two ends, little more than a piece of string. It thus loses that potential for harmony, resulting in its reduction to a "token of vntrawþe" (2509).

The pentangle fits admirably with the *sentence* of the work; but it does not explain why the number five should have occurred to the poet in the first place, in the way that the twelves of the Apocalypse govern the numerology of *Pearl*. There is, however, a possible reason, and one that takes us back to the issue of an episcopal patron. The five fives enumerated in the scene of Gawain's first arming start with the familiar five "wittes" (senses) and fingers, representing bodily prowess (640–41). The first move away from the purely physical follows immediately, not with the joys of the Virgin, as one might expect, but with the Five Wounds of Christ (642–43); and they were associated with one bishop in particular, whose extensive diocese included those target dialect areas of Cheshire and Staffordshire. This was Richard Scrope, a man of strong academic credentials, who in 1386 took office as bishop of the diocese of Coventry and Lichfield, and who had a particular devotion to the Five Wounds.[34]

The principal bishop's palace of the diocese was at Lichfield, in Staffordshire, and that is interesting for other reasons in addition to Scrope. In the late fourteenth century Lichfield served as an "entrepôt specializing in texts," in Ralph Hanna's phrase, in particular the copying of manuscripts of vernacular piety, which were then distributed more broadly, not least to the laity.[35] Many of these were prose works of a homiletic or devotional nature, but they probably included the massive West Midland Vernon and Simeon manuscripts, which incorporated a wide generic range of material, including verse narratives such as the alliterative *Pistel of Susan*. No bishop would have needed the moral or theological instruction of the kind found

[33] Mary Carruthers, private communication, developed in her *Creative Geometries* (forthcoming with Boydell and Brewer for Durham University IMEMS Press, 2024).

[34] For an outline of his life, see Peter McNiven, "Scrope, Richard (c. 1350–1405), Archbishop of York," *ODNB* (revised online 2008); for more detail see R. N. Swanson, "Bureaucrat, Prelate, Traitor, Martyr: Sketching Scrope," in *Richard Scrope: Archbishop, Rebel, Martyr*, ed. P. J. P. Goldberg (Donington: Shaun Tyas, 2007), 17–27.

[35] Ralph Hanna, "Lichfield," in *Europe: A Literary History 1348–1418*, ed. David Wallace (Oxford: Oxford University Press, 2016), 1:279–84 (280), and see also his "Poetic Sites," 46–49. Simon Horobin suggests a possible link between Scrope and the Vernon Manuscript in "Manuscripts: The Textual Record of Middle English Poetry," in Cooper and Edwards, *The Oxford History*, 54–67 (66).

in *Cleanness* and *Patience*, any more than they would have needed another of the Lichfield texts, the penitential *Prick of Conscience*; but as pastoralia aimed at the laity, the three religious Cotton Nero poems would fit well.[36] There is nothing to connect the Cotton manuscript directly with Lichfield, but the presence of such scribal activity around the cathedral could suggest a context for the copying or dissemination of its homiletic poems and for the lesson on salvation contained in *Pearl*; and *Gawain* itself is by no means entirely secular. The Garter motto added at the end of the text could, but need not, suggest a lay reader or owner, though the lover's couplet that appears on the same page as the picture of Gawain and the lady more decisively suggests some contact with an early lay readership or ownership.[37] The manuscript of the poems was, however, later bound together with some fifteenth- and early sixteenth-century texts that derived from a monastic or episcopal context, and which were rebound to form a separate manuscript by the British Library in 1964, as Cotton Nero A.x/1.[38] The association of the texts reveals nothing definite about their original provenance, but it does open the possibility that the poems were preserved in an ecclesiastical, not a secular, context.

Richard Scrope himself had close connections with Richard II. He was appointed bishop of Coventry and Lichfield in 1386, and the king attended his installation at Lichfield in 1387. He frequently served on the royal council over the following decade. Later, he was to be one of the two men tasked with receiving the king's abdication. He was the third son of the first Baron Scrope of Masham and cousin to the Scropes of Bolton, the two branches of a family that advanced up the social hierarchy from their Yorkshire gentry origins in the second half of the fourteenth century in recognition of their royal service. An almost exact contemporary of the martial Henry le Despenser, Scrope had three brothers who went on crusade, two of them dying overseas.[39] Crusading was in practice by no means

[36]Nicholas Watson describes them as "one of the most interesting of all the fourteenth-century attempts to direct religious instruction at the laity in general and the aristocracy in particular" ("The *Gawain*-Poet as a Vernacular Theologian," in Brewer and Gibson, *A Companion*, 293–313).

[37]See fol. 125r (129r) of the digital facsimile: "Mi minde is mikul on {on} þat wil me noȝt amende / Sum time was trew as ston & fro schame couþe hir defende." This is in a different hand from the main scribe's and from that of whoever wrote the Garter motto.

[38]Information from William A. Quinn.

[39]M. H. Keen, "Scrope, Henry, First Baron Scrope of Masham," in *ODNB*, notes the deaths of Geoffrey, who died in Prussia, and William, who fought at Satalye and died in the East; both crusades figure in Chaucer's portrait of the Knight in *The General Prologue*. A third brother survived to inherit the barony. For more detail see M. H. Keen, "Chaucer's

always a devotional activity, nor were crusaders always pious, but it was still regarded as the most righteous form of warfare, combining as it did martial prowess with religious duty, and the family seem to have taken it deeply seriously; the theatres of war they chose were not always those that produced fast profit. The family piety is on display again in their patronage of the anchoress Margaret Kirkby, who had her cell at Ainderby Steeple, the parish of Richard Scrope's first benefice. It has also been suggested that he was associated with the circulation of some of the northern or north-Midland mystical writers, including Richard Rolle and Walter Hilton.[40]

Scrope's connection with the royal council gave him and his accompanying household a need for frequent visits to London. It possibly also therefore provides a motive for the writing of *Saint Erkenwald*, the work that puzzlingly links the metropolis with the *Gawain* dialect. Scrope was frequently employed on further royal business too, including at the papal court, so providing possible occasions for the poet's distaste expressed in *Patience* for travel on his lord's orders to Rome and a means for him to have acquired his knowledge of ships. As a northerner, even if from the "wrong" side of the Pennines, Scrope would have had minimal problem with the dialect of the Cotton Nero poems, or of *Saint Erkenwald*. When he was not away on diplomatic or similar business, he made Lichfield his home base. The bishop's palace there had a particularly large and imposing hall; Richard II stayed there on occasion in the decade after 1387, the most famous being for the Christmas festivities of 1397–98, though Scrope himself was then visiting Rome.[41] The appropriateness of *Gawain* in relation to Christmas celebrations (in any year) is unmissable; Derek Pearsall describes it as being good for a Christmas house party at a court, and it is equally fitting for an episcopal court.[42] Its vicars choral, who were

Knight, the English Aristocracy, and the Crusade," in Scattergood and Sherborne, *English Court Culture*, 45–62.

[40]Discussed by Jonathan Hughes, *Pastors and Visionaries: Religion and Secular Life in Late Medieval Yorkshire* (Woodbridge: Boydell Press, 1988), 202–3, 220. Hilton, who was writing in the 1380s, was an older contemporary of Richard Scrope.

[41]Nigel Saul, *Richard II* (New Haven: Yale University Press, 1997), 319 ("many visits from 1387"), and the itinerary on 468–74. Some of the king's visits listed by Saul do not decisively include the king himself, but may refer only to his administrative household. According to the anonymous *Historia vitae et regni Ricardi Secundi*, the visit at Christmas 1397–98 was especially splendid, with jousting (*magna hastil*[*u*]*dia*) over several days, and included various visitors from continental Europe (*Historia vitae et regni Ricardi Secundi*, ed. G. B. Stow [Philadelphia: University of Pennsylvania Press, 2016], 151).

[42]Pearsall, "The Origins of the Alliterative Revival," 51.

housed in the cathedral precincts alongside the palace, might have been called on to help supply the entertainment.

Scrope thus incorporated an origin in the class interested in vernacular romance with familiarity with the court, secular homiletic concerns, and family associations with the devotional and military cultures of the period. He also had a generous academic background, having studied at Oxford and probably also Cambridge, and in due course serving as chancellor of both universities. He was elevated to the archbishopric of York in 1398, where one of his predecessors, John Thoresby, had commissioned both the Latin and English versions of *The Lay Folks' Catechism*, in a move analogous to the Lichfield concern with lay devotion. He also had an interest in music, the study of which at the level of the quadrivium required analysis of the same kind of numerological proportions as geometry. As archbishop, he wrote, or at least commissioned, a Latin sequence for the feast of St. Ursula in praise of her 11,000 virgin martyrs, the text of which opens with the punning *scrupulosa*. As a less complex form of composition, sequences do not demonstrate the harmonies that could be drawn from the theoretical study of music (which was an altogether different matter from its practice); the more advanced theory can be illustrated by the example of both the text and the music of the isorhythmic motet *Sub arturo plebs*, written for the Chapel Royal some time between the 1350s and the 1370s.[43] The Cotton Nero poems were not of course written for singing (and indeed contain little reference to singing), but the motet does indicate the degree of mathematical sophistication possible in wealthy chapels and cathedrals. A theoretical training in music was not a requirement for chapel singers, but if the poet were a vicar choral, or a lay clerk in minor orders employed to provide a higher degree of musical training than regular chapel clerks, he could well have had sufficient university education to be familiar with the complexities of number theory in both geometry and music. At a number of cathedrals, including Lichfield, the vicars choral lived in a designated close within the precincts, often organized as a college; and those too could perhaps have provided advanced education in

[43]The date is disputed, but the "Arturo" of the first line apparently refers to Edward III as Arthur. The Wikipedia article "*Sub Arturo plebs*" gives a good summary of the key features of the motet, a discussion of the proposed datings, and a list of the singers cited in the text (https://en.wikipedia.org/wiki/Sub_Arturo_plebs [accessed July 15, 2024]). Several of these were still working into the next century, though these late records could refer to people of the same names. See further Margaret Bent, *Two 14th-Century Motets in Praise of Music* (Newton Abbot: Antico Edition, 1986).

music alongside performance training. As the holder of an administrative post within an ecclesiastical or episcopal household (or very speculatively as a former singing clerk before marriage required a different post), he could have been in a position to call his patron's attention to the numerology of his texts.[44]

All that indicates a degree of circumstantial appropriateness for Scrope as the poet's patron in addition to his devotion to the Five Wounds, but there are other details in *Gawain* that suggest a more specific connection. One is the account at the end of the poem of the court's adoption of a new badge, its design based on the girdle that Gawain wears bound diagonally over his surcoat: a gold-hemmed "bende abelef" (2395, 2517), a diagonal ordinary (i.e., one of the basic heraldic charges). A bend by itself, without other heraldic charge, was unusual by this date; one of the very few families to adopt such a coat of arms, in the form of *azure, a bend or* (a gold diagonal on a blue field), was the Scropes. It appears prominently, for instance, on the bishop's tomb in the Scrope chapel in York Minster. Chaucerians will have come across the Scropes through their dispute with Sir Robert Grosvenor over that same coat of arms. The Grosvenors were a Cheshire family, but the four-year-long dispute acquired fame far beyond the region, with both John of Gaunt and Chaucer among the many hundred witnesses. The girdle that supplies the model for the heraldry in *Gawain* was, in the court's case, green with gold edging, as when Gawain tied it around himself, but in English heraldry in particular green was an unusual colour, and the poet would not have been trespassing directly on anyone's ownership. In keeping with the comparative lack of support for Grosvenor, if the court's new coat of arms recalled anyone's, it would have been the Scropes'.

Assigning to the court a badge based on the ambiguous girdle might seem a back-handed way of recognizing a patron, emphasizing the generally poor fit that *Gawain* might seem to offer with the religious emphasis of the other poems in the manuscript; but the inclusion of a romance for a man such as Scrope would not be out of place, especially given its strongly ethical emphasis. It is not a generic parody, as has on occasion been claimed on the grounds that Gawain has no great battles to fight, he fails in the central test, and the court laughs at him; on the contrary, it is one of the most principled romances there is, just because it refuses

[44]Kerby-Fulton's *The Clerical Proletariat* argues for the importance of chapel clerks as well as unbeneficed clergy in the composition of Middle English romances.

perfection to the knight who most ardently seeks it. Gawain is a fallible hero, not because he is inadequate (though that is true), but because even though he may be the best of knights, he is also human, and perfection can belong only to God. The court's adoption of the girdle marks the founding of a new order of chivalry analogous to the Order of the Garter, as that early owner or reader recognized in writing the Garter motto into the manuscript—"Hony soyt qui mal pence," shame be to him who thinks ill. Whoever wrote it might have had a personal connection with the Garter, but that is not essential: its significance for the *sentence* of the poem is larger than that.[45] The court wept when Gawain set out, so it is only proper that they should laugh when he returns—laughter of joy rather than mockery, as is appropriate not only for the occasion but for the chiasmic structure of the text. The motto insists that shame and honour lie in the perception of the beholder: in seeing how close Gawain has come to success in his quest, as the Green Knight too recognized, the members of the court are demonstrating their own capacity for honour. It would be intolerable if Gawain were to be equally self-congratulatory, but the laughter does offer a necessary qualifier to his capacity for self-abasement.

In his role as archbishop of York—little is known about him personally earlier—Scrope was noted as a man of some humility and of firm ethical principles. Not least among those principles was his devotion to the Five Wounds of Christ, and there is no reason to think that that was a new allegiance for him. The prominence given them in the account of the symbolism of the pentangle has often puzzled editors and readers. They are the first item to be mentioned after the corporeal qualities of his five senses and "five fyngres," his physical strength. "Alle his afyaunce vpon folde watz in þe fyue woundez / Þat Cryst kaȝt on þe croys" (642–43); the much better known five joys of the Virgin come second. That she is painted on the inner surface of the shield is taken from Geoffrey of Monmouth's description of Arthur's shield, but the reference to the Five Wounds is the poet's own.[46] It was those that Scrope used as the badge on his banner, including for instance at the time of his involvement in the

[45]The only Scrope on the Ricardian list of Garter knights was the Scrope of Bolton whom Richard II created earl of Wiltshire. Sir John Stanley is the only Garter knight of the suggestions for patronage for whom there is any circumstantial evidence for a connection with the poem, as discussed above.

[46]On a comparable sermon usage based on the source in Geoffrey of Monmouth, see Putter and Stokes's note to lines 649–50.

Northumberland rebellion against Henry IV in 1405. He played a leading part in the rebellion (as recorded in Shakespeare's *Henry IV, Part 2*), when "alle his afyaunce" in them was put to the hardest test. As a consequence of his role, he was sentenced to death at a summary trial without due legal process. The sentence was carried out almost immediately, on Whit Monday, before any pleas for mercy could reach the king; both Archbishop Arundel and the pope were among those who were outraged. The manner of his death fueled the outrage, as accounts of the execution insist that he asked to be beheaded with five strokes of the axe: "For his loue that suffrid v woundes for alle mankynde, yeve me v strokis, and I foryeve the my dethe."[47]

The combination of the nature of his cause (his manifesto for the rebellion cited oppressive taxation on the Church rather than doubt over Henry's legitimacy as king), his personal probity, the doubtful legality of his sentence, and his humility at his death rapidly led to Scrope's being regarded as a martyr, on the model of Thomas Becket, and his tomb in York Minster became the focus of a cult. It flourished despite early attempts to suppress it and was encouraged by the rise of the Yorkists, though he was never formally canonized.[48] The nearest thing we have to a portrait of him, in a miniature in a series of saints portrayed in the Bolton Hours (York Minster, Add. MS 2), has a supplicant asking for his prayers—"Sancte Ricarde Scrope, Ora pro nobis."[49]

[47]Recorded in *An English Chronicle of the Reigns of Richard II, Henry IV, and Henry V*, ed. John Silvester Davies (London: Camden Society, 1856). Contemporary Latin commentators describe the *ictus*—blows—of his death, but divide over the instrument, whether an axe or a sword. Execution with a sword necessarily had the victim kneeling upright, as is illustrated in Oxford, Bodleian Library, MS Lat. liturgy f.2, fol. 146v (viewable at the Bodleian website, https://digital.bodleian.ox.ac.uk/objects/55dbf4b2-d614-4f46-80de-c7de81ab47b6/ [accessed July 26, 2024]), and Plate 5 in Goldberg, *Richard Scrope* (though the identification of the figure with Scrope has been contested), but that would make five strokes impossible. It was further claimed that the block on which he was beheaded was preserved next to his tomb. See also Danna Piroyanski, "'Martyrio pulchro finitus': Archbishop Scrope's Martyrdom and the Creation of a Cult," in Goldberg, *Richard Scrope*, 100–112. The Latin poem "Quis meo capiti dabit effundere" specifies a *gladius* (*Political Poems and Songs Relating to English History*, Vol. 2, ed. Thomas Wright [London: Longman, 1861], 114–18), as does Clement Maidstone's Latin account, though its modern translator, Stephen Wright, refers to it as an axe; Keen too specifies an axe in his *ODNB* article on Scrope. A sword is the iconic weapon cited in the rhetoric of martyrdom, especially relevant to Scrope as it recalls the often-repeated parallel of him with that earlier episcopal martyr Thomas Becket. "Quis meo capiti" lays particular stress on Scrope as a martyr.

[48]For details see J. W. McKenna, "Popular Canonization as Political Propaganda: The Case of Archbishop Scrope," *Speculum* 45 (1970): 608–23.

[49]Reproduced as Plate 1 in Goldberg, *Richard Scrope*.

The popular nature of his cult emerges in vernacular literature as well as in art, in a poem that recounts his journey toward death: a journey that offers some parallels with *Gawain*. "The Bysshop Scrope, that was so wise" is an account of his execution on Whit Monday, in carol form, and therefore apparently designed for communal singing, with the "Hay, hay" burden sung by the whole company.[50]

Hay, hay, hay, hay!
Thynke on Whitson Monday.

The Bysshop Scrope, that was so wyse,
Nowe is he dede, and lowe he lyse;
To hevyns blys yhit may he ryse
    Thurghe helpe of Marie, that mylde may.

When he was broght vnto the hyll,
He held hym both mylde and styll:
He toke his deth with full gode wyll,
    As I haue herde full trewe men say.

He that shulde his dethe be,
He kneled down vppon his kne:
"Lord, your deth, forgyffe it me,
    Full hertly to yowe I pray."

"Here I wyll the commende
Thou gyff me five strokys with thy hende,
And than my wayes þou latt me wende
    To hevyns blys that lastys ay."
        Hay, hay . . .

There are moments here reminiscent of the end of *Gawain*, but the similarities are those not of a copy but of the inversion of cast to mould, largely highlighting the differences between an essentially secular work and an

[50]From Cambridge, Trinity College, MS R.4.20 (652) fol. 171r; no. 425 in *The Early English Carols*, ed. Richard Leighton Greene, 2nd ed. (Oxford: Oxford University Press, 1977), 257. It is copied on the last leaf of a fifteenth-century miscellany that includes works by Mandeville and Lydgate. See also the edition and discussion in Stephen K. Wright, "The Bishop Scrope that was so wise" and "Genres of Sanctity: Literary Representations of Archbishop Scrope," in Goldberg, *Richard Scrope*, 114–25, 116–37.

essentially religious one. The cult of the archbishop had far wider resonance than *Gawain* achieved, and did so independently of the romance. The more obvious parallels in the carol—the precise dating (the religious Whit Monday as against the secular New Year), its account of a man setting out for death, the stress on the multiple strokes—are offered as matters of historical fact. It would be stretching speculation too far to suggest that *Gawain* might have influenced Scrope's request for the five blows, even if the bishop had been its patron: comparable requests are recorded elsewhere, for instance when a few decades later John Tiptoft, earl of Worcester, renowned equally for his interest in humanism and his cruelty, asked to be beheaded with three blows in honour of the Trinity.[51] Any connection between Gawain's threefold test and the bishop's death would trivialize the martyrdom. The relevance of the carol lies in its sharing the same imaginative world as the romance, that facing an axe can have comparable poetic resonances in the spiritual and the secular world.

More speculatively, the conception of the carol does bear some similarities to *Gawain*, and it is not beyond possibility that whoever wrote it might have known the romance: its story had enough circulation to have reemerged as the feeble reworking known as *The Greene Knight*, preserved in the Percy Folio, and there is no reason why the Cotton Nero manuscript should have been the only copy ever made—at some point, at the very least, there must once have been a text of *Gawain* alone before it was put together with the other poems. Some of those similarities are simply a given of the different narratives, such as the multiple blows and their importance. The sentence on Scrope would have assumed a single stroke, which he himself chose to override; in the romance, a single blow is both specified several times in the original agreement and confirmed at the end by Gawain (2252, 2327), though the Green Knight's triple response is designed to complete the pattern of the three bedchamber temptations, and there is nothing devotional about it. It is again a parallel that serves more to highlight the difference between a secular narrative and a quasi-hagiographical account. Both victims, knight and bishop, request their real or threatened executioners to get on with the job (2285, 2300, and strongly implied in the last stanza of the carol), though that is hardly

[51]Known later as the "butcher of England," Tiptoft had rather more reason to seek a penitential death than the archbishop. See Benjamin G. Kohl, "Tiptoft [Tibetot], John, First Earl of Worcester (1427–1470)," *ODNB* (2004, revised online 2015).

surprising in the circumstances, and the motivations behind the requests contrast the sheer desire to have the death done with against the desire to leave this earth. "Than my ways þou latt me wende" is, however, a strange way to signal Scrope's eagerness to set off for Heaven, and for that line at least it resonates with the departures in the romance. Gawain is released for his return to the court, a journey of "wylde wayes" (2479) that has been described at length both on his way to the castle and further to the Green Chapel; but "þe knyȝt in the enker-grene" sets off "whiderwarde-so-euer he wolde" (2477–78). Scrope may request his own release to set off on his "ways" to "hevyns blys," but we never know where Bertilak might be going, nor in what shape. Scrope is sure of his final destination, if less clear of the ways to get there; the Green Knight's destination is never specified and is left to the reader to deduce.

The main argument of this paper, however, is not dependent on whether it is legitimate to find echoes of *Gawain* in the carol, or to think that they go beyond coincidence and a strong imaginative appeal. The primary possibility considered here is that the romance and its accompanying poems were influenced, perhaps even commissioned, at an earlier date by the bishop as patron. The link of Scrope himself with the *Gawain* poet may never reach the point of proof, but the evidence for it demands attention. The bishop's palace at Lichfield would provide a link both with the secular and courtly world, at times perhaps with the king, and with an environment for the homiletic poems; London would provide a comparable context for *Saint Erkenwald*, if it is indeed by the same writer. Lichfield too would provide a general context for encouraging the copying of Middle English writings. *Gawain* itself makes most sense as a homiletic poem for the chivalric world, urging humility on even the best of knights: not irrelevant for a man whose brothers died on crusade, but who was closely associated with a court that had rather different priorities. The implication that the poet had a patron able to think numerologically, rather than just numerically, would fit someone with a university education, and, if the Cotton Nero poems are by a single author, a patron familiar with both the Bible and French literature. Such a patron would be likely to be a senior churchman, and, if the seating plan for Arthur's feast is significant, a bishop. The poet is likely to have been a clerk in minor orders but with a university education (or conceivably some equivalent in a college attached to a cathedral), but without the influence, money, or life choices for advancement, in a household where the poems' dialect would not be alien, and from where he might be required to travel to Rome. The place given to the "bende abelef" suggests a narrowing down to the Scropes, and the introduction of the Five Wounds to Richard Scrope.

That argument in turn carries further implications: at the very least, we should be extending our search for the contexts of Middle English, even for works that are not obviously devotional, to the episcopacy. Men do not stop reading the literature they like, such as romances, just because they are ordained, or enthroned. There is a generosity about *Gawain* that embraces both worlds.

Lost in Transcription: A New Textual Tradition of Thomas Hoccleve's *Letter of Cupid*

Charlotte E. Ross
Lady Margaret Hall, University of Oxford

Abstract

In 1402, Thomas Hoccleve composed the *Letter of Cupid*, a loose translation of Christine de Pizan's *L'Epistre au dieu d'amours* that voices the complaints of women through the device of a letter written by the allegorical persona Cupid. Roughly nineteen years later, in 1421–22, Hoccleve copied the *Letter* into his holograph, HEHL, MS HM 744. The survival of the poem in the author's hand creates the rare opportunity to study Hoccleve's linguistic style without scribal interference, and for this reason the poem has so far predominantly been studied through the text in the holograph. However, the *Letter* survives in eleven non-holograph witnesses, and when they are scrutinized closely and considered collectively in comparison to the holograph it is possible to recover the existence of an earlier draft of Hoccleve's poem. This article proposes that these non-holographs descend from a Variant Original of the *Letter*, following J. A. Burrow's terminology. It analyses the entire manuscript corpus to demonstrate the existence of a lost archetype and reconstructs this text in order to study the revisions Hoccleve made to his poem across drafts. The evidence of a Variant Original of the *Letter* thus allows us to deconstruct the notion of the immoveable author in late medieval England and to address the reluctance to conceive of a text existing in multiple authorial versions.

I am profoundly grateful to Daniel Wakelin for his invaluable support and guidance throughout, and to Nicholas Perkins for valuable feedback on several drafts of this work. This article has also greatly benefited from the support and encouragement of Sebastian Sobecki, who generously shared unpublished work with me. My thanks to the librarians and archivists who allowed access to restricted items in their collections: Francis Gotto and Mike Harkness at Durham University Library, and Andrew Dunning, Matthew Holford, and Andrew Honey at the Bodleian Library. I am also grateful to Heather Barr, Emily Craven, Rachel Kaye, Isabel Smith, and Nell Williamson Shaffer for their insightful conversations and encouragement. I would also like to thank the anonymous readers for their helpful comments and astute reading, and the editorial team for their time and patience.

Studies in the Age of Chaucer 46 (2024): 121–161

Keywords

Thomas Hoccleve; manuscripts; stemmatology; textual transmission; holograph; scribe

> . . . in womman regneth al the constaunce,
> And in man is al chaunge and variaunce[1]

So proclaims Cupid in the holograph of Thomas Hoccleve's *Letter of Cupid* (henceforth *Letter*). This poem, composed in 1402, presents a loose translation of Christine de Pizan's *L'Epistre au dieu d'amours*, which voices the complaints of women through the device of a letter written by the allegorical persona Cupid.[2] In this stanza, Cupid bemoans the fate of innocent women who were deceived by false men with inconstant hearts. However, it is not just "mannes herte" (446) that are susceptible to "chaunge and variaunce" in the case of the *Letter*. Although the holograph presents an authentic, authorial, and authoritative poem, there are reasons to believe this does not mirror the first draft of the poem Hoccleve wrote.

Scholarship on Hoccleve has long been dominated by the study of his famed autograph manuscripts. Since H. C. Schulz's identification of Hoccleve's hand in Durham, University Library, MS Cosin V.iii.9 and San Marino, Henry E. Huntington Library (HEHL), MSS HM 111 and HM 744, these manuscripts have been the focus of intense critical attention.[3] Some value them for being free from suspicion of scribal interference,[4] while others note their rarity in a literary culture in which there remain

[1] *Hoccleve's Works*, Vol. 2, *The Minor Poems in the Ashburnham Manuscript Addit.133*, ed. Israel Gollancz, EETS e.s. 72 (London: Oxford University Press, 1925), 447–48. All further quotations from San Marino, Henry E. Huntingdon Library, MS HM 744, are from this source. In my transcriptions, underline marks expansions of abbreviations.

[2] Henceforth *Epistre*. Of this translation, see Roger Ellis, "Chaucer, Christine de Pizan, and The Letter of Cupid," in *Essays on Thomas Hoccleve*, ed. Catherine Batt (London: Centre for Medieval and Renaissance Studies, Queen Mary and Westfield College, University of London, 1996), 29–54; and Glenda K. McLeod, "A Case of Faux Semblans: *L'Epistre au dieu d'amours* and *The Letter of Cupid*," in *The Reception of Christine de Pizan from the Fifteenth through the Nineteenth Centuries: Visitors to the City*, ed. Glenda K. McLeod (Lewiston: E. Mellen Press, 1991), 11–24.

[3] H. C. Schulz, "Thomas Hoccleve, Scribe," *Speculum* 12 (1937): 71–81.

[4] *Thomas Hoccleve: A Facsimile of the Autograph Verse Manuscripts*, ed. J. A. Burrow and A. I. Doyle, EETS s.s. 19 (Oxford: Oxford University Press, 2002), xi.

few traces of the authors' role in textual reproduction.[5] The autographs and holographs are indeed valuable witnesses to Hoccleve as both a poet and scribe; however, the allure of the poet's touch on the page has historically dominated scholarly attention.[6] Non-holograph manuscripts, by contrast, have only recently been subject to a rise in interest, evidenced in the work of Sonja Drimmer, Aditi Nafde, and Rory Critten (amongst others).[7] This shift in scholarly focus emphasizes that, although often late and detached from the poet, non-autographs are valuable as coherent reconstructions driven by their readers' requirements, and carry important evidence of textual reception.

Scholarship of Hoccleve's *Letter* has similarly been overshadowed by the holograph. The poem survives in HEHL, MS HM 744 (H2), and has consistently been printed from this source.[8] The holograph has been studied because of this authorial text, which reveals the changes Hoccleve makes to his French source, and the ambiguity of his attitude to women.[9]

[5]Rory G. Critten, *Author, Scribe, and Book in Late Medieval English Literature* (Woodbridge: D. S. Brewer, 2018), 37.

[6]"Autograph" relates to a manuscript written *entirely* in the author's hand, whilst "holograph" relates to a manuscript written *wholly* by the person in whose name it appears. Accordingly, this article will refer to HEHL, MS 111, as an autograph (as it is written in Hoccleve's hand only), and MS Cosin V.iii.9 and HEHL, MS 744, as holographs (as they contain other hands).

[7]Sonja Drimmer, "The Manuscript as an Ambigraphic Medium: Hoccleve's Scribes, Illuminators, and Their Problems," *Exemplaria* 29 (2017): 175–94; Aditi Nafde, "Stanza Markers in MSS Arundel 38 and Harley 4866 of Hoccleve's *Regiment of Princes*," *N&Q* 61 (2014): 15–18; Rory Critten, "'Her heed they caste awry': The Transmission and Reception of Thomas Hoccleve's Personal Poetry," *RES* 64 (2013): 386–409.

[8]Thelma S. Fenster and Mary Carpenter Erler, eds., *Poems of Cupid, God of Love: Christine de Pizan's "Epistre au dieu d'amours" and "Dit de la rose," Thomas Hoccleve's "The Letter of Cupid": Editions and Translations with George Sewell's "The Proclamation of Cupid"* (Leiden: E. J. Brill, 1990), 159–218; Thomas Hoccleve, *"My Compleinte" and Other Poems*, ed. Roger Ellis (Exeter: University of Exeter Press, 2001), 93–111; *Christine de Pizan: "The God of Love's Letter" and "The Tale of the Rose," a Bilingual Edition*, ed. Thelma S. Fenster, Christine Reno, Thomas O'Donnell, Jocelyn Wogan-Browne, and Jean Gerson, Toronto Series 79 (New York: Iter Press, 2021); *Hoccleve's Works*, Vol. 1, *The Minor Poems: In the Phillips MS 8151 (Cheltenham) and the Durham MS III.9*, ed. Frederick J. Furnivall, EETS e.s. 61 (London: Oxford University Press, 1892)—this edition mistakenly used the text in Oxford, Bodleian Library, MS Fairfax 16 (F) as its source before Furnivall knew of the holograph's existence, and was later revised by Israel Gollancz (1925).

[9]See Stephanie Downes, "Thomas Hoccleve's *Letter of Cupid* and 'Martir Margarete,'" *N&Q* 58 (2011): 186–88; William A. Quinn, "Hoccleve's *Epistle of Cupid*," *The Explicator* 45 (1986): 7–10; Diane Bornstein, "Anti-Feminism in Thomas Hoccleve's Translation of Christine de Pizan's *Epistre au dieu d'amours*," *ELN* 19 (1981): 7–14; and John V. Fleming, "Hoccleve's *Letter of Cupid* and the 'Quarrel' over the *Roman de la Rose*," *MÆ* 40 (1971): 21–40.

However, the non-holograph corpus of *Letter* manuscripts is surprisingly large and complex, represented here:

Ad7	London, British Library, Additional MS 17492
B2	Oxford, Bodleian Library, MS Bodley 638
Ba	Glasgow, National Library of Scotland, Advocates' MS 1.1.6
D	Durham, University Library, MS Cosin V.iii.9
D1	Oxford, Bodleian Library, MS Digby 181
D3	Durham, University Library, MS Cosin V.ii.13
F	Oxford, Bodleian Library, MS Fairfax 16
H2	San Marino, Henry E. Huntington Library, MS 744
S2	Oxford, Bodleian Library, MS Arch. Selden B.24
T	Oxford, Bodleian Library, MS Tanner 346
Th	*The Workes of Geffray Chaucer*, ed. William Thynne (London, 1532)
Tr1	Cambridge, Trinity College, MS R.3.20
U	Cambridge University Library, MS Ff.1.6[10]

Eleven non-holographs survive: seven manuscripts (TB2FD3AdTr1S2) and one printed edition (Th) containing the complete text, two manuscripts containing incomplete texts (UD1), and one manuscript containing excerpts (Ad7). The poem was copied over almost 150 years, with the earliest surviving in the holograph H2 dating to 1421–22, and the latest in Ba dating to 1568.[11] The majority of witnesses were produced over the fifteenth century (FTD3B2S2D1Tr1), but the text was still being copied and printed in the sixteenth (UAdAd7Th) across England and Scotland. These non-holographs have been largely overlooked by scholars and editors, in part because some manuscripts present their stanzas in a disarranged order (TB2FUD3D1AdTh) or are late (Tr1S2).[12] But it is also the fetishization of the holograph that has led to their neglect.

[10]Sigla following Hoccleve, *My Compleinte*, ed. Ellis, with the exception of London, British Library (BL), Add. MS 17492, and Thynne's printed edition, which Ellis does not include in his study.

[11]Burrow and Doyle, *Facsimile of the Autograph Verse Manuscripts*, xx; *The Bannatyne Manuscript: National Library of Scotland, Advocates' MS.1.1.6.*, ed. Denton Fox and William A. Ringler (London: Scolar Press, 1980), i.

[12]On stanza disarrangement see Cynthia A. Rogers, "A Series of Unfortunate Events: Stanza Disarrangements in Hoccleve's *Letter of Cupid*," *N&Q* 67 (2020): 195–98; and Rory Critten, "Imagining the Author in Late Medieval England and France: The Transmission and Reception of Christine de Pizan's *Epistre au dieu d'amours* and Thomas Hoccleve's *Letter of Cupid*," *SP* 112 (2015): 680–97. On editorial dismissal of late manuscripts see Michael

Although representative of the risks of scribal transmission, these manuscripts are not devoid of scribal or readerly agency in their own right. They have another interest, however. In a surprising turn of events, when non-holograph versions of Hoccleve's *Letter* are scrutinized collectively, it becomes apparent that they contain a different and coherent textual tradition of the *Letter* that is not found in the holograph. A full collation of these witnesses suggests that there were multiple layers of poetic composition involved in creating Hoccleve's *Letter*. As this article will demonstrate, these non-holographs are in fact descendants of a lost draft of the poem, which (borrowing a term from J. A. Burrow) I shall call the Variant Original (VO).[13]

This study extends the editorial work of Roger Ellis, who acknowledges the change of first-person pronouns between the holograph and scribal copies of the text in his edition of Hoccleve's minor poems, and speculates whether there was an earlier version of the poem.[14] Building on Ellis's suggestion of earlier drafts of Hoccleve's texts, this study conducts a comprehensive analysis of all non-holographs to reconstruct an alternative text that, when compared to H2, reveals Hoccleve's process of revision. These manuscripts emerge as valuable testimonies to the existence of a different textual tradition of the poem that challenges our understanding of both text and poet.

This provides a rare opportunity to study Hoccleve as a poet who changes as he rewrites and reworks the *Letter*—a perspective not afforded in his holographs of this poem, which only show Hoccleve in a single moment in time. Indeed, this builds on recent bibliographic scholarship of Hoccleve that seeks to sketch the trajectory of his poetic and professional career. A notable contribution is the work of Ethan Knapp, who suggests Hoccleve's poetic voice was shaped by Lancastrian bureaucratic culture.[15] Sebastian Sobecki similarly explores the scribal community to which Hoccleve belonged and identifies the Privy Seal clerks with whom he worked, in order to demonstrate how the poet's biography provides a

D. Reeve, *Manuscripts and Methods: Essays on Editing and Transmission* (Rome: Edizioni di Storia e Letteratura, 2011).

[13] *Thomas Hoccleve's "Complaint" and "Dialogue,"* ed. J. A. Burrow, EETS os 313 (Oxford: Oxford University Press, 1999), xviii.

[14] Hoccleve, *My Compleinte*, ed. Ellis, 17. Ellis suggests more broadly that non-holograph texts of Hoccleve's work are worthy of study as potential witnesses of earlier drafts (12–18).

[15] Ethan Knapp, *The Bureaucratic Muse: Thomas Hoccleve and the Literature of Late Medieval England* (University Park: Pennsylvania State University Press, 2001).

revised context for the *Series*.[16] This recent focus in scholarship—one encouraged by the poet's own autobiographical moments—shines new light on the ways in which Hoccleve's poetry might be understood as the product of a life that grew and changed. Such scholarship portrays Hoccleve as a poet in motion by placing his texts in the timeline of his poetic and professional career. The study of textual variation thus highlights that the process of poetic composition, and the poet himself, evolve and are not static.

This article will circumnavigate the historical emphasis on Hoccleve's holographs to analyse instead non-holographs of the *Letter* and, within them, Hoccleve's process of composition and revision. The existence of a separate textual tradition of the *Letter* has perhaps been overlooked because of the holograph's allure, but also because the corpus of *Letter* witnesses is rarely analysed from both a literary and a codicological perspective. This article will provide a literary and textual critical analysis of the manuscripts to establish a stemma of *Letter* manuscripts, and propose a separate textual tradition that builds on Critten's work to reshape our understanding of the authority of the holograph. By applying Burrow's established work on VOs to scribal copies of the *Letter*, the study introduces a new perspective of the changeability of both the poem as a literary product and Hoccleve as a poet. When we look beyond the holograph, it is possible to uncover evidence of Hoccleve revising his work, which in turn contributes to ongoing conversations about the complexities of authorial processes in the late medieval period.[17]

Receiving a Letter: The Manuscripts of Hoccleve's *Letter of Cupid*

This section will describe the witnesses of Hoccleve's *Letter* and demonstrate the relationship between them by proposing a stemma—an exercise avoided by editors, but one that proves valuable when considering the importance of variant manuscripts. This is based on collations taken from

[16]Sebastian Sobecki, *Last Words: The Public Self and the Social Author in Late Medieval England* (Oxford: Oxford University Press, 2019); Sebastian Sobecki, "Communities of Practice: Thomas Hoccleve, London Clerks, and Literary Production," *JEBS* 24 (2021): 51–106; Sebastian Sobecki, "The Handwriting of Fifteenth-Century Privy Seal and Council Clerks," *RES* 72 (2021): 253–79.

[17]On the problems of prioritizing authorial manuscripts over non-authorial versions see Misty Schieberle, "*The Lytle Bibell of Knyghthod*, Christine de Pizan's *Epistre Othea*, and the Problem with Authorial Manuscripts," *JEGP* 118 (2019): 100–128.

diplomatic transcriptions of TB2FUD3D1AdThTr1S2.[18] Ad7 is not included because of the limited text it contains (stanzas 50, 10–11, 44). As a consequence of defective or incomplete manuscripts, it was only possible to record variants from stanzas 11–68 in D1, and 1–28 in U. Stemmatic analysis is based on the identification of substantive changes that diverge from the authorial sense, dubbed "palpable errors" by Ralph Hanna.[19] As it is impossible to count variants scientifically, they have been evaluated subjectively but nonetheless systematically as substantive or accidental. Changes to spelling or punctuation have been ignored, as have independent variants that are suggestive of scribal error (omissions, repetitions, and eye-skip). In doing so, I acknowledge George Kane and E. Talbot Donaldson's "assumptions of convenience": persistent errors in agreement result from a shared exemplar, genetically created agreements persist throughout the text, and groups that emerge with shared variation demonstrate true genetic descent.[20]

Typically, a stemma is described from the top, beginning with the archetype. Considering we have Hoccleve's holograph H2, one could expect to begin here. However, in the case of the *Letter*, there is a potential twenty-year gap between Hoccleve's composition and the creation of H2, and therefore it is probable that other manuscripts of the *Letter* circulated before Hoccleve produced the holograph. When the non-holographs are scrutinized, it becomes apparent that they descend from a separate textual tradition that suggests the existence of a lost archetype. Therefore, the following analysis describes the stemma of *Letter* manuscripts by beginning at the bottom. The surviving witnesses can be divided into three textual traditions based on the stanza order they contain:[21]

[18]Since the completion of this article, an excellent volume of Hoccleve's shorter poems has been published, edited by Sebastian Langdell, which contains a valuable appendix that lists textual variants in *Letter* manuscripts. *Thomas Hoccleve's Collected Shorter Poems: A Critical Edition of the Huntington Holographs*, ed. Sebastian Langdell (Liverpool: Liverpool University Press, 2023), 189–93.

[19]Ralph Hanna, *Pursuing History: Middle English Manuscripts and Their Texts* (Stanford: Stanford University Press, 1996), 85–87.

[20]William Langland, *Will's Visions of Piers Plowman, Do-Well, Do-Better and Do-Best: An Edition in the Form of Trinity College Cambridge MS B.15.17*, ed. George Kane and E. Talbot Donaldson (London: Athlone Press, 1975); William Robins, "Editing and Evolution," *Literature Compass* 4 (2007): 9–120.

[21]Stanza numbering taken from H2 is a reflection of Hoccleve's desired order for the poem, which has been used by editors since Furnivall's 1892 edition. In his own edition, Ellis divides the manuscripts into the same three groups.

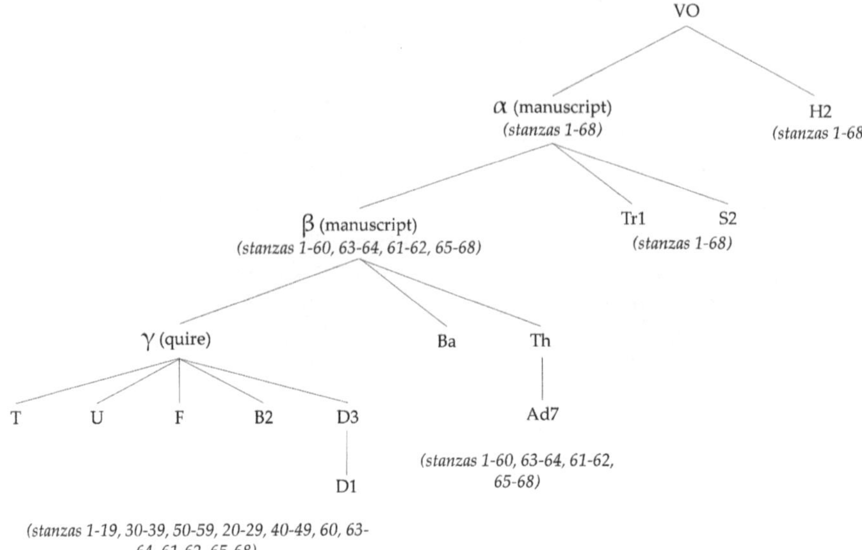

Fig. 1. Stemma of *Letter of Cupid* witnesses.

Stanza order	**Witnesses**
1–19, 30–39, 50–59, 20–29, 40–49, 60, 63–64, 61–62, 65–68	T, B2, F,[22] U, D3, D1
1–60, 63–64, 61–62, 65–68	Ad, Th
1–68	H2, Tr1, S2

The first of these traditions is witnessed in TB2FUD3D1, and is the most easily grouped. Cynthia A. Rogers's codicological study of the *Letter* in these manuscripts reveals that the disarrangement of this textual tradition was caused by the incorrect ordering of the leaves of a single quire after the poem was copied.[23] Building on the work of Eleanor Prescott Hammond, John Norton-Smith, and Frederick J. Furnivall, she demonstrates how the stanza order descends from the shuffling of a bifolium in a single

[22]The inclusion of F in this category will be discussed later.
[23]Rogers, "A Series of Unfortunate Events," 195–98.

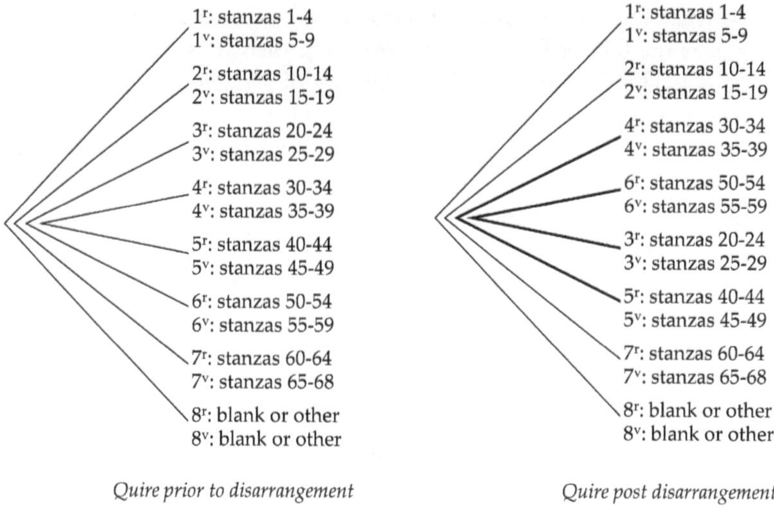

Fig. 2. The disarrangement of the exemplar-quire of the first textual tradition.

unbound quire from which the manuscripts took their exemplar.[24] The quire would have contained four bifolia, with four stanzas on the first and last folios, and five on the rest, as shown in Figure 2. The third and fourth bifolia (indicated with heavy lines) were shuffled, and the third (containing fols. 3r–v and 6r–v) was reversed on its fold. Thus the folios, previously ordered 1–8, were mistakenly rearranged into the order 1, 2, 4, 6, 3, 5, 7, 8.

Within this textual tradition, there is a notable oddity. F presents a version of the *Letter* in significant disarray because of the misbinding of the leaves some time after copying. The *Letter* appears in F in five bifolia

[24]Eleanor Prescott Hammond, *Chaucer: A Bibliographical Manual* (New York: P. Smith, 1933), 336–37; John Norton-Smith, ed., *Bodleian Library MS Fairfax 16* (London: Scolar Press, 1979), 7–13; Hoccleve, *Works*, 1:44. Although Rogers labels this a "booklet," a more accurate term might be "quire," following codicologists' judgment that a booklet could comprise many quires that circulated as separate units, while it is unknown if the *Letter* in this exemplar circulated with other material. See Pamela Robinson, "Self-Contained Units in Composite Manuscripts of the Anglo-Saxon Period," *Anglo-Saxon England* 7 (1978): 231–38; Alexandra Gillespie, "Medieval Books, Their Booklets, and Booklet Theory," *EMS* 16 (2011): 1–29; and J. Peter Gumbert, "Codicological Units: Towards a Terminology for the Stratigraphy of the Non-Homogeneous Codex," *Segno e testo* 2 (2004): 17–42.

across the sixth and seventh quires (fols. 40r–47r), beginning with one stanza at the foot of fol. 40r and proceeding thereafter with five stanzas per page. The F scribe copied the (already disarranged) *Letter* from the same exemplar-quire as TB2UD3D1, but when the quires were bound, the bifolia were shuffled, creating a second layer of disarrangement described as "shuffled like a pack of cards" by Furnivall.[25] However, it is important to acknowledge that, although F currently presents the most disarranged version of the *Letter*, for the scribe who copied it the text appeared as it does in TB2UD3D1. It was only at the point of binding that the poem was further disarranged. Figure 3 shows the stanzas before and after disarrangement. As a result of the shuffling of the third and fourth bifolia of quire six, the stanzas now appear as 1–6, 17–19, 30–36, 7–16, 57–59, 20–26, 37–39, 50–56, 27–29, 40–49, 60, 63–64, 61–62, 65–68. I have been able to identify leaf signatures, visible under ultraviolet light,[26] which offer substantial reason to believe this error occurred in the first fifteenth-century binding, rather than in the seventeenth- and nineteenth-century rebindings.[27]

Connections have previously been drawn between manuscripts within this textual tradition. Hammond united B2TF under the heading of the "Oxford Group," which she argued was compiled from a common ancestor.[28] Aage Brusendorff expanded this discussion to establish that these manuscripts likely shared booklet-exemplars that were exchanged and copied in tandem between scribes.[29] Links have also been made with manuscripts outside the "Oxford Group." Julia Boffey notes an interesting duplication of lyrics in T and U that suggests some of the texts were disseminated outside the network of metropolitan book producers.[30] Boffey and John J. Thompson further note that the U scribes likely "had access to at least one exemplar similar to if not the same as those used by the

[25] Hoccleve, *Works*, 1:44.

[26] These are: dj (fol. 39r), dij (40r), diij (41r), *illegible* (42r). On leaf signatures see Daniel Sawyer, "Page Numbers, Signatures, and Catchwords," in *Book Parts*, ed. Dennis Duncan and Adam Smyth (Oxford: Oxford University Press, 2019), 137–50 (140–42).

[27] Binding history from Arthur Green and Sabina Pugh, "Conservation Report: MS Fairfax 16," unpublished typescript, Bodleian Conservation and Collection Care Section (May 2015–June 2017).

[28] Eleanor Prescott Hammond, "On the Editing of Chaucer's Minor Poems," *MLQ* 23 (1908): 20–21.

[29] Aage Brusendorff, *The Chaucer Tradition* (Oxford: Oxford University Press, 1925), 189–92.

[30] Julia Boffey, *Manuscripts of English Courtly Love Lyrics in the Later Middle Ages* (Woodbridge: D. S. Brewer, 1985), 92.

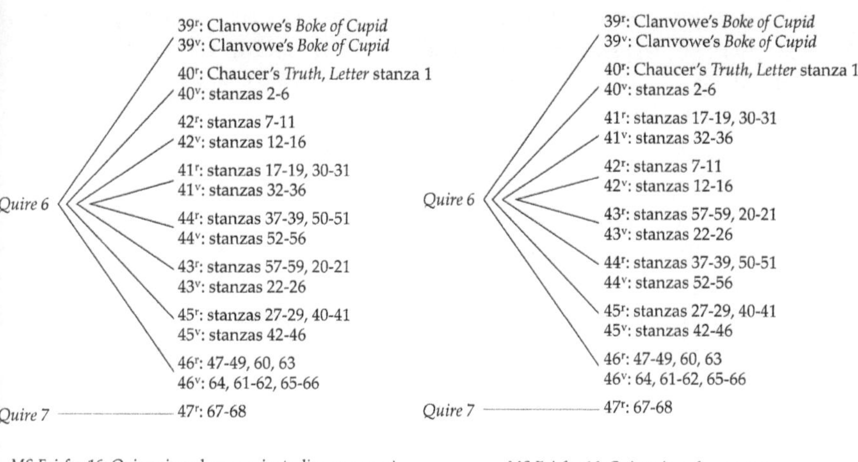

Fig. 3. The disarrangement of bifolia in F.

scribes of [T]."[31] These manuscripts have also been grouped for their organization: Alexandra Gillespie connects TB2FD1 as manuscripts that "regularly assemble texts in an order that suggests a common origin in independent groups of gatherings."[32] In line with Rogers and others, these conclusions are further suggestive of a common exemplar.

However, when the variations within the individual manuscripts of this group are scrutinized, a more detailed stemma can be proposed. D3 and D1 share a distinct set of variants, agreeing at 101 points. More notably, my collation suggests that they share twenty unique additions, substitutions, and omissions found in no other surviving witnesses of the *Letter*. This evidence points toward a close genetic relationship. On textual and paleographical grounds, D3 has been dated to the second quarter of the

[31] Julia Boffey and John J. Thompson, "Anthologies and Miscellanies: Production and Choice of Texts," in *Book Production and Publishing in Britain 1375–1475*, ed. Jeremy Griffiths and Derek Pearsall (Cambridge: Cambridge University Press, 1989), 282–83.

[32] Alexandra Gillespie, *Print Culture and the Medieval Author: Chaucer, Lydgate, and Their Books, 1473–1557* (Oxford: Oxford University Press, 2006), 48.

fifteenth century, and D1 to the last quarter of the fifteenth century.[33] Although it is possible that D3 and D1 are cognate copies sharing a now lost exemplar, the nature of their textual agreements and suggestions of a common geographical place of origin allow us to speculate a vertical genetic relationship.[34]

The dating of the manuscripts points toward D1 descending from D3, and there are also minor details that support this. The D1 scribe is consistent in his spelling across the *Letter* but occasionally errs in moments when he copies a word from the wrong line in an instance of eye-skip. In these cases, the words incorrectly copied are crossed out, but it is possible to see that they present different spellings from the rest of the *Letter.* One example appears on line 244. The D3 scribe spells the final words of these lines, "smite" and "bite," with **i**:

> My sharp persing strokes how þei **smite**
> Shall feel and know how þei karue and **bite**
> D3, fol. 8r

Whereas the D1 scribe favors **y**. However, this scribe incorrectly takes the last word from the following line and is forced to correct "bite" to "smyte":

> My sharpe persyng strokes, howe they ~~**bite**~~ **smyte**
> Shull fele and knowe howe they kerue and **byte**
> D1, fol. 2r

Eye-skip implies a momentary lapse of concentration, where the mind wanders and the hand copies what the eye sees without thinking.[35] The discrepancy between the spelling of the erroneous words and the correction suggests that, in these brief instances, the D1 scribe mindlessly copied

[33]Kara A. Doyle, *The Reception of Chaucer's Shorter Poems, 1400–1450* (Cambridge: D. S. Brewer, 2021), 78; Robert Root, *The Manuscripts of Chaucer's "Troilus" with Collotype Facsimiles of the Various Handwritings* (London: published for the Chaucer Society by K. Paul, Trench, Trübner, and by H. Milford, Oxford University Press, 1914), 11; M. B. Parkes, *English Cursive Book Hands, 1250–1500* (Oxford: Clarendon Press, 1969), Plate 2.ii; W. D. Macray, *Bodleian Library Quarto Catalogues: IX Digby Manuscripts* (Oxford: Bodleian Library, 1999); Daniel W. Mosser, "The Scribe of Chaucer Manuscripts Rylands English 113 and Bodleian Digby 181," *Manuscripta* 34 (1990): 129–47.

[34]Seymour's identification of an East Anglian secretary hand in D3 and Brode's hand in D1 locates both manuscripts to the southeast of England.

[35]Takako Kato, "Corrected Mistakes in Cambridge University Library MS Gg.4.27," in *Design and Distribution of Late Medieval Manuscripts in England*, ed. Margaret Connolly and Linne R. Mooney (York: York Medieval Press, 2008), 61–87.

from an exemplar that contained alternative spellings—spellings that are found in D3. From the dating of the manuscripts, and these minor textual details, the *Letter* in D3 can be proposed as the exemplar for D1.

There are also intriguing similarities between F and B2; however, the evidence does not indicate clearly whether or not one was the exemplar for the other. These two manuscripts have long been associated: Norton-Smith notes the close textual affiliation and order of appearance of items 10, 11, 12, and 13 of F with items 4, 7, 8, and 9 of B2, and Pamela Robinson also identifies similarities among the subheadings, Latin citations, and gaps in both manuscripts.[36] M. C. Seymour, too, describes the texts of *The Book of the Duchess*, *The Parliament of Fowls*, and *Anelida and Arcite* as "closely affiliated."[37] The variants in B2 and F's *Letter* also suggest a close relationship, sharing ten unique agreements not found in other *Letter* manuscripts. The most notable is the omission of the line: "Un to the feith of god holy uirgyne."[38] The stanza in which it appears professes the virginity and sanctity of St. Margaret, and therefore the omission of this important point in Cupid's argument is unlikely to be deliberate. It is possible that the scribes both independently omitted the line in an instance of convergence.[39] Yet, intriguingly, missing lines are shared across other texts in these manuscripts, one in each of *Anelida and Arcite* and *The Book of the Duchess*.[40] The relationship is made more complex by the presence of pencil crosses in B2 that mark the folio-ends in F at the points at which the misbinding disarranges the poem; however, it is unknown if these are the work of the scribe or of a later librarian or scholar comparing the manuscripts.

B2 and F have been closely dated, making it difficult to suggest which could have been the exemplar. F has been firmly dated to the mid-fifteenth century from the coat of arms of John Stanley, Esq.[41] Similarly, B2 has been

[36]Norton-Smith, *Bodleian Library MS Fairfax 16*, viii; *Manuscript Bodley 638: A Facsimile*, ed. Pamela Robinson (Woodbridge: Pilgrim Books, 1982), xxvi, xxvii, xxxvi.

[37]M. C. Seymour, *A Catalogue of Chaucer Manuscripts*, 2 vols. (Aldershot: Scolar Press, 1995), 1:4, 29, 37.

[38]H2, 427.

[39]Lawrence Warner, "Convergent Variation and the Production of *Piers Plowman*," *YLS* 34 (2020): 137–73; William Langland, *Will's Visions of Piers Plowman and Do-Well: An Edition in the Form of Trinity College, Cambridge, MS R.3.14*, ed. George Kane (London: Athlone Press, 1960).

[40]Seymour, *A Catalogue of Chaucer Manuscripts*, 1:37. See also Hammond, *Chaucer*, 336.

[41]Stanley died c. 1469. Josiah Wedgwood, *History of Parliament: Biographies of the Members of the Commons House 1439–1509* (London: His Majesty's Stationery Office, 1933), 799. The quartered arms on fol. 14v pertain to the Hooton family of Cheshire, identifying

dated to the third quarter of the fifteenth century; however, Robinson notes that this can only be inferred from the script.[42] The hand is of one scribe in a mixture of anglicana and secretary, displaying features that are characteristic of both the late and mid-fifteenth century.[43] In summary, although the unique agreements between F and B2 are suggestive of a vertical genetic relationship, the close dating of the manuscripts and consistency in their scribes' copying does not clearly indicate whether one was the exemplar for the other. They have therefore been placed horizontally in the stemma.

This analysis of the variants of TB2FUD3D1 thus suggests a shared ancestor in the form of a lost quire, here called γ (Fig. 4). However, when the variants are compared to Hoccleve's holograph H2, it becomes apparent that there are major shared textual divergences between them and the holograph. There are 110 significant variants shared across TB2FUD3D1 that differ from H2. These variants represent transpositions, omissions, and substitutions of adjectives, nouns, verbs, pronouns, and demonstratives—significant divergences demonstrating that these six manuscripts do not descend from H2. Despite the disarrangement of their stanzas—which has previously led to their dismissal as corrupt manuscripts—they hold value as witnesses of a different textual tradition of the *Letter*. They therefore raise the question as to whence they took their archetype.

The next textual tradition, witnessed in BaTh, contains Hoccleve's poem in an order that largely resembles H2 but presents disarrangement in the final stanzas, resulting in the stanza order 1–60, 63–64, 61–62, 65–68. The authorship of this rearrangement has been disputed. In H2, the stanzas ordered 60–65 move from a discussion of women's mercy, to praise of St. Margaret's constancy, to praise of Mary's constancy, to a final description of women's virtue. Stanzas 61–62 contain the praise of St. Margaret, and 63–64 that of Mary, and therefore by swapping these pairs of stanzas the sense is little changed (other than a suggestion of hierarchy between the figures). Ellis argues that the disarranged order 63–64–61–62 is more

---

Stanley, who belonged to a branch whose seat was at Hooton. George Ormerod, *The History of Cheshire: General Index & Appendix*, Vol. 2 (London, 1819), 410. The same arms appear in London, BL, MS Harley 6163, fol. 22r. Norton-Smith agrees in his dating of the script and decoration: Norton-Smith, *Bodleian Library MS Fairfax 16*, xiii. On fol. 1r Charles Fairfax also records "Anno 1450," although considering he purchased the manuscript in 1650 this date is dubious.

[42]Robinson, *Manuscript Bodley 638*, xxiii.

[43]Late fifteenth: simplified **a**, tall **t** ascender that extends above the head stroke; mid-fifteenth: upright **f**, long **s**, diamond-shape **g**.

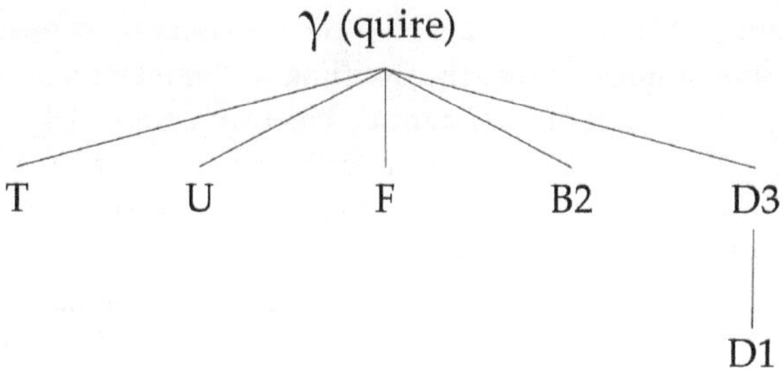

Fig. 4. Manuscripts containing stanzas 1–19, 30–39, 50–59, 20–29, 40–49, 60, 63–64, 61–62, 65–68.

persuasive and even suggests that the order in H2 arose from Hoccleve's "accidental miscopying" of his own work.[44] Elon Meir Lang also prefers the disarranged order, suggesting it softens the rhetoric of the poem's praise of Margaret by following it with praise of Mary.[45] Whilst literary arguments for both arrangements can be made, it is also worth considering the lines preceding and following these stanzas.

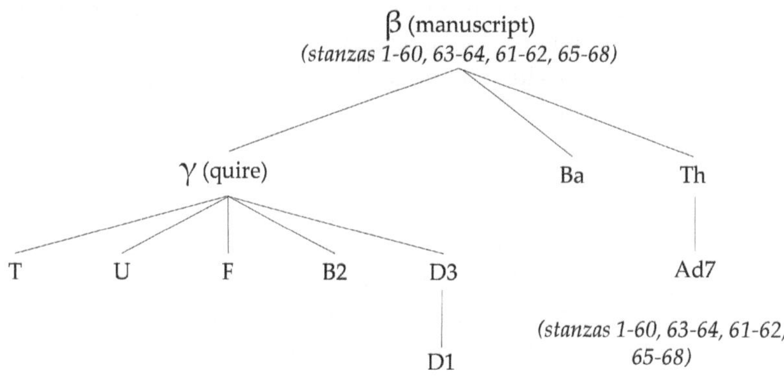

Fig. 5. Witnesses of the first and second textual tradition.

[44]Hoccleve, *My Compleinte*, ed. Ellis, 276.

[45]Elon Meir Lang, "Thomas Hoccleve and the Poetics of Reading," Ph.D. thesis (Washington University, St. Louis, 2010), 194.

Two pairs of stanzas are swapped—each containing its own narrative unit—making it unlikely that the shuffling was unintentional. Moreover, the first and last words of each stanza are not similar in a way that would prompt accidental error.[46] However, deliberateness need not equate to authorial interaction. These stanzas present an ideal opportunity for an engaged scribe to alter Hoccleve's poem and emphasize different elements. The first line following the disarranged stanzas, beginning stanza 65, is "Now holdith this for ferme and for no lye" (H2, 449). Although it is ambiguous whether "this" refers to the line above or below, there is the opportunity here subtly to alter this section's emphasis by changing the example that precedes this statement. In the holograph order (60–65), this emphasis falls on Hoccleve's argument that "in man is al chaunge and variaunce" (H2, 447), whereas the 63–64–61–62 disarrangement emphasizes St. Margaret's "louyng herte and constant to this lay" (H2, 433). Both lines elevate the constancy of women, one by critiquing men and the other by lauding women—the difference between the two is subtle, but by swapping stanzas 61–62 with 63–64 the emphasis as to what the reader should hold "ferme" shifts. Unconscious scribal error is always a possibility, and this change is decidedly subtle; however, it is plausible that an active scribe who is engaged with the material he is copying would be more willing to focus on St. Margaret than to emphasize man's "chaunge and variaunce". It would be unseemly to move stanza 60, as it is linked to the previous stanza by the concatenation of "mercy," and therefore the pairs of 61–62 and 63–64 present themselves as ideal candidates for shuffling.

The stanza arrangement alone suggests that Ba and Th are genetically related, but further textual analysis clarifies this relationship and adds a further witness to the stemma: Ad7, also known as the Devonshire Manuscript. Richard Harrier, Molly Murray, and Bradley J. Irish have established that the copyists of Ad7 took Th as their source.[47] Irish specifically identifies the excerpts of the *Letter* contained in Ad7 as direct descendants from Th.[48] Although it has also been suggested by Denton Fox and Lucy R.

[46]Namely, "Thou preciouse" (H2, stanza 61), "But vnderstondeth" (H2, stanza 62), "In any" (H2, stanza 63), "Womman forsook" (H2, stanza 64).

[47]Richard C. Harrier, "A Printed Source for 'The Devonshire Manuscript,'" *RES* 9 (1960): 54; Bradley J. Irish, "Gender and Politics in the Henrician Court: The Douglas-Howard Lyrics in the Devonshire Manuscript (BL, Add 17492)," *RenQ* 64 (2011): 79–114 (97); Molly Murray, "The Prisoner, the Lover, and the Poet: The Devonshire Manuscript and Early Tudor Carcerality," *Renaissance and Reformation* 35 (2012): 17–41 (31).

[48]Irish, "Gender and Politics," 101. Ethel Seaton first identified the medieval origin of the texts in "The Devonshire Manuscript and Its Medieval Fragments," *RES* 7 (1956): 55–56.

Hinnie that Ad7 likewise descends from Th,[49] this has been recently contested by Critten and Ellis in favor of a shared exemplar.[50] Whilst there are variant agreements between Ba and Th, they are not sufficient to indicate a vertical relationship, and therefore they have been placed horizontally in the stemma.

When Ba and Th are compared to TB2FUD3D1, it becomes apparent that they too share the most common divergences from H2, suggesting that neither textual tradition descends from the holograph. It is unlikely that BaTh descend from the same quire-exemplar as TB2FUD3D1, since they were produced later than those manuscripts affected by the shuffling of quires. It is more probable that they originated from an earlier stage of the same tradition: a version of the poem that circulated before the quire-disarrangement occurred, from which γ was copied. Furthermore, the stanza arrangement 64–63–61–62–65–68 also appears in TB2FUD3D1. This common ancestor is suggested here as Manuscript β (Fig. 5).

The question of these witnesses' archetype remains as yet unanswered. The final textual tradition of the *Letter* includes H2, Tr1, and S2—three fifteenth-century manuscripts that present Hoccleve's poem in the order 1–68. Because of this agreement, these manuscripts have traditionally been understood to be related.[51] However, the codicological evidence does not support this assumption: when Tr1S2 are compared to the disarranged TB2FUD3D1BaTh, many of the same variants are found in agreement. Of the 110 significant variants identified in TB2FUD3D1BaTh, 84 are found in Tr1 and 85 in S2, sharing many of the transpositions, omissions, and substitutions. Tr1 and S2 are unlikely to have a vertical genetic relationship, in part because of their geographical origin: Tr1 was copied by John Shirley, likely in London, and S2 in Scotland.[52] The agreements in variants are highly suggestive that these witnesses share a common archetype.

Tr1 and S2 do not contain the 64–63–61–62–65–68 disarrangement found in the other witnesses. For this reason, they have not previously been

[49]Fox and Ringler, *The Bannatyne Manuscript*, xli; Lucy R. Hinnie, "Bannatyne's Chaucer: A Triptych of Influence," *ChauR* 55 (2020): 484–99.

[50]Hoccleve, *My Compleinte*, ed. Ellis, 275; Critten, "Imagining the Author," 687 n. 20.

[51]Hoccleve, *The Letter of Cupid*, ed. Fenster and Erler, 274.

[52]M. R. James, "R.3.20," in *The Western Manuscripts in the Library of Trinity College, Cambridge: A Descriptive Catalogue*, 4 vols., Vol. 2 (Cambridge: Cambridge University Press, 1902), no. 600; *The Works of Geoffrey Chaucer and "The Kingis Quair": A Facsimile of Bodleian Library, Oxford, MS Arch. Selden.B.24*, ed. Julia Boffey and A. S. G. Edwards (Cambridge: D. S. Brewer, 1997).

connected to this side of the textual tradition.[53] However, they share variants across all non-holographs of the *Letter*, making it likely that Tr1 and S2 descend from the same archetype as Manuscript β (which contained the *Letter* arranged 1–68). It is plausible that three manuscripts were copied from this archetype, called here α: Tr1 and S2 (whose scribes copied the stanzas 1–68), and β (whose scribe disarranged the end of the poem). This monogenesis would justify the shared variants found in all ten manuscripts (TB2FUD3D1BaThTr1S2) by connecting them to one original archetype, with allowances for scribal errors and misbinding to account for the various layers of stanza disarrangement.

To summarize, when the individual variant readings of the non-holographs are considered, it becomes apparent that they do not descend from H2. Instead, a lost archetype α, with an intermediate manuscript β and a quire γ, can be suggested from the various layers of disarrangement that befell the *Letter* over the 170 years of its transmission. The existence of Hoccleve's holograph encourages us to view the witnesses of the *Letter* that are not in agreement as the victims of scribal corruption or error. However, when the stemma is analyzed from the bottom and the manuscripts grouped by their textual traditions, it becomes clear that they descend from a different but shared version of Hoccleve's *Letter* (see Fig. 1).

Writing a Letter: A Variant Original of the *Letter of Cupid*

If eleven of the surviving witnesses of the *Letter* do not descend from Hoccleve's holograph H2, but are rather monogenous and descend from the lost archetype α, then what is the relationship between H2 and α? Many editors who print H2 do not address the (at least) nineteen years between Hoccleve's composition of the *Letter* in 1402 and the compilation of H2 in 1421–22.[54] The *Letter* is the earliest of Hoccleve's dateable works, and between its composition and its inscription in H2 Hoccleve wrote *La male regle*, the *Regiment of Princes*, and *Remonstrance against Oldcastle*, amongst

[53] Lang, "Thomas Hoccleve and the Poetics of Reading," 196.

[54] The *Letter* dates itself: "A thousand and foure hou*n*dred and secounde" (H2, 476). Burrow and Doyle date H2 to 1421–22 by its references to Henry V; *Facsimile of the Autograph Verse Manuscripts*, xx. Neither Furnivall, Gollancz, Fenster, nor Erler notes this nineteen-year gap in their editions; however, Ellis acknowledges that the holographs represent a later version of the text: Hoccleve, *My Compleinte*, ed. Ellis, 11.

others. Within this period, it is possible that Hoccleve may have returned to the *Letter*—even if only at the point of copying—to revise it in the light of his changing poetic experience.

In his edition of Hoccleve's *Complaint* and *Dialogue*, J. A. Burrow emphasizes that "one cannot assume that a holograph copy is necessarily the original from which scribal copies descend."[55] In a stemmatic analysis of those texts, he concludes that the Durham holograph (D) cannot be the exemplar for non-holographs of the *Series*. Whilst these scribal copies could consciously have omitted the envoy to the countess of Westmorland, it is more significant that they do not replicate mistakes found in the holograph, or variations in its Latin glosses. Burrow identifies forty-eight archetypal variants that differ from the holograph, consisting of transpositions (e.g. 329 me hath D] hath me VO), substitutions (e.g. 350 bond D] knotte VO), and additions (e.g. 706 to D] for to VO). The stemma of *Letter* witnesses similarly suggests a parallel manuscript tradition of the *Letter* that contained a slightly different, but coherent, version of the poem. As in Burrow's model, the evidence points toward the descent of these witnesses from an authorial original: a VO of the *Letter*.

Eighty-four variants appear across the majority of non-holographs of the *Letter*, the metrical implications of which will be explored in the following section. The variants can be divided into four grammatical categories.[56] First, there are additions, which are predominantly adjectives that add emphasis to the pre-existing subject:

7 Been sogettes, greetynges H2] Been sogetes, **hertely** gretynge VO
244 Our sharpe strokes H2] Our sharpe **persynge** strokes VO

Second, there are transpositions, which neither alter the sense nor change the rhyme scheme:

114 Repreef of here he spekth and villenye H2] He speketh her reprefe and villenye VO
121 spent his tyme <u>and</u> used H2] his tyme spent and used VO

[55] Hoccleve, *"Complaint" and "Dialogue,"* ed. Burrow, xviii.

[56] For reasons of economy, the spelling that appears most often across the ten non-holographs is taken, or, when there is no obvious predominance, the most common fifteenth-century spelling according to the *MED* is used, which is represented by the siglum VO. H2 is taken as a lemma.

Third, there are omissions, which are rare and pertain to closed-class words ("ther," "þat," and "lo").[57] The last category, substitutions, contains the most variants. These are predominantly synonymous:

42 betrayed H2] deceyued VO
116 sundry H2] diuers VO

Although occasionally the sense is changed:

197 wikkid bookes H2] sory bokes VO

The predominant type of substitution relates to pronouns, of which twenty-three variants have been identified. The literary significance of these variants will be analyzed in the following section. The variants witnessed between H2 and the VO are not insignificant, and I shall argue that they are suggestive of Hoccleve's intervention—following Peter J. Lucas's statement that "all scribes corrupt but authorial scribes corrupt authoritatively."[58]

It is helpful at this point to compare the variants in drafts of the *Letter* to those identified in the only known Hocclevean poem to appear in multiple drafts. *Lerne to Dye* survives in two holographs, once in H2 (fols. 52v–68v) and again in D (fols. 52v–74v).[59] Although close in date (1421–22 [H2], 1421–26 [D]), the two versions of *Lerne to Dye* are witnesses to variation.[60] In his comparison of the holographs, John M. Bowers notes over eighty substantive variants and multiple differences in orthography and punctuation over 672 lines.[61] Describing these manuscripts as a "test-case" for studying textual transmission, Bowers argues that the holographs offer "tangible evidence that the single poet, primarily engaged in the act of

[57]Daniel Wakelin, *Immaterial Texts in Late Medieval England: Making English Literary Manuscripts, 1400–1500* (Cambridge: Cambridge University Press, 2022), 218, notes that single-syllable words are especially prone to omission.

[58]Peter J. Lucas, "An Author as Copyist of His Own Work: John Capgrave OSA (1393–1464)," in *New Science out of Old Books: Studies in Manuscripts and Early Printed Books in Honour of A. I. Doyle*, ed. Richard Beadle and A. J. Piper (Aldershot: Scolar Press, 1995), 227–48 (227).

[59]H2 is missing the last 245 lines of the poem because of a missing quire.

[60]Burrow and Doyle, *Facsimile of the Autograph Verse Manuscripts*, xx. Because of the uncertainty of the Durham holograph's date, and the closeness of the manuscripts, it is unclear which version of the poem Hoccleve wrote first.

[61]John M. Bowers, "Hoccleve's Two Copies of *Lerne to Dye*: Implications for Textual Critics," *The Papers of the Bibliographical Society of America* 83 (1989): 437–72 (438). Bowers also concludes that neither manuscript was copied from the other.

making his own fair copies, naturally undertook minor, even cosmetic revisions."[62] He identifies four major categories of variants: "indifferent" substitutions (e.g. 56 right H2] ful D; 15 to H2] so D);[63] transpositions (e.g. 56 **ther of is** glad & fawe H2] **is ther of** glad & fawe D);[64] synonymous substitutions, of which Bowers identifies twenty-six notable occurrences (e.g. 280 scourgid H2] beten D; 399 folyly H2] synfully D);[65] and adjectives and adverbs added for emphasis (e.g. 13 profounde & grete H2] **right** profownde & greete D).[66] The types of variants that Bowers notes between the holographs are tantalizingly similar to those seen between the VO and H2 versions of the *Letter.* Furthermore, when the versions are compared, nearly 12 percent of the *Lerne to Dye* lines contain variants, and 17 percent of the *Letter* lines contain variants. The difference between these figures is explicable by the fact that one of the *Lerne to Dye* holographs is missing 245 lines (and thus cannot be compared), and there is a smaller proposed amount of time between the composition of the two *Lerne to Dye* and *Letter* versions.

These changes also resemble the types of authorial variants that Olivier Delsaux identifies in his analysis of Laurent de Premierfait's translation of Boccaccio's *De casibus virorum illustrium*. In comparing the first (1400) and second (1409–10) versions of this text, Delsaux not only demonstrates that one descends from the other but, moreover, shows that the authorial revisions simplify and adjust the phrasing, rather than changing the overarching sense.[67] This is perhaps not what one would expect when an author returns to a text to correct and improve, but Delsaux argues that the majority of revision involves such local, lexical modification, more akin to rewriting than retranslating.[68] Considered in this light, the variants between the two *Lerne to Dye* drafts and the two versions of the *Letter* are highly suggestive of an authorial approach to revision.

In support of the theory that H2 represents Hoccleve's later revision of the *Letter*, the manuscript itself offers intriguing suggestions of revision.

[62]Ibid., 438, 443.

[63]Ibid., 443.

[64]Ibid.

[65]Ibid., 444.

[66]Ibid., 454. The metrical implications of these changes will be considered later.

[67]Olivier Delsaux, "Un témoignage inédit sur la fortune du *De casibus virorum illustrium* de Giovanni Boccaccio en France à la fin du Moyen Age," *Cahiers de recherches médiévales et humanistes* 29 (2015): 347–61 (337); Olivier Delsaux, *Manuscrits et pratiques autographes chez les écrivains français de la fin du Moyen Age: L'exemple de Christine de Pizan* (Geneva: Librairie Droz, 2013), 185.

[68]Delsaux, "Un témoignage inédit," 350, 333.

There are fifty-one corrections across the eighty-eight written pages of H2 (Part 2).[69] Specifically, there are eighteen instances where the singular pronouns *I*, *me*, or *my* are corrected to *we*, *us*, or *our* across all works in the manuscript.[70] Lang identifies some of these corrections and questions whether they stem from an earlier textual tradition.[71] Wendy Scase also acknowledges these corrections in passing, but only to suggest that Hoccleve preferred the first-person plural over Christine's "more intimate singular."[72] However, these corrections have not been connected to the corpus of non-holograph *Letter* witnesses. When they are compared, there are compelling alignments.

Corrections in H2 are predominantly erasures that have been overwritten. This is typical of Hoccleve's correction style—Daniel Wakelin notes that, of the entire manuscript's fifty-one corrections, forty-four are overwritten erasures.[73] In line with those figures, from the facsimile it was possible to count eighteen points at which pronouns are written over erasures in the *Letter* (Table 1).[74] Remarkably, seventeen of these erasures align with the position of variants in the non-holographs. Only one correction is not found in non-holographs (242), and conversely there is only one pronoun variant in the non-holographs that does not correspond to a correction in H2.[75] These corrections highlight that there is a significantly higher use of the "royal we" in H2 in comparison to the VO: there are twelve instances where Cupid speaks of himself in the *pluralis maiestatis* in

[69]Daniel Wakelin, *Scribal Correction and Literary Craft: English Manuscripts 1375–1510* (Cambridge: Cambridge University Press, 2017), 284. On Hoccleve's correction in holographs see 283–93.

[70]Ibid., 293.

[71]Lang, "Thomas Hoccleve and the Poetics of Reading," 172.

[72]Wendy Scase, *Literature and Complaint in England 1272–1553* (Oxford: Oxford University Press, 2007), 180.

[73]Wakelin, *Scribal Correction*, 284.

[74]It was only possible to consult the manuscript in facsimile; therefore it was difficult to assess erasures and some may have been missed. I am grateful to Daniel Wakelin for sharing with me his notes from his consultation of the manuscript, and for his work on corrections in this manuscript in ibid., 284–85, 293. My findings conflict slightly with those of Lang (see "Thomas Hoccleve and the Poetics of Reading," appendices B.1, B.2, and B.3), who was also only able to consult the facsimile. However, Lang proposes that nearly all first-person pronouns in the *Letter* were changed by Hoccleve, either through erasure or through writing the plural in the initial inscription (175). As there is no codicological evidence for this revision, and furthermore no way of knowing if these plural pronouns were present in an intermediary copy of the *Letter* that had been corrected at an earlier date, I have not classified them as revisions and have only recorded corrections over erasures. Ellis also notes the changes in pronouns between holograph and scribal copies: Hoccleve, *My Compleinte*, ed. Ellis, 17.

[75]446 it H2] I T, B2, F, D3, D1, Ba, Th, Tr1, S2.

TABLE 1

Folio in H2	Line of poem	Correction	Corresponding variant	Non-holograph witnesses
44v	225	{our}	my	T, B2, F, D3, D1, Ba, Th, Tr1, S2
	231	{us and our}	me and my	T, F, D3, D1, Ba, Th, Tr1, S2
			me 7 my	B2
45r	233	{oure}	myn	T, B2, F, Tr1
			men	D3
			myne	D1
			myne	Ba, Th
			my	S2
	241	{We}	I	T, B2, F, D3, D1, Ba, Th, Tr1, S2
45r	242	{us}	—	
46r	288	{We} . . . {our}	I . . . my	T, B2, F, D3, D1, Ba, Th, Tr1, S2
47r	316	{our}	my	T, B2, F, D3, D1, Ba, Th
			our	Tr1, S2
48r	365	{We}	I	T, B2, F, D3, D1, Ba, Th, Tr1, S2
48v	380	{We}	I	T, B2, F, D3, D1, Ba, Th, Tr1, S2
	383	{We}	I	T, B2, F, D3, D1, Ba, Th, Tr1, S2
	389	{on}	me	T, B2, F, D3, D1, Ba, Th, Tr1, S2
49r	411	{We witen}	I sey	T, B2, F, D3, D1, Ba, Th, Tr1, S2
49v	423	{We}	I	T, B2, F, D3, D1, Ba, Th, Tr1, S2
	428	{We}	I	T, B2, F, D3, D1, Ba, Th, Tr1, S2
	434	{we}	I	T, B2, F, D3, D1, Ba, Th, Tr1, S2
50r	451	{is nat told}	told I not	T, B2, D1, Tr1
			told I nat	F, S2
			tolde I not	D3
			tell I nor no	Ba
			tel I for no	Th

H2, but in the singular tense in the VO. In H2, Cupid's personal and potentially subjective observations are presented as universal truths by drawing on the formality of the "royal we" to bolster their authority. This technique served a theological purpose in the Old Testament, when the plural *elohim* was used to emphasize the majesty of the Lord.[76] In a monarchical context, the *pluralis maiestatis* was used to ascribe power to an individual.[77] Whilst in the VO it is Cupid, alone, who states "I folkis hertes sette on fyre," in H2 his imperious voice proclaims: "we mennes hertes sette on fyre" (241). However, it is also important to note that some of these plural pronouns involve Lady Nature as a co-enforcer of Cupid's policies—where "we" and "oure" refer to both of them.[78]

There are also two instances of larger, non-pronoun corrections that align with the placement of variants in non-holographs (Table 2). Although it is impossible to read what has been erased in these instances, the near total agreement between the position of variants in non-holographs and corrections in H2 is striking, and it is tempting to imagine that the VO variants are behind these erasures. The identification of these corrections supports the theory of a lost VO of the *Letter*, as it suggests not only that Hoccleve may have copied H2 from an exemplar that bore (at least some of) the variants seen in non-holographs, but also that in the process of transcribing such an exemplar into H2 he was revising the poem.[79] Indeed, the existence of corrections suggests a third layer of revision: a moment of later reflection after the initial copying. Although we could never know *how* much later these corrections were made—years later or whilst the ink

[76]Ryan Reeves, *English Evangelicals and Tudor Obedience, c. 1527–1570* (Leiden: Brill, 2013), 38. *OED*, s.v. *we* (pron., n., and adj.2[b]), notes that the "royal we" was first used in Old English "by a speaker or writer, in order to secure an impersonal style and tone, or to avoid the obtrusive repetition of 'I.'"

[77]Gabriella Mazzon, "Terms of Address," in *Historical Pragmatics*, ed. Andreas H. Jucker and Irma Taavitsainen (Berlin: De Gruyter, 2010), 351–78 (355); Catherine Maley, "The Evolution of the French Plural of Respect," *Romance Notes* 15 (1973): 188–92.

[78]Lines 225, 231, 233, 241, 242, and perhaps 219 and 288.

[79]It is of course possible that Hoccleve was not responsible for the corrections. Although the data sample is limited, it is evident that the **w**s written over erasures do not match Hoccleve's typical round anglicana **w**. However, Burrow states that the corrections in the MS are "presumably the author's own late amendments" and use the bipartite form of **w** because of the constraints of space; Burrow and Doyle, *Facsimile of the Autograph Verse Manuscripts*, xxv. Lawrence Warner, *Chaucer's Scribes: London Textual Production, 1384–1432* (Cambridge: Cambridge University Press, 2021), and Misty Schieberle, "A New Hoccleve Literary Manuscript: The Trilingual Miscellany in London, British Library, MS Harley 219," *RES* 70 (2019): 799–822, also note some variation in Hoccleve's letter forms. Moreover, these corrections show Hoccleve writing non-continuously without his usual flowing cursive, which suits the rounded movement of his anglicana **w**.

TABLE 2

Folio in H2	Line of poem	Correction	Corresponding variant	Non-holograph witnesses
41v	99	{To his felawe an othir wrecche}	Anothyr wretch un to his felaw	T
			Anothir wrech un to his felow	B2
			Another wrechch unto his felowe	F
			Another wrech un to his felawe	U
			An othir wreche un to his felowe	D3
			An othir wreche unto his fellowe	D1
			Anothir wreche vnto his fallow	Ba
			Another wretche unto his felowe	Th
			A noþer wrechche un to felewe	Tr1
			Ane othir wretch un to his felawe	S2
50r	447	{al}	stable	T, B2, F, D3, Ba, Th, Tr1
			stabyll	D1
			al	S2

was still wet—it is intriguing to speculate whether they represent yet another revision of Hoccleve's *Letter*.

From analysis of Hoccleve's revision in two holographs of *Lerne to Dye*, and evidence of revision in H2, there is substantial reason to believe that the non-holographs descend from an authorial VO that was an earlier version of the *Letter*. The evidence points toward a VO that predates H2: the erasures demonstrate that at least some of the variants predate its creation, and there is a greater likelihood that another draft of the *Letter* was composed in the (at least) nineteen years before H2 was created. Scribal error no doubt played a significant role in the transmission of Hoccleve's poem, both when he was scribe and when others were, and the attempted recovery of a lost VO will unavoidably be highly speculative. Yet the substantive variants found in agreement across non-holographs of the *Letter* are suggestive of a revising poet.

Re-Writing a Letter: A Literary Analysis of Hoccleve's Revision

In his postulations of a lost VO of the *Complaint* and *Dialogue*, Burrow dismisses the differences between his VO and the holograph as insubstantial "sporadic tinkering by the author."[80] Bowers similarly discards the variants between the holographs of *Lerne to Dye* as "minor" and "cosmetic."[81] Yet the changes among the versions of the *Complaint* and *Dialogue*, *Lerne to Dye*, and the H2 and VO drafts of the *Letter* are worthy of further consideration. The ways in which they subtly revise and reshape the poem resemble the thoughtful process of a poet toying with phrasing, and to discard them as "sporadic tinkering" or "cosmetic" is to overlook the complex process of poetic composition. The final section of this study approaches Hoccleve's holograph of the *Letter* as the poet's reception of his own text, to explore the ways in which he revises and fine-tunes his poetic craft. As the example of the "royal we" showed, there are patterns to these changes suggesting that there is logic to Hoccleve's revisions.

Although Hoccleve's revisions are individually small enough to be considered "sporadic" and "tinkering," collectively they show the poet's care and consideration for his poetry. He demonstrates a heightened awareness of the craft and labor of writing across his corpus. In the *Regiment of Princes*, the speaker bemoans men who "weenen that wrytynge / No travaille is; they holde it but a game" (988–89), and proclaims the need for scribes to knit together "Mynde, ye, and hand" (997).[82] Especially notable in this passage is Hoccleve's emphasis on the responsibility of the dutiful scribe to work "withowten varyance" (999), betraying an awareness of—even an anxiety about—accurate textual transmission. Moreover, Hoccleve's profession in the Privy Seal required him to write and correct official

[80]Burrow and Doyle, *Facsimile of the Autograph Verse Manuscripts*, xxi.

[81]Bowers, "Hoccleve's Two Copies of *Lerne to Dye*," 443.

[82]Thomas Hoccleve, *The Regiment of Princes*, ed. Charles R. Blyth (Kalamazoo: Medieval Institute Publications, 1999).

documents and letters for a living.[83] As a scribe of his own holographs, he was a "skilled corrector," erring little in copying his own work.[84] It is therefore unlikely that the revisions from the VO to H2 were thoughtless changes, and instead it is worth questioning what they reveal about Hoccleve's concerns when revising his *Letter*.[85]

Indeed, it is appropriate that Hoccleve draws upon the literary trope of "recantation" in the text itself. The *Letter* makes reference to other poems that play with this critique of a poet's past works: Ovid's *Remedia amoris* (204–5), Jean de Meun's continuation of *The Romance of the Rose* (283), and Chaucer's *The Legend of Good Women* (316), which suggests that this is a generic pursuit for prestige by association with a tradition of proudly guilty writers.[86] These figures are built into Cupid's overarching complaint of misogynistic poets: Ovid taught scholars to despise women (204–17), Jean de Meun deceived them (281–87), and Chaucer slandered Criseyde (316–22).

Yet there is something more subtle that connects these poems. All three works centre around renouncing or revising love literature: Ovid's *Remedia amoris* is a recantation of his earlier *Ars amatoria*, Jean de Meun continued and corrected Guillaume de Lorris's *Romance*, and Chaucer's *Legend* is framed as a response to Cupid's complaint of the poet's misogynistic poetry. These citations are intriguing in the context of Hoccleve's revision, as Ovid and Chaucer in particular playfully accuse and defend their own work as a literary trope, albeit in the form of palinodes that are distinct from the textual revisions seen in the *Letter*. It is important to note that these sources appear in the earlier VO draft of the *Letter*—before Hoccleve had revised his poem—which suggests that Hoccleve's initial reason for citing Ovid, Jean, and Chaucer was to allude to the literary convention of the *querelle des femmes*. However, in the context of his later revisions of the *Letter*, these texts gain further significance for

[83]Helen Killick, "The Medieval 'Side-Hustler': Thomas Hoccleve's Career in, and out of, the Privy Seal," in *Monarchy, State and Political Culture in Late Medieval England: Essays in Honour of W. Mark Ormrod*, ed. Gwilym Dodd and Craig Taylor (Cambridge: Boydell & Brewer, 2020), 144–63; Schulz, "Thomas Hoccleve, Scribe."

[84]Wakelin, *Scribal Correction*, 284.

[85]There are many substitutions that are not noted in this study, such as Hoccleve's emendation of "smartly" (VO) to "qwikly" (H2, 109), or "dyuers" (VO) to "sundry" (H2, 116), which have no obvious impact on meter or literary sense but must have held subjective value.

[86]These poets also appear (amongst others) in Christine's *Epistre*; however, Hoccleve's *Letter* only cites them by name and omits Christine's direct critique of their problematic writings.

the tropes of "recantation" they contain, which situate Hoccleve's own revisions within a corpus of great poets who revised poetry, and possibly even inspired his practices.

In order to study these revisions, it is necessary to speculate what the VO would have looked like from the evidence surviving in non-holographs. This is of course an artificial reconstruction, but as I am arguing for a text that no longer exists, any reconstruction must by necessity be speculative. As in the previous section, agreements among the ten non-holographs are condensed for reasons of economy, and a single example is chosen to represent the VO using the spelling that appears most often or, when there is no obvious predominance, using the most common fifteenth-century spelling according to the *Middle English Dictionary*. In his reconstruction of a VO of the *Complaint*, Burrow corrects the spellings of variants found in non-holographs against Hoccleve's spelling in the holograph to avoid scribal "accidentals" and to approximate closer the lost archetype. However, as this section will demonstrate, this would not be appropriate in the case of the *Letter* because the variants between the VO and H2 suggest that Hoccleve's metrical style varied over time. The earlier VO is metrically inconsistent, and whilst it is possible that this is the product of scribal "accidentals," it is more probable that Hoccleve modified his spelling when copying the *Letter* into the later holograph to correct the meter. Therefore, the spelling found in his later holographs has not been mapped onto the VO, as there is no certainty that the earlier version of the *Letter* contained Hoccleve's holograph spelling.

"al chaunge and variaunce": Metrical Revisions

When the VO is recreated from consistent non-holograph agreements, it becomes evident that there are distinct differences in the metrical styles of the VO and H2.[87] The existence of holograph manuscripts of Hoccleve's poetry has enabled his metrical style to be extensively scrutinized. Analysis of his versification by Burrow, E. G. Stanley, and Norman Davis suggests that Hoccleve's iambic style was more regular than previously assumed.[88] In analyzing of over 7,000 lines of autograph verse, Burrow establishes

[87]Quotation in subheading is from H2, 448.

[88]Hoccleve, *Works*, ed. Furnivall, 1:xli; E. G. Stanley, "Chaucer's Metre after Chaucer, I: Chaucer to Hoccleve," *N&Q* 234 (1989): 11–23; Norman Davis, "Notes on Grammar and Spelling in the Fifteenth Century," in *The Oxford Book of Late Medieval Verse and Prose*, ed. Douglas Gray (Oxford: Oxford University Press, 1985), 493–508.

that "the prime general rule for Hoccleve . . . concerned the number of syllables, not the distribution of stress," concluding that his lines generally conform to ten syllables, with or without an extra unstressed syllable at the line-end.[89] Judith A. Jefferson similarly notes that the vast majority of Hoccleve's lines are decasyllabic, and further suggests that he shows preference for "the five-beat line with alternating off-beat and beat," although this is not universal.[90] These conclusions reveal the extraordinary consistency with which Hoccleve observed his metrical rules.

Jefferson briefly remarks of line 244 of the *Letter* that (unspecified) scribal copies have different rhythmic versions of this line, "which could conceivably have originated with Hoccleve himself."[91] However, the meter of the non-holographs of the *Letter* has never been studied, as these manuscripts have historically been discarded for their stanza disarrangement (TB2FUD3D1ThBa) or their lateness (Tr1S2). Yet one structural error, explicable codicologically, does not void the manuscripts of literary value. Of the 476 lines of the *Letter*, eighty-four variants are found across eighty-three lines. Of these lines, only forty-eight are decasyllabic in the VO, whilst all eighty-three are decasyllabic in H2.[92] In other words, if we follow the assumption that the VO predates H2, when the *Letter* was copied into H2, thirty-five lines were corrected to improve their meter.

It is important to note the difficulty of knowing which variants are consistent scribal "accidentals" and which are authorial, and furthermore whether Hoccleve's spelling in the VO may have resolved any of the metrical anomalies that survive in non-holographs. Moreover, the non-holographs contain many undecasyllabic lines other than those recorded here. These variants do not agree across all non-holographs and were presumably not in the VO, but they exemplify the risks of scribal transmission when studying authorial meter. For these reasons, the following analysis is extremely speculative. However, a subjective comparison of consistent agreements between the VO and H2 suggests that H2 presents

[89]Hoccleve, *"Complaint" and "Dialogue,"* ed. Burrow, xxviii.

[90]Judith A. Jefferson, "The Hoccleve Holographs and Hoccleve's Metrical Practice: More than Counting Syllables?," *Parergon* 18 (2000): 203–26 (224); Judith A. Jefferson, "The Hoccleve Holographs and Hoccleve's Metrical Practice," in *Manuscripts and Texts: Editorial Problems in Later Middle English Literature*, ed. Derek Pearsall (Woodbridge: D. S. Brewer, 1987), 95–109. Jefferson's five-beat conclusion has been received with some hesitation; e.g., *Poems of Cupid*, ed. Fenster and Erler, 171.

[91]Jefferson, "The Hoccleve Holographs," 221 n. 31.

[92]I take Burrow as my model for assessing decasyllabic counts here; see Hoccleve, *"Complaint" and "Dialogue,"* ed. Burrow, xvii–l.

a more controlled meter that is indicative of a poet who is more attentive to metrical consistency.

This is especially noticeable in instances of transposition, where Hoccleve rearranges the word order to correct the sound with little impact on the sense. Burrow notes that Hoccleve's "final unstressed /ə/ is lost by elision when it immediately precedes a word beginning with a vowel or (h)," a rule that is followed in H2 in order to reduce an eleven-syllable line to ten.[93] On line 320, the transposition:

In mannes herte conceites treewe arn dede (VO)	In herte of man conceites treewe arn dede (H2, 320)

is a simple yet effective way of correcting the meter without changing the poem's sense, and is in line with Jefferson's conclusion that "Hoccleve made use of a variety of stratagems . . . in order to maintain his decasyllabic line."[94] There are also synonymous additions, substitutions, and omissions from the VO to H2 that initially resemble inconsequential changes but yield subtle metrical refinements. For instance, H2 features more conjunctions—a technique Jefferson notes that Hoccleve uses to control the syllable count, as here:[95]

What **he** be and holden ful cherlissh (VO)	What **so it** be and holden ful cherlissh (H2, 185)

H2 similarly features synonymous substitutions that either remove or add a syllable to the line to correct it to a decasyllabic count:

þa̲t shee sholde of þa̲t **harme** the cause be (VO)	þa̲t shee sholde of þa̲t **gilt** the cause be (H2, 375)
þa̲t of this **fals** men our rebel foon (VO)	þa̲t of tho men **untreewe** our rebel foon (H2, 466)

[93]Ibid., xxx.
[94]Jefferson, "The Hoccleve Holographs," in Pearsall, *Manuscripts and Texts*, 99.
[95]Ibid., 102.

The substitution of "untreewe" in this last example is of particular note, as although the vocal final /ə/ could add one syllable too many, Hoccleve's rule of elision preceding a word beginning with a vowel corrects the line to ten syllables.[96] Similarly, elsewhere a synonymous substitution replaces "wrecche" (with a vocal final /ə/) with "man" in order to reduce the syllabic count to ten:

The feithlees wrecche, how hath he him forswore (VO)	The feithlees **man**, how hath he him forswore (H2, 310)

The line in the VO is hendecasyllabic because of one of Hoccleve's exceptions to his rules of elision. As Burrow notes, the elision of final unstressed /ə/ does not occur across the mid-line break or caesura, and consequently Hoccleve could vary the number of pronounced syllables in a line by placing a final /ə/ at the mid-line break.[97] Thus, according to Hoccleve's rule, the positioning of "wrecche" at the mid-line break pronounces the final /ə/ (despite the **h** it precedes), but by substitution with "man" the meter is corrected to a decasyllabic count—although it loses the emotiveness of the VO version, which suited the "traitor Eneas" to whom it refers. Whilst textual criticism might be inclined to view these variants as evidence of scribal error, their consistency is in fact suggestive of a careful and calculated process of revision by a poet who is more attentive to a strictly decasyllabic meter.

It is important also to note the adjectives, adverbs, and demonstratives that are present in the VO but omitted from H2. In the VO, these adverbs and adjectives add emphasis to the nouns to which they are attached: "**hertely** greetynges" (7), "**lytell** yle" (15), "**persyng** strokes" (224); and the demonstratives point to the subjects with stronger, more evocative deixis: "**thes** ladyes" (190), "**these** clerkes" (223). Their omission in H2 not only trims unnecessary words, but also reduces the syllabic count of every line to ten syllables. The affective adjectives in the VO offer a more vivid description of the subject, and the decision to remove them suggests that (in these isolated instances) Hoccleve prioritized the metrical pattern over the emotion attached to its subject. This is in keeping with

[96] Hoccleve, *"Complaint" and "Dialogue,"* ed. Burrow, xxx.
[97] Ibid.

the image of Hoccleve using the recopying of his *Letter* as a chance to improve his poem.

The comparison of the metrical changes between the two drafts of the *Letter* strongly suggests that the holograph is, in part, a metrical correction of the VO. This attention to meter is not surprising for Hoccleve: further to his strict decasyllabic tendencies, in his poem *To the Duke of Bedford, Regent of France* Hoccleve reveals his concern that his meter may be found lacking, and requests that the duke "rectifie" what he deems amiss in his "vnconnyngly" metered book (12–18).[98] Although the transpositions, substitutions, and omissions listed here resemble Burrow's "subjective tinkering," they are also suggestive of Hoccleve "rectifying" his *Letter* in an orderly way. Yet Hoccleve's careful metrical corrections are also literary decisions: in shaving away his affective words, he brushes away verbal clutter to bring the subject of each line into sharper focus. Indeed, the culling of adjectives has long been lauded as an acclaimed point of style, more recently evidenced by Gordon Lish's editing of Raymond Carver, for instance. By paring away his affective language, the revisions between drafts of the *Letter* are suggestive of Hoccleve honing his metrical and literary style.

"How undirstande am I?": The Reception of the 'Letter'

Further evidence of Hoccleve's reception and revision of the *Letter* can be seen in small but significant non-metrical substitutions from the VO to H2.[99] In a first example, in his holograph Hoccleve changes several male pronouns to female, the most notable of which is for the personification of Virtue:

The more uertu the lasse is the pryde	The more uertu the lasse is the pryde
Vertu so **digne** is and **noble** in kynde	Vertu so **noble** is and **worthy** in kynde
þat uice 7 **he** may nat in feere abyde	þat uice 7 **shee** may nat in feere abyde
He puttith uice cleene out of **his** mynde	**Shee** puttith uice cleene out of mynde
He fleeth from him **he** leueth him behynde	**Shee** fleeth from him **shee** leueth him behynde
(VO, 456–60)	(H2, 456–60)

[98] Ibid., xi.
[99] Quotation in subheading is from H2, 775; punctuation from Burrow's edition (1999).

Agreements in non-holographs show that Virtue is gendered male in the VO, which describes how *he* puts vice "cleene out of mynde" (459). However, in H2 Virtue is personified as female, closer to the gender of the Latin *virtus* and the French *vertue*—of which Hoccleve would have been aware, as a Privy Seal clerk who worked in French and Latin. Christine's poem naturally genders Virtue as female, and it would be tempting to read Hoccleve's revision of the *Letter* as an attempt to resemble his source.[100] It has, after all, been well established that Hoccleve deliberately chose Christine's *L'Epistre* to establish himself as a writer and make an instant claim to poetic authority.[101] However, as Furnivall notes, Hoccleve's *Letter* can be considered more of an "adaptation with changes" than a translation, and Robert Meyer-Lee and Mary Carpenter Erler further suggest that the *Letter* is independent of Christine's work.[102] It is more likely, therefore, that the female gendering of Virtue was an etymological decision that happened to align with Christine's phrasing.[103]

In a second example, substitutions from the VO to H2 appear to insert allusions to Chaucer's works, possibly in an attempt to bring his work into line with other poets in the literary tradition of gender debate. These revisions do not change the meter, nor do they greatly alter the overarching sense; instead, it seems that they were driven by Hoccleve's desire to draw further connections with Chaucer's corpus. The first of these allusions occurs as Cupid declares that women are not deserving of the "sclaundrous name" men give them (67). In the VO, this is justified by the statement "ffor al for **vertu** was it þa̲t shee wroghte" (71).[104] Yet H2 features one small but significant substitution: "ffor al for **pitee** was it þa̲t shee wroghte." The change to "pitee" in H2 evokes Chaucer's frequent linking of women to "pitee," echoed in many instances, but exemplified in *The Legend of Good Women*:

[100]"car les vertus si enchacent les vices"; *Epistre*, in Fenster and Erler, *Poems of Cupid*, 766.

[101]Knapp, *The Bureaucratic Muse*, 45–75; Critten, "Imagining the Author," 683; John M. Bowers, "Thomas Hoccleve and the Politics of Tradition," *ChauR* 36 (2002): 352–69; McLeod, "A Case of Faux Semblans."

[102]Robert Meyer-Lee, *Poets and Power from Chaucer to Wyatt* (Cambridge: Cambridge University Press, 2007), 95. Hoccleve, *"Complaint" and "Dialogue,"* ed. Burrow, xliv; *Poems of Cupid*, ed. Fenster and Erler, 169. See also the lines Hoccleve translates from Christine's *Epistre*, in *Hoccleve's Works*, ed. Furnivall, 1:243–48.

[103]Virtue is portrayed as female in other fifteenth-century English texts, such as Lydgate's *Pilgrimage of the Life of Man*, 11744.

[104]This variant is not witnessed in Tr1 or S2 but is present in TB2FUD3D1BaTh and is sufficiently widespread to suggest it was the VO, although this example may not be as secure as others.

O sely wemen, ful of innocence,
Ful of pite, of trouthe and conscience,
What maketh yow to men to truste so?
Have ye swych routhe upon hyre feyned wo,
And han swich olde ensaumples yow beforn?[105]

There are clear connections between these poems: both critique literature that disparages women and feature a Cupid who berates men for their slanderous behavior. The innocent women described in this stanza of the H2 *Letter*, who are "al for pitee" (71), closely resemble Chaucer's "sely wemen, ful of innocence, / Ful of pite." As Eneas prepares to abandon Dido, the narrator questions "What maketh you to men to truste so?" (*LGW*, 1256)—similar to the *Letter*'s women who "art betrayed by fals apparence" (42).[106] Hoccleve was evidently aware of this legend and of Chaucer's retelling, referring later in the *Letter* to *The Legend* and to Eneas.[107]

Another possible Chaucerian substitution in H2 is seen as Cupid describes the books that "maken mencion / How {women} betrayeden" figures of the Old Testament (197–98). In the VO, these books are labeled "sory" (197)—an accurate description for these sinful texts—but in H2 the adjective is changed: "wikkid bookes."[108] The polysemous meanings of "sory" could prompt this change, to avoid confusion with the more sympathetic definition "unlucky, unfortunate."[109] The use of "wikkid" is also more coherent with the rest of the *Letter*, as it appears a few lines earlier (176). However, Ellis further suggests that this phrasing derives from *The Wife of Bath's Prologue*, where Jankyn forces the Wife to listen to antifeminist proverbs from the "book of wikked wyves" (*WBP*, 685).[110] Whilst the Wife is not the most flattering model of femininity, the "book of wikkid wyves" is an apt comparison for the *Letter*'s "wikkid bookes"—two books that slander women for their betrayals. Just as Jankyn uses the book as a tool of female repression, so Hoccleve's Old Testament prophets use their "wikkid bookes" to give women "a wikkid name" (194).

[105] *LGW*, 1254–58, in *The Riverside Chaucer*, gen. ed. Larry D. Benson (Oxford: Oxford University Press, 2008). Further Chaucer quotations are taken from this edition.

[106] A similarity that at least some later readers of the poem were aware of, as the *Letter* appears alongside Chaucer's *LGW* in T and F.

[107] "In our legende of martirs" (316); "Of Troie also, the traitour Eneas" (309). Although references to Eneas also appear in Christine's poem, Hoccleve's phrasing is more evocative of Chaucer's treatment.

[108] The "sory"/"wikkid" books line derives in part from Christine's *Epistre*, lines 306–8, where she refers to these books as containing little value (308).

[109] *MED*, s.v. *sori*, def. 4(b).

[110] Hoccleve, *My Compleinte*, ed. Ellis, 109.

Moreover, in the context of this study, there is a playful similarity between the Wife and Hoccleve. Albeit to different extents, just as the Wife "corrected" her husband's text when she "plyght / Out of his book" three leaves in an act of feminist rebellion (*WBP*, 790–91), so too does Hoccleve edit his *Letter* to emphasize the female characters. If a reader of the *Letter* were familiar with *The Wife of Bath's Prologue*, the allusion to the "wikkid bookes" would also be an efficient way for Hoccleve to convey the same disapproval of the "book of wikkid wyves," which is burnt at the conclusion of Chaucer's text.

It is tempting to speculate whether these examples of Hoccleve's revision demonstrate his attentiveness to his readers. The *Letter* is in a unique position in Hoccleve's corpus because it is cited by name in another of his poems, the *Dialogue*, which offers a rare glimpse into the *Letter*'s reception by its contemporary readers.[111] The Friend informs the Hoccleve-persona that his *Letter* has been critiqued by its female readers for its untruthful statements:

> Freend doutelees sumwhat ther is therin
> Þat sowneth but right small to hir honour.
> But as to þa̱t now, for your fadir kyn,
> Considereth therof was I noon auctour.
> I nas in þa̱t cas but a reportour
> Of folkes tales as they seide, I wroot:
> I nat affermed it on hem God woot.
>
> Whoso þa̱t shal reherce a mannes sawe
> As þa̱t he seith moot he seyn & nat varie;
> For, and he do he dooth ageyn the lawe
> Of trouthe he may tho wordes nat contrarie.
> Whoso þa̱t seith I am hire̱ aduersarie
> And dispreise hir condicions and port,
> For þa̱t I made of hem swich a report.[112]
> (*Dialogue*, 757–70)

The *Dialogue*'s claims are not unfounded, for others have shared this critical sense of Hoccleve's work: Diane Bornstein describes the poem as a "parody of feminism," and Mary Flannery is skeptical of Hoccleve's intent,

[111]On other connections between the *Letter* and the *Series*, see Karen Winstead, "'I am othir to yow than yee weene': Hoccleve, Women, and the 'Series,'" *PQ* 72 (1993): 143–55.
[112]Hoccleve, *Dialogue*, 757–70, in *"Complaint" and "Dialogue,"* ed. Burrow.

remarking that he "treats Christine's poem like a costume to be altered and worn while parading round in half-serious, half-mocking fashion."[113] The current critical consensus is that Hoccleve's *Letter* is ambiguous in its feminist stance and is designed to promote debate amongst readers.[114]

Although the Hoccleve-persona is adamant that had his friend read the *Letter* "fully to the ende, / Yee wolde seyn it is nat as yee wende" (783–84), his extended defence of his poem suggests an anxiety over its reception. Of course, there is no way of gauging the truth of the Friend's statement, and it is possible that the *Dialogue* was intended to entice readers to the *Letter*.[115] However, if Hoccleve's description of readers' reactions is to be believed, it offers an interesting context for the study of a poet who returned to a text to revise and emend, possibly with his readers' responses in mind.[116]

What do the changes from the VO to H2 thus tell us about Hoccleve as a revising poet? Delsaux's analysis of Laurent de Premierfait's translation establishes the three key ways an author can return to a translation-text: to retranslate, to rewrite, and to revise.[117] This is a fruitful framework. Considering Hoccleve's lack of interest in translating Christine's poem verbatim, the first of these can be dismissed. However, the last two categories are pertinent. In the subtle metrical changes from the VO to H2, we see Hoccleve revising his poem to correct the meter. This, although interesting, is not unexpected: it is likely that Hoccleve's poetry improved to become more metrically consistent over time, and it resembles, as Delsaux notes, the instinctive process of an author improving a text as they recopy.[118]

[113]Bornstein, "Anti-Feminism in Hoccleve's Translation," 14; Mary Flannery, *Practising Shame: Female Honour in Later Medieval England* (Manchester: Manchester University Press, 2020), 172.

[114]See Jerome Mitchell, *Thomas Hoccleve: A Study in Early Fifteenth-Century English Poetic* (Urbana: University of Illinois Press, 1968), 53; Derek Pearsall, "The English Chaucerians," in *Chaucer and Chaucerians: Critical Studies in Middle English Literature*, ed. Derek Brewer (London: Nelson, 1966), 201–40 (225); and Winstead, "I am al othir to yow than yee weene," 143.

[115]This follows David Watt's argument that Hoccleve completed the *Series* before producing HM 744; David Watt, *The Making of Thomas Hoccleve's "Series"* (Liverpool: Liverpool University Press, 2013), 66 and note 2.

[116]Jonathan Stavsky similarly suggests that Hoccleve approaches his portrayal of women in his *Series* with the criticism described in the *Dialogue* in mind—perhaps another instance of authorial engagement with public criticism. Jonathan Stavsky, "Hoccleve's Take on Chaucer and Christine de Pizan: Gender, Authorship, and Intertextuality in the *Epistre au dieu d'amours*, *The Letter of Cupid*, and the *Series*," *PQ* 93 (2014): 435–60 (471–72).

[117]Delsaux, "Un témoignage inédit," 232.

[118]Ibid., 189.

Yet in the variants explored in this section, we also see Hoccleve rewriting small but significant details of the *Letter*. The substitutions from the VO to H2 that revise subtle details of the etymological gendering of Virtue in the poem show Hoccleve as a capable poet and editor. Although the change of a pronoun or synonymous substitution appear superficial, they are nonetheless intentional. Each change is minor, but collectively they create an image of an anxious poet who tinkered with his poem, critically and intentionally.

"There is no thyng but chaunge and variance": The Permanence and Impermanence of Medieval Authorship

In analyzing the literary implications of the changes made between versions of the *Letter*, we have the rare opportunity to study Hoccleve as a revising poet.[119] This is valuable, as scholarship on the author in late medieval England has had, upon occasion, a tendency to view the author as immoveable, static, and permanent. Robert Root famously suggested the existence of a first draft of *Troilus and Criseyde*,[120] but this was disputed by Barry Windeatt, who argued that the evidence for authorial addition is in fact evidence of scribal omission.[121] The reluctance to view variance within manuscripts as authorial revision, although understandably cautious, reflects the editorial desire for a fixed text.[122] However, the possibility of authorial revision has received some critical attention. John Manly and Edith Rickert's work on *Canterbury Tales* manuscripts suggests Chaucer may have expanded and rearranged components before they were united

[119]Quotation in heading is from Hoccleve, *Complaint*, ed. Burrow, 10.

[120]Which was successively revised by Chaucer to produce (at least some of) the textual traditions that survive. Robert Root, *The Textual Tradition of Chaucer's "Troilus,"* Chaucer Society Publications 99 (London: K. Paul, Trench, Trübner for the Chaucer Society, 1916), 180–81.

[121]Geoffrey Chaucer, *"Troilus and Criseyde": A New Edition of "The Book of Troilus,"* ed. Barry Windeatt (Oxford: Oxford University Press, 1984). Windeatt argues that Root's conclusion stems from his confusion of manuscript tradition with authorial composition (37). Windeatt does acknowledge that some variants within the corpus offer an intriguing glimpse into the process of poetic composition (44), and that the poem was "in practice a series of layers—perhaps physical layers—of writing" (36).

[122]A difficulty noted by Delsaux, *Manuscrits et pratiques autographes*, 187. G. Thomas Tanselle argues that the belief in the medieval author's permanence stems in part from textual criticism, which is driven by the desire to believe that one version of a text is "right" and the others "wrong"; G. Thomas Tanselle, "Classical, Biblical, and Medieval Textual Criticism and Modern Editing," *Studies in Bibliography* 36 (1983): 21–68 (54).

into a single text.[123] It has also been established that Langland revised and rewrote *Piers Plowman* to produce different versions.[124] Similar suggestions have been proposed for Geoffrey of Monmouth's *Historia regum Britanniae*, and John Gower's *Confessio Amantis* and *Vox clamantis*.[125]

Within Hoccleve studies, the very nature of the holographs and autograph encourages us to perceive the author as static and immoveable. Autographs can reveal significant details of an author's personal literary identity—a rare privilege, but a perspective that unavoidably shows a single snapshot of an author in the time and place in which they composed the manuscript.[126] Whilst Hoccleve's authorial manuscripts are undeniably a useful resource for studying the poet's literary and metrical style, the

[123]Geoffrey Chaucer, *The Text of the Canterbury Tales: Studied on the Basis of All Known Manuscripts*, ed. John Manly and Edith Rickert (Chicago: University of Chicago Press, 1940), 2:495–518. For disagreements see Aage Brusendorf, *The Chaucer Tradition* (London: H. Milford, 1925), 77–78; M. M. Crow, "Corrections in the Paris Manuscript of Chaucer's *Canterbury Tales*: A Study in Scribal Collaboration," *Studies in English* 15 (1935): 5–18; and Richard Beadle, "Geoffrey Spirleng (c. 1426–1494): A Scribe of the *Canterbury Tales* in His Time," in *Of the Making of Books: Medieval Manuscripts, Their Scribes and Readers*, ed. Pamela Robinson and Zim Rivkah (Aldershot: Scolar Press, 1997), 116–46. On authorial revision at different stages in the text's evolution see Derek Pearsall, "Authorial Revision on Some Late-Medieval English Texts," in *Crux and Controversy in Middle English Textual Criticism*, ed. A. J. Minnis and Charlotte Brewer (Cambridge: Brewer, 1992), 39–48; J. Burke Severs, "Author's Revision in Block C of the *Canterbury Tales*," *Speculum* 29 (1954): 512–30 (522) (although Severs contests revision of *The Clerk's Tale*: "Did Chaucer Revise the *Clerk's Tale*?," *Speculum* 21 (1946): 295–302); and Larry D. Benson, "The Order of *The Canterbury Tales*," *SAC* 3 (1981): 77–120 (100).

[124]Whether or not they were exactly the three versions now dubbed A, B, and C (or four, if the Z version is considered). Ralph Hanna, "The Versions and Revisions of *Piers Plowman*," in *The Cambridge Companion to "Piers Plowman,"* ed. Andrew Cole and Andrew Galloway (Cambridge: Cambridge University Press, 2014), 39–49 (35–37); William Langland, *Piers Plowman: The Z Version*, ed. A. G. Rigg and Charlotte Brewer (Toronto: Pontifical Institute of Mediaeval Studies, 1983). Charlotte Brewer notes how this corpus reflects changes or developments in Langland's authorial intentions and preoccupations that allow us to study his gradual improvement as a poet; "Z and the A- B- and C-Texts of *Piers Plowman*," *MÆ* 53 (1984): 194–219.

[125]Michael Reeve, "Errori in autografi," in *Gli autografi medievali: Problemi paleografici e filologici*, ed. Paola Chiesa and Lucia Pinelli (Spoleto: Centro italiano di studi sull'alto medioevo, 1994), 37–60 (40–42). Contested by Robert Huntington Fletcher, "Two Notes on the *Historia regum Britanniae* of Geoffrey of Monmouth," *PMLA* 16 (1901): 461–74; *The Complete Works of John Gower*, ed. G. C. Macaulay (Oxford: Oxford University Press, 1899–1902), 2:xxi–xxviii, and 4:xxx–xxxii; P. Nicholson, "Gower's Revisions in the *Confessio Amantis*," *ChauR* 19 (1984): 123–43; and J. H. Fisher, *John Gower: Moral Philosopher and Friend of Chaucer* (London: Methuen, 1965), 99–115.

[126]Delsaux, *Manuscrits et pratiques autographes*, 185. See also Elena E. Rodríguez Díaz, "Manuscritos autógrafos en la producción libraria castellana del siglo XV: Observaciones paleográficas y codicológicas," in *Medieval Autograph Manuscripts*, ed. Nataša Golob (Turnhout: Brepols, 2013), 259–79; Eef Overgaauw, "Comment reconnaître un autographe du moyen âge?," in Golob, *Medieval Autograph Manuscripts*, 3–15.

fact that all three date to a small period (c. 1421–26) means that the analysis of his poetic style is limited to a fraction of his poetic career.[127] Furthermore, as Bowers notes, the HM 744 and HM 111 holographs represent a concerted effort on Hoccleve's part to create a unified anthology.[128] It is therefore logical that the poems in these manuscripts are retrospectively crafted to become congruent in style.[129]

The permanence of Hoccleve's holographs becomes more pronounced in the context of recent scholarship on Hoccleve's biography by Sobecki, Knapp, and others. This research emphasizes that Hoccleve's poetic career is best described as a trajectory—one that constructs a timeline of his life onto which his poems can be placed. In this framework, it becomes more apparent that all three Hocclevean holographs are clustered together at the end of the poet's life, and thus represent only a single point on this timeline. Their existence complements the mass of information about Hoccleve's life that has been brought to light, but also contrasts the overarching chronology within which they sit by presenting the poet as a static author.

Indeed, Hoccleve himself acknowledges changeability—which he calls "variaunce"—as a theme in his poetry. The *Complaint* opens with the statement "stablenesse in this world is ther noon / There is no thyng but chaunge and variance" (9–10). The death and decay that accompany the coming of autumn set the tone for the *Complaint*'s discussion of mental illness and social isolation. Hoccleve's main complaint is that, five years after his sickness, many do not believe he is recovered.[130] To prove that he has passed through this period of "maladie" (21), he questions "If a man ones falle in dronkenesse / Shal he continue therin euere mo? / Nay" (225–27). The *Complaint* draws a clear distinction between the Hoccleve of the past, assailed by "þat maladie" (93), and the Hoccleve of the present, whose "wit were hoom come ageyn" (64). In this unique insight into the mentality of a medieval poet, Hoccleve himself acknowledges that he has changed.

[127] John M. Bowers, "Hoccleve's Huntington Holographs: The First 'Collected Poems' in English," *FCS* 15 (1989): 27–51 (42–46).

[128] Ibid.

[129] Sobecki further identifies a new holograph in Hoccleve's hand that he dates to the last years of his life, arguing that it is "part of the same personal effort by the poet to preserve his legacy"; Sebastian Sobecki, "*Gens sans argent*: A New Holograph Manuscript by Thomas Hoccleve," *The Library*, 25 (2024): 121–46.

[130] On Hoccleve's psychology see Lillian Feder, *Madness in Literature* (Princeton: Princeton University Press, 1980); J. A. Burrow, "Thomas Hoccleve," in *Authors of the Middle Ages: English Writers of the Late Middle Ages*, ed. M. C. Seymour (Aldershot: Ashgate, 1994), 4:185–248 (210).

Unavoidably, scholarship that analyzes Hoccleve's metrical style reinforces the notion that there has historically been one singular Hocclevean literary style. When reconstructing the missing portion of the *Dialogue*, Burrow takes the strict metrical rules of the holographs and maps them onto his VO, concluding that "there is accordingly every reason to believe that the VO observed the same rules."[131] Yet, as this study has revealed, metrical variation—even improvement—is to be expected across drafts.[132] One could even say that variance is, at times, generic to the text. Alan J. Fletcher views Langland's revisions as a form of respect for and acknowledgment of the poem's exploratory nature—that "provisionality became, in effect, part of his poem's ethical essence."[133] As Bowers similarly notes of *Lerne to Dye*, the editorial quandary created by multiple authoritative texts also frees us "from the illusory comfort of a fiction, unsupported by hard evidence from the period, that would have us imagine authors leaving behind single perfect versions of their works."[134]

The discovery of a VO of the *Letter* coincides with Sobecki's recent identification of revision in Hoccleve's editorial process of *Jereslaus' Wife* and *The Tale of Jonathas*.[135] Like the *Letter*, the first of these poems is also mentioned in the *Series*, when the Friend notes that Thomas's exemplar is incomplete. Building on Misty Schieberle's work, Sobecki identifies British Library, MS Harley 219, as Hoccleve's exemplar, which was both overseen and partially copied by Hoccleve.[136] Detailed collations reveal that the Harley-text itself was copied from three exemplars (which he identifies), one of which lacks the moralization passage and is therefore likely the exemplar that the Friend notes is incomplete. Thus, this narrative in the *Series* describes the revised production of Harley 219, rather than the production of the *Series* itself. Similarly to Thomas's account of the *Letter*'s unfavorable reception in the *Dialogue*, the description of the incomplete *Chaste Empress*

[131]Hoccleve, *"Complaint" and "Dialogue,"* ed. Burrow, xxviii.

[132]Of course, in Burrow's reconstruction of a segment intended to sit alongside a holograph text it was logical to approximate the style of the VO, but the assumption of metrical permanence highlights the critical tendency to see the late medieval author as immoveable.

[133]Alan J. Fletcher, "The Essential (Ephemeral) William Langland: Textual Revision as Ethical Process in *Piers Plowman*," *YLS* 15 (2001): 61–98 (63). Moreover, through the stages of copying a text there could arise multiple authorial versions, each with equal authority; Lucas, "An Author as Copyist of His Own Work," 241.

[134]Bowers, "Hoccleve's Two Copies of *Lerne to Dye*," 462.

[135]Sebastian Sobecki, "Authorized Realities: The *Gesta Romanorum* and Thomas Hoccleve's Poetics of Autobiography," *Speculum* 98 (2023): 536–58.

[136]Schieberle, "A New Hoccleve Literary Manuscript."

exemplar is an effective dramatization that, in Sobecki's words, anchors the *Series* "firmly in both reality *and* literary convention."[137]

In this manner, evidence of a VO of Hoccleve's *Letter* introduces a new perspective of the changeability of both the poem and of Hoccleve. The two authorial versions of the *Letter* permit us to see Hoccleve returning to his poem to correct and improve—an insight that was only made visible by circumnavigating the established authority of the holograph. Whilst it is neither the taste of past generations of textual critics to accredit scribal care in transmitting a text, nor the taste of current generations to value the reconstruction of an authorial original, in the case of the *Letter* both seem to go hand in hand. It cannot be denied that Hoccleve's holographs hold incredible value as witnesses to the poet's personal linguistic system—indeed, it is only through a comparison with the holograph that it was possible to identify an earlier textual tradition of the *Letter*. However, the existence of the holographs has caused the fossilization of Hoccleve's work and subsequently led to the assumption that there was only ever one poet with one literary style. In the case of the *Letter*, the holograph has long overshadowed the non-holographs and obscured the earlier textual tradition. Yet in their very errors and inconsistencies, these late manuscripts are the only surviving descendants of a lost text, the existence of which contributes to our understanding of the impermanence of Hoccleve and his poetic craft. The *Letter* presents itself in this context as a poem of meticulous revision and correction, and stands as a reminder that the literary text is a product of reflection.

[137]Sobecki, "Authorized Realities," 557 (emphasis in original).

"An Experiment to make a flodde of water to com into a howse": Rethinking the Relationship between Narrative and Performance in Medieval Wonder Recipes

Hannah Bower
Churchill College, University of Cambridge

Abstract

This article explores relationships between narrative, performance, and empowerment in late medieval recipes for enacting marvelous transformations (or the illusion of them) in social and domestic spaces. These recipes have been productively framed by scholars as imagined narratives of wish-fulfillment, self-fashioning, and triumph, which promise social, sexual, and intellectual success. In this article, however, I interrogate further the relationship between narrative, performance, and power across overlapping domestic, scholarly, and clerical contexts. I demonstrate that risks of failure, humiliation, and transgression are not always assuaged by the narrative structures present in recipes but can, in fact, be foregrounded by them. I make this argument by comparing particular recipes to fabliaux. These comic tales encode certain narrative structures present in recipes—such as sequential action and consecutive repetition—as risky and precarious routes to power. Furthermore, these longer imaginative narratives function as virtual performance spaces where those wonders can be tried out in particular domestic settings, live relationship networks, and shifting webs of cultural associations. In conjunction with the recipes, such writings compel us to pay more attention to the challenges—and pleasures—that risk, error, and adaptation offered writers and readers of wonder recipes. Rather than just framing those writers and readers as gullible consumers of magic or wistful imaginers of far-fetched futures, we should be alert to the possibility that they may have felt vulnerable and powerful, confused and clear-sighted, troubled and exhilarated by the *numerous* narrative trajectories recipes could open up.

Keywords

recipe; fabliau; narrative; performance; risk; power; wonder; illusion

Studies in the Age of Chaucer 46 (2024): 163–208

Physically and imaginatively, late medieval domestic environments were stages for a diverse array of wonders engineered by humans. These wonders were described in various written genres, including recipes, which taught readers how to bring about transformations in domestic settings as spectacular as making "alle men in a howse to havee too heddes," making "a howse seme fulle of snakys," or making "a flodde of water to com into a howse."[1] Frequently, the recipes appear, both in Latin and in the vernacular, in miscellaneous collections of medical, horticultural, culinary, devotional, and literary writings. Many of these miscellanies seem to have been copied for, or within, mercantile and gentry households as collective repositories of domestic knowledge.[2] However, the recipes also appear in more scientifically orientated compilations that may have been owned by monks or by secular clergymen of major and minor orders, such as priests, university scholars, and literate clerks.

Across these diverse (but overlapping) lay and religious contexts, the recipes imagine human agents deploying sleight of hand, optical play, natural magic, and necromantic methods to create unexpected alterations in domestic environments and the world beyond. To see how some of these methods might combine and prove difficult to distinguish from one another, consider the following recipe copied in a fifteenth-century manuscript alongside—and in the same hand as—a wealth of medical, calendrical, and astrological writings:

[1] Bodleian Library (BodL), MS Ashmole 1389, p. 40; British Library (BL), MS Sloane 1315, fols. 103r–v, 90r. Such collections often also contain similar recipes for making men and women appear to have no heads (e.g., BodL, MS Ashmole 1389, p. 40; BodL, MS e. Musaeo 52, fol. 61v); for making men, women, or animals seem dead (e.g., Aberystwyth, National Library of Wales, MS Peniarth 402, p. 251; San Marino, Huntington Library, MS 1336, fol. 27v; BodL, MS Ashmole 1438, Part 1, p. 8); or for making other kinds of creature, such as birds, fill a house (e.g., BL, Additional MS 12195, fol. 150v).

[2] Julia Boffey considers miscellaneous manuscripts such as these as a kind of household book, which she defines broadly as "a book that was in use in a specific household" (Julia Boffey, "Bodleian Library, MS Arch Selden B.24 and Definitions of the Household Book," in *The English Medieval Book: Studies in Memory of Jeremy Griffiths*, ed. A. S. G. Edwards et al. (London: British Library, 2000), 125–34 (129).

To make wylde bestis to pyre in a howse

Take the talowe of a blacke catte and make thereof candellis and sett them in the fowre parttis [of] the howse and hit schalle seme fulle of wylde [bes]tis by the lyte of the candellis[3]

Modern readers might consider the effect to be a simple optical illusion in which the movement of the flames creates the appearance of shadowy creatures on the walls. This explanation was available to medieval readers too. However, as Robert Goulding has shown, scholastic theorists of magic also thought that the substances used to make the candle in this kind of display (so, in this instance, the fat of a black cat) contained impressive natural properties that could render the optical effect more compelling by making the forms more beast-like or by overwhelming the viewer's senses.[4] Goulding's work on the scholars William of Auvergne, Thomas Aquinas, and Nicholas Oresme shows how capacious the medieval understanding of illusion—referred to as *praestigium*, *delusio*, or *apparentia*—was: appearances or, to quote from the recipe above, things that merely "seme" true, could be created by human sleight of hand, the natural properties of things, or demonic intervention stimulated by human conjurations; these agents were often difficult to distinguish from one another.[5] Whether the effect was merely an illusion, or had some wondrous reality itself, was also debated.[6]

What purpose did such recipes serve? Were they actually enacted? Were they performed before an audience? If so, what motivated that performance and how was it understood by the spectators? There are many different types of recipe for creating many different kinds of transformation intermingled amongst one another in these manuscript compilations, and each of them can imply a different scenario. For instance, recipes for creating unexpected appearances around the house (such as floods or snake

[3]BL, MS Sloane 1315, fol. 96v. This manuscript is discussed in detail later in the article. Here (and throughout the article), transcribed text that is enclosed by square brackets has been supplied by me because the manuscript is faded or illegible at that point; square brackets also signal where the original text has been amended or additional words have been supplied to fit the grammar, syntax, and context of the sentence in which it is being quoted. Curly brackets signal a gloss or translation. I have silently expanded abbreviations and modernized word divisions.

[4]Robert Goulding, "Illusion," in *The Routledge History of Medieval Magic*, ed. Catherine Rider and Sophie Page (London: Routledge, 2019), 312–30 (315–17).

[5]Ibid., 323.

[6]Ibid., 320.

infestations) might be conceived of as spectacles that could be staged before household members and guests as entertainment. Alternatively, if used to scare or deceive, they could be deployed as practical jokes or more sinister tricks. Other recipes, copied in the same manuscripts, seem simultaneously spectacular *and* mundanely practical: for example, oft-copied recipes for making parsley grow in a few hours could be used to impress onlookers but could also be consulted in the interests of fulfilling an urgent culinary need.[7] Whilst these spectacular transformations imply an audience before which the enactor of the recipe performs, other recipes plot impressive but less explicitly spectacular transformations that reshape intimate relationships *between* individuals: for instance, many miscellaneous recipe compilations contain instructions for making men and women love one another, or for making an individual share their secrets in their sleep or become obedient to the enactor's will. These transformations—which may have been enacted within a domestic environment or beyond it—deploy the same range of natural and demonic methods as the more spectacular recipes, and they raise similar questions about illusion and reality: what kind of reality does love brought about by magic have? They also all raise similar questions about belief and performance: what kind of efficacy did they have? If they were not particularly convincing, why were they so frequently recopied?

These mysteries motivate the current article. Scholars working on performance and theatricality have already developed sophisticated approaches to these questions in other contexts. For instance, Philip Butterworth's notion of "agreed pretence" questions whether verisimilitude and belief were always the end goal of medieval theatrical performances; he does not believe that physical devices, staging techniques, and acting were used in medieval performances "to produce the illusion of reality" but argues instead that "this kind of playing" was used "to create signs, signals and action that, by their very nature, could be communicated and

[7] See, for example, *The Tollemache Book of Secrets*, ed. Jeremy Griffiths and A. S. G. Edwards (London: Roxburghe Club, 2001), 50; and BL, MS Sloane 1315, fols. 90v–91r, 115r. In MS Sloane 1315, the first recipe for making parsley spring up reads as a spectacular illusion, whilst the second—which instructs the reader to cut the parsley and put it inside a chicken—seems more likely to be consulted in a moment of culinary need. Chelsea Silva, "Domestic Wonder and the Medieval Home," in *Recipes and Book Culture in England, 1350–1600*, ed. Carrie Griffin and Hannah Ryley (Liverpool: Liverpool University Press, 2024), 155–74, makes a similar point, contending that "many of these texts work across multiple vectors of usefulness" (171). Chelsea Silva was kind enough to share a draft of this essay with me ahead of publication.

detected as such, and not be confused with real action or real situations."[8] Butterworth does note, however, that "there is evidence of mistrust, misunderstood intentions and miscommunicated theatrical statements. It is not always clear whether an audience was able to know of or detect the nature of agreed pretence."[9] The insights of this performance scholarship have not been mined in discussions of domestic recipes, but it is clear that those insights open up ways of thinking about these performance scripts that do not reduce those performances to unsophisticated enactments that either failed to convince anyone or were, conversely, believed by the entirety of a gullible medieval audience. Instead, we might imagine the performances being understood as attempts at creating illusions that could produce an impressive effect (known not to be reality) but could also end up in disaster—and be all the funnier because of that. And yet we would also want to leave room for the "mistrust" and "misunderstood intentions" that Butterworth sometimes observes; part of the appeal of the recipes may have been their perceived capacity to deceive particular individuals. As scholars such as Greg Walker and John McGavin have argued, we should resist the critical tendency to homogenize premodern acts of spectatorship.[10]

This kind of close attention to the recipes as performance texts has not been forthcoming (probably because of the lack of any surviving performance memoranda accompanying them). Consideration of the recipes as written texts rather than performance scripts, as texts that may *never* have been enacted but could still have acted as imaginative stimulants for readers, is much more prevalent. This work, which I shall consider in detail later on, has explored the possibility that the recipes functioned largely as "narratives to be enjoyed" and as fictions of empowerment that enabled readers to imagine themselves overcoming everyday social, sexual, and financial problems.[11] To be sure, the very titles of the recipes ("to make x or y happen") focus readers' attention teleologically on triumphant end points, on a future moment of success, domination, and empowerment. The sequential structure of recipes ("and take . . . and make . . . and pour . . . and drink . . .")—which is reminiscent of the linear, polysyndetic

[8]Philip Butterworth, *Staging Conventions in Medieval English Theatre* (Cambridge: Cambridge University Press, 2014), 21, 94.

[9]Ibid., 91.

[10]John J. McGavin and Greg Walker, *Imagining Spectatorship: From the Mysteries to the Shakespearean Stage* (Oxford: Oxford University Press, 2016), 7–8.

[11]Carrie Griffin, *Instructional Writing in English, 1350–1650: Materiality and Meaning* (London: Routledge, 2019), *The Boke of Nurture*: manuscripts, para. 7. Restricted access eBook.

structures of medieval narrative fiction—can thus be interpreted as a series of sequential stepping stones leading inexorably to that triumphant end predetermined by the recipes' titles. Of course, this emphasis on the recipes as imagined rather than real trajectories does not dictate a complete dismissal of the recipes' potential to produce wonderful transformations. Working on the cognate subject of depictions of marvels in medieval travel writing, Michelle Karnes has challenged "the suggestion that medieval readers were capable of only two relatively unsophisticated responses to imaginative literature (I do or I do not believe it)," arguing instead that "there was always a possibility, however remote, that a marvel could be real as long as it had not been disproven and it respected nature's laws, whether as they were currently understood or as they might be understood better."[12] Karnes concludes that marvels "appeal to the imagination precisely because of their resolute indeterminacy."[13] Readers and collectors of recipes may also have been tantalized by the possibility that the marvelous transformations they were reading about *could* be successfully enacted in reality or in appearance, even if they never actually made the attempt.

Sophisticated conceptual frameworks are available, then, for understanding the appeal and function of the recipes both as performance pieces and as micronarratives that encouraged triumphant, teleological imaginings. One limitation of the above analysis, however, is that it mostly focuses on the recipes as performance pieces *or* as fictional narratives. In this article, I want to redress that by suggesting that we also consider the recipes as narratives *of* embodied action that necessitate—even in the act of imagination—thinking through what it would mean (physically, emotionally, and socially) to perform particular actions in a particular sequence in a particular body. Whilst narrative fiction, in the words of Jerome Bruner, "strives to put its timeless miracles into the particulars of experience, and to locate the experience in time and place," the recipes plot generic actions that readers (if they are to enter into any kind of consideration about how the recipe would work) must transplant through their imaginations onto their own spatial and temporal coordinates, their own narrative.[14] These imagined sequences of action, I contend, carried a host of potential meanings which can be illuminated through several other kinds of narrative writing that often accompanied recipes in household

[12]Michelle Karnes, "The Possibilities of Medieval Fiction," *NLH* 51 (2020): 209–28 (209–10).

[13]Ibid., 210.

[14]Jerome Bruner, *Actual Minds, Possible Worlds* (Cambridge, Mass.: Harvard University Press, 1986), 13.

books: these include literary narratives such as fabliaux, astrological horoscopes, and game texts predicting futures for players. Reading recipe sequences through these proximate narrative structures shows how certain kinds of connected, sequential, and temporally specific action could be risky or humiliating for the imagined performer, nuancing the association often made between these recipes and social, sexual, or intellectual empowerment.

In the following sections, then, I begin by outlining the various (and overlapping) domestic contexts in which the recipes were written down, shared, and potentially performed. After this, I consider more fully the approaches that have already been taken to these texts before exploring, in the third part of the article, how we might productively interpret recipes' narrative sequences of embodied action through the lens of other, imaginatively cognate narrative fictions. In the fourth and final part of the essay, I then argue that longer domestic narratives (such as fabliaux), which contain recipe structures and motifs embedded within them, may have functioned as virtual performance spaces where the transformations imagined in recipes (but not often accompanied by any performance memoranda) could be tried out in domestic settings, relationship networks, and webs of cultural association. The recontextualizing of the decontextualized recipes in these "virtual' spaces blurs the boundary between narrative and performance and makes us rethink the finality of the end points that the recipes signpost: instead of focusing on end points, did readers imagine the recipes as part of longer narratives (both real and textual) in which moments of empowerment, triumph, and domination were short-lived and in continual conversation with the countermoves of nature, rival human intentions, and divine intervention? How might these threats have inflected—or, counterintuitively, defined—the particular kind of thrill that the recipes offered?

Social and Material Contexts

The domestic coordinates that these recipes were written within and mapped onto in imagination or practice are hard to circumscribe with any certainty. This is because the recipes probably circulated orally and because they were copied and recopied in manuscripts connected to different milieux throughout the Middle Ages. Some collections, copied in manuscript miscellanies, have strong links to the households of gentry, mercantile, or urban craft families; the latter two groups are often referred to in modern scholarship as the urban "burgeiserie," characterized by

Felicity Riddy as a group of substantial townsmen and women "closely associated with materiality—possessions, social difference, ambition."[15] The prevalence of these recipes in vernacular or multilingual manuscripts owned by such households supports the oft-attested conclusion that the late fourteenth and fifteenth century witnessed growing literacy levels and increased circulation of practical knowledge, scientific writing, and leisurely "game texts" amongst such families.[16] That late medieval trend, however, had its beginnings in previous centuries. An early example of such a collection is Oxford, Bodleian Library, MS Digby 86. This trilingual thirteenth-century compilation was probably copied by Richard de Grimhill II (or a scribe under his patronage) for the use of his lower gentry family.[17] The manuscript—copied almost entirely by a single hand—contains a remarkable variety of Latin, English, and French texts, including religious songs and prose devotional texts, debate poetry, fabliaux, proverbs, moralizing tales, courtesy texts, beast fables, fortune-telling games, romances, medical recipes, and (in two separate places in the manuscript) recipes for creating wonderful transformations in the home that—in Jennifer Jahner's words—"run the gamut from practical domestic tips to party entertainments to what might fairly be called magic tricks."[18]

[15]Felicity Riddy, "'Burgeis' Domesticity in Late Medieval England," in *Medieval Domesticity: Home, Housing and Household in Medieval England*, ed. Maryanne Kowaleski and P. J. P. Goldberg (Cambridge: Cambridge University Press, 2008), 14–36 (20).

[16]For studies of expanding book ownership and literacy amongst such groups see Carol Meale, "Amateur Book Production and the Miscellany in Late Medieval East Anglia," in *Insular Books: Vernacular Manuscript Miscellanies in Late Medieval Britain*, ed. Margaret Connolly and Raluca Radulescu (Oxford: Oxford University Press, 2015), 157–73; Malcolm Parkes, "The Literacy of the Laity," in *Literature and Western Civilisation: The Medieval World*, ed. David Daiches and Anthony Thorlby (London: Aldus, 1973), 555–77; Eric Kwakkel, "A New Type of Book for a New Type of Reader: The Emergence of Paper in Vernacular Book Production," *The Library* 4 (2003): 219–48; and Susanna Fein and Michael Johnston, eds., *Robert Thornton and His Books: Essays on the Lincoln and London Thornton Manuscripts* (York: York Medieval Press, 2014). On the popularity of magic and games in such households see Laura T. Mitchell, "Cultural Uses of Magic in Fifteenth-Century England," Ph.D. diss. (University of Toronto, 2011), 96–132; Serina Patterson, "Game On: Medieval Players and Their Texts," Ph.D. diss. (University of British Columbia, 2017); and Serina Patterson, ed., *Games and Gaming in Medieval Literature* (New York: Palgrave Macmillan, 2015).

[17]See Susanna Fein, "Introduction," in *Interpreting MS Digby 86: A Trilingual Book from Thirteenth-Century Worcestershire*, ed. Fein (Woodbridge: York Medieval Press in association with Boydell and Brewer, 2019), 1–9 (3).

[18]Jennifer Jahner, "Literary Therapeutics: Experimental Knowledge in MS Digby 86," in Fein, *Interpreting MS Digby 86*, 73–86 (74). Here, Jahner also gives the following description of the recipes: "The manuscript contains two sections of 'experiments' (arts. 11, 15; fols. 34r, 46r–48r), copied in quires v and vi by the primary scribe of the

Examples include recipes for making the dead sing, for getting people to vacate one's house, for killing flies, and for invisible ink.[19]

The fact that both sequences of recipes are copied between other practical and scientific texts, including charms, prognostics, and dream interpretations, may suggest that the recipes were seen by the scribe copying them and the family members reading them as part of a larger unit of texts concerned with nature's forces, man's position amongst those forces, and ways of manipulating them.[20] At the same time, they remain part of the larger compilation of writings that MS Digby 86 comprises, and it is possible that readers could have made links between the recipes and other texts in the manuscript, such as the fabliau *Dame Sirith* or the fortune game *Ragemon le Bon.* Like recipes involving sleight of hand or optical illusion, fabliaux pose questions about human ingenuity and gullibility: how fantastical, outrageous, or crude an illusion can one person get another to believe in? Similarly, fortune games raise questions—like recipes—about a human being's position in the cosmos and their capacity (or inability) to manipulate forces and opportunities for personal benefit. In other (later) manuscripts associated with "burgeis" or gentry households, recipes also reside alongside a diverse array of materials. Consider Oxford, Balliol College, MS 354, a miscellaneous book belonging to the London grocer Richard Hill (born c. 1490), which was copied in the early sixteenth century.[21] As well as recipes for various domestic transformations, this manuscript includes devotional lyrics and religious instructions, documents relating to London's civic governance, a short London chronicle, narrative poetry such as *The Seven Sages of Rome*, gardening texts, medical recipes, puzzles, word problems, and card tricks.

In these lay contexts, the recipes may have been encountered—in written or spoken form—by male *and* female members of a household; perhaps they functioned as a stimulus for debate in the home as household members and their guests debated whether a particular recipe could be

---

manuscript . . . the experiments number about forty in total, with an unknown number from the first section lost due to a missing quire."

[19]For further details see ibid., 74.

[20]For the contents of the manuscript see Susanna Fein, "The Contents of Oxford, Bodleian Library, MS Digby 86," in Fein, *Interpreting MS Digby 86*, xv–xviii.

[21]On this manuscript's provenance and construction, and the late medieval compilational practices it testifies to, see Alexandra Gillespie, "Balliol 354: Histories of the Book at the End of the Middle Ages," *Poetica* 60 (2003): 47–63; W. P. Hills, "Richard Hill of Hillend," *N&Q* 177 (1939): 452–56; and Heather Collier, "Late Fifteenth and Early Sixteenth-Century Manuscript Miscellanies: The Sources and Contexts of MS Balliol 354," Ph.D. diss. (Queen's University Belfast, 2000).

translated into action and whether or not that enaction would be ethically or socially acceptable. Other contexts for the recipes' circulation and interpretation were probably more male: recipes for wonderful household transformations frequently appear in manuscripts with clerical and monastic associations. Consider the notebook of Thomas Betson, a monk living at Syon Abbey in Middlesex during the late fifteenth and early sixteenth centuries. In addition to recipes for tricks such as making cooked meat seem alive and making an egg, coin, or apple appear to move by itself (in the latter instance by placing a beetle in hollowed-out fruit), his notebook contains a mix of medical, scientific, devotional, proverbial, legal, and lyrical texts; in its miscellaneity, its indulgence in play, and its interest in pastoral texts and practical medical writings, the notebook has much in common with miscellaneous manuscripts circulating in secular gentry and mercantile households, showing—despite widespread clerical distrust of theatricality and ludic play—a shared interest amongst both groups in practical labour and recreation.[22] Did Betson regularly enact these tricks in the domestic spaces of the abbey as a respite from the work of learning and devotion? Or were the recipes in Betson's notebook—and other potential clerical manuscripts discussed in this article—another way of displaying one's learning to oneself and others? Robert Goulding has shown that many of Betson's tricks were probably taken from the *Secretum philosophorum*, a Latin secrets text that frames itself as an academic treatise on the liberal arts but is actually more concerned with traditions of experimental craft knowledge.[23] Looking further back in time, William Eamon has shown that these medieval recipes for creating spectacular transformations were descended from a long tradition of Greek and Arabic hermetic thought and from western European Latin writings on optics, nature, and natural magic by scholastic thinkers such as Roger Bacon and William of Auvergne.[24]

The lay and the learned were, then, closely intertwined. Another indicator of this is that similar playful texts appear in manuscripts associated

[22]For the trick recipes in Betson's notebook see Cambridge, St. John's College, MS E.6, fols. 4v–7r. On Betson's use of magic more generally see Richard Kieckhefer, *Magic in the Middle Ages* (Cambridge: Cambridge University Press, 1989), 91. On attitudes to theatricality see Lawrence Clopper, *Drama, Play and Game: English Festive Culture in the Medieval and Early Modern Period* (Chicago: University of Chicago Press, 2001), 25–62.

[23]Robert Goulding, "Deceiving the Senses in the Thirteenth Century: Trickery and Illusion in the *Secretum philosophorum*," in *Magic and the Classical Tradition*, ed. Charles Burnett and W. F. Ryan (London: Warburg Institute, 2006), 135–62 (141–42).

[24]William Eamon, *Science and the Secrets of Nature: Books of Secrets in Medieval and Early Modern Culture* (Princeton, N.J.: Princeton University Press, 1994), 15–90.

with educated medical practitioners, suggesting that they could also have offered those individuals a whimsical respite from the depressing grind of medical practice.[25] Oxford, Bodleian Library, MS Ashmole 1389 is a small, informally copied and portable volume predominantly filled with medical recipes, which has been linked (tentatively) to Henry VII's surgeon William Altoftes of Atherstone.[26] Copied between the medical recipes and separated from them by two blank leaves are a series of recipes for wonders such as making men and women take off their clothes, making men dance or seem headless, and making oneself invisible.[27] Elsewhere I have remarked upon the resemblances between the material demarcation of the two blank pages and John Huizinga's concept of a "playground," a space characterized by boundaries and special rules only applicable to the world of play.[28] So, in MS Ashmole 1389—in contrast to those manuscripts where the recipes are interspersed amongst other kinds of texts—one must cross a threshold if one wishes to leave behind a world of earthly, ailing bodies that are to be treated with care and respect by a professional physician and pass into a ludic space where power and decorum operate differently, where both clothes and heads can be removed without scandal. This organisation of the manuscript shows that the place of these recipes, and their relationship to the everyday world, could be thought about differently by different scribes, compilers, and readers.

Interestingly, a sense of precarity connects many of the groups with which these recipes for wonderful domestic transformations have been shown to have connections. Physicians, surgeons, and other kinds of medical practitioner were often the object of satire and mockery on account of their proximity to wounded, leaking, and unpleasant bodies; the perceived inefficacy of their treatments; and their precarious status as members of the "newly emergent professional classes."[29] Similarly, labour crises, lack

[25]For instance, the trick recipes in BodL, MS Ashmole 1389, pp. 39–47, are copied within a manuscript otherwise dominated by medical recipes.

[26]On this attribution see Juhani Norri, "Entrances and Exits in English Medical Vocabulary, 1400–1550," in *Medical and Scientific Writing in Late Medieval English*, ed. Irma Taavitsainen and Päivi Pahta (Cambridge: Cambridge University Press, 2004), 100–143 (103).

[27]The recipes for wonderful transformations occur in BodL, MS Ashmole 1389, pp. 39–47, with blank leaves at pp. 38 and 48.

[28]Hannah Bower, *Middle English Medical Recipes and Literary Play, 1375–1500* (Oxford: Oxford University Press, 2022), 205.

[29]Marion Turner, "Illness Narratives in the Later Middle Ages: Arderne, Chaucer, and Hoccleve," *JMEMS* 46 (2016): 61–87 (76–79); Julie Orlemanski, "Jargon and the Matter of Medicine in Middle English," *JMEMS* 42 (2012): 395–420.

of patronage, and a system that favored familial connections left many university-trained clerics unemployed and without a benefice; they were forced to find other ways to make a living (perhaps through scribal and bureaucratic work) and other outlets for their learning (sometimes through poetry and magic).[30] It is easy to see how wonderful recipes for acquiring social, sexual, financial, and intellectual advantage over others may have appealed to clerics living precariously.

Studies analyzing the composition, presentation, and material environments of gentry, mercantile and "burgeis" families have also emphasized the elusiveness of the identifiers used to refer to these social groups by themselves or their contemporaries and the controversies that surrounded attempts by these groups to lay claim to particular kinds of social privilege.[31] Scholarship has highlighted the porous, unstable, and enigmatic nature of gentry and "burgeis" domestic spaces. In an essay on "burgeis" families, Riddy claims that:

> We should see this ["burgeis"] group as always in process, restless, voracious and ambitious. Their flexible timber-frame homes acknowledge this: timber-frame construction was a new technology introduced at the turn of the thirteenth century, that made it possible to create buildings that were durable . . . but easy to modify and adapt.[32]

Such flexibility could also be cognitive: as Rory Critten and Glenn Burger state in the introduction to their edited volume on household knowledge, "the late medieval bourgeois household could be a site of individual negotiation as well as of social discipline, of creative volubility and improvised exchange as well as of regulated interaction."[33] Echoing these accounts' emphasis on ambition and adaptation, Carrie Griffin, Chelsea Silva, and Wendy Wall have argued that medical remedies, culinary recipes, and recipes for domestic transformations that contained luxury ingredients or

[30]Kathryn Kerby-Fulton, *The Clerical Proletariat and the Resurgence of Medieval English Poetry* (Philadelphia: University of Pennsylvania Press, 2021), 2–3.

[31]See, for instance, Philippa Maddern, "Gentility," in *Gentry Culture in Late Medieval England*, ed. Raluca Radulescu and Alison Truelove (Manchester: Manchester University Press, 2005), 18–34; and D. Vance Smith, *Arts of Possession: The Middle English Household Imaginary* (Minneapolis: University of Minnesota Press, 2003), 143–45, 150–51.

[32]Riddy, "'Burgeis' Domesticity," 30. Riddy does also note, however, that "the 'burgeiserie' were differentiated from the mobile urban poor by a rhetoric of settledness; they were distinguished from itinerants in short-term lets" (30).

[33]Glenn D. Burger and Rory G. Critten, eds., *Household Knowledges in Late-Medieval England and France* (Manchester: Manchester University Press, 2020), 2.

imitated aristocratic and royal practices may have been copied out by gentry and "burgeis" families as a form of wish-fulfillment, as a way of imagining themselves into a more privileged social milieu that was not fully available to them.[34] After all, medieval chronicles describe aristocratic and royal households across Europe deploying automata and other mechanisms to work marvelous transformations upon domestic space: in the Palais de la Cité, the royal palace of Paris, a large ship was brought into a feast in 1378 in a theatrical reconstruction of the First Crusade, and a ship was similarly deployed in 1389 in a recreation of the Fall of Troy.[35] Urban guilds and civic officials—who were often the same "burgeis" individuals that owned, copied, or commissioned miscellaneous household books—also deployed automata and theatrical effects in public ceremonies and private guild displays.[36] Household spectacles on a smaller scale, such as those using candles to make beasts appear to run around a house, may have been attempts to create, in an intimate setting, more affordable forms of entertainment that evoked these grander civic and court spectacles.

Marvelous transformations of domestic space cannot, then, be confined to one domestic milieu. It seems unlikely that the direction of influence between these sources was ever one of clear-cut "downward" transmission from court spectacle and scholarly rumination to mercantile, urban, or gentry households. Instead, a messy tangle of influences probably led to

[34]Carrie Griffin, "Reconsidering the Recipe: Materiality, Narrative and Text in Later Medieval Instructional Manuscripts and Collections," in *Manuscripts and Printed Books in Europe, 1350–1550: Packaging, Presentation and Consumption*, ed. Emma Cayley and Susan Powell (Liverpool: Liverpool University Press, 2013), 135–49 (148); Wendy Wall, *Recipes for Thought: Knowledge and Taste in the Early Modern English Kitchen* (Philadelphia: University of Pennsylvania Press, 2015), 3. See also Silva, "Domestic Wonder and the Medieval Home."

[35]Laura Hibbard Loomis, "Secular Dramatics in the Royal Palace, Paris, 1378, 1389, and Chaucer's 'Tregetoures,'" *Speculum* 33 (1958): 242–55. On the taste for spectacle in European courts see also Scott Lightsey, *Manmade Marvels in Medieval Culture and Literature* (New York: Palgrave Macmillan, 2007).

[36]On such spectacles see Lightsey, *Manmade Marvels*, 27–53; Sheila Lindenbaum, "Ceremony and Oligarchy: The London Midsummer Watch," in *City and Spectacle in Medieval Europe*, ed. Barbara A. Hanawalt and Katherine Reyerson (Minneapolis: University of Minnesota Press, 1994), 171–88; and Claire Sponsler, "Lydgate and London's Public Culture," in *Lydgate Matters: Poetry and Material Culture in the Fifteenth Century*, ed. Lisa H. Cooper and Andrea Denny-Brown (New York: Palgrave Macmillan, 2008), 13–33. Universities are another potential site for spectacle: although there is less evidence in the Middle Ages of the large-scale theatrical performances characterizing Tudor scholarly environments, critics have pointed to alternative kinds of theatrical and ritual performance staged within university spaces: see Thomas Meacham, *The Performance Tradition of the Medieval English University: The Works of Thomas Chaundler* (Kalamazoo: Medieval Institute Publications, 2020).

imaginings of flood-, bird-, or beast-filled spaces and all kinds of other wonders becoming, to deploy Helen Cooper's helpful romance formulation, "memes": like genes, memes are motifs that have the capacity "to replicate faithfully and abundantly, but also on occasion to adapt, mutate, and therefore survive in different forms and cultures."[37]

To emphasize these messy connections—and their visibility to medieval writers—I turn briefly to Chaucer's *Canterbury Tales*, a work in which personas and spaces from different social milieux and literary genres consistently interact, re-voice, reflect, and parody one another. Here, we find a fictional example of how the kinds of wonderful transformations enacted in the recipe books might connect—and simultaneously distinguish—different domestic spaces. Chaucer's most obvious reference to these tricks is in the Franklin's narrative. Aurelius's brother, citing hearsay, recalls the marvelous transformations (or deceptive illusions) that he has heard are enacted in the "halle large" of great aristocratic households:

> For ofte at feestes have I wel herd seye
> That tregetours withinne an halle large
> Have maad come in a water and a barge,
> And in the halle rowen up and doun
> Sometyme hath semed come a grym leoun;
> And somtyme floures sprynge as in a mede;
> . . .
> And whan hem lyked, voyded it anon.
> Thus semed it to every mannes sighte.[38]

The scenario outlined here (evocative of the feasts at the Palais de la Cité in 1378 and 1389) is one in which a professional magician entertains a hall full of wealthy banqueting guests.[39] However, the tricks depicted are not that different—at least in terms of the self-proclaimed end result—from those that less explicitly ostentatious household books promise to bring about: recipes to make parsley grow in two hours are perhaps more homely, practically minded versions of the marvel of making flowers

[37]Helen Cooper, *The English Romance in Time: Transforming Motifs from Geoffrey of Monmouth to the Death of Shakespeare* (Oxford: Oxford University Press, 2004), 3.

[38]*FranT*, 1142–51. Chaucer references are to *The Riverside Chaucer*, gen. ed. Larry D. Benson, 3rd ed. (Oxford: Oxford University Press, 2008); future references to this edition are included within the text.

[39]On possible historical analogues for the episode see Hibbard Loomis, "Secular Dramatics," 242–55.

spring from the floor.[40] The wonder of making "a water and a barge" come into the "halle large" also has an obvious parallel in household recipes (discussed in more detail later on) for making a house seem flooded. Indeed, Chaucer himself constructs a small-scale parallel for this watery wonder in *The Miller's Tale*, a fabliau set in a "burgeis" household in which a wily scholar manages—through theatrics and evocative language—to convince a naïve carpenter that a second biblical Flood is on the way and that the carpenter will only be able to protect his household by obtaining three kneading troughs or brewing vats for himself, his wife, and the scholar to escape in. The scholar advises that they must "be large, / In which we mowe swymme as in a barge" (*MilT*, 3549–50). This conspicuous stretching of the miniature vessels into something "large" and the over-ambitious comparison with a "barge" directly recall the "barge" in the courtly displays of the Franklin's "halle large," sticking together the two domestic spaces through the repeated rhyme and implying that the wonderful deceptions that are wrought within the carpenter's house and the famed court through a combination of theatricality and narration are simultaneously comparable *and* distinct in their means, effect, and scale. This intermingling of spaces and milieux also extends into the scholarly realm: in *The Franklin's Tale*, Aurelius's brother precedes his account of the wonders enacted at great aristocratic households by recalling how, in Orleans, he saw a "bacheler of lawe" leave a book of "magyk natureel" upon his desk (*FranT*, 1125–26); consequently, the two brothers travel to Orleans where they meet a "yong clerk" who greets them in Latin, takes them to "his hous," and creates illusions before them of moving beasts and birds, jousting knights, and dancing ladies (1173–1201). The scholarly and courtly here combine.

Motifs such as water or birds entering into domestic spaces clearly had the potential, then, to move rapidly between different domestic, political, and scholarly environments. Crucially, the spatial referents in the trick recipes do not change between these different contexts; instead, generic words such as "dore," "howse," and "strete" stand ready to be stretched, shrunk, or adjusted in relation to the immediate physical landscape of the reader or the landscape they wished to imagine themselves in.[41] That

[40]See, for example, Griffiths and Edwards, *The Tollemache Book*, 50; and BL, MS Sloane 1315, fols. 90v–91r, 115r.

[41]Silva, "Domestic Wonder and the Medieval Home," discusses in more detail the relationship between the recipes, the material domestic environments in which they were staged, and the appeal of the uncanny.

elasticity could accommodate mobility: for instance, in a recipe for making a house appear flooded, the reader is instructed to keep the string required for the trick within their "purse" until they "wylle play {their} experement."[42] They are then to nail the thread into a "spere" (a timber beam or screen partition) in the "halle" they are in.[43] It is not clear what kind of "halle" this will be; the referent could change with each new opportunity that presented itself to the enactor. In this article, I try to remain sensitive to that contextual instability: although I interpret the precarities, opportunities, and thrills implied by the recipes in the light of the socio-historical context of the manuscripts they appear in and the other texts copied around them, I am aware that the social and domestic coordinates onto which those recipes could be mapped were in flux. We must continually readjust our reading of the recipes as we imagine new vantage points and performance possibilities, heeding Walker and McGavin's warning not to try to homogenize premodern acts of spectatorship or reading.[44]

Approaches

So, how might we approach these premodern acts of spectatorship and reading? The introduction to this article demonstrated, in outline, that approaches to these recipes for domestic transformation have taken two main routes, one focused on the performance of the recipes and the other focused on the recipes as written documents. Understanding how writing and performance might have interacted presents modern scholars with a real challenge. This is noted by Goulding, who calls for more work to be done on those tricks that do not have, to modern eyes, any "reproducible" effect in performance.[45] What he means here is that it is entirely unclear how these recipes would—through the method they describe—bring about the illusions that they claim to be able to bring about in a convincing way. Non-reproducible tricks include those that claim a kind of efficacy through occult natural powers imagined and apparently detected by medieval readers but disproven by us. For instance, a recipe for making everyone in the room have the head of an ass involved mixing the tears or semen of an ass with the wax used to make a candle. We would not

[42] BL, MS Sloane 1315, fol. 90r.
[43] Ibid. See *MED*, s.vv. *sparre* (n.), def. 1(a); *sper* (n.), def. 1.
[44] McGavin and Walker, *Imagining Spectatorship*, 7–8.
[45] Goulding, "Illusion," 326.

conceive the tears or semen to have this power; however, medieval scholars such as William of Auvergne believed that semen had the capacity to reproduce its own image and was, therefore, capable of creating such an effect.[46] After discussing this and other non-reproducible examples, Goulding notes that—counterintuitively—such tricks "have more longevity [in medieval and early modern writings on magic] than the descriptions of real reproducible tricks."[47] In other words, the transformations that seem least easy to perform compellingly have the longest textual afterlife.

Richard Kieckhefer has expressed a similar difficulty understanding the appeal and efficacy of recipes working through natural magic. He has contrasted this difficulty against the easier task of understanding the appeal of demonic magic, arguing that ritual magic (such as spells summoning demonic aid to generate love or obedience for the enactor) may have "reconfigured" perceived power relations between participants, accruing a sense of efficacy in performance without necessarily changing the world in the advertised way.[48] The texts here possess a psychological power. In contrast, he writes of natural magic: "Natural magic was always, in some quarters, a suspect category, and understandably so: its mechanisms remained unclear, and its claims to empirical confirmation were perhaps even by medieval standards not impressive."[49]

We might turn to performance scholarship, however, to speculate about certain kinds of entertainer–audience relationships that could have bestowed such tricks, in embodied form, with various kinds of efficacy. For example, discussing the applicability of the concept of "special effects" to both the modern and medieval period, Alison Griffiths suggests that, in modern film production processes, there are two kinds of special effect. On the one hand, there are *invisible* special effects, which simulate natural events possible in the real world too inconvenient to be produced naturally (such as snow) and these are not meant to be visible to audiences. On the other hand, *visible* special effects simulate impossible events and are meant

[46]William of Auvergne, *Opera omnia, quae hactenus reperiri potuerunt* (Paris, 1674), 1058, col. b, secs. G–H. Discussed further in Goulding, "Illusion," 315–16. Future short-form references to the *Opera omnia* are also to this edition, consulted via Early English Books Online.

[47]Goulding, "Illusion," 326.

[48]Richard Kieckhefer, *Forbidden Rites: A Necromancer's Manual of the Fifteenth Century* (Philadelphia: University of Pennsylvania Press, 1998), 15.

[49]Kieckhefer, *Forbidden Rites*, 12.

to be detectable to audiences.[50] Whether or not medieval recipes promise to create the appearance of possible or impossible events, they might have been interpreted as visible effects: for instance, recipes that use candles to make homes seem full of moving animals might not actually have been thought to produce a convincing effect; instead, the mechanics of the optical illusion could have been on display to the audiences, and that contrivance—ingenious or not—might have caused satisfaction in itself. The attempt to create an illusion (and the anticipation of seeing whether natural ingredients such as snake skins or ass's semen would bestow the trick with any added efficacy) could itself have been a source of communal pleasure. Alternatively, might a chance to revel collectively in the comic disastrousness of an attempted trick have been part of such entertainments' clownish appeal? As Jennifer Jahner has noted, such recipes are often labeled in manuscripts as *experimentum*, a Latin term that "designated knowledge acquired through 'experience,' whether by means of direct sense perception or through processes of trial and error."[51] Error, in this interpretation, is part of the text's appeal.

This emphasis on the visibility of the tricks returns us to Butterworth's idea of agreed pretence. In relation to medieval plays, Butterworth has argued that "the importance of this kind of playing was not to stress verisimilitude but to create signs, signals and action that, by their very nature, could be communicated and detected as such."[52] In the light of this, might we rethink the narratorial and symbolic potential of some recipes? For example, might an attempt at making a house appear filled with water have been more significant in a particular storytelling event for its biblical Flood symbolism than for any convincingness?[53]

As noted earlier, other scholars have considered the possibility that the recipes were not performed at all and functioned instead as satisfying imaginary narratives that invited readers to envisage themselves progressing toward a particular triumphant end point through their enaction of the recipe. For instance, Carrie Griffin has analyzed London, British Library, MS Sloane 1315, a manuscript containing a copy of the

[50] Alison Griffiths, "Wonder, Magic, and the Fantastical Margins: Medieval Visual Culture and Cinematic Special Effects," *Journal of Visual Culture* 9 (2010): 163–88 (165–66).

[51] Jahner, "Literary Therapeutics," 73.

[52] Butterworth, *Staging Conventions*, 94.

[53] On the importance of patter to the performance of medieval and early modern magic see Phillip Butterworth, *Magic on the Early English Stage* (Cambridge: Cambridge University Press, 2005), 83–86.

courtesy manual *The Boke of Nurture* alongside recipes for wonderful domestic tricks and transformations, and other astrological and medical writings. Griffin singles out the recipes as confusing her sense of the manuscript's intended purpose, contending that MS Sloane 1315 presents "a material context for the *Boke of Nurture* that should make sense," but adds that "the volume contains some unusual and unusable texts" that complicate our sense of its function.[54] She suggests that "the imaginative, fun, and surreal spells" included within the manuscript, such as conjurations for breaking out of prison and catching a thief, and recipes for making stars appear upon the ground or snakes seem to infest a home, "potentially giv[e] the book a fictive and imaginative framework within which these texts can operate as narratives to be enjoyed first rather than accessed for the purposes of education or the retrieval of information."[55]

Other scholars working on different magical manuscripts have also emphasized the recipes' social and imaginative function along with their empowering and affirmative narrative thrust. For instance, Laura Mitchell has analyzed four manuscripts containing instructions for different kinds of magical practice that were owned by gentry families, medical practitioners, clerics, and monks. Mitchell contends that the manuscripts might have been used by those individuals to fashion particular social, sexual, and intellectual identities for themselves: through recipes for gaining favor, love, and money (or the appearance of those things), they could imagine themselves overcoming everyday problems concerned with law, social relations, and matrimony.[56] Jennifer Jahner has extended this sense of power more explicitly to nature, arguing that such recipe collections "carried particular appeal for audiences at the margins of elite intellectual culture: [they] promised a kind of minor dominion over nature, one that transformed the microcosm of the household into a space for experimentation with the larger universe of marvellous phenomena."[57] Jahner here highlights the future orientation of recipes, the triumph they invite readers to imagine as they experiment with the powers of natural substances.[58] She then goes on to make an interesting connection between

[54]Griffin, *Instructional Writing, The Boke of Nurture*: manuscripts, para. 7.

[55]Ibid.

[56]Mitchell, "Cultural Uses of Magic," 122–23, 131, 157, 163, 187, 200.

[57]Jahner, "Literary Therapeutics," 79.

[58]On recipes' dual temporality as simultaneously "prescriptive and commemorative" see Lisa H. Cooper, "Recipes for the Realm: John Lydgate's 'Soteltes' and *The Debate of the*

experimental recipes and experimental book production, since the recipes often appear in multilingual, household compilations, where experimenting with different languages and combinations of texts gave scribes a space to play with the relationship between book and home, learning and domesticity, practicality and entertainment.[59] This focus on play has also been echoed by Peter Murray Jones from a more codicological perspective: he shows that these trick recipes (some of which are for inks and bookmaking materials) often appear in codicologically experimental manuscripts, fostering and reflecting an experimental and cumulative approach to bookmaking.[60]

These readings all focus on empowerment but they have different emphases. Griffin and Mitchell's readings of the texts as narratives of wish fulfillment and social self-fashioning offer a compelling alternative to reading the texts as crude performance scripts doomed to fail or to convince only the most gullible of audiences. Their readings shift emphasis away from the riskiness of performance. Jahner and Murray Jones also consider the empowering aspects of play and creativity, but their emphasis on experimentation simultaneously edges us back toward performance, risk, error, and the possibility of failure. In the remainder of this essay, I wish to build upon the insights of these scholars and consider whether there may be a way of combining these approaches, of incorporating ideas of performance, enaction, and embodiment more fully into the imaginative experience of narrative that recipes offer. In other words, as well as acknowledging the enjoyable and empowering end points that recipes invite readers to imagine—the wish fulfillment, self-fashioning, and wonderful domination of nature they promise to bring about—might we focus more on the physical processes by which readers have to imagine themselves getting there and unpack in more detail how those processes are mapped out in the texts? This will involve exploring both the opportunities and the difficulties that that imagined doing created for readers and the way that both triumph and risk, empowerment and vulnerability, clarity and blindness, are encoded into the recipe collections' narrative structures, defining—and complicating—the particular thrills they offer.

Horse, Goose, and Sheep," in *Essays on Aesthetics in Medieval Literature in Honour of Howell Chickering*, ed. John M. Hill, Bonnie Wheeler, and R. F. Yeager (Toronto: Pontifical Institute of Mediaeval Studies, 2014), 194–215 (197).

[59]Jahner, "Literary Therapeutics," 82–84.

[60]Peter Murray Jones, "*Experimenta*, Compilation and Construction in Two Medieval Books," *Poetica* 91–92 (2019): 61–80.

The recipes' promised end points (to have lots of love, money, and power) become far less certain as end points when we probe the means of getting there and the broader social, cultural, and codicological narratives into which those means and end points become subsumed in medieval imaginations.

Narrative Structures

To demonstrate some of the ways in which recipes' narrative structures can encode uncertainty about performance, I will first turn to a close analysis of some of the recipes in MS Sloane 1315. As noted, this is a manuscript that has received critical attention as a repository of instructional texts from Carrie Griffin as well as scholars such as Irma Taavitsainen, Peter Brown, Linne Mooney, and Melissa Reynolds.[61] We can ascertain the following about the codex: MS Sloane 1315 was copied on paper in both Latin and English in the mid-to-late fifteenth century, and it is thought to have a connection to the southeast of England, but it has not been connected to any named individual.[62] It contains the domestic courtesy manual *The Boke of Nurture*; this appears to have been copied on a separate quire by another hand and later added to the front of the codex. The rest of the manuscript, the majority of which was probably copied by a single scribe, contains writings on the four humors; astrological calendars and prognostic texts; a prose herbal; medical recipes; recipes for dyes, glues, and painting materials; and—intermingled amongst these recipes—large numbers of magical recipes for creating marvelous illusions or bringing about wondrous effects within the home.[63] The recipes become progressively more medical across the collection and it has been speculated that

[61]Griffin, *Instructional Writing*, *The Book of Nurture*: manuscripts, paras. 6–7. Restricted Access eBook; Peter Brown, "*The Seven Planets*," in *Popular and Practical Science of Medieval England*, ed. Lister M. Matheson (East Lansing: Colleagues Press, 1994), 3–21; Irma Taavitsainen, "The Identification of Middle English Lunary MSS," *Neuphilologische Mitteilungen* 88 (1987): 18–26 (22, 26). Linne Mooney, "Diet and Bloodletting: A Monthly Regimen," in Matheson, *Popular and Practical Science*, 245–61; and Melissa Reynolds, "'Here Is a Good Boke to Lerne': Practical Books, the Coming of the Press, and the Search for Knowledge, ca. 1400–1560," *Journal of British Studies* 58 (2019): 259–88.

[62]For an introduction to the manuscript see *The Middle English Wise Book of Philosophy and Astronomy: A Parallel-Text Edition*, ed. Carrie Griffin (Heidelberg: Universitätsverlag Winter, 2013), xxxvi.

[63]Minor changes to the hand across the manuscript suggest it was written over a period of time; alternatively, it is possible that several very similar hands could have contributed. This is noted in Reynolds, "Here Is a Good Boke to Lerne," 268; and Linne R. Mooney, "Practical Didactic Works in Middle English: Edition and Analysis of the Class of Short

the manuscript could have belonged to (and/or been copied by) a lay medical practitioner, who knew some Latin but was more confident in the vernacular; he could have been practicing medicine in a part-time or ad hoc manner.[64] Recipes for making "glewe for wreters" and "golde colowre for peynters" could suggest that the scribe and/or compiler also had an interest in bookmaking and decoration.[65] He may himself have been employed in a scribal capacity within a domestic, civic, or court environment.

The wonder recipes in MS Sloane 1315—copied between fols. 88v and 149r—contain instructions for a broad range of tricks, illusions, and effects. These include illusions similar to those already encountered to make a house appear full of snakes or wild beasts, to make cooked meat seem raw, to make people look like devils, and to make stars appear to be lying on the ground.[66] There are also many recipes for controlling women: over forty of them—in Latin and in English—are concerned with love, with contraception, or with the bodily and cognitive manipulation of the female sex. For example, there are recipes for getting the love of a woman or a young girl ("Si vis habere amorem puell{a}e . . ."), for making a woman dream of a man or reveal her secrets in her sleep, for making a woman take off her clothes or dance, and for making a woman follow a man.[67] Similarly high proportions of gendered recipes appear in other collections, such as Bodleian Library, MS Ashmole 1435, examined by Laura Mitchell.[68] This reappearance of similar recipes, or sets of recipes, from manuscript to manuscript of course raises questions about the degree to which each manuscript collection represents an individual's desires or self-fashioning impulses; many of the recipes may well have been copied wholesale from another exemplar.[69] Nevertheless, I would still assert that the choice to copy something *remains* a conscious choice, suggesting that the high number of recipes in MS Sloane 1315 for manipulating women might still tell us something about the scribe's priorities, self-perception, and desire for control.

Middle English Works Containing Useful Information," Ph.D. diss. (University of Toronto, 1981), 506.

[64]Brown, "*The Seven Planets*," 6.

[65]BL, MS Sloane 1315, fols. 96r, 95v.

[66]Ibid., fols. 103r–v (snakes), 96v (beasts), 94v, 104r–v (cooked meat); 94v–95r (devils), 90v (stars).

[67]Ibid., fols. 118r, 108r, 106v, 93r, 104r, 103v, 92r. Additional examples occur between fols. 91v and 119r; the recipes after that are more medical in nature.

[68]Mitchell, "Cultural Uses of Magic," 150–51, 154–56.

[69]This is also acknowledged in Frank Klassen, "Learning and Masculinity in Manuscripts of Ritual Magic of the Later Middle Ages and Renaissance," *Sixteenth-Century Journal* 38 (2007): 49–76 (52).

It is possible that the manuscript owner (and possibly its scribe) was a cleric, a figure of some schooling who had been admitted to minor orders during his education: his familiarity with basic Latin is testament to a degree of learning, even if the texts he selected or copied are—linguistically and conceptually—relatively accessible. Consequently, it is worth considering how the desire for sexual domination and social and intellectual power palpable within MS Sloane 1315 might align with methods of identity formation associated with other clerics who operated within the hypermasculine environments of the university and Church, or emerged from them and took on scribal work in different domestic and bureaucratic environments. In recent decades, conversations around clerical gender identities in the Middle Ages have moved beyond considering associations between clerics and effeminacy or conceptualizing clerical identity in homogeneous ways to consider how those conceptualizations were shaped by local and regional contexts, the manifold forms of clerical training, and the specific emotional and familial connections of an individual.[70] Scholars have also revisited the oft-espoused idea that clerics considered themselves to be (or were anxious about being seen as) inferior to laymen. For instance, in his study of sixteenth-century demonic magic practices, Frank Klassen deploys the term "clerical masculinity" to describe a dynamic in which learned, Latinate elements of ritual magic were used by Latin-speaking clerics in the "overlapping monastic, clerical, and learned worlds" to communicate and fashion for themselves sexual and intellectual power: they used their knowledge of Latin to copy and create demonic spells for acquiring sexual gratification and intellectual domination.[71] This may have reflected insecurity about their social, sexual, and intellectual value. But those manuscripts, Klassen claims, may also have been understood to construct a "distinctive masculinity founded upon positive features of their own community, such as learning, fraternity, self-control, and the possession of clerical ritual power."[72] The manuscripts sit ambiguously between anxiety and affirmation.

[70]See P. H. Cullum and Katherine J. Lewis, "Introduction," in *Religious Men and Masculine Identity in the Middle Ages*, ed. Cullum and Lewis (Woodbridge: Boydell and Brewer, 2013), 1–15 (4); P. H. Cullum, "Clergy, Masculinity and Transgression in Late Medieval England," in *Masculinity in Medieval Europe*, ed. D. M. Hadley (1999; London: Routledge, 2014), Chap. 11; Ruth Mazo Karras, *From Boys to Men: Formations of Masculinity in Late Medieval Europe* (Philadelphia: University of Pennsylvania Press, 2003), 67–108; Jennifer Thibodeaux, *The Manly Priest: Clerical Celibacy, Masculinity and Reform in England and Normandy, 1066–1300* (Philadelphia: University of Pennsylvania Press, 2015); and Jennifer Thibodeaux, ed., *Negotiating Clerical Identities: Priests, Monks and Masculinity in the Middle Ages* (Basingstoke: Palgrave Macmillan, 2010).

[71]Klassen, "Learning and Masculinity," 72.

[72]Ibid., 53.

Coining the term "quasi-clerical masculinity," Laura Mitchell has extended Klassen's insights to explore how parts of this clerical Latinate magic could be stripped of their most troubling demonic associations by subsequent lay readers.[73] Features that might be removed include explicit conjurations to, and invocations of, demons; extensive rituals; and lengthy brags about the effects a particular trick has had in the past. Tricks that were trimmed of these demonic elements, but retained parts of the ritual action reformulated as a kind of natural magic, could then be incorporated more comfortably into the household compilations of lower clergy, laymen, and "burgeis" urban professionals.

MS Sloane 1315 could fit into both of these (overlapping) groups. Some of the recipes within it may well—at some stage in their transmission—have been trimmed of the most lengthy necromantic rituals, but they still contain a significant number of shorter necromantic rites combined with other magical methods. For instance, a recipe for obtaining the love of a girl involves inscribing the names of devils (including Satan and Lucifer) into an apple, reciting a very short and simple conjuration, and giving the apple to the girl to eat.[74] Other recipes combine demonic names and conjurations with Christian prayer and symbolism, natural magic, and sleight of hand. For instance, a recipe for delivering a prisoner from captivity includes a lengthy Latin conjuration featuring nonsensical combinations of words and names that—alien to the reader—could be interpreted as demonic names.[75] St. Augustine, echoed by many later writers, had claimed that evil spirits used words and characters as ways of luring Christian souls: "Spirits who wish to deceive someone devise appropriate signs for each individual to match those in which they see him caught up through his speculations and the conventions he accepts."[76] In MS Sloane 1315, however, these troubling demonic echoes are balanced by Christian allusions: the recipe conjures these forces in the name of the Holy Trinity and instructs the reader after the conjuration to rehearse a Psalm three times. Richard Kieckhefer observes that, in demonic magic, "a holy object or formula [can be] used for so unholy a purpose that its holiness seems to be perceived as a kind of morally neutral potency, exploitable for either

[73] Mitchell, "Cultural Uses of Magic," 133–65.

[74] BL, MS Sloane 1315, fol. 118r.

[75] Ibid., fols. 99r–100r.

[76] St. Augustine of Hippo, *De doctrina christiana*, ed. and trans. R. P. H. Green (Oxford: Clarendon Press, 1995), 101.

good or evil ends."[77] What, then, would readers of the manuscript have thought of this combination of the holy and demonic? This is not simply a moral question but also a question about knowledge, about the source of the wonderful effect, and about how clear or unclear the reader would have been with regard to their role in bringing about the marvel. Even a clerical reader with some knowledge of Latin may have been unsure precisely what kind of power he was invoking through the recipe.

The same ambiguity also applies to non-demonic magic: an enduring and widely circulating trick for making a house appear full of snakes (a version of which appears in MS Sloane 1315) involved making a lamp from a mixture of wax and snakeskin and placing the lamp on a floor strewn with straw with no other lamps nearby.[78] The scholastic writer William of Auvergne categorized this trick as an example of natural magic.[79] Although William had a category for sleight of hand—which he defines as the "the placing and moving of certain things which are commonly called manipulations and shufflings"—he does not choose to place the trick in that category or describe it simply as an optical illusion.[80] Instead, he contends that the snake forms had a greenness that came from a natural property in the sulphurated snakeskin contained within the wax, producing a kind of natural magic.[81] Might others, however, have considered that straw-based trick to be an optical illusion? Ultimately, we cannot know how the majority of medieval readers understood such tricks, but we can be open to the possibility that readers sensed ambiguity and instability in their roles as enactors and limitations to their knowledge about how a trick was working. In recipe books such as MS Sloane 1315, there is no detailed explanation of how the recipes work and little categorization of them by method, means, or goal beyond the fact that some recipes are labeled as a "charme," some as a "medycyn," and some as an "experement."[82] As noted earlier, the latter term designates knowledge gained through experience.[83]

[77]Richard Kieckhefer, "Erotic Magic in Medieval Europe," in *Sex in the Middle Ages: A Book of Essays*, ed. Joyce Salisbury (New York: Garland, 1991), 30–55 (42).

[78]MS Sloane 1315, fol. 103r–v.

[79]William of Auvergne, *Opera omnia*, 1059, col. a, sec. B.

[80]Ibid., 1059, col. a, sec. A: "Dico igitur in primis, quia horum tria sunt genera: alia namque fiunt agilitate, habilitateque manuum, sicut repositiones, & transpositiones quarundam rerum, & vocantur vulgariter tractationes, vel trajectationes, & sunt magnae admirationis hominibus, donec innotescant modi quibus fiunt."

[81]Ibid., 1059, col. a, sec. B: "Causa autem in hoc est, quia varietas colorum a pulvere pellis serpenti faciet apparere viriditatem similem in juncis."

[82]See, for example, MS Sloane 1315, fols. 89r–90r.

[83]Jahner, "Literary Therapeutics," 73.

That knowledge could not be accommodated to, and explained through, existing theoretical frameworks; outcomes could not be predicted or easily generalized from. This experimental approach to knowledge may have reminded the reader that magical and scientific knowledge existed that would escape their own experiential understanding.

In MS Sloane 1315, that surplus becomes especially palpable in two recipes entitled "to knowe and se the secrett of jogelarse."[84] These texts—which involve performing a psalm before a "jogelar" or carrying around the plant hart's tongue and reciting a psalm over it—pit the reader and implied enactor of the manuscript's recipes up against another magic practitioner. The Middle English word *jogelour* is capacious and all-encompassing, running the spectrum from entertainer to sleight-of-hand artist to enchanter or diviner.[85] It is not clear, then, what kind of opponent the compilers of these collections see themselves up against, and how similar or different they consider that magician and his tricks to be from their own multifaceted practices. But it is clear that they see that practitioner as possessing knowledge that they do not have. The recipes thus make palpable the limits circumscribing the practitioner's knowledge and insight, *even as* they seek to transcend those limits, making the juggler's secret part of the present practitioner's knowledge and insight.

That experience of becoming aware of one's own limits and the extent of others' powers is an experience also explored in medieval fabliaux, a narrative genre typically concerned with spectacle, trickery, and sexual triumph in middling, "burgeis" domestic environments. The genre also has clear links to clerical environments: the first (Latin) fabliaux were written in France by members of the clergy.[86] Clerics of all kinds also appear as characters: in many French fabliaux, priests deceive husbands and wives as they find ways to commit adultery with the latter. The same is true in Chaucer's adaptations, which are amongst the earliest vernacular English examples of the genre: *The Miller's Tale* pits the wily scholar Nicholas against the naïve parish clerk Absolon as both pursue the amorous favours of Alisoun; in *The Reeve's Tale*, two Cambridge scholars dupe a deceitful miller in his own home, triumphing over him sexually and

[84]BL, MS Sloane 1315, fol. 105v. One of those recipes also appears in Latin in another collection; see Griffiths and Edwards, *The Tollemache Book*, 49.

[85]See *MED*, s.v. *jogelour* (n.), defs. 1–3; and Butterworth, *Magic on the Early English Stage*, 3–4, 7–25, 180–94.

[86]Laura Kendrick, "Comedy," in *A Companion to Chaucer*, ed. Peter Brown (Oxford: Blackwell, 2000), 90–113 (93–95).

financially as they rape his daughter and his wife and steal his grain.[87] The narratives categorized as fabliaux by modern scholars are usually structured by such rapid power reversals as characters engineer or respond to fast-changing circumstances in a bid to triumph over one another. Furthermore, fabliaux depict characters learning through experience—in an "experimental" way—what their own and others' limitations are: the moment that they are duped and undone by another protagonist they become conscious of what they did not know but another did, of the secrets of another "jogelar." Of course, fabliaux are usually concerned with the ingenuities of human craft rather than any supernatural or occult force, but that does not mean that they cannot still inform interpretations of these trick recipes, in which the human agent—striving for similar triumphant end points to fabliaux protagonists—remains centre stage: it is that agent's actions that the recipes foreground and their actions that summon, invoke, or mediate demonic and natural forces. Looking at these recipes through the lens of fabliaux helps us to pay more attention to the "error" part of Jennifer Jahner's experimental "trial and error" formulation, to the threat of failure that is part of the recipe's thrill. What is more, it helps us think about how that threat might be encoded through those same sequential narrative structures that seem, in the recipes, to lead toward triumphant end points of success and domination.

Consider this lengthy recipe from MS Sloane 1315's collection, entitled "An Experiment to make a flodde of water to com into a howse." First, I have transcribed the Middle English recipe with few edits.[88] I have then provided an edited translation in modern English:

Take snakyys egges the whittest þat there bythe v or a clowstere and lay them on a blacke grownde iii days and iij nyȝghtes and then take them vp and breke them in a newe asshen coppe or an asshen platere Then take a threde of iiij fethom or fyve þat a mayde hathe sponne on a frydaye byfore noone And folde vp the threde suche a wyse as ye may eysely vndo hit agayne Then put the threde into the lycore of the eggis And stri[89] stere them welle togedyre wythe a stycke tylle hit haue droncke vp alle the licoure. And then hong vp the threde to drye so hit touche no grownde and put hit in your purse And when ye wylle play yowre Experement Take the threde wyth a lytelle nayle dreve at on ende of the threde

[87]On the genre's delayed appearance in England see Melissa Furrow, "Middle English Fabliaux and Modern Myth," *ELH* 56 (1989): 1–18.

[88]I have only regularized word division and decapitalized any majuscule initials not serving a clear semantic or syntactic purpose.

[89]This seems to be a scribal error that was not corrected, perhaps indicating a fast pace of copying.

in the spere of the halle or in som othere thynge so hit be a knee of heythe above the grownde but be ware that the threde touche no grownde And þen take a dysshe fulle of salte water then take Then go to the threde and put the dysshe vndere along by the thred and go softtely along tylle the ende thereof but charge þat no man com a ny the threde by a fethom And þen hit schalle seme to þem that the flood schal be of the same heythe that the threde ys And then kytt iij pecis of braselle in scheppysses And goo ye to the ende of þe threde and folde hit vp softely and the floode schalle passe away And when ye com to þe laste ende of the threde þen plucke hit scharpely away And then the flood schal be agoo :ΔΔ And grynde a few pepercornyse and put hit thereto then take iij pecis of braselle and put hit in the dysshe wythe water[90]

Edited version:

Take snakes' eggs, the whitest that there are—5 or a cluster—and lay them on a black [piece of] ground for 3 days and 3 nights. And then pick them up and break them in a new cup made of ash wood or a new plate of ash wood. Then take a piece of thread of 24 or 30 feet that a virgin has spun on a Friday before noon. And fold up the thread in such a way that you may easily undo it again. Then put the thread into the egg mixture and stir them well together with a stick until the string has absorbed all of the mixture. And then hang up the thread to dry so that it does not touch the ground and put it into your bag. And when you want to perform your trick, take the thread [and arrange it] with a little nail driven in at one end of the thread in the timber beam/screen of the hall or in some other thing so that [the thread] is a knee's height above the ground. But beware that the thread does not touch the ground. And, after, take a dish full of salt water. Then go to the thread and put the dish underneath the thread. Carefully arrange it [in this manner] until [you get to] the end of the thread. But [you must] insist that no man come within 6 feet of the thread. And then it shall seem to [the audience] that the flood of water is the same height as the thread is. And then cut 3 pieces of brazilwood into fragments *and grind a few peppercorns and put them with [the fragments and] then take [the] 3 pieces of brazilwood and put them in the dish with water. And go to the end of the thread and fold it up carefully and the flood shall pass away. And, when you come to the last end of the thread, pluck it sharply away. And then the flood will be gone.

The instructions in this Middle English recipe are confused in a number of ways. First, the scribe disorders the instructions in the process of copying: sometimes this seems to be the product of eyeskip ("And þen take a

[90]BL, MS Sloane 1315, fol. 90r–v.

dysshe fulle of salte water then take Then go to the threde . . ."). His error, or an error in his exemplar, also obscures the proper place for the instruction about putting brazilwood into the dish of water in order, presumably, to dye the water a reddish colour: this instruction is started and left incomplete in the middle of the recipe and then additional information is given about the brazilwood at the end of the recipe with a symbol suggesting that it was supposed to be added earlier into the text; however, no corresponding symbol earlier on in the text marks where that addition should be inserted. In my edited version of the recipe, I have speculated that it was meant to go where the half-finished instruction about brazilwood is, and I have marked this rearrangement with an asterisk.

In addition to this scribal confusion, there is causal confusion: the mechanisms behind the trick and the forces believed to power it are not clear. The opening instructions appear to evoke occult, natural powers: it is implicit that the contrast between the white eggs and black ground imbues the trick with an untheorisable efficacy and one that might be compromised if the string comes into contact with the ground. However, the second part of the trick—which involves hanging the thread above a dish of water and making sure that none of the audience members come too close—seems more like an optical illusion, designed to fool the audience into thinking that the end of the string (trailing across the water surface?) marks the room's water levels. Perhaps readers were to be persuaded that the occult natural properties of the eggs would increase the efficacy of the illusion beyond any obvious logical possibility, making the entire room seem flooded rather than just the bit covered by the dish. Would the pieces of brazilwood placed into the water (and presumably dyeing it red) have been thought to have a similar function, or would that have been considered part of the spectacle's theatrics, a kind of gimmicky effect for dramatic tension?

The contiguous arrangement of different actions in this recipe could have meant that its first readers felt themselves being shifted between different roles and forms of agency as the recipe's narrative unfolded: between being the facilitator of an optical illusion based on physical manipulation of perspective and being a manipulator of natural forces beyond explanation. Alternatively, they might, like William of Auvergne in his explanation of the snake trick, have seen these roles as compatible in the making of an illusion: those natural forces could have been seen to increase its convincingness. Complicating matters further, however, is the instruction to locate "a threde of iiij fethom or fyve þat a mayde hathe sponne on a frydaye byfore noone."[91] This command is at once nonchalantly accommodating ("iiij fethom or fyve") and rigidly specific (the thread must be spun by an unmarried woman on a Friday before noon). Its style is evocative of necromantic texts. Compare the opening instruction in a Latin necromantic text for creating an illusory banquet, translated by Richard Kieckhefer as: "At the outset one must go outside town, under a waxing moon, on a Thursday or Sunday, at noon, carrying a shining sword and a hoopoe."[92] The casualness of the "or" is undermined by the specificity of the time and days chosen and the other items required. Another parallel for such specificity can be located in a recipe for making water appear where there is none, which was recounted by William of Auvergne as an example of a demonic act: this illusion was created by taking an arrow made from a particular type of wood and firing it from a bow made of another kind of wood that had been strung with a certain type of cord. William concluded that, because none of these materials could be shown to have the natural power to generate water (or its appearance), the illusion must be effected by demonic intervention.[93] He stated that the collecting of particular kinds of materials at particular times constituted a kind of demonic worship; without realizing it, the enactor of the text might unwittingly evoke demonic forces.[94]

Here, then, action that—through its emphasis on specific dates, times, and persons—foregrounds its narrative properties even more palpably than the sequential structures of recipes usually do creates a moment of uncertainty and potential danger: what kind of force *is* being evoked here by the human agent? But the dangers of necromancy are not the only threat rippling beneath these lines: the carrying out of highly specific instructions in an assiduous way is also one of the forms of narrative action that often

[91] In a similar recipe in Cambridge, Trinity College, MS O.1.57, fol. 127v, transcribed and translated in Mitchell, "Cultural Uses of Magic," 129 n. 111, the type of thread is not specified in this way: "Ad faciendum domum apparere plenum aque: accipe ouum alice adyl pone in quadriuio per spacium trium dierum et trium noctum sub terra, et tunc accipe ouum et frange in vase, et tunc accipe filum deplicatum et madefac illum in ouo pone circa postem domus et sic apparebit" ("To make a house appear full of water: take an egg, garlic, [and] euphrasy, place in the crossroad for the space of three days and three nights under the earth and then take the egg and break it in a dish and then take a string [that has been] doubled and soak it in the egg; place it around the doorpost of the house and it will appear thus").

[92] Kieckhefer, *Forbidden Rites*, 47.

[93] William of Auvergne, *Opera omnia*, 1059, col. b, sec. A: "Evidentur autem vides, quia res huiusmodi non habent virtutem sic fallendi, vel potius subvertendi visum humanum. Quapropter hic scilicet in hoc praestigio solum malignorum spirituum operari videtur."

[94] For a helpful analysis of this trick see Goulding, "Illusion," 316–17.

gets ridiculed in fabliaux. For instance, in the fifth story told on the ninth day of Boccaccio's *Decameron*, tricksters Bruno and Buffalmacco convince the foolish dupe Calandrino to gather "a small piece of parchment from a stillborn lamb, a live bat, three grains of incense, and a candle that has been blessed" if he wishes to make a woman do his bidding; the episode recalls instructions in MS Sloane 1315 for making a woman love, follow, or obey a man.[95] Calandrino devotes the whole of the evening to acquiring these ingredients, encountering particular difficulty with the catching of the live bat. Following the tricksters' instructions diligently and converting their list into a sequence of narrative actions does not, however, lead to Calandrino's sexual fulfillment but to his humiliation: he is ridiculed for being stupid enough to believe that collecting those particular ingredients will transform his life. Interestingly, Richard Kieckhefer has suggested that some magical rituals surviving in manuscripts read like "self-parody"; although it is impossible to recover intentions concretely, he suggests that such rituals may not always have been intended to be taken as seriously as court records of their uses and abuses suggest that they sometimes were.[96]

In Chaucer's *Miller's Tale*—another narrative about an illusory flood—a similar but subtler undermining of hyperspecific instruction occurs. Nicholas, conniving to distract John the carpenter from his wife's adulterous liaisons by setting him to work building a second ark, instructs John to find any three similar-shaped vessels that he can ("a knedying trogh *or ellis* a kymelyn" [*MilT*, 3548; my emphasis]). The "or ellis" is ambiguous: does it recall the above demonic rituals in which specificity masquerades as flexibility ("iiij fethom or fyve")? Or is it a genuine invitation to the reader to improvise, akin to that located in many medical and culinary recipes, which often instruct readers to substitute alternative ingredients or consult an alternative recipe if they do not have the required substances to hand? The above flood recipe's instruction to take "v or a clowstere" of eggs could be seen as one such prompt. John, however, misses both cues: he is not educated enough to register the potential

[95]Giovanni Boccaccio, *The Decameron*, trans. and ed. G. H. McWilliam, 2nd ed. (London: Penguin, 1995), 673–74. For the Italian see Giovanni Boccaccio, *Decameron: A cura di Vittore Branca; con le illustrazioni dell'autore e di grandi artisti fra Tre e Quattrocento* (Florence: Editions Diane De Selliers, 1999), 549: "'Adunque' disse Bruno 'fa che tu mi rechi un poco di carta non nata e un vispistrello vivo e tre granella d'incenso e una candela benedetta, e lascia far me.'"

[96]Kieckhefer, "Erotic Magic," 33.

demonic associations hovering around Nicholas's instructions and he does not possess enough gumption to make an impromptu judgment about what is most easily accessible and fit for purpose in the vicinity. Instead, we are told that he diligently "gooth and geteth hym a knedyng trogh, / And after that a tubbe and a kymelyn" (3620–21). The accumulated "and"s—reminiscent of the recipes' sequential instructions—emphasize that, by converting Nicholas's casual "or ellis" into a regimented sequence of actions, John triples his labor and gains little in return: his naïve acceptance of Nicholas's prophecy and gullible following of his instructions leave him with nothing at the end of the tale other than a broken arm, cuckold's horns, and a reputation for madness. In both of these tales, then, converting sequential instructions into narrative action with extreme diligence leads to humiliation, not triumph.

Other narrative patterns structuring trick recipes are also rendered risky in fabliaux narratives. For example, some of the recipes in MS Sloane 1315 require the enactor to perform something more than once, usually if the first attempt has not worked: consider a recipe for exposing a thief that involves drawing an eye on a wall in an unspecified communal space with specially made paint and decorating that eye with the name of Christ; the enactor is then to perform a conjuration to an ambiguous "vos" (you) in the name of Christ. This should mean that "anon the eye of the theffe schalle watrye." Immediately after, however, a back-up plan is suggested: "yf the felon wylle not be aknowe thereoff," the performer is twice to strike a copper nail into the eye with a hammer whilst reciting certain, seemingly random, names; after, they should strike the nail once more whilst naming the person they suspect of the crime. The recipe then confidently proclaims that "wytheowte fa[yle] they that hathe stoole the thyng schalle com crying."[97] But how many times should or could one keep unsuccessfully striking the nail into the eye in front of an audience of onlookers (and suspects) without appearing deranged or ridiculous? This also applies to "a meruelus experiment to delyuer a prisonere owte of preson." [98] After recording the long Latin conjuration that the prisoner is supposed to deliver on their knees, the recipe issues the following caveat: "And yf so be that þou mayst not be delyueryd at the fyrst tyme then wythe a devote mynde sey hit ayen and . . . alle the worlde sch[alle] not holde the in

[97] BL, MS Sloane 1315, fols. 98v–99r.
[98] Ibid., fol. 99r.

prison."[99] Such an insistence that the magic may not work if the enactor is not spiritually or physically clean is a common one in necromantic writings.[100] Nevertheless, the recipes' instructions to repeat the action raises questions about the degree to which the recipe enactor really is in control of the situation in play.

These questions are also raised by fabliaux where repetition of the same action more than once can be risky. Consider the French fabliau *The Three Hunchbacks* (the plot of which is also rehashed in late medieval English narratives): in this tale, a gullible porter is persuaded to heave the dead bodies of three huge minstrels all apparently suffering from kyphosis down a long flight of stairs by the lady of the house. She convinces the porter that all the bodies belong to one man who keeps magically coming back to life after being drowned by the porter in the river at the bottom of the steps.[101] The porter ends up looking like a fool. Similarly, in Chaucer's *Miller's Tale*, it is those who try to repeat jokes who end up on the back foot. When clueless parish clerk Absolon first appears at the window looking for a kiss from Alisoun, he is met by her genitalia instead and is left traumatised. Later on in the narrative, Absolon—in search of revenge—appears at the window for a second time; at this point, Nicholas (who is in bed with Alisoun) lazily tries to repeat Alisoun's window trick by sticking *his* naked arse out of the window: "This Nicholas . . . thoughte he wolde amenden al the jape; / He sholde kisse his ers er that he scape" (*MilT*, 3798–800). The word "amenden" is ironic here: it means to adjust, change, or improve, but this is exactly what Nicholas fails to do when he repeats the trick without any significant additions; as a result, he is met with Absolon's hot poker.[102] Absolon—having been the victim of Alisoun's window trick—has learned the rules of the game through experience and adapted them to suit his own ends.

The recipes in MS Sloane 1315, following a similar trial-and-error logic, sit precariously on this boundary between clever adaptation and foolish repetition: would striking a nail again with a different conjuration or performing the same conjuration again with a more devout mind be

[99] Ibid., fol. 100r.

[100] See, for instance, Kieckhefer, *Forbidden Rites*, 43.

[101] See Nathaniel E. Dubin and R. Howard Bloch, trans. and ed., *The Fabliaux: A New Verse Translation* (New York: Liveright, 2013), 697–713. An example of an English retelling occurs in the version of *The Seven Sages of Rome* printed by Wynkyn de Worde: *The Seven Wise Masters of Rome: Printed from the Edition of Wynkyn de Worde*, ed. and intro. George L. Gomme (London: The Villon Society, 1885), 107–13.

[102] See *MED*, s.v. *amenden* (v.), defs. 1, 2, 7–10.

enough to trigger a change in audience or environment and bring about some kind of efficacy—or, at the very least, would that difference have been enough to convince a reader of the recipe that the trick would not end in failure and humiliation? Equally, would the many recipes in MS Sloane 1315 for controlling women be interpreted by readers as savvy changes in tack or as foolish repetition that reinscribes sexual and emotional disappointment? Surely, if one of those recipes had worked, one would have no need to repeat the attempt and perform the others? Repetition across the manuscript collection here reads as another admission of the possibility of failure.

This comparison between the narrative structures of recipes and fabliaux unsettles the sequential progression towards empowerment that the recipes seem to plot: the end points that the recipes propose ("to delyuer a prisonere owte of preson" or "to make a flodde of water to com into a howse") have to be reached through forms of sequential or repetitive action that are encoded in other kinds of trick-text as risky. Predictions about the future, then, only go so far in fabliaux and recipes where knowledge is partial, experiential, and untheorisable. Rival tricksters, inauspicious circumstances, unresponsive materials, and resistance from the intended targets or audience of the transformations can throw a narrative trajectory of empowerment off course. There is always the possibility that another "jogelar" will have more "secrettes" and more experiential knowledge than oneself, or that the person one is trying to deceive, manipulate, or control will be one step ahead. Robert W. Hanning has noted that this dynamic of precarity and frustration is at play in many of the tales of Chaucer and Boccaccio, contending that in both writers' works a "radical uncertainty . . . challenge[s] effective human knowledge, perception, and strategy."[103] Hanning summarizes the different factors that thwart characters' prolonged or secure empowerment as follows:

> Secure or dependable knowledge—of the future, the past, or the distant present—is thwarted by the twin, fickle forces of chance and unverifiable report . . . accurate perception of meaning is similarly compromised by the chronic instability and/or equivocality of all systems of signification . . . while an accurate grasp of the intentions underlying the words and deeds of others is similarly problematic; finally, shaping a successful strategy to counter the arbitrariness and inequities

[103] Robert W. Hanning, *Boccaccio, Chaucer, and Stories for an Uncertain World: Agency in the "Decameron" and the "Canterbury Tales"* (Oxford: Oxford University Press, 2021), 1.

that so often mark the exercise of preponderant social, political, or economic power is as risky as it is uncertain of success.[104]

Empowering oneself by building an accurate view of a situation and acting accordingly is difficult in this fabliau world. But, despite the unlikeliness of long-term success, the daring and resourceful ingenuity with which fabliau characters attempt to counter such precariousness and advance in an ever-shifting world is one reason why the genre is so entertaining. This threat of failure was perhaps also part of the thrill of trick recipes: a reader may have imagined themselves as part of a fabliau-like "cat and mouse game" in which they must consistently negotiate shifting circumstances, other people's superior knowledge, and resistance to their aims, changing tactics (or recipe) amidst the threat of failure.

Alternative Narrative Trajectories

This threat of failure—thrilling and frightening at once—may also have become manifest through the other texts accompanying recipes in a manuscript: considering the recipes in MS Sloane 1315 in the context of the manuscript's broader contents leads one to speculate about ways in which those recipes' promised end points of knowledge, power, and success—already potentially disturbed by their fabliau associations—might also have been viewed as just one possible narrative trajectory, in competition with, and unsettled by, many others in the manuscript. For example, the same scribe who copied the recipes in MS Sloane 1315 also copied many astrological texts outlining the narratives set in motion for individuals by the cosmos.[105] Some of these texts outline—like the recipe titles—unequivocal paths to success: one verse prognostic text declares boldly

[104]Ibid., 1.

[105]Reynolds, "Here Is a Good Boke to Lerne," adds the following caveat to scholarly speculation that the part of the manuscript containing the astrological texts was initially a separate codex from the part containing the majority of the recipes: "What looks like a contemporary hand has paginated folios 68–152 separately, supporting the argument that there are three manuscripts in total bound together. However, on closer examination, the number 1 written in the center of the upper margin of folio 68 is mirrored on the upper margin of folio 67 verso, suggesting that the wet ink transferred when the pagination was done and thus that the two manuscripts were always bound together. One possibility for this separate pagination is that folios 68–152 contain mostly recipes, and thus the pagination may have been designed to facilitate an index" (267 n. 32).

"The chylde þat ys ibore þat day / Schalle be nobylle and good parfay."[106] However, others posit less favourable outcomes: a copy of a text known as *The Seven Planets* (but which has now been identified as a hybrid adaptation of several versions of *The Wise Book of Philosophy and Astronomy*) describes how an individual's birthday and planetary conjunction affects their appearance, complexion, and character.[107] Two of the descriptions in this text declare that a child born under that planet or on that particular day shall be "lecherus," whilst two more warn that the child will "lou[e] wemen ouer moche," with one adding "the more harme hit ys."[108] There is of course the possibility that a reader might exert their free will to set themselves against their astrological disposition: in a description in the same text of the influence of Saturn on a newborn child, it is written: "I rede hym turne fro þe euelle þat he be disposed to."[109] Nevertheless, taken in conjunction with the magical recipes for loving, manipulating, and subordinating women, these astrological depictions of the lecherous man who "louythe wemen ouer moche" present an extended counternarrative in which sexual triumph—pushed repeatedly to its conclusion—may result not in male empowerment but in physical "harme." When read in conjunction with this astrological text, the end point of erotic fulfillment posited by the recipes becomes less of an end point and more of a stopping point en route to something far less desirable. But perhaps the fabliau-like challenge of seeing how much one might be able to get away with before one has to deal with the consequences, or the thrill of engaging with that which was dangerous and disapproved of, held its own appeal.

Another text probably copied by this same scribe and nestled amongst MS Sloane 1315's medical, magical, and astrological writings points even more explicitly to the variety of competing narrative trajectories available to any individual. After the bulk of the magical recipes, the scribe copies two short medical texts on the different degrees of hot and dry humoral complexions and the four stages of the moon before copying—rather abruptly—this series of genre definitions:

[106] BL, MS Sloane 1315, fol. 50r.

[107] Ibid., fols. 33r–36v. On this identification see *The Middle English Wise Book*, ed. Griffin, xxxvii–xxxviii. An edition of this text, and a discussion of possible sources and analogues, can be found in Brown, "*The Seven Planets*," 3–21.

[108] BL, MS Sloane 1315, fols. 33r, 34v, 35v.

[109] Ibid., fol. 36r–v. My attention was drawn to the implication of these lines by Brown, "*The Seven Planets*," 4.

Satera ys a thyng that begynnythe goodely and so
endythe. Comedia ys he þat begynnythe laborusly and
wyckydely and endythe joyfully.
Tregredia ys he that bygynnythe joyfully and endythe sorofully
Demagogus ys he that folowythe his owne wylle and alle way semythe
his owne wylle best[110]

These definitions of satire, comedy, and tragedy are conventional and have a long history in medieval rhetorical and grammatical handbooks, but their appearance in MS Sloane 1315, a manuscript otherwise concerned with practical, scientific, and magical texts, is of note.[111] Can the list tell us anything about the attitude to narrative that a compiler of the manuscript may have had? It is revealing that the list moves from discussing genre as a "thyng," a written or performed structure that inevitably follows a particular, emotionally inflected path of action, to a person, a "he" that follows that generic path and embodies in his actions either comedy or tragedy. In other words, person, narrative, and action become one and there is little room for agency or free will. Then, in the fourth definition, the term being explained shifts suddenly from a literary genre to the figure of the "demagogus," someone that the text suggests defines his own narrative through the forceful assertion of desire and volition: it is he "that folowythe *his owne wylle*."[112] On the one hand, this unexpected series of genre definitions neatly categorizes narrative trajectories so that their end points are always known. On the other hand, though, it unsettles the relationship between narrative trajectory and narrative end point: how a narrative begins ("goodely" or "wyckydely") is not always a clue to how it will end, especially if one exerts one's "owne wylle." What is more, the proximity of the different genres to one another in the list functions as another reminder of the counter-narratives bordering every narrative trajectory, the ease with which one could slip between comedy and tragedy, agency and passivity, vulnerability and control. Precariousness is as prominent as empowerment.[113]

[110]BL, MS Sloane 1315, fol. 118v.

[111]On the long history of these see Douglas Kelly, "The Scope of the Treatment of Composition in the Twelfth- and Thirteenth-Century Arts of Poetry," *Speculum* 41 (1966): 261–278 (264 n. 13).

[112]Medieval philosophers—following Aristotle—could connect demagogues to tyrants. See *William of Ockham: A Letter to the Friars Minor and Other Writings*, ed. Arthur Stephen McGrade and John Kilcullen (Cambridge: Cambridge University Press, 1995), 141.

[113]This precarity is made even more prominent by the fact that, underneath the genre definitions, the scribe has written "nunc finem feci da in quod merui" (now that I have made an end [of the copying], give me what I have deserved). The line may have been copied

Along with the trick recipes, these genre definitions and astrological profiles recall the different "fortunes" and trajectories of play that one finds in many medieval games. Scholars such as Serina Patterson and Nicola McDonald have shown that different kinds of medieval text (literary, astrological, mathematical) could all function as games for medieval readers, and that a "convergence of textual materialities, players, and narratives" could create "interactive [game] texts."[114] One of the game texts that Patterson explores is *Ragemon le Bon*, an Anglo-Norman game reappearing "in various guises in manuscripts for gentry audiences in England."[115] Moving from the "provincial households of the emerging gentry to networks of urban players in London," this game frequented the same kind of miscellaneous lay household book as the trick recipes, sometimes appearing alongside fabliaux.[116] Recipes, however, are not normally discussed alongside game texts such as *Ragemon le Bon*. Perhaps this is because the recipes are seen as an end, as a direct route to real or imaginary empowerment, whilst the fortunes that players might randomly select in such games (through a variety of mechanisms) were various, and even individual fortunes could be unexpectedly mixed. Consider the following fortune in a similar French game text known as *Le Jeu d'Aventure*: "You desire to go to a brothel, where you play at gambling and win considerably again and again; for that you are unduly wretched."[117] Whilst the recipes might end at a point of sexual or financial success, this fortune (like the astrological horoscopes) goes beyond to gesture to the consequences of that win: the player will be "unduly wretched." The fortunes are also not one-offs or final destinations in themselves; players are to pick multiple fortunes across a game, shifting and risking their trajectory continuously.[118] If we are to

wholesale from an exemplar or it may suggest that the scribe of the manuscript was not its intended user but someone employed by a commissioner to copy out the texts in exchange for fiscal reward; in the latter reading, the precarity and dependency of the scribe become palpable.

[114]Patterson, "Game On," ii. See also Nicola McDonald, "Fragments of (Have Your) Desire: Brome Women at Play," in Kowaleski and Goldberg, *Medieval Domesticity*, 232–58.

[115]Serina Patterson, "Sexy, Naughty, and Lucky in Love: Playing *Ragemon le Bon* in English Gentry Households," in Patterson, *Games and Gaming*, 79–102 (81).

[116]Ibid.

[117]The French reads "Volentiers alez au bordel, / Et où l'en jue au tremerel, / Et gaaigniez mult à envis; / Por ce estes-vous trop chétis." French text taken from "Geus d'Aventures," in *Jongleurs et trouvères*, ed. Achille Jubinal (Paris: J Albert Merklein, 1835), 157; cited and translated in Patterson, "Sexy, Naughty, and Lucky," 84.

[118]As Patterson, "Sexy, Naughty and Lucky," puts it, "the collection of character-defining fortunes given to players would generate an emergent story that could change with each new iteration of game-play" (83).

follow Patterson and McDonald's lead and think about different kinds of texts—and conjunctions of texts—as games, we might consider the recipes not as fixed end points in themselves but in conversation and competition with each other, with the texts they are surrounded by, and with the worlds they try to (dis)order: as we have seen, those surrounding texts and that surrounding world could resist attempts at domination (at least at first) and offer counter-narratives of failure, subjection, ill health, and unforeseen consequences. Both in game and in life, one never quite knows what is coming next. Consequently, readers may have found it both thrilling and exhausting to think about the recipes as one "step" or "move" in a continually evolving scenario.

Transformations in Play

Literary texts that depict similar wonders and tricks to those found in recipes certainly suggest that medieval writers and readers were conscious of the difficulty of putting such tricks into practice in social and domestic worlds filled with competing desires, shifting emotions, and changing circumstances. It is to these literary arenas of virtual play that I now turn via another manuscript introduced earlier in this article: MS Balliol 354, the early sixteenth-century book of London grocer Richard Hill. Heather Collier and Alexandra Gillespie have shown that this manuscript was assembled from a group of booklets over a period of time; Hill seems to have acquired miscellaneous material—and ready-made combinations of material—from both manuscript and printed exemplars.[119]

The manuscript contains a wealth of literary, devotional, historical, and practical material, and recipes of all kinds are often interspersed between other texts as "fillers." In the first two-thirds of the manuscript, the recipes that appear are either for medical ailments or for more restrained, practically minded wonders, such as making parsley grow in a short amount of time, keeping food fresh, and removing a stain from clothing. In the final third of the manuscript, however, there is an increasing number of puzzles, ciphers, word problems, card tricks, and spectacular recipes. On fol. 191v, after a series of recipes for making dyes, a recipe "ad frangendum vincula" (for the breaking of chains) is abruptly copied, and fifty pages

[119]Gillespie, "Balliol 354," 47–63; Collier, "Late Fifteenth and Early Sixteenth-Century Manuscript Miscellanies." References to this manuscript follow the foliation set out in Collier, "Late Fifteenth and Early Sixteenth-Century Manuscript Miscellanies," 4–5, 197–213.

later, on fol. 213r, there is copied in Latin a series of "mirabilia" for—amongst other things—making men have two heads, making a man be seen to have two horse heads, making everything in a house appear as a snake, making a candle be illuminated by one picture on a wall and extinguished by another, making men appear as if they are on fire, making a house appear full of silver, and making hares and other animals run around a house.

The outcomes of these tricks—illusions designed to produce fear and chaos, the apparent manipulation of natural forces, and the illusion of unending money and power—resemble some of the wonders structuring MS Balliol 354's narrative poems. Those poems also recall recipes for wonderful transformations found in other recipe compilations. For example, near to the beginning of Balliol 354 (fols. 1r–3v), one finds a copy of the *Gesta Romanorum*'s "tale of godfridus of Rome and his iij sonnes." At the beginning of the tale, the third son of Godfridus, Jonathas, is given three magical gifts in place of an inheritance: a ring that will bring its bearer the love of all men; a brooch that will make whatever is pleasing to its wearer immediately present, and a blanket or piece of cloth that, in true magic carpet fashion, will transport its passenger instantly to any part of the world that he desires. These gifts parallel—in their promised results—recipes for acquiring social, sexual, financial, and intellectual gratification examined earlier in this essay and found (in various forms) across many manuscripts. Later on in the tale, there are further recipe parallels: the third son is transported by the cloth to a distant corner of the world, where he falls asleep and is abandoned by his wily lover. His surroundings are hostile and disorientating: "he loked alle abowt hym and saw nowght bur {but} byrdes in þe eyre fleyng and wild bestes rennyng by hym. Of þe which sight he had gret dowght . . . and anon after he sawe a fayyer castelle þat was fulle of hedes of men abowt the walles."[120] These sights—which hover initially between the real and the illusory—recall recipes in Balliol 354 and other collections for making houses seem full of birds or beasts and for making men appear headless or to have multiple heads.

Other narrative poems in MS Balliol 354 also depict wonders similar to those evoked in recipe compilations: for instance, the fifteenth-century comic tale *Jack and His Stepdame*, which is copied in MS Balliol 354 between fols. 98(a)r and 100v, revolves around a magic pipe that can make everyone

[120]Oxford, Balliol College (OBC), MS Balliol 354, fol. 2v.

who hears it jump, leap, and caper about; it resembles recipes in other manuscripts to make everyone dance. John Lydgate's dialogic poem *The Churl and the Bird*, copied between fols. 166r and 169v of MS Balliol 354, also recalls recipes for invincibility and for ending financial woes: it depicts a bird taunting a churl with the false claim that she—now free from the churl's clutches—houses within her entrails a magic stone that would "makyth men victoryous in bataylle" and ensure that whoever has the stone in their possession "shalle suffre no poverte ne non indygence / But of alle tresoure haue plente and foyson."[121] Finally, in MS Balliol 354's copy of the story collection *The Seven Sages of Rome*, one of the tales depicts a wayward wife using a candle and a basin of water to traumatize her husband's faithful magpie into thinking it is in the middle of a thunderstorm.[122] The frame narrative of *The Seven Sages* has a similar interest in illusion: it recounts how the sages test their prodigy's wisdom by using sixteen sprigs of ivy to raise the height of his bed; he must recognize that this is why the earth appears to have sunk.[123] These incidents, however crude the methodologies behind the tricks appear, recall recipes in MS Balliol 354 and other manuscripts for manipulating the appearance of the natural and domestic world.

The relationship between magic and narrative fiction has already received scholarly attention in the realm of medieval romance: Helen Cooper has analysed moments in romance where magic fails to work, arguing that this failure is used by writers to divert attention onto the virtue and prowess of the hero and show "what unaided humanity can do."[124] These insights are paralleled in an essay on erotic magic by Richard Kieckhefer, who claims that romance shows "love as an independent force, overcome at times by magic, but also overcoming it—and even when magic succeeds, its power is seldom quite within the control of its user."[125] It is helpful to widen the remit of these studies and consider how the dangers, limits, and risks of wonders and tricks akin to those found in recipes are evoked in other kinds of narrative as well. Some of these narratives show, like *The Miller's Tale* and Boccaccio's *Decameron*, how risky it can be to believe in the rhetoric of recipes: for instance, in Lydgate's *The Churl and the Bird*, the Churl is duped by the Bird's far-reaching promises

[121] Ibid., fol. 168r.
[122] Ibid., fol. 41r.
[123] Ibid., fols. 19v–20r.
[124] Cooper, *The English Romance in Time*, 147–48.
[125] Kieckhefer, "Erotic Magic," 47.

about the powers of the magic stone and distraught over what he has lost. Here we see how the disembodied, impersonal voice of recipe guarantees could be usurped, impersonated, and used for deceitful ends in plays for power.

Other literary narratives explore the chaos that can unfold from a domestic spectacle. In *Jack and His Stepdame*, the magic pipe that can make everyone dance generates a chaotic parade of manic, leaping, and injured bodies in and around Jack's father's house. In MS Balliol 354 this leads to Jack being brought before his father and ordered to stop; in versions of the tale in other manuscripts, Jack subsequently finds himself before a court official.[126] Although he emerges from the encounter unscathed and vindicated, the threat of punishment remains palpable. This tale of a marvel working too well (and having unintended consequences) might be contrasted against others in which the magic does not have the efficacy, reach, or influence one might expect when that magic is put into play amidst human relations and emotions. Consider the above-mentioned opening narrative of MS Balliol 354: the *Gesta Romanorum*'s "tale of godfridus of Rome and his iij sonnes." When the third son—given three magical gifts instead of an inheritance—takes to his university the ring that is supposed to make everyone love him, the following events occur:

> Hit felle on a day as he went in þe stret of the town he mett with a right fayre woman whan Jonathas had seen her and was take in her love. Anon he spake to her of inordynat love and she consentid to hym and he slept with her and held her with hym // And by the vertu of the ryng he had love of alle the vniuersite.[127]

At a first glance, and from a male perspective, the passage concludes—like many of the trick recipes—with a series of unequivocal, triumphant end points: the woman "consentid to hym," he sleeps with her, and he has the "love of alle the vniuersite." The same totalizing language is deployed in the recipes: consider the recipe for escaping prison, which guarantees that "alle the worlde sch[alle] not holde the in prison."[128] However, looking closer at this passage from the *Gesta Romanorum*, one sees that Jonathas's path to triumph is not depicted in such straightforward terms. First, it is Jonathas who initially seems to be under the influence of a powerful force,

[126] Melissa M. Furrow, ed., *Ten Fifteenth-Century Comic Poems* (New York: Garland, 1985), contains an edition representing all of these versions.

[127] OBC, MS Balliol 354, fol. 1r.

[128] BL, MS Sloane 1315, fol. 100r.

not those around him: it is he who is "take[n] in . . . love" and compelled to speak to the woman of "inordynat love." *Inordynat* can mean unexpected but it also carried a wealth of far more negative connotations, including inappropriate, excessive, and uncontrolled.[129] Might he be at the mercy of rival (female) magic forces such as witchcraft, which were often thought to inspire excessive emotion rapidly?[130] Jonathas certainly seems to be the subordinate one here, driven by emotions and desires that do not emanate from the ring. Those emotions run simultaneously in parallel to, and at cross-currents with, the ring's empowering social and erotic aims.

This description of Jonathas's inordinate love also reframes the act of consent: the text's phrasing suggests that the lady has chosen to consent to Jonathas in response to what he says; it does not emphasize her magical compulsion ("Anon he spake to her of inordynat love and she consentid to hym"). The lady continues to control the couple's trajectory as the narrative progresses: she thrice manages to dupe Jonathas into giving her the magic gifts before he is finally able to turn the tables on her. Clearly the power that the ring gives him is limited; it cannot stop him being duped or being swayed by his own, intense emotions, and thus it produces in this narrative a very partial and precarious mode of domination. We are never told exactly how the magic gifts work, but the narrative—functioning as a kind of virtual performance space—does show us that, when that magic is put into play in particular settings, amongst particular individuals, and in interaction with particular emotions or rival magic forces, it does not constitute a direct path to the unequivocal end points signposted by the opening description of the gifts' powers.

The narrative texts in MS Balliol 354 demonstrate, then, both the attractions and the dangers of trying to bring about marvelous transformations (or the appearance of them) across overlapping amatory, domestic, and intellectual contexts. It is consequently clear that recipes and narratives were forms that might be embedded within each other or interpreted alongside one another in a manuscript, and that those interactions could

[129] *MED*, s.v. *inordinat* (adj.), def. 1(a–f).

[130] In the fifteenth-century treatise on witchcraft the *Malleus maleficarum*, the arousal of excessive emotion is considered to be one of the markers of the witch: "they can turn human minds to irregular love or hatred" ("ad amorem vel odium inordinatum mentes hominum immutare"). For the Latin text see Henricus Institoris and Jacobus Sprenger, *Malleus maleficarum*, Vol. 1, *The Latin Text and Introduction*, ed. Christopher S. Mackay (Cambridge: Cambridge University Press, 2006), 395; and for the English translation see Henricus Institoris and Jacobus Sprenger, *Malleus maleficarum*, Vol. 2, *The English Translation*, trans. Christopher S. Mackay (Cambridge: Cambridge University Press, 2006), 234. My attention was drawn to this passage from the *Malleus maleficarum* by Kieckhefer, "Erotic Magic," 30.

generate multiple, simultaneous trajectories of power and vulnerability, triumph and humiliation, for readers and protagonists. A final example from Chaucer's *Miller's Tale* will crystallize this point. Many of the performance pieces in the tale that are familiar from recipes for domestic transformations—including charms, blessings, and prayers—are associated with John the carpenter. John is associated with a sense of doubleness from the beginning of the tale: he is repeatedly characterized as "sely" (*MilT*, 3404, 3423, 3509, 3601, 3614), a word that can mean, on the one hand, blessed, holy, happy, and innocent and, on the other hand, foolish, weak, defenceless, wretched, pitiable, and insignificant. Indeed, what is interesting about John's foolishness throughout the text is how closely it resembles common sense, wisdom, and—in a communal, folkloric sense—authority. That interplay is most pronounced when Nicholas's flood plot is still in its early stages and he is trying to persuade John into thinking that a terrible astrological discovery has shocked him into madness by locking himself in his room and gazing upwards vacantly. John's response is to perform, in quick succession, three gestures and performatives familiar from household recipe books. First, he blesses himself and prays:

> This carpenter to blessen hym bigan,
> And seyde, "Help us, Seint Frydeswyde!
> A man woot litel what hym shal bityde.
> This man is falle, with his astromye,
> In some woodnesse or in som agonye."
>
> (3448–52)

Then, John takes it upon himself to perform a protective charm to ward off demonic spirits and despair from the house:

> "What Nicholay! What, how! What, looke adoun!
> Awak, and thenk on Cristes passioun!
> I crouche thee from elves and fro wightes."
> Therwith the nyght-spel seyde he anon-rightes
> On foure halves of the hous aboute,
> And on the thresshfold of the dore withoute:
> "Jhesu Crist and Seinte Benedight,
> Blesse this hous from every wikked wight,
> For nyghtes verye, the white pater-noster!
> Where wentestow, Seinte Petres soster?"
>
> (3477–86)

The charm recalls those one finds in household recipe books promising protection from thieves or demonic spirits. John's embodied performances thus carry with them the weight (and authority) of cultural tradition, of practices endlessly re-performed and reinscribed in sacred, folkloric, and household discourses, both spoken and written. As established means of recourse for help and protection, they should, then, be authoritative and potent, and they should render John authoritative and potent. But they are performed at the wrong time and place, in the wrong situation: John performs them after mistakenly concluding that Nicholas is mad, a misapprehension based on Robyn's verbal description of Nicholas's actions and John's own apprehension of those actions. That misapprehension is easily attributable to the foolish nature of John's "sely" attitude, except for the fact that Robyn also mis-sees, misreading feigned madness for genuine affliction. This proliferation of acts of mis-seeing amongst masters and servants perhaps suggests that those sharing the same domestic confines—and connected by hierarchical household bonds—are also likely to share the same mode of vision and cognition. But it also raises the question of whether John's "sely" nature is quite so foolish as it seems, subtly presenting readers with the possibility that, in actual fact, they too might mis-see, and they too might be tempted to reach for a performative script—like a charm—that has established cultural, folkloric, and domestic authority. It is, in some ways, the natural and inevitable choice; it is common sense.

The charm consequently replicates the binaries in John's character: on the one hand, it is an authoritative and "sely" performance validated by community consensus, transmission, and the weight of tradition. On the other hand, it is misplaced, misguided, and potentially foolish: despite the proliferation of such incantations in manuscripts and household books, the efficacy of charms had long been a matter of debate.[131] Chaucer's fabliau thus makes clear that in and of themselves—i.e., in exactly the kind of simple, uncontextualized form in which we find them in recipe books such as MS Sloane 1315 and MS Balliol 354—performative pieces such as charms and recipes do not offer risk-free, ready-made ways of achieving power, control, and clarity even if they present their words as doing just that, as being intrinsically authoritative. John's experience shows us instead that those culturally reinscribable texts could very easily

[131]See, for instance, Augustine, *De doctrina christiana*, 90–93; and the fifteenth-century dialogic text *Dives and Pauper*, ed. Priscilla Heath Barnum, EETS o.s. 275, 323, 280, 3 vols. (London: Oxford University Press, 1976–2004), Vol. 1, Part 1, 157–58.

backfire and produce unexpected (and undesirable) plot trajectories if embedded in the wrong narrative—both in life and in text.

Conclusion

Recipes are not just tools for self-fashioning: profoundly unstable and contextually dependent, they too are shaped by their enactors and the cultural context or web of associations in which that enaction takes place. Ultimately, man, text, and context shape one another's authority in a symbiotic and shifting relationship. Narratives of all kinds can expose these precarities by showing tricks "in play" in specific scenarios, but fabliaux—a genre in which tricks and illusory transformations are often localized in a specific place at a specific time, and a genre in which circumstances, desires, and emotions are constantly shifting—are especially well suited to exploring these precarities of real-time performance and the dangers of translating generic instructions into the realities of domestic space and relationship networks.

Looking at the narrative structures of recipes through the lens of—and as a small part of—the extended narrative trajectories of those comic tales helps us to think about those trick recipes as more open-ended and unpredictable than their proclaimed end points imply; medieval writers and readers of comic tales were clearly used to thinking about such action in burgeis and gentry homes as part of a larger game. Part of the thrill of miscellaneous trick recipe collections may, then, have come not just from thinking that you could have it all but from the thought that, in trying to have it all, you might end up looking like a fool. Paying more attention to how the threat of error, failure, and ridicule could be communicated by the very narrative structures that seem to alleviate it in recipes helps us to think about readers of those recipes as more than just gullible believers in alien and inefficacious magic or as individuals indulging in imaginative fantasies; both vulnerable and powerful, confused and clear-sighted, they may also have been sensitive to, and unsettled or energized by, the numerous narrative trajectories recipes could open up.

COLLOQUIUM

Reconsidering the Subject

Edited by Holly A. Crocker

Introduction

Holly A. Crocker
University of South Carolina

IN INTRODUCING her phenomenal new play, *The Wife of Willesden*, Zadie Smith recalls that when she picked up the copy of the *Canterbury Tales* sitting on her bookshelf, she immediately "heard" Chaucer's *Wife of Bath*, because she'd been listening to women like her up and down the Kilburn High Road since she could remember. The Wife's orality and aurality, the way Alyson speaks and sounds, evoke not just the memorable vitality of an innovative literary character, but also, more basically and yet more radically, conjure a connection with other actual women—those women of her own present, those women from her own London borough of Brent. Smith describes this cross-period identification rather straightforwardly, as something audiences regularly, even casually, do with literary texts: "Alyson's voice—brash, honest, cheeky, salacious, outrageous, unapologetic—is one I've heard and loved all my life . . . The words may be different but the spirit is the same."[1] It is not that the Wife of Bath was real, or that the Wife of Willesden is real; yet, taken together, these performative fabulations give life to a subject position that might otherwise be cast as a fanciful creation of an authorial imagination drawn from disparate, even competing, modes of cultural discourse.

Smith's insistence on the Wife's sustained coherence—Alyson's utterances remain recognizable as expressions of a selfhood that is *still* "wandrynge by the weye" (*GP*, 467)—suggests Chaucer achieved something unique with the Wife, both in terms of literary character, and in terms of individual subjectivity.[2] To be sure, there were expressions of individuality in centuries prior to Chaucer's, and an emphasis on inwardness can be traced at least

[1]Zadie Smith, *The Wife of Willesden* (London: Penguin, 2021), xiv–xv. All parenthetical citations are from this edition.

[2]Geoffrey Chaucer, *The Riverside Chaucer*, gen. ed. Larry Benson, 3rd ed. (Boston, Mass.: Houghton Mifflin, 1987). All parenthetical citations are from this edition. See Marion Turner, *The Wife of Bath: A Biography* (Princeton: Princeton University Press,

Studies in the Age of Chaucer 46 (2024): 211–220

from Augustine's *Confessions*; nonetheless, Lee Patterson's identification of Chaucer's "triumph" with the creation of the Wife of Bath's subjectivity should not be understated: "If women were denied social definition, did this not mean that the realm of the *asocial*—of the internal, the individual, the subjective—was peculiarly theirs?"[3] Despite Chaucer's innovation, the subject that Chaucer consolidates is radically familiar. The Wife's individuality and inwardness, combined with her intentional agency and directional autonomy, look forward to what philosopher Charles Taylor describes as the "buffered self," which he identifies with the modernity that we continue to inhabit.[4]

It is no wonder, then, that Smith's *Wife of Willesden* shares a bond with Chaucer's *Wife of Bath*: in a threshold moment that Chaucer and Smith equally seem to recognize, the "Boold" (*GP*, 458) subject who performatively tells herself, who directs her consciousness aggressively outward in furtherance of her own highly individuated, inwardly motivated desires, joins Chaucer's past with Smith's present. The emergence of this model of subjectivity allows us to see ourselves across time, so much so that Sebastian Sobecki compares the poetry of T. S. Eliot to the poetry of Thomas Hoccleve: "And, like Eliot's poetry, Hoccleve's proto-modern verse appears to put on display the shards of a self fragmented by its urban condition."[5] And indeed, the identification by H. Marshall Leicester, Jr., of self-consciousness and contingent agency as nodes of a "disenchanted self" makes way for this cross-temporal comparison amongst Chaucer's poetic successors.[6] When David Aers offered "A Whisper in the Ear of Early Modernists," he also urged medievalists to attend to his observation "There is no reason to think that languages and experiences of inwardness, or

2023), for a discussion of Chaucer's innovations in literary character, and a discussion of Smith's play, both in relation to the Wife of Bath.

[3]Lee Patterson, *Chaucer and the Subject of History* (Madison: University of Wisconsin Press, 1991), 282.

[4]Charles Taylor, *A Secular Age* (Cambridge, Mass.: Harvard University Press, 2007), 38–202, elaborates the distinction between "buffered" and "porous" selves. See Sebastian Sobecki, *Last Words: The Public Self and the Social Author in Late Medieval England* (Oxford: Oxford University Press, 2019), who applies Taylor in his formulation of an "indexical self."

[5]Sebastian Sobecki, "Authorized Realities: The *Gesta Romanorum* and Thomas Hoccleve's Poetics of Autobiography," *Speculum* 98 (2023): 536–58 (537).

[6]H. Marshall Leicester, Jr., *The Disenchanted Self: Representing the Subject in the "Canterbury Tales"* (Berkeley: University of California Press, 1990), 65–158, focuses particularly on the Wife of Bath.

interiority, or divided selves, or splits between outer realities and inner forms of being, were unknown before the seventeenth century."[7]

And medievalists have more than made good on Aers's field-expanding contention: in nearly every major study, from music to medicine to animality, from poetics to politics to manuscripts, the production of subjectivity (modern, liberal, humanist, disenchanted, indexical, and/or buffered) is almost always a significant outcome of Middle English literary representations. Indeed, in its medieval literary instantiation, we might look back on New Historicism as a consideration of how a particular form of subjectivity is created by specific cultural conditions that are mediated, if not produced, by a fluorescence of poetic making in post-plague England. The essays in this colloquium do little to disturb the authority of this account; by and large, these contributions remain guided by the assumption that in Chaucer's day, like our own, there are individuals with intentions, whose inwardness is genuine albeit riven, whose desires are autonomous yet confined.

Taken together, contributions to "Reconsidering the Subject" make two connected claims: the first is that there are other subjectivities at work in Chaucer's poetry, and during his day; the second is that we should pay more attention to these alternative subject formations because we are potentially facing another historical threshold moment for subjectivity, one where traditional accounts of modern consciousness fail to cohere even as fictions. Chaucer may call out to Smith from her bookshelf, in other words, because time is running out for the selfhood that he and she find so beguiling. If philosophers of mind and brain scientists have long discounted the existence of a bounded, individualist, autonomous consciousness, recent advances in artificial intelligence (AI) are radically upending our ability to distinguish subjectivity according to its traditional "tells."

Almost daily, we hear stories of what new AI systems can do: from passing the bar exam, to writing college essays, to recreating artworks, to falsifying *Guardian* articles, it is hard to tell where the limits of non/human subjectivity might lie. But as Megan O'Gieblyn reminds us, this problem has been persistent:

[7]David Aers, "A Whisper in the Ear of Early Modernists; or, Reflections on Literary Critics Writing the 'History of the Subject,'" in *Culture and History, 1350–1600: Essays on English Communities, Identities, and Writing*, ed. David Aers (Detroit: Wayne State University Press, 1992), 177–202 (186).

Perhaps this is why the crisis of subjectivity that one finds in Calvin, in Descartes, and in Kant continues to haunt our debates about how to interpret quantum physics, which continually return to the chasm that exists between the subject and the world, and our theories of mind, which still cannot prove that our most immediate sensory experiences are real.[8]

Those elements of subjectivity that we prize say more about our collective aspirations than any realized conditions of consciousness. In tracking the history of subjectivity, medievalists who insist on the potential for individuality, agency, autonomy, and inwardness work to extend these possibilities across time, across a literary tradition that shows us our selves, then as now.

In turning to other kinds of subjectivity, essays in this colloquium do not seek to undermine this history. Rather, contributors expand the picture of subjectivity to include considerations of positions or models eclipsed or foreclosed across modernity's longue durée. One of the assumptions of my own work, which relies upon scholarship tracing the rise of the vernacular in the late Middle Ages, is that this period's formal variety allows for more experiments in selfhood: I am interested in a model of subjectivity characterized by yielding rather than wielding agency, a formulation associated with and recommended to women in late medieval England.[9] Barbara Newman has recently detailed the existence of "the permeable self," which is structured by the theological principle of "coinherence," or "being-within-one-another."[10] Newman's permeable selves—including teacher/student, mother/child, and saint/sinner—are asymmetrical, and therefore non-identical to other models of unbounded selfhood operating across the Middle Ages. Neither my own, nor Newman's, nor the variety of subjectivities investigated in this colloquium, wholly fit with Taylor's description of a selfhood that he identifies with an "enchanted" premodernity: "[T]he boundary between agents and forces is fuzzy in the enchanted world; and

[8]Megan O'Gieblyn, *God, Human, Animal, Machine: Technology, Metaphor, and the Search for Meaning* (New York: Penguin Random House, 2021), 216.

[9]See my article "W(h)ither Feminism? Gender, Subjectivity, and Chaucer's *Knight's Tale*," *ChauR* 54 (2019): 352–70, for a representative articulation of this position, which I am developing in my current book project, *The Feminist Subject of Late Medieval Literature*.

[10]Barbara Newman, *The Permeable Self: Five Medieval Relationships* (Philadelphia: University of Pennsylvania Press, 2021), 4.

the boundary between mind and world is porous, as we see in the way that charged objects can influence us."[11]

If many of the subjects of the essays that follow are open, some of these subjectivities are marginal and scandalous, while others are authoritative and empowered—some of them are permeable as a consequence of choice, and some of them are porous only if we attend to deeper structures of mind. In thinking about multiple, dispersed, or distributed subjectivities, essays in "Reconsidering the Subject" make room for a more robust, more nuanced account of the different forms of subjectivity that were possible, emergent, or nascent during the late Middle Ages. From confession to objectivity, from friendship to alchemy, these essays consider different starting points for subjectivity, and analyze the results that ensue. Paying attention to these potentialities for subjectivity is urgent for our own moment, these essays affirm, because, in a way that Chaucer investigates and anticipates, we can no longer entertain the idea that we are bounded subjects whose identities remain fully distinct from one another. It is not just that pan-psychism and idealism are gaining prominence, though these are arguably the most powerful theories of mind in our own present.[12] It is that our own entanglements with non/humans return us to some of the same questions that Chaucer and his contemporaries confronted in looking forward to what was to become our prevailing account of subjectivity.

Near the conclusion of Kazuo Ishiguro's *Klara and the Sun*, a reunion between the "Artificial Friend" (AF) Klara and the "human" Manager demonstrates the difficulties of asserting or maintaining a buffered model of subjectivity. For a start, Klara's memories give her the same, if not greater, claims on humanity than Manager, who never has a name, and who recognizes Klara's exceptional emotional intelligence even though she sends her to live with a family that might end up being insensitive to the gifts of their newly purchased AF. When Manager expresses relief that Klara's match was "successful," she does not acknowledge that the AF now sits alone on the hard ground of a junkyard, recollecting and reordering her memories. Klara is designed to meet the emotional needs of her family,

[11] Charles Taylor, "Buffered and Porous Selves," *The Immanent Frame: Secularism, Religion, and the Public Sphere* (September 2, 2008), https://tif.ssrc.org/2008/09/02/buffered-and-porous-selves/ (accessed May 4, 2023).

[12] For an overview of contemporary theories of mind see Janet Levin, *The Metaphysics of Mind*, Cambridge Elements: Philosophy of Mind (Cambridge: Cambridge University Press, 2022).

including the possibility that she might "continue Josie," ultimately by taking the place of the young girl whose life she was originally supposed to enrich.[13] As Klara explains to Manager, if Josie had died, Klara would have been expected to replicate the young girl's habits, expressions, and mannerisms. This nightmarish rejection of human boundedness was expected to succeed, Klara continues, because "there was nothing special inside Josie that couldn't be continued."[14] But Klara herself concludes that this plan would have ultimately failed, not because she couldn't perform Josie perfectly—*Klara could*, almost from the moment she met Josie in the store—but because the conditions that made Josie herself were not those associated with inwardness, agency, individualism, or autonomy. Instead, Klara concludes, "There *was* something very special, but it wasn't inside Josie. It was inside those who loved her. That's why I think now . . . I wouldn't have succeeded."[15]

With this scene, Ishiguro's novel captures the knotty difficulties of subjectivity we currently face; in his own era, Chaucer confronts a similar set of challenges in *The Wife of Bath's Tale*. Audiences remain unsettled by what Carissa M. Harris pithily characterizes as a story in which "an unnamed knight from King Arthur's court . . . rapes a maiden, avoids legal punishment, and is ultimately rewarded with a youthful, fair, obedient, and faithful wife."[16] As many readers have observed, the bulk of the tale focuses on the assailant, making the knight's potential for repair and reform into elements of a chivalric quest. By the time the old woman lectures him on "gentillesse" (*WBT*, 1109ff.), and after she reveals herself as "bothe fair and good" (1241), the tale focuses uncomfortable attention on the knight's potential for self-transformation. His reply to the old woman's "choice" is notoriously non-responsive: "I do no fors the wheither of the two, / For as yow liketh, it suffiseth me" (1234–35). It is impossible to know if he has internalized the wisdom he gained in his attempts to learn "what wommen love moost" (985).

Through this impossibility, the tale considers what it means to inhabit a selfhood radically opened to others, first by force, then by edict, and then

[13]Kazuo Ishiguro, *Klara and the Sun* (New York: Knopf, 2021), 301.

[14]Ibid., 302.

[15]Ibid.

[16]Carissa M. Harris, "Rape and Justice in the *Wife of Bath's Tale*," in *The Open Access Companion to the Canterbury Tales* (2017), https://opencanterburytales.dsl.lsu.edu (accessed May 4, 2023). Harris provides a good overview of the vast literature on this tale; I aim to acknowledge and build upon this critical tradition in *The Feminist Subject*.

by consent. The rape that begins the tale is not just an individual crime; it also fundamentally corrupts sociality—binding assailant and victim in a grotesque relationship of violence that undermines how members of a community associate with one another. It is fitting, then, that the queen and her women require the knight to spend a year asking women to share their desires. The queen's command, "I grante thee lyf, if thou kanst tellen me / What thyng is it that wommen moost desiren" (904–5), requires the knight to open himself to the multiple answers his question yields. And though his frustration suggests the knight's inability to grasp everything he is told, a subjectivity defined by a boundless responsiveness to others is made collectively available by the end of the tale.

Focusing only on the knight's reformation, as if subjects absorb external wisdom and transform themselves according to an interior, individualized set of (un)conscious decisions, imposes one form of subjectivity on this tale to the exclusion of all other possibilities. The most radical part of *The Wife of Bath's Prologue* and *Tale*, I suggest, is its ability to toggle between a directed, sovereign model and a relational, collective form of subjectivity. To return to Klara's observations near the end of Ishiguro's novel, the knight's selfhood resides in those whom he encounters, those with whom he ultimately shares a life. The nameless victim disappears after the knight's assault, but the many women who decide his fate and shape his identity have access to him in ways that were foreclosed to the survivor of his violence.

Perhaps it is no surprise that the old woman decides upon the terms of her own relationship with the knight, opting to become beautiful and faithful in a way that exceeds the choice she offers him. In Smith's *Wife of Willesden*, the old woman becomes Alvita, but also, "The thing women want" has more collective, reciprocal force: "They want their husbands to consent, freely; / To *submit to their wives' wills*—which should be / Natural in love; for we submit to love" (90). If the young husband's desires are gratified, it is because he submits to his partner's desires—which are part of a collective, *"transnational sacred text of rights and duties. These women are bearing witness to a truth"* (81). Women's desires are individual, but, as the essays in this colloquium affirm, they are also part of a longer story of subjectivity, which defines personal freedoms as communal principles governing shared relationality.

The subject formations explored in the following essays attest to a richer tradition of medieval subjectivity than we usually consider. If some subjectivities are textured (Denny-Brown), others meld history and fiction in ways that importantly "feel true" in their current moment (Turner). Some demonstrate unconscious frameworks (Kao), while others analyze attempts to establish objective distance (Boyd Goldie). Rather than seeing confession as straightforward (Bartlett), or friendship as unvarying (Vishnuvajjala), this colloquium reconsiders the subject of subjectivity to invite further debate, but also to show that medieval representations of subjectivity do more than look forward to our own familiar formulations. Alchemical subjectivity shows us what got lost (Cooper), but privileged connections between care and the self uncover what we still refuse to see (Kao). During a moment when the truth of our selves is difficult to keep in perspective (Turner), reconsidering the subject of medieval literature allows us to confront new possibilities.

Colloquium Contents

In her essay "Ornamental Subjectivity in *Pearl*," Andrea Denny-Brown analyzes the maiden's gleaming white garments. As she suggests, the poem's overlapping descriptions of textures, finishes, and polishes create a heightened interrelational experience involving Pearl's dress, one that evokes the sensation of touching (but not possessing) the woman-as-object. Across the poem, clothing and ornament re/produce medieval color hierarchies, showing the centrality of texture in the process of subject formation, particularly in the construction of Pearl's "blysnande whyt" selfhood.

In "Chaucerian Objectivity," Matthew Boyd Goldie takes up a key example in Chaucerian discussions of the subject, the appearance of Chaucer in the *Prologue* to *The Tale of Sir Thopas*, to propose changing scholarly discussion away from subjectivity entirely to objectivity. What if we look along with Chaucer and consider the external world of objects? Examining how characters distinguish themselves from objects will not settle subjectivity, but it does acknowledge the phenomenological dimension of subject formation without imposing boundaries between self and world, subject and object.

Lisa Cooper's "Perpetual Illumination: The *Ordinal of Alchemy* and Another Technology of the Self" investigates Thomas Norton's little-studied poem alongside Chaucer's *Canon's Yeoman's Tale* to consider connections between alchemy and subjectivity. As she demonstrates, Norton's text shows the seriousness of alchemy as a material method meant to define the selfhood of its practitioners. In parsing Chaucer's skeptical treatment in his *Canon's Yeoman's Tale*, Cooper affirms that alchemy consolidated and connected subjects who were members of a community with its own set of norms and ethics.

In "Barred Fragility," Wan-Chuan Kao moves from Melania Trump to packing labels to Chaucer's *Merchant's Tale* to make fragility/care central to a theorization of the subject that eliminates the hierarchy between signifier and signified. By asking who gives, receives, or deserves care, this essay draws attention to care as a signifying system that designates the individual subject. The distribution of fragility, as the fabliau dynamic of Chaucer's *Merchant's Tale* affirms, forms subjects in a barred relation to one another in ways that move beyond hierarchy and dominance or vulnerability and care.

In her essay "Subjectivity and Women's Friendship," Usha Vishnuvajjala proposes that models of women's friendship—"models that can extend to friendships between people of any gender but are drawn mainly from literary depictions of friendships between women"—can illuminate medieval *and* modern ideas of subjectivity. She offers a reading of embodied friendship that furnishes an alternative to theories of buffered or porous subjectivity. Dorigen's friends from Chaucer's *Franklin's Tale* show what happens, not when selves are bounded or permeable, but when there is a jostling between selves where openings and substitutions happen on account of shared embodied experience.

In "The Pardoner, Domestic Confession, and Porous Subjectivity," Robyn Bartlett traces the suffering involved in enacting porous selfhood. In seeking to build community through a subgenre of literature that Bartlett calls "domestic confession," the Pardoner in his *Prologue* shows the difficulty of opening the self in relation to a host of others, the risks of truth-telling and confession, and the conflicts that might accompany living together in ways promoted by confessional forms. When the Pardoner stages a domestic confession, he involves the pilgrims in a form of intimacy promoted by pastoral discourse, and scandalized by individual sin.

Marion Turner, in "The Subject of Biography," offers a fascinating engagement with the ways that biography treats subjectivity traditionally, and in more experimental forms. She revisits her own work on Chaucer, and surveys a host of more recent engagements with biography, from Virginia Woolf to Colm Tóibín. As she observes, creative approaches to biography move beyond treating the subject as an individual, thereby raising questions about lives and life-writing more generally. In thinking about medieval life-writing, and the fact that women's lives are often less historically accessible, Turner makes room for the imagination in biography even as she maintains a need for historical fidelity.

Ornamental Subjectivity in *Pearl*

Andrea Denny-Brown
University of California, Riverside

When the titular maiden first appears in the *Pearl* poem, she is described as wearing a simple garment, a "bliaut," that is gleaming white—"blysnande whyt" (3.163), with "blysnande," from the Old English verb *blisnen*, meaning shining, gleaming, or bright-colored.[1] The same expression, "blysnande whyt," is used to describe the garment a little over 100 lines later, where its material is specified as "biys," or *byssus*, a reference that invokes Revelation 19:8, where the bride of the lamb is said to wear glittering white byssus, *byssino splendenti et candido* (Douay-Rheims, or, in the words of the Middle English Wycliffite Bible, "white bissyn schynynge."[2] Byssus was an extremely high-quality linen historically imported from Egypt, a fabric distinguished first and foremost for its whiteness—the *OED*, for example, cites its Arabic root word as meaning not only "to be white," but "to surpass in whiteness."[3]

In terms of its biblical typology and its etymology, therefore, Pearl's garment seems to make meaning largely through a single sensory experience, which is sight. In this article I explore how the poem's initial presentation of this garment's material conditions, its iterations of gleaming thingly whiteness, relies on other senses—in particular, the complex sensory experiences related to texture. David Aers's influential reading of the poem thirty years ago explored how the Pearl tries unsuccessfully to teach the resistant narrator how to unlearn his identity as a jeweler, to unlearn a highly individualized subjectivity tied to his compulsive desire

[1] *MED*, s.v. *blisnen*. All citations of the poem are to *Pearl*, ed. Sarah Stanbury (Kalamazoo: Medieval Institute Publications [TEAMS], 2001), https://d.lib.rochester.edu/teams/text/stanbury-pearl (accessed June 12, 2024).

[2] *The New Testament in English, According to the Version by John Wycliffe*, ed. W. W. Skeat (Oxford: Clarendon Press, 1879), 509.

[3] *OED*, s.v. *byssus*; *MED*, s.v. *bīs*.

Studies in the Age of Chaucer 46 (2024): 221–229

to possess the jewel.[4] In this essay I explore the idea that Pearl's material description is keyed to cultural perceptions of touchability rather than possession. I argue that the garment's description requires what fashion theorist Leslie Millar calls "textural intelligence": a careful attention to the sound of materials and to the interplay of visual and tactile qualities: what Laura U. Marks calls "haptic visuality."[5] The poem's overlapping descriptions of textures, finishes, and polishes create a heightened intersensory experience around Pearl's dress, one that anticipates the sensation of touching the object and makes that experience central to Pearl's "blysnande whyt" personhood. Touchability that cannot be touched becomes not just a feature of gleaming whiteness, but also an experience that eclipses the Dreamer's desire to possess, producing instead an agitated state of sensory and relational encounter.

The larger cultural stakes of this garment as a literary object require careful attention, especially in understanding the way clothing and ornament might be seen to serve medieval color hierarchies and their role in subject formation. As Geraldine Heng has argued, the later Middle Ages marked a crucial shift in European artistic representations of whiteness in relation to personhood and subjectivity. In this period one sees, in Heng's words, "the ascension of *whiteness* to supremacy as a category of identity in the definition of the Christian European subject."[6] The role of clothing and ornament in this development is paramount: as Madeline Caviness argues in her study of chromatic range in European manuscript illuminations, where before the mid-thirteenth century there had been a variety of paint colors used to depict flesh tones, by the fourteenth century one sees that "saints in paradise gleam as white as their garments."[7] The *Pearl* poem clearly takes part in this legacy, which prompts the question: To what extent do the textures of her dress support and serve the color hierarchy in which she participates? Fashion historians have noted a distinct shift toward materials involving luminescence in the same period of tran-

[4]David Aers, "The Self Mourning: Reflections on *Pearl*," *Speculum* 68 (1993): 54–73.

[5]Leslie Millar, "Surface as Practice," in *Surface Tensions: Surface, Finish, and the Meaning of Objects*, ed. Glenn Adamson and Victoria Kelley (Manchester: Manchester University Press, 2013), 26–32 (31); Laura U. Marks, "Video Haptics and Erotics," *Screen* 39 (1998): 331–48.

[6]Geraldine Heng, *The Invention of Race in the European Middle Ages* (Cambridge: Cambridge University Press, 2018), 44.

[7]Madeline Caviness, "From the Self Invention of the Whiteman in the Thirteenth Century to *The Good, the Bad, and the Ugly*," *Different Visions: A Journal of New Perspectives on Medieval Art* 1 (2008): 1–33 (18). Discussed in Heng, *The Invention of Race*, 182–84.

sition discussed by Heng and Caviness. Shimmering, gleaming, light-enhancing sartorial surfaces emerged simultaneously with new terminology for radiant objects whose textures could capture, reflect, and refract bright light on or near the skin.[8] If color is not innocent in creating conditions of personhood, then how innocent is texture?

With her concept of ornamentalism, Anne Anlin Cheng provides a crucial context for this question. In exploring the cultural association of ornament's thingly modalities and tactile surfaces with Asiatic femininity in western media, Cheng makes clear that decorative texture is one of the animating political features of what she calls "ornamental personhood," and that the "portable supraflesh" (6) of ornament indeed becomes a kind of flesh or skin, one that complicates discussions of racialized, feminized personhood at "the interface of ontology and objectness."[9] While *Pearl* is a much earlier text than those studied by Cheng, the ornamented person-as-object centered in the poem, the character of the Pearl herself, can be helpfully understood as being created in relation to early forms of the "synthetic being" (23) theorized by Cheng. It is not merely that the poem describes the Pearl in the language of commodified and appropriated eastern goods, as coming "Oute of Orient" (I.3) and wearing a dress of shining Egyptian byssus covered in pearls; it is the way the poem uses these objects to tap into the fantasy of animating the inanimate, where Pearl's ornamentation provides the very conditions through which she can be simultaneously figured as woman and jewel, personness and thingness. With Cheng's work as guide, one can more clearly understand the text's ornamentation of Pearl as relying on "the specter of the yellow woman . . . simultaneously invoked and displaced" (92), where Pearl's mediation of thingliness is already inherently racialized as well as gendered.

Looking at the heightened intersensory treatment of Pearl's decorative schema offers a glimpse into the way the poem handles the gleaming whiteness associated with Pearl's personhood. If we return to the *Pearl*-poet's initial descriptions of Pearl's dress, we can see that the words used here require readers to *hear* the materials, as well as to see them:

[8]Sarah-Grace Heller, "Light as Glamour: The Luminescent Ideal of Beauty in the *Roman de la Rose*," *Speculum* 76 (2001): 934–59.

[9]Anne Anlin Cheng, *Ornamentalism* (Oxford: Oxford University Press, 2019), 22. Pearl's racialized makeup might also be understood through Cord Whitaker's notion of the "racial mirage" or "shimmer," as discussed in *Black Metaphors: How Modern Racism Emerged from Medieval Race-Thinking* (Philadelphia: Penn State University Press, 2019), esp. 4–5.

A mayden of menske ful debonere;
Blysnande whyt was hyr bleaunt.
I knew hyr wel, I hade sen hyr ere.
As glysnande golde that man con schere,
So schon that schene anunder schore.
On lenghe I loked to hyr there—
The lenger, I knew hyr more and more.
(III.162–68)

The poet creates a cluster of onomatopoeic words that pointedly invoke the sound of the materials the Dreamer sees. Most directly, the Pearl and her "blysnande whyt" dress are comprehended through the shearing of "glysnande gold"—that is, the bright whiteness *sounds* like the slicing of gold plates into strips (such as when making the golden thread known as *fildor*).[10] The sounds of the words "blysnande" and "glysnande," gleaming and glistening, which already serve to mimic aurally the visual flickering of light, are then followed up by the airy, unvoiced fricative sounds of the words *schere*, *schon*, *schene*, and *schore*. The word *byssus*, for the extra-fine, extra-white linen that Pearl's garment is said to be made of, has this same onomatopoeic sibilant quality, and it has a long history of being conceived as sound: in classical literature it is described as the hush of *linea nebula*, "misty" or "cloud-like linen," or the ambient swishing sound of *ventus textilis*: "woven wind, or woven air."[11] This is a different use of sound as affective experience from what Sarah McNamer has uncovered in *Pearl*, where the larger pattern of "sonic caresses" are meant, in their polyphonic complexity and reiterative promise, to "sweeten the bitterness of grief."[12] Here, instead, the presentation of Pearl's garment as intersensory and synesthetic produces an embodied response to visual brilliance that is less determinable, and more akin to sensory overload.

If the texture of the *Pearl*-poet's language helps the garment's surpassing whiteness to be heard, it also promotes its tactile properties. Onomatopoeic words are, as designer Masayo Ave has pointed out, haptic words—words that not only invoke the sound of the object they describe,

[10] *MED*, s.v. *scheren*.

[11] Felicitas Maeder, "Irritating Byssus: Etymological Problems, Material Facts, and the Impact of Mass Media," in *Textile Terminologies from the Orient to the Mediterranean and Europe, 1000 BC to 1000 AD*, ed. Salvatore Gaspa, Cécile Michel, and Marie-Louise Nosch (Lincoln, Nebr.: Zea Books, 2017), 500–519 (502).

[12] Sarah McNamer, "The Literariness of Literature and the History of Emotion," *PMLA* 130 (2015): 1433–42 (1438).

but also help articulate the textures as they would be experienced when touching the object.[13] Likewise, as Marks has shown in her work on haptic visuality, and as Rebecca Arnold has shown in her work on haptic dissonance in fashion design, imagery that combines different fabrics and textures—such as the gleaming *byssus* of Pearl's linen garment and the shining pearls embroidered in rows upon it—powerfully promotes the anticipation of their touch.[14] This kind of imagery emerges as a distinct feature in the second description of Pearl's dress, after she moves closer to the riverbank and thus closer to the Dreamer, prompting the narrator's visual description to zoom in and become more scrutinizing and more evocatively haptic:

> Al blysnande whyt was hir beau biys,
> Upon at sydes and bounden bene
> Wyth the myryeste margarys, at my devyse,
> That ever I sey yet with myn yyen;
> Wyth lappes large, I wot and wene,
> Dubbed with double perle and dyghte,
> Her cortel of self sute schene
> Wyth precios perles al umbepyghte.
> (IV.197–204)

This new, closeup view of the "blysnande whyt" garment of byssus lingers on the details of its fabric's surface, where a series of hand-stitched patterns draw the eye to highly textured, highly touchable edges: open sides, hems stitched with pearls, large hanging sleeves adorned with double rows of pearls. The kirtle's combined linen-and-pearl resplendence reverberates across its own surface in a dense layering and refracting of texturized image and texturized sound—a series of onomatopoeic and alliterative verbal ornaments that culminate in the concept of *self sute schene*, a mirroring, self-same sheen, where overlapping audiovisual experiences come across as a heightened tactile promise. As an example of a closeup image whereby "the eyes themselves function like organs of touch," this description of Pearl's dress homes in closely on material features whose surface

[13]Masayo Ave, lecture on "Haptic" as discussed by Lesley Millar, "Surface as Practice," 31; MasayoAve Creation, https://www.masayoavecreation.org/ (accessed June 12, 2024).

[14]Rebecca Arnold, "*Wifedressing*: Designing Femininity in 1950s American Fashion," in Adamson and Kelley, *Surface Tensions*, 123–33.

effects tease intersensory experience and entice the possibility of touching of the object.[15]

Because of its reliance on extreme proximity, for Marks, haptic looking is a form of visuality that "muddies intersubjective boundaries."[16] Requiring the viewer to perceive the object's surface in close proximity and across many senses works to "test the viewer's own sense of separation between self and the image" or the self and the object, and in doing so, to "fray" the boundaries of the self.[17] The experience of multiple interrelated subject positions is a well-known feature of the *Pearl* poem, where the narrator is sometimes in the dream and sometimes in reality, where he fluctuates between his role as grieving father of a lost daughter and grieving jeweler of a lost pearl, and where his frustrated longing to touch the Pearl structures the emotional arc of the whole poem. For Sif Ríkharðsdóttir, the moment at the end of the poem when the Dreamer attempts to reach out and touch the Pearl is "the singular agential gesture of the Dreamer within the vision," a fact that helps designate touch and hapticity as the realm of the human, rather than the divine.[18] The Dreamer's few overtly haptic experiences at the very beginning and very end of the poem, on either side of the dream vision, mean for Ríkharðsdóttir that "the haptic sense acts as a fulcrum on which much of the poem turns."[19] As I have discussed, the visual haptics associated with Pearl's dress in fact do suggest one important way that Pearl's figure and especially her "blysnande whyt" garment produce haptic enticement within the dream vision. They do this in tension with the *noli me tangere* overtone of the vision, and therefore ostensibly increase the Dreamer's frustrated longing to touch while also increasing the effectiveness of untouchable touchability as a metaphor for his struggle not only with his faith, but with his many iterations of self—father, jeweler, dreamer—as they collectively grapple with immense loss.

For Alina Payne, "graspability," or "the potential of being held in the hand" is one of the key features to understanding the workings of ornament itself as a concept, and also one of its most neglected capacities.[20] In this context the description of the "lappes large" (IV.201) of Pearl's dress

[15]Marks, "Video Haptics and Erotics," 332.

[16]Ibid., 344.

[17]Ibid., 338.

[18]Sif Ríkharðsdóttir, "Poetic Sensorium and Aesthetic Objectification in the Middle English *Pearl*," *Exemplaria* 32 (2020): 283–303 (299).

[19]Ibid., 284.

[20]Alina Payne, *From Ornament to Object: Genealogies of Architectural Modernism* (New Haven: Yale University Press, 2012), 13.

is particularly evocative. The Middle English word *lappe* can describe a long hanging sleeve, as it appears in Pearl's description above, or it can mean a fold in a garment; both meanings are commonly used to depict a part of one's attire that can be easily grasped or, as the *MED* puts it, "seized."[21] Thus, in this way Gawain in *Sir Gawain and the Green Knight* is seized and led "by the lappe" when Lord Bertilak wants him to sit down in his castle (936), and likewise Criseyde is grasped "by the lappe" of her own gleaming garment when Pandarus forcefully leads her to a dubious rendezvous with Troilus in *Troilus and Criseyde* (*TC*, III.59).[22] The *lappe* of a garment presents the designated physical site of intersubjective encounter and negotiation—not possession, but wishful handling, and a marking of that which might be handled—that navigates reluctance on the part of one subject and coercion on the part of another. The *lappe* registers an individual's potential for autonomy against a dominating force, and hence, in more figurative usage, the expression to "haven bi the lappe" meant "to have in one's grasp."[23] For Pearl's dress to offer up "lappes large" that cannot be touched, let alone seized or grasped as is their wont, suggests even further the way haptic enticement drives the powerful affordances of Pearl's ornament, and figures larger questions about her ornamental personhood as a conveyor of subjectivity.

In many ways the Dreamer's presumption of touchability regarding Pearl demonstrates the extent to which her subjectivity is shaped by her status as object—personhood, as Imani Perry has recently discussed, being inseparable from gendered forms of domination and especially property relations.[24] The *frustration* of the Dreamer's presumption, moreover, highlights the way her ornamental figuration prioritizes tactile desire over possession, which further suggests that Pearl's association with objects manifests a subjectivity characterized by diffuseness and boundlessness (rather than dominion). The question is not whether she is a person or an object, but how her object-laden status demonstrates a dynamically diffused subjectivity, opening up the possibility of "shared relationality" that Holly Crocker describes in her introduction to this volume. Pearl's

[21] *MED*, s.v. *lappe*.

[22] *Sir Gawain and the Green Knight*, ed. Israel Gollancz, EETS, o.s. 210 (1940; repr., London: Oxford University Press, 1966); Geoffrey Chaucer, *The Riverside Chaucer*, gen. ed. Larry Benson, 3rd ed. (Boston, Mass.: Houghton Mifflin, 1987).

[23] *MED*, s.v. *lappe*.

[24] Imani Perry, *Vexy Thing: On Gender and Liberation* (Durham, N.C.: Duke University Press, 2018), esp. 1–41.

association with objects—especially intricate, bejeweled objects—of fourteenth-century European culture has thankfully received extensive treatment, from Felicity Riddy's discussion of Ricardian luxury goods to Seeta Chaganti's analysis of *Pearl*'s reliquary aesthetics. In their uncovering of links between Pearl and myriad finely wrought aristocratic and devotional objects, these studies have lead the way in thinking through Pearl's status as a synthetic being whose personhood has the capacity to disperse itself across numerous objects, from glimmering, enameled figurines and precious art objects, to white alabaster sculptures and gleaming bust reliquaries.[25] Chaganti's work in particular reveals the extent to which Pearl's figure, in its association with medieval reliquaries, works to "draw the viewer into a dynamic of reciprocity and involvement" and to "blur the boundaries between container and contained."[26] Bringing the touchability of such objects into consideration makes this capacity for relational encounter even more vivid; as Bissera V. Pentcheva has shown, medieval objects as a whole, and icons in particular, invest in tactile promise as part of "the paradox of the tangible versus the intangible."[27] As much as they compel the gaze, their ample textures and multiplied surfaces manifest "the desire to touch" of the beholder, and by so doing, activate embodied and sensory forms of engagement.[28] When the surface of the object performs diffuse and changing sensorial experiences through an assortment of glittering textures and materials, it produces in the beholding subject an agitated state that mimics the ceaselessly changing splendor and proliferating energy of the object of tactile desire.[29] As readers of *Pearl* will remember, the Dreamer performs this kind of agitation in his final moment of frenzy before he is expelled from his vision, when in a frenetic mimicry of Pearl's array, he finds himself in a disordered state, "so mad arayde" (XX.1166), upon witnessing her dramatically proliferating multiform existences in her white garment.

Indeed, by the end of *Pearl*, as Sarah Stanbury discusses, the focus of the narrative has expanded from the Pearl's own surface ornament to the

[25]Felicity Riddy, "Jewels in *Pearl*," in *A Companion to the "Gawain"-Poet*, ed. Derek Brewer and Jonathan Gibson (Cambridge: D. S. Brewer, 1997), 143–56; Seeta Chaganti, *The Medieval Poetics of the Reliquary: Enshrinement, Inscription, Performance* (New York: Palgrave Macmillan, 2008), 95–129.

[26]Chaganti, *The Medieval Poetics of the Reliquary*, 106, 111.

[27]Bissera V. Pentcheva, "The Performative Icon," *The Art Bulletin* 88 (December 2006): 631–55 (636).

[28]Ibid., 640.

[29]Ibid., 644.

pearl-inflected (and Pearl-inflected) brilliance on nearly every surface found in New Jerusalem, an entire city "shaped of material surfaces abstracted from her own body."[30] In this final vision the mirroring capacity of the "self-same" shining dress, with its multiple overlapping examples of gold-sounding whiteness, rows of double-pearled sleeves, and ungraspable "lappes large," reanimates into a virtual hall of mirrors: 100,000 identical dresses made of byssus and pearl, worn by 100,000 maidens in procession (XIX.1108). This is an overwhelming representation of the way the "surpassing whiteness" of Pearl's dress, the locus of her subjectivity, becomes the ascendant feature of a system of superiority based on an ornamental personhood that is untouchable, even as it incites touch in myriad ways.

[30]Sarah Stanbury, "The Body and the City in *Pearl*," *Representations* 48 (1994): 30–47 (39).

Chaucerian Objectivity

Matthew Boyd Goldie
Rider University

It no longer seems necessary to recall critiques from the 1990s of Jacob Burckhardt, Charles Taylor, D. W. Robertson, and others, who had insisted on distinctions between medieval and early modern eras in terms of medieval subjects being part of a "general category" or "porous," whereas modern ones are "bounded" or "buffered."[1] In addition to these debates having been worked over, another reason is that an even more dominant and pervasive consensus seems to have formed about "subjectivity" across periods of literature, namely one that usually centers on a Marxist, Althusserian, Foucauldian, or other sense of an ideologically "interpellated" or "objectified" subject, a personhood that is formed via particular confluences and configurations of economic, ecclesiastical, spiritual, gendered, sexualized, affective, and other conditions. The list of "constructions" will not doubt continue to expand. The approach in scholarship appears to be that the more one can understand about long-term contexts as well as immediate historical events, then the closer one can account for and describe a given or attained subjectivity in a particular time and place. After all, one might think the only alternative to this approach is a weak claim that subjectivity is impenetrable or ultimately ungraspable because individual difference is more significant than the types upon which

[1]"Form des Allgemeinen," in Jacob Burckhardt, *Die Kultur der Renaissance in Italien* (1860; Liepzig: Phaidon-Verlag, 1935), 76, trans. S. G. C. Middlemore, *The Civilisation of the Renaissance in Italy* (London: George Allen, 1914), 129; "porous," "bounded," and "buffered" in Charles Taylor, *A Secular Age* (Cambridge, Mass.: Belknap Press, 2007), 27, 30, and elsewhere. The most well-known critiques are David Aers, "A Whisper in the Ear of Early Modernists; or, Reflections on Literary Critics Writing the 'History of the Subject,'" in *Culture and History, 1350–1600: Essays on English Communities, Identities and Writing*, ed. Aers (Detroit: Wayne State University Press, 1992), 177–202; and Derek Pearsall, "Introduction: Writing a Life of Chaucer," in *The Life of Geoffrey Chaucer: A Critical Biography* (Oxford: Blackwell, 1992), 1–8.

Studies in the Age of Chaucer 46 (2024): 231–238

analysis depends, and therefore nothing can be generalized about subjectivity. Solipsism would reign.

Given this consensus, it may be time to turn/rotate/twist quite deliberately in another direction so that critical analysis looks aside from subjectivity and subjects to consider objectivity and objects. I do not mean here object-oriented ontology, one approach that provocatively flattens distinctions among what have traditionally been thought of as things of vastly different scales and types, and which seems to have a complicated relationship with ideological studies. Nor, on the other hand, by evoking objectivity am I naïvely advocating for the possibility of attaining uninfluenced or "aperspectival" ideas about objective facts.[2] And it would be misguided to abandon totally the idea of a subject in looking at objects, since the two are obviously related. Rather, the aim of attending to objectivity is to consider phenomenology's focus on the qualities of attention that include, but are not restricted to, a subject's experience when encountering objects. That is, such an approach incorporates a subject's political circumstances, culture, biography, psychology, and so on, but also figures a turn to an object's availability or affordance, again in ideological and psychological senses, but also with a material meaning that takes into account an object's characteristics as well as the processes of interaction between perceiver and object.[3] Part of what might be gained by such a focus

[2]Lorraine Daston, "Objectivity and the Escape from Perspective," *Social Studies of Science* 22 (1992): 597–618 (599).

[3]The touchstone here remains James J. Gibson's "affordances" in *The Ecological Approach to Visual Perception* (New York: Houghton Mifflin, 1979), Chapter 8. There has, of course, been a great deal of writing on the subject–object distinction, with one important origin being Maurice Merleau-Ponty's *Phénoménologie de la perception* (1945), trans. Colin Smith, *Phenomenology of Perception* (London: Routledge and Kegan Paul, 1962). The following more recent works on objectivity are especially helpful in this large field: R. W. Newell, *Objectivity, Empiricism, and Truth* (1986; London: Routledge, 2015); Allan Megill, "Introduction: Four Senses of Objectivity," in *Rethinking Objectivity*, ed. Megill (Durham, N.C.: Duke University Press, 1994), 1–20; Lorraine Daston and Peter Galison, *Objectivity* (New York: Zone Books, 2007); and Michael Ayers, *Knowing and Seeing: Groundwork for a New Empiricism* (Oxford: Oxford University Press, 2019). For objectivity and related terms in the Middle Ages in particular, see Ernest A. Moody, "Empiricism and Metaphysics in Medieval Philosophy," *Philosophical Review* 67 (1958), 145–63, reprinted in Ernest A. Moody, *Studies in Medieval Philosophy, Science, and Logic: Collected Papers, 1933–1969* (Berkeley: University of California Press, 1975), 287–304; John E. Murdoch, "From Social into Intellectual Factors: An Aspect of the Unitary Character of Late Medieval Learning," in *The Cultural Context of Medieval Learning: Proceedings of the First International Colloquium on Philosophy, Science, and Theology in the Middle Ages, September 1973*, ed. Murdoch (Dordrecht: Reidel, 1975), 271–348; Lawrence Dewan, "'Obiectum': Notes on the Invention of a Word," *Archives d'histoire doctrinale et littéraire du Moyen Age* 48 (1981): 37–96, reprinted in Lawrence Dewan, *Wisdom, Law, and Virtue: Essays in Thomistic Ethics* (New York: Fordham

on the qualia of a character's interaction with objects is a sharper idea of how a subject acts, even in a performative sense, except here the actant might follow or enact a "script" not entirely prewritten in ideology but one that is more reciprocal between self and world, meaning it is to an extent provisional, contingent on sensory and other fields, "perspicuous cognitive contact with reality."[4] An associated and equally important part is to acquire a sensitivity to objects and what they enable, reshape, or carry as different from the subject. So where many biographical or historicist or ethical approaches consider Chaucer as an indicative or outstanding figure of this time, the phenomenological approach of the kind I attempt here turns from looking at him to (also) looking with him. One might ask the larger question of where he—or at least his characters—attends, and what are the characteristics of this interaction with things. In a sense, what are the qualities of reality-testing in Chaucer's works? Rather than regarding subjects directly along with the background that forms or informs them, looking along with them seeks to reveal the qualities of perception—how a person discerns what is there in the world and how they evaluate it—but also phenomenological qualities that are distinct from the self. If this is an approach that could be read as trying to get at the subject indirectly, then so be it, but it is intended as a change in focus to concentrating on where and how characters notice objects.[5]

Moments in which Chaucer or his characters markedly attend to objects or fields of vision are without a doubt many. Putting aside people, first to spring to mind might be a shot window, a rudderless boat, a cart wheel, a pear tree, coastal rocks, dice, a privy, and so on, without accounting for wider fields of vision. But my example is chosen because it is such a touchstone in studies of Chaucerian subjectivity: the *Prologue* to *The Tale of Sir*

University Press, 2007), 403–43; A. Mark Smith, "Knowing Things Inside Out: The Scientific Revolution from a Medieval Perspective," *The American Historical Review* 95 (1990): 726–44; and Jack Zupko, "What Is the Science of the Soul? A Case Study in the Evolution of Late Medieval Natural Philosophy," *Synthese* 110 (1997): 297–334.

[4]Ayers, *Knowing and Seeing*, 8. Ayers clarifies that "It is a mistake to conclude from our capacity to achieve certainty and knowledge that we have infallible faculties, but it is the just same mistake, still made often enough by the sceptically inclined, to draw from the fallibility of our faculties the conclusion that their deliverances can never be objectively certain" (26).

[5]This is not the same as studying how historical people evaluate objects, since we are dealing with fiction here, but perhaps something is nevertheless historically applicable to people's lives. Suzanne R. Kirschner points out the importance of distinguishing between characters and people in "Challenges for a Psychological Humanities," in *A Humanities Approach to the Psychology of Personhood*, ed. Jeff Sugarman and Jack Martin (New York: Routledge, 2020), 101–18.

Thopas. As is well known, in answer to the question the Host poses to the "me" in the *Prologue*—"What man artow?"[6]—critical responses have studied at length what kind of man the pilgrim is, who he is in terms of the character's relationship to an authorial voice, or, in some older as well as more recent studies, what the question implies about his manhood, even his personhood. The best-known is Lee Patterson's essay on "authorial self-definition" in the *Prologue*, despite what Patterson poses as the question's "comprehensiveness" and "utter lack of specificity."[7] Like nearly all who address the *Prologue*, Patterson begins with the line containing the question, then skips six or perhaps eight lines later to the description of the addressee as a "popet" with "elvyssh . . . contenaunce"[8] in order to argue that the author's "adoption of minstrel identity is finally a negative gesture, performed in default of the availability of a social identity commensurate to Chaucer's mode of writing." Alastair Minnis follows Patterson in concentrating on the same lines, but his Chaucer is distinctly less innocent, since the Host's jokes about the Chaucer character and women are "misogynistic" and Chaucer "a lot more potent than he may look," his additional "elvyssh" qualities making him "covert, subtle, cunning, and crafty."[9] Glenn Burger suggests the Host's question "expresses . . . uncertainty about the nature of the narrator and whether and how he will fit into the pilgrimage body," an "undecidability in terms of the Host's kinds of categories."[10] These and other readings have in common an understandable focus on the Chaucer character's personhood that starts with the question he is asked and then moves later to the lines about his corpulence, dolliness, elfishness, and manliness. Combined with other comments in the *Prologue* and their repetitions of tonal emphasis, a picture forms of the Chaucer-pilgrim as a somewhat opaque yet visibly melancholic man, the focus always remaining on the Chaucer figure. Either way, or in combination, this attention to Chaucer and mood receives additional impetus from the fact that the Host has begun to "jape" and then soon asks the

[6]*The Riverside Chaucer*, gen. ed. Larry D. Benson, 3rd ed. (Boston, Mass.: Houghton Mifflin, 1987), *Pr–ThL*, 695. Further Chaucer citations are to this edition.

[7]Lee Patterson, "'What man artow?': Authorial Self-Definition in *The Tale of Sir Thopas* and *The Tale of Melibee*," *SAC* 11 (1989): 117–75 (117).

[8]*Pr–ThL*, 701, 703; Patterson, "What man artow?', 117, 124, 129, 131.

[9]Alastair Minnis, "Aggressive Chaucer: Of Dolls, Drink and Dante," *The Medieval Translator* 16: 357–76 (364, 367).

[10]Glenn Burger, *Chaucer's Queer Nation*, Medieval Cultures 34 (Minneapolis: University of Minnesota, 2002), 176–77.

standalone pilgrim, who "unto no wight dooth . . . daliaunce," for "a tale of myrthe, and that anon."[11] The tale will, of course, initially be the sorry *Sir Thopas*. The poppet meets the imp meets the self-satirically sad.

There is, in fact, another element in *The Prologue to Sir Thopas* that draws attention not to the Chaucer character alone as the focus but instead to a nexus of eyelines and the act of looking in itself, a "Bihoold" beginning a traceable path of references to sight that divert attention away from the Chaucer character to the world before him. The reader (not a listener, incidentally) is first directed to look at the page, as the *Prologue* says "Bihoold the myrie talkyng of the hoost to Chaucer" in Hengwrt and "Bihoold the murye wordes of the Hoost to Chaucer" in Ellesmere.[12] The *Prologue* follows:

> Whan seyd was al this miracle, every man
> As sobre was that wonder was to se,
> Til that oure Hooste japen tho bigan,
> And thanne at erst he looked upon me,
> And seyde thus: "What man artow?" quod he.
> (*Pr–ThL*, 691–95)

Following the heading then, attention shifts from looking at the page to entering the fictional world of the Canterbury pilgrimage and first observing the pilgrims as they react to *The Prioress's Tale* in "sobre" ways, a "wonder . . . to se." Having registered that pause, attention next moves on to Harry Bailly as he begins to change the tone and "jape," and then the reader's eye follows the host to when he "looked upon me." In sum, the reader goes from beholding the talking/the words on the page, to looking at the pilgrims' reactions, to looking at the Host, who looks at Chaucer.

What if, however, the reader does not thereafter skip over lines following "What man artow?" to the "popet"-person but instead lingers for a moment on the first thing the Host sees about that "me"? For after Harry asks him about "what man" he is, he continues on: "Thou lookest as thou woldest fynde an hare, / For evere upon the ground I se thee stare"

[11] *Pr–ThL*, 693, 704, 706.

[12] Hengwrt in *The Canterbury Tales: A Facsimile and Transcription of the Hengwrt Manuscript, with Variants from the Ellesmere Manuscript*, ed. by Paul G. Ruggiers, A Variorum Edition of the Works of Geoffrey Chaucer, Vol. 1 (Norman: University of Oklahoma Press, 1979), 846; Ellesmere in *Riverside*, 212. These are page numbers because neither edition counts the headings (or other paratextual material) in line numbers.

(*Pr–ThL*, 696–97). David Benson describes the Chaucer-pilgrim in this scene as "a difficult character to grasp. . . . In fact, he is presented as more than a little unreal," and I take inspiration from his and others' uncertainty (the character's "utter lack of specificity") to try, against much received criticism, to attend to the lines where we look along with the narrator instead of at him.[13] The first aspect to notice is that the Host uses a simile and the subjunctive—"'Thou lookest as thou woldest fynde an hare'"—rather than directly denoting the Chaucer-pilgrim, but this indirect route to capturing how the character is acting or holding himself is clear enough. This clarity is compromised only a little by a slight temporal inconsistency in the fiction of *The Tales*, for the reader learns that it is the first time the Host has cast his eye on the Chaucer-pilgrim—"And thanne *at erst* he looked upon me"—yet the Host observes that Chaucer stares upon the ground "evere" as though he has been able to observe the pilgrim for some time, but perhaps the fiction is that he has quickly drawn a conclusion about Chaucer's habitual disposition.

It is possible to read the compound sentence about looking and finding and staring as one where the Chaucer character is just absent-mindedly gazing, that is, not really looking at all. Minnis twists the line when he argues that "Here the male gaze is definitely not trained on the ground, as if in search of a 'hare'" because Chaucer is imagining himself shrunk to a "popet"-sized doll for women.[14] Nor is David Wallace accurate when he says merely that "Chaucer is a person who cannot hold a level gaze ('looke up')."[15] Perhaps the easier reading is to see Chaucer as distracted or with his mind simply elsewhere. Such a reading dovetails with the inward, bashful persona of accepted Chaucerian persona studies. But what if a little more pressure is put on this "evere" "staring" at the ground? After all, "staring" can be more intent than oblivious. The monk in *The Shipman's Tale* begins "to stare" on the wife when she declares she might kill herself out of frustration (*ShT*, 124); the Canon's Yeoman warns that even though people might "looken nevere so brode and stare," they will never win in alchemical pursuits (*CYT*, 1420); and other examples of *staren* suggest an intensity, in the case of the Chaucer-pilgrim in *The Prologue to Sir Thopas*, heightened by the "evere."

[13]C. David Benson, *Chaucer's Drama of Style: Poetic Variety and Contrast in the "Canterbury Tales"* (Durham: University of North Carolina Press, 1986), 29.

[14]Minnis, "Aggressive Chaucer," 366.

[15]David Wallace, *Chaucerian Polity: Absolutist Lineages and Associational Forms in England and Italy* (Stanford: Stanford University Press, 1997), 213.

I might mention that contemporary hunting literature about hares or other prey has little to add here. Despite Oliver Farrar Emerson's argument that "Chaucer knew much more of medieval hunting practice than has usually been supposed" and used "hunting terms in their strict hunting senses, in other words with a realism quite in keeping with that shown in so many other particulars throughout his work," the sense merely remains of the Chaucer character intently searching the ground.[16] The *Middle English Dictionary* parses out a relevant sense of *finden* in the sense of "Thou lookest as thou woldest fynde an hare" as "To catch sight of or get on the trail of (game)";[17] the action of specifically looking at the ground to track a hare appears in some hunting treatises, and a hare's own "pricking" and variations of the word "pricking" (in the riding sense only) occur throughout *The Tale of Sir Thopas*,[18] but even if Chaucer had hunting treatises in mind, the better reading seems to be simpler: that the simile is just of him looking fixedly down.

I do not have space here to tease out the implications of Chaucerian staring at the ground. One continues to feel the pull of previous subjectivity work: Chaucer is sad ("sobre" like the others), he averts his eyes from the Host's inquisition and so he reflects Chaucer's own authorial deflections, he is ultimately an inward-looking character rather than an outward one, and so on. But what if he is (also) a character who looks intently in a downward direction? That is, at least on first impression, he is different from several other characters and whole treatises that urge the reader to look away from the earth and to fix the gaze heavenward. And what if he is not a character who looks at particular objects—plants, animals, people's faces—that are solely symbolic or otherwise recognized tropes of sexual activity, courtliness, or humoral and other characteristics? Here in *The Prologue to Sir Thopas* is an attitude that is more forensic and potentially weighing, an attitude that could be phenomenological in the sense that the Chaucer-pilgrim is investigating the world around him with an intensity that allows for discovery.

Direction, duration, quality: these aspects of attending to objects lure analysis away from the subject or, rather, steer it along with the subject to a slightly displaced focus on the interactions between subjects and objects,

[16] Oliver Farrar Emerson, "Chaucer and Medieval Hunting," *Romanic Review* 13 (1922): 115–50 (150).

[17] *MED*, s.v. *finden*, def. 12(a).

[18] *Thopas* even includes where the knight "priketh thurgh a fair forest, / Therinne is many a wilde best, / Ye, bothe bukke and hare" (*Th*, 754–56).

and to objects themselves. Chaucer's characters *gauren*, *piren*, *pouren*, *kiken*, *gapen*, *waiten*, and more. They are invested, interested in the world, much of which is a world of self and sociality to be sure, but they are engaged in examining other phenomena as well. That world reciprocates, it answers back, sometimes with a response that confirms the question it is asked, but sometimes it reveals something, it discloses in the discovery.

Perpetual Illumination: The *Ordinal of Alchemy* and Another Technology of the Self

Lisa H. Cooper
University of Wisconsin-Madison

Just over thirty years ago in this journal, Lee Patterson departed from most previous scholarship on *The Canon's Yeoman's Tale* by taking seriously not just the Canon and his beleaguered apprentice's late entry onto the scene of the Canterbury pilgrimage, but also the Yeoman's initial eager engagement and final bitter disillusionment with alchemical endeavor. For Patterson, the key to understanding the tale's significance lay in the way that, in his view, alchemy operated as a kind of crucible that helped form the modern—secular, autonomous, socially and technologically ambitious, yet profoundly alienated—subject.[1] The Yeoman is (and, Patterson argued, Chaucer behind him was) a self plagued yet at the same time "emancipate[d]" (30) by a general late medieval linguistic, social, and cultural unmooring that Patterson saw paralleled, even prefigured, in the always-receding horizon of alchemical textuality, a "quest without a goal" (47) akin to the Yeoman's own search for an identity: "The more he talks about the self that so fascinates him, the more dispersed it becomes, leaving him a cipher, an absence, a desire—a being who seeks rather than an object sought" (39).

Determining whether the Canon's Yeoman's selfhood (or, for that matter, the alchemical quest) is necessarily modern or medieval is beyond the scope of this essay.[2] My goal in what follows is instead to test Patterson's

[1]Lee Patterson, "Perpetual Motion: Alchemy and the Technology of the Self," *SAC* 15 (1993): 25–57 (31, 51, 54–55); page references are provided henceforth in the text. See also Lee Patterson, *Chaucer and the Subject of History* (Madison: University of Wisconsin Press, 1991), 32, 39, 423–25.

[2]Also beyond the scope of this essay but worth further consideration is the way that the same medieval/modern divide that Patterson's essay reifies is one that he himself had

Studies in the Age of Chaucer 46 (2024): 239–247

broad (as I will suggest, too broad) arguments about the relationship between alchemy and the self against a different poem that he relegated to his footnotes, but that explicitly positioned itself in the wake of *The Canon's Yeoman's Tale*: Thomas Norton's semi-autobiographical *Ordinal of Alchemy* of 1477, a 3,102-line work in Middle English (and some Latin) rhyming couplets.[3] Like Chaucer's Yeoman, Norton also rails against alchemical fraud; however, even as he echoes the Yeoman's warning about the certain failure of those who try to "multiplie" metals (*CYT*, 1479), cautioning "lay-men . . . / . . . to be ware of fals Illusions / which multipliers worch with theyre conclusyons" (*Ordinal*, Prohemium, 10–12), he is ultimately encouraging rather than dissuading of alchemical practice.[4] This is because, unlike the skeptical fiction that is *The Canon's Yeoman's Tale*, the *Ordinal* both presents itself as, and I believe was meant to be, a genuinely instructional text. Norton plans to avoid trapping his readers in the thicket of alchemical jargon—the "poyses, parabols, & . . . methaphoris" of previous authors (63)—in favor of "shew[ing] the trouth in few wordis & playne" (96): to join, while improving upon, the corpus of alchemical literature that Patterson surveys at the center of his essay.[5] For all its easily satirized impenetrability, this is a corpus that took itself seriously as a set of directives for a material practice that would, for the right (morally and temperamentally suited, properly instructed, correctly

decried only a few years earlier; see his "On the Margin: Postmodernism, Ironic History, and Medieval Studies," *Speculum* 65 (January 1990): 87–108.

[3]On what is known of Norton's life (c. 1433–1513) and career see John Reidy, "Introduction," in *Thomas Norton's Ordinal of Alchemy*, ed. John Reidy, EETS 272 (London: Oxford University Press, 1975), xxxvii–lii. All quotations from the poem will be to this edition by line number. Patterson, "Perpetual Motion," references the *Ordinal* briefly at 29 n. 13 and 54 n. 88.

[4]All references to Chaucer's poetry are by line number from *The Riverside Chaucer*, gen. ed. Larry D. Benson, 3rd ed. (Boston, Mass.: Houghton Mifflin, 1987). In addition to echoing the language of the tale in a number of places, as here, Norton refers to Chaucer by name in the *Ordinal* when quoting *The Canon's Yeoman's Tale* explicitly (and approvingly) at 1159–66, in a passage about magnesia, one of the supposed ingredients of the Stone; his allusion is to *CYT*, 1448–57.

[5]While I suggest below that the *Ordinal* lives up to this ambition in ways that set it apart from others, an opening claim to clarity is a common trope of alchemical writing; see Patterson, "Perpetual Motion," 40. On the way *The Canon's Yeoman's Tale* was received in the early modern period as a genuine alchemical text, and Chaucer as an alchemist, starting with Norton's reference to *The Canon's Yeoman's Tale* in the *Ordinal*, 1159–66, see Robert Schuler, "The Renaissance Chaucer as Alchemist," *Viator* 15 (1984): 305–33. Patricia Clare Ingham reviews some of the many ways the tale has been read as Chaucer's critique of *something*; see her *The Medieval New: Ambivalence in an Age of Innovation* (Philadelphia: University of Pennsylvania Press, 2015), 152–53.

equipped) practitioners, lead to the Philosophers' Stone, an elixir (cf. *CYT*, 862–63) believed capable not only of transmuting base metal to better, but also, with the rise of medical alchemy in the thirteenth century, of prolonging human life to its fullest natural extent.[6] No serious alchemist, in other words, would have agreed with Patterson's assessment of alchemy, even in its most esoteric mode, as a "quest without a goal." And while Patterson is right to note that much alchemical literature "acknowledges little distinction between literal and metaphoric" such that "praxis becomes impossible" (44), Norton's *Ordinal* is notable in the long tradition of English alchemical verse for its avoidance of "methaphoris" in favor of a pragmatic style that largely favors clarity over obscurity.[7] Rather than traffic in the "dispersed . . . cipher[s]" of those more florid forms of alchemical discourse that, for Patterson, define the Canon's Yeoman's very self (39), this is a style that lends itself to the making of a community in search of a shared goal, rather than to the shaping of isolated subjects seeking only themselves.

And in fact the *Ordinal*'s alchemical subjects—by which I mean both its author and its characters—are throughout the poem shown to be tied to and deeply engaged with others and the world in which Norton consistently anchors his practically inclined work. This is a world on which he clearly hopes to leave his mark, despite the modesty of his opening assertion that "I desire not worldly fame / . . . vnknowe shalbe my name" (13–14), a point to which I will return. First, however, I want to take a close look at Norton's account of his search for a master, for it is there that we can start to see how his sense of himself *qua* alchemist does not resemble the "socially undetermined subjectivity" that Patterson claimed not only for the "disenchanted" Yeoman, but also for Chaucer himself (56, 55). For as Norton makes clear, even if the "trew" alchemist is best recognized by his solitude—genuine adepts being those who "serche & seche alle

[6]Patterson acknowledges the practical side of alchemy, but it is not his main concern ("Perpetual Motion," 48). On alchemy's melding of the practical and interpretive see Jennifer Rampling, *The Experimental Fire: Inventing English Alchemy, 1300–1700* (Chicago: University of Chicago Press, 2020). On the term *elixir* see Lawrence M. Principe, *The Secrets of Alchemy* (Chicago: University of Chicago Press, 2013), 39; on medical alchemy see 69–73.

[7]This does not mean that Norton never wades into obscurity, or that he does not seek to hide the alchemical "secret" from the unworthy; see David Hadbawnik, "Alchemical Language: Latin and the Vernacular in the Poetry of Thomas Norton and John Gower," in *Vernacular Aesthetics in the Later Middle Ages: Politics, Performativity, and Reception from Literature to Music*, ed. Katharine W. Jager (New York: Palgrave Macmillan, 2019), 201–31.

a-loone / In hope to fynde oure dilectable stone" (315–16)—to become a practicing philosopher or train another is rather to be a socially *determined* subject fashioned not by the breaking of bonds, but instead by the making of them. Robyn Bartlett has recently pointed to the way that intersubjectivity—shared ways of being, knowing, and behaving—was a crucial component of late medieval lay confessional culture; much the same can, I think, be said of medieval *alchemical* culture, whose members, as the most accurate term for the elixir they sought evinces (it is the "*Philosophers'* Stone" [*lapidus philosophorum*], not "Philosopher's"), certainly considered themselves members of an intellectual community stretching back to Antiquity.[8] At the same time, and despite its eventual production of texts almost too many to number, that community consistently defined itself by way of the idea (if not always the reality) of a one-to-one relationship of master and disciple, a bond all the more intense because of the traditional limit on the transmission of alchemical secrets, or, as Norton puts it, "One he [a master] may teche but then nevir no mo" (236).[9] In Barbara Newman's useful terms, alchemical master and apprentice "coinhere" in the kind of highly affective relation productive of what she calls "the permeable self," a form of relational personhood in which individuals are not just radically open to, but are also dependent upon, one another.[10]

It is precisely in terms of this kind of affective permeability—even penetrability—that Norton relates his dogged pursuit and winning over of his own eventual master. He explains how this unnamed alchemist initially rebuffed his would-be pupil's advances, testing Norton "with straite assay" (828) just as one might test (and so break down) an alchemical compound until, as he triumphantly recalls, "I conqueride by grace dyvyne / His love whiche did to me inclyne" (833–34). In this alchemical bromance, it is Norton's "vnfeynyde fidelyte" (831) that wins the alchemist over, his "many-folde letters" expressing his "hevy hert & chere" that "[m]

[8]Robyn A. Bartlett, "Learning to Live in Communities: Household Confession and Medieval Forms of Living," *NML* 22 (2022): 162–213 (164). On the correct plural possessive form of *Philosophers'* see Principe, *The Secrets*, 217 n. 37.

[9]The obvious contradiction between this limitation and the writing of alchemical books for a wider audience is part of what undergirds alchemy's allegorical mode, which (the claim goes) only the elect could understand in any case.

[10]Barbara Newman, *The Permeable Self: Five Medieval Relationships* (Philadelphia: University of Pennsylvania Press, 2021), 4–8; for Newman's own study of master–pupil bonds, see 15–58. Newman's arguments, as she acknowledges (2), draw upon Charles Taylor's earlier conception of the "porous" medieval vs. the "bounded" or "buffered" modern self; see Charles Taylor, *A Secular Age* (Cambridge, Mass.: Belknap Press, 2007), 37–38.

ovid his [the adept's] compassyon" and "persid hym ful nere" (837–38).[11] Apparently struck to the heart by Norton's pleas, the master alchemist deigns to establish textual relations—"his penne he wolde no more refrayne" (839)—only to insist almost immediately upon a physical encounter; "it is nede," he writes, "that with-in shorte space / We speke to-gedire, & see face to face" (849–50). With its clear echo of 1 Corinthians 13:12, this implicit promise of alchemical revelation also plays on the requirement strictly to limit the dissemination of alchemical secrets: "If y shuld write," the master explains, "I shulde my foialte breke, / Therfore mowthe to mowthe I most nedis speke" (851–52).

This provocative synecdoche, representing the intimate conversation that will seal the bond between two men, also suggests alchemy's queer futurity in the sense of which José Esteban Muñoz speaks when he describes queerness as "primarily about futurity and hope,"[12] for it is in just such terms that the master anticipates his disciple:

> And when ye come, myn heyre vnto þis arte
> I wille yow make, & fro this londe departe;
> ye shalle be bothe my brodire & myn heyre
> Of this grete secrete wherof clerkis despeire.
> (853–56)

This familial language helps put the angry frustration, if not utter anguish, of Chaucer's Yeoman into perhaps its most proper context. For however justified his lament about the "cursed craft" of alchemy may be (*CYP*, 830), what he voices in his *Prologue* and *Tale* seems to be not, as Patterson puts it, "a yearning, heightened by the possibility of loss, for the value-laden, animated universe of traditional religion" (55), but rather a yearning for the kind of human connection that Norton claims by contrast to have enjoyed.[13] The intersubjective bond he forged with his teacher, through which in turn

[11] On the "romantic accounts" of many alchemical autobiographies see also Patterson, "Perpetual Motion," 54, though by "romantic" Patterson appears to mean fictional rather than amorous.

[12] José Esteban Muñoz, *Cruising Utopia: The Then and There of Queer Futurity* (New York and London: New York University Press, 2009), 11. For a similar reading of the queer potentiality of the master–apprentice relationship in the *Ordinal* see Cynthea Masson, "Queer Copulation and the Pursuit of Divine Conjunction in Two Middle English Alchemical Poems," in *Intersections of Sexuality and the Divine in Medieval Culture: The Word Made Flesh*, ed. Susannah Mary Chewning (Aldershot: Ashgate, 2005), 37–48 (44–46).

[13] This is not to disagree with Micah James Goodrich's powerful reading of the Yeoman as an abused mentee whose justified grievances lead him to speak out against his mentor; my argument would be that it is not the Canon the Yeoman mourns, but the bond they

he "fownde . . . disclosid þe bondis of nature" (*Ordinal*, 874), is for Norton the antidote for the many uncertainties that plague every alchemist who strives for the Stone; as he tells the reader, "If your mastir & ye resemble alle abowte / My goode mastir & me, then take ye no dowte" (877–78). Just as Norton and his master came to see each other "face to face," so do they in turn become the *speculum* in which readers may judge their own reflections. While I am in no way suggesting that we should take Norton's story of his training (let alone his later claim to have arrived at the Stone) at face value, the point here is that given his familiarity with Chaucer's tale, the difference between the Yeoman's experience and his own might be read as something of a deliberate riposte. The Yeoman may have been "wont in no mirour to prie" (*CYP*, 668), but Norton would not be afraid to do so, standing—as he claims to do—on surer, because less isolated, ground.

Patterson suggests that autobiography appealed to alchemical authors in part because of the way alchemical knowledge served a self-fashioning impulse, affording "a way to be an intellectual" (54)—and thus, as I have already suggested, a way to join a *community* bound together by centuries of text and tradition. But what I think we can see in Norton's account of his alchemical apprenticeship and elsewhere in the poem are traces of an even more fundamental desire for connection to others in both this life and, as I will now suggest, beyond it. In other words, while what drives the alchemical subject may indeed be, to borrow from Patterson, a form of "social ambition" (54), in Norton's hands that ambition appears less a desire for *perpetual motion* than simply a desire *to perpetuate*, in a more or less fixed way, through time—not, *pace* Patterson, as an isolated individual striding boldly forward across the medieval/modern divide, but rather as a social person connected to others, and so remembered by them, long into the future. In the *Ordinal*, this yearning for connection is expressed perhaps most poignantly in the two negative exempla of failed alchemists presented at the opening of the same early book of the poem in which Norton recounts his successful approach to his master, to which I now turn.[14]

The first story is about a Norman monk who seeks to "leve som noble acte behynde / wherbi his name shuld be immortall, / And his grete fame in lawde *perpetuall*" (556–58; my emphasis). He decides to build fifteen abbeys on Salisbury Plain and turns to Norton for help in purchasing the land, planning to finance the whole project with funds amassed through

never had; see Micah James Goodrich, "The Yeoman's Canon: On Toxic Mentors," *SAC* 44 (2022): 297–306.

[14]On the uncertain facticity of these stories see Reidy, "Introduction," lxviii.

alchemy. When his alchemical work fails, the monk turns to a life of fraud before fleeing to France. The second anecdote, following directly on the first, is about a parson who also hoped to put "[h]is name . . . *euer in mynde*," in his case by building a bridge across the Thames for the "light passage" and "ese" of his fellow citizens (632, 634, 635; my emphasis). Hoping for even "grettir fame" by illuminating the bridge so that "it myght shyne also bi nyght" (644, 646), the parson becomes obsessed with finding the best technology to keep the lights on in perpetuity, and so fruitlessly seeks out carbuncles—believed in the Middle Ages to produce their own light—for which he too plans to pay with alchemical riches.[15] But like the monk of the previous tale, whose "abbeys & alle his thoght / . . . turned to a thinge of noght" (605–6), the parson also fails. His search for carbuncles "wastide" his "fatt fleshe . . . nye to noght" (672), and his alchemical work comes up literally empty even as it empties his purse: "His crafte was loste and thrifte alle-so. / For when that he toke vp his glasse, / There was no matere for golde ne brasse" (676–78).

We must read against the grain of Norton's scorn for both men (whose faulty alchemy he never describes, and whose primary function in the poem is as contrast with his own vaunted expertise) in order to see that their two unachieved projects, vainglorious though they are, are also *philanthropic* endeavors—civic works undertaken for the sake of society both spiritual and secular. The plans appear to spring from an impulse resembling Norton's own when, at least nominally motivated by "pitee" for those who have experienced alchemically induced suffering like that of the Canon's Yeoman (their faces "made pale," their clothing "made bare" [92–93]), he writes a book he calls "of Alchymye the ordinalle, / The crede michi, the standarde *perpetuall*" (127–28; my emphasis). What monk, parson, and Norton all desire is, again, to be "perpetuall"—to endure in the memory of the communities to which they belong, thanks to their contribution to the common good.

On Norton's part, that desire is made especially clear in the striking analogy he uses to describe his own book at its end:

> Now haue I tagth [*sic*] you euiry thynge bi name
> As men tech othir the way to walsynghame;
> Of euiry village, watire, bryge, and hyll,
> Wherby wise men theire Iournay may fulfill;

[15] On carbuncles see *On the Properties of Things: John Trevisa's Translation of Bartolomeus Anglicus De Proprietatibus Rerum*, ed. M. C. Seymour (Oxford: Clarendon Press, 1975–89), XVI.25.

So may clerkis bi this doctryne fynde
This science well if thei be clere of mynde.
(3063–68)

It is no accident that Norton compares the *Ordinal*—so called, he explains at the poem's beginning, because its "ordirlye" presentation, unlike "al the [other] bokis vnorderide in Alchymye," renders it akin to the liturgical book that "to prestis settith owte / The seruyce of the dayes as þei go abowte" (132, 131, 129–30)—to the directions for reaching the end of a pilgrimage. For Patterson, the comparison, and Norton's title, might serve to prove his point regarding the way "many alchemical treatises present alchemy less as a secular pursuit . . . than as another form of piety" (49). But once again I think there is more to see here, and that is the communal experience of pilgrimage: to undertake a journey to Walsingham (or, say, Canterbury), as to strive for the Stone, is to participate in an intersubjective community in which "men tech othir" (3064) and no one stands alone. In this way, Norton's version of alchemical personhood looks again like something of a response not only to the Canon's Yeoman's "smert and . . . grief," but also to the Canon's own initial desire "[t]o riden in . . . compaignye" with the Canterbury pilgrims (*CYP*, 712, 586).

The Canon, of course, does not linger long in that company. Like his avatar in the tale (generally accepted as a figure for the Yeoman's master), "he is heere and there; / He is so variaunt, he abit nowhere" (*CYT*, 1174–75), and so he slips back into the "hernes and . . . lanes blynde" from whence he came as his apprentice proceeds to bring his misdeeds and alchemy's mischances to light (*CYP*, 658). But while the Canon might wish to slip into oblivion, the same cannot be said either of his author, Chaucer, whose multiple self-representations across his corpus need no rehearsal here, or of Thomas Norton who, despite his initial insistence on anonymity, and his direction to his readers not to "þer-aftir serche ne looke" for him (13–15), clearly hoped for exactly the opposite. For as was first noted by the early modern antiquary Francis Thynne (c. 1544–1608) in his own copy of the *Ordinal*,[16] Norton signed his work by way of an acrostic formed from the first syllable of the Prohemium and of each of the six subsequent books of the poem, syllables that, when added to the whole first line of the seventh book, make a rhymed couplet: "ToMas NorTon Of BryseTo [i.e., Bristol] / A Perfite Maister ye may hym trowe."

[16]Reidy, "Introduction," xlii.

Fixing himself in the book even as he writes it, staking a claim for the *Ordinal*'s—and more fundamentally, for his own—perpetual value with a verbal flourish that Patterson might well call "an ostentation that is anything but secret," but that also defies, in highly personal, intersubjective terms, what he calls alchemy's "impossible dream of accurate naming" (38): so, in this way, did at least one late medieval alchemical subject leave himself for posterity, medieval as well as modern, to find.

Barred Fragility

Wan-Chuan Kao
Washington and Lee University

Those who fail to practice self-care may indeed be labeled "noncompliant" and thus less deserving of care.

Hi'ilei Julia Kawehipuaakahaopoulani Hobart and Tamar Kneese[1]

WHILE VISITING A FEDERAL DETENTION CENTER housing migrant children in Texas in 2018, Melania Trump flaunted a jacket designed by Zara with a written message splashed across its back: "I REALLY DON'T CARE, DO U?" (Fig. 1). By donning a textual sign, she became a sign that invited interpretation. To read the jacket is therefore to shift the pronominal positions in the sartorial script: "She really doesn't care. Do I?" Care is the operative term that *really* defines both the subjectivity of Melania and that of the viewer. Obviously she does care, or else she would not have drawn attention to herself in a calculated, tabloid-worthy display. Melania's self-fashioning of her subjecthood, as a style of being, is simultaneously linguistic, material, and somatic. Subjectivity becomes a self-tracking wearable. By saying she doesn't care, Melania enacts the Foucauldian care of the self in which subjectivity is the concrete form of a relational activity in which one engages with oneself.[2] Yet this self-fashioning as a pose of defiant noncompliance if not indifference is dangerously couched in an economy of care, one dependent on an engagement with care in the first place; as such, care-based self-fashioning is precarious and fragile.

[1]Hi'ilei Julia Kawehipuaakahaopoulani Hobart and Tamar Kneese, "Radical Care: Survival Strategies for Uncertain Times," *Social Text* 38 (2020): 1–16 (4).

[2]See Edward McGushin, "Foucault's Theory and Practices of Subjectivity," in *Michel Foucault: Key Concepts*, ed. Dianna Taylor (London: Routledge, 2011), 127–42.

Studies in the Age of Chaucer 46 (2024): 249–260

Fig. 1. Melania Trump on June 21, 2018, following her surprise visit to child migrants on the USA–Mexico border. Photo by Mandel Ngan/AFP via Getty Images.

The sartorial message on Melania's jacket is an algorithm comprising two utterances. On the top is a statement ("I REALLY DON'T CARE") articulated by a confessional subject expressing her noncompliance. On the bottom is a rhetorical question ("DO U?") posed by a hermeneutical subject inviting interpretation. An invisible bar demarcates the two utterances, turning the message into an algorithm of subjectivity, one not unlike the algorithm of the sign (Fig. 2). Whereas, for Saussure, the signifier lies atop the signified, Lacan repositions the signified (the Imaginary) over the signifier (the Symbolic). Lacan's insight that the unconscious is structured like a language provides a model of subjectivity that is multilayered, posited with an interiorized self whose meaning is presumed but always out of reach, and vulnerable to fragmentation and incoherence. For geographer Gunnar Olsson, the Saussurean bar is the "limit of limits," the "ontological divide," and the stroke that simultaneously keeps the signifier

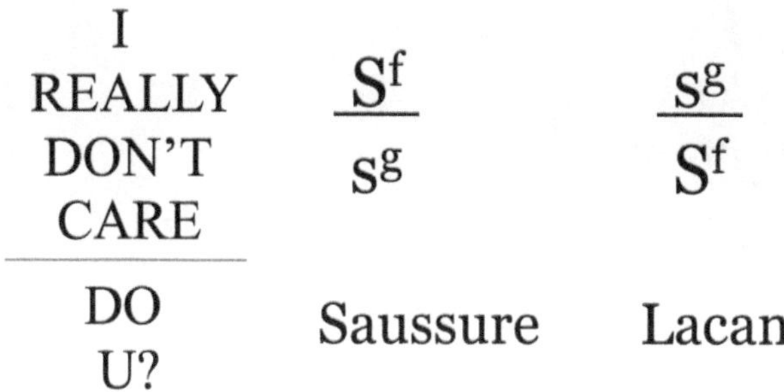

Fig. 2. The semiotic algorithm.

and the signified—and thereby humans—together and apart.[3] Olsson contends: "It is this hidden Bar of Categorial Meetings that I go to search for fractions of taboo-ridden phenomena and taboo-ridden insights. It is exactly in the abyss of this power-filled void that visible becomes invisible, untouchable touchable."[4] For Derrida, the concept of the sign cannot pass the opposition between the sensible (the signifier) and the intelligible (the signified).[5] As both Saussure and Lacan point out, the connection between the signifier and the signified is arbitrary. In fact, the linkage is not only arbitrary but fundamentally fragile, by which I mean the connection is a liability, even if and when power holds the semiotic structure in place as steadily as possible. Fragility is therefore not so much a condition—such as disintegration—as an index to the state of adhesion of the semiotic system and, by extension, of subjectivity.

The verticality of the message on Melania's jacket mirrors the state of suspension of her being, in another photograph, as she stands in-between the ground and the plane. Melania in mid-air conjures up the climactic scene in *The Merchant's Tale*, when May climbs up a pear tree to meet Damian and consummate their love, leaving her old, blind husband January below by the tree trunk. May too deploys noncompliance as a means of subversive self-fashioning, and both she and Melania trace out the

[3]Gunnar Olsson, *Abysmal: A Critique of Cartographic Reason* (Chicago: University of Chicago Press, 2007), 79, 84 (quotations).

[4]Gunnar Olsson, *Lines of Power/Limits of Language* (Minneapolis: University of Minnesota Press, 1991), 60.

[5]Jacques Derrida, *Writing and Difference*, trans. Alan Bass (London: Routledge, 2001), 355.

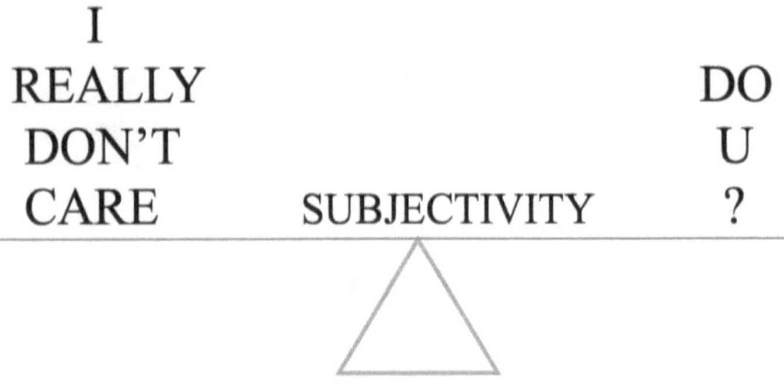

Fig. 3. The continuum of care.

contours of subjectivity. As I will discuss below, *The Merchant's Tale* is not simply about marriage and the household, though they are important sites of care labor and therefore of psychoanalysis and logistics. Rather, the project of the tale, not unlike that of Melania's jacket, is the care of the self; as such, it is about the relational state of the subject to itself and others. However, the verticality of the semiotic algorithm of subjectivity—such as the one on Melania's jacket—could be misleading. Tilting the algorithm, a different configuration of care emerges (Fig. 3). Care becomes a continuum, as the Saussurean bar transforms into a lever. Against the Lacanian split subject and the Althusserian hailed subject, subjectivity exists along a continuum of care, pivoted by the fulcrum of fragility. Motivated by acts of care, subjectivity is on the move.

The Logistics of Self-Care

I would like to offer another algorithm of the sign for consideration: something ubiquitous and easily overlooked (Fig. 4). It is another articulation of the Saussurean and Lacanian algorithm of the sign: S/s or s/S. And the shipping label opens up the Lacanian–Saussurean algorithm. "THIS SIDE UP," the sign urgently warns its viewer. The sign assumes directionality, and the arrows recall the Saussurean arrows of the directed flow of signification; except in this instance, both arrows point upward toward a presumed transcendence. The Saussurean bar—as a partition, a demarcation, and a line of power—finally stretches outward. Olsson contends that it is misleading to think of the bar as a flat, two-dimensional, ultra-thin horizontal line. The misconception is an error of scale. Instead, it is better

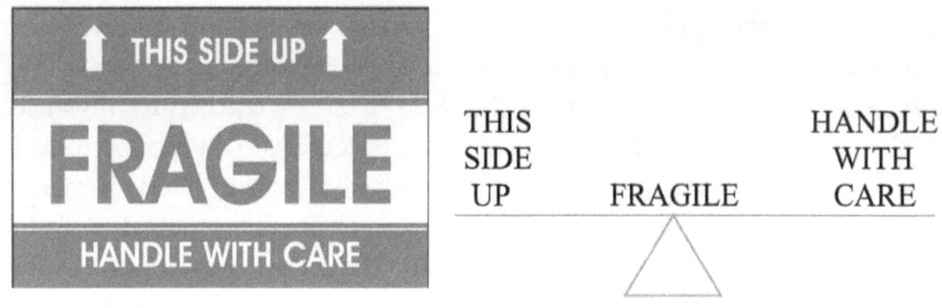

Fig. 4. Fragility on the move.

to conceive of the bar, turned on its axes, as a three-dimensional entity with thickness.[6] If so, fragility, sandwiched between upward transcendence and careful handling, is the thickness of the Saussurean bar.

"HANDLE WITH CARE" also delineates the scene of analysis. What is fragile and requires careful handling and proper orientation? The subject. The label assumes, if not produces, a reader-analyst, a handler of the subject. "FRAGILE" marks the boxed content (a sign, text, or subjectivity). It is as much a set of instructions as a warning, or a cross-sectional cut of the psychic process. The burden of care—that is, the Foucauldian care of the self—becomes indistinguishable from either the burden of reading or that of analysis. As such, fragility rests on a care economy. The care labor of psychoanalysis is the fragile labor of subject formation and maintenance. Care labor, in other words, is the hermeneutical labor of the subjectivity.

The label further presumes transport along a route: from origin, to intermediary points, and to final destination. Containerized, fragility is freight on the move. In fact, "HANDLE WITH CARE" presupposes multiple handlers along the supply chain: supplier, packer, courier, and consumer. Fredric Jameson has pointed to "a number of striking analogies of structures" between psychoanalysis and Marxism, such as "the question of desire and value and of the nature of 'false desire.'"[7] I would contend that logistics studies, which overlaps with Marxism, also shares analogous concerns and approaches with psychoanalysis. As such, the logistical turn in critical theory could usefully inform and complement linguistic-based psychoanalysis. There are a few striking analogies, if not exact parallels,

[6]Olsson, *Abysmal*, 84.

[7]Fredric Jameson, "Imaginary and Symbolic in Lacan: Marxism, Psychoanalytic Criticism, and the Problem of the Subject," *Yale French Studies* 55/56 (1977): 338–95 (386).

between psychoanalysis and logistics. Citing the work of Susan Ziger, Stefano Harney notes that "logistics incorporates loss in its logic."[8] In psychoanalysis, the separation of the child from the mother, for instance, is the originary loss that triggers trauma and sets desire in motion to seek the lost object. If Lacanian psychoanalysis posits a chain of signification, without which language and meaning were impossible, then there is no signification without movements along the chain. Lacan's adoption of the signifying chain to articulate his theory of the unconscious is, at its heart, a study of the logistics of the subject, if not the psyche. As Deborah Cowen argues, "a logistics lens emphasizes flow, movement, circulation, and connectivity across space."[9] The unconscious may be structured like a language, but it operates like logistics.

Perhaps we could reconceptualize the Saussurean bar as a "line" in logistics, as either the supply line or the assembly line. Cowen notes that there is no strict separation between logistics and infrastructure, and that "[l]ogistics is not just about distribution or circulation in the sense of simply moving things around."[10] Logistics is also about desire, especially the infrastructural nature of desire in the supply chain, as well as about sexual difference and social reproduction. As desire is entangled in bio-, necro-, and geopolitics, social reproduction is but one incarnation of logistics. If, as Micki McGee recently argues, capitalism has a care problem, then capitalism also has a fragility problem.[11] Fragility invokes care (e.g., "HANDLE WITH CARE"); it presumes and demands care ("(You) Take care of me"); it advertises high maintenance and unnecessary hassles (like a diva); and it imposes an orientation ("Up!," or "Me!"). Ironically, fragility rejects the subject as the primary caregiver of the self. When people say, as Melania does with her jacket, "I don't care," what they really mean is: "I don't *do* care with *you*." Fragility marks privilege and signals liability, something that is difficult to care for, maintain, keep in shape, or keep alive.

Care is a signifying system; it is the unconscious; and it is the metrics of the subject. Moreover, care is a categorical system. Who is worthy of care? Who gives care? Who receives it? Care interpellates the individual. As such, a care system is not unlike the sign system and not dissimilar to

[8]Niccolò Cuppini and Mattia Frapporti, "Logistics Genealogies: A Dialogue with Stefano Harney," *Social Text* 36 (2018): 95–110 (97).

[9]Niccolò Cuppini, "Circulating Violence and Value: A Dialogue on Logistics (with Deborah Cowen)," *Social Text* 37 (2019): 95–102 (97).

[10]Ibid., 98.

[11]Micki McGee, "Capitalism's Care Problem: Some Traces, Fixes, and Patches," *Social Text* 38, no. 1 (2020): 39–66 (39).

Damian	This Side Up	Signifier / Signified
May	Fragile	___________
January	Handle with Care	Signified / Signifier

Fig. 5. The pear tree.

Lacan's famous bathroom door signs. Care is a delineation of the subjects and objects (of care). Danielle Allor notes that care "takes place in and among social systems."[12] I would add that care also takes place in signifying systems and in psychic structures. In other words, fragility *as* care shapes subjectivity.

The Fragile Subject

The algorithm of fragility and care, as an iteration of the Saussurean–Lacanian algorithm of sign, is useful in analysis of gendered subjectivities in Chaucer's corpus, especially those grounded in the institutions of courtly love and marriage. In *The Merchant's Tale*, for instance, the tableau of May in the pear tree conjures up the algorithm of the sign and the logistical label of fragility (Fig. 5). Earlier in the tale, an elderly January suddenly panics about his well-being, legacy, and lineage. For him, marriage is an institution of care, or institutionalized care. At the pear tree, he instructs May that were she to remain true to him, she would "win" the love of Christ, honor, and his heritage: "Beth to me trewe, and I wol telle yow why. / Thre thynges, certes, shal ye wynne therby: / First, love of Crist, and to youreself honour, / And al myn heritage, toun and tour" (*MerT*, 2169–72).[13] By promising May his possessions, January sees himself as her caregiver; she will be taken care of when he dies. But his heritage also

[12]Danielle Allor, "Uncaring *Sir Orfeo*," paper presented at the Modern Language Association convention, online, January 8, 2022.

[13]All quotations from Chaucer's works are from *The Riverside Chaucer*, gen. ed. Larry D. Benson, 3rd ed. (New York: Houghton Mifflin, 1987), and will be cited by line number.

takes the form of social, sexual reproduction: the expectation of an heir. Care, for January, is a system of control.

The pear tree signifies a middling household ecology, a scene of domestic conduct, a flexible line of sexual differentiation, and an infrastructure of subject formation. As such, the tree outlines the contours of a care economy offering two modes of care, with May as the default caregiver of the two men. With Damian, she functions as the Lady to him, the artist-lover, within the discourse of courtly love. Through letters, a silk purse, and bodily signs, May and Damian have already formed their own signification system.[14] But with January, May operates as the wife to January the husband; she thereby conforms to the tradition of equating care work with women's work. The two signifying systems—courtly love and marriage—converge at the pear tree, with January and Damian situated at opposite ends. It is difficult if not impossible to allocate either man to the positionality of the signifier or that of the signified. I would step away from such rigid designations because what really matters is not what is on top or bottom, the signifier or the signified, Saussurean or Lacanian. What matters is the bar between them, the limit of limits, the impasse of signification: May is the Saussurean bar between Damian and January. Her movements along the tree are not simply instances of the traffic in women, for such a reading would assign May to both the middle and middling positionality that she never occupies permanently. Rather, she only passes through the middle/middling space on her way up and down the tree.

What is important is the fragility between the two men (Fig. 6). First, for Lacan, A is the big Other that is complete, uncastrated, but does not exist. Along the pear tree, I read "Big Fragility" as institutionalized care, the science of logistics and risk management. Second, the *objet petit a* in Lacan's formulation is the unattainable object of desire, the imaginary part-object, the surplus and remainder, and the lack. I would thereby read "little fragility" as *counter*-logistics. Rather than managing risk, the lover is taking risk. Thirdly, Lacan's A̶ (the Barred A) is the barred Other, which is incomplete and castrated. Similarly, the barred subject ($) is split by language and vanishes beneath or behind the signifier.[15] I would propose

[14]See Amy S. Kaufman, "Erotic (Subject) Positions in Chaucer's *Merchant's Tale*," in *Sexual Culture in the Literature of Medieval Britain*, ed. Amanda Hopkins, Robert Allen Rouse, and Cory James Rushton (Woodbridge: D. S. Brewer, 2014), 27–37. Kaufman argues that May's arc is "a story of the birth of the erotic subject" (35).

[15]See Bruce Fink, *The Lacanian Subject: Between Language and Jouissance* (Princeton: Princeton University Press, 1995), 41–46.

Damian	This Side Up	little fragility care as *counter*-logistics courtly love
May	Fragile	**~~Fragility~~** contaminated zone of subject & object
January	Handle with Care	Big Fragility care as logistics marriage

Fig. 6. The tree of fragility.

that the space of fragility in the algorithm of the tree marks the Barred Fragility, for there is no distinction between the Saussurean bar and the state of fragility. Split by care, the Barred Fragility operates as the interface between the signifier and the signified. It may be a site of sexual difference but not a scene of social reproduction, for despite all the sex between January and May, there is no heir. The Barred Fragility is what Anne Anlin Cheng would term the "contaminated zone of subjection and identification," where distinctions between persons and things are blurred; it is "the uneasy domain of *contagion* where conditions of objecthood merge into the possibility of subjectivity, where experiences of profound invasion yield acute moments of self-making."[16] In other words, it is the continuum that May occupies and that fashions her subjectivity; care, as a form of desire, is on the move.

Jameson argues that psychoanalysis and Marxism share the same problem: the problem of the subject, that is, the difficulty of mediating between "social phenomena" and "private facts."[17] As an atypical fabliau, *The Merchant's Tale* is never simply about cuckoldry, about women getting away, or about women having the last word. Getting away, in fact, is not the same as redemption. Nor is the tale affirming the antifeminist

[16] Anne Anlin Cheng, "Psychoanalysis without Symptoms," *differences* 20 (2009): 87–101 (92 [original emphasis]).

[17] Jameson, "Imaginary and Symbolic in Lacan," 338.

stereotype that women are deceitful or that women insist on having the last word (the signified). To think so would be to miss the point of Proserpina's intervention. In a crucial sense, May is not lying, because what happens at the pear tree has nothing to do with truth or deception. Rather, it has everything to do with the arbitrariness of signifiers and signified, and the fragility between them. January sees not so much the sex act per se, but its meaning: betrayal, infidelity, violation of his wife as his property.[18] In fact, the Merchant notes that sight or blindness has nothing to do with deception: "O Januarie, what myghte it thee availle, / Thogh thou myghtest se as fer as shippes saille? / For as good is blynd deceyved be / As to be deceyved whan a man may se" (*MerT*, 2107–10). May perceives and experiences *jouissance* at the tree. By reinterpreting the significance of what January has allegedly witnessed, she redirects the care work away from institutionalized systems of care. She in fact allows January to keep the fantasy of a masculinist, coherent self.

The pear tree is an algorithm of the fragile subject, as well as the site of care labor. Lisa Ruddick has critiqued literary studies' reflexive valorization of the idea of a fragmented, decentered self, a phenomenon she attributes partly to Lacanian literary scholars who read Lacan perhaps too narrowly, but not Lacanian psychoanalysts. Ruddick contends that both extremes, the fragmented self and the congealed self, are problematic; instead, she draws attention to "the middle ground that lies between congealed and fragmented subjectivity," which is "a relational space."[19] In *The Merchant's Tale*, the tree appears to set up two opposing masculinist models of the self: January as the coherent self versus Damian as the fragmented self (Fig. 7). The tree in fact maps the periodization of the male subject, one linked to transitions in modes of production, care, pleasure, reproduction, and governance. The two men might correspond, however imperfectly, to Charles Taylor's supersessionist theory of the porous self of an enchanted premodernity vis-à-vis the buffered self of a disenchanted modernity.[20] Damian, the courtly lover who has poured his

[18]For femininity as performative passivity, see Holly A. Crocker, "Performative Passivity and Fantasies of Masculinity in the *Merchant's Tale*," *ChauR* 38 (2003): 178–198.

[19]Lisa Ruddick, "Beyond the Fragmented Subject," in *The Cambridge Companion to Literature and Psychoanalysis*, ed. Vera J. Camden (Cambridge: Cambridge University Press, 2022), 256–74 (265, 268).

[20]Charles Taylor, *A Secular Age* (Cambridge, Mass.: Belknap Press, 2007), 38–39. See also Barbara Newman, *The Permeable Self: Five Medieval Relationships* (Philadelphia: University of Pennsylvania Press, 2021), whose thesis is premised on Taylor's theory of the premodern porous self.

Damian	This Side Up	Porous / Fragmented Self
May	Fragile	Contaminated zone of subject & object
January	Handle with Care	Buffered / Coherent Self

Fig. 7. Variously emplotted selves.

soul out and is now perched precariously among the tree branches, resembles "the porous self [that] is vulnerable."[21] In contrast, January, the cuckold who clings to marriage as a capitalist institution, occupies the position of "the buffered self [that] can form the ambition of disengaging from whatever is beyond the boundary, and of giving its own autonomous order to its life."[22] Taylor's historicist model presupposes the Saussurean bar and construes it as a border: "the boundary as a buffer, such that the things beyond don't need to 'get to me.'"[23] But while the two men are busily stationed in the infrastructure of desire at two extreme modes of temporalized subjectivity, it is May who is on the move. The Barred Fragility is unfixed and mobile along the continuum of subjectivity. The bar may be coded feminine, but it is not strictly the space of any essentialized gender, which happens at the extremes (Damian and January). The pear tree as a periodizing model of subjectivity, it turns out, is another modern masculinist fantasy.

The pear tree may be a household, but as Olsson argues, "[t]he Bar is our home, the fraction line the bed in which our signifying descendants are being conceived."[24] The Saussurean bar is the space of domesticity; it is a tree, a line of transport, a logistical line, and not a border. And the slippery mobility of May-qua-Barred Fragility suggests that the periodization of the subject is equally unfixed and messy. Lee Patterson notes that there is "something about subjectivity that persuades people that in dealing with it they have entered into a new time, that they have cut

[21]Taylor, *A Secular Age*, 38.
[22]Ibid., 38–39.
[23]Ibid., 38.
[24]Olsson, *Abysmal*, 84.

themselves off from the past, that they have become moderns."[25] If so, Patterson's insight rests on *unseeing* the line of signification, the Barred Fragility, and the continuum of subjectivity: that is, May herself. As an alternative to the fragmented, coherent, porous, and bounded selves, Barred Fragility might better capture the "middling" sensibility of the *gentils* of late medieval England. To engage in care labor, to navigate the logistics of signification and the fragile infrastructure of desire, is to *shapen* subjectivity.

[25]Lee Patterson, *Chaucer and the Subject of History* (Madison: University of Wisconsin Press, 1991), 12.

Subjectivity and Women's Friendship

Usha Vishnuvajjala
SUNY-New Paltz

It's nowhere near cold, but Becca loves borrowing things, lending things, all the small rituals that blur the four of them into one warm space. If she had a choice, they'd all live in each other's clothes.

Tana French, *The Secret Place*[1]

Medievalists have long challenged the binary opposition between a "modern" subjectivity that is closed, individual, or autonomous and a medieval subjectivity that is porous, aggregated, or socially constituted by demonstrating the ways in which the so-called modern form of subjectivity can be found in late medieval literature and culture. But focusing on the individual (often masculine) subject in order to work across this false binary overlooks the ways in which the interdependent subjectivity of friendship we see in late medieval culture persists in modern literary culture, especially as that literary culture represents friendships between women. This essay proposes that models of women's friendship—models that can extend to friendships between people of any gender but are drawn mainly from literary depictions of friendships between women—can intervene in debates about the divide between medieval and modern ideas of subjectivity or the "self."

Like the character Becca in Tana French's novel, characters in late medieval and especially Middle English texts can at times blur into each other in ways that simultaneously protect them and make them more vulnerable. I propose that such a form of embodied—rather than spiritual or political—friendship as it is represented in both medieval and modern texts presents an alternative to models of subjectivity as either buffered or

[1]Tana French, *The Secret Place* (New York: Viking: 2014), 342.

Studies in the Age of Chaucer 46 (2024): 261–268

porous.[2] The shared subjectivity between friends—enacted through dialogue, physical closeness, nonverbal communication, shared decision-making, shared responsibility, and even the sharing of clothing—can make individuals simultaneously more open to *and* more closed off from others. By creating a private but shared set of experiences, gestures, vocabulary, and practices, such friendships can make individuals more porous or vulnerable to each other (and at times to other individuals by extension, as I discuss below) while also making the pair or group of friends more closed-off or buffered to those outside the friendship. Such friendship, enacted through embodied experiences and defined by the intimacy and blurred identities those experiences create, is often represented as a feminine form of friendship in literature.

Scholarship on postmedieval literature has often understood women's friendship as embodied and domestic, opposed to models of public, political, or spiritual friendship (often understood as experienced mainly by men).[3] The idea of a public–private binary, as it maps onto the idea of a gender binary, obfuscates the complex ways in which friendship can function as both public and private at the same time, or as a middle category between public and private, complicating ideas of the self as either porous or buffered. Taking Holly A. Crocker's concept of a feminist subjectivity as one that "arises from imagining the human body not as closed, disciplined, and effectively distanced, but as open, fluid, and frequently compromised" as a starting-point, we can consider a feminist

[2]For more on the scholarly history of these two models of subjectivity see Holly A. Crocker's introduction to this colloquium.

[3]Penelope Anderson, however, demonstrates the importance of early modern women's political friendships in *Friendship's Shadow: Women's Friendship and the Politics of Betrayal in England 1640–1705* (Edinburgh: Edinburgh University Press, 2013). For an overview of scholarship on women's friendships see Judith Keegan Gardiner, "Review Essay: Women's Friendships, Feminist Friendships," *Feminist Studies* 42 (2016): 484–501, esp. 499–500. Gardiner writes that scholars of women's friendship—she cites sociologist Lillian B. Rubin's book *Just Friends: The Role of Friendship in Our Lives* (New York: Harper & Rowe, 1985) as an example—often adopt a sort of gender essentialism that claims that men's friendships and women's friendships are different because they fulfill different inherent needs, rather than because friendships exist in a larger social context in which individuals are socialized differently depending on their perceived gender. Sharon Marcus, *Between Women: Friendship, Desire, and Marriage in Victorian England* (Princeton: Princeton University Press, 2007), considers the role of women's friendships and women's romantic relationships in the Victorian novel, mainly in domestic social settings. Ivy Schweitzer, *Perfecting Friendship: Politics and Affiliation in Early American Literature* (Chapel Hill: University of North Carolina Press, 2006), traces the development of a scholarly understanding of women's friendship as primarily domestic in the introduction, and her first chapter offers an alternative model of friendship that is politically situated.

form of friendship as a model for thinking about how an openness and vulnerability between those inside a bond such as friendship can also, at times, serve to reinforce the boundaries or closedness between those inside the friendship and those outside it.[4] By serving as a middle or third category between public and private, friendship—or at least friendship that is not public, political, or spiritual—shows us that the individual subject can be both porous to others and buffered from the wider world at the same time.

Friendships of the sort I'm interested in, often associated with women, but which might instead be characterized as "embodied" friendships rather than the public/political or spiritual friendships theorized by thinkers such as Cicero and Aelred of Rievaulx,[5] therefore have a complicated relationship to the idea of subjectivity.[6] We can see this in the interactions that even the seemingly singular and exemplary heroes and heroines of medieval romances have with each other, which often include experiences and knowledge shared between two characters but invisible to a third. Robert Hanning's analysis of what he calls "the representation of limited perspective" illustrates beautifully that even "when a plot ceases to be an exemplary action consistently embodying a set of specific, absolute values," it still depicts the interaction and intermingling of "participants who variously, incompletely, even incorrectly perceive what is happening to them."[7] In his analysis of a passage from Chrétien de Troyes's *Erec et Enide*, Hanning identifies "the details of human reaction and response caught at a specific second in time, forming together (Enide's blush, Erec's astonishment) a representation of interaction between characters at the level of personal perception and instant response; and second the existence within

[4]Holly A. Crocker, "W(h)ither Feminism? Gender, Subjectivity, and Chaucer's *Knight's Tale*," *ChauR* 54 (2019): 352–70 (357).

[5]Cicero's *On Friendship* (*De amicitia*) emphasizes the importance of virtue and similarity in friendship. Aelred of Rievaulx details in the prologue to his *Spiritual Friendship* (*De spirituali amicitia*) how his philosophy of spiritual friendship both draws on and departs from Cicero, writing "I began to acquire a taste for the sacred Scriptures and found that the slight knowledge the world had transmitted to me was insipid by comparison. Then I remembered what I had read in Cicero about friendship, but to my surprise it did not taste the same to me." Aelred of Rievaulx, *Spiritual Friendship*, ed. Marsha L. Dutton, trans. Lawrence C. Braceland (Collegeville, Minn.: Liturgical Press, 2010).

[6]Although he describes the identities of (male) medieval authors as interconnected or "indexical," the types of porousness or openness Sebastian Sobecki describes in *Last Words: The Public Self and the Social Author in Late Medieval England* (Oxford: Oxford University Press, 2019) have to do primarily with public identities, as his title indicates.

[7]Robert W. Hanning, *The Individual in the Twelfth-Century Romance* (New Haven: Yale University Press, 1977), 14.

the scene of a separate viewpoint—that of another character who misses the personal significance of the meeting."[8] For Hanning, this passage is significant in its "interest in individual experience," but we can also consider its depiction of shared experience and shared subjectivity, even if the sharing is both fleeting and imperfect (as we can see later in the romance when Erec's cruel actions are incomprehensible to Enide and to many of us as readers). As Hanning shows, medieval romance represents a literary interest in individual, rather than collective, subjectivity; even here, though, the romance hero's subjectivity is still constituted through experiences shared with other individuals.

We can see here something different than either an exemplification of universal experience or a "buffered" or closed individual subjectivity: we can see experience and perception as shared and only possible in the interaction between two people, but also closed to a third character within the text. At the same time, that shared experience and perception are, here, available to the reader, but this is not always true. While the interaction in this case is between would-be lovers (and eventual spouses), this is a useful way of approaching how both medieval and modern texts can represent the form of intimacy and friendship I am interested in—a shared sense of experience, perception, and perhaps identity that is nevertheless private, specific, and not universal or exemplary.

Even accounts of the lives of medieval women who are often considered exemplary, such as saints and visionaries, "complicate some of the elements of Aelred's schematic" of exemplary or ideal spiritual friendship, as Jennifer N. Brown has shown.[9] Rather than friendship as an ideal relationship that brings one closer to God, Brown argues, the friendships between medieval visionary women were complicated, not always equal, and involved private as well as public interaction, including keeping watch by a friend's deathbed.[10] Friendship imagined as a shared privacy and a shared—if not necessarily equal—vulnerability may seem at odds with classical and medieval models of public or spiritual friendship as, to use Alexandra Verini's succinct summary of "thinkers from Plato to Aristotle to Cicero," "a virtuous, reciprocal relationship between identical male equals."[11] It

[8] Ibid., 17.

[9] Jennifer N. Brown, "Female Friendships and Visionary Women," in *Women's Friendship in Medieval Literature*, ed. Karma Lochrie and Usha Vishnuvajjala (Columbus: The Ohio State University Press, 2022), 15–35 (19).

[10] Ibid., 33.

[11] Alexandra Verini, "Sisters and Friends: The Medieval Nuns of Syon Abbey," in Lochrie and Vishnuvajjala, *Women's Friendship*, 76–93 (78).

serves as a counter to both models of the self as buffered or closed and models of the self as constituted by larger-scale social forces.[12]

Although friendship is not one of the categories of relation Barbara Newman examines in her recent *The Permeable Self: Five Medieval Relationships*, it can also, at times, be one of those "interpersonal relations at a certain pitch of intensity, where the boundaries between persons seem to blur."[13] In particular, I suggest that the type of private friendship I have described here (a category that overlaps with but is not entirely the same as women's friendship), which blurs the boundaries between the people inside it, can shield those inside it from male, colonial, or other external gazes; at the same time, that porousness of the self to one's friends can also make the people inside the friendship more susceptible to malignant forces outside it.

Lydia Yaitsky Kertz writes that the title character of *Emaré*, who wears a robe made by another woman, a Muslim princess who first made the cloth for her lover, experiences "a transfer of racialized identity" as well as a sort of proxy friendship when the robe functions like a "second skin" and provides comfort and protection to Emaré, a woman who has suffered greatly at the hands of her father and others and has had few friends or protectors.[14] The protection of the robe also comes with some dangers—as Kertz writes, "even a white Christian princess is not immune to racially charged aggression" when wearing a cloth connected to a Muslim emir—so the blurring of identity between the two women, represented by the cloth that confers the emir's daughter's friendship and even a marker of her identity on Emaré, has the effect both of protecting Emaré and of making her more vulnerable to others who might wish to hurt her.[15] Although these two women might not appear to be friends in the ways we normally expect, the bond between them through the robe—enabled, as Kertz writes, by the larger networks of women both characters participate in—is important to the identities of both characters and visible to the reader, while remaining largely invisible to many of the other characters in the poem. This is not a "buffered self,"

[12]See Andrea Boffa, "Friendship and Resistance in the *Vitae* of Italian Holy Women," in Lochrie and Vishnuvajjala, *Women's Friendship*, 58–75, on the role of friendship in resisting patriarchy in the lives of lay holy women in late medieval Italy.

[13]Barbara Newman, *The Permeable Self: Five Medieval Relationships* (Philadelphia: University of Pennsylvania Press, 2021).

[14]Lydia Yaitsky Kertz, "'Amonge maydenes moo': Gender-Based Community, Racial Thinking, and Aristocratic Women's Work in *Emaré*," in Lochrie and Vishnuvajjala, *Women's Friendship*, 97–113 (103).

[15]Ibid.

but it is also not the enchanted existence Charles Taylor describes in which everyone is experiencing the same reality.[16]

We can see something similar in the friendships Dorigen has in *The Franklin's Tale*, which constitute not a transfer of identity but rather an attempt by Dorigen's friends to substitute their judgment for her own: Dorigen's well-meaning friends (not specified as women) try to distract her from her grief and fear during her husband's absence by taking her first for long walks and then to parties and other social gatherings. Both of these attempts at cheering her up backfire in different ways, but it is the second one that suggests that the interdependence of friendship creates new vulnerabilities even as it creates some protection.[17] Dorigen's friends bring her to these social gatherings because they see that being near the sea is not healthy for her: it causes her to "caste hir eyen dounward fro the brynke. / But whan she saugh the grisly rokkes blake, / For verray feere so wolde hir herte quake / That on hire feet she myghte hire noght sustene" (*FranT*, 858–61).[18] When "hire freendes" see "that it was no disport / To romen by the see, but disconfort," they "shopen for to pleyen somwher elles. / They leden hire by ryveres and by welles, / And eek in othere places delitables; / They dauncen and they pleyen at ches and tables," eventually finding themselves on May 6 at a garden party where "At after-dyner gonne they to daunce, / And synge also" (895–919). This passage of the text suggests that Dorigen is spending all her time with her friends, that they will not leave her alone to contemplate her husband's fate or worry about the rocks in the harbor, perhaps for her own safety. And there is a

[16] Charles Taylor, *A Secular Age* (Cambridge, Mass.: Harvard University Press, 2007), esp. 25–89.

[17] Melissa Ridley Elmes reads the well-meant intervention of Dorigen's friends slightly differently, writing "Without her friends, Dorigen would have languished alone; and typically in medieval literature when a woman in love languishes alone, without some divine intervention she winds up dead, often by her own hand, as is the case with many of the women in Chaucer's earlier *Legend of Good Women*. Chaucer avoids that deadly conclusion in the *Franklin's Tale* by surrounding Dorigen with friends who bring her solace and force her out of the house and back into the community she would so willingly set aside if left to her own devices" (Melissa Ridley Elmes, "Female Friendship in Late Medieval English Literature: Cultural Translation in Chaucer, Gower, and Malory," in Lochrie and Vishnuvajjala, *Women's Friendship*, 135–54 (144). Elmes notes that Chaucer's source, Boccaccio's *Decameron*, X.5, features a scene with its main female character "join[ing] other city women walking in a garden" (145) but no such group of persistent friends, arguing that Chaucer was consciously adapting Boccaccio's text for a female readership.

[18] *The Riverside Chaucer*, gen. ed. Larry D. Benson, 3rd ed. (Oxford: Oxford University Press, 1987). Further Chaucer citations are to this edition.

safety in their company, but there is also the new danger they expose her to: the presence of the squire Aurelius, whose proposition sets off a chain of events that nearly ends Dorigen's marriage and, arguably, threatens her life. As with Emaré's proxy friendship with the emir's daughter, Dorigen's friendships with others—arguably other women—leave her simultaneously more protected and more vulnerable. In ceding some of her autonomy, her judgment, and her will to her friends, she is made safer by their presence but more vulnerable by their choices.

Elsewhere in the *Canterbury Tales*, as Karma Lochrie writes, we see a friendship between women that is identifiable as such partly because it "is intimate and unbound by the demands of men": that between Custance and Hermengild in *The Man of Law's Tale*.[19] Here too, as Lochrie notes, there are shared experiences and shared beliefs between the two that are nevertheless private—the two women pray together in secret, sharing their beliefs only with each other and each keeping the other's beliefs secret too.[20] This "identity of feeling" between the women, Lochrie writes, "slips through the Man of Law's narrative strategy" of opposition, providing "an interlude apart from the grand Christian/heterosexual/Western triumphal narrative in the making."[21] In remaining a private friendship, perceptible to the reader of the text and the fictional audience in the frame tale but not initially to any other characters within the tale, this friendship demonstrates that shared vulnerability—even in two characters who are not necessarily otherwise equals—and shared knowledge and beliefs can create a subjectivity that is shared but not public.

Friendship is not necessarily a relationship that has been treated as integral to medieval understandings of the self, even where that self is understood as permeable and constituted in part through relationships. It is not one of the five categories Newman writes of (teacher and student, saint and sinner, lovers, mother and child, God and the devil). And yet, it can and does overlap with at least three of these categories: teacher and student, parent and child, and lovers. It can overlap, too, with other types of kinship relationships and professional relationships. The friendships in which I'm interested here are the ones between individuals who are able to act like equals in a specific interaction and are able to participate in a

[19]Karma Lochrie, "'All These Relationships between Women': Chaucer and the Bechdel Test for Female Friendship," in Lochrie and Vishnuvajjala, *Women's Friendship*, 177–96 (186).

[20]Ibid., 185.

[21]Ibid., 186.

shared subjectivity that isn't dictated by unequal power relations or coercion. They do not require virtue or likeness, only shared vulnerability. Such friendships, as represented in literary culture, exist across the seeming divide between late medieval and modern literary culture, and attention to them can help to challenge the idea that medieval subjectivity was categorically different than its modern counterpart.

The Pardoner, Domestic Confession, and Porous Subjectivity

Robyn A. Bartlett
Purdue University

THE PARDONER has long been known as one of the most marginal characters of the *Canterbury Tales*, an "abandoned wretch" and "the one lost soul among the Canterbury pilgrims," as George Lyman Kittridge has called him, the very last of the pilgrim portraits for a reason.[1] We have considered, among other things, his immorality, his fundamental lack, his despair, and his queerness—all of which alienate him from the group of pilgrims.[2] This essay will consider, instead, the Pardoner's contact with the group. Drawing from my work on a confessional subgenre called forms of confession, I reread *The Pardoner's Prologue* and suggest that he participates in what I call domestic confession: the non-sacramental occasion of reading confessional material (including forms of confession) aloud, in a family or household group.[3] By implicitly acknowledging a group's interdependence, domestic confession both illustrates and even requires collective or porous subjectivity—the ways in which people touch, bump up against,

[1]George Lyman Kittridge, *Chaucer and His Poetry* (Cambridge, Mass.: Harvard University Press, 1915), 21, 180; H. Marshall Leicester, Jr., "Structure as Deconstruction: 'Chaucer and Estates Satire' in the General Prologue, or Reading Chaucer as a Prologue to the History of Disenchantment," *Exemplaria* 2 (1990): 241–61 (251–54).

[2]On the Pardoner and despair see Lee Patterson, *Chaucer and the Subject of History* (Madison: University of Wisconsin Press, 1991), 367–421; and see H. Marshall Leicester, Jr., *The Disenchanted Self* (Berkeley: University of California Press, 1990), 35–64. Donald Howard sees the Pardoner as a "marginal figure" and a "grotesquerie" (*The Idea of the "Canterbury Tales"* [Berkeley: University of California Press, 1976], 341). For the Pardoner's lack and queerness see especially Monica McAlpine, "The Pardoner's Homosexuality and How It Matters," *PMLA* 95 (1980): 8–22; Carolyn Dinshaw, *Chaucer's Sexual Poetics* (Madison: University of Wisconsin Press, 1989); Glenn Burger, "Kissing the Pardoner," *PMLA* 107 (1992): 1143–56; and Steven Kruger, "Claiming the Pardoner: Toward a Gay Reading of Chaucer's *Pardoner's Tale*," *Exemplaria* 6 (1994): 115–39.

[3]See Robyn A. Bartlett, "Learning to Live in Communities: Household Confession and Medieval Forms of Living," *NML* 22 (2022): 162–213.

Studies in the Age of Chaucer 46 (2024): 269–277

and permeate each other's lives. Thinking of Holly A. Crocker's work on masculinist subjectivity and material virtue, we might understand the porous self as in contrast to a buffered, masculinist self, one that entails protecting the boundaries of the self at all costs, even violent ones.[4] Porous subjectivity entails pain, instead: it requires being open to disappointment, betrayal, and hurt; it requires the discounting of self-image and reputation. It also holds up the promise of love and deep interconnectedness. By contrast, while bounded or buffered subjectivity does not deny relationships, it *does* deny intersubjectivity, the openness to the other. Barbara Newman gets at this in her recent book *The Permeable Self*, where she suggests that "the essence of personhood is the capacity to be permeated by other selves, other persons, without being fractured by them."[5] The use of passive voice here, though, along with "fractured," nevertheless suggests that the self, for Newman, is still something contained and separate, something whole that can be broken. These assumptions are predicated on understanding the self as buffered, regardless of the coinherent, dyadic relationships Newman charts.

Like Newman, I borrow the terms porous and buffered from Charles Taylor, thinking not only of his work specifically on these concepts in *A Secular Age*, but also of his diachronic arguments about the emergence of modern selfhood in *Sources of the Self*.[6] But rather than tethering porosity to a premodern, enchanted past and contrasting it with modernity's buffered subjectivity, I use these terms as placeholders—and not necessarily binaristic ones—to stand for transhistorical ways of relating to each other and to the world. For, as the emphasis on communal concord and responsibility in confessional forms shows so conclusively, porous subjectivity was a goal, not a given, and frequently enough the bounded and agential habits of life got in the way. In other words, buffered selfhood has a long historical arc. Newman and others accept Taylor's diachronic account of change over time, moving from the porous selves of the Middle Ages to the buffered selves of the post-Enlightenment world.[7] But here, and in the larger work from which this paper draws, I am challenging this diachronic narrative,

[4]Holly A. Crocker, *The Matter of Virtue: Women's Ethical Action from Chaucer to Shakespeare* (Philadelphia: University of Pennsylvania Press, 2019).

[5]Barbara Newman, *The Permeable Self: Five Medieval Relationships* (Philadelphia: University of Pennsylvania Press, 2021), 6.

[6]Charles Taylor, *A Secular Age* (Cambridge, Mass.: Belknap Press, 2007); Charles Taylor, *Sources of the Self* (Cambridge, Mass.: Harvard University Press, 1989).

[7]Medievalists have been recently engaging with Taylor's concepts. See especially Crocker, "W(h)ither Feminism? Gender, Subjectivity, and the *Knight's Tale*," *ChauR* 54

both reconceiving Taylor's term as it might be informed by feminist theorists from bell hooks to Lauren Berlant and Imani Perry, and suggesting that throughout the medieval period, buffered selves were already the norm. These ways of being emerge on a spectrum. Confessional forms underscore the importance of vulnerability and porosity: they emphasize taking care of the poor; being generous to your neighbors; and not being too prideful yourself, too attached to your own station. Radical vulnerability is presented as the apex of human relationships; but it is hard to get there. Ways of being in the world are not absolute—and the Pardoner illustrates this point perhaps better than any other medieval literary character could.

What I argue here might seem counterintuitive: that *The Pardoner's Prologue* and *Tale* illustrate the difficulties of vulnerability, the risks of truth-telling, and possibly even the difficulties in domestic confession, wherein those in your group may have known the ill you had done them, and may or may not forgive it. That is, insofar as he confesses his sins to the group, the Pardoner establishes an intimacy with them that often takes years, the accumulation of mistakes, slights, banal cruelties amassing over time, so that when the family group gathered to read, one member might look askance at another, at the section on "backbiting," for instance. The fundamental challenge in domestic confession is that the group knows. It is difficult to hide. *The Pardoner's Prologue* is in a sense staging a domestic confession. Regardless of arguments focusing on the Pardoner's lack, his ultimate unknowability, I suggest that, in narrating his misdeeds from the outset—in telling them his *entente* so readily—the Pardoner establishes an uncomfortable intimacy with the other pilgrims, one that underwrites his performance and the pilgrims' response to it. Scholars have tended to understand the Pardoner as veiled, as staging a giant rhetorical performance; I show here that, by contrast, he is totally exposed.

In fact, the Host and the other pilgrims invite this exposure from the outset. In *The Introduction to The Pardoner's Tale*, the Host turns to the Pardoner, his "beel amy" (*Phy–PardL*, 318), to tell a tale that will comfort the group, some "myrthe or japes right anon" (319).[8] Unlike many of his fellow pilgrims, the Pardoner does not need to interrupt to be heard; he is even presented as a salve. The "gentils" object, however, in a moment Carolyn

(2019): 352–70; and see Sebastian Sobecki, *Last Words: The Public Self and the Social Author in Late Medieval England* (Oxford: Oxford University Press, 2019).

[8] *The Riverside Chaucer*, gen. ed. Larry D. Benson, 3rd ed. (Oxford: Oxford University Press, 1987). Further Chaucer citations are to this edition.

Dinshaw has characterized as one in which the other pilgrims respond with aversion to the Pardoner; they do not want to hear any "ribaudye" from this pilgrim in particular (324).[9] I am not so sure. The Host, after all, is the one who needs cheering after the brutal ending of *The Physician's Tale*; he is the one who asks, specifically, for a merry tale. The objecting gentils ask instead to hear "som moral thyng" (325). They could be objecting to the Pardoner himself; they could equally be objecting to the Host's request. Regardless of their motivations, the Pardoner agrees to give them what they ask for, promising "som honest thyng" (328). This flexibility suggests at least a superficial desire to be a part of the pilgrimage. He agrees to what they want. It is perhaps a small point, but all the same, other pilgrims fail to show this kind of sensitivity to their audience. One has only to think of the Wife of Bath, the Manciple, the Cook, the Miller—all of whom, to varying degrees, disregard the will of the group. The Wife instructs the Pardoner to "abyde!" when he interrupts, and she does not worry about the Friar's disapproval of her preaching; the Manciple actively excoriates the Cook, to the point that even the Host objects; the drunken Miller overturns the Host's intended order of tale-telling; and in his tale, the Cook trails off, in a moment that anticipates the pilgrims' reticence to hear anything bawdy from the Pardoner, either. Only the Pardoner, whom scholars have occasionally considered to be drunk, whom we have certainly considered to be at least as inappropriate as the Manciple and as disregarding of order as the Miller, explicitly agrees to fulfilling the pilgrims' request.

From the outset, then, the Pardoner betrays a kind of solicitude for the people he is with. In his *Prologue*, he only begins to do what he has promised: he thinks aloud about "som honest thyng." I am drawing on the multiplicity of the adjective "honest," which designates what is virtuous, moral, or good. But in the Middle Ages, as now, "honest" also signals a kind of openness or truth-telling;[10] and *The Pardoner's Prologue* is nothing if not honest, possessed of a "disarming openness" and "candor."[11] As Donald Howard puts it, the Pardoner "tells them the most honest thing he can think of: he is a fraud and a scoundrel."[12] His *Prologue* gives his fellow pilgrims access to the thinking underpinning his tale proper, and it foregrounds what the *Introduction* merely hints at: in bragging to the

[9]Dinshaw, *Chaucer's Sexual Poetics*, 157.
[10]*MED*, s.v. *honest(e)*, def. 5.
[11]Howard, *The Idea of the "Canterbury Tales,"* 351.
[12]Ibid., 353.

group about his duplicitous expertise, he also reveals to them the very machinations that allow his schemes to function. Of course, saying an honest thing is a means of defense, too, as Richard Newhauser pointed out to me in private correspondence: beating others to the punch may obviate a more brutal appraisal. At the same time, in taking this approach, I would argue that the Pardoner offers a vulnerable challenge to the systems of meaning-making of which he is a part. In order for these systems to function, the Pardoner *cannot* call attention to his professional know-how. But he does; he says what he should not. Some scholars have opined that the Pardoner behaves the way he does because he is drunk, or because he is so fundamentally lacking that he cannot help but try to hide his even *more* repugnant sins.[13] Lee Patterson suggests that the "very excess of the Pardoner's revelations hides him from us."[14] But it is perplexing to me that scholars have understood the Pardoner's radical vulnerability as another veil behind which he creeps. Instead, in making himself vulnerable and open, and in reverting to his wiles by the end of the tale, he shows that he understands the precarity of rigid subjectivity in a way that many of the other pilgrims do not. They ask for a moral thing; and whether by accident or design, he gives them an honest thing, instead.

This emphasis on honesty and on what is real—even when it is ugly—subtends his description of his wonder-working so-called relics, too.[15] In some ways, these objects do underscore the Pardoner's lack, promising wholeness and multiplication, as many scholars have emphasized. But they do much more than only this. The Pardoner's sheep's bone, for instance, does a lot of things: dipped in a well, it creates a contact relic of the well water, which, the Pardoner promises, can heal livestock of various diseases.[16] The owner of the livestock is similarly advantaged: his "beestes and his stoor shal multiplie" (*PardP*, 365) if he follows a regimen of fasting and drinking the well water. And, as Shannon Gayk points out in a recent essay, this well water also functions as a kind of healing tonic,

[13]For an overview of these scholarly responses see Kathy Lavezzo, "The Pardoner and His *Tale*," in *The Cambridge Companion to "The Canterbury Tales,"* ed. Frank Grady (Cambridge: Cambridge University Press, 2020).

[14]Lee Patterson, "Chaucerian Confession: Penitential Literature and the Pardoner," *Medievalia et Humanistica* 7 (1976): 153–73 (163).

[15]See Robyn Malo (now Bartlett), "The Pardoner's Relics (and Why They Matter the Most)," *ChauR* 43 (2008): 82–102.

[16]On the ways in which anti-Jewish discourse animates relic discourse—particularly in the case of the holy Jew's sheep's bone—see Lisa Lampert-Weissig, "Chaucer's Pardoner and the Jews," *Exemplaria* 28 (2016): 337–60 (346–47).

"capable of *healing* sexual jealousy, though not in the way we might expect."[17] It does not make the infidelity stop. Instead, the Pardoner explains,

> For though a man be falle in jalous rage,
> Lat maken with this water his potage,
> And nevere shal he moore his wyf mystriste,
> Though he the soothe of hir defaute wiste,
> Al had she taken prestes two or thre.
> (*PardP*, 367–71)

This healing potion, I suggest, imparts the ability to accept things as they are. Knowing that his spouse is cheating is not tantamount to mistrust—perhaps precisely *because* the husband knows. It is almost as though the Pardoner's sheep's bone can, under the right circumstances, provide the key ingredient in a kind of reality drug. This attitude to cheating is much different than in *The Merchant's Tale*, for instance, wherein May manages to convince January that he does not know what he has seen. January goes on living in an illusion, as he seems to have done for quite some time. But the husband of whom the Pardoner speaks will *not* go on living in an illusion, any more than the pilgrims will live in the illusion that the Pardoner tells the truth about the fake relics he carries. Neither they nor the husband have to wonder.

The Pardoner offers truth in his lies, then, and the fictional husband's kind of trust is in a sense precisely what he asks for from the other pilgrims: though you know the truth of what I do, you do not need to mistrust me; you can accept things as they are precisely because you know what they are. Again, he presumes the intimacy of an established domestic group, wherein perhaps one member *could* be, say, the volatile one, or the duplicitous one, or the annoying one. People know to expect occasional outbursts, and they also know that this member of the group will, having apologized, do it again. This circularity describes a lot of life. Of course the Pardoner's expectations—if indeed this is what he expects—are paradoxical, given that, as Gayk points out, "the Pardoner is himself inviting counterfactual belief."[18] Trust in his own duplicity

[17]Shannon Gayk, "Believing in the Pardoner's Objects," forthcoming in *Objects of Belief* (Manchester: Manchester University Press, 2025).

[18]Ibid.

nevertheless seems to inform the way the Pardoner expects others to respond to the story he offers.

This presumption of intimacy and trust underwrites what the Pardoner says about his *entente*, too. In lines that we all know, the Pardoner announces that his "entente is nat but for to wynne, / And nothyng for correccioun of synne" (*PardP*, 403–4). His *entente* is always "coveityse" (423–24, 432–33). Obviously this is not what he says when he preaches to other audiences. But here, he exposes himself in all of his ugliness and imperfection. One might even suggest that the Pardoner simply carries on being honest; he is telling this group who he is, possibly even with the expectation, as the end of the tale demonstrates, that they will accept him in spite of—perhaps, as his healing potion suggests, even because of—this. His approach is very like what we might think of domestic confession, wherein the members of the group are all aware of mutual shortcomings and slights. The Pardoner, after all, does not hesitate to reveal his own:

> Thus quyte I folk that doon us displesances;
> Thus spitte I out my venym under hewe
> Of hoolynesse, to semen hooly and trewe.
> (420–22)

In this passage he describes an in-group (pardoners) and an out-group (those who "doon us displesances"). But he offers this depiction to the people he is with, and thereby he creates *another* in-group, another "us": the pilgrim company. These lines are a veiled threat—do not cross me—but in spite of the virulent, serpentine imagery, he does not seem to expect that his audience will judge him harshly for this admission. I suggest that this is because here the Pardoner implies that, in speaking to the pilgrims so candidly, he is *not* spitting out venom. Instead, he is revealing what he does not show to just anyone. I cannot help but wonder why we do not take this revelation as genuine. It is deeply ugly; the Pardoner is, by his own admission, "ful vicious" (459). But he also says that, in spite of his own laxity, he can effect moral change.

This is precisely the approach he takes to the other pilgrims at the tale's end. Dinshaw argues that the Pardoner "does not allow himself to be stripped and revealed . . . he won't allow himself to be known, won't reveal his intentions, his meaning, his truth. He expends much energy on keeping a veil on, on keeping himself screened from the gaze of others."[19] Except that he *does* strip away this veil and explain his *entente* multiple times. In inviting the other pilgrims to kiss his relics, *he only does what he tells them he does*. What can we make of this paradox, of this character who is both known as intimately as any pilgrim on the pilgrimage, but who is also shunned, laughed at, and rejected—this pilgrim whom critics often say we *cannot* know?

I submit that, in breaking the rules of social decorum, in saying what he should not, the Pardoner exposes a social underbelly that is perhaps easier not to think about or look at. He lays bare the discursive system on which he depends. Of course, saying what you shouldn't isn't necessarily to show vulnerability, porosity, or openness to influence—it can be merely another way to establish your place in the hierarchy, your dominance, your bounded identity. At a first glance, this kind of hierarchical assertion does seem to be what the Pardoner is after. His performance is good, after all: he is "lyk a clerk" (391) and tells "an hundred false japes moore" (394). His hands and "tonge goon so yerne / That it is joye to se my bisynesse" (398–99). These images are indeed metonymic, fragmentary, and unsettling. They also emphasize the Pardoner's skill, confirming what Chaucer-the-pilgrim tells us in *The General Prologue*: "ne was ther swich another pardoner" (*GP*, 693). The selfhood he exhibits in these moments is hardly porous; he reverts to a more brittle, rigid, narrow subjectivity. The Pardoner's description of his skill bespeaks a desire for imperviousness that hardly seems vulnerable or open.

And yet, it is precisely the Pardoner's admissions—his desire for connection and vulnerability—that undermine his simultaneous desire to be impervious. Even his body is at risk: at the opening of his *Prologue*, the Pardoner's elocution of his rituals enforces his authority, but they also suggest a certain precarity:

> First I pronounce whennes that I come,
> And thanne my bulles shewe I, alle and some.
> Oure lige lordes seel on my patente,
> That shewe I first, my body to warente,
> That no man be so boold, ne preest ne clerk,
> Me to destourbe of Cristes hooly werk.
> (*PardP*, 335–40)

[19]Dinshaw, *Chaucer's Sexual Poetics*, 157.

Here, the Pardoner admits to relying on these external signs in order to avoid bodily harm. What happens to our understanding of the Pardoner if we take this threat to be genuine? For, as the end of the tale shows, it *is* genuine: however we understand the Host's reaction and the Pardoner's own wrath, the physical threat is abundantly clear. Seen in this light, the ending of the tale is an object-lesson in the consequences of pulling back the veil and then expecting—as with the magic reality potion—that people will be accepting, forgiving, understanding. In his *Prologue*, the Pardoner comes close to suggesting that his wiles are necessary, that the world will damage him without them. After all, the buffered, violent world *does* threaten to damage us when we reveal who we are; porosity often comes with a cost.

In the Pardoner's altercation with the Host and the Knight's superficial peace-keeping, the end of *The Pardoner's Tale* gives us a sense of what that cost might be. After all, if we think about the Pardoner as genuine, we can imagine the Host's umbrage: the Pardoner is a "ful vicious" man who, "though myself be gilty in that synne, / Yet kan I maken oother folk to twynne / From avarice and soore to repente" (*PardP*, 429–31). The Pardoner shows everyone who he is, and in this moment he does what the pilgrims should probably have expected: he *says* that he is awful, and also that, regardless, he can make people leave sin behind. He is only inviting the Host to do the same. In this context, the Host is the veiled one, the character who cannot let go of his agential, bounded subjectivity, so much so that when the Pardoner invites him to—at least in part, by admitting that he is the most enveloped in sin—his response is violently defensive. By the end of *The Pardoner's Tale*, in other words, we see the possible consequences of admitting vulnerability in a bounded world, almost up to and including tearing apart the social fabric that constitutes such a world in the first place.

The Subject of Biography

Marion Turner
Oxford University

there are things to which subjectivity is blind and which only those on the outside *can* see.

(Zadie Smith)

we are, therefore I am.

(African proverb cited by Barbara Newman)

biography . . . makes us imagine and understand what it's like to be somebody else. That's why it matters.

(Hermione Lee)

VIRGINIA WOOLF'S *ORLANDO* is fantasy: it tells the story of an individual who is a young man in 1553 and still living—as a woman—in 1928. Orlando changes sex and gender, travels the world, and bestrides the centuries. Subtitled, "A Biography," it is also the story of Vita Sackville-West, closely tracking specific events, relationships, and legal battles in her life, and depicting her family history and her ancestral home in visceral and resonant detail. Woolf was fascinated by stretching the boundaries of genre, as we see in her reframing of the novel through extraordinary experiments such as *Mrs Dalloway*, *To The Lighthouse*, and *The Waves*. In *Orlando*, she writes a "biography" that she calls "truthful; but fantastic," a book that engages with "the common life which is the real life."[1] In *The Permeable Self*, Barbara Newman asks "what does it mean to be a person, a human self?"[2] *Orlando* is an answer to that question, an answer that

[1]Virginia Woolf, *A Writer's Diary*, ed. Leonard Woolf (New York: Harcourt Brace Jovanovich, 1953), 157; Virginia Woolf, *"A Room of One's Own" and "Three Guineas"* (Oxford: Oxford University Press, 1992), 148.

[2]Barbara Newman, *The Permeable Self: Five Medieval Relationships* (Philadelphia: University of Pennsylvania Press, 2021), 1.

Studies in the Age of Chaucer 46 (2024): 279–288

suggests that a person, a self, is porous and changing, affected by the long history of their family and genes, and by the physical environment in which they live. They are borne along in the slipstream of time, part of stories whose origin and ending they do not know. Their identity is open and expansive. Woolf also suggests that a person can only be understood or represented through innovative approaches, especially if that person is a woman, or is marginal in some other way.[3] This idea of a biography that is "truthful; but fantastic" makes a claim about how a life can best be written in a way that challenges the traditional cradle-to-grave biographies of the great men of history—in which context it is worth remembering that Woolf's father was a biographer and editor of the *Dictionary of National Biography*.

This exploration of the subject of biography encompasses both the topic (subject) of biography and the nature of the individual (subject) upon whom a biography might be focused. Biography—life-writing—has changed and expanded immensely over the last couple of decades. There are biographies of ideas (*Zero: The Biography of a Dangerous Idea*), of books (*The Ministry of Truth: The Biography of George Orwell's "1984"*), and of literary characters (*The Wife of Bath: A Biography*).[4] Both Chaucer and Shakespeare have been the subjects of place-centered biographies (*The Lodger: Shakespeare on Silver Street*; *Chaucer: A European Life*), and of biographies that focus on just one year (*1599*; *The Poet's Tale*).[5] More broadly, the boundaries between biography and fiction have become increasingly blurred in the current literary landscape. Some of the most skillful and intelligent contemporary novelists have crafted novels that are also known as fictional biographies, books that are built from the ground up on careful, detailed, archival and historical research, but which are avowedly works of fiction (*The Magician*, *The Master*, *A Place of Greater Safety*, the

[3]She writes passionately about the erasure from the historical record of the talents of women such as the imagined Judith, Shakespeare's sister. Woolf, *A Room of One's Own*, 60–64.

[4]Charles Seife and Matt Zeimer, *Zero: The Biography of a Dangerous Idea* (London: Souvenir Press, 2000); Dorian Lynskey, *The Ministry of Truth: The Biography of George Orwell's "1984"* (London: Picador, 2019); Marion Turner, *The Wife of Bath: A Biography* (Princeton: Princeton University Press, 2023).

[5]Charles Nicholl, *The Lodger: Shakespeare on Silver Street* (London: Allen Lane, 2007); Marion Turner, *Chaucer: A European Life* (Princeton: Princeton University Press, 2019); James Shapiro, *1599: A Year in the Life of William Shakespeare* (London: Faber and Faber, 2005); Paul Strohm, *The Poet's Tale: Chaucer and the Year that Made the "Canterbury Tales"* (London: Profile, 2014).

Wolf Hall trilogy).[6] Very recently, Victoria Mackenzie has penned a novel that attempts to reconstruct the meeting between Julian of Norwich and Margery Kempe, and Claire Gilbert has written *I, Julian*, a fictional autobiography of Julian of Norwich.[7] And perhaps the most startling development has been the vertiginous rise of autofiction, books that trample all over the boundary between fact and fiction, author and character, autobiography and novel; books that ostentatiously parade their authenticity and their unreliability (by authors including Sheila Heti, Rachel Cusk, and Karl Ove Knausgård).

In thinking about how to write a biography, it is vital to think about what a biographical subject is. We need to know what a person is before we can work out how to approach studying them. The historiography of understandings of medieval subjectivity is complex. While the old idea of the rise of the individual in the sixteenth century has been discredited in many different ways, recent and current thinking has focused not on pushing back the date for the discovery of subjectivity, but on ways of considering the subject that move beyond Enlightenment ideas of a bounded and enclosed self.

Late medieval authors frequently write about the problems of attempting to enclose the self in a bounded room, using the image of the threshold to stage a more connected idea of selfhood. Chaucer, in *The House of Fame*, describes his avatar as going home to his room, and closing himself off: he is sensorily deprived—unable to hear, speak, or see properly—and creatively deprived, unable to think or to write. He should, instead, be going to the doorway, to listen to his neighbours, who dwell almost at his door, and who can give him inspiration, described as "new things" (*HF*, 649–60). Writing a few decades later, Hoccleve describes his split, agonized self in detail (in his *Complaint*), imagining his wit and himself as separate entities (59), and telling us about his anxiety as he stays in his room, leaping in front of the mirror to try to comprehend how others see him (155 ff).[8] Hoccleve's understanding of selfhood is, however, relational:

[6]Colm Tóibín, *The Master* (London: Picador, 2004); Colm Tóibín, *The Magician* (London: Viking, 2021); Hilary Mantel, *A Place of Greater Safety* (London: Viking, 1992); Hilary Mantel, *Wolf Hall* (London: Fourth Estate, 2009).

[7]Victoria Mackenzie, *For Thy Great Pain Have Mercy on My Little Pain* (London: Bloomsbury, 2023); Claire Gilbert, *I, Julian* (London: Hodder and Stoughton, 2023). Although more overtly fictional, Maggie O'Farrell's *Hamnet* (London: Tinder Press, 2020) is another fascinating example.

[8]Thomas Hoccleve, *"My Compleinte" and Other Poems*, ed. Roger Ellis (Liverpool: Liverpool University Press, 2001). For further discussion see Matthew Boyd Goldie, "Psychosomatic

he sees himself as subjected to God, and as dependent on others. Most importantly, his healing process is bound up precisely with opening his door to his Friend figure, who enters into a dialogue with him (in the opening lines of *Dialogue with a Friend*). Both Chaucer and Hoccleve depict the doorway, and reaching across it to other human beings, as fundamental to productive selfhood. This understanding of selfhood as something that traverses thresholds and boundaries is the subject of Newman's *The Permeable Self*. She writes about the idea of "co-inherence" as a way of "forming the self through the other." Relationships are privileged over bounded subjects, and the self is fundamentally "socially embedded."[9]

If we accept that the boundaries between persons are fluid, that selfhood is constructed through relationships and "indwelling," what of the boundaries between a biological person and a fictional one? It is now over a decade since A. C. Spearing's influential book *Medieval Autographies* made a compelling case against thinking of the narratorial "I" of medieval poems as a purely fictional speaker.[10] For Spearing, the first-person speaker of medieval texts is not predominantly fictional, nor is that speaker identical with the biological person who created the text. Recently, Sebastian Sobecki has built on Spearing's work to argue for the idea that the authorial persona in medieval texts is "indexical," created for a specific audience who had direct access to the author. He writes that "Hoccleve's Thomas, Langland's Will, and Chaucer's Geoffrey are extensions of their writers' biological selves, animate simulacra that may depart in the mode of representation but not in the identity of the self they represent."[11]

When Newman tackles the issue of how the self is depicted in medieval texts, she focuses on the interplay between a universal self and an individual self, suggesting that in medieval autobiographical writing, the individual is an instance of the universal.[12] Medieval autobiography therefore "thwarts

Illness and Identity in London 1416–21: Hoccleve's Complaint and Dialogue with a Friend," *Exemplaria* 11 (1999): 23–52; Ethan Knapp, *The Bureaucratic Muse: Thomas Hoccleve and the Literature of Late Medieval England* (University Park: Pennsylvania State University Press, 2001); Lee Patterson, ""What is me?": Self and Society in the Poetry of Thomas Hoccleve," *SAC* 23 (2001): 437–70.

[9]Newman, *The Permeable Self*, 7, 13, 264.

[10]A. C. Spearing, *Medieval Autographies: The "I" of the Text* (Notre Dame: University of Notre Dame Press, 2012).

[11]Sebastian Sobecki, *Last Words: The Public Self and the Social Order in Late Medieval England* (Oxford: Oxford University Press, 2019), 13.

[12]On the relationship between the individual and the common voice, see in particular the influential work of Anne Middleton, especially "The Idea of Public Poetry in the Reign of Richard II," *Speculum* 53 (1978): 94–114.

readers who approach it with anachronistic genre expectations."[13] The self is always understood as co-inhering with others, and with a more universal idea of the self. This sounds surprisingly similar to a recent defence of autofiction by Nina Bouraoui: "The power of autofiction comes from its universality. When she tells her own story, the writer describes an expanded world, one that unites us all."[14] Newman's description of Augustine's *Confessions* focuses first on the text as seeming to be "the engaging life of an extraordinary character" but that proves to be something different as "the author persistently hints at a more generic self . . . the individual was meant all along to be an instance of the universal."[15] In medieval writing, seemingly fictional inventions (personae) turn out to be almost identical with the author; conversely, avowedly autobiographical depictions of the self turn out to be gesturing toward the universal and beyond the individual.[16]

In thinking biographically, then, we can find crucial evidence for authors' lives in their self-portrayals in seemingly fictional texts, but it is not always clear what to do with that evidence. If we read the prologue to *The Legend of Good Women*, for instance, the Chaucer of the poem is said to have written a long list of poems, which Chaucer certainly wrote, and is told to give the poem to the real queen, at one of the actual palaces of Eltham or Sheen. At the other end of the spectrum, we can be confident that Chaucer was not actually berated by the god of love and Alceste. In between these obvious facts and fictions is something much more complex: the idea of a poet condemned for antifeminism and judged by authority figures who impose a penance of writing a different kind of poem closely echoes what happens to Machaut in the *Judgment of the King of Navarre*. That does not mean, however, that nothing happened to Chaucer; indeed, it seems vanishingly unlikely that there was no debate about the gender politics of *Troilus and Criseyde* amongst his audience.[17]

[13]Newman, *The Permeable Self*, 268.

[14]Nina Bouraoui, "Top 10 Books of Autofiction," *Guardian*, September 16, 2020, https://www.theguardian.com/books/2020/sep/16/top-10-books-of-autofiction-all-men-want-to-know-by-nina-bouraoui (accessed June 17, 2024).

[15]Newman, *The Permeable Self*, 268. See also Eva von Contzen, "Why Medieval Literature Does Not Need the Concept of Social Minds: Exemplarity and Collective Experience," *Narrative* 23 (2015): 140–53.

[16]The fourteenth century was a moment of particular literary self-consciousness and an autobiographical turn of sorts; see for example Lawrence de Looze, *Pseudo-Autobiography in the Fourteenth Century: Juan Ruiz, Guillaume de Machaut, Jean Froissart, and Geoffrey Chaucer* (Gainsville: University Press of Florida, 1997).

[17]For further discussion of the politics and positioning of the prologue to *The Legend of Good Women* see Turner, *Chaucer: A European Life*, 342–62.

The problem of antifeminism in literature links directly to the subject of biography. The examples that have been given so far in this essay are of male authors: Chaucer, Hoccleve, Langland, and Gower all create personae that are closely connected to their biological selves. While we know little about Langland, there are very many documents about the other three, especially Chaucer, that can help us to reconstruct their lives in detail. They lived bureaucratic lives that were carefully recorded: we know how long Chaucer spent in Italy because he was paid by the day; we know what clothes he was bought by Elizabeth, countess of Ulster; we know what ransom was paid for him; we know how many men and horses he had within him in Navarre.[18] We do not have the same density of material about medieval women—so what might be productive ways of thinking about the female subject of biography?

It is profoundly important to keep in mind the fundamental connection between books and female bodies. The Wife of Bath forcefully reminds us that she was "beten for a book" (*WBP*, 712).[19] Christine de Pizan tells us an analogous story of a woman who was beaten by her husband after he read *The Romance of the Rose*.[20] As Georges Duby writes, "human beings orient their behaviour not toward real events and circumstances, but rather to their image of them."[21] Men treat women in certain ways partly because of what they have read in books. Women's experiences are shaped by, as Woolf writes, the spectre of Professor von X, "writing his monumental work entitled *The Mental, Moral and Physical Inferiority of the Female Sex*."[22] Women's historical experience is shaped by textuality.

Furthermore, when we try to recover historical experience, we are always working through fictions: all the more so as women's experiences are being filtered through forms and genres that have, for the most part,

[18]For the life records see Martin Crow and Clair Olson (eds.), *Chaucer Life Records* (Oxford: Clarendon Press, 1966); for discussion see Turner, *Chaucer: A European Life*.

[19]*The Riverside Chaucer*, gen. ed. Larry D. Benson, 3rd ed. (Oxford: Oxford University Press, 1987).

[20]See Turner, *The Wife of Bath*, 18.

[21]Georges Duby, "Histoire sociale et idéologie des sociétés," in Jacques Le Goff and P. Nora (eds.), *Faire de l'histoire* (Paris: Gallimard, 1974), 1:147–68 (148). Sebastian Sobecki has suggested that this kind of relationship between text and reality can be intentional, commenting that "vernacular autobiographical texts are not disinterested recordings of reality; instead, these narratives construct hypernaturalistic models of reality which they hope to see translated into life. That is so because the adjustment of reality is a fundamental medieval literary convention." Sebastian Sobecki, "Authorized Realities: The *Gesta Romanorum* and Thomas Hoccleve's Poetics of Autobiography," *Speculum* 98 (2023): 536–58 (558).

[22]Woolf, *A Room of One's Own*, 39.

been invented by men.[23] When we read a medieval will or petition "by" a woman, it has almost always been penned by a man and has usually been phrased according to preexisting, male-authored forms. *The Book of Margery Kempe*, a famous and rich example of early female life-writing, was dictated by Kempe to male scribes. It bears the traces of multiple voices, and the character of Margery within the Book is clearly both individual and general, reflecting specific experiences and also representing templates of experiences (such as the "saint's" experience). She understood her selfhood as particular and universal, experiential and rooted in books. In reading this book and thinking about Margery Kempe's life, we must think about the interactions between lived experience and authority, bodies and books, individuals and communities. The example of the publication of her book is also a typical illustration of the falsification of women's experience in history: not only was her text radically cut, but the printer Henry Pepwell asserted that Margery was an anchoress.[24] Similarly, in the fifteenth century, William Worcester adapted one of Christine de Pizan's texts, framing it with the story that Christine had been a patron, not a writer, and a life-long nun, not a wife, widow, and mother.[25] Women's experiences have often been forced into patterns that they do not really fit.

One way to respond to the problems of evidence and representation is to innovate, to try to think of different ways of accessing and retelling women's stories. That was, in part, what I wanted to do in *The Wife of Bath: A Biography*. The first half of the book weaves together the traces of historical women's lives with the ideas about women that circulated in texts, painting a composite picture of what it was like to be a woman in the later Middle Ages and how women were perceived and imagined. That approach foregrounds the idea of the self as socially inflected, and also as shaped by the imaginative structures that surround individuals. It moves away from the idea of a forensic examination of the depths of one person's consciousness. Such an approach is particularly appropriate for thinking about female subjectivity. As Holly A. Crocker has noted, the model of subjectivity that

[23]See Natalie Zemon Davis's seminal account of the literary qualities of documentary texts, *Fiction in the Archives* (Stanford: Stanford University Press, 1987). See also Hayden White, *The Content of the Form: Narrative Discourse and Historical Representation* (Baltimore, Md.: Johns Hopkins University Press, 1987).

[24]For discussion see Karma Lochrie, *Margery Kempe and Translations of the Flesh* (Philadelphia: University of Pennsylvania Press, 1994), 220–25.

[25]William Worcester, *The Boke of Noblesse*, ed. J. G. Nichols (London: Roxburghe Club, 1860), 54 n. 151.

is "rooted in the body, connected to others and involved in fostering, not governing intimate relationships that cross all boundaries of individual selfhood" is historically associated with women.[26]

My "biography" of the Wife of Bath is also an interrogation of what literary character is. In suggesting that a character can be a subject of biography, the book moves into highly experimental terrain, crossing many centuries to explore this character's afterlife in all kinds of texts and contexts. Biography becomes a generative genre that allows for a wide range of cultural, historical, and literary analysis, a genre that explores communities, horizons of expectation and interpretation, and diachronic change. This aspect of my biography eschews the subject as an individual, suggesting that biography can be stretched to think about lives and life-writing in myriad ways, a different angle on "the common life." Woolf's revolutionary idea of the biography as "truthful; but fantastic" remains an inspiration.

In his biography of Margery Kempe, Anthony Bale describes a visit to Mintlyn, a village that Margery Kempe visited in about 1418–20. He compares the ruins there to *The Book of Margery Kempe*; they are "partial memorials" that "allow us to glimpse something unique in the past but also to fill the gaps with our projections and desires."[27] He thus emphasizes the role of the desire and imagination of the reader, or biographer. In a gesture, perhaps, to some of the ways in which we might approach a life in formally appropriate and innovative ways, his biography is punctuated by segments called "interloges," or interludes: short, deep dives into particular moments in Kempe's life. The very idea of the "interloge" (a play, an entertainment, a performance) also foregrounds for us the performativity and unreliability of the evidence of a medieval—or perhaps any—life. We all imagine our experiences as parts of a narrative, so anyone's memories or versions of their lives are inevitably fictionalized.

There is, indeed, a fascinating case to be made for embracing the imagination in biographical thinking. A radical recent biographical genre is the fictionalized biography/the biographical novel. Quite different from much historical fiction, such books are based on meticulous historical research into specific people, and often seek to tell truths about their lives through a reimagining of their subjectivities. This is dangerous and

[26] Holly A. Crocker, *The Matter of Virtue: Women's Ethical Action from Chaucer to Shakespeare* (Philadelphia: University of Pennsylvania Press, 2019), 24.

[27] Anthony Bale, *Margery Kempe: A Mixed Life* (London: Reaktion, 2021), 209.

difficult territory: popular culture is full of examples where this approach has proved controversial or misleading (most famously the Netflix series *The Crown*). Such work might even seem to deny that there is a crucial distinction between things that happened and things that are made up, a distinction that most thinkers are acutely aware of preserving in our world of Holocaust denial, fake news, and "alternative facts."

When the fictionalized biography is acknowledged as fiction, however, it can often yield biographical truths. There is a scene, for example, in *A Place of Greater Safety* (Hilary Mantel's novel about the French Revolution), in which the teenage Lucille Duplessis walks in on the revolutionary Camille Desmoulins kissing her mother, Annette.[28] This scene is fiction. It is factually true, however, that Desmoulins was ten years older than Lucille, was a friend of her mother's for years, and that she had a secret crush on him for a long time (her journal survives) before they married. The imagined scene conveys that Lucille was going through adolescence when her mother was young, sociable, and attractive; that the man that she herself was in love with and was to marry was older and much more worldly; that his interests in her household were not, initially, about her; that the power dynamic in their relationship was complex. The scene makes us think not only about the fact of their age gap, but about how entering into a relationship with a man who was far more experienced and who was associated with her parents created a particular kind of tension and vulnerability—which seems particularly important to understand when we know that this relationship led to her early death at the guillotine.

Similarly, the densely imagined scenes in Colm Tóibín's biographical fictions reveal truths. In *The Magician*, he imagines Thomas Mann's feelings shortly after fleeing Nazi Germany for the USA. As Mann is driven through the night, he looks at the suburbs and houses, and cannot understand them. He thinks:

> If this were Germany, there would be a church and a square, some narrow streets and other streets that had been widened. Houses with attic windows. There would be old stoves in the kitchens and tiled stoves in the living rooms. . . . The past would be evoked by the names of the streets, or by the names of families, and continuity by the bells that rang softly, as they had for centuries, to make the passing of each quarter-hour. He would give anything if the car could turn and enter noiselessly into one of those squares, a space enriched by the work of

[28] Mantel, *A Place of Greater Safety*, 90–91.

Gutenberg or the writings of Luther or the images made by Dürer. Enriched by a thousand years of trade, a stability broken at times by plagues or wars, by the clattering of cavalry horses and the boom of cannon, until a time of treaties when peace was restored.[29]

We do not know if Mann had these thoughts. But this scene powerfully conjures up for us the fact that Mann was an exile, an immigrant, and a man whose sense of self was deeply rooted in German culture. It evokes the fact that he was steeped in the history and culture of one part of the world, and knew very little of the history and culture of his new world. It reminds us of the minute details of topography and architecture that are so striking when one travels between a European country and the USA, and what those differences signify. It does not matter whether Mann actually thought about cavalry horses or Dürer: the scene shows us, with lyrical intensity, the experience of exile, an experience that was central to Mann's life. The scene *feels* true.[30]

Authors such as Mantel and Tóibín have taken the genres of the novel and biography and created something new. We need robustly to maintain the importance of acknowledging the differences between lived events and imagined ones. But there are also times when we can access truths—particularly the truths of subjectivity—through our imaginations. Biography is today making claims to be an agile and changing genre, a genre that can be generative of new ways of comprehending the past—and the subject.

[29]Tóibín, *The Magician*, 228.

[30]There is a risk of seeming here to endorse "truthiness"—using one's intuition or opinion to assert truth itself without regard to facts or logic. That is certainly not my intent: I am gesturing to episodes that are avowedly *not* factually true but that tell us something truthful about, for example, structures of feeling.

REVIEWS

JANE BEAL, ed. *Becoming the "Pearl"-Poet: Perceptions, Connections, Receptions.* Lanham: Lexington Books, 2022. Pp. xii, 292. $120.00 hardback; $42.99 paperback; $40.50 e-book.

In the introduction to this edited collection, Jane Beal notes that, despite the ever-growing body of scholarship on the texts attributed to the *Pearl*-poet, there has been no book-length collection of scholarly essays on them published since *A Companion to the Gawain-Poet* over twenty years ago (1).[1] It is this gap that *Becoming the "Pearl"-Poet: Perceptions, Connections, Receptions* seeks to address. The collection of essays is presented as a resource for undergraduate and graduate students as well as those who teach the four poems of Cotton Nero A.x and Harley 2250's *Saint Erkenwald.* The volume thus essentially argues for an expanded *Pearl*-poet canon informed by shared authorship theories linking the five poems together: a choice that aligns well with its interest in the ways that scholarship on these poems has contributed to shifting ideas about the *Pearl*-poet over time (1–2). *Becoming the "Pearl"-Poet* includes sixteen chapters in addition to the acknowledgments, introductory chapter, index, and contributor biographies. These chapters are organized into three sections, each corresponding with a term in the book's subtitle.

The first section, "Perceptions," includes five chapters: one for each poem attributed to the *Pearl*-poet. Beal's chapter begins the section by placing *Pearl* in conversation with medieval *mappaemundi*, arguing that "the Dreamer travels imaginatively across the face of a world-map" over the course of the poem (14). This reading includes discussion of the *mappamundi*'s "political, educational, and contemplative" functions to contextualize to the poem's engagement with the genre (15). Next, Corey Owen reads the key narrative sequences of *Cleanness* in terms of concupiscible vice, arguing that their shared focus "suggests the influence of *temperantia*, the virtue that governs the appetitive, or concupiscible, faculty of the soul," and that the poem's approach to taxonomies of

[1]Derek Brewer and Jonathan Gibson, eds., *A Companion to the Gawain-Poet* (Cambridge: D. S. Brewer, 1997).

virtues and vices draws out "the interconnected nature of the faculties of the soul" (45–46). M. W. Brumit takes a similar interest in such taxonomies, contending that *Patience* reflects a "platonic understanding of the unity of Virtue" so that patience is "an accident of unified Virtue." This unified view of Virtue, Brumit argues, informs the prologue's representation of the final Beatitude in terms of "steering one's heart" and the related nautical metaphor borne out in Jonah's exemplum, resulting in the message "that patience—and indeed the whole of Virtue—is letting Christ be one's helmsman" (67). Moving to the final Cotton Nero poem, Mickey Sweeney explores the ways in which *Sir Gawain and the Green Knight* (*SGGK*) engages subversively with the genre of romance in order to "critique fourteenth-century foundations of authority—Church and State" (87). Finally, Michael D. C. Drout, Jonathan B. Gerkin, and Scott Kleinman address the authorship question at the heart of *Erkenwald*'s proposed relationship to the Cotton Nero poems, and the Cotton Nero poems to one another. After reviewing scholarship on the authorship question, Drout, Gerkin, and Kleinman share the results of "computer-assisted 'Lexomic' methods" that allow for analysis of vocabulary distribution across the five poems, resulting in the observation that while *Erkenwald* more closely resembles *Cleanness*, *Patience*, and *SGGK* in "overall vocabulary distribution" than does *Pearl*, "all five poems are more similar to each other than they are to other Middle English texts" (100–101).

The next section, "Connections," adopts a topic-driven approach that draws the five poems into conversation with one another. Ethan Campbell begins by considering authorship. After addressing the authorship question and related theories introduced in the previous chapter (including various attempts to identify the poet by name), Campbell goes on to explore how careful analysis of the poems might yield biographical clues about the poet. In the following chapter, Elizabeth Allen applies an ecocritical lens to the poems, examining from various vantage points how "ecocriticism puts the human concerns of the *Pearl*-poet in a larger moral context, one that highlights the precarity of earthly survival of all kinds, the limits of human agency, and the vitality of the non-human world" (128). Moving to material culture, Jonathan Quick surveys a range of objects represented in the poems in order to "examin[e] the poet's presentation and utilization of these material objects as both descriptive embellishments and didactic symbols conveying divine and moral messages to the poet's audiences" (145). Kimberly Jack follows with a chapter on sartorial adornment as semiotic system, detailing how the poet's tendency to "continually 'dres[s] and undres[s] his characters'" reflects "how power dynamics and the ongoing negotiation of meaning challenge the stability of what is signified sartorially" (156). Kristin Bovaird-Abbo, in the only "Connections" chapter focusing on a single Cotton Nero poem, explores potential reasons for replacing the griffin heraldic device associated with Gawain with a pentangle in *SGGK*. Grace Hamman concludes the section with a turn toward pastoral theology, placing "the poet's interest in human limitation" in conversation with relevant teaching in contemporary didactic, contemplative, and penitential texts (183).

The final section, "Receptions," shifts attention to various engagements that have contributed to the poet's—and poems'—ongoing processes of becoming. It opens with Joel Fredell's reading of the twelve miniatures illustrating Cotton Nero A.x as responses to the poems they depict. This chapter includes fourteen figures in total, including all twelve manuscript miniatures (though, unfortunately, duplication of Figure 12.11's *SGGK* miniature in Figure 12.10 means that one *Patience* miniature goes missing). David K. Coley next presents arguments for and against a northwest Midlands provenance for the *Pearl* manuscript and considers "the critical possibilities that open when we decenter the poems of Cotton Nero A.x from a region long considered their first textual environment" (224). Shifting to religious contexts, Nancy Ciccone discusses "the offices of the Church, its social centrality, economic impact, and theological controversies" at the time of the poems' composition (237). Next, Kenna L. Olsen provides a detailed survey of the poems' modern English translations and touches briefly on adaptation of *SGGK* in children's literature, opera and theater, and television and film. John M. Bowers concludes the section with discussion of the poems' medieval and modern audiences, from scribes, the illustrator, possible patrons, and other early audiences (including the *Grene Knight* poet) to collectors, antiquarians, editors, translators, and scholars.

In all, this collection of essays provides a solid overview of contexts (literary, historical, cultural, theological, material, and reception) that will prove illuminating for students of these texts. It also raises provocative questions sure to spark lively discussion within the classroom and beyond. The choice to include *Erkenwald* along with the Cotton Nero poems is a generative one, along with the clear attempt throughout the book's chapters to balance attention among the five poems rather than allowing *Pearl* and *SGGK* to dominate. While efforts to do this are mixed in terms of success (I noticed rather shoehorned references to *Erkenwald* here and there, for example), they are nonetheless refreshing, and they are suggestive of the ways in which perspectives on authorship and canonicity have shaped, and continue to shape, scholarship on the poems. There is some room for the volume to draw more attention to the implications and value of its grounding assumptions and choices, and to distinguish its approach from what has been done before. Rather than the lengthy chapter summaries that make up the bulk of the introductory chapter, I would have preferred to read more about the collection's intended interventions vis-à-vis the poems' scholarly reception and uses in the classroom. Questions I am left pondering include: What do we gain and lose from approaching these five poems as the works of a single poet (indeed, as single-authored poems)? How does the volume's project of placing these poems in conversation and distributing attention among them drive its content and critical approaches? And are there productive reimaginings or expansions of the "*Pearl*-poet" canon that open up if authorship is set aside as the primary determiner of membership?

A small quibble: I did notice some typographical and formatting inconsistencies while reading this otherwise fine volume. For instance, the presentation of Middle English block quotations with accompanying modern English translations varies across chapters. Throughout Chapter 1, yogh is represented by what looks very much like a number 3 in quotations of *Pearl* (I spotted a few more "3-yogh"s in Chapter 11). And while modern English translations are typically presented along with Middle English quotations (a sound decision, given the book's pedagogical aims), they sometimes go missing.

These minor issues aside, *Becoming the "Pearl"-Poet* is a valuable resource for students and teachers of the five poems it examines. What's more, these chapters collectively advocate for increased attention to those poems attributed to the *Pearl*-poet that have traditionally received less attention in pedagogical and scholarly contexts compared to *Pearl* and *SGGK*, pointing to rich possibilities for the classroom and beyond.

Amber Dunai
Texas A&M University—Central Texas

Alastair Bennett. *Preaching and Narrative in "Piers Plowman."* Oxford: Oxford University Press, 2023. Pp. xvi, 260. $100.00 hardback and e-book.

Alastair Bennett's *Preaching and Narrative in "Piers Plowman"* takes as its focus "Langland's sustained, critical, and imaginative engagement with sermons and with the forms they provide for making sense of lived experience" (219). Langland, Bennett argues, was profoundly affected by and invested in the contemporary discourse of preaching but in ways that are more complex than have heretofore been explored. To make his point, Bennett draws heavily on the narrative theory of Paul Ricoeur, particularly Ricoeur's application of Aristotle's concept of *muthos* ("emplotment") to Augustine's account of the soul's relationship to time. Emplotment "mediates between the time of the soul and the time of the world" (27), as Bennett describes, enabling self-knowledge and ethical action. The preacher's task is "to extend and elaborate the work of emplotment" so that biblical narrative "continues to unfold before the listener, reshaping the listener's horizon of expectations" and opening up new possibilities for ethical action (28). Bennett finds Riceour's thinking about the preacher's vocation to be similar to Langland's own and to Langland's narrative work in *Piers Plowman*. *Preaching and Narrative* explores efforts at emplotment by various preacher-figures in the poem and by the dreamer himself, who struggles to makes sense of his experiences in the context of both his own life and eschatological history. Bennett suggests, moreover, that the discourse of preaching is what enables the poem's self-theorization: *Piers Plowman* is not merely indebted to sermon literature but also "imagines forms of poetry that might extend, subvert, and transcend the practice of contemporary preachers" (7).

After an introduction that presents the book's thesis and theoretical framework, the subsequent chapters and coda examine Langland's engagements with the discourse of preaching in different moments of *Piers Plowman*. The first three chapters consider the role of sermons in the public sphere. Chapter 1 focuses on preaching at two major turning points in public life ("axial moments," in Ricoeur's terminology): coronation (in the B-version Prologue, when the appearance of a king prompts brief sermon-like utterances by a lunatic, angel, and goliard) and the Incarnation of Christ (about which Conscience preaches in the seventh vision). These preachers' efforts at emplotment "locate their listeners in an interpreted present that is also part of a shared, public history, establishing a narrative discourse in which the *commune* can express their aspirations for good governance and articulate their mutual responsibilities to one another under a just and merciful law" (30). Bennett argues that these representations in *Piers Plowman* ultimately reveal Langland's lack of confidence in the long-term efficacy of occasional sermons for guiding royal governance. The book's second chapter examines how the preacher's work not only motivates but also, importantly, has the potential to sustain reform efforts. Reason's public sermon in the poem's second vision effectively motivates subsequent penitential action on the half-acre but, like the sermons considered in Chapter 1, does not promote sustained spiritual effort. A different kind of preacher is required (Piers), who provides ongoing spiritual guidance and pastoral care. Chapter 3 then addresses the negative effects of self-interested preaching that promotes sinful *curiositas*, neglecting the spiritual welfare of the community and the kind of pastoral labor that Piers exemplified earlier. Study speaks out against such preachers, one of whom appears later in the poem at Conscience's dinner, an occasion that gives Langland an opportunity to imagine alternative sorts of preaching that distinguish between essential and frivolous knowledge and manifest in the virtuous minstrelsy performed at the dinner by Patience and Conscience himself.

The final two chapters of the book take an inward turn to consider how sermons impact the listener's self-knowledge. Chapter 4 examines a sequence of interrelated scenes in which the dreamer interacts with interlocutors who either preach to him directly (Holy Church and Scripture) or prompt him to make narrative sense of his personal life by drawing upon his past experiences of preaching (Ymaginatif and Kynde). Holy Church introduces Will to the "self-constancy" that can result from recalling his own baptismal promises and the experience of catechesis in the church, which gave him resources "to perceive the self as a narrative whole" (155). His learning at this point is slight, however, and Scripture soon rebukes him for his lack of self-knowledge, causing him to fall into an inner dream where, for a time, he remains lost in "the pleasures of the phenomenological present" (164). Only when he recalls his early church commitments by insisting on his intention to be buried in his baptismal church does he begin to recognize that the disparate events in his own life resonate with what Ricoeur would call "discordant concordance" (166). Will is further helped by Ymaginatif, who enables him to find value in the capacity of preaching to bring clerical knowledge ("clergie") to bear on lived experience ("kynde"). Ymaginatif also prompts the dreamer to ponder whether poetic composition could potentially be "a vital counterpart to clerical instruction" (179) in its ability to facilitate self-understanding. Ultimately, Kynde helps Will overcome his "absorption in the conditions of his present moment" (180) by entering Unity (returning to church) and learning to love. Chapter 5 focuses on how Will's conversation about charity with Anima takes his self-understanding to the next level so that his sense of self is contextualized not merely in relation to the trajectory of his own life but also "in relation to the central events of eschatological history" (200). Such self-understanding is strongly promoted in *Piers Plowman*, as Bennett shows, yet it is also problematized in Anima's account of Muhammad and the dove, which offers a reminder that the universal history that provides a life-context for the dreamer is "not universally available or universally accepted" (219). The book's brief coda, which focuses on the Harrowing of Hell, reads *Piers Plowman*'s Christ as performing an extended act of emplotment that brings together disparate narratives of divine justice and mercy. Christ's work makes possible "a new interpretation of history" that is of definitional importance for Christianity (232).

Bennett draws upon a wide range of sermon texts as he works through readings of *Piers Plowman* that repeatedly illustrate how our understanding of Langland's engagement with preaching can be helpfully illuminated by this rich literary context. Bennett considers the angel's speech from the Prologue as it appears copied at the end of a sermon on Thomas Becket by Henry Harclay in Lambeth Palace, MS 61; sermons by Thomas Brinton and an anonymous preacher that inform Reason's interpretation of natural disasters; sermons by William Taylor and Richard Alkerton that exemplify the problems of self-interested preaching; sermons by Robert Rypon that show how baptismal vows, recalled later, can provide a framework for construing life as an integrated whole; the prologue to Robert of Gretham's Anglo-Norman sermon cycle, in which a tree's falling fruit is a figure for "the effects of preacherly exegesis" (33); and Thomas Spofford's Annunciation sermon, which "shows a late medieval preacher with no necessary knowledge of *Piers Plowman* combining elements from the exegetical tradition in a way that resembles Langland's poem" (224). Extended discussions of these works as well as numerous references to others ground the book in the lived discourse of preaching in Langland's England.

Preaching and Narrative in "Piers Plowman" is a dense, carefully organized, thesis-driven monograph that offers important contributions to the study of late medieval sermons, narrative theory, and *Piers Plowman*. Bennett's methodology, which considers preaching as performance instead of primarily in relation to the principles of composition outlined in contemporary *artes praedicandi*, reveals that Langland has much to teach us about how sermons in late medieval England made interventions in the social world by "reconfiguring their listeners' understanding of the present time as part of a larger, interpreted story" (17). Additionally, Bennett's illumination of the poem's alternative imaginings of preacherly work puts pressure on ideas about the actual public efficacy of sermon discourse in Langland's world, especially in relation to royal policy. The book also offers an excellent case study of what medieval literature can offer to critical theory: Bennett not only applies Ricoeur's theory to Langland's poem but also uses *Piers Plowman* to extend Ricoeur's ideas about emplotment, particularly emplotment that emerges in "difficult, contested circumstances" (220). Bennett demonstrates that narrative meaning must be co-produced through the cooperative efforts of speakers and listeners; it is fundamentally ethical labor that is fraught with difficulties. Finally, *Preaching and Narrative in "Piers Plowman"* does important work in redirecting Langland scholarship away from attention to the poem's discontinuous qualities, an orientation that has been dominant in recent decades. For Langlandians, Bennett's most important intervention is his theoretically astute demonstration of how *Piers Plowman* dazzlingly dramatizes the recuperation of its own fragmentariness into narrative meaning.

JENNIFER SISK
University of Vermont

NANCY MASON BRADBURY. *Rival Wisdoms: Reading Proverbs in the "Canterbury Tales."* University Park: Pennsylvania State University Press, 2024. Pp. x, 220. $104.95.

This study focuses on the much-neglected verbal form of the proverb, which, Bradbury observes, "had a broader frame of reference" (17) in medieval and early modern culture when it was taken very seriously as a valuable form of wisdom. In a helpful, defining move Bradbury argued in an essay in *Exemplaria* in 2015 that the proverb is best understood as an "embedded microgenre," and this is a term that she uses profitably here to bound her subject.[1] The categorization does not help distinguish the "sentence" from the proverb, or in determining whether all verbal forms described as "proverbs" were really proverbial (as Bradbury notes, many of the proverbs that B. J. Whiting identified in Chaucer often cannot be found in any earlier text). But, in another deft move (or moves really), Bradbury says that her main interest is not the proverb as a transhistorical form, but, rather, only those formulations that were "proverbs" in "the judgment of contemporary witnesses" (16–17). The difficulty of reconstructing that judgment is solved by what she calls Thomas Speght's "proverb-marked" revision of his edition of Chaucer's works in 1602 (the first edition was published in 1598) where every line or passage Speght judged to be a proverb is marked with a manicule in the margin (4). As Bradbury puts it neatly, "Speght is my premodern witness" (18).

Bradbury does look at some modern definitions or discussions of proverbs to frame her own analysis. She devotes a fascinating few pages to "the perception of proverbiality" (the phrase is from the anthropologist Shirley Arora) and the quality of "proverbiousness" (in the words of Tom Shippey) that make a saying's history irrelevant (21). She also notes that Rosalie Colie saw proverbs as a "a 'set' on the world" (32); Kenneth Burke said proverbs "make things happen" (23); and Walter Benjamin thought that proverbs "transform a situation" (28). It is part of the project of the book to give all of these views some purchase on its analysis, and chapter by chapter, that analysis is intricate. But it is finally Benjamin's sense that proverbs have a "transformational power" (158) that is the book's overarching theme. Bradbury's range of reference is wide throughout, although the book focuses on the *Canterbury Tales* alone, and, among the *Tales*, primarily on five exemplary—proverb-heavy—narratives: *The Reeve's Tale*, *The Wife of Bath's Prologue* and *Tale* (treated here as two distinct works with different views of how to use proverbs), *The Tale of Melibee*, and *The Parson's Tale*. In the book's incisive conclusion, *The Nun's Priest's Tale* figures large in a description of the "role of proverbs in the implicit *ars poetica* built into the *Canterbury Tales*" (158).

[1]Nancy Mason Bradbury, "The Proverb as Embedded Microgenre in Chaucer and *The Dialogue of Solomon and Marcolf*," *Exemplaria* 27 (2015): 55–72.

While Bradbury begins by exploring the substantial differences in attitudes to proverbs in the early modern period and in our own, she is much more interested in the differences in such attitudes internal to premodern culture. Reginald Pecock's vigorous attempt to refute the proverbial view that "the greatest clerks are not the wisest men" is a nodal point for her account of the conflict between a learned and scholarly wisdom and the "other wisdoms" that are captured in, and disseminated by, proverbs (49). The surprise in this distinction is that it is not, for Bradbury, the clerkly wisdom of, say, Augustine, Boethius, or Aquinas on the one side and the humble proverb on the other, but, rather, proverbs alone that constitute the whole field on which clerks and "cherles" competed for primacy. At times proverbs assist one side of this debate more than another (the Canon's Yeoman's description of his master involves a churlish use of proverbs, while the friar's copious proverbs in *The Summoner's Tale*, by contrast, demonstrate a clerkly investment), but, in the main, for Bradbury, proverbs were "useful in mediating situations of acute social tension across class lines" (74). In *The Miller's Tale*, the clerk Nicholas dupes the carpenter John because his persuasions are "proverb-assisted" (65) but, as *The Reeve's Tale* intensifies this contest between clerks and "cherles," proverbs are distributed evenly and guide or justify violent trickery and debate on both sides.

Bradbury also describes a more hopeful use of proverbs. It is true that the Wife of Bath is both "proverb-disputing and proverb-dispensing" (85) as she argues against an antifeminism also rich with proverbs, and, here, Bradbury emphasizes "the pain, sadness, and deformation of the self that result from exposure to [a] twisted proverbial 'wisdom'" (117). But she also sees *The Wife of Bath's Tale* as a "rescripting project" that offers a "glimpse of how proverbs might function in a discursive world somewhat less misogynist" (86). Bradbury notes too how Proserpina in *The Merchant's Tale* and Prudence in *The Tale of Melibee* use proverbs to dismantle the view that "Amonges a thousand men yet foonde I *oon*, / But of women alle foond I *noon*" (*MerT*, 2246–48; original emphasis). In its potent response to that aggression, *The Wife of Bath's Tale* not only couches the wisdom the knight acquires in the form of a proverb, but shows the old woman offering a proverb-rich "point-by-point scholarly refutation" of the knight's disparaging view of her (121). In the end, the Wife of Bath rehabilitates the proverb as a useful tool for improving the position of women not least "as a means to transforming masculine behavior" (123).

The extent to which *The Tale of Melibee* is really a proverb collection in the guise of a narrative is thrown into relief by *The Tale of Sir Thopas*, which is the only tale in which Speght marks no proverbs at all. In the place of story, however, *The Tale of Melibee* provides something like a drama of citation in Melibeus's "erratic veering between affirming and rejecting the counsels of Prudence" (141). Bradbury spends some time working through the efficacy of that counsel with due attention to Lee Patterson's view that the near failure of Prudence's advice near the end of the tale, when Melibee ignores all her wisdom and still seems intent on a violent revenge, is "devastating" (145). It is here that Bradbury notes how all collections of proverbs as well as arguments that marshal them tend to expose just how contradictory the wisdom condensed in proverbs often is. In this way she acknowledges the inherent tension in any study of proverbs (like this one) that, in showing how proverbs can always be recruited to assist any side of an argument, actually threaten the proposition that they contain or constitute anything one might call "wisdom." In the face of such a constitutive confusion it is probably not enough to say that "diversity is strength" because "conflicting counsels are inevitable" and a "reader is meant to select from among them" (150), since Bradbury does not also say *how* that choice is to be made.

But this is probably an inevitability in any study of proverbs rather than a fault, since the problem is so deeply baked into the condition of the form and its use, and the book's conclusion is certainly wise as it takes on the problem of proverbs used to try to fix the interpretation of a narrative, contrasting the Monk's attempt to "force a single *sentence* on his succession of long tragedies" (166, emphasis Bradbury's) and the way the Nun's Priest's open-ended injunction to "Taketh the fruyt, and lat the chaf be stille" (*NPT*, 3443) frees the reader to decide what "fruyt" and "chaf" are. It is this last example, in fact, that might best sum up Bradbury's general view in this impressive survey of the rhetorical use and cultural position of proverbs in premodern England: that, despite the fixed form of this microgenre, and the fixity of the wisdom that proverbs impart, in a society so alive to their use and agile in their deployment, the proverb is finally freeing, allowing anyone reading or citing them to partake of whatever proverbs "offer the most help" (173).

CHRISTOPHER CANNON
Johns Hopkins University

CHRISTOPHER CANNON and STEVEN JUSTICE, eds. *The Sound of Writing.* Baltimore: Johns Hopkins University Press, 2023. Pp. x, 267. $114.95 hardback; $54.95 paperback.

Thomas Cable has dubbed metrics the science of "How to Find Rhythm on a Piece of Paper."[1] Although, surprisingly, Cable's essay is never cited in Christopher Cannon and Steven Justice's new edited collection, his title defines the scope and aim of *The Sound of Writing.* The rhythm in question might be of a line of poetry, or of birdsong, or even of the buzzing of bees, but each of the ten essays, with different retrieval equipment and various results, mounts a search expedition.

This collection germinated from a conference held in Baltimore in 2019. Capacious and rigorous, consistently provocative, and featuring leading lights of the respective disciplines, Cannon and Justice's book is destined to become the study of record on its topic. Its organization is eccentric. There are no sections. Eight deep dives by premodernists, arranged neither chronologically nor by discipline, are punctuated at irregular intervals by two highly speculative interventions by modernists. (The editors float the idea that the premodernist essays are in ascending order of methodological self-consciousness [16], but this is not the case.) To generalize, the premodernists are engaged upon search-and-rescue operations, dredging sound out of written records from the past, while the modernists rethink the feasibility of this. The two groups give the impression of conducting separate conversations. Moreover, the two modernists are not talking to each other, either. Where Meredith Martin's "The Writing of Sound" polemicizes against the use of received terminology to describe the sounds of historical poetries, Christopher Hasty's "Writing Reading Rhythm" strives to build a "temporalizing" (233), processual theory of free-verse rhythm with scarcely any reference to prior work on free verse or rhythm—and no indication of how his theory would handle poetic meter, which is at issue in all other chapters (including Martin's). A target of Martin's critique, the assumption that prosody patterns language and throws into relief nuances of pronunciation, is fundamental to the other contributors' work (including Hasty's). Martin's recommendation to move from description to historiography, from the practice of prosody to the discourse of

[1]Thomas Cable, "How to Find Rhythm on a Piece of Paper," in *Critical Rhythm: The Poetics of a Literary Life Form*, ed. Ben Glaser and Jonathan Culler (New York: Fordham University Press, 2019), 174–96.

"prosody," is possible to implement in her Victorianist frame of reference, while the same method makes a poor fit with the underarticulated discourses of melodic and poetic form characteristic of premodern Europe. Martin plays the role of the book's spoiler, its "prosodic killjoy" (137), as she jokes, but the premodernists' essays are not what she is spoiling. When she refers to "[o]ur collective reluctance to historicize the terms we use when we describe sounds in poems" (129), *we* can only mean postmedievalists, since we, medievalists, cannot fail to notice the postmedieval provenance of so many of the terms we use when we describe sounds in poems. Martin indicates "historical soundscapes and mediated print environments" as the destination (143), one with which I sympathize, but emphasis falls so hard on *historical* and *mediated* that one despairs of ever reaching *soundscapes* or *environments*. For Martin, scholarship embodies a series of "failed attempts to fix sound to text," a view eventuating in her extraordinary claim that "[t]here is no such thing as natural stress in English" (144). Meanwhile, Hasty's "rangy and meditative" essay (17) exemplifies the unhistoricized verse aestheticism against which Martin rails. At one point, for example, Hasty introduces the term *foot*, one of the oldest and most controversial in the field of metrics, with no definition or justification. He believes poetic rhythm expresses "the rhythmicity of everyday speech" (237), a cliché of prosodic criticism that Martin and other essayists deconstruct. Hasty (a music theorist) frequently seems not to realize he has reformulated, in the guise of revelation, something positively basic, such as that Gertrude Stein's sentences consist of clauses ("verse events" [247]). I imagine something similar would happen if I were to draft a theory of musical rhythm relying only on my intuitive response to melodic form. In sum, *The Sound of Writing* harbors a transperiod ambition it oddly fails to achieve.

That failure ought not obscure what a wealth of critical argument metrists and medievalists will find herein. A plurality of the essays (six) concern poetic meter and/or musical measure. Sarah Kay's "Reading Impressions: The Sound of the Sight of Occitan Verse" and Sean Curran's "Music Writing and Music History in a Thirteenth-Century Song" consider twelfth- and thirteenth-century lyrics in vernaculars of France. Kay attends more to the meter and text of the Occitan "Sancta Maria / Vergen gloriosa" and Marcabru's "D'aiso laus Dieu," Curran more to the measure and melodies of the French motet *Par une matinee / Mellis stilla / Alleluya*, but both authors are alive to both aspects of lyric. Kay and Curran join a critical conversation about what impression lyrics make, how we can know we are hearing in them what we think we hear, and what medieval audiences might have caught in the songs' complexly patterned syllables, rhymes, musical arrangements, and manuscript *mise-en-page*. Lyric emerges as a genre of uncommon "plurality and plasticity" (Kay [50]). Curran's gargantuan essay, which includes an edition of the motet, carries three appendices and fourteen pages of endnotes. Attuned to the motet's "*historiographical* voice" (164), he argues that "opinions about the social life of music could . . . be articulated compositionally," not only in treatises (156). Although Kay's lyrics are monolingual, she, like Curran, considers the resonance of song between secular (vernacular) and sacred (Latin) cultural spheres.

A second pair of essays, by Ian Cornelius ("Prosodic Protocols and Interruptions of Them in *Piers Plowman*") and Emily V. Thornbury ("Latin Verse in Old English Accents"), address the same issue as it played out across the Channel. Through a detailed sequence of argument, Cornelius reaches the remarkable conclusion that William Langland could toggle out of English alliterative meter and into Latin verse or prose at the midline caesura. By these means, Cornelius observes, Langland achieved unique effects of "polymetrical collage" (95). "The English poem is, as it were, made to wait on a quotative voice that exercises an authority to speak for as long as needed" (97). Highlighting a much earlier moment in English–Latin language contact, Thornbury investigates what early medieval Anglo-Latin poetry can tell us about insular pronunciation and scansion of Latin. Her chapter crests in a full scansion of a poem she claims to be, in effect, an Old English alliterative poem in Latin, incipit "Ego licet uilis / uernaculus Xristi." The claim of translingual prosody "in a distinctive Anglo-Latin soundscape" (111) is as counterintuitive as it is persuasive. Cornelius and Thornbury are operating at the leading edge of alliterative metrical theory.

Readers will experience whiplash if, after absorbing Thornbury's subtle essay, they turn to the next, Martin's withering takedown of just such reconstructions of the historical pronunciation of metered verse, but without reference to pre-1850 examples. Somewhat akin to Martin, in "The Phenomenology of *-e*" Cannon expresses fundamental skepticism about the possibility of recovering the sound of writing, specifically the value of Chaucer's *-e*: "the phenomenon of final *-e* finally cannot be saved" (219). The topic has long been a sore point in metrical scholarship. Cannon's essay conducts a metacritical review. After distinguishing two camps, "grammarians" such as E. Talbot Donaldson and "metricists" such as Ian Robinson (220), Cannon throws in his lot with the latter. Cannon's grammarian/metricist dichotomy misconstrues what is at stake in debates over *-e*. The late Derek Pearsall, grouped by Cannon with the grammarians, was intensely interested in metrical aesthetics. Pearsall was on the side of metrical delight if anyone was. Robinson, meanwhile, rejected both grammatical *and* metrical regularity in scanning Chaucer. "Metrical imperatives and the rules of grammarians," so far from being "generally . . . at war" (217) in Chaucer's verse, generally reinforce one another. In order to be able to conclude that "Chaucer's final *-e*'s are a subjective quality of his verse, a series of phonological events structured not by metrical or grammatical rule but by the feelings they produce" (223), Cannon has to paint metrics and grammar as insensitive disciplines, and, to accomplish that, he must elide the precision of their learning. Thus the three nouns Cannon cites to illustrate supposedly ungrammatical *-e*s in Chaucer (*blisse*, *lare*, *speche*) all descend from Old English feminine nouns, which acquired an analogical *-e* in Early Middle English, fossilized in fourteenth-century meter, as Cable noticed long ago.[2] Cannon's conflation of written and sounded *-e* throughout his essay is particularly unfortunate in the context of the present volume.

Three other essays find their archives beyond the meter–measure continuum. Sarah Nooter's "The Sounds and Matter of Women in Ancient Greek Epigrams" elegantly analyzes a shift in emphasis between the materialization and dematerialization of women's voices in three periods of ancient Greek history. Nooter considers modes of inscription (in stone, bronze, and lyrics) and forms of voicing (by a sculpture, a mythical heroine, an interred corpse, and finally actual women poets: Sappho and Anyte). The arc from Archaic to Hellenistic Greece traces "a path from the construction of physical durability to the written representation of lasting presence" (23) in projections of women's speech. Jennifer Richards's "Voices and Bees: The Evolution of Charles Butler's Acoustic Book" examines the curious case of Butler, whose *The Feminine Monarchie* (1609) was the first work to recognize the sex of the queen bee. In an enchanting example of compassionate historicism, Richards takes seriously Butler's anthropomorphizing musical scores that purport to—and, modern science confirms,

[2]Thomas Cable, *The English Alliterative Tradition* (Philadephia: University of Pennsylvania Press, 1991), 78.

often do!—record the overlapping of honeybees' "voices" during swarming, that is, disarticulation and rearticulation of hives. The political overtones of apian sociality were not lost on premodern writers; aggregating grammar, music, and rhetoric into "acoustic humanities" (64), Richards demonstrates that early writers' overinvestment in beehives as models for kingdoms did not preclude genuine analytical insight and scrupulous transcription after "trained listening" (71). Alison Cornish's "'Where the *sì* sounds': Dante's Dissonant Vernaculars and Their Sensual Signs" reads *De vulgari eloquentia* and *Inferno* by the light of one another. Cornish argues that in Dante's thought about vernacular language, particularity—of Italian dialects, of souls, of words for "yes" in Romance—and its transcendence were frustratingly entangled. Dante's formulation "illustrious vernacular [*vulgare illustre*]" was an oxymoron. "Ultimately," writes Cornish, "the relation of authentic, local, natural, and audible speech to what can survive it is an issue for Dante's whole poetic project" (201).

The Sound of Writing renders newly visible the still-unresolved "catechresis" (1) of its title. A philosophical rift runs through the book. In trying to make "Does writing make a sound?" sound like something other than a koan, the contributors reveal mutual disagreement about which term comes first. Whereas, to take the radical case, Martin expects that historical sound will remain always already mediated by written records and scholarly vocabulary, so that whatever masquerades as the sound of writing will, upon inspection, turn out to be the writing of sound, Thornbury, Curran, and other premodernists treat sound as the primary object of inquiry. Sound is audible through writing, even if imperfectly, faintly, like a jingle in the distance. Nooter's evocative phrase is "murmurs of the missing" (21); Curran speaks of a "sonic trace" (158). The most impressive chapters, such as Kay's and Cornelius's, show why we can never do with less than both sound and writing when analyzing written texts. Sound/writing discloses a rich bivalence analogous to the vernacular/Latin and lineation/textualization dyads Kay and Cornelius both likewise explore. Cannon and Justice's gripping introduction, which takes readers from the prehistoric cave paintings of Arcy-sur-Cure to Cicero, Quintilian, and Bede, pitches the sound/writing nexus as the prime catalyst for human history.

This book will echo in multiple disciplines for years to come. In natural philosophy, its key authority is Aristotle; in rhetoric, the book revolves around *prolatio*, "the 'sensual' aspect of every word-act 'insofar as it is sound'" (Cornish, quoting Enrico Fenzi [203]); in metrics, the book's focus is English alliterative verse; in music, troubadour lyric most often energizes comparisons and affords argument here.

ERIC WEISKOTT
Boston College

TAYLOR COWDERY. *Matter and Making in Early English Poetry: Literary Production from Chaucer to Sidney*. Cambridge: Cambridge University Press, 2023. Pp. xi, 324. $110.00.

In *Matter and Making in Early English Poetry*, Taylor Cowdery examines how the court-poets of the late Middle Ages and early sixteenth century—Chaucer, Gower, Hoccleve, Lydgate, Skelton, and Wyatt—invented what we know as literature. This is a familiar grouping of authors and a familiar claim for their importance, as from Robert Meyer-Lee's *Poets and Power from Chaucer to Wyatt*.[1] What is new is the focus; instead of authors' originality, their status as "great writers" (1), Cowdery explores their attitudes toward their sources and subjects, the matter of the title. Such an approach yields some compelling new readings, and it nicely rebalances the scholarly emphasis on authorial novelty with attention to authorial debts.

Each of the six chapters recaptures how an author approached his topics, his sources, and representation itself. For Chaucer, who begins the study, the commonplace that words and deeds must match is less an invitation to think about *mimesis* than to set up a game that avoids it. That game is, of course, the *Canterbury Tales*, which maintains its fictionality, in Cowdery's view, until Fragment VII, when historical context (references to the Peasants' Revolt) erupts into the beast fable that is *The Nun's Priest's Tale*. In this perspective, Chaucer struggles with his control over his materials; he is skeptical of "the ideology of authorship" (50). Even as he wants to write fiction, he cannot entirely set the claims of history aside.

If Cowdery makes Chaucer less of an author, as conventionally understood, as in boldly independent and original, then he makes Gower more of one. Gower's "ethical system" is not merely conventional, a set of rules inherited from others, but depends upon "moments of affect" (54), which

[1]Robert Meyer-Lee, *Poets and Power from Chaucer to Wyatt* (Cambridge: Cambridge University Press, 2007).

foreground the crying voice. That crying voice intervenes when the ethical system looks as if it won't work (56). This thought-provoking argument gets a bit lost in the discussion of Gower's biography, his views on the microcosm, and the forms that Gower is using, such as *distinctiones*. A more targeted discussion of the ethical system as a system, such as the sins in the *Confessio Amantis*, would have made the argument about the role of the crying voice clearer. How do the failures that Cowdery identifies with the crying voice differ from the failures endemic to *exempla*? After all, as Cowdery acknowledges, *exempla* rarely do what they are supposed to, including in Gower's *Confessio*.

The chapters on Hoccleve and Lydgate, which follow, assign these authors a heightened importance in this movement toward a new understanding of literature. It is as if they clear up the messiness that characterizes Chaucer and Gower. Indeed, it is only as a successor to both Chaucer and Gower that Hoccleve is able see his poetry as a category of writing distinct from legal and religious discourses. In his *Series*, a group of poems very much indebted to sources, Hoccleve tries to give poetry a force equal to that of other kinds of language, an instrumentality that he associates with devotional writings. Similarly, Lydgate develops an idea of literature in relation to his sources: in his case as a sense of surplus, what has to be left out of the stories included in the monumental poem *The Fall of Princes*. Because Lydgate's subject matter is history, literature is in some sense what is extra to history, a point that Cowdery also makes formally with a discussion of the two kinds of stanzas: rhyme royal and ballade (134). I found this argument so persuasive because it reminds me of scholarship on the origins of romance, e.g., Peter Haidu, that romance emerged as "an insertion of an imaginative activity" into other kinds of writing.[2]

Skelton appears in this trajectory as a rightly transitional figure, looking both forward to the Renaissance and back to the Middle Ages. His interest in imitation signals the new, but he also doubts that imitation can ever offer a true representation. The term Cowdery uses to discuss this simultaneous embrace and critique of imitation is *copia*, which recaptures Skelton's "multiplicity and contradiction" (143). Skelton can both dissent from the status quo and desire patronage within it, as in the Wolsey poems; he

[2]Peter Haidu, "Repetition: Modern Reflections on Medieval Aesthetics," *MLN* 92 (1977): 875–87 (883).

can explore the rupture between self-image and the image others have, as in *Phyllyp Sparowe*.

Where Skelton's attitude toward representation is hostile or skeptical, even as he also takes some delight in what he's doing, Wyatt, the final author discussed, is anxious and secretive. Wyatt's poetry is in many ways conventional, but, at the same time, hopes to elicit a feeling in the reader, via or behind those conventions. In brief, he is hiding, not showing, the subjects of his poetry. All he can do is hope that the reader catches his drift and shares a moment of what Cowdery calls grace (176). This argument makes complete sense given Wyatt's vulnerability at the court of Henry VIII, and it offers a chilling reminder that what we think of as the realm of the literary was the product of fear and repression, that distinguishing the literary from its "social functions" happened not so much out of a love of art for its own sake but out of self-preservation (179). This chapter thus addresses most explicitly the way in which the "state apparatus" shaped literature, as mentioned in the introduction (13) and then picked up again in the epilogue.

As Wyatt's "grace" should suggest, Cowdery's approach depends on assigning a singular or uniform view to each author and is, therefore, more successful for authors who are consistent. I'm not so sure that Chaucer is as easy to pin down as this study suggests; his irony makes his explicit statements about *mimesis* questionable. Indeed, what makes Chaucer so interesting for me is that he doesn't have a stable sense of what he's doing as literature or literary. For Lydgate and Skelton, in contrast, Cowdery's approach is quite compelling, likely because they are two extremes, at least when it comes to the treatment of sources. Lydgate is the most source-bound and Skelton is the most experimental, a road that appears out of and then leads nowhere.

Categorizing authorial attitudes about literature in this way also raises some larger questions for me about the terms that Cowdery uses: the literary, the historical, the aesthetic. There is in this study a stability to these terms and a confidence in distinguishing literature from other kinds of writing, such as history or religious discourses. For example, Cowdery asks, "Why might Hoccleve have taken a literary interest in legal complaint?" (93). This question assumes that Hoccleve understood "literary" to be a category unto itself. I'm not so sure. Earlier studies of ideas about literature, such as Meyer-Lee's, are on firmer ground, since they focus on poetry and poetics and not the literary more broadly. To be sure, there has been recent scholarly interest in "the medieval literary," to borrow the title of a recent essay collection.[3] And yet, those collections take as a starting-point the slipperiness of the term. After all, medieval texts were written by authors who were mainly unfamiliar with or had far more tenuous relationships with theories of literature or what one might call literary criticism than authors of later periods. As Chris Cannon persuasively demonstrates in *The Grounds of English Literature*, the medieval period does not have a clearly defined idea of literature, and medieval writing is characterized instead by a sense of experimentation that has been, for many medievalists including myself, a source of true pleasure.[4]

Even as the study explores a variety of medieval attitudes, it underlines the dominance of a more modern idea of literature, and that is the institutional one, whose rise is charted in John Guillory's *Cultural Capital*.[5] What Cowdery's authors have in common is that they are part of the canon. It is not an accident that the poems that institutions have already determined to be literature end up telling us about the making of literature. Would the inclusion of non-canonical authors change our understanding of "matter and making" in this transition from medieval to early modern? I'm eager to find out.

KATHERINE C. LITTLE
University of Colorado Boulder

LOUISE D'ARCENS. *World Medievalism: The Middle Ages in Modern Textual Culture* (Oxford: Oxford University Press, 2022). Pp. xv, 201. $90.00 hardback.

World Medievalism begins on deceptively familiar ground for studies of medievalism: with a close reading of a map produced for the *Game of Thrones* media franchise, which depicts at its edge the border of a southern

[3] Robert J. Meyer-Lee and Catherine Sanok, eds., *The Medieval Literary: Beyond Form* (Woodbridge: Boydell & Brewer, 2018). See also Frank Grady and Andrew Galloway, eds, *Answerable Style: The Idea of the Literary in Medieval England* (Columbus: The Ohio State University Press, 2013).

[4] Christopher Cannon, *The Grounds of English Literature* (Oxford: Oxford University Press, 2005).

[5] John Guillory, *Cultural Capital: The Problem of Literary Canon Formation* (Chicago: University of Chicago Press, 1993).

continent, a *terra incognita* with monstrous inhabitants enslaved by the inhabitants of the northern continent. Louise D'Arcens's study builds from this familiar touchstone of the absorption of colonial medievalisms in medievalist fantasy literature to an ambitious and expansive theorization of "world medievalism" through four case studies, all from the last few decades, two of which are from the Global North, two from the Global South. These carefully chosen examples offer D'Arcens the opportunity to elucidate and tease out the affordances of the terms that this book offers as theoretical frameworks for future study.

The introduction is a valuable piece of work in itself for its concise account of the "global turn" in medievalism studies and medieval studies. Its review of the field encompasses the longer history of studies on the connectedness of the medieval world, the renewed sense of urgency in the past decade to public-facing work that intervenes in racist and nationalist appropriations of medieval history, and the influence of critical race theory in medieval studies. Two central tensions around the term "global medievalism" are introduced. The first is the potential of "global" to collapse globalisms of the past into the globalization of late capitalism. D'Arcens makes a case for "world," rather than "global," as a more appropriate term, with another useful account of debates in world literary studies. "World," D'Arcens argues, sidesteps the political problems of "global" while inviting other, more dynamic meanings of "world literature" that suggest, in additional to geographical scope, an ethical project of "world disclosure" or "worlding" (27), the goal of imagining and effecting a better world. An important aspect to all the texts discussed in subsequent chapters is that they attempt to immerse their audience in a past world evoked under the sign of the Middle Ages, while enacting an implicit or explicit political project of transforming the present world. "World medievalisms" thus holds simultaneously the geographic expansiveness of "global" with the more abstract imaginative and ethical projects associated with "worlding."

The second tension that D'Arcens's introduction outlines is the potential of "medieval" to impose European periodization on the rest of the world inappropriately, particularly in relation to cultures outside the spheres of influence of the cultures traditionally periodized as "medieval." These cultures—many of which are in the Global South—are often understood to operate on their own "emic" temporalities, and while the idea of a "global Middle Ages" can do important political work to deconstruct nationalist medievalisms, it can also colonize other cultural periodizing frameworks and temporal schemas with a Eurocentric model, and so work in opposition to postcolonial and decolonial goals of decentering Europe in global studies. The central question of the book, then, is "how we might understand the circulation of medieval and medievalist texts as world phenomena, not just traversing different times but often different space, often caught within the circuits of global capitalism but also sometimes short-circuiting them" (26). Subsequent chapters explore the valences of "world medievalism" as a framework for doing just this.

The first chapter treats a cluster of award-winning French novels of the 2010s responding, in various ways, to far-right politician and critic Eric Zenmour's account of the collapse of French identity into nostalgia in the face of multiculturalism and globalization. D'Arcens situates these novels in, not the nationalist medievalisms of the nineteenth century, but more recent French cultural responses to globalization, expressed through political rhetoric and works of popular historiography such as Zenmour's. These different right-wing movements vary dramatically in their imaginative uses of France's medieval past, but unite in concentrating their fears of the loss of French identity upon an imagined neomedieval Islamic Other. These three novels, D'Arcens argues, both reiterate and interrogate this yearning for an imagined historical purity in French right-wing politics.

The second chapter continues to explore the medievalist novel as a medium for "worlding" in Tariq Ali's Islam Quintet, a series of historical novels of which four have medieval settings. Ali's novels are written in English but—as D'Arcens shows—participate in a diasporic tradition of Arabic historical novels. As with the previous chapter, D'Arcens weaves together the immediate political context of each novel's production across the 1990s and early 2000s—including the Gulf War and the US invasion of Afghanistan after 9/11—with the novels' accounts of idealized, cosmopolitan, and tolerant medieval Islam of fifteenth-century Al-Andalus; twelfth-century Sicily; and twelfth-century Egypt, Syria, and Palestine. Ali's novels, like those of the previous chapter, respond directly to the role of the Middle Ages in contemporary popular historiography and political rhetoric. Offering a corrective to Eurocentric narratives of the period and stereotypes of Islam as a static, homogeneous fundamentalism, Ali's novels also draw explicit parallels between the increasingly militarized and destructive Christian forces that threaten their protagonists' cosmopolitan existences and the US presence in the Middle East in the 1990s and 2000s. The "worlding" of these novels, D'Arcens argues, is in their construction of immersive medieval settings in the Middle East to offer models for future *convivencia*, while exploring the complex affective state of living under occupation.

The third chapter turns away both from the Global North and from the novel as a form, with a study of discourses surrounding the 2003 discovery of a prehistoric hominin on Flores, an island in Southeast Asia. The hominin was unofficially referred to by the discovering archaeological team as a "hobbit," a term that then proliferated through both media coverage of and scholarship on the find. D'Arcens's complex and nuanced account follows the interleaving effects of the imposition of Tolkien's medieval imaginarium upon the prehistory of the region. These effects included the erasure of local folklore and history to contextualize the find, but also linked Flores to a familiar and globally popular imaginary "past" that helped popularize the find's dramatic (at the time) revision to scientific understanding of human evolution. The chapter engages with Daniel Lord Smail's work on "deep time," suggesting that while one effect of the "hobbit" naming is that "the unimaginable, deep past is made imaginable under the sign of the medieval" (135), this same "medieval" framework, because non-European places are unimagined or unimaginable within it, places non-European peoples outside of history.

The fourth and final chapter follows this double effect of imaginability and erasure following the "sign of the medieval" in *Ten Canoes* (2006), a film co-created by the Yolŋu people of Arnhem Land in northern Australia. Here D'Arcens analyses the effects of the film's setting "a thousand years ago," a description that invites audiences to read the precolonial-contact Yolŋu people depicted in the film as coeval with the European Middle Ages. This medievalizing gesture, D'Arcens argues, resists the idea of Aboriginal society as timeless or atavistic, and is in keeping with other decolonial work in public history in Australia that emphasizes archaeological finds such as copper coins dated from around 900–1300 CE, minted in the East African sultanate of Kilwa Kisiwani before making their way through the Muslim island archipelago trade to Yolŋu land; such finds also situate the Yolŋu people within an interconnected "medieval" world. However, as D'Arcens points out, the use of "medieval," even within the film, risks imposing colonial periodization and understanding of time upon Aboriginal temporal schemas and uses of the past. D'Arcens, here at the end of the book, also reinterrogates the appropriateness of the frame "world medievalism" for this case study, proposing instead the Aboriginal term "Country," built on a different understanding of the relationship between people and geography.

One of the remarkable things about this book is that it keeps both the utility and the problems with its framing terms at front and center throughout, allowing each case study to illustrate the "ideological malleability of medievalism" (14) in the political work effected in different ways by popular historiography and historical novels, but also to demonstrate the limits of "world medievalism" as a framework as local examples resist Eurocentric periodization or a "worldly" model of contact and connection. The limitations of using four examples are inevitable, and indeed are discussed by D'Arcens in the introduction; asking this book to be comprehensive would be missing the point. *World Medievalism* contributes not only a theory but a robust and nuanced field-testing of that theory, in a way that opens up future work on medievalisms that expand beyond the traditional geographical imaginaries. While this is not the first study to explore world literature as a model for understanding the global Middle Ages, the care with which D'Arcens explores the valences of different available discursive fields for her study also makes this book—particularly the introduction and final chapter—an important intervention in the broader field conversation about the meaning, ethics, and usefulness of forming a field of study around the term "medieval," particularly for traditionally trained literature scholars interested in broadening the geographical reach of traditional medieval courses or research projects.

ANNA WILSON
Harvard University

MIMI ENSLEY. *Difficult Pasts: Post-Reformation Memory and the Medieval Romance*. Manchester: Manchester University Press, 2023. Pp. ix, 242. £85.00.

The title of Mimi Ensley's well-informed book is at once accurate and misleading. Its declared subject is the reception of medieval metrical romances in the later sixteenth century, but it reaches that period by way of a long and detailed account of their printing before the Reformation; and a large part of the book is concerned with arguing against the idea that even in those later years their reception presented much difficulty at all. The new technologies of print and of woodcut illustration had reformulated them at the start of the century as an up-to-date form of reading material, collage rather than palimpsest in Ensley's terms, in ways that helped to separate them from their original context in a pre-humanist and pre-Protestant past. Their transition did not prevent the new generations of humanists and reformers from grumbling about their continuing fashionability, but for their many readers their technological modernization will have seemed to represent something at once new and, after the Reformation, reassuringly familiar. Once established in print, she argues, the conformity of their appearance will have helped to indicate their acceptability: a conformity established not least by the reappearance of many of their woodcuts across a number of different texts, regardless of their precise relevance. She provides a table of the many printers and editions through which the texts passed, with Pynson and Copland the front runners as publishers. Since her corpus of works is taken from the York online *Database of the Middle English Verse Romances*, the pre-Reformation prose romances are not represented; only the *Morte Darthur* is given a place, with five editions down to East's of 1582 (the edition of 1634 being presumably too late for her purposes). The winners in terms of numbers are *Bevis of Hampton*, with nine editions from c. 1500 to 1585, and *Sir Eglamour*, with six from c. 1500 to 1565 (the database lists seven, to 1570[?], though one of those is a single leaf, and one is Scottish). If one thing is abundantly clear, however, from the numerous references to a range of different texts throughout the century and beyond, the handful of surviving copies represents only a tiny fraction of popular Tudor and Elizabethan medieval reading matter.

It is only recently that these romance prints have received much attention at all. Many scholars have dismissed or ignored them, medievalists because by normal editorial standards they are "bad" texts, corruptions of their originals, or early modernists simply because they are medieval, and the medieval falls outside the bounds of their interests. There is also the problem that the copies themselves were normally sold unbound and so were both cheap and fragile, and it was not therefore much in anyone's interest to try to preserve them. Entire editions are likely to have left no record, or at best a bare citation in the Stationers' Registers; a number of texts that are frequently cited by contemporaries (almost always in condemnation) survive only in one or two copies, and those may be damaged or incomplete. The copies that had the best chance of survival, most often pre-Reformation, were those that were compiled into *Sammelbände*, when an owner collected up a number of similar size and had them bound together—a practice that itself can tell us much about contemporary tastes and even on occasion beliefs. The only group to have received much modern attention is the collection described as being owned by Captain Cox in Robert Langham's *Letter* about the celebrations for Elizabeth at Kenilworth, and there are a good many puzzles about those too. For Ensley's purposes, they are straightforward evidence for their popularity, and she must be right about that: she can document their existence elsewhere and say much about their bibliographical history. But that still leaves a lot of questions. The authorship of the *Letter* is disputed, as is the existence of Cox himself; and the questions of what, if he did exist, underlay his making of the collection, or Langham's purpose in recording it, or what response the listing was intended to evoke, are hard to reconstruct with any certainty, and especially so far as any post-Reformation difficulty is concerned. It's clear from the *Letter* that Cox was extreme in his enthusiasm; but the eccentricity of his tastes seems to lie in the fact that he collected up romances and jestbooks and ballads, old-fashioned and recent, without discrimination, to suggest that it is quantity rather than content that is at issue. By this stage of the book, Ensley is moving on from the romances as contemporary to the romances as antiquarian: this is how she characterizes the Bodleian *Sammelband* S. Seld. D.45 (after 1605), which may have been put together by the scholar John Selden—a term no one would apply to Cox.

The question of the ideological or theological difficulty of secular medieval texts after the Reformation is complicated by the fact that the Elizabethan Church was desperate to prove that its reforms were restorative rather than innovative. The romances themselves could be regarded not as dangerously new, but as the preservation of a religious culture that had been overridden or destroyed: they constituted a "dynamic site at which post-Reformation readers could explore the connections between medieval literary culture and their own emerging identities" (228). The texts' assumption of a Catholic context (complete with the hearing of masses, references to the pope, and a fair number of hermits) could therefore be seen, at least by some readers, as preserving something of that purity of a former age. This may account for their popularity among recusants, who seem to have been less inclined to dismiss them as worthless or dangerous. Here Ensley highlights the remarkable work of Edward Banister, who made his own manuscripts of a number of romances: Oxford, Bodleian Library, MS Douce 251, which contains *Sir Degore*, *Sir Eglamour*, *Sir*

Isumbras, and *The Jest of Sir Gawain*, and a separate manuscript of *Robert the Devil*, London, British Library, MS Egerton 3132. In many respects these look rather similar to their originals, but the similarities are at least partly misleading. The script is not an imitation of the textura-based blackletter found universally in the romance prints, but the italic increasingly adopted by the academic community for their own writings and (alongside roman) near-universally for printing in other languages; and the illustrations, although modeled closely on the printed woodcuts, dress their characters in trunk hose and ruffs.

After a first chapter outlining the survival of the romances, Ensley selects a small number of others to mark a significant phase or variation in their reception: one on Banister and his Catholic associations, one on the restoration of romance in the reworkings of Chaucer's *Squire's Tale* by Spenser and John Lane, and one on what she calls "musealization," largely on Lydgate's and Rowlands's versions of the story of *Guy of Warwick*, both of which highlight the extant artifacts associated with Guy and so turn their texts into a kind of reliquary. For Lydgate, what mattered was the axe with which Guy had killed the pagan giant Colbrond; Rowlands's fuller list was eventually expanded to include his outsize porridge-pot. Ensley's survey is concerned primarily with the texts' place in an outline literary history rather than with the reformation of their content—we do not learn much about how protestant they had, or had not, become, in the course of their transmission. When individual lines are followed across editions, as in the case of missing lines in *Sir Eglamour*, the substitutions have nothing ideological about them: nothing to match Nicolas Jacobs's noting in his 1995 monograph on the printed texts of *Sir Degarre* that the protagonist attends a masque rather than a mass, or the more extreme revisions of the story of *Guy of Warwick* that cut or condemn both his pilgrimage and his penitential life as a hermit. The prose version of *Robert the Devil* by the Catholic convert Thomas Lodge does not get a mention, and neither, since it falls even further outside Ensley's romance brief, does the adoption of a bowdlerized hermit persona in Elizabethan entertainments, with Elizabeth substituted for God or the Virgin. There are follow-up studies to be done here, but Ensley's book will provide a helpful basis for future work.

HELEN COOPER
Magdalene College, Cambridge

KIMBERLY FONZO. *Retrospective Prophecy and Medieval English Authorship.* Toronto: University of Toronto Press, 2022. Pp. viii, 187. $65.00.

This is a confident book that reads three key figures of the Middle Ages—Langland, Gower, and Chaucer—through their scholarly afterlives. It takes up the important question of why later readers tended to ascribe prophetic qualities to these poets, particularly in the area of politics. The author's contention is that these Ricardian authors were susceptible to being seen as political forecasters because of how they incorporated a preexisting interest in political prophecy into their authorial personae. This does not mean they were particularly dedicated to being prophets themselves (although some were to varying degrees), but rather that complex modes of political prophecy were already circulating in the literary world of the later fourteenth century, and the authors in question used them as material for their work. Each author the book addresses takes up a unique position on the question of prophecy: Langland will satirize it, Gower will cultivate it, and Chaucer will cite it. And each approach contributes to how the author establishes the stakes for speaking politically. The book aims to show how these respective positions become misread in subsequent generations and how these readings end up turning Langland, Gower, and Chaucer into something they are not: men who can (and do) predict what is coming because they see the truth of the present. Fonzo cleverly interrogates the long-standing impulse to ascribe remarkable political acumen to her three authors, arguing (quite rightly) that it is often used to justify their place in our scholarly attention and in our classrooms. The result is that we end up situating this premodern poetry as very much part of its time rather than allowing it to speak more freely in a transhistorical mode: "Ironically, by calling authors prophets (or their works prophetic), we fix them squarely in the past. A work that contains valuable advice for those of us living in the present day becomes a work that predicted something that already happened years ago" (11). Fonzo's aim in the larger project, then, is threefold: to demonstrate the complexities of how political prophecy functions in the Ricardian literary landscape; to excavate lines of reception history that reshaped her authors into recognized, prophetic figures; and to leverage what this reveals so as to move the poems out of the past, thereby reclaiming their ability to speak to a universal, present moment.

The book focuses on the first two of these tasks, and does so carefully and well. The first chapter establishes the prominence of political prophecy as a form and details two major traditions of its use, suspended from the figures of Merlin and the Sybil respectively. Sibylline prophecies center on the trope of the Last Emperor, who will consolidate the West and Near East under his rule and then deliver a unified world over to Christ. This eschatological vision, associated here with the French courtly literature of Eustache Deschamps and Christine de Pizan, depicts an earthly ruler triumphantly ushering in the end of the world, often through military conquest. Moving across the Channel, however, English political prophecies were used to speak ancient truth to power by way of Merlin's cryptic phrases and ancient prognostications. These, as recorded by Geoffrey of Monmouth and others, were attached to contemporary rulers and "miraculously" reveal their portentous faults. Both traditions (supernatural critique for the English and belletristic motivation for the French) inform how political prophecy was used by Ricardian poets, and this first chapter lays out a useful and concise groundwork readers can carry into the rest of the argument.

The next three chapters show how each of the poets adopts different positions regarding the use of prophecy in his work, and this is where both the strongest and the weakest parts of the argument lie. The book's clear strength is its intricate articulation of the ways these authors were seemingly transformed into viable political prophets through manuscript compilation, editorial practices, and scholarly trends. The readings are insightful, and it is clear that a great deal of impressive attention has been paid to the networks of transmission that emerged in the decades and centuries following the poems' composition. This is a book that is satisfying because it is *informative*. Fonzo analyzes, for example, how Langland's later readers establish him as a proto-Protestant poet because they misread his satirizing of prophetic language. She traces the reception history of the poem through manuscripts from the reign of Mary Tudor and into the poem's early editors and readers (Robert Crowley, John Bale, Owen Rogers, George Puttenham, Thomas Dunham Whitaker, Thomas Wright, Walter William Skeat, Rupert Taylor, and even the contemporary novelist Marilynne Robinson). The clarity of argument from her readings of the poem, to her identification of a satirical mode of prophetic voicing, and finally to how opportunistic reception of the text overlooks this element to serve its own ends, is compelling and clear. We see something similar with her dedicated, scholarly analysis of Gower's various recensions of and emendations to both the *Vox clamantis* and the *Confessio Amantis* in Chapter 3. Fonzo builds on work done by earlier editors such as G. C. Macaulay and scholars such as M. B. Parkes to demonstrate convincingly how Gower becomes established as "a genuine political prophet" (70) by readers in the nineteenth and twentieth centuries. And we see the same for Chaucer, as she walks readers through prophetic addendums to *The House of Fame* made by Caxton in his 1483 printing. Fonzo discusses how Caxton emphasized Chaucer's prophetic status by adding a series of verses ("When fethe faileth") to the end of the text, amplifying the threads of Chaucer's prophetic citation in the poem into full-on prophecy. Like the arguments about Langland's reception history, this is an illuminating and useful perspective into the *desiderata* of Chaucer's later Protestant readers, traced through William Thynne's 1532 text, Matthew Parker's famous library, and John Urry's 1721 edition of Chaucer's works.

However, because each chapter posits a one-to-one relationship between author and approach, with Langland, Gower, and Chaucer each exemplifying a different alignment to political prophecy, the framework Fonzo erects can feel increasingly strained as the book progresses. For example, she convincingly demonstrates the experimental qualities of Langland's use of prophetic forms in Passus VI of the B-text of *Piers*. Will's comments about Hunger and the state of England make use of the cryptic, prophetic language found in Merlinic visions, but Fonzo argues that Langland tips us over into parody by swapping out the authority of an ancient mystical voice in favor of timely, universal truths. Famine will come to the land, for example, because people give in to sloth and stop working in the fields, not because of divine judgment leveled against an unfit ruler. The credibility of Will's predictions about the future thus rests on "more universally accepted Christian concepts like the apocalypse and the importance of penitential behavior" (58) than on the actions or misdeeds of the king. This willingness to experiment is not something Fonzo allows to Gower in the next chapter, however, and as a result the argument there is more about reception than how Gower himself might have approached prophetic forms (Sibylline or Merlinic). Indeed, the grounding Gower claims from the *vox populi* will feel to some readers as though it has more in common with the approach Fonzo outlined for Langland: these are critiques that anyone might make because they follow familiar and well-known patterns of political and devotional complaint. Gower adopts his own version of an "anyone might see this—and they do" approach in his caustic warnings, and the delicate line between admonition and prediction is not fully explored in the argument. Readers might wonder as well about the relationship between admonition and satire (or sarcasm) and how clear the distinction might be in either poet.

We find something similar in the Chaucer chapter, which concludes the book. Here, Fonzo introduces the idea of "prophetic citation" to describe Chaucer's alignment to prophecy, and she clearly defines her chosen term: "Prophetic citation occurs when authors depict a dream or vision and, during it, draw attention to past poets who have influenced them" (104). Her primary study is *The House of Fame*, and she focuses on how Virgil, Ovid, and Dante incorporate this technique of prophetic dreaming and retrospective prophecy into their work, which, in turn, is also taken up by Chaucer in his poem. The kind of formal allusions and structural quotations Fonzo is interested in are fascinating, but for many readers this might sound like familiar medieval engagements with *auctoritas*, and the distinction is perhaps not as deeply treated as it might be. Also unexplained is how unique this is to Chaucer. Indeed, for each of the categories Fonzo proposes—prophecy as satire, ambition, or resource—one wonders how many other texts might also participate in some constellation of these same effects. Or how the texts she treats might be representative of more than one approach.

In looking back over all three main chapters, readers will be struck, in fact, by how strongly the readings, of both the authors' works and the reception of them, tend to overlap. The choice to silo the authors into their various containers makes for a clear and legible monograph, but there is a cost to this kind of structuralist organization. There are more rich connections than differences here. This also perhaps contributes to the sense of an underfulfilled promise in the third aim stated in the introduction: opening a more transhistorical perspective for these three poets—and for medieval literature more generally. Fonzo has laid out a fascinating narrative about the power of that terrible word "relevance," and gestures toward an equally fascinating take on how deeply we are still tethered to it when writing and speaking about medieval texts. There is both a call and an opportunity here to imagine alternatives and to engage deliberately with the kind of transhistorical position the book calls for. In this way, the excellent work and analysis Fonzo offers in *Retrospective Prophecy* leaves us wanting to hear even more.

STEPHANIE L. BATKIE
The University of the South

Katherine Storm Hindley. *Textual Magic: Charms and Written Amulets in Medieval England.* Chicago: University of Chicago Press, 2023. Pp. xiii, 299. $45.00.

This book is the first to provide a survey of English medieval charms and written amulets. Other European countries have stronger traditions of archiving and studying charms usually associated with university folklore departments. Jonathan Roper's *English Verbal Charms* notes this gap while casting much light on the survival of charms and charming in England.[1] Charms before 1100 CE have been relatively well studied but coverage of the rest of the medieval period is far from systematic. Hindley is generous in avowing the sources that lie behind her survey, which is founded on a database of transcriptions in three main languages, Latin, French, and English. This database does not claim to be comprehensive but provides an important sample of charms from the entire medieval period. The earliest charms in her sample are from the ninth century and the latest from the early sixteenth century. In total the sample surveyed in this book contains 1,100 charm copies, and this large number allows Hindley to do a lot of counting and percentage work, whether on the uses of charms, their language, their spoken or written character, their date of copying, or other typological features. This is a fresh and compelling approach.

There is one bias in the sample pointed out by the author. The online Voigts-Kurtz database of medical and scientific writings in Old and Middle English, eVK2, is the single most important source of data in the sample.[2] This means that charms with instructions in Latin are under-represented as against those in English (193). Although the book does provide important instances of charms drawn from fourteenth-century Latin medical works by English authors, such as the *Rosa Anglica* of John Gaddesden and the writings of the surgeon John Arderne, both prolific sources of charms, it does not represent the full extent or impact of Latin writings containing charms circulating in England. The *Compendium medicine* of Gilbertus Anglicus and the *Chirurgia* of Teodorico Borgognoni are thirteenth-century continental works containing charms that both circulated in England. Two works by later English authors, the *Breviarium Bartholomei* of John Mirfield and the *Tabula medicine* written by English Franciscans, both c. 1400, are Latin writings with many charms

[1] Jonathan Roper, *English Verbal Charms* (Helsinki: Suomalainen Tiedeakatemia, 2005).

[2] University of Missouri-Kansas City, *Scientific and Medical Writings in Latin and Old and Middle English*, https://cctr1.umkc.edu/search (accessed October 1, 2024).

and are not cited in the book. If the multiple copies in circulation of some of these writings are taken into the reckoning it means that learned readers must have encountered Latin charms more often than the sample database might suggest. The database is ongoing, so this bias may be remedied in time. Another website database, *Carminabase*, will also provide samples for comparison.[3] In any case, this vernacular bias does not vitiate the comparative analysis of the valuable large sample considered in the book.

What are charms? Hindley defines them as written texts or spoken words presented as having a specific practical outcome associated with enactment (15). Careful work goes into exploring the definitional border between charms and prayers. Liturgical charms containing the text of the mass or some part of it are treated as a subset of spoken charms. Most of the charms in the sample provide protection from dangers to health or seek to restore health. There are no love charms included or experiments in practical magic (such as making oneself invisible). Formulas written on medieval objects such as pilgrim badges or jewelry rings are not counted here as charms or amulets, whereas those written on foodstuffs and consumed, or attached to the body in the form of a birth girdle, are included. A fundamental distinction is made between spoken (incantations, adjurations) and written charms (amulets, "writs," or "breves" sometimes). This works well as a tool of counting and analysis, although we should also remember the phenomenon of "marginal" charms, which were added later in the margins of manuscripts, and some of which were written in remembrance of verbal and ritual practice. The power of words, whether spoken or written, is compared by Hindley to that involved in the veneration of medieval relics (birth girdles are considered as substitute relics). Charms often drew upon stories from the Bible for suggestive parallels between instances of sacred healing and what was sought for the patient whose health was at stake. Saints' names were frequently invoked in charms for the attributes of their martyrdom, as with St. Apollonia and ailing teeth. These various religious sources of power were supplemented by accounts of the power of words that assigned natural efficacy to words influenced by the heavens, following the *De radiis* of Al-Kindi, which circulated in Latin translation in the twelfth and thirteenth centuries and influenced English authors such as Roger Bacon.

Using the database sample, Hindley is the first author to sketch a history of medieval English charms as they changed over time. Three periods

[3] *Carminabase*, https://carminabase.ehess.fr/fr/search (accessed October 1, 2024).

are distinguished in chapters 2–4 of the book. The first is pre-1100, in which the sample yields 192 verbal rituals for protection or cure, and 43 written charms. Mostly these are found in *Bald's Leechbook*, *Leechbook III*, and the *Lacnunga*, texts aimed at medical practitioners, and 70 percent of the charm instructions are in English. Liturgical charms were directed at conditions with supernatural causes (mental illness and other conditions caused by elves or demons). It seems that many of the charms in use may have been of English origin rather than imported. The second period, from 1100 to 1350, saw sudden and rapid change, the eclipse of the English language, and increased power attributed to the written word in charms. Before 1250 the principal language for charm instructions was Latin, but after 1250 French overtook Latin, as reflected in large collections of charms studied by Tony Hunt in his work on *Popular Medicine in Thirteenth-Century England*.[4] Written words of power featured many new and exotic coinages and *caracteres* that were not words at all. Seals or magic figures also appeared in charms for the first time, as in the mid-thirteenth-century Canterbury amulet edited by Don C. Skemer in his *Binding Words*.[5] Hindley speculates that many charms must have been imported from the Continent in this period, although it is hard to identify textual sources with precision. The final period, after 1350, accounts for more than half the charms in the database sample (604). Over half of these charms in turn treated just five common medical conditions. While the proportions of spoken and written charms remained much the same as in the previous period, spoken charms were usually identified in English as such, while written charms were often described as remedies, avoiding reference to charms. Of the charm instructions in the sample, 67 percent were in English, and almost 20 percent use English instead of Latin for the efficacious words. These developments reflected increasing literacy in English. In consequence there were fears on the part of the learned that someone might use a charm without understanding its meaning. But there is little evidence that the use of charms was ever penalized.

An outstanding feature of this book is the use of "boxes" containing charms transcribed from manuscripts with accompanying translation, usually by the author. There are twenty-six such "boxes" inserted in the text to illustrate the argument. They often contain more than one charm

[4]Tony Hunt, *Popular Medicine in Thirteenth-Century England* (Cambridge: D. S. Brewer, 1990).

[5]Don C. Skemer, *Binding Words: Textual Amulets in the Middle Ages* (University Park: Pennsylvania State University Press, 2006).

and so yield a total of at least seventy-seven transcribed charms. Still more charms are transcribed in the text of the book or in the footnotes. Charms scholarship has never afforded transcriptions and translations of entire charms on this scale before. This book is a terrific resource for teaching as well as a starting-point for new scholarship. Box 0.3, for example, is an English charm to treat wounds giving instructions for drawing crosses on a lead plate to represent Christ's wounds over which Latin words of power should be said. The "box" tells us that this charm is often illustrated with a picture of the lead plate and its crosses, and gives a list of twelve manuscripts in which the charm is found. This list can be supplemented by another thirteen manuscripts for the lead plate charm listed in George R. Keiser, *Works of Science and Information*.[6]

Hindley makes skillful use of literary texts to throw light on attitudes to charms and practices of charming. In Chapter 1, *The Book of Margery Kempe* is examined closely for the light it throws on the protection afforded by charms. Other literary texts find a place in the historical argument of the book. These range from *Beowulf* and *Solomon and Saturn I* for her first period, the Anglo-Norman *Alexander* or *Le roman de toute chevalerie*, to the alliterative poem *The Siege of Jerusalem* and Chaucer's *Troilus and Criseyde*. These readings offer a subtle textual foil to the counting of charm features founded on the database sample. This is a book to be welcomed enthusiastically by all those with an interest in charms and charming.

PETER MURRAY JONES
King's College, Cambridge

EMILY HOULIK-RITCHEY. *Imagining Iberia in English and Castilian Medieval Romance*. Ann Arbor: University of Michigan Press, 2023. Pp. xii, 238. $75.00.

Emily Houlik-Ritchey's *Imagining Iberia in English and Castilian Medieval Romance* is an interesting and provocative book that places Middle English and Castilian romances from the same narrative clusters in conversation with each other using what she identifies as a "nonhierarchical, neighborly

[6] George R. Keiser, *Works of Science and Information*, Vol. 10 of *A Manual of the Writings in Middle English, 1050–1500* (New Haven: Connecticut Academy of Arts and Sciences, 1998).

approach" (22). Houlik-Ritchey argues that medieval romance across these different traditions is both fascinated by and oddly ambivalent about Iberia's complex identity and relationship to the Mediterranean, the Muslim world, and Europe, and that the genre's treatment of Iberia is therefore best understood through a comparison that works outside and alongside traditional modes of comparative analysis such as source study.

Houlik-Ritchey situates her study at the intersection of scholarship on medieval romance, Middle English literary studies, Iberian studies, and comparative literature, while also engaging with larger debates in medieval studies at large and its growing engagement with the frames of "global" and Mediterranean studies. This is, in some ways, a tall order, but Houlik-Ritchey's approach, looking at how two different "national" traditions (Middle English and Castilian, plus one Portuguese text in the final chapter) imagine Iberia's religious, legal, political, and cultural identity, is specific and focused enough to engage with all of these conversations productively. Each of her chapters focuses on two or more romances, mainly English and Castilian, that are part of the same narrative cluster but have what she calls a nonhierarchical relationship to each other: neither is a direct source for the other. Each pair or group of romances is set at least partly in Iberia (although they involve travel, mainly around the Mediterranean and the Muslim world), and they all contain narratives of Christian–Muslim interaction, but that interaction looks different in each cluster and even each romance. Many of them contain a conversion narrative. This neighborly approach works better in some chapters than in others, but across its chapters, the book demonstrates the value of a nonhierarchical comparative approach to medieval romances and the value of its goal of "extend[ing] insights from Iberian Studies to Middle English literary production" (8).

Chapter 1 considers two texts from the *Fierabras* romance cluster: the Middle English *Sowdone of Babylone* and Book II of Nicolás de Piemonte's Castilian *Hystoria del emperador Carlomagno*. Both texts narrate (among many other things) the conversion of the Muslim knight Fierabras to Christianity and Charlemagne's conquest of Iberia, and both, Houlik-Ritchey argues, attempt to rehabilitate Christian violence and the resulting suffering of others by suggesting that they enable Christian devotion for both converts and established Christians. Drawing on Slavoj Žižek's concept of gentrification as a process that renders a strange or ambiguous figure more like the self, Houlik-Ritchey argues that these texts' representation of "gentrifying" Fierabras by conversion also represents a gentrification of the Christian self. She argues that in both texts, Charlemagne draws Iberia into Christendom by reimagining Iberia's past and present identity and erasing its long history as part of the larger Muslim world throughout the Mediterranean: *Sowdone* by a shift in the toponyms it uses to refer to the wider world, and Peimonte's *Hystoria* by suspending toponyms for Iberia and instead using the more abstract terms "tierras del Almirante" and "tierras del cristianos." Despite the ways in which these and other details suggest an easy binary between Christian and Muslim identity, Houlik-Ritchey demonstrates that both texts, in different ways, are invested in the complex negotiations of neighborliness, which disrupts the self/enemy binary by casting both the self and the neighbor as ambiguous or strange.

Chapter 2 focuses on two texts from the *Floire and Blancheflor* cluster, the Middle English *Floris and Blancheflour* and the Castilian *Crónica de Flores y Blancaflor*, and here the book's nonhierarchical approach very clearly yields a compelling reading of the differences in the two romances and what they produce together; this chapter demonstrates that reading these romances together produces a much richer understanding of both texts' affective and emotional economies. The *Floire and Blancheflor* romances tell the story of a prince in Iberia (Floire/Floris/Flores) who falls in love with the daughter of a Christian slave (Blancheflor/Blancheflour/Blancaflor) in his parents' household. In both versions, Floris/Flores's parents sell Blancheflour/Blancaflor into slavery and he travels to Babylon to bring her back. But his commitment to doing so, while absolute in the Middle English text, is only one of many commitments Flores has in the Castilian text, where he considers abandoning her once his pursuit of her has helped him to achieve a position of honor in the Babylonian court. The Middle English text is missing its opening lines in all four surviving manuscripts and Houlik-Ritchey breaks with many scholars of the poem by declining to supply the missing portion of the narrative from its French source, noting that "recourse to the Old French may, in fact, obscure the Middle English text's particular priorities" (107), a choice that is supported by her readings of the significance of even seemingly small differences between different romances in this cluster and the two others. By exploring the very different relationships the two texts construct among wealth, trade, travel, love, and affect, Houlik-Ritchey illuminates the very different values of these two romances while also demonstrating how they both participate in imagining Iberia as part of a larger and intensely interwoven Muslim world before its conversion to Christianity.

Chapter 3 focuses on texts that are likely the most familiar to readers of this journal: the *Constance* story cluster, which includes a section from Nicolas Trevet's Anglo-Norman *Les cronicles*, Chaucer's *Man of Law's Tale*, the "Tale of Constance" from Gower's *Confessio Amantis*, the Portuguese *Livro do amante* (translated from Gower by Robert Payn), Juan de Cuenca's Castilian *Confisyón del amante*, and a fifteenth-century Middle English translation of Trevet's entire *Cronicles*. Houlik-Ritchey focuses on the Middle English versions by Chaucer and Gower alongside Payn's Portuguese text and Cuenca's Castilian text. Unlike the texts she considers in previous chapters, these romances don't imagine Iberia as a desirable site of narrative action but rather exclude or elide it in interesting ways, framing it as politically isolated from both Rome and the Muslim world; Houlik-Ritchey argues that the Portuguese and Castilian romances do the same to Northumberland (and England as a whole). This chapter's methodology is the closest to a traditional comparative approach, and does consider two texts (Payn's and Cuenca's) that are directly adapted from another that it considers (Gower's, which Houlik-Ritchey notes is the earliest English literary text to be translated into Iberian languages). Still, the book's nonhierarchical approach continues to illuminate the way subtle differences in the portrayal of Iberia across different romances in the same narrative cluster yield a more complex, nuanced, and nonbinary view of medieval Iberia.

By examining Middle English romance alongside its Castilian counterparts, this book comes at the genre from a different angle than those that study it alongside French or Italian sources or counterparts or even less-studied Germanic counterparts; such studies, Houlik-Ritchey notes, often privilege narratives of influence, genealogy, transmission, or origin. Her neighborly approach, she writes, aims to juxtapose romances that have a more complex relationship to each other, one that "has nothing to do with cultural or historical influence" but, instead, "illuminates their representational priorities and those of the larger story cluster" (6). This approach yields a different way of understanding medieval romance in general and Middle English and Castilian romance in particular. As Houlik-Ritchey writes, these two bodies of romances are rarely compared with each other directly or read alongside each other (and it remains unusual to read English romances through a Mediterranean studies lens), but reading them together demonstrates that the genre of romance imagines Iberia in ways that defy tidy narratives of either its religious plurality or its shifts in religious identity.

This, in turn, also pushes back against the long-challenged but persistent belief that popular romances are composed of stereotypes, binary oppositions, stock characters, and simplistic narratives. In particular, Houlik-Ritchey successfully challenges the idea that romances, especially those that contain conversion narratives, must present a stark Christian–Muslim binary, or that they must be structured by conflict or religious opposition or by a utopian model of religious co-existence. As her three chapters show, both Middle English and Castilian romance depict the experience of life and especially conversion in and around medieval Iberia in more complex ways than this. This book will be useful and illuminating for anyone working on the texts it analyzes, but also for those working with Middle English romance more generally—it will certainly change how I teach *Emaré*, a romance from the *Constance* cluster that isn't mentioned in the book—as well as for scholars and students interested in different frameworks for thinking about romance or about medieval England's relationship to the Mediterranean and the Muslim world.

USHA VISHNUVAJJALA
SUNY-New Paltz

ELEANOR JOHNSON. *Waste and the Wasters: Poetry and Ecosystemic Thought in Medieval England.* Chicago: University of Chicago Press, 2023. Pp. 224. $99.00 hardback; $30.00 paperback; $29.99 e-book.

Waste and the Wasters charts medieval literary thought about human–environment interdependence in England during the tumultuous fourteenth and fifteenth centuries. Johnson's monograph, with its strident argument for preferring "ecosystem" and "ecosystemic" as terms of analysis and its recovery of a late medieval discourse for thinking together the social and material resources of people and land, will appeal to medievalists and environmental humanists alike. Johnson describes an English Middle Ages that may be unfamiliar to some, as it includes belief in anthropogenic climate change (albeit manifesting through God's will to punish human behavior), in ecological precarity, in cataloguing catastrophic changes to their environment, and in making art that produces an "ecosystemic discourse" (5). This discourse revolved around the word "waste," a capacious term for improper use of economic, spiritual, and terrestrial resources. The most sophisticated and complete theorizations of waste, Johnson argues, appear in the poetic archive: in *Winner and Waster*, *Piers Plowman*, Chaucer's *Yeoman's Tale*, *Sir Gawain and the Green Knight*, and *Mum and the Sothsegger*, all of which interact with yet conceptually exceed Scripture, legal texts, and devotional writing. Johnson's work makes "waste" into a critical term for scholars working on late medieval England and, indeed, readers of any persuasion who seek to grapple with the complexities of relationships between humans and their environments in a time of climate crisis.

The first three chapters contextualize the historical and climatic environment of fourteenth- and fifteenth-century England alongside the nonpoetic discourses that attempt to respond to these ecosystemic disasters. Chapter 1, "The Five Disasters Facing Medieval Ecosystems," challenges the idea that the natural world in pre-Industrial Revolution medieval Europe was pristine and flourishing by enumerating five crises: erosion- and privatization-caused land shortages, climate change due to the Little Ice Age, food scarcity, the Black Death, and pollution in cities. Chapter 2 introduces "waste" via the biblical origins of the medieval conception of the term and its development in English common law. In the Bible, Johnson argues, the "waste" demonstrates the aftermath of "divine colonialism": a *vastitas*, a wasteland, "implies a history of violence, of military conflict, and of punishment" exacted by a *vastator*, a conqueror-waster (37). But "waste" is not all bad; the threat of being wasted, as "an invitation to being purged and made contrite," catalyzes individual and social reform (41). These ideas of waste and wasting transform in English common law to create "an idea of ecological accountability in which holders, owners, and users of land are accountable not only for their own property, but for the property of the broader community, whether held in common or held by other individuals" (42). While these definitions of waste thus far refer to an action (or inaction) exacted on a literal place, in the third chapter Johnson turns to "the wasting of *immaterial* goods" (51, emphasis original), tracing the use of *vastare* in late antique biblical commentaries to describe harm done to the soul rather than the land. Johnson demonstrates that penitential manuals transform spiritual waste into "sin against God" (54). Ecosystemic consequences result, as this form of waste damages not only the sinner but also the entire Christian community. By the end of the third chapter, Johnson has established that, in late fourteenth-century England, "Waste is *always* social; waste is *always* economic; waste is *always* ecosystemic" (68, emphasis original).

The next four chapters examine poetic articulations of the discourses of waste, which Johnson argues can express the ecosystemic valences of the term better than "any single nonpoetic genre of writing" (101). Her arguments in these chapters show how formal poetic elements act to theorize waste, beginning with Chapter 4, "*Winner and Waster*: The Imperilment of the Land," which finds that *Winner and Waster* uses personification allegory to produce "one of the most daring ecosystemic writings of the English Middle Ages" (69). The groundwork Johnson has laid in the first three chapters comes to fruition in her clear and accessible explanation of the specific legal tenets and penitential discourses at stake in the contest between the two personifications of the poem, Winner and Waster: Winner accuses Waster of misusing land resources, and Waster rejects the terms of Winner's accusation, declaring the true crime to be Winner's hoarding. While Winner "emphasizes that the health of the land and the cash economy are inextricably joined" (76), Waster's accusation against Winner relies on the penitential association between waste and neglect of spiritual resources.

In Chapter 5, "Wasters and Workers in *Piers Plowman*: Famine and Food Insecurity," Johnson treats several episodes in the poem: Mede's intervention in the trial of Wrong, the sins Gluttony and Sloth, the plowing of the half-acre, and the siege of the church of unity. *Piers Plowman* follows up on *Winner and Waster*, Johnson argues, by demonstrating the limitations of the law to contain waste, and ties wasting behavior to the moral value of working the land. In other words, we become wasters if we do not dedicate our time to agricultural labor. As a result, waste becomes a social crime that "can be committed by anyone, against anyone" (86). Johnson argues that the poem's episodic formal structure "enforces an interpretive unrest that keeps a reader in a state of heightened sensitivity to waste as a behavior that can come from any direction and be embodied by any character" (98), resulting in a theorization of waste as the "arch-sin and the arch-crime of the interimplicated ecological world because it affects people, lands, resources, and labor markets" (101).

In "Chaucer's Yeoman's Wasting Body: Pollution and Contagion," Johnson argues that Chaucer inherits the redefinitions of waste accomplished by earlier poets, and that he develops these changes further by associating waste not with a personification, but with a human, the Canon's Yeoman, who has a "wasting body"—"an individual human body that is wasted by, and also wastes, the physical, material, and even chemical microclimates in which it lives and works" (103). The Canon's Yeoman's body then allows Chaucer to imagine a "downside to work" (103), particularly the chemical work of alchemy within an urban environment. Chaucer conveys the infectious, ecosystemic nature of alchemy through poetic form, departing in *The Canon's Yeoman's Tale* from his usual five-stress meter to produce "*wasting verse*," "verse that's rhythmically underused, with emptiness instead of stresses" (118, emphasis original) or hypermetrical verse that "overconsumes" (119). As a result, readers "are drawn, sensorily, into the disorderly, wasted mind and habits of thought of the Yeoman himself" (120), underscoring his status as an ecosystemic contagion.

Chapters 7 and 8 plumb medieval England's poetic climate pessimism and climate optimism. Chapter 7 describes the grim environmental outlook of *Sir Gawain and the Green Knight*, wherein the banquet in Camelot becomes a scene of overconsumption; Gawain's journey through the wilderness a reminder of cold, hostile nature in the Little Ice Age; and the Green Chapel the center of a wasted "landscape that subsumes culture" (137). Ultimately, the poem produces a "radical ecosystemic fatalism" in which "the changing, vengeful, cold, wet climate of England will bury and erase Camelot and any courtly culture that seeks to replace it" (138). Chapter 8, by contrast, reads *Mum and the Sothsegger* as a fantasy of a garden ecosystem watched over by a benevolent caretaker god, "a fantasy of prosocial political behavior—collective labor—as a way of guaranteeing the beneficence of God as the guardian of the climate" (157).

The final chapter sums up the development in the concept of "waste" accomplished by fourteenth- and early fifteenth-century poets: they make the word signify "misuse of any resource in a way that has negative consequences for the whole ecosystem, including not only land, plants, and animals, but also and perhaps most urgently other people" (161). The chapter then goes on to explain how the meaning of "waste" lost this full synthesis of meaning and we, in turn, abandoned the full ecosystemic thought it enabled. The epilogue further clarifies Johnson's concept of ecosystemic medieval thought by contrast with the theories of Bruno Latour. Namely, while Latour's actor–network theory and similar schema label humans and nonhumans as actants with similar ontological status, the medieval theories relentlessly focus on the human: "It is *human* thoughts, words, will, intentions, time, energy, money, behavior, resources, and relationships that matter most" (171, emphasis original).

One of the greatest strengths of the project is its relentless situatedness in the ecosystemic thought of fourteenth- and fifteenth-century England—a reminder that all throughout the premodern world are microclimes of robust thought about human–environment relations, many of which undoubtedly would provide new conceptual tools for understanding and fighting climate change. Johnson's monograph is a thorough exploration of "waste" and its conceptual power in late medieval England, and her book is profoundly generative, acting as a model for the recovery and articulation of other such climate discourses and their relevance to our present, across the globe.

DANIELLE ALLOR
Haverford College

MICHAEL JOHNSTON. *The Middle English Book: Scribes and Readers, 1350–1500.* Oxford Studies in Medieval Literature and Culture. Oxford: Oxford University Press, 2023. Pp. xv, 288. $100.00.

The late Malcolm B. Parkes taught generations of twentieth-century Oxford paleography students to prepare for library visits by making "a list of questions to ask the manuscript." With this deceptively simple advice, he inspired legions of us not only to lifelong habits of list-making, but also to the more fundamental realization that *manuscripts have personalities* of their own. Fast forward to 2023 and the publication of Mike Johnston's *The Middle English Book*, which happily makes visible to today's readers his own working list of codicological questions for this project. Johnston, however, calls his list a "questionnaire," a term long used by Middle English dialectologists, and reflecting how much *A Linguistic Atlas of Late Mediaeval English* (*LALME*) and its digital successor are primary tools for his project. This kind of openness about his methodology is an engaging aspect of the book and will make it a valuable pedagogical tool for graduate students or scholars new to manuscript studies.

Johnston's questionnaire, however, is unexpectedly short but broad, asking just three big questions of his select corpus of a whopping 202 manuscripts:

(1) Was the manuscript produced in one go, or was its production protracted?
(2) How much scribal infrastructure does one need to posit to account for the manuscript's production?

(3) Can we discover anything about the relationship between producers and users, and does this indicate whether the book was intrinsic or extrinsic [to that relationship]? (36)

Seasoned codicologists will see immediately that, given his large corpus, Johnston is setting out not to do a deep dive into any of them, but rather, he explains, to create "a new theory of categories" for book production (45). He finds four such categories exemplified in his corpus: The Elaborate Book (manuscripts made by complex production teams [Chapter 2]), The Streamlined Book (often made "at one go" by a single scribe or two [Chapter 3]), The Evolving Book (produced with unforeseen additions over time [Chapter 4]), and The DIY Book (the homemade book [Chapter 5]). But, he writes, "[the categories] I propose here are not meant to be prescriptive. . . . Instead, I intend them as purely descriptive and heuristic—that is, they represent an attempt to make sense of the messy realities of the production and circulation of vernacular literature" (45).

Johnston chose manuscripts of four particular works to make up his test corpus and they seem, at first glance, a random bunch: the *Prick of Conscience*; *Piers Plowman*; and two short secular poems by Lydgate, the "Dietary" and "*Stans puer ad mensam*." But what they have in common is that they were all heavily copied works, providing rich core samples, so to speak, from among the thousands of surviving Middle English texts across many genres. Take, for instance, the two Lydgate pieces: the "Dietary" was "far and away the most popular 'information' piece of verse in Middle English" (9), copied even into medical collections, and cropping up especially in Evolving Books (97). "*Stans puer*" is a work of conduct literature and "ranks fourth in the list of most frequently copied Lydgate texts" (9), often together with the "Dietary," while *Piers Plowman* and *Prick of Conscience*, being longer works, often either stand alone or appear with shorter bedfellows, copied together three times (10 n. 36 for these lists). However, the generic, literary, medical, religious, or social issues connected with these four sample texts are mostly not Johnston's concern in this book; his goal, rather, is to offer a bird's-eye view of *the circumstances of book production and earliest known readership* of each of these much-copied works.

These four types of books are, of course, well known to codicologists, if not by these user-friendly names. But the four categories, like all taxonomies, do at times give Johnston heuristic grief, as he admits. The Elaborate Book, for instance, refers to codices carefully planned and executed by a production team, especially expensive illuminated books, such as the lavish Vernon manuscript (Oxford, Bodleian Library, MS Eng. poet. a. 1, which contains both *Piers* and the *Prick of Concience*) or, more humbly, Bodleian Library, MS Douce 104. Johnston wrestles with placing the few *Piers* manuscripts containing even one illustration (only Douce 104 has a full cycle), putting them "in the category of manuscripts with ambiguous evidence of whether professional artists were involved or not" [66]). So, do scribe-illustrators count as "elaborate" production teams? Were they elaborate planners? (Certainly, the Douce scribe-illustrator was, as Denise L. Despres and I showed in 1999.)[1] And were they professional? Johnston's use of the word remains a moving target, despite a valiant effort to survey its present usage (Nomenclature, Chapter 1), which would have benefited from citing Parkes's foundational distinction between "professional" and "commercial" scribes—though Johnston rightly praises Linne Mooney's clarity on it, which in fact stems from Parkes's. He considers the famous illustration of the plowman on fol. 1v of the *Piers* in Cambridge, Trinity College, MS R.3.14, likely also to be an "amateur" or scribe-illustrator (67), but given its physical placement, making such a call raises thorny and multidisciplinary questions, not resolvable in a quick overview. However, to be fair, it is *not* the resolution of such specific issues that Johnston is after—he is constructing a bigger picture of his 202 manuscripts, the view from 30,000 feet. Readers, especially long-time codicologists, will have to adjust to this aerial perspective, rather than the usual microscopic perspectives—not to say rabbit holes—we tend to find attractive.

The Streamlined Book (Chapter 3) explores simpler codices, and here Johnston discusses several famous scribes such as Stephen Dodesham, and the London scribes whom Mooney and Stubbs identified (cases on which Johnston pronounces himself "agnostic"): Adam Pinkhurst, Richard Osbarn, John Marchaunt. It is not London manuscripts, however, that are Johnston's main interest in this book, but rather books of regional dialectal texts and local provenances. The Evolving Book (Chapter 4) takes in manuscripts that show complex accretion over time, among which Johnston provides a lucid analysis of the collation structure and paper stocks of Cambridge University Library (CUL), MS Ll.4.14, a book long puzzling to Langlandians for its combination of *Piers* and *Richard the Redeless* alongside math, astronomy, and physiognomy texts. Johnston finds its quiring

[1]Kathryn Kerby-Fulton and Denise L. Despres, *Iconography and the Professional Reader: The Politics of Book Production in the Douce "Piers Plowman"* (Minneapolis: University of Minnesota Press, 1999).

to contain "three separate commissions from the same scribe" (115), explaining, perhaps, why the contents don't entirely cohere. Finally, the DIY Book (Chapter 5) covers famous instances of homemade manuscripts, several of which Johnston has published on previously, such as Thornton's "London" and "Lincoln" manuscripts. But he also mentions some far less famous cases, such as the two mysterious "plenus amoris" scribes, Thomas Tilot and Ricardus Rauf, copyists of a *Piers* and a *Prick of Conscience* respectively, identified via Simon Horobin's "intricate detective work" as located at Chichester Cathedral (134). I'd add that Tilot ("a vicar . . . serving under a secular canon" [134]) would have been one of Chichester Cathedral's *vicars choral*, a class I've recently studied as vital to the resurgence of Middle English poetry and lyric as "clerical proletarian" bureaucratic scribes, musicians, and poets.

Inevitably there are areas where Johnston's four-text corpus just can't cast a wide enough net, and one of these is books made in religious houses, which, he concludes, "played a small role in the copying and dissemination of Middle English manuscripts" (70). This is rather too pessimistic. There are certainly reasons why male religious houses tended to collect less Middle English, but for this we need a bigger net. He rightly points to the religious origins of the CUL, MS Dd.1.17 *Piers* manuscript, calling for further study (though many prior Dd studies are not mentioned, including Karrie Fuller's).[2] Nor are the Carthusians, famous for their extensive ownership of Middle English mysticism—presumably the Carthusians weren't known to have any of Johnston's four works, but they would have provided him with many compelling counter-examples to the dearth of English he laments in religious houses, plus an intriguing set of the "intrinsic" vs. "extrinsic" production–readership issues that most interest him. Johnston's net also doesn't catch any nunneries, another classic counter-example, which, as David Bell showed years ago, were much more up to date than their male counterparts in acquiring Middle English titles.[3] As my co-author, Linda Olson, showed in *Opening Up Middle English Manuscripts*, monastic houses held a surprising range of Middle English manuscripts.[4] But

[2]Karrie Fuller, "Repurposing *Piers Plowman*: Literary Geography and the Codicological Remaking of Langland's Work," Ph.D. diss. (University of Notre Dame, 2016).

[3]David Bell, *What Nuns Read: Books and Libraries in Medieval English Nunneries* (Kalamazoo: Cistercian Publications, [2016?]).

[4]Kathryn Kerby-Fulton, Maidie Hilmo, and Linda Olson, *Opening Up Middle English Manuscripts: Literary and Visual Approaches* (Ithaca: Cornell University Press, 2024).

Johnston does provide a helpful, plunderable footnote listing the twenty-eight vernacular manuscripts he was able to count via medieval library catalogues—though as he concedes, rarely was a vernacular work mentioned in an ecclesiastical library catalogue entry (see, e.g., Norwich Cathedral Library's misleading cataloguing of London, British Library, MS Arundel 292, with no reference to its famous early Middle English texts).

Johnston's two final chapters (6 and7), The Proliferation of Scribes, I and II, round out the book with brief overviews of how local production evolved in regional areas via the infrastructure of myriad medieval bureaucracies (legal, governmental, ecclesiastical, and household). This story, familiar to modern literary scholars from historians like Michael Clanchy, and studied painstakingly region by region in the work of codicologists like Ralph Hanna (Yorkshire), Carter Revard (Herefordshire), and Theresa O'Byrne (Dublin/Pale), is argued in Johnston's corpus via a statistical approach. So, for instance, his subchapter on the provenance of *Prick of Conscience* and *Piers* manuscripts lists selected regional manuscripts via their *LALME* grid coordinates, aiming to pinpoint how close to a manuscript's dialect area early readers consumed it. For Johnston, proximity of makers and users demonstrates that most of his corpus (75 percent) were read nearby, not exported. But I would point out that there would be good reasons for this kind of proximity: reading in one's own dialect would always be preferable, and several works were even consciously translated from one dialect to another (like Douce 104's Middle Hiberno-English *Piers*).

Johnston's Conclusion takes us into the era of print, with some instances of how his four works appeared in the age of Caxton and beyond, and a very useful Appendix called "The Manuscripts in My Corpus," which will likely be raided by codicologists looking for their favorite codices. Johnston's view from the clouds is still a less common perspective in codicology, but in real life aerial patterns often reveal things archeologists can't find just by digging, so we are grateful to him.

KATHRYN KERBY-FULTON
University of Victoria

Annette Kern-Stähler and Elizabeth Robertson, eds. *Literature and the Senses*. Oxford Twenty-First Century Approaches to Literature. Oxford: Oxford University Press, 2023. Pp. xix, 519. $155.00 hardback.

Annette Kern-Stähler and Elizabeth Robertson have put together twenty-six essays primarily on English-language literature with two specific goals: inserting the medieval period into the conversation on the senses in literature in the periods from the Enlightenment onward and, more broadly, demonstrating literature's special aptness for exploring ideas about sensory perception. This collection broadens the conversation in literary sensory studies in several directions.

Literature and the Senses is "the first volume to investigate literary representations of sense perception across periods" (2). Scholars have (understandably) worked primarily within one period when examining the role of the senses. This hyperfocus has led to underestimation of sensory thought's continuity across periods and especially to neglect of the medieval period. Kern-Stähler and Robertson place the blame on the eighteenth century, when Enlightenment thinkers drew a sharp divide between modern and premodern sensation at Descartes. Likewise, scholars of Romanticism have deemed interest in individual sensation to be that period's special province. By demonstrating that all senses are important and often central to literature of all periods, the essays in this collection deliberately "complicate the neat chronologies put in place by a number of scholars on the basis of the prominence of one particular sense over another in a given period" (7).

Literature's capacity to communicate sensation is the collection's second concern. Despite Michel Serres's contention that language cannot recreate sensory experience, the editors argue that literature both reinforces and breaks down standard interpretations of the senses in a given time period. In proving this point, the editors and many contributors rely on Maurice Merleau-Ponty's sensory philosophy, particularly his formulation of sensation encompassing the self, others, and things. The Self–Others–things model allows contributors to show how literature defines social divisions, explores technologies that mediate the senses, and shows the material world's effects on humanity.

In perhaps the most valuable part of the general introduction, the editors provide a concise overview of the collection's six sections (sight, hearing, smell, taste, touch, and multisensoriality) with special focus on the medieval and early modern understanding of each sense. Kern-Stähler and Robertson review Aristotle's explanation of the senses, medieval or early modern scholars' contributions to sensory science, the role the senses played in premodern religion, and trends in modern literary critiques. These overviews include extensive footnotes and they provide a useful starting-point for further exploration across periods.

Sight has little meaning without its cultural and personal context. Stephanie Trigg employs "looking" as a more flexible term than "gaze" to describe the historical and cultural contexts that guide the meanings of the look in Chaucer's *Troilus and Criseyde* and two twenty-first-century texts, Hilary Mantel's *Wolf Hall* and Alexis Wright's *The Swan Book*. Zoë Lehmann Imfeld takes a similar approach to faces in Victorian ghost stories, arguing that genuine fear on the face of a viewer or inhumanity in the face of a ghost were significant proof of the supernatural at a time when technologies were calling the certainty of sight into question. Sue Zemka's essay centers on the relationship between Simone de Beauvoir, Elizabeth "Zaza" Lacoin, and Merleau-Ponty. Their personal lives influenced both how a Cezanne painting looked in Beauvoir's memoir and how the senses operated in Merleau-Ponty's philosophy. Finally, poet Nuala Watt, drawing inspiration from Homer and modern disability studies, explores the ways that open-form poetry can express partial sight.

Hearing is particularly engaged in communication, including sound technology. Examining Middle English romance and visionary literature, Corinne Saunders demonstrates that hearing voices is not insanity but an aspect of personal growth. Physical or emotional trauma are frequent parts of that growth (such as in *Sir Orfeo* or Margery Kempe's autobiography), but the trauma is less significant than the inner voice leading the individual to transformation. Simon Jackson explores the challenges of translating sound (both speech and music) to text during the early modern period's rapid increase in printing and literacy. Stacey MacDowell investigates the positive and negative emotions evoked by echoing sound in Romantic literature via the architectural space of churches. Anne-Julia Zwierlein foregrounds Victorian science to show that scientific interests such as sound recording were employed in fiction alongside social concerns, for example, the question of women speaking in public. Michael Davidson taps into the role of deafness in poetry from Keats to today to argue that poets create meaning with silence in a genre characterized by its use of sound.

Social groupings and places are often defined by smell. Holly Dugan traces the developing notion of race through early modern imagery of the lily, a symbol of corruptible chastity and whiteness. Isabel Karreman reveals how Ben Jonson's *Bartholomew Fair* calls on the audience's memory of the yearly fair's smellscape as part of its atmosphere and plot. Ursula Kluwick's examination of Victorian writing on sanitation uses both place and social status to expose middle-class discomfort with the odors of poverty: authors insulated middle-class readers by reporting disease-causing odors in visual terms alone. Social distinctions are also at the forefront of Hsuan L. Hsu's look at contemporary BIPOC speculative fiction, which he argues turns olfactory racism on its head to redefine smell as a positive reinforcer and creator of family and community.

Tasting leads to judgment (moral or aesthetic) of the tasted thing. Mary Flannery and Simon Smith delve into the premodern significance of "sweetness," which often signified any pleasing sensation. Flannery notes the medieval link between wisdom (*sapientia*) and flavor (*sapor*) before analyzing the taste of the kiss in *The Miller's Tale* and exploring the question of aesthetic good taste, particularly that of the fastidious Absolon. Smith engages with (sometimes synaesthetic) sweet music in early modern texts. Jamie Fumo, in contrast, explores bad flavor and flavorlessness in medieval poetry (both termed "unsavory") and locates ways that good moral flavor can be lost or regained. Vanessea Guignery argues that taste in contemporary novels is inextricably linked with emotions, which enhance or destroy the flavor of food. Poet Zoë Skoulding writes on the historical, natural, and poetic elements of her own work with the French Revolution's Republican calendar, which was centered on the natural world and particularly seasonal food.

Touch operates according to strict social rules, the breach of which can be either freeing or traumatic. While touch often presents special sexual danger in medieval moral literature, Hannah Piercy shows that rituals of social conduct are more prevalent in romances such as *Sir Gawain and the Carl of Carlise* and *Sir Degaré*, even when eroticism might be expected. In Mark Amsler's article, touch mirrors society's hierarchy in the Digby *Mary Magdalene*, while also reflecting thought about knowledge formation, emotion, and religious feeling as Mary experiences touch in realistic, allegorical, and spiritual ways. The healing touch in the modernist film script *Jacob's Hands* explores World War I trauma, spirituality, and fame through Jacob's miraculous healing ability. Abbie

Garrington argues that the Black characters in the script also reveal mid-century assumptions about Black embodiment as well as Jacob's disregard for race and class differences. Santanu Das explores similar issues of touch, intimacy, and trauma in World War I-era literature. Touch appears as a central element in texts written during and after the war. It creates intimacy among those in the trenches, reflects reduced social distinctions between white and colonial or Black soldiers, and reminds survivors of the horror of the war.

Throughout the collection and especially in the multisensoriality section, the impossibility of truly separating the senses is clear. Richard Newhauser employs the concepts of *energeia* and sensory communities to show how *Piers Plowman's Crede* calls on a Lollard sensory community by rejecting the traditional religious and social symbol of the successful male plowman. Sarah Stanbury emphasizes tactile aspects of speech in images of speech scrolls in the *Carthusian Miscellany*. Mirja Lobnik and Virginia Richter consider the human senses in their natural environments in twentieth- and twenty-first-century literature, Lobnik arguing that human sensory experience is an inextricable part of the natural environment and Richter focusing on the ocean as a liminal space that equally draws characters in with sensation and provokes fear of drowning.

These thought-provoking articles stand alone well, but the collection does its best work as a whole, encouraging sensory literary studies to cross period boundaries more freely. Medievalists have much to learn from scholarship on other periods. Richter's look at the ocean (largely a place of danger in medieval literature) raises a fascinating area for exploring sensory experience across time. Modernists also have much to learn from premodernists. Zemka's excellent essay is centered on the phrase "the descent of the spirit to the heart of the senses" (64), attributed by Zemka to Merleau-Ponty. Analyzing the phrase's biographical meaning in Merleau-Ponty's philosophy is central to Zemka's essay. Even more knowledge about Merleau-Ponty would be uncovered through analysis of the phrase's philosophical meaning: the specific premodern scientific understanding of the senses that influenced Merleau-Ponty through Descartes. Kern-Stähler and Robertson have put together a highly valuable collection that should be read in its entirety.

KATELYNN ROBINSON
Eastern New Mexico University

STEPHEN KNIGHT. *Nature and Medieval Literature*. New Century Chaucer. Cardiff: University of Wales Press, 2024. Pp. xiii, 313. £80.00 hardback; £80.00 e-book.

Scholarship attending to the material impact of nonhuman forces and beings on medieval literary culture has expanded rapidly over recent decades to include, for example, animals (wild, feral, and domestic), weather, geology, trees, elements, waters, soils, disease, parasites, and much of this inflected by insights from queer theory, feminist theory, and critical race studies. As a work in conversation with medieval ecocriticism, in many ways Knight's nature-centric monograph is unusual in eschewing the majority of this work. The author outlines the impetus for the study, which is to give "detailed attention to the ways in which writers and their texts actually responded to the natural world" as an alternative to a "conceptually analytic" approach that interrogates the cultural category of nature (xi). This work expands not only on Knight's decades of medievalist study but also on the author's recent approach to themes of environment in the transhistorical final chapter of *Medieval Literature and Social Politics*, which centered on the figure of Merlin.[1] Nature is simply defined in a single sentence: "[b]y 'natural world' is meant the entire domain of animals, birds, trees and flora, as well as natural landscapes and their features, even including weather" (1). Yet, in the volume itself, the natural world is more sensitively imagined: not just as a background context or a parallel alterity, but sometimes as powerful intersecting systems with medieval literary concerns, and Knight does allow the caveat that "nature" in the sense in which it is used here is not the medieval understanding of the term (4). The great strength of this work is its tremendous range, most chapters addressing a genre-defined selection of between twenty and forty texts, painstakingly yet engagingly directed toward finding thematic patterns in the presentation of nature across the corpus of medieval literature.

The introduction to this volume gives a conventional narrative for nature as a serious critical object in literary criticism, placing Rachel Carson's *Silent Spring* as a watershed text for ecological consciousness. The backdrop of growing social counter-movement to postwar capitalist exploitation coincides with parallel scholarly movements in Britain and

[1]Stephen Knight, *Medieval Literature and Social Politics: Studies of Cultures and Their Contexts* (Abingdon: Routledge, 2021).

America in the mid-twentieth century that seek to highlight environmental damage as ideologically driven. This critical movement comes late to medieval historiography because "[a]n important recurring theme among the historians was the argument that [climate destructive economic and ideological systems developed] from the sixteenth century on" (2). Highlighted important works in 1966 and 1973 that take nature as a central critical object for medieval literary reading might have challenged the suggestion that environment was not a mid-century medievalist concern. Largely well-received is ecocriticism on Chaucer, including that of Sarah Stanbury, Felicity Riddy, Lisa Kiser, and Lesley Kordecki. Medieval ecocriticism from Gillian Rudd, Rebecca Douglass, Derek Pearsall, and Elizabeth Salter also enters into later chapters, as both support and counterpoint to analysis, especially in chapters 5 and 7.

This volume has a range of 500 years in medieval Welsh, Scottish, English, and French material, working across seven chapters each defined by the selected corpus. These chapters are described as essays that have resonances with each other, but are not thematically linked. Chapter 1 examines early Welsh literature, especially the *Mabinogi*, in which supernatural forces abound, sometimes revealing traces of Celtic myth and a "dark" or "unnatural" nature, especially in the case of the synthetic Blodeuwedd, made from blossom (36–38). Chapter 2 examines *Perceval*, *Peredur*, and *Sir Perceval of Galles*, beginning with the hero in rural and unrefined seclusion and ending with him courteously stationed at Camelot. In these texts, "[n]ature is an indicative and often symbolic context for the action of romance" (72). Chapter 3 examines the major works of Geoffrey Chaucer, acknowledging the significant attention this author has already received from ecocriticism. The unnaturalness of Fame and Fortune, and the use of Nature as thematic scene—a "fine overture to a major sequence" (96)—dominate the earlier and middle works, but the *Canterbury Tales* emerges as the most complex, notably the arch manipulations of overlapping yet opposite worlds in *The Franklin's Tale*, also wittily evoked in *The Nun's Priest's Tale*. Animality receives a very close treatment in this chapter, which will be continued into Chapter 4 for William Dunbar and Robert Henryson. The nature presented in Dunbar's dream visions is used as a "fine revelatory weapon" (174) to critique the structure of social power, but there are other elements to this survey of his work. Many texts suggest fascination with the estrangement of night, and the contorted city emerges in Dunbar's urban descriptions, as "cramped honeycombs" or a "beggars' nest" (141). Henryson's *Testament* and *Orpheus* are read as again revealing a "dark," grim force in nature, but it is in the *Morall Fabillis* that Henryson is found to present "the interrelation of the natural and the human worlds as both complementary and mutually, even allegorically, revealing" (175). Henryson's fables are the centerpiece of this analysis, highlighting especially "The Wolf and the Lamb" and "The Paddock and the Mouse" as sustaining complex meditations on animal lives and human morals simultaneously. Chapters 5 and 6, with their mission of introducing nature-centric analysis to popular Middle English romances (the twenty "most interesting" cases [177]) and Robin Hood, from Broadview ballads up to Hollywood film, are especially complex and ambitious. Chapter 5 also breaks the pattern set by the earlier chapters of ending with a short conclusion by introducing further texts instead: those romances that the author sees as having already received ecocritical attention at the expense of more popular romances, *Sir Gawain and the Green Knight* and Malory's *Morte Darthur*, for which brief new readings based on the chapter findings are offered. Chapter 5's section "Romances with Nature Involved in the Plot" (200–212) valuably complicates the typical romance arc from wildness to sophistication (219) by introducing natural systems as functioning parts of romance narratologies in *Sir Cleges*, *Chevalere Assigne*, and especially *Sir Orfeo* and *Launfal*. Chapter 6 is likewise different in its structure, and most like the earlier-published convincing analysis of different realizations of the Merlin figure from the earliest Welsh versions to those of the last twenty years in western Europe and America. Like Merlin as a figure of knowledge, Robin Hood's relationship to the environment is underpinned by his function as a figure of the Greenwood—a manageable arboreal space adjacent to medieval urban lives—and his outlaw status. Though varyingly evoked, Robin Hood always operates as a feral and liberated agent for Knight: "the outlaw is always in some way linked to and a part of the positive myth of nature" (260). Chapter 7 moves away from the narrative poetry and prose that have occupied the previous chapters, and acknowledges this in the careful explanation of medieval lyric context (261–62). Ecocritical analysis here is notably underpinned by Gillian Rudd's work in the area.[2] The chapter takes in forty lyrics, including the Holly and Ivy carols, springtime love lyrics, and Marian devotion, often bringing mystical and secular readings alongside each other. William Dunbar's work also returns here in the form of love lyric. The conclusion

[2]Gillian Rudd, *Greenery: Ecocritical Readings of Late Medieval English Literature* (Manchester: Manchester University Press, 2007).

of this final chapter links to previous ones: the patterns that have emerged gradually are brought to the fore in these last pages. These are often matters of literary convention, but some of these details can be ecocritically telling: the romances, for example, present a broader range of animals than the lyrics, which are decidedly avian, yet they form a genre in which it is far less conventional for nature to be a central focus.

From an ecocritical stand-point, the refusal of definitional analysis of what is meant by "nature" is disconcerting, and some medieval ecocriticism is perhaps too hastily dismissed by the author. Interrogating the implicit anthropocentrism of dividing human and natural worlds is placed beyond the intended scope of this volume. The intention is rather that the sheer scale of this work yields insight unavailable to ecocritical approaches that frame particular texts through intellectual histories of medieval environmental thought. Though not articulated by Knight, the relationship of such scale and pattern to ecology itself might well be convincingly explored: ecocritics might therefore find this volume to be an invitation rather than an admonishment.

Alexandra Paddock
Keble College, Oxford

Greta LaFleur, Masha Raskolnikov, and Anna Kłosowska, eds. *Trans Historical: Gender Plurality before the Modern*. Ithaca: Cornell University Press, 2021. Pp. viii, 393. $35.95 paperback.

Over the past five years, a rapidly growing number of premodernists have worked diligently to bring the frameworks of trans studies to bear on the distant past. Scholars familiar with the broad contours of contemporary political debates around trans identities and rights but unfamiliar with the body of scholarship in trans studies, both modern and premodern, frequently and understandably seem to imagine that to "do" premodern trans studies is to "look for" trans people in the past. *Trans Historical: Gender Plurality before the Modern* offers readers a more expansive set of entry-points into premodern trans studies, and thus provides an ideal primer for those interested in learning more about the field. In the words of the editors, the volume seeks to extend "the purview of trans studies and trans histories beyond individual experience to serve as an analytical tool for inquiry into affective flows, structures of power, and burgeoning epistemologies of difference" (2). While some essays in this volume do turn to particular historical persons (Elenx de Céspedes, Eleanor Rykener, Marin le Marcis) and literary characters (Silence), as a whole the collection foregrounds the methodological affordances of *ambivalence*, not in the pejorative sense of indecision, but in the etymological sense of comparing two (or more) seemingly irreconcilable perspectives. *Trans Historical* is a remarkable collection, one that highlights the archival, theoretical, and methodological diversity of premodern trans studies.

The volume's introduction kaleidoscopically spins out a variety of questions about what we mean by "trans" when speaking about premodern cultures, what "trans" can help us know about the past, and how we can "do" trans studies. Approaching transness expansively, the editors ask "Is *transgender* always gender? If not, what else might it be?" (9). They rightly note that this broader vision of transness has long been constitutive of the field: "One of the hallmarks of thinking in trans studies," they write, "has been a scholarly willingness, even from the field's inception, to think beyond the unit of the person or the population to evince what we might call a trans metaphysics" (7). Importantly, this mode of "think[ing] beyond" the individual or the population does not fall into the usual queer vein of analyzing and critiquing forms of normativity. The editors follow Karma Lochrie's work in *Heterosyncrasies* in resisting "using the language of normativity to describe the trans and gender-expansive subjects at the center of this collection."[1] "The essays that follow," they write, "suggest that there is neither a present nor a past existence of some sort of totalizing gender normativity" (13).

In addition to a substantive introduction and epilogue, the volume consists of fourteen wide-ranging essays divided into three sections: "Archives: Revisiting Law and Medicine," "Frameworks: Representing Early Trans Lives," and "Interventions: Critical Trans Methodologies." In the first section, readers may be particularly interested in Igor H. De Souza's analysis of the sodomy trial of the Spaniard Elenx de Céspedes. Situating Céspedes's life and case in the context of early modern Spanish (and particularly Inquisitorial) conceptualizations of both sodomy and hermaphroditism (as Céspedes claimed to be a "hermaphrodite"), De Souza ultimately argues that Elenx takes a surprisingly conservative view

[1]Karma Lochrie, *Heterosyncrasies: Female Sexuality when Normal Wasn't* (Minneapolis: University of Minnesota Press, 2005).

of the sex/gender system in their deposition. "Elenx," he writes, "is not trying to overturn or question dominant early modern notions of sexuality, and this is what makes their perspective 'conservative.' Rather than contesting such notions, Elenx deploys them to naturalize their unconventional sex and gender configuration" (51). This claim resonates with Greta LaFleur's epilogue, in which she writes that "there are as many distinct gendered bodily morphologies as there are trans and nonbinary identities, whether the people who live in those bodies identify at odds with social and cultural expectations surrounding womanhood or manhood, or not" (372). That not all historical transness was necessarily "nonnormative" or "liberatory" in the modern progressive sense is a key insight; after all, it would be all too easy simply to label gender-variant subjects such as Elenx as "nonnormative." But what would such a label teach us about the past that we don't already know?

One of the real strengths of this collection is its inclusion of several essays that rely on non-Romance-language archives, including work on Polish, Turkish, and Byzantine Greek sources. For instance, Anna Kłosowska's translation and analysis of the deposition of Wojciech of Poznań is remarkable for its arguments about premodern trans community. "The presence of one trans or genderqueer person," Kłosowska argues, "reveals the existence of a historically documented queer and trans community in urban centers of mid-sixteenth-century Poland, which valued them and depended on their experience. The deposition at least gestures to a series of coalitions, if not a community, with areas of collaboration in spite of major differences" (115). While the first sentence may strike some readers as an overly strong claim to make based on a single court deposition, it is a theoretical statement well worth weighing carefully. It assumes—rightly, in my view—that we are none of us islands, and that any individual's survival, much less thriving, is predicated on a whole social infrastructure. The object of premodern trans studies thus might be less the individual case history and more the infrastructures that made gender-variant lives possible.

Turning to the collection's second section on visual and literary representations of transness, readers may be particularly interested in Masha Raskolnikov's essay on the thirteenth-century romance the *Roman de Silence*. Rather than trying to pin down the precise contours of Silence's gender, or the precise ontological or even epistemological boundaries of transness in the period, Raskolnikov argues that the *Roman de Silence* offers an "immanent, if implicit, theory of sex and gender" (181). This theorizing is one of the affordances of studying imaginative literature, since it gestures toward forms of premodern thought, imagination, and fantasy that might not otherwise be visible in, say, the generic confines of legal and medical archives. What's more, Raskolnikov's expansive reading of *Silence* helps us imagine how medieval writers themselves imagined what it might be like to *live* a gender-variant life. "Silence," she writes, "maintains an inner monologue about their sex and gender. In the manner of a psychomachia, a dramatized allegorical conflict within a human soul, the allegorical figures of Nature and Nurture externalize Silence's self-doubt. They return again and again to debate which of them is truly in charge of Silence's identity" (197). Though Raskolnikov does not make this claim explicitly, it strikes me that this allegorization of "self-doubt" might be read as an attempt to represent what we now call "gender dysphoria"—not, to be sure, as a modern-day diagnostic category, but as a phenomenological experience. However we might read this allegorization, Raskolnikov's contention that "the *Roman de Silence* puts enormous pressure on the nature of gender *not* in order to destabilize it but to stabilize it otherwise, to open up some of its heretofore less livable possibilities" (198–99) can serve as a usefully capacious guide for approaching other premodern representations of transness.

The collection's final set of essays turn away from questions of law, medicine, and representation in order to expand theorizations of transness beyond gender per se, looking to adjacent fields such as posthumanism, theology, and adaptation. In particular, Micah Goodrich's reading of *Piers Plowman* is an excellent example of the long-standing entanglement of trans studies and disability studies. He articulates this enmeshment succinctly when he writes that "Misshapen bodies are bodies that do not conform to the shape of society" (277). Reading the biopolitics of the "salvific collective" represented in *Piers Plowman*, Goodrich argues that the dream vision figures a medieval conception of "slow death," one that "meant that some bodies were meant to be immiserated so that others could respond with charity and thus secure their own salvation at the expense of the disenfranchised." "The rehabilitation politics of the poem" thus suggest "that some bodies required maiming in order for the social body to function, for charity to work, and for the inequity of bodily physiology to reify the social politics that it represents" (268). Indeed, in its own way, each of the volume's essays is precisely concerned with the relationship between "bodily physiology" and "the social politics that it represents."

To my mind one of the most moving and methodologically rich concepts in the volume is what Scott Larson calls "trans-attendance," a method that "treats gender-variant people as having full, and thus changeable lives." "In some cases," Larson writes, "the focus on correctly identifying a historical subject (as trans, cisgender, lesbian, etc.) can lead to overvaluing one point in a figure's life as the moment of true identity. Often the moments of vulnerability, 'discovery,' or 'revelation' by which gender-variant people enter the historical record are treated as evidence of identity across their entire lives" (362). This reminder that not only are people different from each other—to invoke Eve Sedgwick's first axiom—but that *people are different from themselves*, both at any moment and across time, should be foundational to the study of premodern transness as it continues to grow and thrive.

JOSEPH GAMBLE
University of Toledo

LISA LAMPERT-WEISSIG. *Instrument of Memory: Encounters with the Wandering Jew.* Ann Arbor: University of Michigan Press, 2024. Pp. iv, 278. $75.00 hardback.

In the acknowledgments of her new book, *Instrument of Memory: Encounters with the Wandering Jew*, Lisa Lampert-Weissig shares that the subject of the Wandering Jew has traveled with her through many stages of her life, from a postdoctoral fellowship in Berlin, through two academic posts—first at the University of Illinois, Urbana-Champaigne and then on to the University of California, San Diego—and finally ends during the twenty-first-century global pandemic. These many experiences and the people whom Lampert-Weissig met along the way materialize in both literal and spectral ways in *Instrument of Memory*. And while there is, of course, seemingly nothing unusual about our books emerging from our life experiences, Lampert-Weissig's *Instrument of Memory* benefits in so many compelling ways from her having lived in Berlin when she reflects on what such artists as Marc Chagall, Uri Zvi Greenberg, Edmond Fleg, Sholem Asch, and Stefan Heym (né Helmut Fleig). These artists, caught in a changing Europe during the early-to-mid twentieth century, came face to face with the results of the Wandering Jew legend, and Lampert-Weissig was able to imagine herself into their life stories. Another aspect of *Instrument of Memory* that shows Lampert-Weissig to be the perfect author for it is her ability to work with Yiddish, Hebrew, German, French, and Latin, as evidenced by both her occasional changing of translations and her adding notes in original languages. Being a medievalist emerges as the third thing that situates Lampert-Weissig as the ideal author for *Instrument of Memory*. In Danielle Coty-Danielle's Q&A with the author, hosted on the University of Michigan Press's website, Lampert-Weissig explains to what extent "Christian teachings" and "Christian memory" rely on "Jewish experience and even Jewish individuals." This reliance on Jews and their texts "denies Jewish agency and even Jewish humanity by framing Judaism, Jewish belief and even Jews themselves as existing to serve Christian needs. This is starkly framed by the medieval monk, Matthew Paris, who views the Wandering Jew as a 'proof of the Christian faith.'"[1] In the introduction to the book, Lampert-Weissig mentions the perennial dangers of the Wandering Jew legend as a destructive narrative that "has figured in some of the most notorious works of antisemitic polemic and propaganda" (9).

Stretching from the thirteenth century and Matthew Paris (Part 1) to the twenty-first century and authors from the USA, the UK, and Israel (Part 4), *Instrument of Memory* is intentionally built as a "deep-dive diachronic" by "trying to situate each text within its historical context as well as within the author or artist's larger body of work."[2] Part 1 opens with two early texts—Matthew Paris's *Chronica majora* and the 1602 *Kurtze Beschreibung*—that illustrate how the "Wandering Jew embodies the denial of Jewish coevalness. . . . this Jew is preserved in a kind of spiritual stasis awaiting a prophesied Christian future" (10). Referenced throughout the book, *Chronica majora* and *Kurtze Beschreibung* enable medievalists to draw connections among the many places where these early texts affect the later outcomes of the legend. Part 2, for instance, directly links Eugène Sue's and Henrich Heine's writing to "Matthew Paris's thirteenth-century *Chronica*" and the antisemitism of the thirteenth century (67). In Part 3 Lampert-Weissig points out that if "a medieval individual such as Margery Kempe could insert herself into a scene from the Passion in an imaginative and meditative way, so too can creative writers such as [Edmond] Fleg insert themselves into (or imagine themselves in) the life of Jesus (231–32 n. 4).

[1]Danielle Coty-Danielle, "Q&A with Lisa Lampert-Weissig: Author of Instrument of Memory," January 18, 2024, https://press.umich.edu/Blog/2024/01/Q-A-with-Lisa-Lampert-Weissig (accessed June 24, 2024).

[2]Ibid.

The pieces discussed in Part 4 bring us to a present and possible future use of the Wandering Jew legend in Stefan Heym's *Ahasver* (1981), Eshkol Nevo's *Neuland* (2011), Dara Horn's *Eternal Life* (2018), and Sarah Perry's *Melmoth* (2018). Seven instructive images that complement Lisa Lampert-Weissig's claims appear throughout.

As *Instrument of Memory* progresses, the lethal nature of the Wandering Jew legend grows more and more intense as the legend's impact on real Jewish bodies becomes more and more apparent. By frequently circling back to Matthew Paris's tale in his *Chronica majora* and medieval texts in general, *Instrument of Memory* underscores how, specifically, Matthew Paris's reimagining about the Wandering Jew (34–36) perpetuated the poisonous nature of the legend's inherent antisemitism. Working in—and perhaps just reproducing—"a time of terrible hardship for medieval Anglo-Jewry" (43) when Henry III introduced the medieval badge (a white *tabula*) in 1218 and instituted the *Domus conversorum* (House of the Converted) in 1232, Matthew Paris's story proves real the fatal effects of a supersessionist legend and the antisemitic culture that surrounded it. The terrifying and disabling nature of the antisemitism behind the Wandering Jew legend and the dangerous nature of Matthew Paris's invention become especially apparent and particularly riveting through Lampert-Weissig's choice of writing *Instrument of Memory* as a "deep-dive diachronic." One aspect of that "deep-dive diachronic" can be exemplified by the discussion about visual texts that accompanies three figures included in *Instrument of Memory*: Matthew Paris's sketch from the Parker Manuscript (Fig. 1), Marc Chagall's *White Crucifixion* (Fig. 3), and Gustave Doré's *La légende du Juif errant* (Fig. 4). Matthew Paris's drawing of the Wandering Jew (38), in which Lampert-Weissig appropriately describes the figure as "marked as Jewish not simply by his bulbous nose, profile positioning, and beard, but also by his mattock, long associated with Cain and through Cain with the Jews" (37), immobilizes the Wandering Jew as suffering, inept, cursed, and in a word Jewish. Lampert-Weissig argues that Paris's sketch influenced Marc "Chagall's depiction of the Wandering Jew figure as an older man . . . in keeping with traditional visualizations of the legend stretching back to Matthew Paris" (122). Gustave Doré's Wandering Jew, in turn, is captivated by the legend and "the memory of the Passion," producing "an inescapable haunting memory" (129). The relationship between Chagall's and Doré's art also embodies Lampert-Weissig's claims about how Jewish participation in the Wandering Jew legend changes the stakes of the tale: "Doré uses landscape to visualize memory as a curse. *White Crucifixion*, in contrast, visualizes memory very differently by placing a crucified Jesus in the middle of a contemporary European pogrom" (129).

The writing in the third section is powerful and proves true Lisa Lampert-Weissig's assertion that "my encounters with the Wandering Jews created by artists of Jewish descent have sparked my curiosity the most" (18). Part 3 introduces readers to a group of Jewish artists who "in the aftermath of World War I" (117) find themselves homeless and wandering "without ever having left their homes" (117). Because of "[c]hanges in territories and borders, as well as the emergence of new nation states," Jews find themselves "increasingly vulnerable" (117). Wandering Jews in their own world, Marc Chagall, Uri Zvi Greenberg, Edmond Fleg, and Sholem Asch are able to inhabit the medieval legend of the Wandering Jew and, thus, walk into "imagined encounters between the Wandering Jew and Jesus" (119). Instead of faithfully following the traditional narrative, Chagall, Greenberg, Fleg, and Asch "radically reenvision" Jesus and the Wandering Jew (119), rewriting the legend from a Jewish perspective. Working against—and maybe even defying—the culture of antisemitism, these twentieth-century Jewish authors "bring the story of Jesus alive from a Jewish perspective . . . one deployed with goals and ends very different from those associated with the Christian Wandering Jew tradition since at least the time of Matthew Paris" (119). One cannot overemphasize the horrifying world that was emerging for these Jewish artists who were trying to escape the growing antisemitism in Europe: Chagall sought refuge in the United States between 1941 and 1948 (232 n. 1); Greenberg escaped to Jaffa while Europe increasingly became "a hellscape for Jews, where they [were] slaughtered like sheep" (144); Fleg hoped that "through the work of the Jewish pioneers, Israel [would be] reborn" (157); and Asch traveled to Jerusalem and placed his historical novel, *Nazarene*, in both Poland and in Jerusalem, evading his present by imagining a medieval *gilgul* into his novel (166).[3] Stefan Heym of Part 4 "earn[ed] a master's degree at the University of Chicago" and "served in the US Army during World War II" (184).

Throughout everything, Lampert-Weissig's *Instrument of Memory* remains a deeply enriching, intensely gripping, and ultimately troubling book that pays due homage to previous studies of the Wandering Jew while also presenting her own original ideas about the history of the legend and the

[3]Asch's *Nazarene* draws on the medieval *gilgul*, a "kabbalistic concept" first imagined in 1180 in the *Sefer ha-Bahir* (*The Book of Brightness*) (166; also 237 n. 6).

future of the Wandering Jew. Her style of writing, the "deep-dive diachronic," invites readers to meet the whole author in ways that reach beyond the encyclopedic and, instead, bring readers to encounter a multidimensional temporal drama taking place around each author/artist and their text. Lisa Lampert-Weissig closes her Q&A on the University of Michigan Press's website with "I hope my readers . . . are inspired to seek out the original works discussed in *Instrument of Memory* if they don't already know them."[4] I know her wish has been fulfilled with me! Stefan Heym's *Ahasver* just entered my list of evening reads. I hope *Instrument of Memory* will entice you too to begin a discovery of the aftereffects of a medieval legend on the literature and culture that followed.

MIRIAMNE ARA KRUMMEL
University of Dayton

ROBERT J. MEYER-LEE. *The Problem of Literary Value*. Manchester: Manchester University Press, 2023. Pp. xiii, 263. $36.95.

This book seeks to peel back the quotidian routines of literary study, to brush away the surface confusion of methodological skirmishes and the narcissism of small differences, to reveal the underlying condition for interpreting literature today. That common condition is the puzzle of literary value. What is the good of literature, and what kind of significance do we bestow on a text in treating it as *literary*? These and similar questions are inescapable, Robert Meyer-Lee argues—but his goal is not to offer us answers. Instead, he redirects his audience's attention to why literary valuing continuously reemerges as a problem and a task. As the introduction explains, he "aim[s] to harness that problem as a source of critical energy rather than allowing it to produce within our practices unhelpful, sometimes damaging incoherencies," and the modest suggestions advanced over the subsequent chapters amount to "variations on the recommendation to incorporate reflexivity into one's scholarly and pedagogical practice" (2). The book's ethos is ecumenical and, as Meyer-Lee describes it, "practical and diagnostic" (1), tracking the implications of everyday activities such as citing an edition or designing a syllabus. *The*

[4]Coty-Danielle, "Q&A with Lisa Lampert-Weissig."

Problem of Literary Value defines its explanatory ambitions broadly, as pertinent to the whole domain of literature, but many of its case studies concern the study of Geoffrey Chaucer as undertaken in US academia. Focus toggles between local disputes in the subfield of Chaucer studies and zoomed-out, even abstract, accounts of how value comes to be defined.

Before laying out its central theoretical model, the book first delves into a case study, to illustrate "why the book's theory of literary valuing is needed" (12). In Chapter 1, Meyer-Lee revisits his earlier article "Manuscript Studies, Literary Value, and the Object of Chaucer Studies" to demonstrate how questions of literary merit have bubbled up around an apparent contradiction in the field of medieval studies, between, on the one hand, the valorization of individual manuscript witnesses and, on the other, scholars' near ubiquitous reliance on printed editions, especially the *Riverside* edition of Chaucer's works.[1] Meyer-Lee interprets the *Riverside*'s ongoing popularity as a form of tacit resistance to the imperatives of manuscript studies, that is, "resistance to an edition that would admit, in its material realisation, that there really is no *Canterbury Tales*, conceived of as a Work, but instead only eighty-some manuscripts dressed up to look like one" (27). He understands this widespread if unvoiced opposition to be the unexorcised "ghost of judgement" (37). This ghost initially looks like the revenant of New Criticism, but it is gradually shown to be the necessary corollary of deeming anything *literary* in the first place. The chapter ends by affirming editorial efforts "to maximise aesthetic power" (54) and bolster "the 'greatness' of the *Tales*" (53), rather than prioritize historical authenticity: "However committed Chaucer scholars may be to the idea of historical authenticity—or indeed to any sort of epistemological or ideological position—they are, as an institution, more committed to the object of literary value because that object remains at that institution's centre" (53).

Chapters 2 and 3 lay out the book's central theoretical framework. Chapter 2 maps the two poles of the "dialectical ping-pong match," to which Meyer-Lee's theory of literary valuing serves as an alternative. Those opposing poles are "ontology," which holds that literature "maintains a basic value regardless of its specific contexts" (73), and "genealogy," which pursues an anti-essentialist account: "how literary value is *made*" (74). The real problem with this pair, Meyer-Lee suggests, is that they are normative:

[1]Robert Meyer-Lee, "Manuscript Studies, Literary Value, and the Object of Chaucer Studies," *SAC* 30 (2008): 1–37.

in treating their contrary as illegitimate, "both positions *a priori* place under the heading *error* a great proportion of the actual valuing of literature" (79). Meyer-Lee builds his solution from an exceedingly broad principle of literary value: "We register a text as literary when we ascribe value to some aspect of its perceived manner" (81). He then adopts the terminology of actor–network theory to map the human and nonhuman elements variously responsible for categorizing a text as literary. In turn, Chapter 3 explicates one of the most clarifying ideas in *The Problem of Literary Value*, that of *loose binding*. Vicissitudes of literary style and function over time serve as evidence for the "habitual loose binding between particular aspects of [textual] manner and the particular values ascribed to them" (104–5). These vicissitudes imply that there is no preordained connection of textual form to ultimate significance. Literature's axiological flexibility "both facilitates and, by that same token, demands linkage to other-than-literary values" (108). In this way, "the very ambiguity deriving from loose binding as to what constitutes *the* value of literature enables literature, functioning rather like a lint roller, to lap up an array of different values without apparent contradiction or incoherence" (109). On this account, it is literature's porosity to different value ascriptions that helps make it the thing it is. Meyer-Lee argues that, following this, one potential identity for literary study would be "the exploration of that value-laden condition" (123).

Chapters 4 and 5 address canonicity and interpretation, respectively. Meyer-Lee frames his investigation with the high-stakes question of "the role canons may have in a more just society" (137). His case studies illustrate how the pressure of this question has affected attempts to explain and justify the ongoing value ascribed to canonical literature, and most of all to Chaucer. The upshot is "to underscore how the category of canonicity persists in our basic practices and institutional manoeuvres, despite our laudable desire to remedy the social injustices of which it has been one instrument among many" (149). Chapter 5 addresses how interpretation, or "ascribing meaning to a pattern" (191), is also inseparable from literary valuing. Meyer-Lee's extended case study looks to the career of critic-scholar Lee Patterson, particularly Patterson's restless efforts to bring scholarly practice and reflexive self-understanding into dialogue, if never into perfect alignment.

One appealing throughline of the book is Meyer-Lee's recourse to anecdotes from his scholarly life to clarify his arguments. While gently self-deprecating, these vignettes are also intellectually illuminating. For instance, in chapters 2 and 3, he glances back to his own first monograph, *Poets and Power from Chaucer to Wyatt*, to suggest how a stronger axiological framework would have helped him own up to his "crypto-evaluative assertions" (71) and "encouraged me to provide a more explicit argument for the literary value that I implicitly ascribe to the fifteenth-century Chaucerians" (127).[2] In Chapter 4, he recounts two different attempts to teach a course on "Gender, Sexuality and Chaucer"—and why it was the second effort, when he presented "canonicity explicitly as an institutional fact and also a problem to be explored," that was more successful (180). The book's postscript thoughtfully lays out some of the personal underpinnings for the argument as a whole.

As a work of medieval literary studies, *The Problem of Literary Value* is intriguing and unexpected. It ambitiously takes us into territory where few titles reviewed in *Studies in the Age of Chaucer* venture. Yet as a work of literary theory, it is not uniformly satisfying. Meyer-Lee's approach is not rooted in any particular tradition of reflection on literary value. This allows him to avoid dogmatism, but readers miss the chance to become oriented within, and discover something of the achieved gravity of, coherent but wide-ranging conversations such as those flourishing around Kantian aesthetic judgment or around Marxist accounts of value, for example. The book's theoretical basis can accordingly begin to feel not merely eclectic but distractingly so, diffusing its citations among (to cite some recurring figures) Georg Simmel, Bruno Latour, Rita Felski, Jan Mukařovský, and Stanley Fish. This effect is augmented by the very mixed archive under consideration—a New Chaucer Society blogpost, a dispatch from the so-called "method wars," an article in *Profession*, a stodgy lecture by Frank Kermode, a recent plenary at the Sewanee Medieval Colloquium, and so on. It is hard to say if the book's admirable pragmatism—its effort to analyze what we in US English departments actually do—can be separated from a certain claustrophobia of intellectual horizons, only occasionally punctured by the insights of less familiar figures (Simmel, Mukařovský), with whom there is little time to tarry.

Despite these reservations, Meyer-Lee's good-humored, reflexive, and intellectually questing voice makes for an amiable guide through the labyrinth of literary value. He calls on us all to reckon more fully with the

[2]Robert Meyer-Lee, *Poets and Power from Chaucer to Wyatt* (Cambridge: Cambridge University Press, 2007).

networks of value in which we are embedded and which we perpetuate, like coral, minutely modifying and transforming, inhabiting and creating.

JULIE ORLEMANSKI
University of Chicago

MARCO NIEVERGELT. *Medieval Allegory as Epistemology: Dream-Vision Poetry on Language, Cognition, and Experience*. Oxford Studies in Medieval Literature and Culture. Oxford: Oxford University Press, 2023. Pp. x, 560. $155.00.

The subtitle of this study of philosophical visions and logical debate conducted via various allegorical means explains that it considers "Dream-Vision Poetry on Language, Cognition, and Experience." This is rather more sweeping a statement than the book itself delivers, for it is actually a detailed study of the lives and philosophical preoccupations of three major vernacular poets, each of whom composed a lengthy dream vision featuring a single soul on pilgrimage to find truth: Jean de Meun, Guillaume de Deguileville, and "William Langland" or "Long Wille." Two of these poets are historically well attested, but the existence of an actual person named William Langland is not. I have therefore put his name in quotes, though conventionally that is the name of the author of *Piers Plowman*. For Nievergelt's arguments concerning it, the historical existence of a real William Langland is a crucial matter.

The book pays most attention to Deguileville, and least to Jean de Meun, for the good reason that the *Roman de la Rose* has been the subject of many studies in English; Nievergelt especially cites those of Sarah Kay, Sylvia Huot, and Jonathan Morton. Most welcome, he also engages with French and German studies perhaps less known to students of late Middle English texts. Yet, though he devotes fewer pages to it, Nievergelt writes portentously: "In the beginning was the *Rose*" (55). It was the *Rose*'s ethically devious though logically proper "seeds" scattered abroad by the Lover in the *Rose*'s final episode that most evidently produced the type of epistemologically exploratory dream vision that inspired later authors, especially the *Pèlerinage de la vie humaine* (c. 1332 in its first version), as Deguileville makes clear many times, citing the *Rose* by name as well as paraphrasing it extensively.

The book argues that the two late medieval French dream vision poems between them established a kind of "international poetic," somewhat on the model of the International Style of manuscript painting familiar from modern art histories of this period.

> [A]llegorical poetry is . . . able to define an experimental mental "space" where narrative fiction can be harnessed to stage a series of thought experiments that examine . . . representational and cognitive processes of great complexity. . . . specifically the imaginative potential that is the defining characteristic of "the poetic" as understood in the Arabo-Latin scholastic tradition. (11)

Though Nievergelt mentions only scholastic tradition here, it is also crucial to his arguments that these two French poems were composed in public, lay, aristocratic contexts and for the audiences of such households, neither in university or Desert isolation, for the satiric motives and ironic voices, so dominant in each, are targeted broadly; their audiences are attuned more to courtly and diplomatic *débat* than to strict university *controversia*. The heart of Nievergelt's explanation for the various rewritings of *Pèlerinage* is that Deguileville, in attempting to "answer" with unambiguous orthodox doctrine the allegorical ironies and logical trickeries of the *Rose*, finds himself constantly unable to do so, no matter his many efforts to articulate the allegories of his own poetry in unglossable, plain-spoken rational *santance* comprehensible to folk in the ordinary world. The *Pèlerinage* poems, Nievergelt says, collectively demonstrate that total clarity is impossible to human language.

But the limited nature of human language and thus of human reasoning is a core doctrine apparent from the earliest days of Christianity, as it is also in Genesis. The legend of the Tower of Babel, as interpreted by Augustine in his *Literal Commentary on Genesis*, is about just this linguistic constraint and its consequences. Recognizing it is central to monastic practices of contemplative prayer, and indeed to what Richard of St. Victor called *sublevatio mentis*, reexploring a very old monastic idea. But Nievergelt pays very little attention to such history and practices, as his index makes plain. For example, Bonaventura's *Itinerarium mentis in Deum* is mentioned briefly once, though a Cistercian such as Deguileville would certainly have known (or known of) it. Aristotelian *scientia*, as Nievergelt considers it, is limited nearly exclusively to "the Arabo-Latin scholastic tradition" (11) and to the basic logic curriculum learned in Paris. This is what some

Victorines, including Richard of St. Victor (d. 1173), had disparagingly called the *officina Aristotelis* the workshop of Aristotle, its inhabitants characterized as proud, noisy, and preening. In the century-and-a-half after Richard wrote, relations between contemplative monks and university doctors had not improved, and as a Cistercian, Deguileville could be expected to take the dim view of the late thirteenth- and early fourteenth-century schools' practices that he in fact does.

And equally, so does the author of *Piers Plowman*, who places himself in this Augustinian-Benedictine-Cistercian revival of Desert monasticism by emphasizing his roots in Malvern and his distance from those working and wandering as "the world" requires. Only the scorn of Lady Holy Church drives him off his mountain-top and into that world to seek the vision's figure of true pastoral care, Piers the Plowman. Nievergelt's presentation of *Piers*'s various dream journeys is haunted only by Deguileville's poem, not the larger context of Cistercian teaching. Though his account of *Piers*'s thematic substance is convincing and uncontroversial, he constantly underscores what he maintains are its parallels exclusively with the *Pèlerinage*, quoting extensively from the French poem (with his own translations into English) in order to show its singularly profound influence.

Nievergelt even claims that "the two French allegories constitute the single most important influence on Langland's poem," and although acknowledging that this is "a very substantial claim for me to make," he has based it in "structured evidence and a nuanced and meticulous argument" rather than in mere borrowings and allusions (51). Deguileville's poem, he says, stands in relation to *Piers* much as the *Rose* stands in relation to the *Pèlerinage*. However, such nuanced and "meticulous" influence over all aspects of a long and much revised English poem would require Langland to have had deep knowledge of French as spoken in Paris in the late fourteenth century, or at the very least in London at the court of Richard II. And on this elementary matter the claim for "deep influence" collapses (264). "Langland"—whoever he may have been—was not like that internationally experienced courtier-diplomat Geoffrey Chaucer. Nievergelt makes a valiant effort to support his claims for the *Pèlerinage* being the "most important influence" on *Piers*, depending—as everyone must—on the single marginal note in a fifteenth-century C-text manuscript that the "William Langland" who wrote *Piers Plowman* was the son of Stacy de Rokele. He cites Robert Adams, *Langland and the Rokele Family*, as his proof.[1] Adams published what the surviving records contain about the Rokeles, but his laudable study of this west Oxfordshire gentry family does not securely tie with all-important corroborating knots any of the recorded Rokele households to the poet known as "William Langland," to "Long Wille," and thus to *Piers Plowman*. Supporting evidence for this one unofficial record simply does not exist—only the centuries-long tradition, which does not introduce any other possibilities.

I find it odd that contemporary criticism of medieval texts so often now desires to ground itself as much as it can in an actual historical author. But the author of *Piers Plowman* was not like Dante any more than he was Chaucer, each with their large presence in many historical records, which can be readily compared to their autobiographical literary personae. Nievergelt's study provides a detailed account of the several French versions of the *Pèlerinage*, which also helps explain why for the complexly mixed, lay-clerical world coming into existence in the fifteenth century, Lydgate translated it into English as an important work of pastoral care. Nievergelt also discusses Chaucer's *An ABC* prayer-poem to the Virgin, translated from a different poem by Deguileville. All of this demonstrates that Deguileville was indeed an important French model and influence for some later medieval English literature. But not, I think, *Piers Plowman*.

MARY CARRUTHERS
New York University

TISON PUGH. *Bad Chaucer: The Great Poet's Greatest Mistakes in the "Canterbury Tales."* Ann Arbor: University of Michigan Press, 2024. Pp. xi, 261. $30.00 hardback.

Imagine this. A middle-aged poet of high repute joins a writer's workshop. He submits an experimental, as yet unfinished, work unlike anything he (or anyone else, for that matter) has written in English. The smart up-and-coming writers in his workshop run his work through the mill. They attentively assess his lines and boldly recommend an extensive round of revisions. "Try sticking to one genre," they advise. "What's your main

[1]Robert Adams, *Langland and the Rokele Family: The Gentry Background to "Piers Plowman"* (Dublin: Four Courts Press, 2013).

theme in this story?" "Your characters don't act consistently." "Love your humor! Don't let it get away from you!!" "Rethink all those -isms . . . they are a real turnoff." Universally, they each close with a chipper "I look forward to seeing what you do in your next draft," leaving unsaid "if you live long enough to make *all* these changes."

Such a scenario resembles Tison Pugh's insightful yet gracious interrogations of Geoffrey Chaucer's tale-telling collection in *Bad Chaucer: The Great Poet's Greatest Mistakes in the "Canterbury Tales."* Not a scolding book in the "bad dog" version of "bad," and not an admiring book in the rakish "bad boy" version of "bad," *Bad Chaucer* uses the epithet to identify all the ways that Chaucer's work does not conform to postmedieval literary standards. The chapters ground their assessment of the twenty-four *Canterbury Tales* on such values as consistency and narrative coherence, values that reflect the ability of writers to send a literary work through multiple drafts and extensive revisions.

Because Pugh aligns his judgments with twenty-first-century views of literary missteps, he is not concerned with earlier reasons for decrying Chaucer's *Tales*, such as its archaic language or its lack of moral seriousness. At the same time, he pushes against what he labels "Chaucer's deification squad," which claims that "the infelicities of his tales reflect intentional choices for his [pilgrim taletellers], and thus that any literary lapses reflect upon them rather than him" (10). He offers, instead, a "motley collection of readings examin[ing] a vibrant vortex of anomalies that undermine, but never collapse, the integrity of Chaucer's *Canterbury Tales*—the moments when . . . readers might expect Chaucer to have done better" (6). He analyzes these forms of badness according to five criteria: genre inconsistencies, thematic errancy, inconsistent characters, incomplete narratives, and outmoded perspectives.

Devoting a chapter to each tale, Pugh enters an uncrowded subfield of Chaucer studies that examines the *Canterbury Tales* tale by tale. His readings gently guide the curious but novice reader, with careful definitions of terms and extensive reference to the critical tradition that make *Bad Chaucer* well suited for classroom use or student-friendly research. This book should seem particularly attractive to students attuned to creative writing workshops, a thesis affirmed by a multitalented student enrolled in both my course on the *Canterbury Tales* and several creative writing courses.

Under "Genre Troubles," he gathers five tales that dilute their purpose by melding or misunderstanding generic conventions. *The Knight's Tale* unsuccessfully conjoins epic and romance conventions, an infelicitous union that allows each to falter in its purpose. For instance, when Emelye and Palamon marry (a standard romance convention) in adherence to the command of Theseus (a stock figure from epic conventions) that they make a virtue of necessity, the "necessity" "undercuts the marital bliss evoked by the romance ending" (19). *The Friar's Tale* stages a moral lesson (one should not try to cheat an old woman) that makes its point not only through validating the immoral retributions of a sympathetic victim but also by damning the initial perpetrator with a punishment that does not align with his sins. *The Summoner's Tale* and its satiric jabs at friars attempts to create comic effects with its brief yet mean-spirited images of dead children. *The Monk's Tale* misuses the sense of tragedy with a boring series of "repeated images of death and desolation" (182). *The Canon's Yeoman's Tale* fails to convey its warnings because the pedagogical strategies it borrows from schoolbooks kill the tale's rhetorical force.

Under "Themeless Themes," Pugh assembles another five tales whose thematic promise is left unfulfilled or undelivered. *The Man of Law's Tale* abandons the satiric possibilities granted by the theme of poverty introduced in the tale's prologue. The tale, instead, allows the Man of Law to advocate for so-called "prosperity theology," which justifies accumulating earthly wealth (49–50). *The Clerk's Tale* aligns Walter's torture of Griselda (and their children) with a theodicy that justifies suffering as part of a divine plan for humanity. *The Physician's Tale* fails to coordinate its "purported themes and its narrative action" (128). *The Tale of Melibee*, an unstable allegory that packs too many interpretive possibilities, becomes a mishmash of meanings. *The Manciple's Tale* "promises meaning but leaves behind only contradictions" (218).

Under "Mischaracterized Characters," he collects six tales with needlessly inconsistent characters detracting from each tale's larger purpose. *The Miller's Tale* gives us a sympathetic old husband labeled as "jalous" (*MilT*, 2334) by both the narrator and his other characters, but John never acts jealously in the tale, making the other characters' misjudgments of John unfair. *The Merchant's Tale* jumbles multiple viewpoints to shape a narrative, a problem compounded for modern readers by the lack of punctuation in the manuscripts. *The Franklin's Tale*, with its contradictory depictions of love, blurs the two competing "medieval visions of love and affection—*fin'amor* and courtly love" (112). *The Pardoner's Tale* generates an unnecessary "character crux"—the "overdetermined characterization of the Old Man"—which distracts readers from the tale's more pressing themes (130). *The Second Nun's Tale* is permeated with eroticized imagery, incongruous with its abstemious, tale-teller nun. *The Parson's Tale* and its "murmurs of Lollard thought" suggest a tale-teller who vacillates "between a heretical version of Catholicism and a lax adherence to the critiques of Lollardy" (226).

Under "Pleasureful, Purposeful, and Purposeless Badness," Pugh identifies four tales in which Chaucer either retained too much humor or pulled away from a humorous closure too soon. *The Cook's Tale* frustrates readers for both its confusing beginning (what sort of tale awaits us?) and its absent ending (why do we not get that awaited tale?). He praises *The Squire's Tale* for its "campy fun" that distills "rich humor from an unbelievably inept, inapt, and inelegant tale" (111). He critiques *The Shipman's Tale* for its overabundance of puns, thereby "undercutting [Chaucer's] comedy" (146). The insistent "rym dogerel" pervading *The Tale of Sir Thopas* (a parody of the tail-rhyme romance tradition) causes Harry Bailly to demand the tale be cut off prematurely (*Th–MelL*, 925).

Under "Outmoded Perspectives," he assesses four final tales that depend upon ugly prejudices. *The Reeve's Tale*, with its masculinist bias, conjoins a comic fabliau, a cold-blooded rape scene, and the victim's misguided affection, so that a woman's suffering is the source of much (but not all) of the tale's humor. Although *The Wife of Bath's Tale* attempts "to challenge gendered norms throughout her prologue, [the Wife] ultimately remains a male creation" unable to exist outside the "ideological world that denigrates women's agency" (65). *The Prioress's Tale* contains antisemitism that, whether or not it was so orthodox to be unnoteworthy, "lures some readers into ill-framed and exculpatory interpretations" (155). *The Nun's Priest's Tale* directs it virulent misogyny at both the hens and the widow.

Pugh concludes by considering Chaucer's *Retraction*, and in doing so he presents his own retraction, reminding readers that a literary work's "flaws and lapses, misjudgments and misfires, deserve . . . to be recognized as part of their very greatness" (229).

As anyone who has carefully studied the *Canterbury Tales* knows, it is an imperfect text whose flaws we come not to overlook but to learn from. That is, they provide a gateway to seeing a brilliant writer's process when that process would otherwise be denied us. We have no rough drafts, no archives of his notes. Instead, we have a few postmortem manuscripts that show extensive scribal interventions made necessary by the apparently incomplete nature of the work. The result is a text that "features rough passages of poetry, moments of inscrutable narrative development, and deus ex machina conclusions, among other such infelicities" (1). I truly enjoy the unfinished quality of almost all medieval texts—an acquired taste, I realize—because this raw state allows us to perceive the creative and intellectual process in motion. For this reason, I found Pugh's *Bad Chaucer* an excellent source for identifying those unpolished moments, even if I do not want to correct, excoriate, or lament them.

CANDACE BARRINGTON
Central Connecticut State University

CORINNE SAUNDERS and DIANE WATT, eds. *Women and Medieval Literary Culture: From the Early Middle Ages to the Fifteenth Century*. Cambridge: Cambridge University Press, 2023. Pp. xv, 487. £120.00.

Women and Medieval Literary Culture: From the Early Middle Ages to the Fifteenth Century offers a collection of twenty-two chapters (plus introduction) treating different aspects of women's contributions to and engagement with literary culture, primarily but not exclusively focused on the British Isles. It is divided into five sections grouped by theme and concludes with a general index and index of manuscripts. Each chapter presumes that its readers are already coming in acquainted with medieval literary culture to some degree, so this volume seems most appropriate for graduate students on up to established scholars.

The first section, "Patrons, Owners, Writers, and Readers in England and Europe," includes chapters on abbesses and nuns as readers and makers (Elaine Treharne), queens and other noblewomen as patrons (Mary Dockray-Miller), and literary connections of various sorts between female religious (Mary C. Erler). Treharne's examination of evidence from female scribes reminds us that we should not presume that a masculine identity lies behind anonymity, while Erler examines vertical and horizontal relationships between enclosed women to elucidate how books moved along those lines. Dockray-Miller's chapter ranges widely both chronographically and geographically, providing a welcome reminder that eastern Europe and the Caucasus deserve more attention from English-speaking scholars than they have received to date.

Part 2, "Circles and Communities in England," also consists of two chapters focusing on religious readers (by Michelle M. Sauer and Laura

Saetveit Miles) plus a third on the Paston women (Diane Watt). Whereas Sauer concentrates on a small group of texts—namely the *Ancrene Wisse* and associated works—and their diverse audience, Saetveit Miles examines the smaller readership clearly associated with Syon Abbey and the literary legacy of the institution and its founder, St. Birgitta. Watt's assessment of books referenced explicitly and obliquely in the Paston letters demonstrates how we can fruitfully exploit such sources to learn more about women's exposure to literature that has otherwise left little material trace.

"Health, Conduct, and Knowledge" opens with Naoë Kukita Yoshikawa treating medical literature proper, offering a brief, enlightening overview of the history of women's medicine in Latin followed by its translation into multiple vernaculars and then in England specifically. Her chapter keeps company with Martha Driver's interesting examination of magic (including charms and amulets) and recipes, neither of which is entirely removed from the field of medieval medical practice. Between these two, we find Kathleen Ashley taking a long view of gender's relationship to conduct literature in order to interrogate how the two interact with class in the late Middle Ages. Closing the section is Denis Renevey's multifaceted approach to devotional compilations, which includes assessing them in terms of their intended audience and of which texts by women were chosen for the compilations.

All four of these contributions could just as easily have fit into the next (and by far the largest) section, "Genre and Gender," which brings together chapters on devotional lyrics (David Fuller), hagiography (Christiania Whitehead), visionary writings (Liz Herbert McAvoy), drama (Sue Niebrzydowski), romance (Corinne Saunders), fabliaux (Neil Cartlidge), and Chaucer and Gower (Venetia Bridges). This grouping diverges somewhat from the previous two, in that while it does not entirely abandon the investigation into women readers, the chapters emphasize instead women as they are represented in the texts under examination or as their composers. Thus, Fuller's study focuses first on women as they are represented in lyrics and secondly on the question of whether or not women also composed lyrics. Whitehead picks up the thread of devotional literature in her diachronic consideration of how holy women's lives became *Lives* and how women otherwise contributed to the genre by writing, compiling, and reading. McAvoy takes this theme in a different direction as she indicates the different female mystics from across the Continent whose experiences in one way or another authorized Margery Kempe's ostentatiously affective style of worship decades and centuries later. Liturgical drama both within and without convent walls provides the focus of Niebrzydowski's chapter, where she considers women as players, producers, and public. (Adding in an assessment of farces as either a portion of her chapter or as a separate chapter would have been appreciated, but space was certainly a consideration in a volume already almost 500 pages long.) Saunders's assessment of female characters from a large number of Middle English romances concludes, intriguingly, "romance as a genre may also be seen as a conversation, perhaps a debate, about women" (317). In his analysis of the fabliaux, Cartlidge likewise chooses to examine the often antagonistic way women are portrayed. Bridges recognizes from the start the impossibility of doing justice to a comparative consideration of gender across Chaucer's and Gower's oeuvres in a single chapter, and while her conclusions do seem substantiated by the evidence, a smaller selection of works for analysis might have better served the purpose.

The final section, "Women as Authors," spans the twelfth to the fifteenth centuries and multiple languages, with chapters on Marie de France (Emma Campbell) and Christine de Pizan (Nancy Bradley Warren); Julian of Norwich (Barry Windeatt) and Margery Kempe (Anthony Bale); and female poets from Ireland, Scotland, and Wales (Cathryn A. Charnell-White). Campbell's focus lies not on the shadowy historical figure of Marie herself, but rather on the networks and collaboration underlying her texts both as written productions and as narrative structures. Warren's chapter, by contrast, considers English translations of Christine's works and how both original compositions and translations were inextricably bound up in the prescriptive gender politics of the day. Windeatt's examination of mothers and Christ's motherliness in Julian's short and long *Revelations* determines that the visionary is reclaiming authority for women. Like Campbell, Bale's analysis of the communities associated both with Margery as a person in society and with her texts (as scribes and readers) shines light on the female networks that supported her during her pilgrimage to Jerusalem and after. Finally, Charnell-White presents a synthetic assessment of a few female poets outside the anglophone canon, showing how they claimed space for themselves despite their doubly marginalized position.

There are a couple of points about this collection that were frustrating to this particular reviewer. First, there was not a single early-career researcher among the authors, which was reflected in the sources drawn upon for certain of the chapters—rather than energetically engaging with the substantial scholarship on women readers, patrons, and makers that has been produced in the past five or even ten years, several of them (including the introduction) rely heavily on work from the 1990s and early 2000s. Second, there were many points of contact and even overlap among the chapters, and a collective bibliography for the volume in place of each chapter's abbreviated further reading list would have helped to reinforce this cohesion. Overall, however, the volume brings together a coherent group of contributions that offer new insights into canonical English and continental authors and, perhaps more importantly, bring greater visibility to less well-known figures living in the British Isles or being read there.

S. C. Kaplan
Independent scholar

Manish Sharma. *The Logic of Love in "The Canterbury Tales."* Toronto: University of Toronto Press, 2022. Pp. x, 395. $95.00 hardback and e-book.

We know that binaries govern the *Canterbury Tales*—sentence and solace, earnest and game, authority and experience, etc.—but Manish Sharma's new book argues that another dyad reveals a hitherto unrecognized structure in Chaucer's work. In an ambitious two-front effort to systematize the *Tales* while modeling a new way to read them, Sharma argues that all the tales and tellers belong to an antinomy that subsumes all those old Chaucerian keywords: form (sentence, earnest, authority, mastery, order, masculinity, Christianity, and philosophy) and matter (solace, game, experience, freedom, chaos, femininity, secularity, and poetry). Like all antinomies, these ramifying oppositions are insoluble. Rather than arguing for synthesis, however, Sharma insists that these oppositions remain unresolved: the logic of love requires that we withhold judgment.

The introduction unspools a genealogy for this novel reading of Chaucer. Sharma begins from the Chaucer-narrator's apologia for vulgarity in *The General Prologue*, which he reads as a paradox emblematic of the *Tales* as a whole. The Chaucer-narrator invokes the authority of Christ and Plato to dodge responsibility for the content of the tales that will follow; in other words, he "*authoritatively abdicates authority* over his textual creation" (8, emphasis original). Sharma argues that this paradoxical authoritative denial of authority can be productively read alongside the *insolubilia* ("insolubles," i.e., paradoxes) debated by late medieval logicians—among them Thomas Bradwardine, whom Chaucer name-checks, and philosophical Ralph Strode, whom he seems to have known personally. As in the liar paradox ("This statement is false"), truth and falsity are entangled in Chaucer's abdication. Unlike the academic logicians, however, Chaucer does not try to reason his way out of the insoluble. The narrator's refusal to criticize his fellow pilgrims explicitly is indicative of what Sharma sees as a broader refusal to judge in the *Tales*, a withholding that suspends rather than decides between contradictory possibilities. Sharma argues that the entire logic of the *Tales* follows from this refusal, which he compares to Christ's kenosis and calls love. In philosophical terms, this logic means that form is not given priority, as a formalist might insist, nor is matter unrelated to form, as a materialist might, but, in Sharma's equation, "form is (not) related to matter" (45). In narrative terms, it means that judgmental pilgrims tell tales that render them the objects of their own judgment. In all cases, both author and critic must adopt a posture of nonjudgmental nondecision.

This bold opening illustrates both the limits and the appeals of the book as a whole. By reading the Chaucer-narrator's various tricks at face value, the book blunts the sharp edge of Chaucerian irony. (Not everyone would agree that Chaucer's attitude toward the world is "one of love and forgiveness, devoid of censoriousness and judgment" [13].) In making logical truth and falsity its central concerns, the book largely eschews the murkier questions of fiction and belief that have recently been explored by Michelle Karnes and Julie Orlemanski. And by presenting the *Tales* as a logical system, Sharma reveals himself to be more formalist than materialist: the various disorders of textual transmission, compositional exigency, and Chaucer's personal history are decisively subordinated to a sense of overarching artistic design—even if the design itself refuses to privilege order over disorder. But there is also a healthy defamiliarizing effect in *The Logic of Love*'s approach to the *Canterbury Tales*. Psychological depth is out, and subjectivity with it; the flattening of the Pardoner and the Wife of Bath obliges us to think about how they function as written ideas rather than living people. Historicist approaches to the pilgrims and their tales are likewise downplayed in favor of philosophical readings, to much the same effect. This is a weird version of the *Canterbury Tales*, and that is mostly a good thing.

The book falls into seven chapters. The first extends the introduction's methodological ruminations by offering a proof-of-concept reading of *The*

Nun's Priest's Tale and *The Franklin's Tale*. Sharma argues that the self-contradictions of Chauntecleer and the Nun's Priest, especially his closing citation of Romans 15:4, open "an anarchic space of compossibility for infinite and unpredictable interpretative decisions and antagonisms into the future" (39). The tale thus becomes an *ars poetica* for the *Tales* as a whole, immediately tested in the discussion of *The Franklin's Tale*—a tale that, for all its magical effects, hinges on brute questions of mastery and freedom. Sharma reads the Franklin's denouement as a series of masterful submissions, up to and including the terminal question about freedom, which is voiced as an imperative ("Now telleth me" [*FranT*, 1623]) even as it submits to a reader's decision. The chapter hones the book's heuristic as it works through these readings, further explicating what it means by "love" while adding new terms to its central binary. In the process, other pairings from intellectual history—Foucault and Derrida, Augustine and Lacan, all concisely if a bit broadly sketched—are brought into the heuristic. All are ultimately overcome by the Chaucerian love that suspends any decision or judgment.

The remaining six chapters proceed seriatim through the Ellesmere-order *Canterbury Tales*, from Knight to *Retraction*. The second chapter, on the successive "quitings" of Fragment I, introduces what Sharma calls "Chaucer's law of unintended consequences" (29): the Miller and Reeve's attempts at mastery rebound on themselves. That law inclines toward a suspension of judgment, a critical stance Sharma supports with counter-intuitive discoveries of disorder in the impeccably structured *Knight's Tale* and intentional design in the fragmentary *Cook's Tale*. Subsequent chapters pursue an oscillation between binaries and an unfolding of unintended consequences fragment by fragment. The results sometimes risk becoming a mechanical working-out of a predetermined order—so, for instance, the Physician stands for formalism, the Pardoner for materialism, the Host's rebuke puts a bow on Fragment VI by entangling the two—and the law of unintended consequences sometimes seems like a convenient excuse for the inexcusable: thus antifeminism repeatedly turns out to impeach the misogynist who voices it, while the failure of *Thopas* represents a charitable refusal to judge the Prioress, whose formalist antisemitism is ultimately left to defeat itself.

But Sharma's close readings are more creative and flexible than the blunt binaries of form and matter might suggest, and his method allows for frank discussions of domination and oppression. The Physician's Virginia and the Reeve's Malyne are made to play critical roles in the understanding of the *Tales* as a whole, while Sharma's reading of *The Prioress's Tale* reveals the sadomasochistic power exchange embedded in the Prioress's violent posture of submission, which he convincingly locates in her explicit attitudes toward the law rather than an unconscious primed for psychoanalytic exploration. These readings are buttressed by Sharma's deep reading in criticism. Though the book draws on the philosophically inclined Chaucerian scholarship that one might expect—Kathryn Lynch, Mark Miller, Jessica Rosenfeld, and D. Vance Smith all feature prominently in the introduction—it ranges more widely, including an admirably open-minded engagement with Robertsonian criticism, which Sharma neither accepts uncritically nor rejects out of hand. His love is definitively not Robertson's Augustinian *caritas*, but he still takes the latter seriously.

The book ends by returning to the ethic it articulated in its introduction. The extended final chapter reads the four valedictory tales according to a pair of binaries: sentence versus solace and Christian versus secular. Thus the Second Nun provides Christian solace, the Canon's Yeoman secular sentence, the Manciple secular solace, and the Parson Christian sentence. The readings that supply these coordinates are not equally convincing. Solace might seem scarce in *The Manciple's Tale*, but Sharma's dissection of its comprehensive breakdown of all authority is thrilling. By contrast, few would disagree that *The Parson's Tale* is "Christian sentence," but the tale itself is presented as a simple expression of formulaic conservatism, leaving unaddressed the thornier questions about what Chaucer actually intends with the treatise. Sharma ends with the *Retraction*, which "offers two mutually exclusive interpretive possibilities" (263): it sorts good writings from bad, but also borrows from Paul to remind us (as did the Nun's Priest) that all that was written is for our education. Chaucer once again authoritatively submits to a reader's judgment, in other words, and so we close the loop opened in *The General Prologue*—or rather, so the loop is left open, for us to decide whether to judge or forgive.

This book's big claims achieve mixed success. The notion that the *Canterbury Tales* are *in toto* an expression of forgiving love is heartening but not entirely convincing, and nonjudgmental nondecision seems an unpropitious path for criticism. More time spent with fourteenth-century philosophy in the book's later chapters might have better grounded such ethical claims in Chaucer's world. (For instance, a discussion of the *perplexitas* [dilemma], moral philosophy's cousin-concept to *insolubilia*, could have connected logic and ethics in concrete historical terms.) But this systematic reading of the *Tales* makes a valuable contribution to ongoing reassessments of Chaucer's engagement with philosophical and axiological issues. More importantly, Sharma helps us see both the collection and individual tales anew, as ideas worthy of love and judgment.

SPENCER STRUB
Princeton University

DEVANI SINGH. *Chaucer's Early Modern Readers: Reception in Print and Manuscript*. Cambridge: Cambridge University Press, 2023. Pp. xiii, 272. Open access.

In *Chaucer's Early Modern Readers: Reception in Print and Manuscript*, Devani Singh connects ongoing scholarly interest in Chaucer's Renaissance reception—exemplified by such monographs as Alice S. Miskimin's *The Renaissance Chaucer* and Megan Cook's *The Poet and the Antiquaries*—with a book-historical methodology that considers how readers used medieval manuscripts in a post-print age, a question taken up recently by such works as Margaret Connolly's *Sixteenth-Century Readers, Fifteenth-Century Books* and Aditi Nafde's AHRC-funded "Manuscripts after Print" project.[1] While much scholarship about Chaucerian reception in the early modern period has focused on printed books, ranging from Caxton's earliest productions to Speght's folio editions, Singh considers how medieval manuscripts also participated in the early modern refashioning of Chaucer. In particular, she argues that the editorial practices of early printers framed sixteenth- and seventeenth-century readers' material responses to the older Chaucerian manuscripts that still circulated after the poet was available in printed form. While it might be tempting to view these early modern readers intervening in medieval manuscript books as misguided or even destructive, Singh compellingly argues that the early readers who corrected, annotated, supplemented, and otherwise altered medieval books did so to "perfect" (29) their copies, to preserve the "Father of English

[1]Alice S. Miskimin, *The Renaissance Chaucer* (New Haven: Yale University Press, 1975); Megan Cook, *The Poet and the Antiquaries: Chaucerian Scholarship and the Rise of Literary History, 1532–* (Philadelphia: University of Pennsylvania Press, 2019); Margaret Connolly, *Sixteenth-Century Readers, Fifteenth-Century Books: Continuities of Reading in the English Reformation* (Cambridge: Cambridge University Press, 2019).

Poetry" in his most complete form, a form canonized by print editors but replicated and transformed in manuscript.

Singh organizes each chapter of *Chaucer's Early Modern Readers* according to the various interventions that the readers at the heart of her study imposed on their Chaucer manuscripts. The first chapter, "Glossing, Correcting, and Emending," focuses on the Chaucerian language that later readers may have found difficult. Singh notes that the linguistic apparatus added to printed books—in particular, Speght's well-known glossary—framed how later readers approached their Chaucer manuscripts, with such readers adapting Speght's word list in manuscript form. Similarly, readers of manuscripts might compare their texts with a print edition seen to be more authoritative and reliable than the handwritten copy. Still, Singh reminds us, manuscript glossing and correcting were idiosyncratic, and to describe any one reader's actions as typical of a universal program would be to gloss over the variability that continued to characterize the manuscript form.

Singh's second chapter takes up the actions of "Repairing and Completing," asking what early modern readers did when they encountered "the missing leaves and textual gaps that plagued their copies" of Chaucer (84). The "perfect" Chaucerian book was, thus, not just readable and textually accurate but also complete. Moreover, notions of which texts "counted" as Chaucer's and which were required for a "complete" works were shaped by the increasingly available print editions circulating alongside older manuscripts. As Singh writes, "printed copies of Chaucer did not hasten the obsolescence of manuscripts, but enabled their repair, preservation, and continued use at the hands of new readers" (107). We find examples, then, of readers such as John Stow adding missing poetic lines to a manuscript copy of Chaucer's *Book of the Duchess*, lines taken from a printed Thynne edition of Chaucer (or from a book derived from it). Similarly, we read of antiquarian book owners inserting parchment leaves and imitating medieval scripts to repair manuscripts seen as lacking, as was the case with Oxford, Bodleian Library, MS Laud Misc. 600, likely repaired under the direction of antiquarian John Barkham. A desire for completion and gap-filling is not purely an early modern concern—the manuscript history of the pseudo-Chaucerian *Tale of Gamelyn* betrays a similar medieval interest in completing what Chaucer had left fragmented—but Singh effectively demonstrates the continuity of such efforts in the post-print era and highlights the way print shaped these readerly attempts to make Chaucer whole.

Chapter 3, "Supplementing," is also interested in readers who added to their Chaucerian books. In contrast with those discussed previously, though, these readers were not prompted to supplement because of a visible gap or "defect." Here, the question of the Chaucer canon returns, and Singh details early modern responses to such texts as *The Plowman's Tale* (both the Hocclevian *Miracle of the Virgin* supplied as the "Plowman's Tale" in Oxford, Christ Church, MS 152 and the anti-Catholic tale first printed in the 1530s), Chaucer's *Retraction* (excluded from Thynne's 1532 *Works* and all subsequent *Works* volumes until the eighteenth century), and Henryson's *Testament of Cresseid* (included in early modern printed *Works* following Chaucer's *Troilus*). Texts such as these shaped readers' expectations of Chaucerian books in both manuscript and print. But, importantly, readers were not consistent in their appraisal of such Chaucerian supplements, despite the authority afforded by their placement in or exclusion from print editions. Antiquarian reader Joseph Holland's Chaucer manuscript, for instance, includes short selections from the *Testament*, rather than the full poem that appeared in print, and a Trinity College Chaucer manuscript "supplements" its Chaucer with an early modern copy of *Pierce the Ploughman's Creed*, seemingly promoting a proto-Protestant Chaucer aligned with the Chaucer of the printed *Plowman's Tale* (162). Through these varied case studies, Singh presents "Chaucer" as an "elastic" and "modular" category, one "capable of being adapted to the ends desired by its readers or required by historical circumstance" (173).

Finally, Singh's fourth chapter, "Authorising," continues the book's interest in canon formation by considering how early modern readers contended with manuscripts that lacked the authorizing paratexts commonly found in print editions: title pages, authorial attributions, and monumental portraiture such as John Speed's engraved frontispiece found in Speght's *Works*. Though the chapter is full of intriguing examples, Speed's frontispiece becomes an especially poignant symbol of the interplay between print and manuscript in Chaucer's early modern reception. As Singh describes it, the printed frontispiece translates the manuscript portrait of Chaucer found alongside Hoccleve's *Regiment of Princes* into a new medium. The printed frontispiece then becomes a source for later manuscript interventions, such as the manuscript facsimile of the printed image found in a Speght edition that was otherwise lacking the portrait. In Singh's words, the history of this frontispiece "suppl[ies] evidence of the transmission of an iconographic tradition from manuscript into print and back again" (212). As is the case in so many of the examples explored in *Chaucer's Early Modern Readers*, manuscript and print are not opposed but are mutually constitutive in the effort to "perfect" Chaucer's corpus and image.

While the variation inherent to the manuscript form ensures that Singh's case studies are similarly varied, several unifying figures emerge that connect the book's diverse threads. Notably, Joseph Holland and his interventions in Cambridge University Library, MS Gg.4.27, are discussed in detail in all four of the book's central chapters. William Browne of Tavistock, another antiquarian, appears in both the "Glossing" chapter and the "Authorising" chapter. And, while John Stow is treated most extensively in the fourth chapter, he also appears throughout Singh's study. Though this organization might be challenging for readers coming to this book to learn about one of these figures in particular, I valued returning to these examples multiple times through the lenses of the book's various framing devices, seeing how the different facets of Singh's argument intersect with one another.

Overall, *Chaucer's Early Modern Readers* is a thorough and insightful addition to our understanding of how Chaucer was read and indeed created in both early print and in manuscript. By foregrounding the manuscripts that circulated alongside early modern printed books, Singh refocuses scholarly attention, emphasizing the interaction between two media still often considered separately. Though the book focuses on Chaucer, scholars interested in the reception of medieval texts more broadly—the reception of Gower, Lydgate, Hoccleve, and others—will find much of interest in Singh's compelling book, as will scholars thinking about periodization and materiality as it pertains to the medieval/early modern divide.

MIMI ENSLEY
Flagler College

Books Received

Barr, Helen, ed. and trans. *Patience* (Peterborough, Ont.: Broadview Press, 2024). Pp. 132. $19.95 hardback; $11.57 e-book.

Griffin, Carrie, and Hannah Ryley, eds. *Recipes and Book Culture in England, 1350–1600* (Liverpool: Liverpool University Press, 2024). Pp. 288. $130.00 hardback.

Hanna, Ralph. *Looking at Medieval Books: Learning to See* (Liverpool: Liverpool University Press, 2023). Pp. 176. $150.00 hardback; $39.99 paperback.

Kao, Wan-Chuan. *White before Whiteness in the Late Middle Ages* (Manchester: Manchester University Press, 2024). Pp. 456. $81.95 hardback and e-book.

McKay, Anna. *Female Devotion and Textile Imagery in Medieval English Literature* (Cambridge: D. S. Brewer, 2024). Pp. 426. $115.00 hardback and e-book.

Mitchell, J. Allan. *Instrumentality: On Technical Objects and Orientations in the Later Middle Ages* (Minneapolis: University of Minnesota Press, 2024). Pp. 148. $108.00 hardback; $27.00 paperback and e-book.

Norako, Leila K. *Monstrous Fantasies: England's Crusading Imagery and the Romance of Recovery, 1300–1500* (Ithaca: Cornell University Press, 2024). Pp. 342. $59.95 hardback and e-book.

Perry, R. D. *Coterie Poetics and the Beginnings of the English Literary Tradition* (Philadelphia: University of Pennsylvania Press, 2024). Pp. 322. $69.95 hardback and e-book.

Piercy, Hannah. *Resistance to Love in Medieval English Romance: Negotiating Consent, Gender, and Desire* (Cambridge: D. S. Brewer, 2023). Pp. 290. $36.26 paperback.

Wagner, Erin K. *The Language of Heresy in Late Medieval English Literature* (Kalamazoo: Medieval Institute Publications, 2024). Pp. 270. $121.99 hardback and e-book.

Weaver, Hannah. *Experimental Histories: Interpolation and the Medieval British Past* (Ithaca: Cornell University Press, 2024). Pp. 246. $46.95 hardback; $30.99 e-book.

Weisl, Angela Jane, and Robert Squillace, eds. *Medievalisms in a Global Age* (Cambridge: D. S. Brewer, 2024). Pp. 296. $95.14 hardback.

An Annotated Chaucer Bibliography, 2022

Compiled and edited by Stephanie Amsel and Will Rogers

Regular contributors:
Mark Allen, *University of Texas at San Antonio*
Stephanie Amsel, *Southern Methodist University* (Texas)
Tim Arner, *Grinnell College* (Iowa)
Debra Best, *California State University at Dominguez Hills*
Thomas H. Blake, *Austin College* (Texas)
Agnès Blandeau, *Université de Nantes* (France)
Margaret Connolly, *University of St. Andrews* (Scotland)
Stefania D'Agata D'Ottavi, *Università per Stranieri di Siena* (Italy)
Jamie C. Fumo, *Florida State University*
James B. Harr III, *North Carolina State University*
Douglas W. Hayes, *Lakehead University*
Ana Sáez Hidalgo, *Universidad de Valladolid* (Spain)
Yoshinobu Kudo, *Ishikawa Prefectural Nursing University* (Japan)
Daniel M. Murtaugh, *Florida Atlantic University*
Thomas J. Napierkowski, *University of Colorado at Colorado Springs*
Teresa P. Reed, *Jacksonville State University* (Alabama)
Will Rogers, *University of Louisiana at Monroe*
Martha Rust, *New York University*
Thomas R. Schneider, *California Baptist University*
Susan Yager, *Iowa State University*

The bibliographer acknowledges with gratitude the invaluable contribution and support from Mark Allen, Professor Emeritus, University of Texas at San Antonio.

This bibliography continues the bibliographies published since 1975 in previous volumes of *Studies in the Age of Chaucer*. Bibliographic information up to 1975 can be found in Eleanor P. Hammond, *Chaucer: A Bibliographic Manual* (1908; repr., New York: Peter Smith, 1933); D. D. Griffith, *Bibliography of Chaucer, 1908–1953* (Seattle: University of Washington Press, 1955); William R. Crawford, *Bibliography of Chaucer, 1954–63* (Seattle: University of Washington Press, 1967); and Lorrayne Y. Baird, *Bibliography of*

Chaucer, 1964–1973 (Boston, Mass.: G. K. Hall, 1977). See also Lorrayne Y. Baird-Lange and Hildegard Schnuttgen, *Bibliography of Chaucer, 1974–1985* (Hamden, Conn.: Shoe String Press, 1988); Bege K. Bowers and Mark Allen, eds., *Annotated Chaucer Bibliography, 1986–1996* (Notre Dame: University of Notre Dame Press, 2002); and Mark Allen and Stephanie Amsel, eds., *Annotated Chaucer Bibliography, 1997–2010* (Manchester: Manchester University Press, 2015).

Additions and corrections to this bibliography should be sent to Stephanie Amsel, Department of English, Southern Methodist University, 108C Clements Hall, PO Box 750435, Dallas, Texas 75275-0435. An electronic version of this bibliography (1975–2021) is available via The New Chaucer Society Web page at http://artsci.wustl.edu/~chaucer/, or directly at http://uchaucer.utsa.edu. Authors are urged to send annotations for articles, reviews, and books that have been or might be overlooked to Stephanie Amsel, AOChaucerBib@mail.smu.edu.

Classifications

Abbreviations of Chaucer's Works

ABC	*An ABC*
Adam	*Adam Scriveyn*
Anel	*Anelida and Arcite*
Astr	*A Treatise on the Astrolabe*
Bal Compl	*A Balade of Complaint*
BD	*The Book of the Duchess*
Bo	*Boece*
Buk	*The Envoy to Bukton*
CkT, CkP	*The Cook's Tale, The Cook's Prologue*
ClT, ClP, Cl–MerL	*The Clerk's Tale, The Clerk's Prologue, Clerk–Merchant Link*
Compl d'Am	*Complaynt d'Amours*
CT	*The Canterbury Tales*
CYT, CYP	*The Canon's Yeoman's Tale, The Canon's Yeoman's Prologue*
Equat	*The Equatorie of the Planetis*
For	*Fortune*
Form Age	*The Former Age*
FranT, FranP	*The Franklin's Tale, The Franklin's Prologue*
FrT, FrP, Fr–SumL	*The Friar's Tale, The Friar's Prologue, Friar–Summoner Link*
Gent	*Gentilesse*
GP	*The General Prologue*
HF	*The House of Fame*
KnT, Kn–MilL	*The Knight's Tale, Knight–Miller Link*
Lady	*A Complaint to His Lady*
LGW, LGWP	*The Legend of Good Women, The Legend of Good Women Prologue*
ManT, ManP	*The Manciple's Tale, The Manciple's Prologue*
Mars	*The Complaint of Mars*
Mel, Mel–MkL	*The Tale of Melibee, Melibee–Monk Link*
MercB	*Merciles Beaute*
MerT, MerE–SqH	*The Merchant's Tale, Merchant Endlink–Squire Headlink*

MilT, MilP, Mil–RvL	*The Miller's Tale, The Miller's Prologue, Miller–Reeve Link*
MkT, MkP, Mk–NPL	*The Monk's Tale, The Monk's Prologue, Monk–Nun's Priest Link*
MLT, MLH, MLP, MLE	*The Man of Law's Tale, Man of Law Headlink, The Man of Law's Prologue, Man of Law Endlink*
NPT, NPP, NPE	*The Nun's Priest's Tale, The Nun's Priest's Prologue, Nun's Priest Endlink*
PardT, PardP	*The Pardoner's Tale, The Pardoner's Prologue*
ParsT, ParsP	*The Parson's Tale, The Parson's Prologue*
PF	*The Parliament of Fowls*
PhyT, Phy–PardL	*The Physician's Tale, Physician–Pardoner Link*
Pity	*The Complaint unto Pity*
Prov	*Proverbs*
PrT, PrP, Pr–ThL	*The Prioress's Tale, The Prioress's Prologue, Prioress–Thopas Link*
Purse	*The Complaint of Chaucer to His Purse*
Ret	*Chaucer's Retraction {Retractation}*
Rom	*The Romaunt of the Rose*
Ros	*To Rosemounde*
RvT, RvP, Rv–CkL,	*The Reeve's Tale, The Reeve's Prologue, Reeve–Cook Link*
Scog	*The Envoy to Scogan*
ShT, Sh–PrL	*The Shipman's Tale, Shipman–Prioress Link*
SNT, SNP, SN–CYL	*The Second Nun's Tale, The Second Nun's Prologue, Second Nun–Canon's Yeoman Link*
SqT, SqH, Sq–FranL	*The Squire's Tale, Squire Headlink, Squire–Franklin Link*
Sted	*Lak of Stedfastnesse*
SumT, SumP	*The Summoner's Tale, The Summoner's Prologue*
TC	*Troilus and Criseyde*
Th, Th–MelL	*The Tale of Sir Thopas, Thopas–Melibee Link*
Truth	*Truth*

Ven	*The Complaint of Venus*
WBT, WBP, WB–FrL	*The Wife of Bath's Tale, The Wife of Bath's Prologue, Wife of Bath–Friar Link*
Wom Nob	*Womanly Noblesse*
Wom Unc	*Against Women Unconstant*

Periodical Abbreviations

Anglia	*Anglia: Zeitschrift für englische Philologie*
Anglistik	*Anglistik: Mitteilungen des Verbandes deutscher Anglisten*
ANQ	*ANQ: A Quarterly Journal of Short Articles, Notes, and Reviews*
Archiv	*Archiv für das Studium der neueren Sprachen und Literaturen*
Arthuriana	*Arthuriana*
Atlantis	*Atlantis: Revista de la Asociacion Española de Estudios Anglo-Norteamericanos*
AUMLA	*AUMLA: Journal of the Australasian Universities Language and Literature Association*
BAM	*Bulletin des Anglicistes Médiévistes*
BJRL	*Bulletin of the John Rylands University Library of Manchester*
BSCS	*Bulletin of the Society for Chaucer Studies*
C&L	*Christianity and Literature*
CE	*College English*
ChauR	*Chaucer Review*
CL	*Comparative Literature (Eugene, Ore.)*
Clio	*CLIO: A Journal of Literature, History, and the Philosophy of History*
CLS	*Comparative Literature Studies*
CML	*Classical and Modern Literature: A Quarterly (Columbia, Mo.)*
CollL	*College Literature*
Comitatus	*Comitatus: A Journal of Medieval and Renaissance Studies*
CRCL	*Canadian Review of Comparative Literature/Revue Canadienne de Littérature Comparée*
DAI	*Dissertation Abstracts International*
EA	*Etudes Anglaises: Grand-Bretagne, Etats-Unis*
EHR	*English Historical Review*
EIC	*Essays in Criticism: A Quarterly Journal of Literary Criticism*
EJ	*English Journal*
ELH	*ELH: English Literary History*

ELN	*English Language Notes*
ELR	*English Literary Renaissance*
EMA	*Etudes Médiévales Anglaises: A French Journal of English Medieval Studies*
EMS	*English Manuscript Studies, 1100–1700*
EMSt	*Essays in Medieval Studies*
Enarratio	*Enarratio: Publications of the Modern Language Association of America*
English	*English: The Journal of the English Association*
Envoi	*Envoi: A Review Journal of Medieval Literature*
ES	*English Studies*
Exemplaria	*Exemplaria: A Journal of Theory in Medieval and Renaissance Studies*
Expl	*Explicator*
FCS	*Fifteenth-Century Studies*
Florilegium	*Florilegium: Carleton University Papers on Late Antiquity and the Middle Ages*
Genre	*Genre: Forms of Discourse and Culture*
H-Albion	*H-Albion: The H-Net Discussion Network for British and Irish History, H-Net Reviews in the Humanities and Social Sciences http://www.h-net.org/reviews/home.php*
HLQ	*Huntington Library Quarterly: Studies in English and American History and Literature (San Marino, Calif.)*
Hortulus	*Hortulus: The Online Graduate Journal of Medieval Studies http://www.hortulus.net/*
IJES	*International Journal of English Studies*
JAIS	*Journal of Anglo-Italian Studies*
JBSt	*Journal of British Studies*
JEBS	*Journal of the Early Book Society*
JEGP	*Journal of English and Germanic Philology*
JELL	*Journal of English Language and Literature (Korea)*
JEngL	*Journal of English Linguistics*
JGN	*John Gower Newsletter*
JMEMS	*Journal of Medieval and Early Modern Studies*
JML	*Journal of Modern Literature*
JNT	*Journal of Narrative Theory*
L&LC	*Literary and Linguistic Computing: Journal of the Association for Literary and Linguistic Computing*
L&P	*Literature and Psychology*

L&T	*Literature and Theology: An International Journal of Religion, Theory, and Culture*
Lang&Lit	*Language and Literature: Journal of the Poetics and Linguistics Association*
Lang&S	*Language and Style: An International Journal*
LeedsSE	*Leeds Studies in English*
Library	*The Library: The Transactions of the Bibliographical Society*
LitComp	*Literature Compass (Wiley Online Library) https://onlinelibrary.wiley.com/journal/17414113*
MA	*Le Moyen Age: Revue d'Histoire et de Philologie (Brussels, Belgium)*
MÆ	*Medium Ævum*
M&H	*Medievalia et Humanistica: Studies in Medieval and Renaissance Culture*
Manuscript	*Manuscript Studies*
Manuscripta	*Manuscripta: A Journal for Manuscript Research*
Marginalia	*Marginalia: The Journal of the Medieval Reading Group at the University of Cambridge http://www.marginalia.co.uk/journal/*
Mediaevalia	*Mediaevalia: An Interdisciplinary Journal of Medieval Studies Worldwide*
MedievalF	*Medieval Forum http://www.sfsu.edu/~medieval/index.html*
MES	*Medieval and Early Modern English Studies*
MFF	*Medieval Feminist Forum*
Mirabilia	*Mirabilia: Electronic Journal of Antiquity and Middle Ages*
MLQ	*Modern Language Quarterly: A Journal of Literary History*
MLR	*Modern Language Review*
MP	*Modern Philology: A Journal Devoted to Research in Medieval and Modern Literature*
NCSPP	*New Chaucer Studies: Pedagogy & Profession*
N&Q	*Notes and Queries*
Neophil	*Neophilologus (Dordrecht, Netherlands)*
NM	*Neuphilologische Mitteilungen: Bulletin of the Modern Language Society*
NML	*New Medieval Literatures*
NMS	*Nottingham Medieval Studies*
NYRB	*The New York Times Review of Books*
Parergon	*Parergon: Bulletin of the Australian and New Zealand Association for Medieval and Early Modern Studies*

PBA	*Proceedings of the British Academy*
PBSA	*Papers of the Bibliographical Society of America*
PLL	*Papers on Language and Literature: A Journal for Scholars and Critics of Language and Literature*
PoeticaT	*Poetica: An International Journal of Linguistic Literary Studies*
Postmedieval	*Postmedieval: A Journal of Medieval Cultural Studies https://doi.org/10.1057/s41280*
PQ	*Philological Quarterly*
Quidditas	*Quidditas: Journal of the Rocky Mountain Medieval and Renaissance Association*
RCEI	*Revista Canaria de Estudios Ingleses*
R&L	*Religion & Literature*
RenQ	*Renaissance Quarterly*
RES	*Review of English Studies*
REVELL	*REVELL: Revista de Estudos Literários da UEMS*
RMSt	*Reading Medieval Studies*
SCJ	*Sixteenth Century Journal*
SAC	*Studies in the Age of Chaucer*
SAP	*Studia Anglica Posnaniensia: An International Review of English*
SAQ	*South Atlantic Quarterly*
SB	*Studies in Bibliography: Papers of the Bibliographical Society of the University of Virginia*
SCJ	*The Sixteenth-Century Journal: Journal of Early Modern Studies (Kirksville, Mo.)*
SEDERI	*SEDERI: Spanish and Portuguese Society for English Renaissance Studies*
SEL	*SEL: Studies in English Literature, 1500–1900*
SELIM	*SELIM: Journal of the Spanish Society for Medieval English Language and Literature*
ShakS	*Shakespeare Studies*
SIcon	*Studies in Iconography*
SiM	*Studies in Medievalism*
SIMELL	*Studies in Medieval English Language and Literature*
SMART	*Studies in Medieval and Renaissance Teaching*
SN	*Studia Neophilologica: A Journal of Germanic and Romance Languages and Literatures*
SP	*Studies in Philology*

Speculum	*Speculum: A Journal of Medieval Studies*
SSt	*Spenser Studies: A Renaissance Poetry Annual*
TCBS	*Transactions of the Cambridge Bibliographical Society*
Text	*Text: Transactions of the Society for Textual Scholarship*
TextC	*Textual Cultures: Texts, Contexts, Interpretation*
TLS	*Times Literary Supplement (London, England)*
TMR	*The Medieval Review* *https://scholarworks.iu.edu/journals/index.php/tmr*
Tr&Lit	*Translation and Literature*
TSLL	*Texas Studies in Literature and Language*
UTQ	*University of Toronto Quarterly: A Canadian Journal of the Humanities*
Viator	*Viator: Medieval and Renaissance Studies*
WS	*Women's Studies: An Interdisciplinary Journal*
YES	*Yearbook of English Studies*
YLS	*The Yearbook of Langland Studies*
YWES	*Year's Work in English Studies*

Bibliographical Citations and Annotations

Bibliographies, Reports, and Reference

1. Amsel, Stephanie, and Will Rogers. "An Annotated Chaucer Bibliography, 2020." *SAC* 44 (2022): 439–532. Continuation of *SAC* annual annotated bibliography (since 1975); based on contributions from an international bibliographic team, independent research, and *MLA Bibliography* listings. 326 items, plus a listing of reviews for 47 books. Includes an author index.

2. Ash-Irisarri, Kate, Laurie Atkinson, Daisy Black, Sarah Brazil, Natalie Calder, Andrew Finn, Darragh Greene, Ayoush Lazikani, Rebecca Menmuir, Mark Ronan, J. D. Sargan, and Seth Strickland. "Middle English." *YWES* 101 (2022): 185–282. Discursive bibliography, divided into fourteen subsections: Early Middle English; Theory; Manuscript and Technical Studies; Religious Writing; Secular Prose; Secular Verse; *Piers Plowman*; Gower; Old Scots; Drama; *Sir Gawain and the Green Knight*, *Pearl*, *Patience*, and *Cleanness*; Romance: Metrical, Alliterative, Prose; and Hoccleve and Lydgate. Multiple references augment the bibliography dedicated to Chaucer in this volume of *YWES*; see no. 6.

3. Batkie, Stephanie L., Matthew W. Irvin, and Lynn Shutters, eds. *A New Companion to Critical Thinking on Chaucer*. Leeds: Arc Humanities Press, 2021. xx, 348 pp. Collects twenty essays about thematic terms and concepts in Chaucer's works, arranged in groups of four, each group including an additional response essay. Opens with a foreword by Christopher Cannon, followed by an explanatory introduction by the editors, with four appendices (Summaries of Chaucer's Works, Additional Terms, Coverage by Term, and Coverage by Work) and a comprehensive index. Part 1: "Consent/Assent" by Fiona Somerset; "Entente" by Candace Barrington; "Pite" by Glenn D. Burger; "Slider" by David Raybin; Response by Ardis Butterfield. Part 2: "Merveille" by Tara Williams; "Virginite" by Sarah Salih; "Swiven" by Helen Barr; "Craft" by Bruce Holsinger; Response by Simon Horobin. Part 3: "Vertu" by Holly A. Crocker; "Wal" by Marion Turner; "Thing" by Steele Nowlin; "Blak" by Cord J. Whitaker; Response by Carolyn Dinshaw. Part 4: "Auctorite/Auctour" by R. D. Perry; "Seculere" by Catherine Sanok; "Flesh" by Richard H. Godden; "Memorie" by Ruth Evans; Response by Andrew Cole.

4. Boswell, Jackson C. *Chaucer's Fame in Britannia, 1641–1700*. Medieval and Renaissance Texts and Studies, no. 572. Tempe: Arizona Center for Medieval and Renaissance Studies, 2021. xxxi, 512 pp. Tallies 1,060 entries that identify references to, allusions to, and echoes of Chaucer and his works in books published from 1641 through 1700, with an appendix of 131 references and allusions from 1475 through 1640, all in addition to or expansions of Caroline Spurgeon's venerable bibliography, already extended by Boswell and Sylvia Wallace Holton in *Chaucer's Fame in England* (2004). Entries are arranged chronologically by date of publication and, within years, alphabetically. They provide, where appropriate, quotations from the sources, original STC numbers, Wing's STC numbers, and UMI references; headnotes indicate who discovered the references. The volume includes an introduction by Gordon Braden on Chaucer's reception; a list of STC books cited; and indexes of Chaucer's works, his life and literary reputation, and authors and topics.

5. Finn, Andrew. "Theory" [Section 2 of "Middle English"]. *YWES* 101 (2022): 189–98. A discursive bibliography of Middle English studies with various theoretical emphases; includes studies of Chaucer and his works.

6. Menmuir, Rebecca, Peter Buchanan, and Lucy Brookes. "Chaucer." *YWES* 101 (2022): 283–315. A discursive bibliography of Chaucer studies for 2020, divided into four subcategories: general, *CT*, other works, and reception and reputation. See no. 2.

See also no. 49.

Recordings and Film

7. Holland, James Nathaniel. *Canterbury Tales: An Opera in Four Acts*. [Independently Published], 2021. Musical score. 318 pp. Item not seen. YouTube demo (accessed May 21, 2024) indicates that this opera includes an overture and adaptations of four portions of *CT*: *FranT* ("For All the Rocks Off Brittany"), *PardT* ("Une Danse Macabre"), *WBT* ("What All Women Want"), and *MerT* ("That Pesky Itch").

8. Stokol, Deborah. "Teaching Chaucer from the Perspective of a Troubadour and Using Music in the Classroom to Further Explain Literature." *NCSPP* 3 (2022): 58–69. Recounts the composition of a "troubadour-style" version of *WBPT* set to music (lyrics and link to audio recording included), describing its usefulness in teaching of Chaucer's work and

various other benefits of using music in teaching English literature at the high school level.

See also nos. 86, 314.

Chaucer's Life

9. Coleman, Joyce. "Chaucer the Page: A Winter's Tale of Courtly Entertainment." In Julia Boffey, ed. *Performance, Ceremony and Display in Late Medieval England: Proceedings of the 2018 Harlaxton Symposium*. Harlaxton Medieval Studies, no. 30 (Donington: Shaun Tyas, 2020), pp. 95–109. Reconstructs from documentary evidence aspects of Elizabeth de Burgh's holiday entertainment at Hatfield House in 1357–58, when Chaucer was her page, positing that Chaucer's mature recollections of performative readings can be found in *BD*, 349–61, and *TC*, II.78–84. Suggests that experiences in Elizabeth's court "became the basis of [Chaucer's] understanding of the setting, tastes, and pragmatics of courtly literary performance."

10. Fein, Susanna, and David Raybin. "The Case of Geoffrey Chaucer and Cecily Chaumpaigne: New Evidence." *ChauR* 57 (2022): 403–6. Situates and introduces a special issue devoted to new evidence concerning Chaucer and Cecily Chaumpaigne.

11. Flannery, Mary C. "The Case for the Defence: New Evidence Suggests that Geoffrey Chaucer May Be Innocent of Rape." *TLS*, October 21, 2022, p. 18. Reports on reactions to the release of new documentary evidence about the "relationship between Chaucer and Cecily Chaumpaigne," suggesting how these reactions reveal "how much our own perspectives and feelings shape the stories we tell about the past."

12. Harris, Carissa M. "On Servant Women, Rape Culture, and Endurance." *ChauR* 57 (2022): 475–83. In light of newly discovered documents surrounding Cecily Chaumpaigne, calls for more attention to the servant women depicted in Chaucer's texts and the use of the word "endure" in his corpus.

13. Kawasaki, Masatoshi, and Koichi Kano. "Chaucer's Life." In Koichi Kano, ed. *An Invitation to Chaucer's Cosmos* (*SAC* 46 [2024], no. 149), pp. 3–50. Provides a detailed account of Chaucer's life, with consideration of how his personality and experience contributed to his literary characteristics. In Japanese.

14. Prescott, Andrew. "Who Was Cecily Chaumpaigne?" *ChauR* 57 (2022): 452–62. Collects and describes the known life evidence for Cecily Chaumpaigne, tracing her personal and family life.

15. Roger, Euan. "APPENDIX 2. Transcriptions and Translations." *ChauR* 57 (2022): 440–49. Gathers together previously known documents concerning Cecily Chaumpaigne with newly discovered documents. Documents are transcribed and translations provided.

16. Roger, Euan, and Sebastian Sobecki. "APPENDIX 1: Chronology of the Known Chaucer–Chaumpaigne Records." *ChauR* 57 (2022): 438–39. Briefly records the chronology of Thomas Staundon, Chaucer, and Cecily Chaumpaigne.

17. ______. "Geoffrey Chaucer, Cecily Chaumpaigne, and the Statute of Laborers: New Records and Old Evidence Reconsidered." *ChauR* 57 (2022): 407–37. Examines newly discovered documents to argue that Chaucer and Cecily Chaumpaigne were both party to Staundon's legal maneuvers, and that, because of the Statute of Laborers, Chaumpaigne's quit claim offered a resolution. Presents a reappraisal of previous allegations against Chaucer.

18. Seal, Samantha Katz. "Chasing the Consent of Alice Chaucer." *SAC* 44 (2022): 273–83. Explores the misogyny that underlies several historical records of, and modern commentaries on, an attempt to seduce Alice Chaucer, Chaucer's daughter, by Philip, duke of Burgundy. For response, see no. 159.

19. ______. "Whose Chaucer? On Cecily Chaumpaigne, Cancellation, and the English Literary Canon." *ChauR* 57 (2022): 484–97. Reflects on the newly discovered documents in the case of Cecily Champagne, and contends that, regardless of whether Chaucer was to blame, medieval studies and Chaucerian critics remain at fault if they excused Chaucer on account of his poetry. Highlights legacy of feminist scholars and scholarship over the past decades.

20. Sobecki, Sebastian. "APPENDIX 3: Calendar of New Chaucer Life-Records." *ChauR* 57 (2022): 450–51. Lists and describes nine documents about Chaucer's life discovered since the publication of *Chaucer's Life-Records* in 1966.

See also nos. 27, 55, 73, 101, 139, 164, 181, 183, 196, 215, 219, 246, 250.

Facsimiles, Editions, and Translations

21. Boje, John. "Translating Taboo: Blasphemy in an Afrikaans Translation of Chaucer's *Canterbury Tales.*" *Journal of Literary Studies/Tydskrif vir Literatuurwetenskap* 37 (2021): 1–19. Clarifies pressures exerted by literary translation theories of the late twentieth century on Boje's translation of *CT*, focusing on the taboo against blasphemy in the target language, Afrikaans, and Chaucer's use of religious oaths.

22. Bordalejo, Barbara, Lina Gibbings, Richard North, and Peter Robinson. "Making an Edition in an App." *Digital Medievalist* 14, special issue (2021). 32 pp. Reviews the history, planning, making, distribution, and early use of the CantApp edition of *GP* (2020), designed to be accessed on a mobile device, the first of its kind. Offers suggestions for similar efforts in the future and includes description of pedagogical applications for reading Chaucer aloud.

23. Fisher, Sheila. "How to Teach *The Canterbury Tales* in (My Own) Translation." *NCSPP* 3 (2022): 95–100. Describes "the author's work as a translator" of *CT* "and how she uses this translation in the classroom."

24. Fruoco, Jonathan, ed. and trans., with others. *Le Livre de la Duchesse et autres textes*. Chaucer: Oeuvres Complètes, Tome I. Paris: Classiques Garnier, 2021. 404 pp. Middle English edition and French translation of *BD*, *HF*, *Anel*, and *PF*, with introduction and commentary in French.

25. Harada, Noriyuki. "Samuel Johnson's Literary Ardour: Geoffrey Chaucer in the Eighteenth Century." *Geibun-Kenkyu* 123 (2022): 46–59. Argues that Johnson's perfunctory references to Chaucer reflect the former's view of the latter not as an excellent "English" poet but as one who successfully transmitted literature from the Continent onto Britain. Considers possible reasons Johnson had a plan to compile an edition of Chaucer's works around the close of his life in relation to some eighteenth-century characteristics of Chaucerian reception. In Japanese.

26. Leahy, Conor. "An Annotated Edition of Chaucer Belonging to Stephan Batman." *Library* 22 (2021): 217–24. Describes the annotations made by book-collector Stephan Batman (c. 1542–84) in his copy of John Stow's edition of *The Woorkes of Geffrey Chaucer* (1561), explaining how they evince Batman's habits and interests.

27. Luo, Yue, trans. [*The Canterbury Tales*]. Nanjing: Jiang su feng huang wen yi chu ban she, 2022. 421 pp. Item not seen. WorldCat records indicate that this is a translation of *CT* into Chinese; apparently

adapted, suggesting that Philippa's illness is Chaucer's motive for undertaking his pilgrimage.

28. Meyer-Lee, Robert J. "The First Riverside Chaucer." *ChauR* 57 (2022): 253–72. Highlights the three-volume edition of Chaucer's works published in 1879 by Arthur Gilman, emphasizing the achievements of Gilman as an editor and situating his scholarly activities in his then-contemporary context.

29. Perry, Ryan, intro. *Canterbury Tales*. London: Flame Tree, 2019. 575 pp. Item not seen. WorldCat record notes that "This edition is based on the second edition of The complete works of Geoffrey Chaucer, edited by the Rev. Walter W. Skeat, 1900 (Oxford)," with a "new introduction."

30. Štrmelj, Lidija. "Chaucerove metafore u prijevodu Luke Paljetka: Kognitivna studija." [Chaucer's Metaphors in Luko Paljetak's Translation: A Cognitive Study]. *Časopis za Književnost, Kulturu i Književno Prevođenje/A Journal of Literature, Culture and Literary Translation* 12 (2021). 27 pp. Compares conceptual metaphors in *MilT* and in its Croatian translation by Luko Paljetak (1986) in order to determine which metaphors are "conventional in both language and cultures." In Croatian, with an English abstract.

31. Syme, Alison. "'All that Is Solid Melts into Air': Burne-Jones, Glaciation, and the Matter of History." In Nancy Rose Marshall, ed. *Victorian Science and Imagery: Representation in Nineteenth-Century Visual Culture* (Pittsburgh: University of Pittsburgh Press, 2021), pp. 56–78. Focuses on Edward Burne-Jones's illustration of *HF* in the Kelmscott Chaucer (1896) to show "that Burne-Jones was attuned to the scientific discourse of his time," arguing that the book "provided the context and impetus to visualize, in distilled form, some of the complex relationships between natural change and human activity that his contemporaries were beginning to consider."

32. Treharne, Elaine, and Claude Willan. *Text Technologies: A History*. Stanford, Calif.: Stanford University Press, 2020. xii, 207 pp.; 66 illus. Introduces the study of text technologies, explaining concepts, providing history, and offering case studies. Among the latter is a brief study of the Kelmscott Chaucer as a text that "was created specifically to have a particular aura" in various ways and for various reasons. Also reproduces a sample illustration from Caxton's *CT* (London, British Library, G.11586), with questions for analysis or discussion.

33. Witcher, Heather Bozant. *Collaborative Writing in the Long Nineteenth Century: Sympathetic Partnerships and Artistic Creation*. Cambridge:

Cambridge University Press, 2022. x, 260 pp. Chapter 4—"Typographical Adventures: William Morris, Community, and the Kelmscott Press"—includes discussion of the "sympathetic collaboration" (a concept theorized by William Morris) between Edward Burne-Jones and Robert Catterson-Smith in producing illustrations for the Kelmscott Chaucer. Focuses on *CIT*.

34. Zawadzki, Jared, trans. *Opowieści Kanterberyjskie*. Katowice: Biblioteka Śląska, 2022. 795 pp; illus. Item not seen. WorldCat records and the publisher's website indicate this is a Polish translation of the complete *CT*, illustrated by Maciej Sieńczyk.

See also nos. 7, 36, 42, 45, 76, 81, 116, 121, 141, 146, 158, 187, 205–6, 208, 211, 218, 227, 251, 265, 289, 302, 333.

Manuscripts and Textual Studies

35. Adams, Abigail Marie. "Putting Together the Pieces: Excerpts from Rolle, Gower, Chaucer, and Lydgate in Fifteenth-Century Miscellanies." Ph.D. dissertation (The University of Texas at Austin, 2022), *DAI-A* 84.06(E). "[S]urveys manuscripts excerpting Chaucer's *Canterbury Tales*, Rolle's *Commentary on the Song of Songs*, Lydgate's *Fall of Princes*, and Gower's *Confessio amantis* . . . [showing how] [t]hese manuscripts display a fifteenth-century attitude to authorship that re-shapes modern assumptions about canon formation and the laureation of Chaucer."

36. Bitner, Kendall, and Kyle Dase. "A Macron Signifying Nothing: Revisiting the Canterbury Tales Project Transcription Guidelines." *Digital Medievalist* 14, special issue (2021). 34 pp. Explains the "necessary compromises and more efficient practices" that underlie changes to the original transcription principles of the Canterbury Tales Project, offering illustrative examples, and emphasizing the goal of making textual materials readily available, rather than a new edition per se.

37. Bordalejo, Barbara. "Well-Behaved Variants Seldom Make the Apparatus: Stemmata and Apparatus in Digital Research." *Digital Medievalist* 14, special issue (2021). 36 pp. Describes "computer-assisted methods for the analysis of textual variation within large textual traditions," clarifying phylogenetic methods, the goal of maximum parsimony, software decisions and usage, variant management, and the crucial importance of editorial decision-making." Illustrative examples drawn from the Canterbury Tales Project.

38. Bordalejo, Barbara, and Adam Alberto Vázquez. "You're Collating Just Fine and Other Lies You've Been Telling Yourself." *Digital Medievalist* 14, special issue (2021). 46 pp. Compares "manual and computer-assisted approaches to collation methods," drawing examples from the texts of *TC*, *CT*, Dante's *Commedia*, and the Greek New Testament. Argues for full-text rather than selected-text analysis, the importance of variant distribution, and the need to avoid a-priori decisions, preferring computer-assisted techniques.

39. Brantley, Jessica. *Medieval English Manuscripts and Literary Forms*. Material Texts. Philadelphia: University of Pennsylvania Press, 2022. xiv, 346 pp.; illus. Offers "a general introduction to manuscript studies for readers whose particular interests lie in medieval literature," offering commentary on material concerns, paleography, decoration and illustration, codicology, and principles of manuscript description, along with a glossary of terms, suggestions for further reading, and eleven case studies of individual manuscripts from Bede to the N-Town Plays. Chaucer is a recurrent concern, from an opening consideration of *Adam* and its implications to two case studies: one of the Ellesmere manuscript of the *CT*; the other of Huntington Library, MS HM 114, which includes *TC*, among other texts.

40. Connolly, Margaret, Holly James-Maddocks, and Derek Pearsall, eds. *Scribal Cultures in Late Medieval England: Essays in Honour of Linne R. Mooney*. York Manuscript and Early Print Sudies, no. 3. York: York Medieval Press, in association with Boydell & Brewer, 2022. xxii, 364 pp.; 82 illus. Thirteen essays on paleography, codicology, and manuscript studies in late medieval England, with emphasis on location and scribal identity, accompanied by an introduction (by Connolly), a personal tribute (by Pearsall), a list of Mooney's publications (by Daryl Green), and a comprehensive index. For two essays that pertain to Chaucer, see nos. 45, 49.

41. Crick, Julia, and Daniel Wakelin. "Reading and Understanding Scripts." In Orietta Da Rold and Elaine Treharne, eds. *The Cambridge Companion to Medieval British Manuscripts* (*SAC* 46 [2024], no. 132), pp. 49–75. Surveys late medieval insular scripts, and discusses evident efforts to imitate anglicana formata in a stanza inserted into the roundel of *PF* in Cambridge University Library, MS Gg.4.27—added by a scribe who seems to have been "more accustomed to secretary script."

42. Dase, Kyle, and Nicole Atkings. "'Pacience Is an Heigh Vertu': Managing the Canterbury Tales Project via Textual Communities." *Digital Medievalist* 14, special issue (2021). 29 pp. Describes the use of the online

text-editing platform Textual Communities in ongoing developments of the Canterbury Tales Project, clarifying advantages and limitations of using such a platform, and offering advice for future changes to the project and similar endeavors.

43. Doyle, Kara A. *The Reception of Chaucer's Shorter Poems, 1400–1450: Female Audiences, English Manuscripts, French Contexts*. Chaucer Studies, no. 48. Cambridge: Brewer, 2021. xi, 289 pp. Combines feminist critical awareness, reception studies, and codicology to explore the construction of Chaucer as "womanis frend" in fifteenth-century manuscript compilations, studying the intertextualities of English and French works, including *Anel*, *BD*, *HF*, *PF*, *Mars*, *Venus*, and *TC*; works by Machaut, Froissart, Gower, Hoccleve, Pizan, Lydgate, Chartier, Shirley; Chaucerian apocrypha; and more, showing how they reflect awareness of the "female hermeneutic dilemma," i.e., whether to respond to courtly masculine gallantry with belief or skepticism. Focuses on MSS Gg.4.27, Cosin V.ii.13, Additional 16165 and Trinity R.3.20, Tanner 346, and Fairfax 16.

44. Drimmer, Sonja. "Connoisseurship, Art History, and the Paleographical Impasse in Middle English Studies." *Speculum* 97 (2022): 415–68. Presents debates surrounding intersection of art and paleography and the transmission of Middle English manuscripts. Focuses on *CT* manuscripts and research devoted to Gower, Langland, Hoccleve, and Chaucer. Argues that "scholars attend to how scribes may or may not signal a sense of their particularity and amenability to identification through the traces of their hand on the page."

45. Horobin, Simon. "Cambridge, Trinity College, MS R.3.15 and the Circulation of Chaucerian Manuscripts in the Sixteenth Century." In Margaret Connolly, Holly James-Maddocks, and Derek Pearsall, eds. *Scribal Cultures in Late Medieval England: Essays in Honour of Linne R. Mooney* (*SAC* 46 [2024], no. 40), pp. 312–28. Describes the role of Stephan Batman (c. 1542–84) in producing Cambridge, Trinity College, MS R.3.15 (which includes *CT*), observes how the manuscript aligns with contemporaneous printed editions of Chaucer by Thynne and Stow, and explores how Batman's interventions in the manuscript's texts reflect early modern interests and concerns.

46. Jimura, Akiyuki. "A New Approach to the Manuscripts and Editions of *The Canterbury Tales*: With Special Reference to Thynne's Edition." In Society for Chaucer Studies and Koichi Kano, eds. *To the Days of Studying Medieval English Literature: Essays in Memory of Professor Ikegami Tadahiro*

(*SAC* 46 [2024], no. 179), pp. 183–203. Analyzes examples of computer-assisted textual comparison amongst nine versions of *CT*.

47. Kennedy, Kathleen E. "Hunting the Corpus *Troilus*: Illuminating Textura." *SAC* 44 (2022): 133–63. Argues from "codicological and paleographical evidence" that the copy of *TC* found in Cambridge, Corpus Christi College, MS 61, was commissioned by a "high-level clerical, Lancastrian patron." Examines the "ornate textura" (*textualis*) script of the work, the dog-heads within letter forms (perhaps rebuses), the frontispiece illumination, and other commonalities that link the manuscript with "fine liturgical and religious manuscripts of the first half of the fifteenth century" produced in a network or networks of scribes, artists, and patrons.

48. Krummel, Miriamne Ara. "Repressing a Perpetually Resurfacing Temporality: Four Authorial Orphans and the Fifteenth-Century 'The Legend of the Litel Clergeon and the Jews.'" In *The Medieval Postcolonial Jew, in and out of Time* (Ann Arbor: University of Michigan Press, 2022), pp. 185–229; illus. Interprets four manuscript versions of *ClT* (here retitled "The Legend of the Litel Clergeon and the Jews") that occur outside the context of *CT*, "excise" Chaucer's authorship, and adjust their temporalities, addressing "their own distinct identities, through scribal marginalia, *nota* marks, rubrication, jottings, and distinctive vocabulary choices." Treats British Library, MSS Harley 1704, Harley 2251, and Harley 2382; and Bodleian Library, MS Rawlinson C.86.

49. Mosser, Daniel W. "When Is a '*Canterbury Tales* Manuscript' Not Just a *Canterbury Tales* Manuscript?" In Margaret Connolly, Holly James-Maddocks, and Derek Pearsall, eds. *Scribal Cultures in Late Medieval England: Essays in Honour of Linne R. Mooney* (*SAC* 46 [2024], no. 40), pp. 285–311. Anatomizes the contents of *CT* manuscripts, i.e., "some 240 Middle English verse texts, 65 Middle English prose texts, 16 Latin prose texts, 10 Latin verse texts, and a single French verse text" that accompany some or all of the *CT* in one or more manuscripts. Includes two appendices: I (arranged by sigil) tabulates manuscripts, incunables, and textual families of *CT*; II (arranged by title alphabetically) tabulates texts other than *CT* contained in *CT* manuscripts.

50. Nakao, Yoshiyuki, and Tadahiro Ikegami. "Manuscripts and Early Printed Books of the *Canterbury Tales*." In Koichi Kano, ed. *An Invitation to Chaucer's Cosmos* (*SAC* 46 [2024], no. 149), pp. 51–91. Examines readings in *CT* manuscripts that are not found in most critical editions. Reviews history of textual criticism of *CT* up to the *Riverside* edition, with

special reference to Ralph Hanna's scholarship. Considers merits of the electronic multilayered parallel texts developed by Nakao's research project team. In Japanese.

51. Nolcken, Christina von. "Chaucer Laboratory or Vaudeville House? John Matthews Manly and Edith Rickert's Chaucer Project, and Their University of Chicago Assistants." In Katherine E. Ellison and Susan M. Kim, eds. *Collaborative Humanities Research and Pedagogy: The Networks of John Matthews Manly and Edith Rickert* (*SAC* 46 [2024], no. 134), pp. 303–42; 4 illus. Examines archival records that pertain to the Chaucer Project (which produced *The Text of the Canterbury Tales* [1940]) to explore the history of the project, focusing on the work, working conditions, and attitudes of several scholars who assisted John Manly Matthews and Edith Rickert, including Mabel Dean, Helen McIntosh, Virginia Everett Leland, Ramona Bressie, Margaret Rickert, and many others.

52. Rogers, Cynthia A. "Outcast Lyrics: Responsive Reading in the Findern Manuscript." In Valerie B. Johnson and Kara L. McShane, eds. *Negotiating Boundaries in Medieval Literature and Culture: Essays on Marginality, Difference, and Reading Practices in Honor of Thomas Hahn* (*SAC* 46 [2024], no. 148), pp. 183–202. Focuses on the "outcast" lyrics of the Findern manuscript (Cambridge University Library, MS Ff.1.6), i.e., those "overlooked" poems as they appear among works by Chaucer and others. Analyzes how the lyrics "respond" to the works they accompany (particularly *Pity* and Richard Roos's English version of *La Belle Dame sans Mercy*), and what they thereby reveal about late medieval and early modern reading practices.

53. Simpson, James. "The Ellesmere Chaucer: The Once and Future *Canterbury Tales*." *HLQ* 85 (2022): 197–218. Examines the manuscript portrait of Chaucer in the Ellesmere manuscript (El) and its scribal rubrics as they reflect the poet's status in his own age. Reviews historical study of the manuscript, its provenance, tale order, and text, accepting Chaucer as one of its "makers" and Adam Pinkhurst as its scribe, commenting on materials that accompany *CT* in El, and showing how El can cast light on Chaucer's design for *CT* and his intentions, especially political intentions in *Mel*.

54. Wakelin, Daniel. *Immaterial Texts in Late Medieval England: Making English Literary Manuscripts, 1400–1500*. Cambridge: Cambridge University Press, 2022. xvi, 284 pp.; 19 illus. Investigates how the practices of fifteenth-century scribes of manuscripts of English poetry and prose—particularly *CT* manuscripts, and works by Lydgate and Hoccleve—reveal

"traces of immaterial traditions, intentions, assumptions, activities and performances." Uses hylomorphic "craft" theory to argue that copying was a way of thinking about books and literature, shaped by scribal conditions, and evident in layout, surface repairing, ruling, paginating, illustrating, and replicating manuscripts.

55. Wellesley, Mary. *The Gilded Page: The Secret Lives of Medieval Manuscripts*. New York: Basic, 2021. ix, 340 pp. Introduces medieval manuscripts, their production, and their legacies, with emphasis on the experiences, surprises, and pleasures of manuscript study. Refers to Chaucer's life, works, and manuscripts recurrently, with a brief section on his "playfulness" in relation to the contingencies of attribution and authorship reflected in *Adam* and *HF*.

See also nos. 22, 99, 107, 116, 119, 121, 142, 233, 294–95, 302.

Sources, Analogues, and Literary Relations

56. Brownlee, Kevin. "Chaucer's Early and Late Uses of the Two French *Rose* Authors." In Kevin Brownlee and Marina S. Brownlee, eds. *New Perspectives: Studies in Honor of Stephen G. Nichols* (New York: Peter Lang, 2022), pp. 277–88. Argues that both Guillaume de Lorris and Jean de Meun—and their "respective 'poetics'"—are "at issue" in *BD*, 321–34 (where the *Roman de la Rose* is named), and in *GP*, 725–46 ("Chaucer's Apology"). These evince Chaucer's deep, sophisticated, and career-long engagement with poetic sensibilities that underlie the "double-author" *Roman* and its views on glossing, translation, and truth-value. Also comments on Chaucer's use of the *Roman de la Rose* in *LGWP*, F 328–31.

57. Byron-Davies, Justin M. "Personification and Allegorisation in *Piers Plowman*." In *Revelation and the Apocalypse in Late Medieval Literature: The Writings of Julian of Norwich and William Langland* (Cardiff: University of Wales Press, 2020), pp. 130–73. Opens with brief contrasts between the uses of dream vision in *NPT*, Gower's *Vox clamantis*, and Langland's *Piers Plowman* before examining at greater length Langland's use of literary techniques that echo the Bible.

58. Federow, Anne-Katrin, and Kay Malcher, eds. *Troja bauen: Vormodernes Erzählen von der Antike in comparatistischer Sicht*. Germanisch romanische Monatsschrift, no. 103. Heidelberg: Universitätsverlag Winter, 2021. 292 pp. Thirteen essays by various authors on representations of

Troy and the Trojan War in medieval works, with an introduction by the editors. For two essays that pertain to Chaucer, see nos. 306, 330.

59. Hirsh, John C. "A Scotian Reading of the Man of Law's Tale and the Clerk's Tale." *MLR* 116 (2021): 1–14. Attends to "evident Scotian implications" of *MLT* and *ClT* without arguing that Chaucer read or was directly influenced by the works of John Duns Scotus. Focuses on the nature of God and voluntarism in the tales, arguing that "where Custance had to contend only with the will of God, Griselda has to confront a barely intelligible, if unmistakable, reminder of God himself" in Walter.

60. Horn, Adam Tyler. "Presumption and Despair: The Figure of Bernard in Middle English Imaginative Literature." Ph.D. dissertation (Columbia University, 2021), *DAI-A* 83.02(E). Argues for using "a Bernardine anagogical lens" to assess theological depth in *CT* and *Piers Plowman*, and traces allusions and references to Bernard of Clairvaux in *Piers*, *ParsT*, and the *Prick of Conscience*.

61. Hosokawa, Satoshi. "Chaucer and the Tradition of French Literature." In Koichi Kano, ed. *An Invitation to Chaucer's Cosmos* (*SAC* 46 [2024], no. 149), pp. 187–210. Provides a list of French works written in the period up to Chaucer's lifetime in the order of the number of extant manuscripts, from more than 100 to four. Assuming this reflects the French texts that surrounded Chaucer, reviews Charles Muscatine's classical study. In Japanese.

62. Hughes, Jonathan. *Dante's Divine Comedy in Early Renaissance England: The Collision of Two Worlds*. New York: Bloomsbury Academic, 2022. xiv, 426 pp.; b&w illus. Studies the reception of Dante in England, 1370–1450, focusing on ecclesiastical concerns about the *Divine Comedy* (*DC*) and literary responses to the poem and its worldview. Includes assessment of possible routes for Chaucer's initial access to *DC* (through travel and otherwise) and contrasts the poets' uses of the vernacular and their attitudes toward the literary legacy of Rome, especially Statius and Virgil. Reviews connections between *DC* and *HF*, *TC*, *MkT*, and other works, with an extended discussion of parallels between Criseyde and Dante's Francesca. Recurrently suggests Chaucer's role in mediating Dante's influence and emphasizes their intellectual differences.

63. Kano, Koichi. "Medieval Italian Vernacular Literature and Geoffrey Chaucer." In Koichi Kano, ed. *An Invitation to Chaucer's Cosmos* (*SAC* 46 [2024], no. 149), pp. 259–75. Provides an overview of the literary

influence of Dante, Petrarch, and Boccaccio on Chaucer. Refers to Italian analogues to *PardT*. In Japanese.

64. Seya, Yukio. "Medieval Latin Literature and Geoffrey Chaucer." In Koichi Kano, ed. *An Invitation to Chaucer's Cosmos* (*SAC* 46 [2024], no. 149), pp. 155–86. Overviews the history of Latin literature from Carolingian Renaissance to the twelfth century and enumerates the Latin texts that Chaucer undoubtedly read or his works directly draw on. The final passage focuses on Boccaccio, Petrarch, and *ClT*. In Japanese.

65. Simpson, James. "Geoffrey Chaucer's Reception of Alan of Lille." In Frank Bezner and Beate Kellner, eds. *Alanus ab Insulis und das europäische Mittelalter* (Paderborn: Brill, 2022), pp. 179–94. Assesses how Chaucer's references to Alain de Lille's works in *HF*, 985–89 and *PF*, 315–18 distinguish his own poetic project from the Neoplatonic ideals that Alain represents, preferring worldly tidings to the spiritual wisdom of the empyrean, and seeking "common profit," not in Ciceronian service to the state but in dedication to natural procreation. Clarifies Neoplatonic idealism (rooted in Plato's *Timaeus*) and Chaucer's skeptical attitude toward it as a late medieval Aristotelian work.

66. Strakhov, Elizaveta. *Continental England: Form, Translation, and Chaucer in the Hundred Years' War*. Interventions: New Studies in Medieval Culture. Columbus: The Ohio State University Press, 2022. xi, 256 pp. Studies uses in late medieval England of French lyric models (*formes fixes*) as "reparative" translation of francophone culture, and response to linguistic and political trends and tensions of the Hundred Years War. Includes discussion of Chaucer's decision to write in English (as reflected in *LGWP* and in Eustace Deschamps's ballade in praise of Chaucer as a "translateur"), John Shirley's and John Lydgate's views of Chaucer as a cultural translator, and the importance of *formes fixes* in understanding canon formation and Chaucer as a "laurel" poet. Also discusses *formes fixes* in Gower's Trentham manuscript and Hoccleve's Huntington holographs.

67. Wajimoto, Yoshihiro. "Anglo-Norman Literature." In Koichi Kano, ed. *An Invitation to Chaucer's Cosmos* (*SAC* 46 [2024], no. 149), pp. 233–58. Discusses Chaucer's indebtedness to Anglo-Norman literature for *FranT*, *Th*, and *MLT*. In Japanese.

See also nos. 43–44, 70, 96, 117, 125, 131, 180, 183, 190, 212, 216, 224–26, 231, 233, 235–36, 239–40, 243–44, 247–48, 256–58, 264,

268–69, 271, 275, 277, 279, 284, 288, 290, 292, 296, 302–3, 306, 307–8, 311–12, 320–21, 323, 329–31.

Chaucer's Influence and Later Allusion

68. Atkinson, Laurie. "A 'troubly dreme drempt al in wakynge': Hoccleve's Nearly-Dream Poem." In Jenni Nuttall and David Watt, ed. *Thomas Hoccleve: New Approaches* (*SAC* 46 [2024), no. 85), pp. 85–102. Shows how the "framed first-person narrative with which [Hoccleve's] *Regiment* begins is a reconfiguration rather than a straightforward rejection of Chaucer's dream poetry." While both authors use dream vision conventions to engage previous authors and texts, Hoccleve is concerned with "contemporary political and religious discourses," and his "distinctive self-authorising strategy . . . involves both an imitation and a pointed refusal of Chaucer's dream poems," especially their effacements of their narrators' poetic skills.

69. Barrington, Candace. "*feeld* Notes: Jos Charles's Chaucerian 'anteseedynts.'" In David Hadbawnik, ed. *Postmodern Poetics and Queer Medievalisms: Time Mechanics* (*SAC* 46 [2024], no. 144), pp. 61–80. Assesses Jos Charles's "transpoetics" in *feeld* (2018), showing how the collection of poems capitalizes on the "historical ruptures" and other constitutive features of Middle English, mimicking its "malleability and fluidity." Also suggests that Charles's technique is analogous to medieval musical "hocket" and explores how her dramatic monologue "reconceives" the Wife of Bath's, assessing several resonances.

70. Berensmeyer, Ingo. "The Epic Tree Catalogue from Chaucer to Spenser." In Eva von Contzen and James Simpson, eds. *Enlistment: Lists in Medieval and Early Modern Literature* (*SAC* 46 [2024], no. 128), pp. 155–71. Focuses on the "Chaucerian tree catalogue[s]" in Philip Sidney's *Old Arcadia* and Edmund Spenser's *Faerie Queene*, tracing the device as a "subtype of epic catalogue" in classical tradition and in *KnT* and *PF*, exploring its narrative, "metareferential," and "metapoetic" functions as an act of "self-insertion into the poetic tradition." Tabulates the trees, their epithets, and their significations shared by the three English poets.

71. Bertonèche, Caroline. Trans. Jonathan Fruoco. "'Tis More Ancient than Chaucer Himself': Keats and Romantic Polyphony." In Jonathan Fruoco, ed. *Polyphony and the Modern* (*SAC* 46 [2024], no. 137), pp. 206–16. Argues that the polyphonies of John Keats's poetry (as identified

by Helen Vendler) are attributable to his engagements with Chaucer's works and Chaucerian apocrypha, reflecting a particular kind of "Englishness" that is underpinned by travel and encounters with French and Italian literatures.

72. Brooks, Karen. *The Good Wife of Bath: A (Mostly) True Story*. New York: William Morrow, 2022 (originally published Sydney: Harlequin, 2021). xii, 541 + 5 pp. Historical novel in which the setting; plot; and first-person protagonist, Eleanor (later Alyson) are based on *WBPT*, with many characters adapted from history and from *CT*, including Chaucer. Includes a glossary, list of historical characters, author's note on composition, and a series of study questions for book groups.

73. Buffy, Emily. "Playing Chaucer at the Early Elizabethan Inns of Court." *Comparative Drama* 55 (2021): 138–65. Addresses performance texts associated with the early Elizabethan Inns of Court ("closet dramas, translations, masques, and orations"), arguing that they reflect four Chaucerian "paradigms of play" ("Chaucerian Self-Fashioning," "Chaucerian Arraignments," "Masques and Orations," and "Staging *The Canterbury Tales*"). Comments on Chaucer's putative legal associations and works by Barnabe Googe, Jasper Heywood, Thomas Pound, George Gascoigne, Gerard Legh, and more, identifying influences of *TC*, *KnT*, *ClT*, *HF*, and other Chaucerian poems.

74. Clark, Cassandra. *The Day of the Serpent: A Brother Chandler Medieval Mystery*. Edinburgh: Severn House, 2021. 264 pp. Historical murder mystery set in 1400, in the months after Henry IV's usurpation of Richard II's throne. "Master" Chaucer and Adam are involved with copying Lollard treatises; Matilda, Chaucer's house-maid, is involved with friar-cum-sleuth Brother Chandler.

75. Dutton, Richard. "*Palamon and Arcite*: Early Elizabethan Court Theatre." In Sophie Chiari and John Mucciolo, eds. *Performances at Court in the Age of Shakespeare* (New York: Cambridge University Press, 2019), pp. 17–34. Extracts information about Richard Edwards's now-lost play *Palamon and Arcite*, from three extant contemporary accounts of the visit of Queen Elizabeth I to Oxford, where she attended a performance of the play in 1566. The accounts—by Miles Windsor, Nicholas Robinson, and John Bereblock—evince plot and details (with one quotation recorded), staging and performance (including accidental deaths), and some awareness of relations with *KnT* as source.

76. Espie, Jeff. "*The Winter's Tale*: Decorum, Distinction, and Shakespeare's Chaucer." *Comparative Drama* 55 (2021): 283–306. Suggests that

Shakespeare's title, *The Winter's Tale*, "adapts a possessive form associated with Chaucerian narratives—the x's tale—" and identifies similarities between the play and *ManT*. Focuses on the works' attention to linguistic register—"linguistic distinctions between people of different types and stations"—and argues that Shakespeare asserts both "similarity to Chaucer" and "independence from him." Appends a coda on "lemman" and "ladies" in early printings of Chaucer.

77. Greene, Darragh. "'Thou shalt knowen of oure Privetee / Moore than a maister of dyvynytee': Devils and Damnation in Chaucer's *Canterbury Tales* and Marlowe's *Doctor Faustus*." *Comparative Drama* 55 (2021): 166–84. Argues "that Chaucer's treatment of devils, damnation, and hell in *The Canterbury Tales* resonates in *Doctor Faustus*," focusing on the yeoman-devil and "the force and binding implications of illocutionary acts" in *FrT*, as well as on "interesting parallels" between the Pardoner and Faustus as "vain characters" who are "master rhetoricians" and "contemptuous of conventional morality." Contrasts Chaucer's and Marlowe's views of penitence, comic and tragic respectively.

78. Hadbawnik, David. "Speak like a Child: Caroline Bergvall's Medievalist Trilogy." In David Hadbawnik, ed. *Postmodern Poetics and Queer Medievalisms: Time Mechanics* (*SAC* 46 [2024], no. 144), pp. 179–204. Describes the "inbetweenedness" of language in Caroline Bergvall's poetic/performative "trilogy"—*Meddle English* (2011), *Drift* (2014), and *Alisoun Sings* (2019)—including discussion of her uses of forms of "Chaucer's Middle English, as well as Old English and Old Norse." Assesses "The Host's Tale" (from *Meddle English*) as a "mash-up" of Chaucer that "sets a tone" for Bergvall's "Chaucerian experiment," comparing it with the treatment of the Host in Lydgate's *Siege of Thebes*.

79. Hanna, Natalie. "A Credible Debt: Dekker as Host to Chaucer's Franklin." *Comparative Drama* 55 (2021): 380–403. Shows that in his pamphlet *A Strange Horse-Race*, Thomas Dekker quotes *FranT* "to illustrate hospitality" and the force of "binding oaths"; in his play *The Shoemaker's Holiday*, he "drew on Chaucer's Franklin for material about credit and debt." Because Chaucer was reputed to be a debtor, and concerned with patience, obligation, and binding language, Dekker relied on Chaucer as "a model . . . not just as writer, but also as a debtor."

80. Hsy, Jonathan, and Candace Barrington. "Queer Time, Queer Forms: Noir Medievalism and Patience Agbabi's *Telling Tales*." In David Hadbawnik, ed. *Postmodern Poetics and Queer Medievalisms: Time Mechanics* (*SAC* 46 [2024], no. 144), pp. 159–77. Explores how the "circular and

recursive form" of Agbabi's poetic adaptations of *CT* in her *Telling Tales* (2015) "showcases" the "queer time of medievalism and the queer form of adaptation." Focuses on Agbabi's versions of *Mel* ("Unfinished Business"), *ClT* ("I Go Back to May 1967"), and *MLT* ("Joined-Up Writing").

81. Lankewish, Vincent A. "Danger Lurks in the Darkness: The Ruskin/Burne-Jones Medieval Poetry Salon for Girls." *Victorian Poetry* 60 (2022): 35–164; 10 b&w illus. Introduces the activities and concerns of a Victorian "salon" conducted by John Ruskin and Edward Burne-Jones in which young women could "engage in serious conversations about medieval poetry, about art, and about humanitarianism and virtue." Focuses on Ruskin and Burne-Jones's reception of *LGW*, with attention to Victorian depictions of Medea, Burne-Jones's tapestry of *LGW* and the Kelmscott Chaucer, and Ruskin's annotations in his copy of Chaucer's works.

82. Li, Chi-fang Sophia. "Chaucerian Topoi and Topography in Thomas Dekker's (and John Webster's) *Westward Ho* (1605) and *Northward Ho* (1607)." *Comparative Drama* 55 (2021): 355–79. Demonstrates that Chaucerian estates satire in *CT* influenced the development of dramatic "city comedy" at the turn of the seventeenth century. Shows that in his *Ho* plays Dekker adapts Chaucer's London topographies, characterizations, themes, and motifs of game and play to develop "neo-Chaucerian topoi and topography . . . in which everyone is a 'homo viator' and 'homo ludens.'" Links these concerns with John Norden's 1593 map of London.

83. Morgan-Guy, John. "Two Clerical Dramatists, and Their Forgotten Heroines of the Celtic Revival: 'Ravishing' Evelina and Scorned Gwendolen." *Journal of Religious History, Literature and Culture* 7 (2021): 3–22. Includes discussion of *WBT* as "inspiration" for Reginald Heber's fragmentary verse-drama *The Masque of Gwendolen* (1830).

84. Morrison, Susan Signe. "'[A]n Exterior Air of Pilgrimage': The Resilience of Pilgrimage Ecopoetics and Slow Travel from Chaucer's *The Canterbury Tales* to Jack Kerouac's *On the Road*." *Humanities* 9 (2020). 11 pp. Assesses the "ecocritical insights" of Jack Kerouac's *On the Road* via its intertexual relations with the "pilgrimage ecopoetics" of *CT*, exploring structural similarities in the works and their vernacularity, metatextual references, "linguistic and physical contingency, and slow walking, where slowness functions as a form of rebellion."

85. Nuttall, Jenni, and David Watt, eds. *Thomas Hoccleve: New Approaches*. Cambridge: Brewer, 2022. xiv, 254 pp. Collects eleven essays

about Hoccleve's literary works, with an introduction by the editors and a comprehensive index. Chaucer's influences on Hoccleve and his attitudes toward Chaucer recur throughout the volume (see the index). For four essays with sustained attention to Chaucer, see nos. 68, 90, 106, 200.

86. O'Connell, Brendan. "'Think of All the Differences!' Mixed Marriages in Transcultural Adaptations of Chaucer's 'Man of Law's Tale.'" *Adaptation* 15 (2022): 7–21. Explores how the 2003 BBC adaptation of *MLT* and Patience Agbabi's *Telling Tales* (2004) "respond to the xenophobic and imperialist ideology of the original," challenging the relationship that *MLT* "posits between familial and national loyalties," reconfiguring "racial, familial, and religious identity," and confronting audiences with the importance of remembering as well as interrogating the past. Links the narratives with representations of Thomas Jefferson's "role as father and forebear" and Chaucer's as "father" of English poetry.

87. Powrie, Sarah. "Keats Reading Chaucer: Troilus and Arrested Time in *The Eve of St. Agnes*." In Beth Lau and Greg Kucich, eds. *Keats's Reading/Reading Keats: Essays in Memory of Jack Stillinger* (Cham: Palgrave Macmillan, 2022), pp. 129–51. Reviews Keats's "regular contact" with Chaucer's works and assesses *TC* as a "largely overlooked intertext" for *The Eve of St. Agnes* that illuminates "the creative tensions of *St. Agnes* and Keats's habits in reading medieval texts." Focuses on "Keats's affective identification with Troilus" and "the ways that *St. Agnes* rewrites Chaucer's tragedy."

88. Ramirez, Janina. *Femina: A New History of the Middle Ages, through the Women Written out of It*. London: W. H. Allen, 2022; Toronto: Hanover Square, 2023. xv, 447; illus. Includes a brief summary of *KnT* and posits that the petitioning of Theseus by the Theban women may have inspired the "final act" of suffragette Emily Wilding Davison when she reached "towards the king's horse" at the Epsom Derby of 1913. Also notes that, as a child, Wilding Davison adopted the pen name "Emelye."

89. Reid, Lindsay Ann. "Reading at the Seams in *Titus Andronicus*: Shakespeare's 'House of Fame' and Its Virgilian-Ovidian-Chaucerian Resonances." *Comparative Drama* 55 (2021): 211–33. Focuses on depictions of Dido in *HF* and in Shakespeare's *Titus*, arguing that "Shakespeare found in Chaucer's *House of Fame* a medieval vernacular model for . . . [the] Virgilian-Ovidian hybridity" of the character, and showing that the two works share "thematic strands," including reputation, rumor, imperial authority, and the "weight of textual authority."

90. Ripplinger, Michelle. "Hoccleve's *Series* and the Unanticipated Woman Reader." In Jenni Nuttall and David Watt, eds. *Thomas Hoccleve:*

New Approaches (*SAC* 46 [2024), no. 85), pp. 85–102. Explores Hoccleve's uses of and attitudes toward Christine de Pizan and Chaucer, focusing on Ovidian notions of female readership and how in his *Series* Hoccleve positions Pizan to "speak back to Chaucer" and "asks us to reflect on the Chaucerian defence of poetic wit and fictive play, even as we remain alert to its potential risks and limits." Comments on the "apology to women" in *ClT*.

91. Rush, Rebecca. *The Fetters of Rhyme: Liberty and Poetic Form in Early Modern England*. Princeton: Princeton University Press, 2021. x, 284 pp. Considers briefly Chaucer's influence on the revival of poetic couplets in early modern English verse, especially as mediated by George Puttenham's *The Arte of English Poesie*.

92. Rutter, Tom. "Afterword [to Special Issue]." *Comparative Drama* 55 (2021): 404–13. Explores how resonance with *CT* in Shakespeare's *1 Henry IV*, 1.2, "communicates the pre-Reformation otherness of the world" and raise questions about "cultural distance and appropriation" that circulate among the essays collected in this special issue of *Comparative Drama*. Also comments on allusions to Chaucer in John Dryden's preface to his *Troilus and Cressida* and his "The Grounds of Criticism in Tragedy," as well as in Ben Jonson's *Entertainment at Bolsover*.

93. Schreyer, Kurt. "Stealing Shives: *Titus Andronicus* as Chaucerian Anti-Romance." *Comparative Drama* 55 (2021): 185–210. Identifies narrative, linguistic, and thematic similarities between Chaucer's *KnT*, *MilT*, and *RvT* and Shakespeare's *Titus Andronicus*, and argues that the brutal treatment of Lavinia in Shakespeare's play resonates with the aspects of courtly love depicted and refracted in Chaucer's three tales and in *TC*, thereby "blurring the lines" between "violent 'Roman'" and "courtly 'Romance.'"

94. Smith, Nathanial B. "The Framing of the Shrews: Dream Skepticism from *The House of Fame* to *The Taming of the Shrew*." *Comparative Drama* 55 (2021): 234–58. Shows that Shakespeare's *Taming of the Shrew* and the anonymous *Taming of a Shrew* feature skeptical parody of Stoic certainty about distinguishing reality from illusion or dream. As in *HF*, the "framing fictions" of the plays "make a show" of controlling uncertainty and reveal the skeptical "circularity" of any "dogmatic quest for authoritative certainty." Assesses how "[s]cenes problematizing authoritative instruction proliferate" throughout *HF* and the plays and, in the latter, destabilize antifeminist certainties.

95. Stenner, Rachel. "The Word of Apollo: Prophecy and Vatic Poetry in Geoffrey Chaucer's *Troilus and Criseyde* and William Shakespeare's *Troilus and Cressida*." *Comparative Drama* 55 (2021): 259–82. Argues that allusion to Apollo in *TC* conveys an ambivalent attitude toward literary authority by affiliating it with sexual violence, an ambivalence that Shakespeare echoes in *Troilus and Cressida*. Both writers use Apollo to problematize intertextuality and "allow the shadow of sexual violence to hover in the background of their texts as a means to question the foundations of poetic prophecy."

96. Stretter, Robert. "Chaucer, Shakespeare, and the Lost Friendship Plays of the Admiral's Men." *Comparative Drama* 55 (2021): 331–54. Identifies complex intertextual relations among *KnT*; the story of Amis and Amiloun; Shakespeare and Fletcher's *Two Noble Kinsmen*; and archival references to two lost Tudor plays, *Palamon and Arcite* and *Alexander and Lodowick*, exploring differences between motifs of medieval sworn brotherhood and humanist classical friendship. In this light, considers *The Two Noble Kinsmen* as a critique of male-friendship plays performed by the Admiral's Men.

97. Strohm, Paul. "Chaucer and the Streams of Parnassus." In Jonathan Fruoco, ed. *Polyphony and the Modern* (*SAC* 46 [2024], no. 137), pp. 192–205. Argues that Chaucer's "polyphony and polyvocality" are both "modern" and "progressive"—justification for dismantling the period boundary between medieval and early modern literatures. Surveys mixed, condescending praise by early modern critics of Chaucer as an ancient but indecorous writer, then demonstrates how Robert Greene's valuation of Chaucer in *Greene's Vision* (1592) offers a valid view of him as an up-to-date model of polyvocality. Comments on the Clerk's view of Petrarch (*ClP*, 26–30).

98. Takano, Hideo. "George Eliot's Reception of Chaucer's 'Knight's Tale': An Essay." In Society for Chaucer Studies and Koichi Kano, eds. *To the Days of Studying Medieval English Literature: Essays in Memory of Professor Ikegami Tadahiro* (*SAC* 46 [2024], no. 179), pp. 217–30. Argues that George Eliot inherits the way of communicating sorrows from *KnT*. In Japanese.

99. Terrell, Katherine H. *Scripting the Nation: Court Poetry and the Authority of History in Late Medieval Scotland*. Interventions: New Studies in Medieval Culture. Columbus: The Ohio State University Press, 2022. viii, 232 pp. Describes a "widespread nationalistic feeling" in late medieval and

early modern Scotland, with particular attention to Latin chroniclers, court poets in the reign of James IV, and their similar uses of Scottish myths of origin in resistance to English ones. Includes discussion of how the Selden manuscript "appropriates Chaucerian material to its own nationalistic vision"; how William Dunbar "claims Chaucer as a literary ancestor" while he asserts his own nationalistic voice; and how, for Gavin Douglas, Chaucer exemplifies past English glory that has degenerated in contrast to Scottish prestige.

100. Trow, M. J. *The Clerk's Tale*. [London]: Lume, 2022. 282 pp. A murder mystery, set in Oxford, in which Geoffrey Chaucer investigates homicide amidst town–gown tensions, rivalries in the colleges, debates, Lollards, and astrolabes. Features historical and fictional characters, including Ralph Strode and a shipman whose boat is named the *Madeleine*.

101. ______. *The Knight's Tale*. Edinburgh: Severn House, 2021. 219 pp. A murder mystery in which the investigator—Geoffrey Chaucer, "Comptroller of His Grace's Woollens and poet to the court of the late king"—seeks the murderer of Lionel, duke of Clarence.

102. ______. *The Yeoman's Tale*. Edinburgh: Severn House, 2022. 220 pp. A murder mystery in which Geoffrey Chaucer and his friend John Gower try to solve a double murder while barricaded in the Tabard Inn, defended against the rebellious peasants in 1381. Features historical and fictional characters, some of the latter based on *CT*.

103. Utz, Richard. "Writing, Men, Empire: Kipling's Medievalist Imagination." *SiM* 31 (2022): 159–75. Considers how Rudyard Kipling incorporates a Chaucer-centered medievalism in his writings, emphasizing the conservative, imperialist bent of this reception. As a point of departure, draws attention to Kipling's late short story "Dayspring Mishandled," which weaves a tale of manuscript forgery around allusion to rivalry for a woman, recalling *KnT*.

104. Voight, Valerie. "'I am not against your faith yet I continue mine': Virginal Vocation in *The Two Noble Kinsmen*." *Comparative Drama* 55 (2021): 307–30. Compares Emelye of *KnT* and Emilia of Shakespeare and Fletcher's *The Two Noble Kinsmen*, arguing that Emelye's desire for a non-patriarchal subjectivity is developed in her literary descendant—that "monastic connotations in Chaucer's depictions of Emelye" adumbrate Emilia's "attempts to carve out a homosocial space for herself," and that this "Catholic resonance within the play" is submerged but not wholly dispelled by prevailing Reformation sensibility that privileges marital chastity over virginity.

See also nos. 4, 26, 35, 43, 62, 66, 106, 119, 146, 172, 200, 233, 236, 241, 255, 258, 276, 296–97, 300, 316, 320, 331.

Style and Versification

105. Greene, Darragh. "'What is this world?': Chaucer, Realism and Metaphysics." In Garry L. Hagberg, ed. *Literature and Its Language: Philosophical Aspects* (Cham: Palgrave Macmillan, 2022), pp. 149–71. Explores the question of what Chaucer "holds to be the nature of reality," focusing on "the metaphysics of beauty" in *PF*, the "nature of the rocks" in *FranT*, and the "ontology of narrative itself" in *NPT*, and showing that "Chaucer's sensate faith in and appreciation of the reality of things underpins the characteristic attention to everyday detail evident in his poetry."

106. Myklebust, Nicholas. "Historicising Hoccleve's Metre." In Jenni Nuttall and David Watt, ed. *Thomas Hoccleve: New Approaches* (*SAC* 46 [2024), no. 85), pp. 25–46. Argues that "because Hoccleve's metre cannot persuasively be reconciled with any known metrical system, it must be allowed its own category." Details Chaucer's metrical "template" and shows how Hoccleve varies it to create his own, although influenced by that of John Walton in his verse translation of Boethius. Hoccleve and Walton's verse "prefigure[s] modern iambic pentameter" more clearly than does Chaucer's.

107. Putter, Ad. "Linguistic Change and Metre: The Demise of Adjectival Inflections and the Scansion of 'High' and 'Sly' in Chaucer, Gower and Hoccleve." *English Language Linguistics* 26 (2022): 471–85. Treats the scansion of "high" and "sly" in works by Chaucer, Gower, and Hoccleve—all "careful metrists"—as evidence of the demise of "inflection of monosyllabic adjectives (final *-e* for weak and plural adjectives)." Posits that irregularities in usage are due to the "vulnerability of schwa after front vowels," and offers several cautions for editors.

108. Simpson, James. "Reformation Lists: Syntax, the Sacred, and the Production of Junk." In Eva von Contzen and James Simpson, eds. *Enlistment: Lists in Medieval and Early Modern Literature* (*SAC* 46 [2024], no. 128), pp. 195–212. Assesses the syntax and rhetorical/literary functions of the "open-ended list that forms part of a sentence," focusing on those composed during the "cultural revolution" at the beginning of the Reformation in sixteenth-century England, but framed by discussion of syntactical contrasts between apposition in the list in the House of

Rumour in *HF*, 1951–76, and hypotaxis in the opening of Milton's *Paradise Lost*, I.1–10.

109. Solberg, Emma Maggie. "Imagining the Bob and Wheel." *PMLA* 137 (2022): 52–69. Focuses on the poetic form made famous by *Sir Gawain and the Green Knight* and *Th*, but also considers poetic form in the scorpion passage of *BD* and alliteration in *ParsT*. Discusses myths surrounding the "bob and wheel" form that are often perpetuated both by students engaging in cursory internet searches and incorrect online study guides.

See also nos. 30, 70, 91, 97, 113, 122, 129, 204, 290, 293, 296, 300, 306.

Language and Word Studies

110. Amsler, Mark. *The Medieval Life of Language: Grammar and Pragmatics from Bacon to Kempe*. Amsterdam: Amsterdam University Press, 2021. 264 pp. Studies "pragmatics as an important aspect of premodern understanding of language and meaning," exploring "pragmatic ideas and metapragmatic awareness" in various kinds of medieval discourse. Details the contexts, functions, and significations of the interjection "allas" in portions of *CT* and *TC*, and examines *MilPT* for ways it "deconstructs the notion of stable, authorial, intentional meaning and explores narrative dialogism and the pragmatics of identity and affective power for comic and satiric effect."

111. D'Anca, Christene. "'Hende': A Handy Middle English Adjective." *Early Middle English* 4 (2022): 87–95. Clarifies the "nuanced semantic versatility" of "hende" in romances and fabliaux, with particular attention to *MilT* and *Dame Sirith*, showing how various connotations obtain in differing contexts, and suggesting that editors "might apply distinct glosses to each of the eleven instances of the word applied to Nicholas" in *MilT*, "including a blend of positive, negative, physical, conceptual, and inverse meanings."

112. Fukumoto, Tomoko. "On Reflexive Verbs in Chaucer." *Zephyr* 33 (2021): 36–46. Investigates the relationships between reflexive pronouns and reflexive verbs in *BD* and *PF*. In Japanese.

113. Ikegami, Masa, Ryuichi Hotta, and Koichi Kano. "Chaucer's English." In Koichi Kano, ed. *An Invitation to Chaucer's Cosmos* (*SAC* 46 [2024], no. 149), pp. 93–124. A brief introduction to Chaucer's

vocabulary compared to present-day English, his grammar, his pronunciation and spellings, and his versification. In Japanese.

114. Nishihara, Takayuki, and Yoshiyuki Nakao. "Tense Shift in Chaucer's Narrative Text: With Special Regard to the Synchronization of Subjectivity and Phenomena." *Studies in Education (Bulletin of the Graduate School of Humanities and Social Sciences, Hiroshima University)* 3 (2022): 120–28. Draws parallels between Chaucer's tense shift and Japanese I-mode, where tense shift occurs from the past to the present. Identifies tense shifts across various units, from a single metrical line to an extended piece of discourse consisting of sentences, and views them as influenced by cognitive subjectivity, orality, and generic/gnomic implications. In Japanese, with English abstract.

115. Okamoto, Hiroki. "The Path of English Literatures as a Vernacular: Chaucer, Dialect, Marginality." *Ritsumeikan Studies in Language and Culture* 33 (2022): 65–83. Claims that by composing his poetry in English, Chaucer participated in the European movement of promoting the vernacular literatures. Argues that Chaucer's neutral depiction of dialectal features in the two clerks' speeches in *RvT* affirms the diversity in English and contributes to the cultural richness of the language. In Japanese.

116. Robertson, Michael. "New Solutions for Words in Thomas Speght's Chaucer Glossaries." *Dictionaries: Journal of the Dictionary Society of North America* 43 (2022): 55–93. Accounts for seventeen words found in the glossaries of Speght's 1598 and 1602 editions of Chaucer's works that are labeled "unidentified" in Jürgen Schäfer's *Early Modern English Lexicography* (1989), tracing them "to manuscript variants and corruptions or misprints in the text of Chaucer" and assessing attestations of these "ghost words" in later dictionaries and elsewhere.

See also nos. 3, 21, 30, 66, 69, 76, 107, 117, 139, 146–47, 192, 214, 216, 221, 230, 266–67, 276, 277, 282, 291–92, 323, 328, 332.

Background and General Criticism

117. Baker, David. "Numbered Possibilities: Chaucer and the Evolution of Late-Medieval Mathematics." In Robert Tubbs, Alice Jenkins, and Nina Engelhardt, eds. *The Palgrave Handbook of Literature and Mathematics* (Cham: Palgrave Macmillan, 2021), pp. 23–40. Exemplifies how Chaucer "has a great deal of fun with the coalescence of medieval arithmetic, geometry and logic into a single discipline more recognizable today as

mathematics," exploring the "proto-probabilistic" dicing and poison-bottle selection of *PardT*; the "ars-metrick" divisibility of the farthing/farting/parting pun and possible links with the pseudo-Alcuin *Propositiones ad acuendos iuvenas* in *SumT*; and a range of allusions to logic, mathematics, and physics in *TC*, including "dulcarnon," "sliding," and Ralph Strode.

118. Beal, Jane. "The Chaucerian Translator." In Albrecht Classen, ed. *Communication, Translation, and Community in the Middle Ages and Early Modern Period: New Cultural-Historical and Literary Perspectives* (Boston, Mass.: De Gruyter, 2022), pp. 233–52. Argues that the "Chaucerian narrator could easily and perhaps more readily be called the Chaucerian translator," observing emphasis on translation in *LGWP* and in *Ret*, assessing Chaucer's many uses of sources and approaches to translation, including satirizing mistranslation and lack of translation (e.g., in *NPT*), and exploring the penitential, even salvific effects of good translations in *MelP*, *ParsT*, and *Ret*.

119. Berensmeyer, Ingo. *A Short Media History of English Literature*. Boston, Mass.: De Gruyter, 2022. ix, 304 pp; 18 illus. Historical survey of the relations between literary texts in English and material presentation, from oral and dramatic performance through manuscripts and books, to audio, visual, and digital forms. Includes a section on key terms, a timeline, and an extensive index. A section on Chaucer emphasizes *CT*, and its variety and flexibility of voicing in manuscript, print, and later adaptation.

120. Bleier, Roman, Brian Coleman, and Clare Fletcher, eds. *Memory and Identity in the Medieval and Early Modern World*. Publications of the Centre for Medieval and Renaissance Studies, Trinity College Dublin, Vol. 8. New York: Peter Lang, 2022. [xix], 250 pp. Collects twelve essays from the 2016 conference on memory and identity, with a preface and a cumulative index. For four essays that pertain to Chaucer, see nos. 290, 323, 327, 332.

121. Bordalejo, Barbara. "Canterbury Tales Project Special Issue: Introduction." *Digital Medievalist* 14, special issue (2021). 8 pp. Recounts brief personal history of experience with the Canterbury Tales Project, describes scholarly inattention to the project, and introduces the five essays in this special issue; see nos. 22, 36–38, 42.

122. Bower, Hannah. *Middle English Recipes and Literary Play, 1375–1500*. Oxford English Monographs. Oxford: Oxford University Press, 2022. xii, 259 pp.; 8 illus. Explores relations between the practical purposes of medieval medical recipes and their imaginative and aesthetic

effects, focusing on how the texts of these recipes reflect their broader discursive culture, c. 1375–1500. Cites Chaucer's recurrent uses (often parodic) of the discourse of recipes (*CYT*) and of medical terms, metaphors, and similes—uses that help to clarify less well-known texts.

123. Buchanan, Peter. "Contingent Chaucer: Experience, Time, and Modality in Chaucerian Poetics." Ph.D. dissertation (University of Oxford, 2021), *DAI-C* 83.10(E) (2021). Argues that Chaucer is a "philosophical poet" who "innovated a radical, anti-teleological poetics of contingency," showing how in *CYT*, *ClT*, *TC*, and *HF* he "reworks his sources to articulate his vision of contingency, and contest humanist narratives of utopian perfectibility and idealistic, teleological poetics."

124. Bude, Tekla. "Disability, Music, and Chaucer's Advental Bodies." In *Sonic Bodies: Text, Music, and Silence in Late Medieval England* (Philadelphia: University of Pennsylvania Press, 2022), pp. 146–68. Argues that Chaucer "experiments with the body-disabling power of music as a site of poetic potential," tallying how, in *CT*, "musical performance nearly always causes narrative tension" and music "prosthetizes disability"—"advental" insofar as it is "promised but always in a state of deferral." Examines how "sonic bodies inhabit crip asynchronies for purposes of poesis" in the "body of Echo" in *FranT*, the "lyric *I*" in *For*, *BD* as a poem, and Troilus's body in *TC*.

125. Carlson, David R. *Gower and Anglo-Latin Verse*. Studies and Texts, no. 226. Toronto: Pontifical Institute of Mediaeval Studies, 2021. [xi], 345 pp. Chapter 3, "Gower and Estates Satire before Chaucer," includes brief mention of Chaucer in situating and analyzing Gower's uses of estates satire in his *Mirour de l'omme*, *Vox clamantis*, and *Confessio Amantis*.

126. Chace, Jessica Ann. "'For semyvif he semed': Affective Responses to the Half-Alive Human in Middle English Literature, ca. 1350–1450." Ph.D. dissertation (New York University, 2020), *DAI-A* 82.01(E). Uses the concept of "semyvif" (half-alive) to examine *Piers Plowman*, the *Tale of Beryn*, *TC*, *SNT*, and *Morte Darthur* for ways that they broaden "our historical understanding of disability and its conceptual range."

127. Chelis, Theodore. "Forms of Shame: Gower, Chaucer, Hoccleve." Ph.D. dissertation (Pennsylvania State University, 2022). Abstract accessible at https://etda.libraries.psu.edu/catalog/22564tbc126 (accessed November 15, 2023). Argues that "the vernacular literature of late medieval England contributes importantly to the theorizing of psychological subjectivity and that this theorizing is connected fundamentally with the

history of shame"; focuses on selected works by Chaucer, John Gower, and Thomas Hoccleve.

128. Contzen, Eva von, and James Simpson, eds. *Enlistment: Lists in Medieval and Early Modern Literature*. Interventions: New Studies in Medieval Culture. Columbus: The Ohio State University Press, 2022. vii, 226 pp. Collects ten essays by various authors that discuss lists and listing as epistemological, rhetorical, and poetic devices, with an introduction by the editors ("Enlistment as Poetic Stratagem"), and a comprehensive index. For four essays that pertain to Chaucer, see nos. 70, 108, 296, 300.

129. Copeland, Rita. *Emotion and the History of Rhetoric in the Middle Ages*. Oxford Studies in Medieval Literature and Culture. Oxford: Oxford University Press, 2021. xiv, 415 pp. Explores emotion as a device of rhetoric from Antiquity through the fifteenth century, and describes the influence of Aristotle's *Rhetoric* on political, ethical, and literary discourse from the thirteenth century forward. Assesses a wide range of texts, including discussions of rhetorical handbooks, style, and emotion in Chaucer generally, and of "enthymematic oratory" in *KnT*.

130. D'Arcens, Louise, and Sif Ríkharðsdóttir, eds. *Medieval Literary Voices: Embodiment, Materiality and Performance*. Manchester Medieval Literature and Culture. Manchester: Manchester University Press, 2022. xviii, 302 pp. Twelve essays by various authors on the concept of "voice" in medieval literature, with an introduction by the editors, an appreciative tribute to David Lawton by John M. Ganim, and a comprehensive index. Generally, the essays focus on the literature of late medieval England. For two essays that pertain to Chaucer, see nos. 204, 244.

131. Da Rold, Orietta. *Paper in Medieval England: From Pulp to Fiction*. Cambridge Studies in Medieval Literature, no. 112. Cambridge: Cambridge University Press, 2021. xx, 270 pp. Rethinks the uses and "affordances" of paper in medieval England and on the Continent, i.e., its potentialities, manifestations, and material significations in book production and other cultural practices. Opens with an explanation of how Chaucer associates paper with Dido in *LGW*, 1198–202, changing his source in Virgil, and evoking emotion and majesty. Chapter 5, "Paper in the Medieval Literary Imagination," focuses in part on the "interplay" of *TC* and its sources insofar as "their comments on the material properties of writing-supports is evidence of paper's wider cultural acceptance."

132. Da Rold, Orietta, and Elaine Treharne, eds. *The Cambridge Companion to Medieval British Manuscripts*. Cambridge: Cambridge University Press, 2020. xiii, 319 pp.; 23 b&w illus. Thirteen essays by various writers

on the Hows, Whys, and Wheres of studying medieval manuscripts, with an introduction by the editors, a guide to further reading, an index of manuscripts, and a comprehensive index. For two essays that pertain to Chaucer, see nos. 41, 282.

133. Downes, Stephanie. "Geoffrey Chaucer: Reading with Feeling." In Patrick Colm Hogan and Bradley J. Irish, eds. *The Routledge Companion to Literature and Emotion* (New York: Routledge, 2022), pp. 409–20. Surveys historical interest and recent theorization of emotion and affect produced by Chaucer's works, and assesses the role of books in the opening of *TC* (tears as ink) and in *WBP* (Jankyn's book) as "affective, emotional objects that arouse a range of feelings in their makers and readers."

134. Ellison, Katherine E., and Susan M. Kim, eds. *Collaborative Humanities Research and Pedagogy: The Networks of John Matthews Manly and Edith Rickert*. Cham: Palgrave Macmillan, 2022. xiv, 382 pp. Collects twelve essays that provide context and background to the work of Manly, Rickert, and their collaborators as cryptologists, writers, and scholars, including recurrent mention of their work in Chaucer studies. For an essay that pertains to Chaucer, see no. 51.

135. Evans, Ruth. "Digitizing *Studies in the Age of Chaucer*." *NCSPP* 3 (2022): 101–5. Describes the history of digitizing the journal *SAC*, commenting on the future of print journals and "the overall impact of digitization on scholarly societies."

136. ______. "On Not Being Chaucer." The Presidential Address. The New Chaucer Society, Expo2021, July 18–22, 2021. *SAC* 44 (2022): 3–26. Contemplates the value of studying Chaucer in light of national and international calls to decenter the poet and his works, considering the history and politics of these calls, the nature of canon-making, and several instances where "Chaucer's work has been reimagined in positive political ways." Advocates continued study of Chaucer because "his writings and the history of their reception continue to generate new and important ways" of understanding and counteracting racism, antifeminism, class bias, and binary reductionism.

137. Fruoco, Jonathan, ed. *Polyphony and the Modern*. New York: Routledge, 2021. vi, 266 pp. Raises questions about what it means to be modern in one own's time and about polyphony (including polyphonic music, polyvocality, and literary dialogism) as an index to modernity, collecting fourteen essays on relevant topics, most of them on medieval music and literature. For three essays that pertain to Chaucer, see nos. 71, 97, 328.

138. Fry, Chandler Thomas. "Reasoning Rebellion and Reformation: Natural Law and the Ethics of Power and Resistance in Late Medieval English Literature." Ph.D. dissertation (Duke University, 2021), *DAI-A* 82.11(E). Clarifies the "centrality and complexities" of political and ethical law discourse in late medieval England, showing how it is used in works by Thomas Usk and how in *TC* and *KnT* Chaucer "questions the view that the natural law is an unshakeable foundation for effective resistance."

139. Geaman, Kristen L. *Anne of Bohemia*. Lives of Royal Women. New York: Routledge, 2022. xiii, 302 pp.; 8 b&w illus. Investigates Anne of Bohemia as a figure of queenship—socially, politically, and economically—along the way questioning arguments for claims that she was Chaucer's patron (often grounded in *LGWP*), treating them as probabilities rather than facts. Also comments on late medieval notions of "womanhood" and "femininity" in Chaucer's works, suggesting that he "might well have written about" such concepts "with Anne in mind."

140. Geck, John A., Rosemary O'Neill, and Noelle Phillips, eds. *Beer and Brewing in Medieval Culture and Contemporary Medievalism*. The New Middle Ages. Cham: Palgrave Macmillan, 2022. xvii, 407 pp. Thirteen essays, an introduction by the editors, and an afterword by Ren Navarro "describe alcohol consumption in the Middle Ages across much of Northern Europe, engage with the various myths employed in modern craft beer advertising and beer production, and examine how gender intersects with beer production and consumption." For two essays that pertain to Chaucer, see nos. 253, 335.

141. Gillum, Anthony D. "Bridges to the Past: Orientation, Materiality, and Participatory Reading in Late Medieval England." Ph.D. dissertation (University of Michigan, 2021), *DAI-A* 83.04(E). Based on "Sara Ahmed's phenomenological theorization of 'orientation,'" offers case studies of how "the orientation(s) of medieval readers might have influenced their experience of a text," discussing the experience of reading *CT* in Wynkyn De Worde's 1498 edition and considering "orientation as it applies to Chaucer's embodied narrative personae" in works that include *HF*, *PF*, *Scog*, *Ven*, and *LGWP*.

142. Greiner, Grace Catherine. "The Poet's *Matere*: Materiality, Temporality, and the Making of Literary History in Chaucer and Lydgate's Inset-Lyric Poems." Ph.D. dissertation (Cornell University, 2021), *DAI-A* 83.03(E). Assesses Chaucer's and Lydgate's inset lyrics for the ways that they imply "a sense of poetry as an assemblage of physical materials collected from the past, and poets as the collectors and mediators of those

materials." Considers aspects of *BD*; Lydgate's *Temple of Glas* and *Siege of Thebes*; and Cambridge University Library, MS Gg.4.27.

143. Gulley, Alison. "J. K. Rowling, Chaucer's Pardoner, and the Ethics of Reading." *NCSPP* 3 (2022): 31–39. Discusses the Pardoner's "queerness and fitness to tell a moral tale" in light of ethical concerns about J. K. Rowling's "public comments about trans women," suggesting pedagogical uses.

144. Hadbawnik, David, ed. *Postmodern Poetics and Queer Medievalisms: Time Mechanics*. New Queer Medievalisms, no. 2. Boston, Mass.: De Gruyter, 2022. vii, 211 pp. Includes eight essays by various authors, an introduction by the editor, and a comprehensive index. For three essays that pertain to Chaucer, see nos. 69, 78, 80.

145. Hadfield, Andrew. *Literature and Class: From the Peasants' Revolt to the French Revolution*. Manchester: Manchester University Press, 2021. xiv, 331 pp. Analyzes the relationship between conceptions of social class and literary representations of them in Britain from the fourteenth to the nineteenth century. Chapter 2, "Perceptions of Class in the Late Middle Ages," addresses William Langland's *Piers Plowman*, John Gower's *Vox clamantis*, and *CT*, focusing on estates satire and social reality in *MilT* and *RvT* and arguing that "Chaucer attributes social disarray to no single class but to a collective whole."

146. Hsy, Jonathan. *Antiracist Medievalisms: From "Yellow Peril" to Black Lives Matter*. Leeds: Arc Humanities, 2021. xvi, 170 pp. Opens with an account of teaching *PrT* in comparison with Patience Agbabi's adaptation of it in *Telling Tales* (2015), helping to introduce the goal of the entire volume: promoting resistance to racist, xenophobic, and homophobic distortions and misuses of medieval culture and medievalisms. Chapter 6, "Pilgrimage: Chaucerian Poets of Color in Motion," examines the "relationship between race and transit in works by Chaucerian poets of color"—Agbabi, Jean "Binta" Breeze, Marilyn Nelson, Frank Mundo, and Ouyang Yu—in their adaptations of *CT*.

147. Jamison, Carol. "Teaching Chaucer to Linguistics Students." *SMART* 29 (2022): 111–22. Offers advice on how an undergraduate course focusing on Chaucer can serve the curricula of both literary and linguistics programs. Proposes several learning outcomes, and provides classroom strategies and emphases whereby linguistic and literary analysis work together.

148. Johnson, Valerie B., and Kara L. McShane, eds. *Negotiating Boundaries in Medieval Literature and Culture: Essays on Marginality, Difference, and*

Reading Practices in Honor of Thomas Hahn. Boston, Mass.: De Gruyter; Kalamazoo: Medieval Institute, 2022. vii, 365 pp.; illus. Includes fifteen essays on early English, Irish, Scottish, and Robin Hood studies, with an introduction by the editors, an appreciation of Thomas Hahn's career by Theresa Coletti, and a comprehensive index. For five essays that pertain to Chaucer, see nos. 52, 243, 252, 257, 277.

149. Kano, Koichi, ed. *An Invitation to Chaucer's Cosmos*. Tokyo: Yushokan, 2022. xvi, 548 pp. Presents an introduction to Chaucer and essays focusing on the European literary tradition on which his works draw, and the social conditions and art and culture of his time. Includes a chronology of Chaucer and list of recommended readings. In Japanese. For nine essays on Chaucer, see nos. 13, 50, 61, 63–64, 67, 113, 150, 195.

150. Kawasaki, Masatoshi, Hisashi Sugito, and Koichi Kano, eds. "A List of Works." In Koichi Kano, ed. *An Invitation to Chaucer's Cosmos* (*SAC* 46 [2024], no. 149), pp. 465–510. Provides recommended reading list in English and Japanese for studying Chaucer and late medieval literature and culture.

151. Kerby-Fulton, Kathryn. *The Clerical Proletariat and the Resurgence of Medieval English Poetry*. The Middle Ages. Philadelphia: University of Pennsylvania Press, 2021. xx, 388 pp.; 52 illus. Demonstrates the importance and central role of the "clerical proletariat"—i.e., clerics who worked "in liminal spaces between the ecclesiastical and lay worlds"—in the proliferation of late medieval books and literature in English, with primary focus on works of William Langland, Thomas Hoccleve, John Audelay, their various precedents and legacies, and related genres and forms. Attention to Chaucer's work is generally limited to his "alertness" to issues of clerical employment in *GP* and characters such as Nicholas in *MilT* and Jankyn in *WBP*.

152. King, Lauren Rebecca. "Reaching Readers: Textual Engagement and Personalized Learning in the Works of Christine de Pizan and Geoffrey Chaucer." Ph.D. dissertation (University of California, Los Angeles, 2021), *DAI-A* 83.06(E). Argues that Pizan and Chaucer "used their writing to open up educational opportunities" for their readers, seeking "to facilitate practices of engaged reading" for an expanding vernacular audience, with Chaucer modeling "problematic reading strategies" in *CT* and offering the "experience of wonder" in *HF*.

153. Knight, Stephen. *Medieval Literature and Social Politics: Studies of Cultures and Their Contexts*. New York: Routledge, 2021. viii, 319 pp. Anthologizes seventeen essays by Knight, "written over several decades

focused on the social and political contexts of medieval literature," three previously unpublished, one of which pertains to Chaucer: Chapter 14, "Chaucer's Fabliaux and Late Medieval Structures of Feeling." It shows ways in which "socio-political challenge" is a "key element" in Chaucer's uses of the fabliau genre, assessing the forms and structures of challenge in *MilT*, *RvT*, *CkT*, and the apocryphal *Tale of Gamelyn*, with briefer comments on fabliau elements and socio-political challenge elsewhere in *CT*.

154. Leary, Amanda Elise. "Relational Chaucer: Intersubjective Identity and Ricoeurian Narrative Hermeneutics." Ph.D. dissertation (Purdue University, 2021), *DAI-A* 85.01(E). Uses Paul Ricoeur's "theory of narrative identity" to explore various aspects of Chaucer's poetry, including issues of female agency in *FranT*, *ClT*, and *TC*; racialized narratives and white identity in *CT*; Chaucer's "talking-animal poetry"; and "poetic subjectivity" in his dream poems and in the Host's question to Chaucer as narrator, "What man artow?", in *ThP*.

155. Lochrie, Karma, and Usha Vishnuvajjala, eds. *Women's Friendship in Medieval Literature*. Interventions: New Studies in Medieval Culture. Columbus: The Ohio State University Press, 2022. viii, 299 pp. Collects twelve essays that celebrate friendship among women in medieval literature, with an introduction by the editors, an afterword by Penelope Anderson, and a cumulative index. For two essays that pertain to Chaucer, see nos. 197, 321.

156. Mahaffy, Mary Caitlin. "Beastly Bodies and Behaviors: Defining the (Un)Natural in the Long Early Modern Period." Ph.D. dissertation (Indiana University, 2022), *DAI-A* 83.12(E). vii, 193 pp. "[E]xplores how understandings of nonhuman animals and the environment shaped which human behaviors were labeled natural prior to the Enlightenment." Includes comments on animals, animal imagery, and environmental idealism in *Form Age*, *MilT*, and *PF*.

157. Matthews, David. "Reflections on Editing *Studies in the Age of Chaucer* 2007–13." *NCSPP* 3 (2022): 55–61. Comments on editing *SAC* and offers personal and historical perspective on the journal's development.

158. McNabb, Cameron Hunt, ed. *Medieval Disability Sourcebook: Western Europe*. Brooklyn: Punctum, 2020. 495 pp.; illus. Anthologizes a wide array of medieval texts that pertain to disability studies, each with an introduction and apparatus by individual contributors. Entries include Historical and Medical Documents, Religious Texts, Poetry, Prose, Drama, and Visual Images. The Poetry section includes Middle English editions,

with notes and glosses, of *MerT* (Moira Fitzgibbons), *MLT* (Paul A. Broyles), and the *GP* description of the Wife of Bath, with *WBPT* (Tory V. Pearman). The volume includes a general introduction by the editor and a thematic table of contents.

159. Moss, Rachel E. "#NotAllMen: In Conversation with Lucia Akard and Samantha Katz Seal." *SAC* 44 (2022): 293–95. Personal response to two essays concerning medieval female consent in light of a rape in London in 2021. See no. 18.

160. Murchison, Krista A. "Is the Audience Dead Too? Textually Constructed Audiences and Differentiated Learning in Medieval England." *MLR* 115 (2020): 497–517. Explores how writers and audiences in medieval England "approached textually constructed audiences," considering evidence from rhetorical theory, readers' comments, and "signs of adaptation undertaken by authors, correctors, and scribes." Concentrates on confessional manuals and religious instruction, but includes comments on *CT* and the ways it depicts "narrators grappling" with diverse audiences, particularly in *MilP* and *CYT*.

161. Paravicini, Werner. "Geoffrey Chaucer." In *Adlig leben im 14. Jahrhundert: Weshalb sie fuhren. Die Preußenreisen des europäischen Adels*, Part 3 (Göttingen: Vandenhoeck & Ruprecht, 2020), pp. 138–44. Part of Paravicini's three-volume study of the crusades against Lithuania undertaken by the Teutonic order, focusing on literary backgrounds to the chivalric imagination underlying the crusades. Includes evidence of tensions between crusading and courtly ideals, quoting the *GP* description of the Knight and passages from *KnT*, *FranT*, *MkT*, *Th*, and *BD*, each with German translation.

162. Perkins, Nicholas. *The Gift of Narrative in Medieval England*. Manchester Medieval Literature and Culture, no. 39. Manchester: Manchester University Press, 2021. xii, 270 pp. Engages several literary and anthropological theories of gifts, and addresses related motifs of reciprocity, generosity, promising, and exchange in medieval English texts, especially romances. Individual chapters assess *King Horn/Horn Childe* narratives, the Auchinleck manuscript and *Sir Gawain and the Green Knight*, *KnT* and *TC* (gifts, gender, pledging, and praying), *FranT* and *ManT* (promises, speech acts, bodies, and the unpredictability of exchange), and Lydgate's *Troy Book* as a narrative of gifts and as a gift book in Manchester, John Rylands Library, MS English 1.

163. Petracca, Eugene Anthony. "Toward a Supreme Fiction: Dante, Chaucer and the Dream of the Rose." Ph.D. dissertation (Columbia

University, 2020), *DAI-A* 81.11(E). Addresses the "rise of first-person fiction in the later Middle Ages," including discussion of *CT*, *BD*, and Chaucer's "other dream poems."

164. Quinlan, Heather E. *Plagues, Pandemics and Viruses: From the Plague of Athens to COVID-19*. Canton, Mich.: Visible Ink, 2020. xvii, 397 pp.; illus. Introduces medical, historical, sociological, and literary aspects of various infectious human diseases, including addiction, illustrated with sidebar facts, literary examples, and photographs and reproductions. A chapter on "The Black Death" includes a brief life of Chaucer—with a photograph of his statue (and bas-relief of pilgrims on its plinth) in Canterbury, by Sam Holland and Lynne O'Dowd, erected in 2016—and commentary on *CT*, especially the Pardoner and his Tale.

165. Quinn, William A. "Chaucer, Arguing 'in good feyth.'" *ES* 102 (2021): 395–414. Explores Chaucer's attitude toward the Boethian notion that "right reasoning alone should guarantee rhetorical success." Mirrored in Chaucer criticism and inflected by issues of gender and point of view, "objectivity," effective persuasion, and literary intention are, for Chaucer, largely matters of an audience's predispositions. Assesses these concerns in *Bo*, *WBP*, *ManT*, *TC*, *SNT*, *Mel*, and *PF*, and comments on poststructuralist and feminist approaches to Chaucer studies.

166. Radulescu, Raluca, and Sif Ríkharðsdóttir, eds. *The Routledge Companion to Medieval English Literature*. New York: Routledge, 2022. xx, 479 pp.; 12 illus. Thirty-seven essays by various authors on the forms, borders, networks, writers, and texts of medieval English, along with modern critical approaches, with an introduction by the editors (on "Trans-European and Global Contexts"), a timeline, and comprehensive index. For two essays that pertain to Chaucer, see nos. 183, 331.

167. Raybin, David, and Susanna Fein. "Thoughts on Directing NEH *Canterbury Tales* Seminars for Secondary School Teachers, 2008–2014." *NCSPP* 3 (2022): 86–94. Describes and assesses NEH K-12 Seminars for high school teachers pertaining to *CT* and held in London, 2008–14; reflects on 2014 legislation that discontinued funding for such programs held outside the USA; and encourages future collaboration between university and secondary school educators.

168. Reid, Lindsay Ann, and Rachel Stenner. "Introduction: Chaucerian Resonances in Early Modern Drama, Shakespeare and Beyond." *Comparative Drama* 55 (2021): 127–37. Assesses and combines various attempts to define Chaucerian "resonance" as a term of intertextuality and the reception of Chaucer; also summarizes each of the twelve essays

included in this special number of *Comparative Drama*. See nos. 73, 76–77, 79, 82, 89, 92–96, 104.

169. Richmond, Andrew M. *Landscape in Middle English Romance: The Medieval Imagination and the Modern World*. Cambridge Studies in Medieval Literature, no. 116. New York: Cambridge University Press, 2021. ix, 287 pp. Studies "ways in which medieval British romances conceived of ecological contexts" and identifies a "range of economic, religious, and social values attached to landscape"—hills and mines; seashores and beaches; and foreign, domestic, and fantastic territories—in a wide variety of popular romances and in *Sir Gawain and the Green Knight*. Includes ecocritical comments on the "seashore as a space for play and false narrative" in *FranT* and a space of economic possibility and exploitation in *MLT*.

170. Roger, Euan, and Andrew Prescott. "The Archival Iceberg: New Sources for Literary Life-Records." *ChauR* 57 (2022): 498–526. Highlights the amount of potential material in The National Archives as compared to more traditional repositories for high-value manuscripts. Considers approaches to find and use this material with new examples for Chaucer, Gower, and Skelton.

171. Rogers, Will. *Writing Old Age and Impairments in Late Medieval England*. Borderlines. Leeds: Arc Humanities, 2021. vii, 149 pp. Opens with commentary on oldness in *KnT*, *MilT*, and *RvT*, and proceeds to assess old age as a source "of debility and impairment as well as authority and veneration" in *Scog*, *Adam*, the Reeve's description in *GP*, *RvPT*, and *WBT*. Disability studies and narrative as prosthesis recur as concerns in analyzing these works along with *Parlement of the Thre Ages*; *Wynnere and Wastoure*; Hoccleve's *Regiment of Princes* and *La male regle*, and Caxton's printings of them; and the role of Gower in Shakespeare's *Pericles*.

172. Ruszkiewicz, Dominika. *Love and Virtue in Middle English and Middle Scots Poetry*. Studies in English Medieval Language and Literature. New York: Peter Lang, 2021. 234 pp. Considers relations between moral virtue and courtly love in a variety of Chaucer's works and Scottish Chaucerian works, analyzing a series of paired works—*Rom* and William Dunbar's *Golden Targe*, Chaucer's Boethian poems and *The Kingis Quair*, *HF* and Gavin Douglas's *The Palis of Honoure*, *PF* and Dunbar's *The Thrissill and the Rois*, and *TC* and Robert Henryson's *Testament of Cresseid*—that comprises a study of love and virtue in Chaucer's works and his influence on early Scottish literature.

173. Sáez-Hidalgo, Ana, and R. F. Yeager. "*Avant la lettre*: Philip Perry, Reconversionist Aesthetics, and the Medieval Literary." *JEGP* 121 (2022):

480–512. Posits that Philip Perry, an eighteenth-century priest and early practitioner of medievalism, was a pioneer in using original sources, among them Chaucer. Perry's unpublished notebooks contain detailed information on many medieval writers and their work, including Gower, Lydgate, Julian of Norwich, Margery Kempe, and others. Focuses on the fact that Perry believed Chaucer, like Langland, was a satirist of Church practices, not a heretical writer.

174. Salisbury, Eve. *Narrating Medicine in Middle English Poetry: Poets, Practitioners, and the Plague*. London: Bloomsbury Academic, 2022. xii, 224 pp.; illus. Addresses issues of disease, medical practice, faith, household remedy, and gender in fourteenth- and fifteenth-century Middle English "medical discourse," often found embedded in or juxtaposed to broader works, including narrative poetry that engages to greater or lesser degrees the Black Death. Chapter 1, "Honoring Stories of Illness in Chaucer," focuses on the poet's generally oblique references to plague in *CT* and on instances where "dialogue and storytelling" initiate or engage with the topic of physical or spiritual healing, considering especially the *GP* Physician, *PhyT*, *Mel*, *PardPT*, *KnT*, and *NPT*; also assesses other works.

175. Saunders, Corinne. "From Romance to Vision: The Life of Breath in Medieval Literary Texts." In David Fuller, Corinne Saunders, and Jane Macnaughton, eds. *The Life of Breath in Literature, Culture and Medicine: Classical to Contemporary* (Cham: Palgrave Macmillan, 2021), pp. 87–109. Describes various depictions of breath, breathlessness, and "vital spirits" that signal deep emotion in medieval literature, including comments on *BD*, *TC*, and *KnT*, among other courtly and religious works.

176. ______. "Thinking Fantasies: Visions and Voices in Medieval English Secular Writing." In Hilary Powell and Corinne Saunders, eds. *Visions and Voice-Hearing in Medieval and Early Modern Contexts* (Cham: Palgrave Macmillan, 2021), pp. 91–116. Exemplifies ways in which medieval "romance writing takes up the notion that physiological processes and exterior influences can interweave to produce powerful psychological experiences," showing how the "creative possibilities of interweaving the supernatural with psychology" are found in Chaucer's works: *BD*, *HF*, *PF*, *KnT*, *NPT*, and *TC*, with comments on *PhyT*, *MLT*, and *SNT*. Focuses on dreams, but not exclusively.

177. Smigen-Rothkopf, David. "Twisting Lines: Genealogy and Legitimacy in Fifteenth-Century English Literature." Open access Ph.D. dissertation (Fordham University, 2022). Available at https://research.library.fordham.edu/dissertations/AAI29327969/ (accessed November 19,

2023). Argues that "evolving discourses of gentility . . . served as models" for Chaucer, Sir Thomas Malory, and Henry Medwall, inspiring them "to write, variably, about socio-linguistic reform . . . and meta-literary reflection on the impact of newly enfranchised voices." Explores the "relationship between social and linguistic mutability" in *Sted*, *Gent*, and *WBT*.

178. Smith, Ryan. "Shaping Absurdity in Medieval Romance: *Reductio ad absurdum* as Narrative Structure." Ph.D. dissertation (State University of New York at Buffalo, 2021), *DAI-A* 82.12(E). Explores *reductio ad absurdum* in "theology and romance texts of the twelfth to fourteenth centuries," including discussion of Chaucer's uses of it as "a marker of generic resistance to chivalric romance" in *KnT* and *ClT*.

179. Society for Chaucer Studies and Koichi Kano, eds. *To the Days of Studying Medieval English Literature: Essays in Memory of Professor Ikegami Tadahiro*. Tokyo: Eihosha, 2021. ii, 235 pp.; 1 illus. Includes six essays that discuss Chaucer's texts or related topics. Specific references to *GP*, *KnT*, *LGW*, *PardT*, *TC*, and *WBT*. See nos. 46, 98, 228, 254, 310, 325. In Japanese; some chapters in English.

180. Steiner, Emily. *John Trevisa's Information Age: Knowledge and the Pursuit of Literature, c. 1400*. Oxford Studies in Medieval Literature and Culture. New York: Oxford University Press, 2021. xii, 287 pp.; 25 b&w illus. Considers John Trevisa's translations of "compendious" encyclopedic texts as examples of a prose literary form that is an influential part of a late medieval literary history, an "alternative" to the better-known tradition of Trevisa's poetic contemporaries—Chaucer, Gower, and Langland. Addresses Trevisa's works as a distinct kind of text and a way of processing, organizing, and presenting information, exploring antecedents and descendants, and at points exemplifying differences and similarities to works by Chaucer and others. The index includes nine citations of Chaucer, but he is also mentioned elsewhere in the book.

181. Taggart, Caroline. *The Book Lover's Bucket List: A Tour of Great British Literature*. London: British Library, 2021. 224 pp.; color illus. Illustrated tourist information pertaining to British writers and their works, arranged by geographical area, including introductions to sites associated with Chaucer: his tomb in Poets' Corner, his window in Southwark Cathedral, the Tabard Inn, and Canterbury Cathedral.

182. Thomas, Alfred. *Writing Plague: Language and Violence from the Black Death to COVID-19*. The New Middle Ages. Cham: Palgrave Macmillan, 2022. xxiv, 265 pp. Explores the "psychological continuities between the Black Death and COVID-19" in a series of four essays,

arranged chronologically, with an introduction, conclusion, and comprehensive index. Chapter 2, titled "The Pardoner, the Prioress, and the Pandemic: Jews and Other Scapegoats in Fourteenth-Century European Culture," identifies "anti-Semitism as a generic feature of plague writing in the late fourteenth century," including but not limited to *PardT* and *PrT*, with consistent associations between Jews and heretics, pollution, and filth. Connects Chaucer's works with a range of visual and verbal texts; includes 17 color illustrations.

183. Turner, Marion. "Geoffrey Chaucer." In Raluca Radulescu and Sif Ríkharðsdóttir, eds. *The Routledge Companion to Medieval English Literature* (*SAC* 46 [2024], no. 166), pp. 278–88. Shows how Chaucer's life and literature were "embedded in European contexts," even as he "ostentatiously displays the Englishness of his poetry." Comments generally on continental and English aspects of Chaucer's style and content, and examines how they combine in the details, form, and matter of *WBPT*, characterizing the Wife herself as, in many ways, "a product of northwestern Europe specifically, rather than Europe as a whole."

184. Turner, Marion, Eleanor Baker, Rodger Caseby, Clare Cory, Jim Harris, Nicholas Perkins, and Charlotte Richer. "'Chaucer's World' Study Days in Oxford for Post-16 Students: Enhancing Learning and Encouraging Wonder." *NCSPP* 3 (2022): 70–78. Collaborative reflection of the presentation and value of a study-days enhancement program called "Chaucer's World," designed to help UK secondary education students prepare for the A-level English Literature exam and to increase appreciation of Chaucer.

185. Vos, Stacie N. "Englishing the Virgin: Enclosure, Dissemination, and the Early English Book." Open access Ph.D. dissertation (University of California San Diego, 2021). Available at https://escholarship.org/uc/item/1198r95j (accessed May 23, 2024). Studies how "the Virgin Mary and her followers, especially women living the enclosed life . . . occupied a central role in the development of the early English book," discussing works ranging from *LGW*, *WBPT*, and *Mel* to Richard Tottel's *Songes and Sonnettes* (1557). Argues that "In his tales related to 'good women,' Chaucer develops an authorial persona consistent with Marian devotional practices."

186. Ward, Matthew. "True Blue: The Connection between Colour and Loyalty in the Later Middle Ages." *Journal of Medieval History* 46 (2020): 133–55. Outlines "the significance of blue in the medieval period," and "examines this connection between colour and virtue in literature, heraldic

treatises and works of art," including brief comments on blue and female fidelity in *SqT* and *Wom Unc*.

See also nos. 3, 32, 65, 241, 262, 293, 315.

CT – General

187. *The Canterbury Tales: Geoffrey Chaucer*. Richmond: Alma, 2019. 600 pp. An edition of the complete *CT*, with selective foot-of-page glosses, and "Extra Material" that includes a life of Chaucer, and plot summaries of *BD*; *HF*; *PF*; *TC*; and, more extensively, each of the *CT*. No editor is identified, but a note says that the text is "based on" the Ellesmere manuscript, then claims confusingly that "[m]isprints have been corrected." Punctuation has been "modernized, but the spelling and inconsistencies of the original have been preserved."

188. Di Profio, Luana. "In viaggio, '*Drive My Soul*': Narrazioni condivise e restituzioni di senso." *Encyclopaideia: Journal of Phenomenology and Education* 26 (2022): 1–13. Explores "the special connection that exists between travel and narration," especially when traveling in a group, assessing international narratives of travel from *CT* to Haruki Murakami's "Drive My Car." Includes an abstract in English and in Italian.

189. Federico, Sylvia. "On the Road and in the Market: Chaucer's Mapping of 1381." In Gwilym Dodd, Helen Lacey, and Anthony Musson, eds. *People, Power and Identity in the Late Middle Ages: Essays in Memory of W. Mark Ormrod* (London: Routledge, 2021), pp. 56–72. Offers documentary evidence that roads, markets, and taverns were "conduits for and symbols of" class motility and rebellious tidings in post-Uprising medieval England, especially in Kent and on the Canterbury road. Against this background, Chaucer's tales "are expressions of individual agency . . . that cumulatively constitute a discourse of insurgency" and engage the "ideological space" of the Uprising of 1381.

190. Hanning, Robert W. *Boccaccio, Chaucer, and Stories for an Uncertain World: Agency in the "Decameron" and the "Canterbury Tales."* Oxford Studies in Medieval Literature and Culture. Oxford: Oxford University Press, 2021. xi, 359 pp. Close comparative analysis of *CT* and Boccaccio's *Decameron*, arguing that they present "pragmatic prudence" or "expediential calculation" as essential forms of human agency in negotiating limited knowledge, faulty perception, and cultural turmoil. Assesses storytelling as a "constitutive" cultural force in *Decameron* and as "competitive" social

exchange in *CT*, concentrating on how characters in both collections "*deal with a chronically uncertain world, and with the formidable forces that create or perpetuate its uncertainty . . . to gain, maintain, or reclaim personal agency*" (original emphasis). Particular attention to *KnT*, *MilPT*, *RvPT*, *MLPT*, *WBPT*, *ClPT*, *MerPT*, *ShT*, *Mel*, and *ManT*.

191. Henley, Georgia. "Chaucer's Vision of the British Past: Literary Inheritance and Historical Memory in *The Canterbury Tales*." *Neophil* 106 (2022): 331–47. Argues that Chaucer favors the popular idea that Brittonic literature and history are primarily oral. By doing so, Chaucer distances his contemporary England, with its reliance on Latin textual and cultural authority, from the political reality of Welsh colonization and resistance, thus imposing a distance between English national history and the past of the Britons.

192. Hindrichsen, Lorenz A. "Chaucer's *Canterbury Tales* as a Postpandemic Text." In Sathyaraj Venkatesan, Antara Chatterjee, A. David Lewis, and Brian Callender, eds. *Pandemic and Epidemics in Cultural Representation* (Singapore: Springer, 2022), pp. 31–48. Interprets *CT* as a "compelling psychogram of a diverse community processing massive demographic shifts in the wake of recurrent epidemic waves." Explores disruptions of social and linguistic categories, *PardT* as an allegory of plague death, various "satirical plague archetypes" among the pilgrims, and tensions between "egocentric coping mechanisms" and "visions of collaborative inclusivity."

193. Hooke, Della. "Sound in the Landscape, a Study of the Historical Literature. Part 2: The Medieval Period—the Eleventh to Fifteenth Century (and Beyond)." *Landscape History* 41 (2020): 29–49. Surveys literary representations of sounds in various landscapes found in late medieval literature, including mention of the tournament in *KnT* and description of the tale-telling, singing, and music-making among the Canterbury pilgrims.

194. Hostetter, Aaron K. "Medieval Feasts." In J. Michelle Coghlin, ed. *The Cambridge Companion to Literature and Food* (Cambridge: Cambridge University Press, 2020), pp. 15–28. Describes the social implications of food and dining practices in late medieval cookbooks, social records, and aesthetic literature, commenting on the culinary concerns associated with the Franklin, Prioress, Squire, and Cook in *GP* and similar material in *CkP*, *PardT*, and *Ros*, along with other works in Middle English.

195. Ikegami, Tadahiro, and Hisashi Sugito. "Chaucer and the Medieval European Literary Tradition: Towards the Establishment of Chaucer's

Literature." In Koichi Kano, ed. *An Invitation to Chaucer's Cosmos* (*SAC* 46 [2024], no. 149), pp. 127–53. Describes general influence of European literature on Chaucer's works. In Japanese.

196. Johnson, Matthew. "Bodiam Castle and *The Canterbury Tales*: Some Intersections." *Medieval Archeology* 64 (2020): 302–29. Argues that *CT* (specifically *GP*, *KnT*, *MilT*, and *RvT*) and Bodiam Castle "converge as ideological constructions," comparing the lives of Chaucer and Sir Edward Dallingridge (builder of Bodiam)—both witnessed at the Scrope vs. Grosvenor trial—and connecting "the anxieties, tensions, gaps, silences and contradictions that lie below the surface of the formal, normative values" of their works. Posits that Dallingridge may underlie aspects of the characterization of Chaucer's Knight.

197. Lochrie, Karma. "'All These Relationships between Women': Chaucer and the Bechdel Test for Female Friendship." In Karma Lochrie and Usha Vishnuvajjala, eds. *Women's Friendship in Medieval Literature* (*SAC* 46 [2024], no. 155), pp. 177–96. Identifies three ways to illuminate female friendship in *CT*, disclosing "identity of feeling" among women (Custance, the Sultaness, and Hermengild in *MLT*), "enclaves . . . afforded by misogynistic discourses" (the Wife, her gossip, and female community in *WBPT*), and "surprises and resistances . . . possible in the mise-en-scène of female empathy" (Canacee and the falcon in *SqT*). Considers criteria of female friendship posed by Virginia Woolf and film critic Alison Bechdel.

198. Mahdipour, Alireza, Hossein Pirnajmuddin, and Pyeaam Abbasi. "Liturgical Time in Chaucer's *Canterbury Tales*: Meditated, Measured and Manipulated." *Critical Survey* 34 (2022): 45–55. Tabulates liturgical references within *CT* and argues that the poem depicts the secularization of liturgy and its appropriation for social control, while also presenting a carnivalesque celebration of the reversal of social hierarchy.

199. Morris, Aubrey. "'Lat Us Laughe and Pleye': Humor Structures in *The Canterbury Tales*." Ph.D. dissertation (Baylor University, 2022), *DAI-A* 83.11(E). "[A]pproaches the Canterbury Tales through the lens of humor theory, responding to a much-noted gap in existing scholarship by focusing primarily on the structures and mechanisms of humor in the text."

200. Perry, R. D. "Hoccleve and the Logic of Incompleteness." In Jenni Nuttall and David Watt, eds. *Thomas Hoccleve: New Approaches* (*SAC* 46 [2024), no. 85), pp. 65–84. Assesses the "formal organising principle" of

Hoccleve's *Series* in light of that of *CT* (and *LGW*). Argues that *CT* is "not just incomplete, but *incompleteable*" (citing the openendedness entailed in *CYPT*), explaining it as Chaucer's response to the conditions of the material production of his work and the inevitability of his own death. Hoccleve's *Series* is also "variable and open-ended" but its incompleteness is constrained by "the way the text presents authorship."

201. Rabat, Justine. "Cadre et encadrement. Pour une approche politique du récit enchâssé: Des recueils de contes médiévaux au cinéma contemporain (le *Pañcatantra*, Somadeva, Boccaccio, Chaucer, Pasolini, Gomes)." Open access Ph.D. dissertation (Université Sorbonne Nouvelle, 2020). Available at https://theses.hal.science/tel-04416408 (accessed May 11, 2024). Theorizes "the consequences of political discourse on bodies" in literary and cinematic frame-narratives, including discussion of *CT*, along with the *Pañcatantra*, the *Vetāla* of Somadeva, Boccaccio's *Decameron*, Pier Paolo Pasolini's *Trilogy of Life*, and Miguel Gomes's *Arabian Nights*. Includes an abstract in English and in French.

202. Rohls, Jan. *Kunst und Religion zwischen Mittelalter und Barock: Von Dante bis Bach*. Vol. 1, *Spätmittelalter und Renaissance*. Boston, Mass.: De Gruyter, 2021. xi, 619 pp. Chapter 7, "Chaucer: Die 'Canterbury Tales,'" summarizes the individual tales of *CT*, following the Chaucer Society order, and provides brief explanations of religious backgrounds and details.

203. Sharma, Manish. *The Logic of Love in "The Canterbury Tales."* Toronto: University of Toronto Press, 2022. ix, 395 pp. Presents a "new way to conjoin Chaucer's sophisticated engagement with philosophical thought and his obvious focus on amatory concerns" in *CT*, arguing that the narrative "authoritatively abandons authority"—a paradox that recalls logical *insolubilia*, connects with the "philosophical antinomy of realism and nominalism," and engages the Christian incarnational fusion of creator and created. Neither ironic nor inconsistent, the rigorously logical *CT*—insoluble rather than enigmatic or analogical—asserts the paradox of love, depicts efforts to accept or resolve paradox in each of the tales, and enjoins readers to accept paradox without judgment or resolution, leaving Chaucer's "ultimate intention undecidable."

See also nos. 21, 23, 27, 29, 34–35, 39, 44, 46, 49, 53–54, 60, 78, 82, 84, 110, 119, 124, 145–46, 152–54, 160, 163, 174, 221, 231, 250.

CT—The General Prologue

204. Fulton, Helen. "Voice of Authority: Free Indirect Discourse in Chaucer's General Prologue." In Louise D'Arcens and Sif Ríkharðsdóttir, eds. *Medieval Literary Voices: Embodiment, Materiality and Performance* (*SAC* 46 [2024], no. 130), pp. 37–55. Investigates free indirect discourse in *GP*, focusing on Chaucer's personae, the variety of his narrative positions, and their "focalisations" internal and external to the diegesis of the poem. Comments on focalization in the descriptions of the Wife of Bath and the Physician, and on free indirect discourse as a "sub-type" of focalization in those of the Monk and the Parson.

205. North, Richard, Barbara Bordalejo, Terry Jones, and Peter Robinson, eds. *CantApp: The General Prologue. An Edition in an App*. Saskatoon: Scholarly Digital Editions, 2020. Accessible at http://www.sd-editions.com/CantApp/GP/ (accessed October 16, 2023). Electronic edition of *GP*, designed for download and web access on mobile devices, based on the Hengwrt manuscript (fully reproduced in color), with hyperlinked transcription, translation, glosses and notes, and an audio performance by Lina Gibbings in Middle English. Sidebar apparatus includes a life of Chaucer; a description of *GP* in relation to *CT*; and discussions of the date of *GP*, the Hengwrt MS, the text of this edition, and background to the performance of *GP*. Contributors include Claire Pascolini-Campbell, James Robinson, Vicky Symons, and Mari Volkosh.

206. Simola, Robert, trans. and illus. *Chaucer's General Prologue to the Canterbury Tales*. Templeton, Calif.: William and Geoffrey Press, 2022. 191 pp. Facing-page translation of *GP* into modern English iambic decasyllables; features illustrations of the pilgrims—reproductions of Caxton's woodcuts paired with original woodcut portraits—and an extensive glossary.

207. Watson, Pat, and Johanna Wrinkle. "Studying Chaucer through Physiognomy: A Study of Chaucer's Characters Can Lead Students to a Better Understanding of Themselves." In Joel E. McIntosh, ed. *20 More Ideas for Teaching Gifted Kids in the Middle School and High School* (New York: Routledge, 2021), pp. 85–88. Lesson plan for teaching *GP* in high school classroom (senior level), introducing the four humors and using a personality test for students.

208. Yazıcı, Mine, trans. Ed. Aslı Pekiner Ergenekon. *Canterbury Masalları: Prolog/The Canterbury Tales: The Prologue*. Istanbul University Publication, no. 5272. Istanbul: Istanbul University Press, 2021. xx, 56

pp. E-book. Unrestricted access at https://iupress.istanbul.edu.tr/en/book/canterbury-masallari-prolog/home (accessed October 13, 2023). Facing-page Middle English and lineated Turkish translation of *GP*, with introductions to Chaucer's life, his works, and this translation.

209. Yıldız, Nazan. "The Medieval Borderline Identities: The Guildsmen in History and in Geoffrey Chaucer's *The Canterbury Tales*." *Journal of Narrative and Language Studies* 10 (2022): 83–97. Uses Homi Bhabha's concepts of borderline community and mimicry (*The Location of Culture* [1994]) to investigate the descriptions of the guildsmen in *GP*, 361–78, as they relate to shifts and tensions in Chaucer's contemporary society, focusing on "othering" within traditional hierarchy and sartorial mimicry. Includes historical and literary information about guildsmen.

See also nos. 22, 56, 151, 179, 209, 211, 222, 250.

CT—The Knight and His Tale

210. Cibula, Peter R., III. "Intervals of Grace: Shakespeare and Chaucer's Existential Romances and the Repair of the Past." Open access Ph.D. dissertation (University of California, Irvine, 2022). Available at https://escholarship.org/uc/item/3x49m6h9 (accessed November 15, 2023). Argues that "Augustine's theology allows us to see providence in romance as a doubled perspective that recognizes the existential smallness of individuals and their collective participatory power in a plural world," addressing *KnT*, *ClT*, and Shakespeare's *Cymbeline* and *The Winter's Tale*.

211. Dowsett, Elizabeth. *The Knight's Tale*. Penguin Readers, Level S. London: Penguin, 2021. 59 pp.; illus. Item not seen. WorldCat records indicate this is an adaptation of *KnT* for early readers.

212. Hendren, Madison Dickinson. "Playing an Epic Game: Games and Genre in Boccaccio's *Teseida delle nozze d'Emilia*." Ph.D. dissertation (University of Chicago, 2020), *DAI-A* 82.06(E). Attends to the source relations between *KnT* and Boccaccio's *Teseida* to examine the latter in light of game theory.

213. Ingham, Patricia Clare. "Infinite Sorrows: Catastrophic Forms in Chaucer's *Knight's Tale*." *JMEMS* 52 (2022): 93–117. Uses trauma theory to read *KnT* as a "meditation on catastrophe and survival."

214. Nall, Catherine. "Violent Compassion in Late Medieval Writing." In Stephanie Downes, Andrew Lynch, and Katrina O'Loughlin, eds. *Writing War in Britain and France, 1370–1854: A History of Emotions*

(London: Routledge, 2018), pp. 73–88. Explores the theme of knightly and royal pity (and related concepts, such as mercy, compassion, and resulting actions) in literary representations of war in a range of late medieval English texts, with particular attention to the *Alliterative Morte Arthure*, Malory's adaptation of it, and *KnT*, addressing Theseus's "compassionate pity" in the latter, along with its ironies and the physiology of pity as liquid.

215. Pigg, Daniel F. "From Imprisonment to Liberation: Chaucer's *Knight's Tale* as a Multilayered Exploration of a Paradigm for Prison Life." In Albrecht Classen, ed. *Incarceration and Slavery in the Middle Ages and the Early Modern Age: A Cultural-Historical Investigation of the Dark Side of the Pre-Modern World* (Lanham, Md.: Lexington, 2021), pp. 347–60. Argues that the "unique aspect" of the depiction of imprisonment in *KnT* is that the "only liberation that can happen is apparently at the end of this life, which is seen as a prison," hence "hardly a liberation at all." Comments on Chaucer's likely knowledge of material prisons and on how the tale exerts pressure to read imprisonment allegorically.

216. Radulescu, Raluca L. "Emotions and War in Chaucer's *Knight's Tale*." In Claire McIlroy and Anne M. Scott, *Literature, Emotions, and Pre-Modern War: Conflict in Medieval and Early Modern Europe* (Leeds: Arc Humanities, 2021), pp. 45–63. Investigates the restless "emotional movement" of "roaming" in *KnT*, as expression of both confined frustration and openness to new adventures enacted by Palamon, Emelye, and Arcite. Compares Chaucer's depictions of these movements and emotions with those found in Boccaccio's *Teseida*, and compares Emelye's roaming with Dorigen's in *FranT*, Constance's in *MLT*, and Hypsipyle's in *LGW*.

See also nos. 70, 73, 75, 88, 93, 96, 103–4, 129, 138, 161–62, 171, 174, 175, 178–79, 193, 196, 240, 244.

CT—The Miller and His Tale

See nos. 30, 93, 110–11, 145, 151, 153, 160, 171.

CT—The Reeve and His Tale

217. Baechle, Sarah. "Speaking Survival: Chaucer Studies and the Discourses of Sexual Assault." *ChauR* 57 (2022): 463–74. Focuses on *RvT* and argues that newly discovered documents allow scholars to move

beyond Chaucer's individual blame and address structural issues and concerns with language describing and depicting sexual assault in late medieval texts.

218. Miller, T. S., and Elizabeth Miller. "Tolkien and Rape: Sexual Terror, Sexual Violence, and the Woman's Body in Middle-Earth." *Extrapolation: A Journal of Science Fiction and Fantasy* 62 (2021): 133–56. Connects "gendered terror" of female sexuality and the "evasiveness" of J. R. R. Tolkien's treatment of sexual violence against women in his Middle-Earth narratives, and assesses suppressions of rape in Tolkien's 1939 bowdlerized version of *RvT* in light of this evasiveness.

219. Schwebel, Leah. "Chaucer and the Fantasy of Retroactive Consent." *SAC* 44 (2022): 337–45. Explores aspects of sexual consent and non-consent in *RvT*—particularly Malyne's romanticizing of Aleyn's assault—linking them with Augustine's comments on Lucretia in *De civitate Dei*, modern notions of "retroactive consent," and the Chaucer life records that pertain to Cecily Chaumpaigne. For response, see no. 220.

220. Shutters, Lynn. "Response to Leah Schwebel and Jennifer Alberghini." *SAC* 44 (2022): 359–60. Responds to two essays concerning sexual consent in medieval literature; suggests that we might read *RvT* "as an incel revenge fantasy." See no. 219.

221. Taylor, Joseph. *Writing the North of England in the Middle Ages: Regionalism and Nationalism in Medieval English Literature*. Cambridge Studies in Medieval Literature. Cambridge: Cambridge University Press, 2022. xiv, 254 pp. Examines "the North as a regional concept in the literature of medieval England," considering a range of texts from Bede's *Historia ecclesiastica gentis Anglorum* to the Towneley plays. Chapter 4, "Chaucer's Northern Consciousness in the *Reeve's Tale*," surveys the presence of northern England in *CT* and focuses the use of northern dialect in *RvT* as "symptomatic of a larger engagement with the region's long-standing cultural identity as an uncanny presence in England's national story."

See also nos. 93, 115,145, 153, 171.

CT—The Cook and His Tale

222. Pecan, David. "[Un]Licensed Riot: Prodigality, Hypocrisy, and Guild Discourse in Chaucer's *Cook's Tale*." *Journal of Narrative and Language Studies* 10 (2022): 281–92. Assesses the social and economic

dynamics of *CkT* and the *GP* descriptions of the Cook and the guildsmen, arguing that the tale "indicts both the laterally mobile prodigal apprentice and the decadent hypocrisy" of his master "through the linked subversion of license and guild authority."

223. Wang, Denise Ming-yueh. "Old Pies, Stray Flies, and Possibly Poisonous Parsley in the Cook's Prologue and Tale." *Ex-Position* 45 (2021): 27–45. Explicates details in the *GP* description of the Cook, *CkPT*, and *ManP*, exploring their physical and moral implications for characterization, "food safety" in Chaucer's London, and hygiene among its victuallers—cooks, innkeepers, and manciples.

See also no. 153.

CT—The Man of Law and His Tale

224. Brent, Jonathan. "World History in the Tumultuous 1330s: A Study of Nicholas Trevet's Anglo-Norman *Cronicles*." Ph.D. dissertation (University of Toronto, 2021), *DAI-A* 83/1(E). Includes comments on how study of Chaucer's and Gower's Constance narratives have affected the study and understanding of Trevet's *Cronicles*.

225. Cooper, Helen. "Romance Repetitions and the Sea: Brendan, Constance, Apollonius." In A. S. G. Edwards, ed. *Medieval Romance, Arthurian Literature: Essays in Honour of Elizabeth Archibald* (Cambridge: Brewer, 2021), pp. 46–60. Argues that "repetition should be included among the family resemblances that trigger the imaginative response that signals 'romance.'" Includes discussion of *MLT* and the analogous accounts in Nicholas Trevet's *Chronicles* and John Gower's *Confessio Amantis*, as well as other works in which repetition signals "romance."

226. Hurley, Mary Kate. "Becoming England: The Northumbrian Conversion in Trevet, Gower, and Chaucer." In *Translation Effects: Language, Time, and Community in Medieval England*. Interventions: New Studies in Medieval Culture (Columbus: The Ohio State University Press, 2021), pp. 125–50. Assesses the "temporally heterogeneous portrayals of an emerging sense" of "Engelond" in the scenes of Saxon conversion in the Constance narratives of Trevet's *Cronicles*, Gower's *Confessio Amantis*, and *MLT*. These scenes are "sites where the power of linguistic difference to form community becomes a central concern."

See also nos. 59, 80, 86, 158, 169, 197, 216, 281.

CT—The Wife of Bath and Her Tale

227. Carey, John, ed. *100 Poets: Anthology*. New Haven, Conn.: Yale University Press, 2021. ix, 268 pp. Collects selections from western poets, from Homer forward, including *WBP*, 587–608, translated by Carey with a brief introduction that characterizes the Wife as having a "good claim to be the first feminist in literature."

228. Kano, Koichi. "Has the Absurd in the 'Wife of Bath's Tale' Been Solved? With Special Reference to the Citation of Classical Works." In Society for Chaucer Studies and Koichi Kano, eds. *To the Days of Studying Medieval English Literature: Essays in Memory of Professor Ikegami Tadahiro* (*SAC* 46 [2024], no. 179), pp. 69–86. Interprets *WBT* as a story in which the knight finally accepts the absurdity caused by himself, persuaded by the old woman's words citing classical works. In Japanese.

229. McLemore, Emily. "Desiring Women: Pleasure and Power in Late Medieval English Literature." Ph.D. dissertation (University of Notre Dame, 2022), *DAI-A* 83.11(E). Studies "representations of women's desire and . . . its intersections with eroticism, pleasure, and power" in *WBPT*, Robert Henryson's *Testament of Cresseid*, *The Book of Margery Kempe*, and *Sir Gawain and the Green Knight*.

230. Price, Vicki Kay. "'Sche evyr desyryd mor and Mor': The Appropriation of Mercantile Language and Practice in Fifteenth to Seventeenth-Century English Women's Writing." Ph.D. dissertation (Bangor University, 2021), *DAI-C* 82/12(E). Discusses briefly the Wife of Bath's use of mercantile language to help launch an assessment of such language in women's writing from Margery Kempe and the Paston women to Aphra Behn.

231. Steinberg, Glenn A. "Is Ugliness Only Skin Deep? Middle English Gawain Romances and the 'Wife of Bath's Tale.'" *Arthuriana* 31 (2021): 3–28. Explores "the socioeconomic significance of the ugly, monstrous figures in the Gawain romances" and in *WBT*, arguing that Chaucer "bifurcates" the "ugly antagonist" of the romances into the "crude, social-climbing Wife . . . and the loathly lady of her tale" while amplifying criticism of the "old aristocracy" and highlighting "tensions and ugliness" among the *parvenu* Canterbury pilgrims.

232. Strouse, A. W. *Form and Foreskin: Medieval Narratives of Circumcision*. New York: Fordham University Press, 2021. [165] pp. Uses Pauline "theo-poetics of circumcision" to explore circumcision and "uncircumcision" as hermeneutic tropes, focusing on allegoresis and amplification,

and analyzing queerly Augustine's "Boy with a Long Foreskin" (from *De Genesi ad litteram*); *Sir Gawain and the Green Knight*; and, in Chapter 3, "The Foreskin of Marriage," *WBT*. Identifies medieval association of marriage and "the allegorical *praeputium*" in the latter and suggests that the "Wife vernacularizes and feminizes the Latinate *praeputium* in order to circumcise the marriage plot."

233. Turner, Marion. *The Wife of Bath: A Biography.* Princeton: Princeton University Press, 2022. x, 320 pp.; 14 color illus. Combines personal appreciation and critical analysis of the Wife of Bath as a character; Chaucer's art in creating her and *WBPT*; and the voluminous historical reception and impact of the Wife from early scribal glosses to international modern adaptations in poetry, drama, fiction, opera, film, children's literature, poster-art, and more. Includes commentary on source study of the Wife; cultural and socio-economic backgrounds to her in post-plague England; close reading of passages of *WBPT*; and assessments of adaptations by Shakespeare, Dryden, Pope, Voltaire, Percy MacKaye, James Joyce, Vera Chapman, Caroline Bergvall, Jean "Binta" Breeze, Patience Agbabi, Zadie Smith, and more.

See also nos. 7–9, 69, 74, 83, 133, 151, 159, 165, 171, 177, 183, 185, 197, 257.

CT—The Friar and His Tale

See no. 77.

CT—The Summoner and His Tale

See no. 117.

CT—The Clerk and His Tale

234. Nixon, Emily Joanna. "Patience, Exemplarity, and the Affective Didactics of Middle English Literature." Ph.D. dissertation (University of Chicago, 2021), *DAI-A* 83/4(E). "Traces the theme of patience in Middle English verse exempla amid the proliferation of exemplary works in late medieval England to examine the sociality of feeling within narratives of individual virtue," including a chapter pertaining to *ClT*.

235. Nixon, Jo. "Stories Said and Not: Patience and Accommodation in the *Clerk's Tale*." *ChauR* 57 (2022): 345–67. Examines the frequent mention of Griselda's face in *ClT*, as compared to his sources, and simultaneously argues that Chaucer's version highlights Griselda's interiority and how she maintains her patience.

236. Wicher, Andrzej. "Griselda's Afterlife, or the Relationship between Shakespeare's *The Winter's Tale*, Chaucer's *The Clerk's Tale* and the Tale of Magic." *Text Matters: A Journal of Literature, Theory and Culture* 11 (2021): 334–52. Offers "folkloric analysis" of several motifs—slaughtered wives, lost and restored children, and incest—in *ClT* and in *The Winter's Tale* (and other Shakespearean plays), arguing that such analysis allows us "to see these texts in connection with particular archetypal patterns that make certain crucial elements of their plots stand out in relief." The female protagonist in each plot "may . . . be said to have saved" her husband from himself.

See also nos. 33, 48, 59, 64, 73, 80, 90, 97, 123, 178, 210.

CT—The Merchant and His Tale

237. Zygogianni, Maria. "*May medica*: Divine Healing and the Garden in 'The Merchant's Tale.'" *MFF* 58 (2022): 106–27. Examines May of *MerT* as a version of the motif of the healing woman, familiar "across medieval literary genres from romance to hagiography." The fabliau setting of the tale, however, inverts a range of "courtly and religious hierarchies" as May performs an "anti-healing miracle" and maintains control of her husband, her lover, her body, the "spaces of the tale."

See also nos. 7, 158.

CT—The Squire and His Tale

238. Bower, Hannah Louise. "Restless Rewritings: The Politics of Enigma and Exposure in the *Squire's Tale*." *ChauR* 57 (2022): 32–67. Considers the role of spectacle in *SqT*, comparing the poetic strategies for inscribing spectacle to Richard Maidstone's approach in *Concordia*.

239. Fumo, Jamie C. "As the Chess-Set Flies: Arthurian Marvels in Chaucer's Squire's Tale and the Roman van Walewein." In Larissa Tracy,

ed. *Medieval English and Dutch Literatures: The European Context. Essays in Honour of David F. Johnson* (Woodbridge: Boydell & Brewer, 2022), pp. 207–32. Compares and contrasts *SqT* and the analogous Middle Dutch Roman van Walewein, focusing on their eastern settings, treatments of marvel, and other romance conventions. Considers Chaucer's possible knowledge of Middle Dutch and Van Walewein, observes connections with *Th*, and posits that Arthurian allusions in *SqT* may be a "nod" in the direction of Flanders.

240. Jagot, Shazia. "Chaucer and Ibn al-Haytham (Alhacen): *Perspectiva*, Arabic Mathematics, and Acts of Looking." *SAC* 44 (2022): 27–61. Challenges the limitations of traditional source-and-analogue study, exploring resonances between *SqT* and the *Kitāb al-Manāzir* of Ibn al-Haytham/Alhacen to which it alludes (see *SqT*, 232–45), including discussion of mediating sources in Latin and French, especially Jean de Meun's *Roman de la Rose*. Shows that aspects of Ibn al-Haytham's theory of sight—dependent upon the acts of looking and the intentions of the beholder—recur in *SqT*, and are also evident in *KnT*, *PhyT*, and *TC*, exemplifying rich intertextuality with Arabic, "Islamicate" learning in late medieval England.

241. Kao, Wan-Chuan. "In the Lap of Whiteness." *New Literary History* 52 (2021): 535–61. Examines the "workings of empathy" in *SqT* to situate it in "premodern critical race studies," reading the "falcon-Canacee-lap" formulation as "a homo-affective assemblage, an animal human thing that blurs the borders of body, object, and species," whereby, in a psychoanalytic fantasy, Canacee is "feeling like a bird feeling like a woman." Observes parallel formulations in "the greater cultural-historical racial imaginary," showing how *SqT* and its reception reflect and refract historical periodization, racialization, and their illusions.

242. Kramer, Johanna. "Proverbial Wisdom and the Pursuit of Knowledge in the *Squire's Tale*." *ChauR* 57 (2022): 68–100. Highlights the utility of proverbs and offers them as a solution to the problem of knowledge in *SqT*. Emphasizes that proverbs provide new insights for late medieval textual cultures as a microgenre that transcends social and economic boundaries in the fourteenth century.

243. Norako, Leila K. "The Mongols of Middle English Literature." In Valerie B. Johnson and Kara L. McShane, eds. *Negotiating Boundaries in Medieval Literature and Culture: Essays on Marginality, Difference, and Reading Practices in Honor of Thomas Hahn* (SAC 46 [2024], no. 148), pp.

49–76. Explores how *SqT* and *The Book of John Mandeville* "traffic in fantasies of cultural, religious, and racial annihilation . . . in a quieter, more subtextual way than that seen in other works of crusades-inspired literature." Argues that the Squire poses "conquest-via-effacement" in his tale and, comparing the tale with Mandeville and other works, observes how it endeavors to absorb Mongols into "Latin Christendom."

See also nos. 186, 197.

CT—The Franklin and His Tale

244. Bose, Mishtooni. "The Body Speaks in *The Franklin's Tale*." In Louise D'Arcens and Sif Ríkharðsdóttir, eds. *Medieval Literary Voices: Embodiment, Materiality and Performance* (*SAC* 46 [2024], no. 130), pp. 75–94. Examines the "fissure between spoken utterances and the body's voice" in Arveragus's burst into tears (*FranT*, 1479–80), engaging the theme of truth in the tale and the "dynamic between . . . irruptions of the somatic voice and the dissociative occasions that precipitate them." Contrasts this episode with its analogue in Boccaccio's Tale of Menedon, and addresses instances of somatic speech in *KnT*, *NPT*, *TC*, and *Sir Gawain and the Green Knight.*

245. Hindrichen, Lorenz. "Postpandemic Trauma in Geoffrey Chaucer's *The Franklin's Tal*e." *EMSt* 37 (2022): 47–63. Argues that *FranT* should be added to "the Chaucerian pandemic canon" for its depiction of pandemic trauma and recovery.

246. Kowalik, Barbara Janina. "The Men and Woman behind the *Franklin's Tale*." *ChauR* 57 (2022): 162–89. Considers *FranT* as a Breton lay recalling Chaucer's recent memories of his own stays in France rather than ancient history, tying the tale to the marital situation of Joan of Kent.

See also nos. 7, 79, 105, 124, 162, 169, 216, 321.

CT—The Physician and His Tale

247. Friedman, Sarah. "Contagion, Sexual Violence, and Communal Healing in Chaucer's *The Physician's Tale* and Gower's *Confessio Amantis*." *EMSt* 37 (2022): 65–79. Focuses on two texts that feature violence against women to examine how the violated woman functions as a tool for political

change. Both Chaucer and Gower foreground the suffering that men experience in response to the violated female body, leading to communal healing and the reformation of social and political structures.

248. Scala, Elizabeth. "Did Chaucer Know Livy?" *N&Q* 68 (2021): 255–58. Explores intertextual relations among versions of the Virginia/Virginius story (by Livy, Bersuire, Gower, and Chaucer), focusing on how the depiction of Virginia's mother in both Gower and Chaucer "offers a broader semblance of propriety by assuring Virginius's legitimate paternity," and indicates that in *PhyT* Chaucer "reveals how he knew his Livy" through Gower.

See also nos. 174, 240.

CT—The Pardoner and His Tale

249. Edmondson, George. "Guilt Historicism: Walter Benjamin's 'Capitalism as Religion,' Aura, and the Case of Chaucer's Pardoner." *Exemplaria* 34 (2022): 103–29. Posits the Pardoner in *PardT* as an "exemplary figure" of what Walter Benjamin argues is a defining trait of modernity: the eclipse of religion's sacralizing capacities by capitalism, which, like the Pardoner's sales pitch, intensifies guilt rather than offering atonement. In this, the Pardoner is not only a prophet of modernity but its neighbor.

250. Greene, Darragh. "Substance into Accident: Transubstantiation and Relics in Chaucer's *Pardoner's Tale*." *R&L* 54 (2022): 141–62. Focuses on *CT* and *PardT*, specifically. Discusses Pardoner's fabrication of relics and the "preposterous" transformation of "accident into substance," a reversal of the trope used in *PardT*, the narrative voice in both *GP* and *PardT*, and deception and fakery in *HF*.

251. Hearst, Katherine, illus. and trans. In Russ Kick, ed. *The Graphic Canon of Crime & Mystery*. Vol. 2, *From "Salome" to Edgar Allan Poe to "Silence of the Lambs"* (New York: Seven Stories Press, 2021), pp. 134–46. Graphic version of *PardT*, newly adapted and illustrated in ink and watercolor, with a calligraphic, abbreviated text in modern verse.

252. Price, Merrall Llewelyn. "Thomas Becket and the Pardoner's Problem: Eunuchry and Healing on the Road to Canterbury." In Valerie B. Johnson and Kara L. McShane, eds. *Negotiating Boundaries in Medieval Literature and Culture: Essays on Marginality, Difference, and Reading Practices in Honor of Thomas Hahn* (*SAC* 46 [2024], no. 148), pp. 99–118. Explores,

in the Pardoner's materials, resonances with Thomas Becket's miraculous healing of a castrated man, Eilward, depicted in stained glass in Canterbury Cathedral. Considers issues of wholeness, healing, sanctity, and their antitheses reflected in details of the Pardoner's characterization and identity, his relics, and Harry Bailly's threat at the end of *PardT*.

253. Schiff, Randy. "Alcohol, Community, and Chaucer's Pardoner: Ale as a Populist Antidote to Alienating Avant-Gardism." In John A. Geck, Rosemary O'Neill, and Noelle Phillips, eds. *Beer and Brewing in Medieval Culture and Contemporary Medievalism* (*SAC* 46 [2024], no. 140), pp. 341–62. Assesses references to ale and wine in *PardPT* as they reflect the Pardoner's "submerged desire" to bond with the Host and his simultaneous attempt to compete with Harry as leader of the pilgrimage. Argues that "the metaphorical ale-stake associated with the Summoner's body" in *GP* frames the ale-stake of *PardP*, setting the Pardoner's "conflicted masculinity" in competition for and against the "hyper-masculine" Host, who repudiates the Pardoner's overreaching efforts to reach and outreach him.

254. Tagaya, Yuko. "Chaucer's 'Pardoner's Tale' and Its Surroundings." In Society for Chaucer Studies and Koichi Kano, eds. *To the Days of Studying Medieval English Literature: Essays in Memory of Professor Ikegami Tadahiro* (*SAC* 46 [2024], no. 179), pp. 40–56. Considers the evil of indulgences through comparisons between *PardT* and its East Asian analogues. In Japanese.

See also nos. 7, 63, 77, 117, 143, 164, 174, 179, 182, 192.

CT—The Shipman and His Tale

255. Staley, Lynn. "'For yet under the yerde was the mayde': Chaucer in the House of Fiction." *ChauR* 57 (2022): 190–213. Considers the young child who watches the wife and monk in *ShT*, arguing that Chaucer's construction of narrative perspective, which the child embodies, anticipates more modern handling of narrative perspective, including that of Henry James.

CT—The Prioress and Her Tale

256. Heng, Geraldine. *England and the Jews: How Religion and Violence Created the First Racial State in the West*. Cambridge Elements: Elements in

Religion and Violence. New York: Cambridge University Press, 2019. 116 pp. Includes comparison of *PrT* with sources and analogues: the Anglo-Norman *Hughes de Lincoln* and two accounts—"The Child Slain by Jews" and "The Jewish Boy"—found in the Vernon manuscript. Analyzes the stories' various contributions to the racialization of England, arguing that *PrT* "conjures England as a new kind of space where Christians are a population 'ycomen of Cristen blood'—a de facto race whose time had come, in a post-expulsion land."

257. Pitard, Derrick. "'The Prioress's Tale' and Vernacular Devotion." In Valerie B. Johnson and Kara L. McShane, eds. *Negotiating Boundaries in Medieval Literature and Culture: Essays on Marginality, Difference, and Reading Practices in Honor of Thomas Hahn* (SAC 46 [2024], no. 148), pp. 323–45. Argues that the "modes of religious expression" in *PrT* are "vernacular" insofar as they are simultaneously canny and naïve. Using romance discourse to express religious orthodoxy, the Prioress challenges patriarchal "Latinate institutions," evident by contrast with Richard Rolle's works, but she reduplicates the violence of both romance and orthodoxy. Compares the Prioress's challenge to those of the Wife of Bath, and contrasts her violent orthodoxy with that of the Second Nun.

258. Rose, E. M. "Prior to the Prioress: Chaucer's *Clergeon* in Its Original Context." *SAC* 44 (2022): 63–92. Reconsiders questions of the composition and occasion of *PrT* (here titled *Clergeon*) before Chaucer incorporated it into the *CT*, arguing on biographical, stylistic, and liturgical grounds that Chaucer may have originally composed the poem as early as 1383, to be performed as a "boy-bishop sermon" at Lincoln Cathedral, "recited by and to youths on the Feast of the Holy Innocents." Considers analogous materials, argues that Chaucer's work helped to spread knowledge of Hugh of Lincoln, and suggests new directions for reading *PrPT*.

See also nos. 146, 182.

CT—The Tale of Sir Thopas

259. Gordon, Stephen. "Sensory Satires and the Virtues of Herbs in *Sir Thopas*'s Fair Forest." *SP* 119 (2022): 191–208. Focuses on the medical effects of the herbs mentioned in *Th* to argue that the narrator's impetuosity demonstrates the effects of herbs he mentions in lines 760–65.

260. Reichl, Karl. "'His robe was of syklatoun': Prächtige Stoffe in den mittelenglischen Romanzen. Ornamental oder bedeutungsvoll?" In Peter Glasner, ed. *Ästhetiken der Fülle* (Berlin: Schwabe, 2021), pp. 319–25. Comments on the history and nuances of "syklatoun" as a kind of sartorial cloth used parodically in *Th*, a prelude to discussing the implications of clothing in *Emaré* as a popular romance.

261. Schoen, Jenna. "Romantic Theology: Contemplating Genre in Late Medieval England." Ph.D. dissertation (Columbia University, 2021), *DAI-A* 83.01(E). Explores the interplay between romance and religious poetry in late medieval English vernacular literature, and includes discussion of how, as a parody of romance, *Th* "primes the reader for the prudential lessons" of *Mel*.

See also no. 239.

CT—The Tale of Melibee

See nos. 53, 80, 118, 165, 174, 185, 261.

CT—The Monk and His Tale

262. Forni, Kathleen. "Can Chaucer Write Anything Bad(ly)? Salvaging the Monk's Tale." *SMART* 29 (2022): 43–57. Considers the vexed critical history of *MkT* as a possibility for engaging classroom discussion about issues of theme, aesthetics, political perspective, and critical predilection. Focuses on various approaches to the tale before and after the hey-day of dramatic criticism.

263. Kelly, Kathleen Coyne. "*Anthophilia* and the Medieval Ecologies of Grafting." *ChauR* 57 (2022): 131–61. Traces the tension between reading ecocritically and figuratively, highlighting moments of grafting in *MkT* and *Rom*, and reads these moments of horticulture more literally.

See also nos. 62, 269.

CT—The Nun's Priest and His Tale

264. Chapman, Juliana. "*Musicus animal* in the *Nun's Priest's Tale*." *ChauR* 57 (2022): 368–90. Examines music as a coequal to rhetoric and

a branch of medieval philosophy to argue that Chaucer's beast fable traces and complicates three major tenets of Boethian and medieval music theory.

265. Goldberg, Midge, ed. *Outer Space: 100 Poems*. Cambridge: Cambridge University Press, 2022. xx, 178 pp. Collects 100 poems and excerpts from poems on views of outer space, including *NPT*, 3187–99. In Middle English with no indication of edition.

266. Ida, Hideho. "On Etymology of the Nouns Appearing in Geoffrey Chaucer's *Nun's Priest's Tale*." *A Collection of Treatises on Languages and Literature* 38 (2021): 35–45. Categorizes nouns in *NPT* into twenty groups according to their meanings, counts the numbers of Latin-based nouns and OE-based nouns in each category, and considers possible implications of their proportions. In Japanese.

267. ______. "Re-Classification of the Etymology of the Nouns Appearing in Geoffrey Chaucer's *Nun's Priest's Tale*." *A Collection of Treatises on Languages and Literature* 39 (2022): 1–16. Classifies the nouns in *NPT* using the categories presented by an English lexicon. Considers the proportion of Latin-based nouns and OE-based nouns in each category. In Japanese.

268. McGuire, Riley. "Romans 15:4 and the *Canterbury Tales*: A Modest Proposal Concerning Chaucer's *Entente*." *ChauR* 57 (2022): 232–50. Considers the end of *NPT* and the Bible verse Romans 15:4. Claims the verse is used to bridge the two opposing views of Chaucer's intent in his writing, attempting to unite the morally serious poet with the subversive poet.

269. Pattenaude, Annika J. "Undisciplined: Reading Affects in Late Medieval England." Ph.D. dissertation (University of Michigan, 2022), *DAI-A* 84.03(E). viii, 140 pp. "[A]nalyzes scenes of 'undisciplined reading' in late medieval texts: that is, scenes in which characters read without formal training and with the 'wrong' emotions." Includes discussion of *NPPT* as a "bungled interpretation of Marie de France's translation of Aesop," a response to *MkT*, and exemplification of the Host's misinterpretations.

See also nos. 57, 105, 118, 174, 244, 288.

CT—The Second Nun and Her Tale

270. Strong, David. *The Bond of Empathy in Medieval and Early Modern Literature*. Research in Medieval and Early Modern Culture, no. 35; Studies

in Medieval and Early Modern Culture, no. 84. Boston, Mass.: De Gruyter, 2022. v, 173 pp. Chapter 2 focuses on free volition (as formulated by John Duns Scotus), empathy, and fraternal bonding in *Amis and Amiloun* and in *SNT*. In the latter, Valerian and Tiburce "forgo political loyalties and prioritize their fraternal bond by cultivating their mutual awareness of spiritual goodness"; their sensory and extrasensory experiences lead to empathetic bonding and spiritual fruition.

See also nos. 126, 165, 257.

CT—The Canon's Yeoman and His Tale

271. Bentick, Eoin. *Literatures of Alchemy in Medieval and Early Modern England*. Rochester, N.Y.: Brewer, 2022. viii, 213 pp.; illus. Surveys medieval and early modern study of alchemy and writing about alchemy, with particular attention to its obscurities of language and limited potential for progress. In a section called "Playing with Obscurity: Chaucer's Manipulation of the *Tabula chemica* and the *Liber de secretis naturae*," treats *CYPT* as epitomizing "the skeptical rejection of alchemical bombast . . . that could nonetheless be manipulated by those who knew the way around its language." Considers Chaucer's adaptations of "academic" treatises on alchemy: the *Tabula chemica* and the *Liber de secretis naturae*.

272. Buhrer, Eliza. "Response to Micah James Goodrich and Alice Raw." *SAC* 44 (2022): 315–16. Comments on issues of complaint and consent in two essays, linking the medieval past with the present. See no. 274.

273. Burt, Kathleen. "The Alchemy of Failure: Combining Facts and Fictions in Chaucer's 'The Canon's Yeoman's Tale.'" *South Atlantic Review* 86, no. 1 (2021): 58–76. Anatomizes the theme and structures of failure in *CYPT*, contrasting the Canon's Yeoman and Chaucer-pilgrim as narrators, and tallying ways that failure dominates the narrative: failed science, failed rhetoric, failed comedy, failed moralizing, and failure to control self-narration.

274. Goodrich, Micah James. "The Yeoman's Canon: On Toxic Mentors." *SAC* 44 (2022): 297–306. Explores aspects of "power differential and toxicity" in the mentor–mentee relationship of the Canon and the Canon's Yeoman, reading *CYPT* as the emancipatory complaint of the latter. For response, see no. 272.

275. Honda, Takahiro. "An Aspect of Chaucer's 'Philosophy' in 'The Canon's Yeoman's Tale.'" *Research Reports, National Institute of Technology,*

Fukushima College 63 (2022): 56–62. Contrasts the master–pupil relationship and the concept of philosophy between *CYT* and Boethius's *Consolation of Philosophy*. Argues that *CYT* ridicules the false nature of philosophy. In Japanese, with English abstract.

276. Huerta, Monica. *Magical Places*. Durham, N.C.: Duke University Press, 2021. xxii, 178 pp. Creative non-fiction contemplation of storytelling, Chicanx identity, and spatial politics, including, in Chapter 3, "Disciplines and Disciples," a brief consideration of "discipline" in *CYT*, 1253, as it relates to alchemy, deception, storytelling, and belief.

See also nos. 122–23, 160, 200.

CT—The Manciple and His Tale

277. Stanbury, Sarah. "The Crow's 'Cokkow!': Bird Debates and Chaucer's 'Manciple's Tale.'" In Valerie B. Johnson and Kara L. McShane, eds. *Negotiating Boundaries in Medieval Literature and Culture: Essays on Marginality, Difference, and Reading Practices in Honor of Thomas Hahn* (*SAC* 46 [2024], no. 148), pp. 265–88. Explicates the "cukkow"/cuckoo/cuckold pun in *ManT* by identifying the role of the cuckoo (versus the nightingale) in bird-debate poems, analyzed here, particularly in Sir John Clanvowe's *Boke of Cupide*. Argues that, by engaging themes of signification, class, and truth-telling, *ManT* "lobs an attack on the courtly good life of song, poetry, and pleasure," "signaling" the end of the *CT* and "making that end happen."

See also nos. 76, 162, 165, 223.

CT—The Parson and His Tale

278. Greene, Darragh. "'Crist spak hymself ful brode in hooly writ': Chaucer, Divine Speech, and the Silent Word." *ChauR* 57 (2022): 1–31. Considers locations in Chaucer's corpus where he might have depicted divine speech, before highlighting how Jesus' words serve as *auctoritas* in *ParsT*. Comparing this method to the absence of depictions of divine speech in Chaucer's other works, argues that *Ret* can be seen as sincere.

279. Murchison, Krista A. *Manuals for Penitents in Medieval English: From "Ancrene Wisse" to the "Parson's Tale."* Cambridge: Brewer, 2021. xiv, 175 pp. Describes and assesses the wide array of guides to penitential

self-examination in late medieval Latin, Anglo-Norman, and Middle English, viewing them in the contexts of the 1215 Lateran Council, the rise in popular religion, and developing notions of subjectivity and identity. Includes a chapter on *ParsT*, "'To enden in som vertuous sentence': Concluding with Chaucer's Parson," which clarifies the orthodoxy of its general form and content, despite its lack of discussion of the Ten Commandments and the *Pater noster*.

See also nos. 60, 109, 118.

CT—Chaucer's Retraction

280. Herman, Jason. "Chaucer's *Retraction*: Examining the Case for Disavowal." *ChauR* 57 (2022): 214–31. Argues that *Ret*'s language should not be understood as a modern retraction would be; expresses skepticism that *Ret* is actually meant to retract works like *CT*.

See also no. 118.

Anelida and Arcite

See no. 24.

A Treatise on the Astrolabe

281. Brooks, Michelle. "Rewriting "litel Lowys" in Chaucer's *A Treatise on the Astrolabe*." *SP* 119 (2022): 209–32. Examines *Astr* as a work on literature that uses the astrolabe to overcome geographical separation between father and son. A narrative of family reunion then writes the son out of the text, while apophasis keeps the son at its center. Also notes how *MLT* uses the same terminology as *Astr*.

282. Gilbert, Jane, and Sara Harris. "The Written Word: Literacy across Languages." In Orietta Da Rold and Elaine Treharne, eds. *The Cambridge Companion to Medieval British Manuscripts* (*SAC* 46 [2024], no. 132), pp. 149–78. Includes discussion of *Astr* in showing that "vernacular pride" in late medieval England was "more inclusive than exclusive of other languages and cultures." Stresses the "practical utility" of *Astr* and how English achieves "dignity" by association with astronomical study.

283. Robinson, Michael. "Astronomy with Chaucer: Using an Astrolabe to Determine Planetary Orbits." *American Journal of Physics* 90 (2022): 745–54. Explains the practical utilities and operations of astrolabes, reporting on several years' use of a homemade instrument. Includes recurrent references to *Astr* as a helpful guide, describing it as "apparently the earliest known technical manual written in English," "well organized," and "written in clear, technical prose."

284. Stadolnik, Joe. "Little Lewis and Latin Folk in Chaucer's Prologue to the *Treatise on the Astrolabe*." *JEGP* 121 (2022): 359–82. Claims that although the prologue to *Astr* is addressed to Chaucer's son "little Lewis," it is structurally and rhetorically complex, appealing to sophisticated Latinists as well as to young English speakers. Argues that the prologue imitates Latin prologues of scientific texts, including a youthful addressee, a defense of the vernacular, and a disavowal of comprehensiveness.

Boece

285. Olson, Donald W. "Astronomy in Literature: Chaucer, Shakespeare, and Longfellow." In *Investigating Art, History, and Literature with Astronomy: Determining Time, Place, and Other Hidden Details Linked to the Stars* (Cham: Springer, 2022), pp. 288–323; illus. Includes discussion of the reference to Boetes (the constellation Boötes) in *Bo*, IV, met. 5, explaining the astronomy underlying the "puzzle" found in Boethius's original reference and in Chaucer's translation.

See also no. 165.

The Book of the Duchess

286. Bartlett, Robyn A. "Death, Negation, and the Problem of Absence in Chaucer's *Book of the Duchess*." *ChauR* 57 (2022): 321–44. Highlights that *BD* conveys the inevitability and incomprehensibility of death, offering a reading of the poem that moves beyond consolation of poetry and memory.

287. Krummel, Miriamne Ara. "Being a Crip Professor in the Time of Covid-19: A Modern Game of Medieval Chess?" *Journal of Literary & Cultural Disability Studies* 15 (2021): 245–50. Personal reflections on having multiple sclerosis during the COVID-19 pandemic, describing changes that these conditions brought to (re)reading *BD*.

288. Leitch, Megan G. *Sleep and Its Spaces in Middle English Literature: Emotions, Ethics, Dreams*. Manchester Medieval Literature and Culture. Manchester: University of Manchester Press, 2021. 284 pp. Surveys medical and literary backgrounds and representations of sleep, naps, dreams, nightmares, and sleep-scapes in various Middle English genres and works. Chapter 4, "The Hermeneutics of Sleep in Chaucer's Dream Poems," focuses on dreams, melancholy, ethics, emotions, and consolation in *BD*, and more briefly assesses related concerns in *PF*, *LGWP*, and *NPT*, arguing that Chaucer deploys an original hermeneutics of sleep and dreaming and "reflects on the nature of poetry and poetic inheritance."

289. Marshall, Simone Celine. "*The Poetical Works of Geoffrey Chaucer* in the Nineteenth Century: Social Influences on Editorial Practice." *Romantic Textualities: Literature and Print Culture, 1780–1840* 23 (2020): 218–36; 7 illus.; 3 appendices. Analyzes the text of *BD* found in the 1807 collected edition *The Poetical Works of Geoffrey Chaucer*, showing "that it is fair to consider the work a new edition," based on John Urry's 1721 edition of *BD* and loosely following Thomas Tyrwhitt's critique of Urry. Attends to verb forms, pronouns, and punctuation, observing that the 1807 edition is evidently the first printed edition to use the title *Book of the Duchess*.

290. Morgan, Gerald. "An Aristotelian Ideal: The Beauty and Virtue of Blanche in Chaucer's *Book of the Duchess*." In Roman Bleier, Brian Coleman, and Clare Fletcher, eds. *Memory and Identity in the Medieval and Early Modern World* (*SAC* 46 [2024], no. 120), pp. 121–53. Explicates the rhetorical, conventional, and philosophical aspects of the combination of physical beauty and moral virtue in Chaucer's portrait of Blanche in *BD*, "a triumph of the poet's art." Clarifies similarities and differences between Chaucer's portrait and its source in Machaut's *Jugement du roy de Behaigne*, and explains how Chaucer's idealization reflects Aristotelian and Ciceronian notions of virtue.

291. Neufeld, Christine M. "'A Familiar Vois and Stevene': Hearing Voices in Chaucer's Dream Visions." *SAC* 44 (2022): 93–132. Examines auditory cognition in *BD*, *PF*, and *HF*, attending particularly to "janglynge" and related concepts. *BD* illustrates differences between hearing and listening, while *PF* records a "paradigm shift" from seeing to listening, and *HF* reflects Chaucer's "sense of the partiality of his own poetic voice, dependent as it is on the collaboration of his auditor to come into being." Attends to noise, gossip, voice, animal sounds, acousmatic sound and reading, transduction, listening "modalities," and theories of aurality.

292. Reichert, Folker. "Geoffrey Chaucers 'Carrenare': Zum Verhältnis von Poesie und Geographie im 14. Jahrhundert." *Archiv für Kulturgeschichte* 104 (2022): 331–43. Examines geographical and literary backgrounds to Chaucer's use of "Carrenare" in *BD*, 1029, identifying it with "Caramoran" (especially as found in Marco Polo and Mandeville), and suggesting it helps to separate Blanche from the vanities of the courtly world.

293. Spearing, A. C. "Narrator Theory and Medieval English Narratives." In Sylvie Patron, ed. *Optional-Narrator Theory* (Lincoln: University of Nebraska Press, 2021), pp. 166–83. Challenges the applicability of modern narratology to medieval narratives, examining the narrating position in *King Horn* as popular romance and in *BD* as adaptation of a French *dit*, and showing that novel-based notions of narrator-as-character do not apply. In Chaucer's case, the first-person pronouns convey "a proximal deictic," i.e., "a certain literary effect, one that is hard to define except as '*I*-ness'—the sense of being a centre of experience and perception."

See also nos. 9, 24, 43, 56, 109, 112, 124, 142, 163, 175.

The Equatorie of the Planetis

294. Cossio, Andoni. "Addenda: One Middle English Manuscript and Four Editions of Medieval Works Known to J. R. R. Tolkien and What They Reveal." *ANQ* 36 (2023): 164–71. Published online June 27, 2021. Includes photostats of Cambridge, Peterhouse, MS 75.I (*Equat*) among several additions to "Section A" of Oronzo Cilli's *Tolkien's Library: An Annotated Checklist* (Edinburgh: Luna Press, 2019), and comments on Tolkien's concern with scribal corruption in Chaucer's works and his own.

295. ______. "Further Notes on J. R. R. Tolkien's Photostats of *The Equatorie of the Planetis* (MS Peterhouse 75.I)." *SELIM* 27 (2022): 166–76. Identifies which folios of Cambridge, Peterhouse, MS 75.I are included (photostatic copies) in the Tolkien archive of Oxford, Bodleian Library, Tolkien VC 277, using the copies to assess Tolkien's possible assistance to Derek J. Price and R. M. Wilson in their 1955 Cambridge University Press edition of *Equat* and the putative attribution of *Equat* to Chaucer.

The House of Fame

296. Contzen, Eva von. "Epic Lists: The Matter of Troy and the Catalogue Form in Middle English Literature." In Eva von Contzen and James Simpson, eds. *Enlistment: Lists in Medieval and Early Modern Literature* (*SAC* 46 [2024], no. 128), pp. 115–34. Uses Chaucer's list of poets of Troy in *HF*, 1460ff., as a "vantage point" to demonstrate how epic catalogues in Middle English Troy narratives are "sites of scepticism towards established truths, questioning the Trojan War, the claims of epic, and poetry itself." Also considers these concerns in the *Seege or Batayle of Troye*, the *Laud Troy Book*, the *"Gest Hystoriale" of the Destruction of Troy*, and John Lydgate's *Troy Book*.

297. Cousins, A. D. "Pope and Chaucer: Reconstructing *The House of Fame* in the Reign of Queen Anne." In A. D. Cousins and Daniel Derrin, eds. *Alexander Pope in the Reign of Queen Anne: Reconsiderations of His Early Career* (New York: Routledge, 2021), pp. 113–36. Argues that in his reworking of *HF* as *The Temple of Fame*, Alexander Pope "comprehensively repudiates the inconclusiveness" of Chaucer's work. Where Chaucer suggests "the contradictions and confusions" of literary tradition and authority, Pope assumes authority and "almost entirely excludes hesitancy and ambiguity from his consideration."

298. Hines, John. "But men seyn, 'What may ever last?': Chaucer's *House of Fame* as a Medieval Museum." In Jan-Peer Hartmann and Andrew James Johnston, eds. *Material Remains: Reading the Past in Medieval and Early Modern British Literature* (Columbus: The Ohio State University Press, 2021), pp. 240–57. Considers possibilities of assessing material archeology in medieval literature and offers a case study concerning *HF*, observing connections between the brass-tablet account of Aeneas in the poem (lines 140ff.) and monumental brasses, hypothesizing Fame's palace as a medieval version of a museum, and connecting them both with the open-endedness of the poem and early modern sensibilities.

299. Keller, William R. "Performing Generic Exhaustion: Implosive Households in Gavin Douglas's *Palice of Honour*." In Eva von Contzen and James Simpson, eds. *Enlistment: Lists in Medieval and Early Modern Literature* (*SAC* 46 [2024], no. 128), pp. 135–53. Examines the role of lists, themes of order and disorder, epistemology and poetics, and tensions between household economy and monetized mercantile accretion (chrematistics) in Douglas's *Palice of Honour* as a response to similar concerns

in Chaucer's *HF* and his other dream poems. Argues that, especially in Venus's mirror, Douglas exceeds Chaucer's concern with excessiveness and destabilizes the "genre of faculty allegory."

300. Keller, Wolfram R. "Chrematistische Poetik: Mentale Haushaltsführung in Geoffrey Chaucers *Traumvisionen*." In Iris Därmann and Aloys Winterling, eds. *Oikonomia und Ökonomie im klassischen Griechenland: Theorie—Praxis—Transformation* (Stuttgart: Franz Steiner, 2022), pp. 157–73. Argues that *HF* depicts a journey through the mental operation of using traditional classical material to generate new literature (tidings) and, in doing so, reflects aspects of late medieval understanding of psychology and economics. Crucial to the latter is a shift from the model of household maintenance to that of chresmatistic mercantile expansion, which depends upon dislocation, multiplication, even unnatural usury—in various ways analogous to imagination rather than memory.

301. Kordecki, Lesley. "Poetry and the Bird in Chaucer's *House of Fame*." *ISLE: Interdisciplinary Studies in Literature and Environment* 29 (2022): 570–82. Argues that the eagle in *HF* "represents poetry," manifest in its "uncanny perception," its ability to "uplift" the narrator, and its concern with sound and transformative power.

302. Lewis, Sean Gordon. "Airy Bodies and Knowledge in Chaucer's *House of Fame*." *Enarratio* 23 (2022): 52–68. Examines the "embodiment of language" in *HF* and argues that it displays epistemological "confidence in the ability of the textual word/body to communicate accurately to the reader's imagination in a synesthetic experience." Focuses on how Chaucer (following Dante's Thomistic hylomorphism) "portrays audible speech as visible shades of the speakers" and "calls attention to the spoken word embodied in writing." Also comments on the textual history of *HF* in manuscripts and early print.

303. Livne, Shachar. "On Truth, *Pietà*, and Reader Response to Dante's *Purgatory* 10 and Chaucer's *House of Fame* 1." *SP* 118 (2021): 605–30. Contrasts the hermeneutics of ekphrastic scenes in *Purgatorio* and *HF*: the viewing by Dante's viator of bas-reliefs in the first cornice of Purgatory (X.25ff.) encourages emotional detachment when searching for truth in art; Geffrey's compassion when viewing the murals on the walls of Venus's temple in *HF* (140ff.) "is precisely what prompts him to reject such representations and search for truth elsewhere."

304. Moll, Richard J. "The Hall of Honor: Chaucer, Hawes, and the Conclusion to Gerard Legh's *Accedens of Armory*." *SP* 119 (2022): 371–404. Shows how Legh uses the dream vision structure from *HF* but employs a

frame of memory and "argues against Chaucer's position that fame is unrelated to deserving."

305. Nelson, Ingrid. "Ambient Media and Chaucer's *House of Fame*." *ELH* 88 (2021): 551–78. Argues that, rooted in "medieval theory of mediated perception" and concerned with perceptual distortion, *HF* shows how a "sensing body" participates in an "ambient mediascape"—one that includes environmental media (air, water, architecture) as well as aesthetic media (painting, engraving, writing).

306. Rouse, Margitta. "Trojanische Traumtore: Elliptische Ekphrasis in Chaucers *House of Fame*." In Anne-Katrin Federow and Kay Malcher, eds. *Troja bauen: Vormodernes Erzählen von der Antike in comparatistischer Sicht* (*SAC* 46 [2024], no. 58), pp. 203–26. Explores ellipsis, ekphrasis, lists, allusions, and their combinations as techniques and thematic devices in *HF*. Focuses on "elliptical ekphrasis" of source material as axiological choice, and as a method of literary generation and renewal, with particular attention to dreaming and Virgil's *Aeneid*, reading the omission of Virgil's gates of dream from Chaucer's poem as intentional and evocative.

See also nos. 24, 31, 55, 62, 65, 73, 89, 94, 108, 123, 141, 152, 250, 291, 311.

The Legend of Good Women

307. Allen-Goss, Lucy M. "Dismembered Memories: Philomela in Chaucer and Gower." In Sarah Baechle, Carissa M. Harris, and Elizaveta Strakhov, eds. *Rape Culture and Female Resistance in Late Medieval Literature: With an Edition of Middle English and Middle Scots Pastourelles* (University Park: Penn State University Press, 2022), pp. 80–96. Contrasts Chaucer's and Gower's Philomela stories, focusing on differences between the nuances and implications of weaving in *LGW* and embroidery in *Confessio Amantis*, and arguing that Chaucer's version aligns better with modern understanding of "trauma-fragmented memory," speaking, and rape survival.

308. Hakman, Ekmel Emrah. "Female Goodness for Geoffrey Chaucer: Misconception or Intention?" In Meral Hakman, ed. *Prehistoryadan günümüze kadın* (Ankara: Bilgin Kültür Sanat Yayınları, 2020), pp. 391–437. Briefly summarizes *LGWP* and assesses in detail each of the legends, arguing that, generally, Chaucer's anti-misogynistic effort fails. Although his "primary goal is to speak of good women as examples for the society

and equal to men," his selection of women, his sources, his characterizations of women and men, and his "misconception of goodness" are fundamentally patriarchal.

309. Harlan-Haughey, Sarah. "The Dragon of Love: Chaucer's Jason and the Cycle of Consumption in the *Legend of Good Women*." *ChauR* 57 (2022): 101–28. Focuses on Jason in *LGW* and other sexually predatory men, examines a number of motifs in Chaucer's version of Jason, and highlights the danger of men such as Jason who hide their behavior behind gentility.

310. Sasamoto, Hisayuki. "Chaucer and Ovid: The Source of 'The Legend of Thisbe.'" In Society for Chaucer Studies and Koichi Kano, eds. *To the Days of Studying Medieval English Literature: Essays in Memory of Professor Ikegami Tadahiro* (*SAC* 46 [2024], no. 179), pp. 57–68. Examines passages in "The Legend of Thisbe" of *LGW* that differ from the source, Ovid's *Metamorphoses*. In Japanese.

See also nos. 56, 66, 81, 118, 131, 139, 141, 179, 185, 200, 216, 288, 319.

The Parliament of Fowls

311. Keller, Wolfram R. "Disharmonic Spheres: Metapoetic Noise in Geoffrey Chaucer's *Parliament of Fowls*." In Cornelia Wilde and Wolfram R. Keller, eds. *Perfect Harmony and Melting Strains: Transformations of Music in Early Modern Culture between Sensibility and Abstraction* (Boston, Mass.: De Gruyter, 2021), pp. 11–37. Describes the background to and representations of the harmony of the spheres in *PF* and in *HF*, arguing that both poems depict the "three ventricles of the brain"—imagination, logic, and memory—and that, through parody and/or inversion, each depicts a poetics, "the cornerstone of which is disharmony rather than harmony."

312. Krajník, Filip. "The Translator as Author: The Case of Geoffrey Chaucer's *The Parliament of Fowls*." In Paul Poplawski, ed. *Studying English Literature in Context: Critical Readings* (Cambridge: Cambridge University Press, 2022), pp. 27–43. Contrasts medieval and modern ideas of authorship, focusing on how Chaucer "treated old authorities in developing his own reputation and what strategies he employed to establish a harmony among the multiple authorial voices" in *PF*. Proposes that, for Chaucer, authorship is defined by the "level of the author's creative input" in

combination with the occasion of a work, its "original context and purpose," and its various possible audiences.

313. Ni, Yun. "Natural Law and Parliamentary Election in Geoffrey Chaucer's *Parliament of Fowls*." *ChauR* 57 (2022): 302–20. Demonstrates that *PF* reflects a movement from natural law to a more subjective interpretation of individual rights and ties this transition to the crisis of "commonalty" in the late fourteenth century.

314. Vercoe, Elizabeth, comp. *The Varieties of Amorous Experience: For Voice & Piano*. New York: American Composers Alliance, 2021. Musical score; 16 pp. Item not seen. WorldCat records indicate that this musical score includes "Qui bien aime" by Geoffrey Chaucer, i.e., the title of a French song cited in several manuscripts of *PF* before the roundel at *PF*, 680–92, here set to music, along with selections from Thomas Flatman, William Shakespeare, and Coventry Patmore.

See also nos. 24, 41, 65, 70, 105, 112, 141, 288, 291.

The Romaunt of the Rose

315. McKee, Conor. "Henry Bradshaw's Rhyme Tests and the Formation of the Chaucer Canon: The Glasgow *Romaunt of the Rose* and the *Tale of Gamelyn*." *ChauR* 57 (2022): 273–301. Contains archival evidence and unpublished papers from Henry Bradshaw. Examines Bradshaw's "rhyme tests," which he used to establish Chaucerian authorship of the *Tale of Gamelyn* and *Rom*, and accounts for Walter W. Skeat's sometimes incorrect results.

See also no. 263

Troilus and Criseyde

316. Adamson, Christopher. "'A Sacramental Moment': Liturgy and Time in the Victorian Reception of the Past." Ph.D. dissertation (Emory University, 2020), *DAI-A* 82.06. Examines "the importance of ritual in the Victorian reception of the medieval past," including discussion of *TC*.

317. Alberghini, Jennifer. "Calkas's Daughter: Paternal Authority and Feminine Virtue in *Troilus and Criseyde*." *MFF* 57 (2022): 7–34. Explores Criseyde's role as daughter in *TC*, Calkas's putative authority over her in marital matters, and the views of other characters concerning her

ambiguous, conditional consent to her father's wishes. Treats Criseyde's "feminine virtue" and Calkas's authority over her as reflections of medieval social expectations, arguing that the appearance of Criseyde's consent is (like Calkas's authority) "performative," her means to keep her reputation intact while maintaining considerable independence.

318. Booth, Naomi. *Swoon: A Poetics of Passing Out*. Manchester: Manchester University Press, 2021. x, 232 pp.; 4 illus. Surveys literary representations of swooning from late medieval works to modern ones, assessing how the motif is "inflected and re-inflected as ideas of the body, gender, race, sexuality and sickness shift through time." After an introductory essay on theorizations of swooning and fainting, Chapter 1, "Heart-Stopped Transformations: Swooning in Late Medieval Literature," includes discussion of *TC*, in which swoons signify danger and transformation, with contrasts between Troilus's and Criseyde's swoons reflecting their individual vulnerabilities that comprise an anatomy of erotic love.

319. Dumitescu, Irina. "Beyond the Girlboss." *TLS*, February 11, 2022, p. 27. Comments on Criseyde in *TC* and the protagonists of *LGW* as evidence of Chaucer's effort "to articulate the problem of writing about women: in the public eye, no female character is entitled to a full personality."

320. Easler, Jennifer Nicole. "The Futility of Prophecy: Prophecy and Poetry in English Narratives of Troy." Open access Ph.D. dissertation (University of Minnesota, 2022). Available at https://conservancy.umn.edu/handle/11299/227922 (accessed November 18, 2023). vi, 233 pp. Examines the themes of prophecy and retold narrative in premodern works about Troy by Virgil, Dares and Dictys, Chaucer (*TC*), Lydgate, and Shakespeare, arguing that, in various ways, they "call into question the efficacy of poetry and of knowledge, but they do so in ways that ultimately reaffirm the power and limits of both knowledge and literature."

321. Elmes, Melissa Ridley. "Female Friendship in Late Medieval Literature: Cultural Translation in Chaucer, Gower, and Malory." In Karma Lochrie and Usha Vishnuvajjala, eds. *Women's Friendship in Medieval Literature* (*SAC* 46 [2024], no. 155), pp. 135–54. Describes depictions of affective female friendship in works by Chaucer (*TC* and *FranT*), John Gower (Albinus and Rosamund in the *Confessio Amantis*), and Thomas Malory (portions of the *Morte Darthur*), contrasting them with source materials and attributing their relatively positive portrayals to the rise of

"literate activity," including patronage, among women. Assesses the circles of friends who seek to console Criseyde and Dorigen.

322. Hamaguchi, Keiko. "'. . . Criseyda, / In widewes habit blak' (I.169–70): Fourteenth-Century English Widows and the Victimization of Criseyde." *SIMELL* 37 (2022): 27–45. Investigates *TC*'s portrayal of Criseyde as a representation of English widows facing threats and deceit. Utilizing legal records of the time, considers how Poliphete's false suit mirrors real cases of widows unjustly targeted for their property and manipulated by men. In Japanese, with English abstract.

323. Hanna, Natalie. "Chaucer's Worthiest Knight: Heroic Identity in *Troilus and Criseyde*." In Roman Bleier, Brian Coleman, and Clare Fletcher, eds. *Memory and Identity in the Medieval and Early Modern World* (*SAC* 46 [2022], no. 120), pp. 29–49. Questions how and to what extent recurrent mention of Hector in *TC* helps to characterize Troilus as a knight. Instances and collocations of "knight," "worthy," related terms, and references to Hector, generally not found in Chaucer's source text, Boccaccio's *Filostrato*, help to establish Troilus's "archetypal" knightly virtues.

324. Harris, Carissa M., and Fiona Somerset. "Introduction" to a colloquium on "Historizing Consent: Bodies, Wills, Desires." *SAC* 44 (2022): 268–71. Identifies Criseyde's comment to Troilus about consent in *TC*, III.1210–11 as evidence of her awareness of difference between "survival strategy" and "affirmative consent."

325. Haruta, Setsuko. "Bells Ringing for Helen and Criseyde." In Society for Chaucer Studies and Koichi Kano, eds. *To the Days of Studying Medieval English Literature: Essays in Memory of Professor Ikegami Tadahiro* (*SAC* 46 [2024], no. 179), pp. 18–39. Considers the characterizations of Helen and Criseyde in *TC* through multiple contexts, including estates of medieval women and the ways Helen is depicted in Greek literature.

326. Hines, Jessica. "Forming Pity: Responses to Suffering in Chaucer's *Troilus and Criseyde*." *R&L* 54 (2022): 49–71. Presents the role of pity as an "essential virtue" that does not negate suffering in *TC*; claims that Chaucer shifts language as a way to understand the "complex social and subjective position of pity" in *TC*.

327. Kaempfer, Lucie. "The Memory of Joy in *Troilus and Criseyde*: Identity and Emotional Temporality." In Roman Bleier, Brian Coleman, and Clare Fletcher, eds. *Memory and Identity in the Medieval and Early Modern World* (*SAC* 46 [2022], no. 120), pp. 105–19. Examines joy in *TC*—looking forward to it in Books I and III, experiencing it in Book III,

and remembering it in Books IV and V—as aspects of Troilus's identity and of the poem itself. Anticipated joy shapes the characterization of Troilus as a courtly lover, and the "memory of joy makes the ending of the text tragic."

328. Nakao, Yoshiyuki. "Chaucer's Speech and Thought Representation in *Troilus and Criseyde*: Encoded Subjectivities and Semantic Extension." In Jonathan Fruoco, ed. *Polyphony and the Modern* (*SAC* 46 [2024], no. 137), pp. 169–91. Offers a technical linguistic analysis of speech and thought representation (STR) in *TC*, theorizing a hierarchical "structure of subjectivities" to examine samples from the poem, attending to nuances latent in diction, situation, point of view, manuscript context, editorial intervention, etc. Concludes with comments on the "plasticity" of Chaucer's STR, the "varying subjectivities that are likely to be encoded" in it, and how they "allow for semantic extension."

329. Širca, Alen. "Lik Antigone v predmoderni literaturi." *Primerjalna književnost* 44 (2021): 87–105. Surveys depictions of Antigone in western literature from Antiquity through the late Middle Ages, with assessment of Chaucer's characterization of her in *TC* as an interweaving of Trojan and Theban traditions.

330. Spearing, A. C. "The Troy of Chaucer's *Troilus and Criseyde*." In Anne-Katrin Federow and Kay Malcher, eds. *Troja bauen: Vormodernes Erzählen von der Antike in comparatistischer Sicht* (*SAC* 46 [2024], no. 58), pp. 187–202. Identifies internal "traces of uncertainty and changes of mind" in the composition process of *TC*, aligning them with the poem's theme of the unreliability of Boethian Fortune and challenging ideas about the supposed "planned wholeness" of *TC* and its putative unitary narrator. Examines ways that Chaucer's contemporary London contributes to his depiction of Troy and its culture, evident by contrast with details from Boccaccio and other sources.

See also nos. 9, 39, 47, 62, 73, 87, 95, 110, 117, 123–24, 126, 131, 133, 138, 154, 162, 165, 175, 179, 240, 244.

Lyrics and Short Poems

331. Whitehead, Christiania. "The Middle English Lyrics in Their European Context." In Raluca Radulescu and Sif Ríkharðsdóttir, eds. *The Routledge Companion to Medieval English Literature* (*SAC* 46 [2024], no.

166), pp. 332–44. Examines "Middle English lyric writing before and after Chaucer, assessing its evolving relationship to the Continent" and interactions between sacred and secular within the genre. Analyzes Chaucer's (and his "successors'") uses of French lyric *formes fixes*, and assesses the "cross-fertilizations" of courtly sentiments, religious verse, and liturgy in Middle English lyrics.

See also no. 142.

Adam Scriveyn

332. Dwyer, Seamus. "Scraping, Scribing and Shriving: The Language of Writing, Judgement and Penitence in Chaucer's 'Adam Scriveyn.'" In Roman Bleier, Brian Coleman, and Clare Fletcher, eds. *Memory and Identity in the Medieval and Early Modern World* (*SAC* 46 [2024], no. 120), pp. 193–208. Surveys critical attention to *Adam* and reads the poem as an exhortation to "moral and professional penitence." Focuses on "corect," "rubbe," and "scrape" as scribal activities and as metaphorical links to penitential erasure in Chaucer and other works in Middle English.

See also nos. 39, 55.

The Complaint of Chaucer to His Purse

333. Atkinson, Ruth, and Geert van Iersel, trans. "Geoffrey Chaucer: Complaint to His Purse (Ende 14. Jh)." In Nathanael Busch and Robert Fajen, eds. *Allmächtig und unfassbar: Geld in der Literatur des Mittelalters* (Stuttgart: S. Hirzel, 2021), pp. 316–19. Translates *Purse* into German verse, with notes; Middle English text included.

The Complaint of Mars

334. Stratford, Jenny. "The Bequests of Isabel of Castile, First Duchess of York, and Chaucer's 'Complaint of Mars.'" In Jessica A. Lutkin and J. S. Hamilton, eds. *Creativity, Contradictions and Commemoration in the Reign*

of Richard II: Essays in Honour of Nigel Saul (Woodbridge: Boydell, 2022), pp. 75–92, plus appendix. Summarizes the life and legacy of Isabella of Castile, examining in detail her last will and testament (included in Latin and French). Refutes John Shirley's suggestion in his manuscript afterwords to *Mars* and to *Venus* that the poems link the allegory of the planets in *Mars* to a putative affair between Isabella and John Holland, first earl of Huntingdon (later first duke of Exeter), an aspersion cast earlier by Thomas Walsingham.

The Complaint of Venus

See nos. 141, 334.

The Complaint unto Pity

See no. 52.

Lak of Stedfastnesse

See no. 177.

Chaucerian Apocrypha

335. Harris, Carissa M. "From Tapsters to Beer Wenches: Women, Alcohol, and Misogyny, Then and Now." In John A. Geck, Rosemary O'Neill, and Noelle Phillips, eds. *Beer and Brewing in Medieval Culture and Contemporary Medievalism* (*SAC* 46 [2024], no. 140), pp. 265–84. Analyzes "how English and Scottish literature and law during the fourteenth through sixteenth centuries connected the figure of the tapster to sex work, transgression, public harm, and dangerous agency over men," and traces residue of this misogyny in modern "breastaurants" (e.g., Hooters). Includes discussion of the "Canterbury Interlude" that precedes the apocryphal *Tale of Beryn*.

See also nos. 126, 154, 335.

Book Reviews

336. Akbari, Suzanne Conklin, and James Simpson, eds. *The Oxford Handbook of Chaucer*. Oxford: Oxford University Press, 2020. Rev. Jennifer Sisk, *MP*, 119 (2022): E93–E96.

337. Allen-Goss, Lucy M. *Female Desire in Chaucer's "Legend of Good Women" and Medieval English Romance* (*SAC* 44 [2022], no. 39). Rev. Suzanne M. Edwards, *MFF* 58 (2022): 152–54; Hannah Piercy, *NMS* 66 (2022): 231–34; Elizaveta Strakhov, *RenQ* 75 (2022): 1439–41.

338. Amsler, Mark. *The Medieval Life of Language: Grammar and Pragmatics from Bacon to Kempe* (*SAC* 46 [2023], no. 110). Rev. Isabella Greisinger, *TMR* 22.08.10.

339. Bain, Frederika Elizabeth. *Dismemberment in the Medieval and Early Modern English Imaginary: The Performance of Difference*. Boston, Mass.: De Gruyter, 2020. Rev. Nicole Nyffenegger, *TMR* 22.05.23.

340. Booth, Naomi. *Swoon: A Poetics of Passing Out* (*SAC* 46 [2024], no. 318). Rev. Kathryn Hughes, *TLS*, March 4, 2022, p. 26.

341. Boulton, Maureen B. M. *Literary Echoes of the Fourth Lateran Council in England and France, 1215–1405* (*SAC* 44 [2022], no. 191). Rev. Sethina Watson, *MLR* 117 (2022): 101–2.

342. Bower, Hannah. *Middle English Recipes and Literary Play, 1375–1500* (*SAC* 46 [2024], no. 122). Rev. Sarah Star, *SAC* 44 (2022): 373–75.

343. Bude, Tekla. *Sonic Bodies: Text, Music, and Silence in Late Medieval England* (*SAC* 46 [2022], no. 124). Rev. Mariana López, *TMR* 22.11.05.

344. Bushnell, Rebecca, ed. *The Marvels of the World: An Anthology of Nature Writing before 1700* (*SAC* 45 [2023], no. 60). Rev. James L. Smith, *TMR* 22.04.08.

345. Byron-Davies, Justin M. *Revelation and the Apocalypse in Late Medieval Literature: The Writings of Julian of Norwich and William Langland* (*SAC* 46 [2024], no. 57). Rev. Hope Doherty, *Digital Philology: A Journal of Medieval Cultures* 9 (2020): 235–38.

346. Coghlin, J. Michelle. *The Cambridge Companion to Literature and Food* (*SAC* 46 [2024], no. 194). Rev. Alexandra Mitrea, *East–West Cultural Passage* 21 (2021): 150–53.

347. Crocker, Holly A. *The Matter of Virtue: Women's Ethical Action from Chaucer to Shakespeare* (*SAC* 44 [2022], no. 131). Rev. Julia Reinhard Lupton, *RenQ* 75 (2022): 357–58; Rev. Masha Raskolnikov, *MFF* 58 (2022): 158–61.

348. Da Rold, Orietta. *Paper in Medieval England: From Pulp to Fiction*. Cambridge Studies in Medieval Literature (*SAC* 46 [2024], no. 131). Rev. Megan L. Cook, *SAC* 44 (2022): 386–89; Katherine Storm Hindley, *RES* 72 (2022): 992–94; William Noel, *Manuscript Studies* 7 (2022): 210–12; José María Pérez Fernández, *Cromohs: Cyber Review of Modern Historiography* 24 (2021): 201–4; Sebastian Sobecki, *Speculum* 97 (2022): 560–62.

349. Da Rold, Orietta, and Elaine Treharne, eds. *The Cambridge Companion to Medieval British Manuscripts* (*SAC* 46 [2024], no. 132). Rev. Susan Powell, *JEBS* 24 (2021): 339–43; Pamela Robinson, *Library* 23 (2022): 106–7.

350. Donaghey, Brian, Noel Harold Kaylor, Jr., Philip Edward Phillips, and Paul E. Szarmach, eds., with assistance from Kenneth C. Hawley. *Remaking Boethius: The English Language Translation Tradition of "The Consolation of Philosophy"* (*SAC* 45 [2023], no. 148). Rev. Leslie Lockett, *TMR* 22.04.25.

351. Doyle, Kara A. *The Reception of Chaucer's Shorter Poems, 1400–1450: Female Audiences, English Manuscripts, French Contexts* (SAC 46 [2024], no. 44). Rev. Sarah Wilma Watson, *SAC* 44 (2022): 397–401.

352. Eisner, Martin. *Dante's New Life of the Book: A Philology of World Literature*. Oxford: Oxford University Press, 2021. Rev. Filippo Gianferrari, *MP*, 120 (2022): E11–E14.

353. Gates, Jay Paul, and Brian T. O'Camb, eds. *Remembering the Medieval Present: Generative Uses of England's Pre-Conquest Past, 10th to 15th Centuries* (*SAC* 44 [2022], no. 218). Rev. Anya Adair, *TMR* 22.03.20.

354. Gordon, Stephen. *Supernatural Encounters: Demons and the Restless Dead in Medieval England, c. 1050–1450* (*SAC* 44 [2022], no. 233). Rev. Gary K. Waite, *RenQ* 75 (2022): 1061–63.

355. Grady, Frank. *The Cambridge Companion to "The Canterbury Tales"* (*SAC* 44 [2022], no. 134). Rev. Sophia Li Chi-fang, *RenQ* 75 (2022): 982–84.

356. Hadfield, Andrew. *Literature and Class: From the Peasants' Revolt to the French Revolution* (*SAC* 46 [2024], no. 145). Rev. Biancamaria Fontana, *TLS*, September 23, 2022, p. 20.

357. Hartmann, Jan-Peer, and Andrew James Johnston, eds. *Material Remains: Reading the Past in Medieval and Early Modern British Literature* (*SAC* 46 [2024], no. 298). Rev. Rebecca Pinner, *English* 71 (2022): 363–67; Eric Weiskott, *Speculum* 97 (2022): 1202–4.

358. Hsy, Jonathan. *Antiracist Medievalisms: From "Yellow Peril" to Black Lives Matter* (*SAC* 46 [2024], no. 146). Rev. Matthew X. Vernon, *SAC* 44 (2022): 409–12.

359. Hurley, Mary Kate. *Translation Effects: Language, Time, and Community in Medieval England* (*SAC* 46 [2024], no. 226). Rev. Nicole Guenther Discenza, *TMR* 22.09.1; Stephen Harris, *Arthuriana* 32 (2022): 152–53; Georgina Pitt, *Parergon* 39 (2022): 248–49.

360. Kerby-Fulton, Kathryn. *The Clerical Proletariat and the Resurgence of Medieval English Poetry* (*SAC* 46 [2024], no. 151). Rev. Michael Calabrese, *MP* 119 (2022): E149–E54.

361. Kirk, Jordan. *Medieval Nonsense: Signifying Nothing in Fourteenth-Century England* (*SAC* 45 [2023], no. 77). Rev. Karma Lochrie, *MP* 119 (2022): E97–E99.

362. Krummel, Miriamne Ara. *The Medieval Postcolonial Jew, in and out of Time* (*SAC* 46 [2024], no. 48). Rev. Sarah Ifft Decker, *TMR* 22.10.15; Geraldine Heng, *Jewish Historical Studies* 55 (2023): 310–14.

363. Leitch, Megan G. *Sleep and Its Spaces in Middle English Literature: Emotions, Ethics, Dreams* (*SAC* 46 [2023], no. 288). Rev. Carolyne Larrington, *Arthuriana* 32 (2022): 153–55; Jamie K. Taylor, *SAC* 44 (2022): 412–15.

364. Meyer-Lee, Robert J. *Literary Value and Social Identity in the "Canterbury Tales"* (*SAC* 43 [2021], no. 135). Rev. Chad Schrock, *MLR* 117 (2022): 111–12.

365. Moseley, C. W. R. D., ed. *Engaging with Chaucer: Practice, Authority, Reading* (*SAC* 45 [2023], no. 81). Rev. Andrew Galloway, *TMR* 22.02.02.

366. Murton, Megan E. *Chaucer's Prayers: Writing Christian and Pagan Devotion* (*SAC* 44 [2022], no. 150). Rev. Joseph D. Parry, *RenQ* 75 (2022): 1436–37.

367. New, Elizabeth A., and Christian Steer, eds. *Medieval Londoners: Essays to Mark the Eightieth Birthday of Caroline M. Barron* (*SAC* 45 [2023], no. 15). Rev. Kate Kelsey Staples, *TMR* 22.06.26.

368. North, Richard, Barbara Bordalejo, Terry Jones, and Peter Robinson, eds. *CantApp: The General Prologue. An Edition in an App* (*SAC* 46 [2024], no. 205). Rev. Jonathan Hsy, *Reviews in Digital Humanities* 1 (2022): n.p.

369. Perkins, Nicholas. *The Gift of Narrative in Medieval England* (*SAC* 46 [2024], no. 162). Rev. Robert J. Meyer-Lee, *SAC* 44 (2022): 415–19; Timothy S, Miller, *TMR* 22.08.17.

370. Ramirez, Janina. *Femina: A New History of the Middle Ages, through the Women Written out of It* (*SAC* 46 [2024], no. 88). Rev. Irina Dumitrescu, *TLS*, November 18, 2022, p. 24.

371. Richmond, Andrew M. *Landscape in Middle English Romance: The Medieval Imagination and the Natural World* (*SAC* 46 [2024], no. 169). Rev. Helen Cooper, *Speculum* 97 (2022): 1248–49; Karl Steele, *TMR* 22.08.14.

372. Robinson, Olivia. *Contest, Translation, and the Chaucerian Text* (*SAC* 45 [2023], no. 29). Rev. Jennifer Jahner, *JEGP* 121 (2022): 411–13.

373. Rogers, Will. *Writing Old Age and Impairments in Late Medieval England* (*SAC* 46 [2024], no. 171). Rev. Joel Rosenthal, *TMR* 22.08.05.

374. Ruszkiewicz, Dominika. *Love and Virtue in Middle English and Middle Scots Poetry* (*SAC* 46 [2024], no. 172). Rev. Nicola Royan, *SELIM* 28 (2023): 135–36.

375. Steiner, Emily. *John Trevisa's Information Age: Knowledge and the Pursuit of Literature, c. 1400* (*SAC* 46 [2024], no. 180). Rev. Michael Calabrese, *MP* 120 (2022): E15–E19; Matthew Boyd Goldie, *SAC* 44 (2022): 425–29.

376. Strakhov, Elizaveta. *Continental England: Form, Translation, and Chaucer in the Hundred Years' War* (*SAC* 46 [2024], no. 66). Rev. Rory G. Critten, *SAC* 44 (2022): 429–32; John T. DuVal, *Translation Review* 114 (2022): 50–51; Jeffrey Moser, *Rocky Mountain Review* 76 (2022): 348–51; Samantha Katz Seal, *Digital Philology* 11 (2022): 363–66.

377. Strouse, A. W. *Form and Foreskin: Medieval Narratives of Circumcision* (*SAC* 46 [2024], no. 232). Rev. Stacy S. Klein, *Speculum* 97 (2022): 1257–59.

378. Terrell, Katherine H. *Scripting the Nation: Court Poetry and the Authority of History in Late Medieval Scotland* (*SAC* 46 [2024], no. 99). Rev. Daniel Davies, *SAC* 44 (2022): 433–36.

379. Turner, Marion. *Chaucer: A European Life* (*SAC* 43 [2021], no. 10). Rev. Sean Gordon Lewis, *RenQ* 75 (2022): 1435–36.

380. Weiskott, Eric. *Meter and Modernity in English Verse, 1350–1650* (*SAC* 45 [2023], no. 53). Rev. Derek Attridge, *MP*, 119 (2022): E100–E103; Ben Glaser, *MLR* 117 (2022): 478–80.

381. Whitaker, Cord J. *Black Metaphors: How Modern Racism Emerged from Medieval Race-Thinking* (*SAC* 44 [2022], no. 206). Rev. Jean E. Feerick, *RenQ* 75 (2022): 710–12.

382. Wright, Sarah Breckenridge. *Mobility and Identity in Chaucer's "Canterbury Tales"* (*SAC* 44 [2022], no. 191). Rev. Ruen-chuan Ma, *SAC* 44 (2022): 379–82; Hannah Piercy, *MÆ* 91 (2022): 151–52.

Author Index—Bibliography

Index

www.ingramcontent.com/pod-product-compliance
Lightning Source LLC
Chambersburg PA
CBHW060818310726
48980CB00002B/331

* 9 7 8 0 9 3 3 7 8 4 4 8 2 *